THE STONE OF AUTHORITY COMPLETE SET

THE STONE CYCLE COMPLETE SETS BOOK 2

THE STONE CYCLE COMPLETE SETS SERIES

The Stone of Knowing Complete Set (The Stone Cycle Complete Sets Book 1), *comprising*

- The Stone of Knowing (The Stone Cycle Book 1)
- The Cost of Knowing (The Stone Cycle Book 2)
- The Seer: A Prequel to The Stone of Knowing (The Stone Cycle)

The Stone of Authority Complete Set (The Stone Cycle Complete Sets Book 2), *comprising*

- The Stone of Authority (The Stone Cycle Book 3)
- The Struggle for Authority (The Stone Cycle Book 4)

The Stone of Vitality Complete Set (The Stone Cycle Complete Sets Book 3), *comprising*

- The Stone of Vitality (The Stone Cycle Book 5)
- The Hope of Vitality (The Stone Cycle Book 6)

THE STONE OF AUTHORITY COMPLETE SET

THE STONE CYCLE COMPLETE SETS
BOOK 2

ALLAN N. PACKER

LUMINANT PUBLICATIONS

The Stone of Authority Complete Set

The Stone Cycle Complete Sets Book 2

Comprising:
The Stone of Authority (The Stone Cycle Book 3)
The Struggle for Authority (The Stone Cycle Book 4)

First edition (v1.0) published in 2024
by Luminant Publications

ISBN 978-1-923218-10-9

Luminant Publications
PO Box 305
Greenacres, South Australia 5086

http://www.allanpacker.com

Cover Design by Karri Klawiter
Map illustration by Brian Plush

'The Stone of Authority' Dedication

To Merilyn, my best friend and the joy of my life. I'm still amazed and grateful that you chose me.

'The Struggle for Authority' Dedication

To Julie and Chris, true friends as well as family through the changing seasons of life.

Baron Island
Savage Strait
Castel
Castel Citadel
Deadman's Pass
Steffan's Citadel
Maranelle
Arv
Duchy
of
Erestor
N
W
E
S
Arvenon
& surrounding Kingdoms

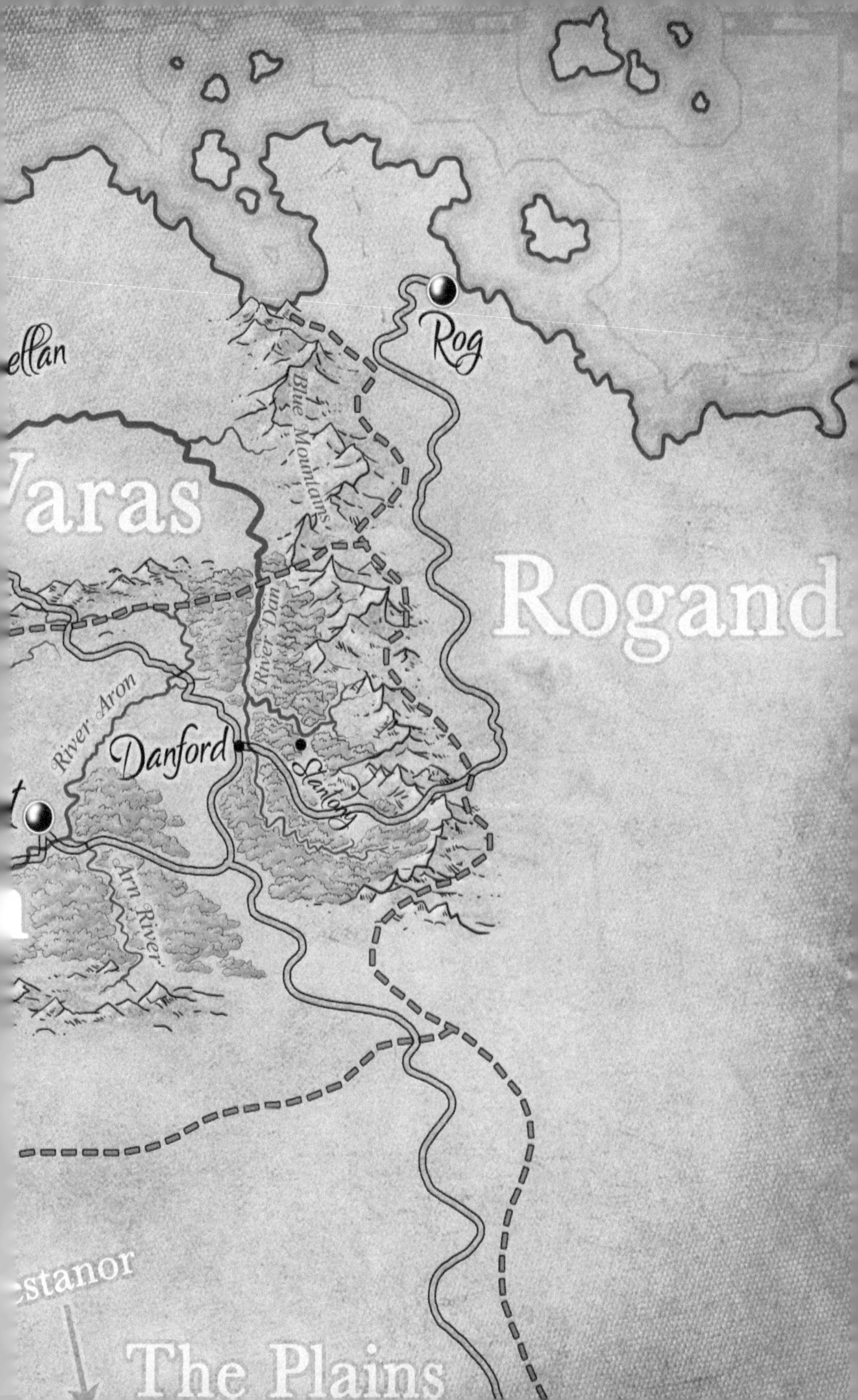
ellan
Rog
Blue Mountains
Varas
Rogand
River Dan
River Aron
Danford
Stanlony
Arn River
estanor
The Plains

PART I

THE STONE OF AUTHORITY

THE STONE CYCLE BOOK 3

VOLUME 1—STORM CLOUDS GATHER

PROLOGUE

Almost 30 years before Thomas Stablehand finds the Stone of Knowing,
The future King Steffan has just been born in Arvenon;
Rogand is ruled by King Ugar;
The Seer has begun to make a name for herself in Lestanor

The eagle soared high on the midday thermals, attentive to the tiniest movement in the desert terrain below. It ignored the little figures and the beasts of burden beside the colorful tents around the oasis. Humans held no interest for it. The monarch of the skies cared nothing for their hopes and fears or the rise and fall of their kingdoms.

The majestic predator glided effortlessly over the series of low hills above the oasis. Sometimes reptiles or rodents were foolish enough to risk exposure in the open. They provided a tasty snack.

A solitary figure briefly caught its eye as a young tent dweller picked his way slowly down the slope of a small hill. The eagle watched dispassionately as the ground suddenly opened up, swallowing the figure in a puff of dust.

Serenely indifferent to the fate of the hapless creature below, the hunter wheeled south, searching for less unsettled hunting grounds.

A RICHLY DRESSED youth sat beneath the eagle as it glided off into the distance. The crown prince fidgeted uncomfortably, struggling to keep every inch of his body sheltered within the shade of a large rock. His idleness was shattered momentarily as something repulsive slithered past, almost startling him out of his wits. It was only a lizard, but he frowned in irritation anyway as he anxiously scanned the dirt nearby.

The tents of the royal caravan lay clustered before him, workers scurrying around them like ants. Prince Agon knew he could be sitting in luxury down there, away from the dust and the heat and creeping things. He would be waited on by bustling servants whose sole purpose in life was to satisfy his every desire. But it would be insufferably boring. And it would also bring him within reach of his father's foul temper.

Thankfully he had managed to slip away, right under the noses of the royal guards. His father would punish them cruelly for their negligence, but he didn't care. It served them right.

Only moments before, a faint cry—quickly cut off—had interrupted his musing. It sounded like a cry for help. Most likely it came from Vilkami, his boyhood companion.

The pointless meanderings of the youth must have finally landed him in some kind of trouble. Agon's first instinct had been to wonder whether he himself might also be in danger. He quickly concluded that he had little cause for concern. The most deadly predators in this region were humans like himself, and they shunned the outdoors in the heat of the day. Apart from serpents, the only other truly dangerous creatures here were nocturnal.

Perhaps Vilkami had disturbed a snake. The prince yawned. The young idiot could bleat all he liked—losing him would hardly be a great loss.

There was a time when Agon might have called the overeager

sixteen-year-old his friend. That was back before he knew better. He had long since realized that a prince didn't have friends. He only had servants.

Just one month earlier Prince Agon had celebrated his eighteenth birthday, attended by the greatest noblemen from across the land, each of them bowing low as they presented him their gifts. He was the most important person in the kingdom, and therefore in the world. The one exception was his father, as the old fool never tired of reminding him.

He spat into the dust. King Ugar's day would come, no matter how often his noblemen greeted him with "Great king, may you live forever!"

Another cry came to him faintly. "Agon! Over here!"

He sat up straight this time, frowning in anger. No one, not even his most faithful boyhood companion, had the right to address him by name. Perhaps he had overlooked such behavior when he was a child, but no more. The young cur needed to learn there was a price to pay for daring to be familiar with the crown prince of Rogand.

Agon got up and set off haughtily in the direction of the voice. Wrathful as he was, he wasn't going to hurry. He had no need to scamper about like a servant.

The moment he left the shade he began to feel uncomfortably hot. The desert might be cold at night, but it was sweltering during the day. He had journeyed with his father and a bevy of royal attendants into the far south of Rogand, and the colder climate of the capital, Rog, seemed a world away. Their reason for being here was a mystery to him. It undoubtedly had something to do with Lestanor, though, since Rogand's border with Lestanor was not far from their current location.

He squinted up at the sun as he walked. The glowing orb in the sky appeared to be making common cause with the boy in failing to show due respect for his royal station. It irked him greatly, not least because he knew he could do nothing whatever about it.

Ahead of him a series of low hills rose out of the desert. The eager summons had come from that direction. The voice had since gone silent—perhaps something had happened to Vilkami. His lip curled in a smirk of satisfaction at the thought. He always enjoyed it when other people suffered.

Then a horrible notion occurred to him—what if the boy had discovered something? Agon quickened his step. He had incontestable rights to whatever it was, and he needed to be on hand promptly to assert those rights.

Cresting the hill he spotted a section of hillside—halfway down the slope—where the earth had caved in. Dust drifted up into the air from around it. There was no sign of his companion.

"Vilkami! Where are you?" he called.

"Down here," a faint voice replied.

Agon knelt beside the hole and tried to peer in. It was too dark to see much of anything in there. "What are you doing?"

"I was investigating a small opening in the hillside," a muffled voice replied. "Then the ground collapsed, and I fell in."

"What's down there?"

"It's a tomb of some kind. A very old one."

Agon shuddered. The idea of falling through the dark into an unknown tomb unnerved him. Vilkami, however, had a peculiar taste for the macabre. He was probably enjoying it.

"Have you found anything interesting?" asked the prince.

"Maybe. I'm not sure."

"Can you get out?"

"I think so."

Agon heard a scrabbling sound, and further sections of the hillside disappeared into the hole. He moved hastily back from the edge.

A head appeared, and Vilkami struggled slowly out of the ground. Trees must once have stood on this hillside, because a tangled mass of ancient roots was providing him with a precarious ladder.

The youth came out covered in dirt from head to toe.

"What's that in your belt?" Agon asked him.

Vilkami brushed himself off. Then he reached down carefully and withdrew a sheathed sword from his belt. "I found it in there. I couldn't really see what it was like." He began to dust it off, and a scabbard richly encrusted with jewels slowly emerged from beneath the clinging detritus of the ages. He slid the sword from the scabbard to reveal a shiny blade without hint of rust or tarnish. The edge was still sharp and true—he tried it on his tunic, and the blade sliced cleanly through the fabric.

A glint came into Agon's eye. The sword was finely crafted—the workmanship was clearly superior. It was exquisite, quite unlike anything he had ever seen. And it fully aroused his insatiable lust.

"What else is down there?" he asked.

Vilkami peered uncertainly into the hole. The idea of going back clearly didn't appeal to him.

"Are you scared to risk your precious life?" Agon asked, a sneer on his lips.

His companion stiffened. "I'm not scared!"

"Climb down, then. I'll hold the sword for you," said Agon.

Vilkami looked very uncertain. After a few moments he reluctantly handed over the sword and climbed back into the hole. He was gone for some time before emerging once again.

"What did you find?"

"It was hard to see in the dark. There wasn't much else down there. Mostly a lot of old bones. And this." In his hand he held a small stone.

Exposed to the sun once more after uncounted years, the tiny object dazzled Agon's eyes, splashes of bright red shining brilliantly out of a gray surface. The stone was thin and flat and almost perfectly round. It was shaped like a miniature version of the low circular loaves that bakers pulled from their ovens every day.

It appeared to be little more than a colorful rock, but there was something mesmerizing about it. The prince wanted it, and he intended to get it.

Vilkami held out his hand for the sword.

"The sword is mine," Agon told him. "You gave it to me."

"Only to hold!" Vilkami retorted indignantly. "While I went back into the hole for you!" Outrage twisted his face.

The prince shrugged. "You didn't say that. You gave it to me, and that's the end of it."

The youth's features contorted as he struggled to master his fury.

Agon watched on thoughtfully. "I'll offer you an exchange," the prince finally said. "The sword for that stone."

Vilkami's face flushed, and he frowned angrily.

Agon smiled to himself. No doubt the young fool thought that since he had found the objects, they belonged to him. He would soon discover otherwise.

After a long pause Vilkami finally nodded. "I agree to the exchange. You can have the stone."

In spite of his words, he seemed reluctant to give it up. He stared hesitantly at the brightly colored object in his hand.

"Well?" demanded the prince impatiently.

Vilkami looked down at the stone once more, then he slowly held out his hand, the stone resting in his open palm. At the same time he stretched out his other hand for the sword.

Agon reached out greedily, his fist closing over the stone. A smug smile twisted his face.

He made no move to honor his end of the bargain.

Vilkami continued to hold out his hand. "Give me the sword," he said fiercely. "You gave your word."

"I changed my mind," Agon said in a bored tone.

"I'll tell my father!"

"'I'll tell my father,'" Agon echoed in a high pitched whine. "I'm so terrified! Ha! As if that old dotard could do anything about it." He snorted scornfully. "The sword is mine anyway. And the stone. Whatever's found here rightly belongs to ME."

He leaned forward, sneering. "Look and learn, little boy. It's time you grew up. Your father will be gone before long, and his title will be yours. You won't have a daddy to run to then.

"I've just done you a princely favor—I've demonstrated a lesson I learned from my father. He taught me that nothing worthwhile in life ever comes as a gift. People always expect something in return. If you want it, then you pay for it, or you take it. The strongest get to take whatever they want. The weak don't matter."

Then his voice hardened. "Don't think this advice is free. It's payment—in full—for anything you've ever done to benefit me. And don't threaten me again, Vilkami. I won't overlook it a second time.

"Oh, and one other thing. As far as you're concerned, I don't have a name. To you I am 'Your Highness'. Don't ever forget it."

With that he spun on his heel and headed in the direction of the royal caravan.

VILKAMI WATCHED HIM GO, blinking back tears of helpless rage. For years he had borne the brunt of Agon's petty cruelty. He had loathed the prince for as long as he could remember, and that seed had slowly been ripening into a passionate hatred.

The future king enjoyed every advantage that came with royal blood—power, prestige, and the divine right to do pretty much anything he pleased. Why had the gods bestowed all this on a person with no more honor than a snake?

He hated everything about Agon. It was surely a punishment from the dark gods to be stranded in this barren desert with him. Every day he asked himself why he was here.

He knew the answer, of course, and he could only grind his teeth in frustration. The king went wherever he pleased, and Vilkami's father—powerful nobleman though he was—followed him like a faithful hound.

And, if he was honest with himself, he was no better. He had always tagged along behind the prince like an obedient puppy.

Vilkami had been born to the nobility, but Agon showed no more consideration to him than he would to a servant. It was time he began learning from his persecutor.

From now on everything would change. "His Highness" might eventually find himself trembling at some of the changes.

The prince had taught him that nothing mattered except power. So Vilkami would learn the ways of power. And he would play by the prince's rules. He would use power ruthlessly, and use it for his own gain.

He would do whatever the prince demanded, but first he would search tirelessly for the way of doing it that would benefit him most.

Vanity was not one of his weaknesses. He had never cared about appearances—he was willing to abase himself and refer to the prince as "Your Highness" if that was what it took. And when Agon eventually became king he was prepared to abase himself even more. When Vilkami came into his own inheritance, he would become Agon's most dependable nobleman.

But he would never forget what had happened here today. Sooner or later an opportunity would arrive for the tables to be turned, and he would pay Agon back in full—for every insult and every humiliation he had endured over the years. His lips twisted in satisfaction as he indulged in vengeful daydreams.

Before long the heat dragged him back to the present.

He pictured again the peculiar stone from the tomb. The prince had defrauded him of it. Royalty or not, the sheer arrogance of Agon's deception infuriated him. He would take it back, and the mysterious sword with it. He had found them, and they belonged to him.

His thoughts were drawn irresistibly back to the stone. Someone important had been laid to rest in that tomb—no ordinary person could ever have owned such a sword. And the other object buried with him had been the stone. He sensed that its unusual appearance was not its only notable characteristic. The stone was significant—he was sure of it. It possessed a strangely alluring quality, and handing it over had been surprisingly difficult.

He wondered if old histories might refer to such an object. He derived endless fascination from poking around in decaying scrolls. The priests of the dark gods loved to hoard ancient documents, and his father had already used his connections to arrange access for him to their main library. He would begin a search there as soon as he returned to Rog.

He couldn't lose himself in the future, though. As he reluctantly dragged his thoughts back to the present, the pain of his humiliation flooded his awareness.

Standing in the heat and the dust, he reached a momentous decision. Taking back what rightly belonged to him would just be the beginning. He vowed to himself that he wouldn't stop until he had found a way to eliminate Agon, however long it took.

Vilkami had no particular desire to become king of Rogand. The title of Lord Drettroth—along with all the wealth, power, and prestige that came with it—had apparently satisfied his forebears well enough, and he fully expected it to satisfy him too.

He wanted revenge.

He would be subtle, and he would be stealthy, but from that day forward he would never rest until he saw the crown pried from Agon's unworthy head.

1

Two weeks after the Battle of Torbury Scarp

King Agon of Rogand paced impatiently, fuming as he waited for his senior agents to arrive. Although the sun had yet to clear the horizon, the first hints of daylight were already visible in the small audience room that adjoined the grand reception hall of his palace in the capital, Rog.

Lorik and Jorvan were the best agents he had. That simply meant that the king placed high expectations on them. It didn't mean that he should be required to wait on their pleasure.

Their appearance did little to improve Agon's mood, even though they came at first light as instructed. He didn't offer them a seat.

"What have you learned about the death of Drettroth?" he demanded. "I expect answers!"

The two men bowed low before daring to speak. "Great king, may you live forever!" began Lorik, the older man.

"Get on with it!" snapped the king.

"Lord Drettroth was poisoned, Your Majesty," Lorik told him.

"Poisoned."

Agon was careful not to show it, but he was shocked at the news. Such a death was surely ironic given that Drettroth had made a particular study of poisons and used them to silence many of his own opponents.

"Who poisoned him?"

"A dispatch rider discovered his lordship's body, Your Majesty," Jorvan replied. "A youth, most likely Lord Drettroth's food taster, was lying dead nearby, also poisoned. His lordship had been run through, apparently with his own sword, although he appeared to have been poisoned first, which would explain why he couldn't defend himself. The dispatch rider found a monk in the same room, in the act of unchaining a prisoner, so he assumed that the monk had killed both Lord Drettroth and his food taster."

"Where is the monk?"

"The dispatch rider killed him, Your Majesty," Jorvan replied.

"Who was the prisoner?"

"An Arvenian youth," said Jorvan. "The monk succeeded in freeing him, and he escaped in the confusion."

Agon scowled in annoyance.

"How did Drettroth allow himself to be poisoned by a monk?" growled the king.

"We believe it was actually the food taster who poisoned Lord Drettroth," said Lorik. "He would have needed to consume the poison himself, which is why he also died. But he managed to free the monk first. And the monk in turn freed the youth before he was killed by the dispatch rider."

"Why did Drettroth imprison the youth?" Agon asked.

"Apparently he had something Lord Drettroth wanted, Your Majesty," said Lorik. "An item his lordship wanted very badly. His lordship expended a prodigious amount of effort to capture the youth and the monk. He sent agents throughout Arvenon searching for them, and also deployed several regiments for the purpose."

Agon's eyebrows furrowed. He knew nothing of this. What had Drettroth been playing at?

"What item did the youth have that Drettroth wanted?"

"The object of his attention seems to have been a small stone, Your Majesty," Lorik replied.

"A stone?" Agon glared at them, shaking his head in contempt. "Do you think I am stupid?"

"Of course not, Your Majesty!" Jorvan replied. He reached for a pile of scrolls with a trembling hand, selected one, and passed it to the king. "We also dismissed it as nothing more than hearsay at first," he said. "Until we read this scroll. We found it among Lord Drettroth's papers."

The scroll was old and appeared brittle. Agon unrolled it carefully and peered down at it. Almost at once his head snapped up again, and he fixed them in a glare. "Do you expect me to read this?"

The agent looked at him blankly.

"It's written in Arvenian!" snapped Agon.

Jorvan stared at him in confusion. "Would Your Majesty care for us to prepare a translation?" he stammered uncertainly.

"I have no need of a translation, you fool!" Agon's eyes narrowed as he stared at them. "You have the audacity to confront me with the language of my bitter enemies, and then you pretend surprise at my reaction?"

Both men stared at him, open mouthed in fear.

He shook his head in disgust. "You'd better pray it's worth my while," he snarled.

Ignoring the men he turned to the scroll and silently began to read. "*Three talismans of great potency are abroad in the world, uncelebrated, unrecognized, and hidden from any certain knowledge. Perhaps I alone know their true history, long forgotten with the passing of many scores of years...*"

At first he scanned the handwriting dismissively. But as he progressed further through the scroll his eyes widened, and his heart began to race. He sped to the end, then started again from the beginning, this time reading slowly and carefully.

Finally he looked up. "Where did Drettroth find this?" he asked.

"We think he might have discovered the scroll here in Rog, Your Majesty," suggested Jorvan, "in the temple library."

"It seems that Lord Drettroth spent many hours there," Lorik added. "The library holds a large number of documents, some of them very ancient. They also have a substantial collection of scrolls written in Arvenian and other languages."

"Who has seen these scrolls?" the king demanded.

"Apart from Your Majesty, no one except us," Lorik replied.

Agon's eyes narrowed. "For your own sakes you'd better keep it that way!" he said. "That applies to this entire investigation."

The men both bowed low.

"You are dismissed," the king told them. "But do not leave the palace. I want you on hand the minute I call!"

The men scurried away.

Agon's memory had begun to stir as he read the scroll. The moment he fully grasped the implications of its words, his excitement had intensified until he was struggling to conceal his agitation from his agents.

The Stone of Authority described in the scroll sounded remarkably like the stone Vilkami had handed over so many years ago. Could that object, long forgotten, truly deliver the powers claimed by the scroll? He felt certain that Drettroth had thought so. From the moment he asked himself that question, nothing mattered to him except finding the missing stone.

The problem was that years had passed since Agon had last seen it. He had been aware from the beginning that Vilkami desperately wanted both the stone and the sword he had found with it. The little brat would have snatched them back the moment an opportunity presented itself. So Agon kept them well hidden. After he returned to Rog, he placed both objects in a secret and very secure hiding place for safe keeping. Then he had forgotten about them. The sword had obvious value, but he had little real interest in either artifact beyond making sure that Vilkami couldn't have them.

It occurred to him now to wonder if Vilkami had somehow contrived to ferret them out in the years since he came into his inheritance as Lord Drettroth. But it couldn't be so. The scroll had described three stones and the powers associated with each of them. It would have been obvious to Agon if Drettroth possessed any such powers.

No, the stone must have remained wherever he had hidden it. The problem was that having disregarded it for so long, he no longer had any clear memory about the location of the hiding place.

AGON STRUGGLED to master his agitation as he waited for Lorik and Jorvan to return to his audience room. He couldn't sit—he was pacing restlessly back and forth like a caged lion.

For days he had searched in vain for the stone. He had upended both his current and his previous apartments without finding a trace of it, and his jangled nerves had long since frayed to tatters. Already today he'd demanded the heads of three of his servants. That must surely have brought the total to fifteen this week.

He could not afford to have these two decapitated though. Not yet. They still had information he needed.

He began breathing slowly and deeply in an attempt to calm himself.

When the men finally entered the room he saw that they were visibly trembling. Agon felt his rage welling up inside him as he witnessed their obvious terror. Hadn't he appointed these men because of their reputation for remaining calm in a crisis? He was surrounded by incompetent fools.

Even as he opened his mouth to spew out his fury, his reason somehow asserted itself. He remembered that he still needed these agents.

With a mighty effort he restrained himself. Gritting his teeth, he snapped his mouth shut without saying a word.

They stood there paralyzed, staring at him wide-eyed in mortal dread. Staring back, he realized he needed to greet them—normally if at all possible.

"Welcome," he sputtered. "You are...welcome." He peeled back his lips to reveal his teeth. It probably didn't look much like a smile, but it was the best he could manage.

He waved them to a pair of seats, and they sank into them. The agents still trembled with fear, although they seemed visibly relieved at his unexpected restraint. Agon didn't find it hard to imagine what was being said about him around the palace.

He thrust such trifles from his mind. There were important matters to address.

He began with a question that had been plaguing him over the last few days.

"You told me that Drettroth went to great effort to capture an Arvenian youth, because he believed the youth had one of the stones mentioned in the scroll," said Agon, managing to speak evenly again. "Which stone?"

He knew that Drettroth could not have been on the trail of the Stone of Authority. The nobleman would have been well aware that the stone was already accounted for.

The men continued to stare at him, wide-eyed. Neither of them said a word.

"Well?" he snapped. His irritability was bubbling away just below the surface, and it took a conscious effort to keep it down.

Lorik finally found his voice. "Great king, may you live forever!" he began. "We believe that Lord Drettroth was looking for the stone that the scroll refers to as the Stone of Knowing."

The king's heart beat faster. From the moment he had read the scroll, the Stone of Knowing was the one he lusted after the most. Could it truly have been almost within Drettroth's grasp?

"What makes you think it was that particular stone?" he asked. He kept his tone mild, but danger lurked below the surface. Lorik had dared to raise the king's expectations, and the man would suffer if he'd done so without good reason.

Lorik bowed respectfully before replying. "Our investigations have revealed that almost twenty years ago Lord Drettroth sent a number of his men to capture a woman renowned as a seer. If she had this stone, its powers could have made her appear to be a seer.

We believe that Lord Drettroth might have drawn a similar conclusion."

"And what happened?" the king demanded.

"The men were unsuccessful, Your Majesty," he replied. "The woman eluded them. The trail went cold in Arvenon. It seems that Lord Drettroth's special interest in Arvenon began at that time."

Agon's eyes narrowed. How had the ambitious army commander managed to conceal all this from his king? *What other games were you playing, Drettroth?*

"How did you learn of this seer?" the king asked.

"Lord Drettroth immediately executed all of the men involved. But a few of them deserted rather than return home. We were able to track one of them down. We pried the whole story from him before he died."

Agon grunted in satisfaction. These men were good.

"So this youth somehow acquired the stone. What do we know of him?" he asked.

"One of Lord Drettroth's agents tracked down the youth and the monk in Arvenon, after the invasion. We have interviewed the agent. He discovered the fugitives hiding in a monastery. Lord Drettroth personally went there with two regiments of soldiers. His men demolished the monastery, but the youth and the monk escaped. They were eventually captured some weeks later."

"So this youth—you have his name and description?"

"Yes, Your Majesty. We believe that his name is 'Tomas'. And we have a reasonably complete description of what he looks like."

Agon scowled as he considered these revelations about his army commander. Drettroth had persuaded him that the annexation of Arvenon would multiply the power and the glory of Rogand, and in particular that it would elevate King Agon. The nobleman had brazenly traded on the king's lust for power. Agon was furious to discover that he had been manipulated.

All along Drettroth had been pursuing an agenda of his own—he must have been laughing at Agon behind his hand the entire time.

The king licked his lips, imagining what he would have done to the commander if he had still been alive.

"What efforts have you made to find the youth and retrieve the stone?" Agon asked.

"We have attempted nothing, Your Majesty," Lorik replied innocently. "We've been awaiting your instructions."

The man was almost certainly lying. His face projected calm, but Agon could see the veins in his neck standing out. And those veins were throbbing. It was hardly surprising. How could any normal man resist the lure of such a prize?

"No further response is required on your part," the king replied haughtily. "I will give the matter more thought before deciding on a course of action."

He would select an entirely different set of agents to renew the search for the youth. He would tell them no more than they absolutely needed to know. It wouldn't serve his purposes if they fully understood what they were searching for.

"I want a report, and I want it in writing," the king ordered. "Every detail of your investigations and everything you have learned. I expect it to be completed in two days."

The men bowed, and he dismissed them.

The agents would not include everything in their report, of course. They were far too clever for that. But it made no difference. Agon would personally squeeze every last detail from them.

He would have no further use for Lorik and Jorvan after that. They knew too much. From the time of their first meeting a few days earlier, Agon had arranged for them to come under constant observation. They had been monitored every minute, day and night. He immediately issued instructions for the watch on them to be doubled.

KING AGON SAT on the floor laughing maniacally. The Stone of Authority was his. He had found it at last.

There had been moments when he feared the stone would

remain lost forever—he had never been more ecstatic about being proven wrong.

The problem had arisen because he acquired the stone when he was crown prince. The crown prince occupied a lesser wing of the sprawling castle that was now the royal palace. The moment Agon became king he had relocated to the king's much more luxurious private apartments. His old accommodations were soon forgotten. He hadn't spared a thought for them in years.

That day—and not for the first time—Agon had focused his search on the suite he once occupied as crown prince. The rooms lay silent and empty, neglected by all except the servants who periodically cleaned and dusted against a day when the suite might be needed again.

He had been leaning on the wall of the little balcony, staring out across a small garden. In a corner of the garden stood an ancient tree, one that he had climbed many times in his youth.

A memory came to him of a young Vilkami falling from that tree and breaking his arm. The injured youth had been too scared to tell anyone that his fall was not an accident. Who would have listened if he revealed that his future king had deliberately pushed him out of the tree? Agon chortled out loud as he recalled it. The broken arm had been just one of the indignities Agon visited upon his supposed friend.

Neither Vilkami—nor Lord Drettroth as he later became—ever found an effective way to pay Agon back. But Agon could not deny that the nobleman had come dangerously close to changing that situation. If Drettroth had taken control of the Stone of Knowing, the balance of power would have massively tilted in his favor.

As Agon gazed at the tree, another memory sprang suddenly to mind. A low stone wall stood behind its spreading limbs, and among the stones he had once discovered a hollow cavity. He remembered occasionally hiding small treasures in there.

Agon immediately dismissed every servant from that wing of the palace. Racing outside he hurried to the stone wall and worked feverishly to locate and expose the cavity. When he at last discovered it, he saw to his excitement that a long metal box lay inside it. The memories came rushing back. He had concealed the box within the wall after placing the sword and the small stone inside it.

Impatiently he wrested the rusted container from the cavity.

He was shaking with excitement when he carried the box inside. After taking a deep breath, he forced open the lid.

Within the box lay the ancient sword, just as he had left it. Beneath it, folded into an old piece of cloth, he found the Stone of Authority.

Grasping it in his hand, he threw back his head and began to howl with laughter. His body shook, and the tears ran down his cheeks. He hadn't been so deliriously happy for years. Not since pushing Vilkami out of the tree. The thought set him off again.

Eventually his body became calm, and his laughter turned to gloating. Everything was about to change in Rogand.

From the moment he ascended the throne, he had found himself surrounded by ambitious schemers. The Rogandan nobility was little more than a pit of vipers, awash with poisonous intrigue. Now, after years of wrestling with the nobles and the priests, he dared to hope that he could bypass completely the power plays and the political maneuvering. He bared his teeth with anticipation at the thought.

The scroll had made it very clear what he should expect from the stone. It was time to stop gloating and to try it out.

2

Five months after the Battle of Torbury Scarp

The crowds bumped and jostled together, forced shoulder to shoulder as they attempted to pass through the narrow entrance at the gates of Arnost. The guards stationed on either side of the entryway gazed on with bored indifference as the human tide ebbed and flowed. It was just another market day at the capital of Arvenon.

A weary traveler approached the gates, leading a donkey. His weathered brown cloak was topped by a broad rimmed hat that covered his face, and he plodded forward with head down, looking neither to the left nor to the right.

His animal bore an unusual burden—an old crone, perched in the saddle uncomfortably with bent back and misshapen shoulders. Her face was concealed by the expansive hood that crowned her black cloak.

Having arrived at the gates the wayfarer halted. His hat swung slowly from side to side as he quietly scanned the faces around him, alert to any possibility of danger. Annoyed at the obstruction, the other travelers called out impatiently, pushing and shoving as they attempted to force their way past him and his donkey. He ignored them.

Apparently finding nothing to interest him, and seeing that the guards were about to intervene, the traveler lowered his head once more and shuffled forward, disappearing through the gates with the donkey and its unsightly passenger in tow.

The main thoroughfare was no less crowded inside, but the wayfarer soon abandoned the main road in favor of a broad alley that wound its way steadily into the heart of the city. He soon turned aside to a narrow road that led upward until he stood directly beneath the walls of the castle.

To one side lay a pair of wooden gates. He pushed them open and entered the courtyard that lay beyond, closing the gates behind the donkey. A small stone cottage lay before him, with smoke drifting lazily upward from its chimney.

He came and positioned himself beside the donkey, glancing pensively up at its rider. Then he stood silently, as if deep in thought, making no move to approach the door of the cottage. He had remained there unmoving for some time when the door opened abruptly.

A man emerged, coming to a sudden halt when confronted with the spectacle before him. The newcomer frowned, seemingly more in revulsion than in puzzlement.

"Who are you, and what is your business here?" he asked brusquely.

"Hello, Father," the traveler replied quietly. "It's your son, Thomas."

Axel Stablehand stood in stunned silence, contemplating the extraordinary prospect before him. Then his face hardened, and he frowned. "You've chosen a strange way to return home, Thomas," he said.

Thomas stiffened, and his misshapen companion reached down

quickly and placed a gentle hand on his arm. He glanced up at her, then stood silent for a moment as he composed himself.

"Is my mother at home?" he asked.

"Yes, of course she is."

"Then may we come in?"

His father cast a sharp glance at the dark figure on the donkey before addressing Thomas. "Why should you need permission?" he asked roughly. "It's your home."

Thomas might have responded in kind, but the gentle pressure on his arm persuaded him otherwise.

The older man turned and opened the door again. He stared at them over his shoulder for a moment before disappearing inside, leaving the door ajar behind him.

Thomas watched him go. He shook his head once. His father was mistaken—this wasn't his home. Not anymore.

After removing his hat, Thomas helped his companion down from the donkey and led her into the cottage.

The first thing he saw upon entering the main room was the startled face of his mother. She took one look at him, then she burst into tears. Rushing to him, she enfolded him in her embrace, sobbing loudly. After a few moments she composed herself and stepped away, holding him at arm's length and studying his face. Finally she smiled in contentment.

Apparently allowing herself to register at last that he wasn't alone, she turned uncertainly toward his companion.

"Mother and Father, this is Elena, the girl I am going to marry."

His father's expression plainly showed his shock and distaste. His mother swallowed, then smiled resolutely. "You are very welcome, my dear!" she said brightly.

Turning to her husband, she saw the look on his face. She frowned. "Could you please fetch us some fresh water from the well, Axel?" she asked firmly.

Thomas suppressed a smile as his father obediently headed outside. His mother's question might have sounded like a request, but both he and his father knew better.

He turned to Elena. "It's safe here," he assured her.

She nodded, then quickly proceeded to shed her cloak and the bundles hidden beneath it.

Finally she stepped away from the pile at her feet. She looked anxiously toward Thomas. Then she faced his mother, her beautiful face flushed and uncertain. "Thank you very much for your welcome," she said softly. "I am very privileged to be able to meet Thomas's parents at last."

The incredible transformation in her appearance must have been no less shocking to Thomas's mother than it had been to him when he first witnessed it. But his mother put him to shame, recovering herself almost immediately.

"Well, now! What a blessed sight you are for these old eyes of mine!" she said, shaking her head in astonishment. "I don't doubt there's quite a tale to be told here."

She reached out and took Elena's hands. "I'm Marya," she said, beaming across at her, "and you truly are very welcome in our home, Elena. You must be tired after your journey. And hungry, too, I don't doubt."

She released Elena's hands and began bustling about, setting up stools at the table, gathering bowls, and stoking the fire.

Thomas turned to Elena and grinned. "She likes you," he whispered.

Elena returned a nervous smile.

The door opened, and Axel reappeared. When he spotted Elena he almost dropped the pail of water. His glance flitted around the room, as if he was trying to locate the old crone. Finally, seeing the robe lying on the floor, he turned to Elena with face flushed.

Thomas decided not to prolong the agony. "Father, this is Elena. Without her disguise."

The stable master reddened with embarrassment, and Thomas realized with a start that he couldn't remember ever witnessing such a reaction from his father.

Thomas addressed his companion. "Elena, this is my father, Axel. He is stable master to the king."

She looked up at Thomas's father, her face pale but determined. "It is a great honor to meet you," she said earnestly.

Axel flushed briefly again. He had not earned the courtesy she was showing him, and it was obvious to Thomas that he was well aware of it.

"I...I am...pleased to meet you, too," he finally blurted.

Thomas suppressed a snort when he saw the look on his mother's face. His father would undoubtedly gain the benefit of a few of her insights when they were next alone.

"Please! Sit down, all of you!" Marya said cheerily, clearly unwilling to tolerate her husband's blundering for another moment.

"Tell us where you've been Thomas, and what you've been doing! Will visited us some weeks ago, and he told us that you were safe and that we should be very proud of you. He wouldn't say any more than that. I've missed you so much, and every day I've been waiting to hear from you!"

"I'm sorry I couldn't come sooner," said Thomas. He had long anticipated this interaction, but had never been able to settle on exactly what to say to account for his prolonged absence.

He hadn't reckoned on Elena.

"Please don't be angry with Thomas," she exclaimed. "It's me who's to blame!" She spoke with such disarming sincerity that his mother's face immediately lit up with an understanding smile. Even his father's frown softened slightly.

"Thomas only delayed coming to Arnost so that I could come with him, too. We waited until spring arrived so it would be easier to travel. I've been so much looking forward to meeting Thomas's parents! My father and I have a great deal to thank you for. Thomas has been such a help to us!"

His mother flushed with pleasure.

"We've come to rely on him very much," she continued. "He saved my father's life when he was dangerously ill with fever. Did you know he had skills as a healer?"

His mother shook her head in surprise.

"And when the Rogandans came, he led them away to protect us. He was so brave!"

"Well, just look at you now!" said Marya with a smile. "What young man wouldn't want to protect you?"

"Oh no, you don't understand!" she exclaimed. "He thought I was an ugly hunchback. Like when you first saw me."

Marya raised her eyebrows in astonishment.

"Thomas led them away, and he was injured and captured as a result! He was taken to their leader's fortress. They would have killed him if he hadn't managed to escape."

Thomas watched her, wide-eyed. Who could resist her? Certainly not his mother—she was hanging on Elena's every word.

"And he persuaded you to marry him?" Axel's question probably sounded more abrupt than he intended.

A delicate blush came to her lovely cheeks. "I don't think he needed to do a good deal of persuading," she said, lowering her eyelids bashfully.

She was incredible. Thomas marveled anew at the fact that she had promised herself to him.

"So we're going to have a wedding," said Marya enthusiastically. "That's just wonderful! I understand that you have connections now, Thomas. Perhaps you'll be allowed to hold the ceremony in the cathedral!"

"The cathedral?" he replied in alarm. "Please, Mother! I'm a commoner. You know as well as I do that commoners don't marry in the cathedral. Our wedding will be small and very quiet. If a church isn't available, we can marry here at home. All we need is a priest to bless the marriage."

"Nonsense," said Marya. "We'll find a church for you, don't you worry."

Axel faced Elena. "You mentioned your father," he said evenly, apparently managing at last to regain some composure. "Did he travel with you to Arnost?"

"Yes," Elena replied. "We parted just before we entered the city.

He didn't want to intrude on Thomas's homecoming. He is hoping to meet you, though."

"We would very much like to meet him, too," Marya assured her. "And what about your mother?"

"She died when I was quite young. My father raised me on his own."

"I'm so sorry to hear that, dear," said Thomas's mother. She reached out and took Elena's hand. "I've never had a daughter, and you don't have a mother. Perhaps we can be friends."

"I would like that very much."

Marya positively glowed. There was no need at all to guess about her opinion of Elena.

Thomas glanced across at his father, and saw that a distant look had come to his eye.

"You might be wondering where Simon is, Thomas," he said. "I don't know myself. He just vanished during the siege. I've heard nothing of him since. I don't suppose you've learned anything of him in your travels?"

Thomas had been anticipating this conversation too, and once again he hadn't decided what to say. This time Elena couldn't help him out.

Thomas knew he had to tell his father something—Axel Stablehand might have been the person who cared most about the youth. And Thomas was determined to acknowledge Simon's courage.

"I actually met Simon—when I was imprisoned at the fortress of the Rogandan leader. I escaped largely thanks to him. Simon behaved very heroically during his time there. I'm sorry to have to tell you, though, that he did not survive."

Axel frowned in disbelief. "He's dead? How did he come to be at the Rogandan fortress?"

Thomas paused, determined to ignore his father's tone. What would his father say if he told him that Simon had left Arnost solely to betray Thomas to the Rogandan leader? How could he explain that Simon had been pressed into that leader's service as his food taster, and that he had lost his own life when he fatally poisoned his master? It would raise too many questions—awkward questions that Thomas was either unwilling or unable to answer.

"The Rogandans captured him outside the city walls. As to how and why he came to be there, those are questions that only he could properly answer."

His father stared at him. "You said he was a hero."

"He was. It was through his efforts that the Rogandan leader was killed. Unfortunately Simon also died as a result."

"Who else knows this?"

"Will Prentis knows. I don't know if he has told the king."

Axel looked at Thomas with narrowed eyes. But he said no more and asked no further questions.

Thomas could not help wondering what he was thinking. But he had never used the Stone of Knowing to spy on his father's thoughts, and he didn't plan to start now.

A NEW DAWN broke over Arnost, sending the sun's rays peeping into the house containing Axel and Marya and their two guests. Marya had set up blankets for her son in the main living area to allow Elena to sleep in his old room.

Thomas had slept badly.

His parents' house was pleasant and familiar, but it held too many mixed memories for him. He missed the rough comforts of the cabin in the woods.

When the four of them were sitting around the little table breaking their fast with newly baked bread and fresh milk, Thomas turned to his father. "Could you please let Will know that we are here?"

"I'll get one of the stable boys to pass on a message," Axel returned gruffly.

Thomas responded with immediate alarm. "Please don't do that! I don't want anyone else to know we're here."

"Why not?" Axel demanded.

Thomas groaned inwardly. He had left Arnost out of fear that his secret would be exposed. The last thing he wanted now was to advertise his return. He couldn't say that, though.

If he refused to answer his father's question it would lead him onto a familiar path, one that wouldn't go anywhere good.

"I'm sure Thomas is thinking of me," Elena interjected, blushing faintly. "He knows I'm dreadfully shy."

His father subsided. "Don't worry," he said. "I'll tell Will myself."

"Thank you so much!" she replied with evident relief.

Thomas had a far greater need for concealment than Elena did, but once again she'd come to his rescue.

The look on her face had clearly softened Axel. Her shyness was charming rather than awkward—it only made her more endearing.

The contrast between Axel's reaction to Elena and his reaction to his own son could not have been more striking. His father plainly saw no particular reason for secrecy when Thomas requested it. Nevertheless, he'd readily agreed to it for Elena's sake.

Thomas had come here to introduce Elena to his parents, and as expected she'd made a good impression on both of them. But he'd also hoped to make a new beginning with his father. That wasn't proving at all straightforward.

Axel sought out Will and delivered the message. Will responded immediately with the proposal that Thomas and Elena meet him later that afternoon in the castle. He suggested the familiar small tower room that Will, Rufe, and Thomas had used as a hideaway in the days before the Rogandan invasion.

At the appointed time Thomas set off with Elena to find the upper room in the tower. They entered the castle through a small postern door and stayed away from heavily trafficked passageways. Both of them wore cloaks and kept their faces concealed.

Will and Rufe were waiting for them when they arrived.

"Thomas! Elena! It's good to see you both again," said Will, a broad smile creasing his scarred face. Rufe, too, greeted them with a warmth and a gentleness that belied his intimidating stature.

Thomas was more delighted than he could express to see his friends again.

"We've heard rumors about you, Will," he said with a smile. "I hear you're an important person now. Well, even more important than you were before, if that's possible."

Will dismissed the comment with a wave of his hand. "To my old friends I'll always just be Will," he said, "whatever happens."

"I hear the two of you are planning a wedding," Rufe said to Thomas and Elena with a grin. "Will you hold it here in Arnost? We'd love to attend if we're invited."

"We would be honored to have you!" Thomas assured him.

Elena said least of all in the energetic conversation that followed, but Thomas noticed her looking on with a contented smile.

After a while Will interrupted them. "There's someone who would like to meet you both," he said.

"Who?" asked Thomas curiously.

"You'll find out very soon. We're expecting her at any moment," Will replied with a grin.

"Her?" asked Thomas, raising an eyebrow. "Is there a lady in your life now, Will?"

The question drew a loud guffaw from both Will and Rufe. "No!" they replied.

As if on cue, a youthful face appeared in the doorway. Seeing Will and Rufe, a smile covered her face as the owner stepped into the room.

"Your Majesty," said Will and Rufe in unison, bowing deeply.

"Your Majesty," echoed Elena, performing a more than serviceable curtsy.

Thomas realized he was standing upright, staring at her with his jaws wide. He snapped his mouth shut and bent low.

"Your Majesty, I would like to present Elena and Thomas," said Will smoothly. "Elena and Thomas, you have the honor of finding yourselves in the presence of Queen Essanda."

Thomas had seen the queen before, but this was his first opportunity to observe her up close. She was indeed a girl. But the merry eyes twinkling out at them seemed somehow older, as if she had witnessed things that aged her prematurely. Knowing a little of her role in the Battle of Torbury Scarp, Thomas was not surprised.

The queen turned to Thomas. "I'm told you were present when Lord Drettroth was brought down," she said admiringly.

"Yes, Your Majesty. I can't take any credit for it, though."

She smiled. "I've heard you were very brave."

Thomas didn't know what to say.

Seeing his discomfort, she turned to Elena. The youthful queen gazed at her silently for a long moment. "I know many elegant young ladies," she said. "But you seem somehow different."

Elena blushed deeply.

A shy smile covered the queen's face. "Would you be willing to spend some time in my company?"

She seemed surprisingly vulnerable as she asked the question, and Thomas had to remind himself that she was scarcely older than a child. Observing the way she conducted herself, even putting to one side her remarkable reputation, it was easy to forget her real age and think of her as a mature young woman.

Elena must have sensed her hesitation, too, because her own shyness quickly gave way to her instinctive kindness. "It would be a great privilege, Your Majesty," she said, extending a warm smile of her own in return.

The queen took her arm, and they disappeared down the tower steps together, the queen already beginning to whisper conspiratorially as if Elena was an old friend.

Queen Essanda led Elena to a small room in her private apartments that featured two windows overlooking a distant forest. The room was illuminated cheerfully by the afternoon sun, and they sat down together in two well worn but comfortable chairs. The young queen chattered away cheerfully, and Elena soon found herself relaxing in her presence. She immediately saw that her hostess wanted to be treated as a normal person, not as a lofty monarch needing to maintain an appropriate distance.

While walking to the queen's private apartments, Elena had once again concealed her face beneath the hood of her cloak. She removed the cloak only when they were out of sight indoors.

"Why do you hide your face in public, Elena?" the queen asked her curiously. "I'm surrounded by young women who love to parade themselves, and none of them are half as beautiful as you."

It was a frank question, but Elena could see that the queen had no desire to make her uncomfortable. She simply seemed puzzled.

"I'm very shy, Your Majesty. My father and I have lived alone in the woods for many years, and I'm not accustomed to being out among people. Most of my life has been very sheltered."

The queen sighed. "I will never look like you," she said wistfully. "I know my husband cares about me very much, but I sometimes wonder if he'll find me attractive when I'm fully grown."

"I don't think you need to worry, Your Majesty," Elena said with a ready smile. "You have lovely features! Besides, attraction isn't just about appearance. Thomas fell in love with me when he thought I was ugly."

"How could he possibly think you were ugly?"

"I wore a disguise, and he'd never seen me without it. My face was always covered, and I looked like I was deformed."

The queen didn't try to hide her astonishment. "But why?"

"When I was growing up, people thought I was a witch."

"Because you had a beautiful face?"

Elena could only shrug.

The queen sighed. "Some people have said nasty things about me because I went to the battle at Torbury Scarp."

"But Your Majesty!" said Elena, completely astonished. "Thomas told me the battle would have been lost without you!"

It was the queen's turn to shrug. "People don't seem to like it if you're different. If it made you worse than others, I could understand it. But they seem just as unhappy if you're different in a good way."

Elena shook her head. "I'm not sure I understand people very well," she said. "Apart from my father anyway. And I think I'm starting to get to know Thomas." She felt herself blushing faintly.

Queen Essanda smiled. "Learning comes from living. Or so my father has always said." Then her face took on an earnest look. "I've been told you probably won't stay in Arnost for long."

Elena nodded a confirmation.

"I would like to see more of you while you're here," said the queen. She hesitated for a moment, then she seemed to come to a decision. "I have some questions I'd like to ask you. There are things I need to talk about with...with a woman. Someone who isn't one of my maids." She spread her arms helplessly. "I don't have a mother to talk to."

"I'm not sure I'll be able to answer your questions," Elena replied awkwardly. "I've grown up without a mother myself." Then she brightened. "Thomas's mother would understand—she's already given me some helpful advice. I could ask her." Seeing the hesitation on the young queen's face, she hastily added, "Without mentioning you, of course!"

The queen nodded. After a pause she said, "You don't have to meet with me of course. Only if you'd like to."

"It would be an honor to spend time with you, Your Majesty," Elena replied. Then she added self-consciously, "And I would enjoy it, too."

Queen Essanda released a breath and smiled. "It's settled, then," she said. "I often have official duties to perform, but I will send you a message."

The queen provided directions to the tower room, and Elena hurried back with her face hidden. She felt considerable relief when she found herself once more in the presence of Thomas and Will and Rufe.

Thomas smiled at her and raised his eyebrows questioningly. She smiled back and gave him a look that said, "All is well. I'll tell you everything that happened later."

THE DAYS PASSED QUICKLY. The queen was true to her word and sent often for Elena. As they became more relaxed in each other's presence they spoke of personal things as well as everyday matters, and the two of them became firm friends.

If Elena could have known, her friendship provided a refreshing change for the queen. At her young age Queen Essanda had already found herself overwhelmed with the subtle and less than subtle maneuvering for power and position that was a constant feature of court life. Elena expected nothing from the queen, and so was able to satisfy that most basic of human needs—the need for a soul mate, a trustworthy friend who saw her as a person, not as a potential rung on the ladder of power and influence.

THE DAY after Thomas and Elena arrived in Arnost, they brought Rubin to meet Thomas's parents. Thomas felt anxious about the meeting, but the outcome exceeded his expectations. Rubin was as even-tempered by nature as Axel was abrupt, but both men were skillful and practical in their own way and they found plenty of common ground.

Rubin was soon spending most days with Axel in the stables. His confidence around horses increased in leaps and bounds. And Axel became noticeably less terse than usual.

3

After several months living in the forest with Rubin, Elena, and Thomas, Haldek had no interest in remaining there alone when his companions set out to visit Thomas's parents. He was devoted to Elena, and the idea of her leaving the safety of her isolated refuge alarmed him considerably. Reluctant though he was to travel openly in Arvenon so soon after the end of the war with Rogand, he immediately decided to join the little party. There was also talk of a wedding, and he wasn't willing to miss that under any circumstances.

As far as Haldek was concerned, he was going as Elena's protector. He liked to describe himself as her uncle, but he could scarcely have cared about her more if she were his own daughter.

When he learned that their destination was Arnost, he was dismayed. He had no expectation that any Rogandan would receive a welcome there. He had last seen the city as a soldier in the army besieging it. None of the residents of Arnost could possibly know that, of course. But he knew it.

When they eventually arrived in Arnost, Haldek was pleased to be there for one reason only—he hoped to see Will again. When the two men had last met, Haldek had been facing a future that seemed bleak indeed. Now he could never remember feeling so contented.

Will had been entirely responsible for the change. Haldek was plodding back to Rogand on foot with a band of other demoralized Rogandan soldiers when he encountered the Arvenian army commander. After the decisive defeat of the Rogandan army at the Battle of Torbury Scarp, Haldek was anxious to leave Arvenon as quietly and unobtrusively as possible. He had been tired, miserable, and hungry when Will's men flushed him out.

Will had been riding in search of Elena and Rubin, accompanied by a group of his soldiers and Thomas. He singled Haldek out and separated him from his companions, attaching him instead to his own party. Haldek had no idea why. But he was forever grateful.

THE FORMER ROGANDAN soldier didn't know it, but Will was acting purely out of gratitude.

He did not recognize the commander as someone he had ever met before, and Will did nothing to enlighten him. But he recognized Haldek immediately. The Rogandan had twice assisted him at crucial moments—once at Lord Drettroth's wooden fortress in the wilderness, and once when Will appeared in the Rogandan army camp outside Arnost in the guise of a priest.

Will later encouraged Rubin, Elena, and Thomas to allow Haldek to join them in their forest refuge near the town of Tallesford. They had done so willingly and quickly came to appreciate him as a genial and capable companion.

RUBIN AND HALDEK had entered Arnost the same day as Thomas and Elena, and Rubin quickly found a cheap room in a small inn to share with Haldek. The following day Thomas took Rubin to meet his parents. Haldek did not join them.

Haldek was grateful for the opportunity to hide himself away. In the secluded cabin in the forest there was no reason for his Rogandan heritage to cause a problem. Openly wandering around in the capital of Arvenon was another matter entirely. His Arvenian language skills had been improving steadily, but he spoke with a thick accent that he knew would betray him as a foreigner. Arvenian merchants traveled widely in Rogand before the recent war, and there would undoubtedly be more than a few who would recognize his accent. His features were distinctively Rogandan, too.

Haldek was determined to limit his forays beyond the four walls of the inn where he was staying with Rubin. But he still needed somewhere to eat and to enjoy an ale. The inn's public serving room proved ideal. The food was barely passable, and the ale was watered down, but the lighting was dim and neither the staff nor other customers appeared to be overly curious.

A couple of days after they arrived, Haldek rose early and headed downstairs alone to break his fast. Few other customers were in the public room at that time of the day, but his eyes were drawn to a couple of men dressed as merchants sitting in a shadowy corner of the room, well away from the bar and the entrance to the inn. There was a furtiveness about them that roused his interest—their demeanor suggested they had something to hide. He chose a table that was near them without being too close. Having ordered some food, he pulled his hooded cloak about him and leaned back in his chair.

Snatches of conversation from the men made him instantly alert. They were speaking Rogandan. Unable to hear them clearly, he strained his ears to catch anything he possibly could of their conversation. He heard the words "Castel", "Varas", and "Agon", and he thought he also heard "murder".

He leaned a little closer, and in doing so accidentally knocked against another chair, causing it to scrape loudly on the flagstone floor. The men looked up abruptly and peered at Haldek for a moment. After exchanging a sharp glance, they rose to their feet and quickly left the inn.

Haldek restrained his immediate urge to get up and follow them. For all he knew they would be waiting outside the inn watching to see if anyone followed them. Hasty action might put him in danger, and drawing attention to himself in a strange city was the last thing he wanted to do.

Haldek hastened back upstairs to his room, where he found Rubin still resting.

"I am hearing something," he said, the words tumbling out roughly as he struggled to speak quickly in his accented Arvenian. "We must see Will at once. It cannot wait!"

Rubin stared at him in surprise for a moment, then nodded his head and got up. They were downstairs and outside in a couple of minutes, but it wasn't quick enough for Haldek. As they headed for the castle, he glanced around him for any sign of the men. But he acknowledged to himself that he probably wouldn't recognize them in the light of day. Their faces had barely been visible in the inn, and their clothing was little different from that of any merchant.

When they arrived at the castle, Rubin approached one of the guards and asked to see Will Prentis. The guard looked them up and down disdainfully. His gaze lingered suspiciously on Haldek, then he turned to Rubin with a frown.

"Who wants to see him?" he asked skeptically.

"Tell him that Rubin and Haldek need to meet with him."

"The commander is a busy man. Come back tomorrow."

"He will want to see us," Rubin replied firmly. "And he will not be pleased if you delay our meeting." He studied the face of the guard carefully through narrowed eyes as if committing his features to memory.

The guard frowned again, but after a moment's hesitation he turned aside and spoke quietly to one of the other guards before disappearing into the castle.

After a short delay, another soldier appeared with the guard and greeted Rubin and Haldek courteously.

"Please follow me. The commander is busy at the moment, but he will see you as soon as he is available."

Before many minutes had passed, Will did indeed appear, with Rufe beside him. Both of them greeted the two men warmly.

"Rubin! It's good to see you again," said Will. "Are you and Elena both well?"

"We are! I know you must be busy—thank you for seeing us so quickly."

Will gave a friendly nod in response, then he turned to Haldek.

"Uncle!" he said loudly. "It's been far too long since I saw you last!"

"Welcome to Arnost, Haldek!" said Rufe enthusiastically.

Haldek was bemused by the greeting. But he quickly guessed the purpose behind Will's little charade. A number of soldiers were standing within hearing range. They would undoubtedly spread the word that Will's "uncle" was in town.

Haldek had once asked Will how he came to be so fluent in Rogandan. Will had explained that he had been adopted by his uncle as a small child, and raised by him and his Rogandan wife. Will's aunt was responsible for his fluency in Rogandan. Haldek had the impression that the aunt had little else to commend her, but she had certainly done a thorough job as a language teacher. Perhaps she might have made a poor sister for Haldek, but he nevertheless clearly understood the value of being seen as Will's long lost uncle.

Haldek knew that after defeating the Rogandan invaders, Will was held in the highest esteem by all Arvenians, from the king down. The commander was trading on that credibility to transform Haldek's obvious Rogandan heritage from a liability into an asset.

A wave of gratitude flooded over the Rogandan. He didn't understand the reason why Will was being so considerate to him, but it made him more appreciative than ever of the Arvenian commander.

"We have something we need to tell you," Rubin said quietly.

Will nodded to Rufe, and the giant guardsman led them all to a small room that boasted several comfortable chairs. Rufe ushered them in and pointed to a seat. Then he shut the door.

Will looked at them curiously. "What is it I need to hear?" he asked. "It sounded important."

Rubin leaned forward. "Haldek overheard some merchants. They were speaking Rogandan." He indicated to Haldek that he should continue.

"I am only hearing a bit," Haldek said. "But they talk about Castel, Varas, Agon, and murder."

Will raised his eyebrows. He turned to Rufe. "Could you please bring Thomas?" he asked. "You may find him at the stables. I'd like him to hear this conversation as well."

Rufe set off without delay.

Will turned back to Rubin and Haldek. "While Rufe is gone," he said with a smile, "you can catch me up on all your news."

RUFE DID INDEED FIND Thomas in the stables.

Thomas was spending a large part of each day working with his father and Rubin, while Elena helped his mother. The two women were getting along famously. That was no surprise. What was more surprising was that his father had become less abrupt when speaking to Thomas. Perhaps Axel's exposure to Rubin was having an effect.

When Rufe arrived he greeted Axel before turning to Thomas. "Can I tear you away from your work here, Thomas? Will would like you to join him as soon as possible."

Thomas raised an inquiring eyebrow toward his father.

"You go, Thomas," his father said. "I can continue on here."

"What's happening?" Thomas asked Rufe as they hurried back to Will.

"Haldek heard some men talking in Rogandan. Will wants you to be there when Haldek tells us what happened."

Thomas thought he understood. Will probably wanted him to use the stone to ensure that no details were lost. While they were walking he unobtrusively retrieved the stone from his pouch.

When they arrived Will greeted them with a smile.

"What is he good for?" Haldek asked, jerking a thumb at Thomas. "He speaks terrible Rogandan." He winked at Thomas as he said it.

Will laughed. "Just ignore him if you like. Tell us what happened."

Haldek switched to Rogandan and began describing the men and their conversation as best he could. While he talked, Thomas studied him closely, working hard to limit his focus to the recent incident.

"We will send some men to try to find these merchants," Will said, switching back to Arvenian. "I am grateful to you, Haldek. Your alertness might prove significant."

"I'm heading over to work with Axel in the stables," said Rubin. "Would you like to come with me, Haldek?"

"No, I head back to the inn," Haldek replied.

"On your own?" asked Thomas.

"I am just fine," Haldek insisted.

As Rubin and Haldek left, Will had a few quiet words with Rufe. The guardsman left the room as well, leaving only Thomas and Will.

"Did you learn anything useful?" Will asked.

"Yes. I was able to see their faces, and in more detail than from Haldek's description. I think I would recognize them if I saw them."

"Did you understand any more of what they were saying?"

"No," Thomas replied regretfully. "Haldek wasn't close enough to hear much of their conversation."

"Was he being too cautious? Or are the men worth investigating?"

"I think he was right to be concerned. I don't know what they are doing here, but I suspect these men are much more than simple merchants."

"Thank you, Thomas. Once again you have proved your unique value to the kingdom."

WHILE WILL and Thomas were questioning Haldek, three men sat huddled together in a dark corner of a quiet tavern in Arnost. They were sipping ale from large mugs. One of them was a thickset man with a scar across his chin. He sat opposite the other two men, one with a thin angular face and another with a crooked nose. To any casual observer they would have appeared to be a group of friends enjoying a well earned break after a hard day's work. Anyone sitting close enough to overhear their conversation, though, would not have understood a word unless they happened to be conversant in Rogandan.

The thin faced man was talking. "The Rogandan went to the castle with another man," he said. "I followed them. When they arrived they asked to see Will Prentis." He spat on the rough stone floor as he voiced the name.

The thickset man frowned. "Who is this Rogandan? What have you been able to find out about him?"

Bent Nose shrugged. "We know nothing about him. I overheard some of the guards talking, and supposedly Will Prentis has a Rogandan uncle visiting him." He snorted dismissively. "I don't believe the story for a minute. He's clearly a traitor."

"Interrogate him. No need to be gentle. Find out what he's doing here and what he's up to."

Thin Face smiled—an ugly smile with no trace of humor in it.

Gulping down the last of their ale, the three men pushed themselves to their feet and left the tavern. Once on the street they pulled their hoods down low over their faces and slipped away in different directions.

HALDEK LEFT the castle and headed back into the city. He kept his head down, careful to mind his own business. He didn't want trouble.

Sensing the underlying tension in his body as he walked, he consciously worked at calming himself. His edginess wasn't just because he was a foreigner in a strange city. He had never found it easy to relax around crowds and noise. In recent months he had come to realize that the peacefulness and seclusion of the forest was the only setting he could truly call home.

He had never lost his sense of wonder at the sights and the sounds of a city, though. Urchins dashed in and out of alleyways, street sellers loudly hawked their wares, and ordinary people called greetings to each other as they went about their business. Occasionally a lord or a lady passed by in a carriage, dressed in their finery. The garments of the nobility splashed reds, blues, and yellows onto a scene dominated by the brown wood and whitewashed walls of the buildings and the dull fabrics and hardwearing leather of the commoners' clothing. Arnost might be a foreign city, but it had much in common with any large city in his native land.

As he approached the inn, the road narrowed, and the houses on either side drew closer together. With the prospect of hot food and a mug of ale occupying his attention, he paid no mind to his surroundings.

Suddenly he was grabbed from behind and pulled into an alley. He registered a brief glimpse of two men before a blow to the head sent him staggering.

"What do we have here?" said a harsh voice. "A traitor, up at the castle making common cause with these vermin. Likely a deserter, too. We know how to deal with scum like you!"

Another blow to the head almost caused him to black out. Then pain dragged him back to awareness as punches began to rain on his body.

Haldek reacted instinctively, aiming a vicious kick at the shins of one of his attackers. The man cried out in annoyance and drew back.

Haldek used the respite to land blows of his own on the other attacker. Gathering all his strength, he aimed a knockout punch at the second man's head. His target swung away at the last moment, and his blow went wide. With Haldek's arm fully extended, the attacker leaned in swiftly and punched him hard in the midriff. Completely winded, Haldek doubled over, gasping for air. Something heavy hit him on the head, and everything went dark.

HALDEK WOKE to find himself in unfamiliar surroundings. Colorful paintings of cherubs gazed down at him from an ornate ceiling.

"Where am I?" he asked the cherubs. His head was pounding, and he ached all over.

Rufe's face appeared above him. "It's good to see you awake again, Haldek. You've been beaten up pretty badly."

Haldek tried to sit up and almost passed out with the pain. He lay back down again.

"Rest!" ordered a voice that seemed to belong to Will. The commander's face appeared over him as well.

"Do you know who the men were?" Rufe asked.

Haldek shook his head, wincing as the pounding in his skull increased in intensity.

"How you find me?" he asked weakly.

"I asked Rufe to keep an eye on you," said Will.

"And a good thing he did," Rufe added. "They probably would have killed you if I hadn't disturbed them."

"You catch them?" asked Haldek, unable to stifle the groan that escaped with his question.

"Unfortunately not," Rufe replied. "They took off fairly quickly. Do you know who they were? Were they the men you overheard in the inn? Or were they local robbers who didn't like the look of you?"

Haldek closed his eyes and drew in a slow breath. Then he opened his eyes again. "They are Rogandan."

"Are you sure?" asked Will.

"Yes. No doubts about it. They speak to me."

Haldek slowly repeated what they had said.

"Were they the men from the inn?"

"Maybe. I have no chance to see faces."

"From now on you're staying at the castle," said Will. "And you won't be walking around in the city on your own again."

THE THREE STRANGERS had once more retreated to a quiet corner of the tavern.

"We cornered our Rogandan friend. We were interrupted before we got anything out of him," said Thin Face.

"We've been asking plenty of questions, though," said Bent Nose. "He's been seen with a youth. And with a girl who is always cloaked. The youth—and the girl—are staying beside the royal stables."

"There are vague rumors about the youth," Thin Face added. "Someone who sounds a bit like him attended a meeting of the Council of Lords during the siege. The meeting supposedly ended in uproar."

"Something strange is going on," said the thickset man with a scowl. "Have all of them watched closely. Especially the Rogandan and the youth. I want to know everything they do and everywhere they go. Stay well away from them, though. That includes the Rogandan! Pay the local street rats to do the snooping for you. Make sure you stay out of sight!"

Both of them nodded.

"We're going to need more money," said Thin Face. "To pay our informants."

The dull clink of coins could be heard as two bulging bags were pushed up onto the table. Thin Face and Bent Nose each took a bag and hid them away in their cloaks.

A moment later, all three men were gone.

WILL STOOD with King Steffan in an inner chamber in the castle. The room was the king's location of choice for private audiences, and Will had become very familiar with it. He had just finished delivering a full report to the king of everything that Haldek had discovered.

King Steffan frowned. "Do you believe the story of this Rogandan friend of yours? Haldek, isn't it?"

"Yes, Sire. I have no doubt whatsoever about it."

The king raised his eyebrows. "No doubt at all? Well, you usually seem to know what you're talking about, Will, so I'll take your word for it."

A thoughtful look came over his face. “Are these men here for a reason? Or are they just merchants with a bad attitude?”

Will shrugged helplessly. “Without proof I can’t be certain,” he acknowledged. “But I don’t want to assume the best and miss something important. I’d rather assume the worst and be proven wrong.”

The king nodded. “Find some of our soldiers who speak Rogandan, and send them into the marketplace. Make sure they do it quietly. It’s possible they might discover something.”

“Yes, Your Majesty.”

Will bowed and withdrew.

Before two hours had passed, Will had chosen twenty reliable soldiers and sent them off with clear instructions. The men set off in twos and threes and spread out around the city. They paused to browse among the wares in the marketplace, they sat quietly on wooden stools in busy inns and quiet taverns and watched and listened as they sipped their ale. All day and into the night they kept a vigilant eye out for anything unusual. The following day they did the same.

They witnessed noisy merrymaking and drunken brawls, and apprehended several pickpockets.

They discovered no sign at all of the Rogandan merchants.

4

Elena had no mother of her own to help prepare her for her wedding, but Thomas's mother stepped into the gap with eager delight. Having delivered only a son, Marya never expected to share such an experience with a daughter. Now finding herself in precisely that situation, she could barely contain her excitement. She leaped in with unbounded enthusiasm and every ounce of her restless energy.

A small church and a priest were quickly secured for the event, and Marya began planning a special meal at her home to follow. The guest list was small. Thomas and Elena could not invite extended family members—none of their relatives lived anywhere near Arnost. The wedding would be celebrated by the immediate families, a few close neighbors, and some of Thomas's friends from the army. Of those who had traveled with Thomas during the Rogandan invasion, only Will, Rufe, and Nestor were in Arnost. All three of them readily accepted the invitation to attend.

Marya began the food preparation several days in advance, helped by Elena. They chattered away merrily as they worked, and both of them seemed equally excited to be sharing the effort with the other.

Whenever Thomas had the opportunity, he stole a few minutes to watch them at work. It pleased him immensely that Elena and his mother were getting along so well.

Just two days before the big event, he found them sitting together at the kitchen table, taking a welcome break from their preparations. He slipped onto a stool beside them.

"Axel has given me some coins for the wedding feast," Marya was telling Elena excitedly. "Tomorrow we will buy a few treats at the market."

Elena's eyes widened.

"My only regret," his mother continued, "is that we're not able to provide you with a suitably magnificent gown." She shook her head sadly.

"Oh, I don't mind at all," Elena replied contentedly. "I'm very happy with the dress I have." She beamed a smile at Thomas, who smiled back encouragingly. However humble her garments might be, he never doubted he would truthfully be able to proclaim her the most beautiful bride in the world.

His musing was interrupted by a voice at the door of the cottage. "Is the mistress at home?"

"Come in!" called Marya.

An old woman appeared in the doorway. "Beggin' your pardon," she said, "but I have a package for the lady of the house from Her Majesty."

The visitor handed it to the astonished Marya, then left immediately.

Marya laid the package on the table. "I have no idea what this could be," she said, bemused.

Whatever it held, its contents had been wrapped in fine paper. Unable to bring herself to wantonly destroy such delicate and expensive material, Marya carefully began to unwrap it. Then she caught a glimpse of what lay inside, and her hands froze in shock. She looked up at Thomas and Elena, her eyes wide.

Then abruptly she recovered herself. Frowning down at Thomas on his stool, she waved him away impatiently. “Off you go, then! Now! This is women’s business!”

When he didn’t immediately move, she put her hands on her hips and glared fiercely at him. “Out! Be off with you!” she cried, pointing to the door.

He finally got the message, and she wasted no time in bustling him out of the cottage.

Thomas stood outside shaking his head in bewilderment. Then he shrugged. Turning on his heel he headed for the stables, chased all the way by the sound of excited squeals from the kitchen.

On the day of the wedding, Marya ejected her son from the cottage almost from the moment he woke. Thomas hadn’t been entirely abandoned though. Rubin, Haldek, and his father had established themselves in one of the stable buildings, and he joined them there. The men had brought with them everything they needed to dress themselves for the wedding, and Marya had sent ample food supplies with Axel. Before long Will, Rufe, and Nestor arrived as well, bringing with them a small cask of ale.

Every necessary ingredient was on hand for a merry party. The three soldiers were soon entertaining the men with tales from their travels. To Thomas’s dismay, most of the stories were at his expense.

“I remember the time when Brother Vangellis was ill,” said Will. “Thomas was sent off to find feverwort.”

“Yes, and he came back with a poisonous plant,” said Rufe, grinning hugely.

“Our female companion was not at all impressed,” chortled Nestor. “She let him know exactly what she thought about it.”

All three soldiers laughed uproariously.

Will leaned in close to Thomas, a huge grin on his face. Then he whispered in his ear, “Shall I tell them what she said that day when she was riding in front of you?”

Seeing the horrified look on Thomas’s face, he laughed and slapped him on the back.

After a steady flow of embarrassing yarns, Rubin clearly decided that his future son-in-law had been punished enough. "You might not know it, but Thomas used feverwort to save my life," he said seriously.

"I'm not at all surprised," said Will. "The truth is that we could never have managed without Thomas."

Rufe and Nestor agreed wholeheartedly. It clearly took some effort for them to swallow their grins, but they nevertheless accepted the change in tone cheerfully.

"There never was a better horse master for the army," Rufe asserted soberly, every trace of irony extinguished from his tone. "He got Will back into the saddle after his injury at Danford. At the time I couldn't imagine Will ever being able to ride confidently again. Thomas proved me wrong."

The remainder of their time together passed very agreeably for Thomas. His companions succeeded admirably in making him feel valued.

Before long it was time to go. Rubin left them, and the others escorted Thomas to the church. He felt conspicuous and awkward in his new doublet and breeches, and his friends didn't help by grinning at his discomfort.

As the big moment approached Thomas's nerves began to surface, and he broke out in a sweat. Apparently deciding to take pity on him, Will threw an arm around Thomas's shoulder and proceeded in low tones to relate a juicy tale about Rufe. He reported that a determined young woman had singled out the giant guardsman as the man of her dreams, untroubled by his lack of interest in her bountiful charms.

Will provided a hilarious account of Rufe's frantic and often futile attempts to avoid her, succeeding so completely in distracting Thomas that at first the groom failed to notice that wedding guests were filing into the church. Thomas tried hard to put on an appropriately solemn demeanor as he redirected his attention to the guests. All of them were known to him, and when they caught his eye they beamed him smiles of encouragement.

A slight girl that he didn't recognize also slipped into the church, choosing to sit at the back. She glanced briefly in his direction, but her face was covered by a hood, and he wasn't able to make eye contact. She was clearly at pains not to be known.

His brows drew together briefly in puzzlement. He knew very few girls, and none of them were close enough friends to be invited to his wedding. Then with a shock he realized who it must be. A brief glimpse of soldiers outside the church confirmed it. The uninvited guest was no lesser personage than Queen Essanda.

This new discovery might have melted his courage away entirely, but at that moment his bride appeared. A hooded cloak had apparently concealed her wedding finery on her way to the church, but as she entered the porch her father helped her out of it. Then she stepped through the door, her delicate hand resting on her father's arm.

Thomas stood with Will at his side, and he heard a gasp escape from his friend. He understood Will's reaction entirely.

Elena took his breath away. He had expected her to be clad in a simple dress with bold colors, much like every other bride he had ever glimpsed. Instead she wore a delicate gown made from a pale fabric he did not recognize. She was beyond beautiful. This was her day, and she shone with a wondrous radiance.

His family and friends stood to honor the bride. But the groom ceased to be aware of them. As Elena and her father made their stately progress toward the altar, Thomas saw only the face of his bride, illuminated with a joyful smile—a smile intended for him alone.

Dazzled as he was by her beauty, he remembered again what had first attracted him to her. Believing her to be surpassingly ugly, he had been captured by the beauty of her spirit. She was gracious, she was guileless, and she was unfailingly kind.

The most amazing thing about this day was that she had entrusted her heart to his keeping. He could never deserve her, but he would always strive to be worthy of her.

The ceremony passed in a blur. He only knew that he could have drowned in his joy.

Vows were spoken, and the newlyweds received a blessing from the priest. Then the congratulations flowed freely as their friends and family shared in their delight.

Only as they were leaving the church did it occur to Thomas to look for the young queen. There was no sign of her. She had slipped away as unobtrusively as she had entered.

A SMALL CROWD had gathered when the wedding party arrived, cheering the bride heartily the moment they caught sight of her.

One observer in particular had looked on with eager interest. He noted that the Rogandan traitor had finally emerged from the safety of the castle, and that he was appearing in the company of both Will Prentis and Rufe Sarjant. His eyes narrowed when he saw the queen's guards escorting her to the church.

The youthful groom and the stunning young woman at his side would warrant further attention.

The moment the ceremony finished and the church had emptied, he had eased his way through the crowd and stole away. Neither his arrival nor his departure attracted attention. Just as he intended.

MARYA HAD LAID out a tempting feast for the wedding party under a shelter beside the stables. Freshly baked bread rolls, meat dishes featuring fish and fowl, tasty sweetmeats, and even dried fruit from Lestanor adorned the tables. Ale, too, was available in plenty. Everyone was soon eating and drinking heartily.

The well wishers might have been few in number, but they kept Thomas and Elena busy.

Elena was smiling and laughing with Thomas's father when his mother bustled up to him. She enveloped her son in a joyous embrace.

"What do you think of your bride's dress?" she asked him breathlessly.

"It's magnificent!" said Thomas, gazing in admiration at his beautiful wife.

"The dress was a gift," gushed his mother. "From no lesser person than Queen Essanda! I even met her at the wedding! Elena was expecting to wed in a much more simple garment. She's such a humble person, after all, in spite of her looks. But the queen said it was fitting for Elena to be seen in her full beauty on her wedding day. So she personally arranged for a silk gown to be made! Silk! Just look at it! Who could have imagined such a thing?"

Thomas gazed at it, feeling like he was seeing it properly for the first time. He saw a brocaded bodice above an expanse of shining lace, but the fabric and design meant little to him. He did notice the way the garment flowed around her, though, serving to accentuate the shapeliness of her figure.

Even he could see that the dress was elegant without being overstated. The overall effect was magnificent. It was a regal gift.

Thomas could not take his eyes off his bride. Everything about her captivated him, from her graceful movements to her shy laugh. The knowledge that she would be his partner for life filled him with amazement. How had he become the one to receive her love?

With his own joy overflowing, he remembered he needed to spare a thought for other people.

From time to time he had caught a glimpse of his new father-in-law glancing wistfully at Elena. He couldn't help wondering if the sight of Rubin's radiant daughter was bringing to mind visions of his own departed wife.

He headed over to speak with him.

"I was wondering if the wedding has brought back memories for you," he began tentatively, hoping he wasn't being insensitive.

Rubin smiled at him encouragingly. "It has. Happy memories. Elena's mother was beautiful, inside and out, just as her daughter is."

Rubin had become a second father to Thomas in the months he had spent with them. "I hope you know how grateful I am to you," Thomas said. "You've helped and encouraged me more than I can say."

Rubin responded with a smile, reaching out a gentle hand and clapping Thomas on the shoulder.

Elena soon joined them, and a tear came to Rubin's eye as he embraced his daughter. Thomas quietly left the two of them alone together.

Thomas found himself near Haldek, who called out to him with a beaming smile, "Congratulations!"

"Thank you," he replied with a grin.

He wondered if Haldek might be missing their quiet home in the forest.

"Does all this feel strange?" he asked, waving a hand vaguely across the celebrations.

The Rogandan gave him a knowing smile. "You are smarter than you look," he said with a wink. He shrugged. "I am not loving change," he acknowledged. "But it is good anyway. Sometimes. Very soon, you, Elena, Rubin, me—all of us are going to the forest again. Then I am happy."

Thomas attempted a response in Rogandan, and his friend was soon laughing at his stumbling attempts. After a while Will joined them, and Thomas left them to converse freely in Haldek's mother tongue.

Thomas noticed that his father was not currently engaged in conversation. He couldn't help wondering what the stable master was thinking and feeling at that moment. The stone, secure in the pouch at his waist, could have answered the question, but he refused to even consider using it to pry into the thoughts of anyone close to him.

The time had come to talk to his father. He felt awkward and apprehensive, but there were things he needed to say. He approached him with as much confidence as he could muster.

"I know I haven't always been as grateful and appreciative as a son ought to be, and I'm sorry for that," he said. Then sucking in a deep breath, he added, "I love you, Father."

He'd done it. He relaxed, slowly releasing the breath.

Axel was too astonished to reply. He stood there uncomfortably for a moment, then thumped Thomas on the back and turned away to get another ale.

Thomas noticed that Elena had witnessed the interaction. She shot him a knowing smile. He raised his eyebrows and shrugged. He'd tried.

He saw that his mother had also been watching, her hand to her mouth. Elena joined her mother-in-law and placed an arm around her. Marya responded by leaning her head on Elena's shoulder.

Then Rufe and Nestor approached Thomas, and his attention was drawn away.

He eventually began to think the celebrations would never end. But the time finally came for the revelers to send off the bride and the groom. Thomas's parents had offered the newlyweds their cottage for their first night, and Marya had set up a bed for Axel and herself in one of the stable buildings.

Everyone walked them to the door of the cottage. Final good wishes and warm embraces were accompanied by cheeky winks from Will and his friends. Then all of them departed and went their separate ways.

FINALLY ALONE INSIDE THE COTTAGE, Elena looked across at Thomas and began to giggle. Taken aback, he felt a deep blush rising to his face. What could possibly be prompting such a reaction?

The giggles died on her lips when she saw his confusion. Taking his hands, she gazed up at him earnestly. "Please pay no mind to me, Thomas," she said. "I think I must be nervous."

Thomas could certainly relate to that.

Rubin had offered Thomas some tips in the lead up to his wedding. He had also received a different kind of preparation for marriage during his time in the wilderness with Brother Vangellis.

Although the monk had been single all his life, he had seen the fruit—both sweet and bitter—of many marriages over the years, and in response to Thomas's curiosity he had freely shared many valuable insights with his young friend.

Thomas later discovered that his mother, never one to be troubled by shyness, had also held a number of frank conversations with her future daughter-in-law.

As a result, both of them had some inkling of what might await them on the journey of life stretching out before them. They were also prepared, at least in part, for the delicate dance that was their first night together.

In spite of all the words of preparation and encouragement, though, Thomas found himself standing red faced and awkward before his bride. Elena decided to help. With a self-conscious smile, she bent low over the candle and snuffed it out. Then she reached out and drew him to herself.

When finally they settled themselves side by side, wide-eyed and breathless, Thomas could only wonder if greater happiness was even possible.

At that moment Thomas might have been tempted to think that he was now a man in every way that mattered. But he knew that a lifetime of responsibilities came with the steps he had taken.

Young as he was, he had boldly reached for the mantle of manhood. Time alone would reveal if he proved worthy of it.

5

One month after the Battle of Torbury Scarp

King Agon gave his horse its head, reveling in the sensation of the sun on his face and the wind in his hair. The nobleman at his side was hard pressed to keep up.

Lord Krasmir, one of Rogand's most wealthy and powerful barons, had come to the palace in response to the king's summons. It was possible that the baron had no desire to spend the afternoon galloping across the extensive grounds surrounding the royal palace. The king neither knew nor cared. Over the preceding weeks Agon had watched on in growing excitement as the stone brought about complete turnarounds in the attitudes of a number of lesser men. The time had come to test it on an unusually difficult subject.

King Agon gradually slowed his horse to a walk and pulled in closer to his riding companion. The man was heavy set and roughly clad. Agon looked at him in disgust—the nobleman dressed himself little better than a hairy animal, for all his wealth. In poor light Krasmir could have been mistaken for a bear.

Never before had Agon chosen to spend an afternoon with Krasmir, not least because the man had a reputation as a callous beast. The king had no cause for apprehension, though—not with a squadron of soldiers following closely behind the two men. The captain of the royal guard left nothing to chance.

Agon had something very specific to say to Krasmir.

"I've decided to levy a new tax on the western barons, Lord Krasmir," said Agon casually. "I wanted you to be the first to know about it."

The nobleman glowered at him through bushy brows.

"You can thank the late Lord Drettroth for this initiative," Agon told him darkly. "He was the one who emptied the royal coffers. All that effort and expense to support his little adventure in Arvenon, and I have nothing whatever to show for it!" He raised an empty hand to the heavens.

"What is the nature of this tax?...Your Majesty," Krasmir asked. He managed to make his words sound more like a snarl than a question, and his addition of the royal title was belated enough to be pointed.

"Think of it as an 'Excess Assets' tax," the king replied evenly. "I'm glad to tell you that only those who possess enormous resources will be required to participate. Barons with lesser means will need to wait for another opportunity."

Krasmir's frown deepened. "What rate of tax are you proposing?"

Agon smiled genially. "Just twenty percent of income. In addition to existing taxes, of course."

Krasmir was too stunned to reply.

"And only for the next five years," the king added.

Agon watched with malevolent satisfaction as a storm began brewing on the baron's face. He knew what the baron would be thinking. Drettroth's armies had tramped through Krasmir's lands on their way to invade Arvenon. As they passed, the soldiers had heedlessly stripped the fields of cattle and sheep, and much else besides. After they were defeated, the surviving rabble had slunk back the same way, desperate and hungry. They'd taken whatever they could without giving it a moment's thought.

Krasmir had suffered more than most. And that was before taking his manpower losses into consideration. Many of his able-bodied men had been forcibly enlisted in the army; more than half of them had not returned. Slapping the new tax on Krasmir was entirely unreasonable—deliciously so.

The nobleman finally found his voice. "The Great Council will have something to say about this!" he snarled.

Agon smiled to himself. The baron's response was predictable. Rogand's council of lords could not actually override a royal decree, although only kings who were supremely powerful—or completely stupid—ignored the council entirely.

"The Great Council has already endorsed the tax wholeheartedly," Agon returned, affecting a bored tone. "Regrettably you were absent during the session. I am told you were unavoidably detained."

Krasmir preferred to pull political strings in private, so he rarely bothered to attend council meetings. That meant he had no one to blame but himself.

The nobleman pulled savagely on his reins, prompting his horse to rear with a high pitched scream. Agon's mount backed away in alarm.

Fearing a confrontation, members of the royal guard thundered up with swords drawn.

Agon waved a hand lazily to indicate all was well. "Lord Krasmir's horse seems to have been startled by a bee," he ventured.

He nodded to Krasmir with an indulgent smile. "I wish you a pleasant afternoon, My Lord."

With that, he turned his horse toward the palace and galloped away.

THE FOLLOWING morning Agon sat in council with his advisors. None of the king's advisors were bold enough or stupid enough to actually offer him advice, but Agon found their pearls of wisdom quite entertaining at times.

"Lord Krasmir is reportedly furious, Your Majesty," one of the advisors suggested. "He is even said to be threatening revolt."

Agon smiled condescendingly. In spite of Krasmir's unpredictability, the nobleman offered no real surprises to the king. Krasmir was a volatile brute—a man after his own heart.

"Would it be wise to approach him with caution?" the advisor concluded. "Even animals can be dangerous when cornered."

The advisor's attempt at wise counsel came across to Agon as comical. The king shook his head in disgust. There was a reason he rarely met with his so-called advisors. These toads could barely boast a working brain between them. They simply didn't get it.

The king was not at all shocked by Krasmir's reaction—it was exactly what he had anticipated. Agon had conceived the tax with the baron in mind. It was hardly surprising that the Great Council had so readily endorsed it. None of the other noblemen were affected by it.

"What will you do, Your Majesty?" another of the toads asked anxiously.

Agon looked at him pityingly. "What will I do? I will invite Krasmir to join me in the procession to the temple tomorrow."

ONCE EACH YEAR the king was expected to lead a procession to the gates of the main temple in Rog. Agon found all such rituals extremely tiresome. Nevertheless he went through the motions, as his predecessors had done before him.

This particular day was a holiday throughout Rogand in honor of the dark gods. The day began and ended with a feast, and no one was expected to work on that day, not even slaves.

It hardly needed to be said that someone must feed the animals, milk the cows, build the fires, fetch water, prepare food, serve at the feast, and tend to every whim of the masters. Apart from that, slaves were not expected to work.

As soon as the sun reached the halfway point in its journey from noon to sunset, the festivities began in earnest. Led by the king and an immaculately presented contingent of the royal guard, the procession started at the palace and descended to the huge central market square before climbing again to the gates of the temple. The streets had been adorned with flowers to honor the dark gods—white lilies for Nehrvina the Awful, and red and white carnations for Malzakh the Destroyer. In keeping with tradition, crudely constructed effigies of corpses painted white were carried on the shoulders of the crowd.

The people marched slowly through the streets in eerie silence, their numbers swelling each time the procession passed a new district of the city. All but the poorest had clad themselves symbolically in funeral attire—black from the waist down, and white above the waist.

The king soon found himself at the head of a massive column that stretched behind him all the way to the central market and beyond.

Finally the column approached the gates of the main temple. Inside the grounds lay an imposing and ominous looking structure shaped like a gigantic mausoleum. However the procession came to a halt before it passed the temple gates.

A large delegation of priests waited at the gates bearing flaming torches. The priests were clad in dark cloaks with black leather belts and shoes. Large cowls covered their heads, and the faces that protruded from beneath the cowls bore long streaks of deep blue paint.

As soon as the procession stopped, the crowd began passing forward the effigies. They flowed in a seemingly endless stream until a massive pile of dummy corpses had risen before the gates. As one man the priests stepped forward and threw their torches onto the pile. A moment later the king and members of his royal guard hurled pitchers of oil onto the blaze.

The flames roared upward into the sky, and the crowd erupted in a deafening cheer. Handheld drums and cymbals appeared among the people, and men and women were soon dancing with abandon from one end of the column to the other, shrieking out the names of their dark gods as they spun and twirled to the hypnotic beat of the drums.

As soon as the flames began to die down the king and his party turned away from the temple and set out for the feast awaiting them at the palace. The crowd gradually dispersed behind them as people headed for their homes and the prospect of abundant food, cheap wine, and bawdy songs.

Throughout the procession, Krasmir marched at the king's right hand. The baron was too angry to speak—he had reportedly been incandescent with fury since learning of the tax—but he nevertheless accompanied the king as commanded.

Agon was not at all concerned by Krasmir's silence. He had nothing to say to the baron himself. Apart from ensuring that the nobleman constantly hovered nearby, the king ignored him completely.

The two men parted the moment they reached the palace. The king did not offer the courtesy of a farewell.

THE FOLLOWING days proceeded in a similar fashion. Before long Agon was spending so much time with Krasmir that people began referring to the baron as the king's shadow.

After two weeks had elapsed, Agon decided that the right moment must surely have arrived. He had come to heartily loathe the baron's company, and he was impatient to sever the cord as soon as possible.

Since announcing the tax to Krasmir, Agon had never referred to it again. He did so now.

"It has been suggested to me that you had reservations about the new Excess Assets tax, My Lord. Was that report accurate?"

Krasmir turned to his sovereign. "I have no objection to the tax, Your Majesty," he replied.

For a fleeting moment as the baron was saying it, he looked confused. He appeared thoroughly convinced that the tax was worthwhile, yet some part of him seemed baffled by his own ready acceptance of it. The moment of confusion quickly passed, though, and his face cleared.

"I was hoping you would see it that way," said Agon mildly.

Krasmir returned a stern nod.

Agon said nothing more, keeping his face expressionless. Inwardly he was shouting with glee.

In the weeks before his first approach to Krasmir, Agon had witnessed with growing excitement the stone's influence on a few carefully selected subjects. Nothing remained but to present it with the greatest available challenge. Drettroth would have been the perfect candidate, except that he was dead and buried. Agon accordingly turned his attention to the most difficult of his barons—Lord Krasmir.

The man possessed a fierce and independent spirit. He bowed the knee to his king in public, but his will belonged to him alone. Inwardly he yielded to no one.

The king knew from the scroll that the Stone of Authority did not take effect instantly—prolonged exposure was needed. Consequently, having enraged and alienated the baron, the king found a myriad of excuses to make constant contact with the nobleman. A furious and bemused Krasmir had no way of knowing that Agon's real intent was to bring him under the influence of the stone.

The results had been nothing short of spectacular. The king had looked on in awe as Lord Krasmir's way of thinking was slowly transformed before his eyes. Nothing now prevented Agon from fully exploiting the power of the Stone of Authority.

The only remaining question was where to focus his attention next.

Before he had come close to exhausting the possibilities of the Stone of Authority, Agon was already dreaming of bigger things.

Giddy as the stone's power had made him, he quickly became hungry for more—much more.

With Lord Krasmir confirmed as his obedient puppy, the king devoted himself to recruiting a new set of agents to pursue the Stone of Knowing. He sent them to Arvenon with instructions for their leader, a man named Biel, to return regularly to deliver a report.

The moment he was informed that Biel had returned to Rog for the first time, the king summoned him to the audience room adjoining his grand reception hall.

"What progress have you made in tracking down this Tomas?" Agon demanded.

His agent bowed respectfully. "We have not yet identified any person matching his description in Arnost, Your Majesty. But we are vigorously pursuing our investigations. We have people watching the gates, and we are establishing a network of informants throughout the city. There is some suggestion he was involved at the royal stables at one time, so we will watch the stables as well."

"Bring me news," Agon warned him. "And do it soon if you want to keep your head."

The man began to sweat visibly. Agon dismissed him before disgust made him do something he might later regret.

He would give Biel and his men ample time to prove their worth. If they failed to deliver on the king's expectations, he would replace them without a second thought. His patience had a limit.

But if they should succeed...

With two such stones under his control, he would become almost invincible. It was hardly surprising that his lust for the Stone of Knowing was increasingly consuming his waking thoughts and troubling his sleep.

WITH THE STONE OF AUTHORITY secured and a search underway for the Stone of Knowing, a new issue began to loom large in Agon's mind. Opportunities beyond his wildest imaginings had already fallen within his grasp. But Agon was now in middle age. It was becoming clear that his own life span would eventually prove to be his undoing.

The Stone of Vitality could prolong his life—if he could somehow get his hands on it. This final stone would not grant him immortality though. It would merely delay the inevitable.

Given all this, his thoughts were increasingly drawn to another scroll buried in the midst of Lorik and Jorvan's pile. It appeared to have been authored by Drettroth. The text was rambling and even incoherent in places, and its content was bafflingly theological in nature. But Agon understood the general idea well enough.

The deceased nobleman had seen the Stone of Vitality merely as a stepping stone. Apparently he believed he had discovered a way to completely overcome the limitations of mortality. Endless delving into old scrolls had led him to a startling conclusion: for the right price, a limitless life span could be purchased from the dark gods.

Drettroth intended to invoke an arcane and sinister ritual that involved human sacrifice on a grand scale. Although he had not detailed the actual ritual in his scroll, he did make it clear that the outcome would be to extend his life in exchange for prematurely ending the lives of others. The price would not be cheap—a steady flow of victims would be needed. Drettroth expected the tally to run into the tens of thousands.

The king was beginning to grasp the reason why Drettroth was so eager to annex Arvenon and the surrounding kingdoms. Having stripped them bare, he would probably have turned south to Lestanor. Eventually he might even have turned east to Rogand itself.

The very notion of such a bargain was utterly absurd. But was it more absurd than the idea that a tiny stone could convey unimaginable power?

Agon would have given a great deal to be able to discuss the scroll with its author. But Drettroth was beyond such concerns. The king might have analyzed the scroll with Lorik and Jorvan if he hadn't already executed them. Only one other way to test Drettroth's conclusions had presented itself. He would need to consult with the High Priest at the temple in Rog.

The very thought left him cold. It still gave him shivers to recall his childhood responses to the priests. Their appearance, their behavior, their very existence—everything about them was profoundly disturbing.

Agon still vividly remembered his first visit to the temple as a child. His nostrils began to twitch uncomfortably as he recalled the sickly atmosphere inside the building. In his childish imagination the temple seemed more like a tomb than a place of worship. Within a few minutes of entering, he had emptied his stomach violently onto the dull stone floor. He had still been retching helplessly as he was carried outside. His father had been furious.

He had learned to master his reactions while among the priests, but his occasional encounters with the High Priest sent a chill up his spine, even as a grown man.

Still more disconcerting, His Eminence never left his temple. He made exceptions for no one, not even the king.

Much as it galled him to admit it, Agon could not force the High Priest to do anything. When he was crown prince his father had tried to impress upon him the principle that a kingdom was only as strong as its foundations. The Kingdom of Rogand rested on the foundation of three powerful institutions—the throne, the nobility, and the priesthood. Agon could no more afford to alienate the priests than he could wish away the nobles.

It might have been possible to bend the High Priest to Agon's will using the Stone of Authority. But the king was not willing to spend the number of days required in the High Priest's presence, and he was certain that the priest would never consent to it anyway.

THE HIGH PRIEST agreed to meet Agon at the temple, and when the day arrived the king set off accompanied by a large contingent of the royal guards. The soldiers were on hand to bolster his courage more than to protect him.

The streets bore no resemblance to their appearance the last time he had made his way through Rog. The procession was no more than a memory now, and filth and squalor had replaced the flowers and the revelers.

Beggars stepped forward eagerly as he approached. As soon as they became aware of the identity of the rider, they scurried away like rats from a flame. Agon stared fixedly ahead, steadfastly refusing to countenance any sight he didn't wish to see.

As soon as Agon arrived at the gates of the temple compound, he dismounted. His men did the same.

He was met by a thickset priest clad in black.

"I bid Your Majesty welcome to this sacred place," the priest said with a bow. "Please, follow me."

Agon proceeded through the gates, followed closely by his men.

"Not the soldiers," the priest said sharply. "They must wait outside."

The men drew back at once.

The king's first reaction was an angry scowl. Then he reminded himself he had come seeking information.

"Wait for me here," he instructed his captain before turning and following the priest.

Agon had visited the temple many times, but never alone. The entrance to the temple building felt no less dark and foreboding than on his previous visits, and Agon paused awkwardly at the threshold before trailing in behind the priest. The light inside was dim, the vast space illuminated only by small clusters of candles that guttered and flickered feebly. A heavy smell permeated the air—a cloying union of incense, smoke, and blood.

His guide led him past a group of priests who appeared to be in a trance. They aimed an empty stare in the king's direction, and he returned their gaze, noticing in the dim light that fresh blood mingled freely with the blue paint on their faces. He tore his gaze away in distaste.

The priest ushered him into a small room where the High Priest sat in an ornate wooden chair. His guide then left without a word.

By that time, Agon's mind was reeling. The otherness of this place overwhelmed him. He was the king. He understood the subtle ways of power and the complexities confronting anyone bold enough to rule a people. But he felt adrift in this temple, far beyond his depth. He had no comprehension of the dark gods, nor did he understand what motivated the men who devoted their lives to ministering to them.

He labored to push all such thoughts from his mind.

"Welcome, Sire," said the High Priest. "What has brought you before me?" He nodded Agon to a seat. He did not get up from his own chair.

A flush of annoyance rose in Agon. The High Priest might rule in this place, but he had no need to flaunt it.

He forced his displeasure down and seated himself. "Thank you, Your Eminence. I have come to you with a delicate question."

The High Priest did not immediately respond. Agon peered at him curiously. The man's skin had the appearance of leather, and the wrinkles on his face were deeply creased. He had already been old when Agon was a child, and he seemed little different today.

The king wondered briefly if the man opposite him possessed the Stone of Vitality. He soon rejected the idea. The High Priest might appear almost ageless, but nothing about him conveyed the vaguest hint of vitality.

"What is your question?" the High Priest finally asked.

"Do the dark gods offer any possibility of relief from the curse of mortality?"

Agon winced as he said it. Surely the question must seem foolish to the priest.

The High Priest did not treat his query with scorn. "You are not the first person to ask me such a question," he observed.

"Lord Drettroth?" the king responded immediately.

His Eminence did not reply. He simply gazed expressionlessly at Agon with his timeworn eyes.

As the seconds ticked away, the king began to fidget. He was accustomed to others feeling uneasy in his presence. Nothing about this place felt normal, though.

Still the High Priest remained silent. As time continued to pass, Agon's need to fill the emptiness became a compulsion.

"Is there a ritual that grants long life in exchange for a sacrifice?" he blurted out.

No answer was forthcoming. Agon shifted awkwardly in his chair, trying hard not to squirm.

After what felt like an eternity, the High Priest's mouth slowly opened. "Nehrvina the Awful grants life. And she reclaims it when she chooses," he droned.

What did that mean? It certainly didn't answer the question.

Agon squinted across at the High Priest, and a frown began to form on his brow. How had His Eminence managed to preserve his own life for so long? And if the High Priest himself was indeed benefiting from such a ritual, how likely would he be to confess his secret?

Was it possible that Drettroth had asked himself the same questions?

The king decided to try again. "Does Her Awful Majesty ever choose to extend the life of a favored person?"

A long pause followed. Agon began to feel lightheaded. Was it the incense in the air, or was it the disconcerting gaze of the High Priest? He shook his head in an attempt to clear it. It was becoming difficult to focus his thoughts.

Once again the High Priest's mouth opened. "Her ways are inscrutable," he slowly pronounced.

Another non-answer. It was increasingly obvious to Agon that he would learn nothing useful here.

When his vision began to swim he decided he'd had enough. He needed to get out of there before he collapsed.

Pushing himself to his feet, he stumbled to the door of the small room. The High Priest sat unmoving, watching his departure dispassionately. Neither man uttered a word of farewell.

Agon lurched unsteadily through the temple and staggered out of the entrance into the open air. Once clear of the building he bent low and placed his hands on his knees, sucking in great gulps of fresh air.

A small group of priests wandered past and glanced at him curiously. He ignored them.

When he had recovered sufficiently he stood upright again and made his way to the gate.

His men were waiting for him there. None of them commented on his appearance—they wouldn't be so foolish. All of them mounted their horses. Agon rode away without a backward glance.

The further he went from the temple grounds, the more normal Agon began to feel. Slowly his head started to clear.

He had left without answers. What had been going through Drettroth's mind when he emerged from his own interview with the High Priest?

Nothing had been said to confirm or deny Drettroth's idea of a bargain with the dark gods. Perhaps no confirmation was needed though. The High Priest's longevity might itself provide the answer. Surely his great age could not be natural. Agon felt sure he had stumbled upon something significant.

The specifics of the ritual were still a mystery, which left important questions unanswered. The king promised himself he would carefully revisit the pile of scrolls inherited from his former army commander.

His spirits rose higher as the temple slipped further away behind him. In spite of his unsettling experience with the High Priest and the unsatisfying outcome of the interview, Agon saw no reason at all to feel discouraged.

6

Six months after the Battle of Torbury Scarp

A brand new sunrise saw King Agon of Rogand standing silently on the balcony of his private apartments, gazing sourly across the extensive woodlands that surrounded his palace. From this vantage point he could see beyond the palace grounds to the capital city of Rog that lay below them. In the far distance he caught a glimpse of the walls that encircled the city.

Birdsong rose from the trees to compete with the muffled din of the city that penetrated the palace's borders. The palace might be a haven from the squalor of the capital below, but the city's proximity provided the king with a daily reminder of the reality that lay just beyond his privileged existence. Agon had no interest in any such reminder, and he had instructed his servants to find a way to block out the sights and sounds of the city. It annoyed him intensely that they had so far failed to satisfy his demands. Perhaps it was time to lop off a couple of heads. That might provide the necessary motivation and focus.

Turning away from the city, he reentered his rooms.

His personal slave hovered nearby, as always.

"I haven't seen you in a while, Ennawi," said the king. "Have you missed me?" He smiled ironically.

The slave did not respond.

"I've been busy," Agon continued. "Not something that could ever be said about you."

The king glanced at Ennawi scornfully. "I hear that my servants have been whispering. They regard you with universal contempt. They simply cannot understand why I retain a person incapable of performing any kind of useful service."

Ennawi offered no response. He could not have answered even if he wanted to of course—having no tongue, he was incapable of speech.

The king had never made any secret about his attitude toward Ennawi—anyone within earshot knew that the royal vitriol was directed at him more than at any other person. Yet whatever Agon said, and however loudly he shouted it, the slave simply ignored it.

Agon couldn't help admiring his composure—no other person who ignored the king had ever lived to see another sunrise. Ennawi was extremely bold or extremely stupid. Either way he was beyond fortunate. Many slaves had come and gone; Ennawi had outlasted them all.

Regardless of the whispers, Ennawi seemed determined to reinforce the widely held view of his usefulness. Silent and unmoving, he simply stood there.

Agon shrugged. How could such a slave be useful anyway? A person without hands was good for almost nothing.

Ennawi was certainly reliable though—he was always there without ever being in the way. Most curious of all, while he was unarguably the most attentive of Agon's servants, he gave no sign of understanding a single word the king said.

Agon did not tolerate idleness in those who attended him. Nevertheless, he tolerated Ennawi.

He came and stood before the slave, studying him silently. Then he shrugged. "Others can think what they like," he murmured. "I'm the king, and I do whatever I please."

The status of his slaves held no lasting interest for Agon, and he soon pushed the issue from his mind. Already his thoughts were taking him in a different direction—there were matters he needed to address. Important matters.

He hastened away from his private rooms without sparing a further thought for Ennawi.

AGON HAD BARELY VANISHED before another slave hurried into the apartments in his wake. The king did not notice her arrival. He never did—she made certain of that.

Spotting Ennawi near the balcony, she immediately bustled across to him.

The woman, Nistinaa, had been Ennawi's carer since before he came to the king. The two slaves were not related, but over the years she had come to care for him as a mother cherishes a son.

Agon had encountered Nistinaa only once, and the contact had been brief. She was well into middle age and no beauty, and the king had looked straight through her. She had no desire to meet him a second time.

She scanned Ennawi carefully. "So he hasn't struck you again," she said with a little grunt of satisfaction.

A bowl appeared in her hand, and she began to spoon food into his mouth. He chewed and swallowed instinctively, offering no hint that he even registered her presence. She was not perturbed by his apparent indifference.

Finally she held up a small vial filled with a dark blue liquid. The appearance of the liquid finally earned her a reaction. His eyes flickered briefly, betraying what she knew to be distaste. She tut-tutted once, raising an eyebrow. He responded by tilting back his head obediently and drinking.

She patted him lightly on the shoulder and smiled sadly up at his impassive face. Then, after whispering a few quiet words of encouragement, she slipped away as quietly as she had come.

DAYLIGHT WAS ALMOST SPENT by the time Agon laid aside his pressing business and returned to his private chambers. He found Ennawi exactly where he had left him. If the slave had moved during the time he was gone, it wasn't obvious.

"My new army commander is no better than the fool I executed last month," he snarled. "I'll give him another week to muster up some intelligence, then I'll have his head!"

He scowled in anger. "Where is Drettroth when I need him?"

Picking up a delicate marble statuette, he hurled it at the far wall. The object shattered into smaller pieces that scattered across the floor. The act of destruction calmed him for reasons he couldn't fathom.

"Drettroth might have loathed me, but he served me well. He only did it to boost his own power and influence of course." He smiled mirthlessly. "I respect that in a person."

He gazed at the slave thoughtfully. "Drettroth might be dead and buried, but he wasn't a complete failure. He did at least give me the Stone of Authority, back when we were youths. I don't pretend it was an ungrudging gift. But I wanted it, and when I want something badly enough I always get it."

Ennawi appeared unmoved by this information.

The king picked up a bunch of grapes from a bowl and began rhythmically popping the dark purple juice balls into his mouth. He chewed them carefully, then he spat out the pips in random locations. He made a mental note to punish his servants appropriately if they failed to locate and remove them all.

"It was Drettroth who learned the truth about the stone. And he hid it from me! But I've discovered his secrets, and I've mastered the stone. The world is about to change!"

He looked pityingly at the slave and shook his head. "Someone like you could never understand how difficult it is to be king, Ennawi. I'm tired of doing things the hard way. I deserve this stone."

The human statue didn't move.

"It's just the beginning. My stone isn't the only one—there's another even more useful one called the Stone of Knowing. I have agents searching throughout Arvenon. In Varas and Castel as well. I intend to find it!"

Agon rubbed his hands together. "With both stones under my control, I'll be unstoppable."

Was that a flicker in Ennawi's eyes?

Agon peered attentively at the slave for a few moments before shaking his head. He was imagining things.

His mind turned to another subject, and he stood brooding for a while.

Eventually he faced Ennawi again. "My nobles have been whispering behind my back. They're saying I need an heir. Perhaps they think that manipulating a prince will be easier than manipulating me."

He snorted. "A crown prince might make the nobles happy, but any intelligent king knows that princes are liabilities. They have a nasty habit of becoming impatient."

He shot a shrewd glance at Ennawi. "I should know. My father died of natural causes—every one of his physicians said so. I made very certain it looked that way," he added with a sly wink.

"There's plenty of time for me to father an heir. It can wait until I'm in my dotage. But I've got a better idea. I've decided to live forever."

He leaned in close to the slave. "Drettroth believed he could do a deal with the dark gods—rivers of blood in return for a life without end. I like the sound of Drettroth's deal," he whispered conspiratorially.

"Every day my nobles exclaim, 'May you live forever'. Given the number of times they say it, it must surely be their fondest wish. So I'm going to grant that wish."

He came and stood before Ennawi, his eyes searching the face of the slave. “I would like to live forever,” he said. “I would like it a lot.”

He peered intently into the other’s eyes, vigilant to detect the faintest hint of a response. “Would you like me to live forever, Ennawi?” he asked softly.

The human statue did not move. Not one of his muscles betrayed a single twitch.

7

Eight months after the Battle of Torbury Scarp

The sun had begun its downward journey in the sky when Ander at last cleared the foothills. He found himself at the base of a steep path that wound its way steadily up the side of a small mountain. His horse was just as weary as he was, but he didn't hesitate to guide it onto the path.

It had been dark when he last traveled this path several months earlier. He remembered it well, and the memories were not comfortable.

Part way up the mountain the path emptied onto a broad plateau. It had been the place where Will Prentis ran Brother Vangellis to ground. Needing a guide, the army commander had forcibly dragged the fallen monk away from his sanctuary. Memories flooded over Ander, sweeping him back to the tumultuous events that followed. A great deal more than Brother Vangellis's life had changed when the monk began to reengage with the world.

Once he reached the top of the path, Ander peered around,

frowning. He had expected to find buildings here encircled by a wall with a large wooden gate—the monastery of St. Rodrig the Martyr. Nothing remained now except blackened timbers and broken fragments of stone.

Ander dismounted and picked around for a while in the ruins. It seemed abundantly clear what had happened. The Rogandans had come, and they'd left nothing standing when they departed.

The monastery had never been what he was seeking, though. He had come in search of the monks.

In particular he sought an old man with a long gray beard and bright eyes. After all that had happened in the months that had followed, he still recalled the penetrating gaze of Brother Elias. He had told himself at the time that the old monk was weak, but he was willing to consider a different interpretation now. He remembered a wiry frame and a gentle manner, but even then he had sensed a toughness and wisdom beneath that exterior.

Ander had pinned great hopes on finding Brother Elias here.

He was not dismayed, though. There were no recent graves anywhere in sight, nor scattered bones picked clean by the vultures and bleached by the sun. The monks must have received some kind of warning before the Rogandans arrived. It seemed apparent that they had fled in time.

Ander glanced up at the sun, now sitting low above the horizon. With dusk almost upon him, he began to prepare for a night among the ruins.

There would have been villages in the area, although the Rogandans had probably destroyed them as well. But farmers should have returned by now, and they would have information to share.

He would begin searching for the monks in the morning.

ANDER ROSE with the dawn and guided his horse back down the mountain path. Before long he came upon a small flock of goats tended by a young boy.

The little goatherd froze the moment he spotted the soldier. He stood rooted to the ground, staring wide-eyed at the horseman and trembling with nervous apprehension.

Ander pushed down his anger at this apparent reminder of the ongoing legacy of the Rogandan invasion. There was a time when the goatherd's reaction might have seemed odd. But after the months of war and turmoil that lay behind them, he had become accustomed to such fearfulness. He wondered what the boy might have witnessed.

"Hello," he said, trying to speak in a gentle tone. The boy probably saw him for what he was—a war hardened soldier—but he was determined to make an attempt at being unthreatening.

The boy offered no reply.

"Do you know where the monks have gone? The ones who lived up the mountain." He gestured toward the path.

The goatherd still didn't respond verbally, but he pointed away to the southwest, beyond some low hills.

Ander returned a civil nod.

Wanting to relieve the boy of his anxiety, he set off immediately, heading southwest.

Before long four armed riders came into view. As soon as they spotted him they diverted in his direction. Ander had been around for long enough to sense trouble when it headed his way. He began to wonder if the young goatherd's anxiety had more to do with bandits than with the Rogandans.

When the riders reached him they flowed smoothly around him until he was surrounded.

"Good morning," said Ander evenly. "I'm looking for some monks. Perhaps you can give me directions."

One of the men wore a calculating expression. He appeared to be their leader. "What do you want with the monks?" he demanded.

"I'm planning to join them."

His announcement earned him snorts of derision from all the men.

"He might be big, but he's soft," one of them pronounced with a sneer.

"You won't need that horse if you're joining the monks," said the leader. “They’ve already donated to us anything they had of value. Hand the horse over now, and we might let you go with nothing worse than a beating.”

Ander shook his head.

“Why don’t we fight him for it?” asked one of the men eagerly.

The leader responded with a mocking nod. “I suppose that would be more sporting,” he sneered. “He doesn’t have a sword. We can use staffs.”

One of the men dismounted. Leaving his sword sheathed, he reached up and loosed a staff secured to his saddle.

With no other option available, Ander dismounted and faced him. “Where’s my staff?” he asked.

His question drew a guffaw from the men. “You don’t get a staff,” the leader replied. He nodded to a second member of his band, and the man slid from the saddle grasping a staff of his own.

The two men circled Ander with broad grins on their faces. One of them poked his staff tauntingly in Ander’s direction. Then the other man aimed a stinging blow at Ander’s legs, intending to bring him down.

Leaning swiftly aside, Ander reached out to grab the staff as it swept past. Then he yanked the staff hard, pulling its owner off his feet. The second man came for him at once. As the new attacker raised his staff to strike, Ander pulled the downed man to his feet and swung him around to face his comrade. Ander’s human shield took a glancing blow to the head and collapsed to the ground the moment the big soldier released him.

Before the two mounted men could react, Ander grasped the fallen man’s staff and strode in to aim a crushing blow at his other opponent. The man brought his own staff up in time to defend himself but went down hard when Ander struck him a second time.

With both of his men out of the fight and the unarmed stranger untouched, the leader apparently decided he had seen enough sport. Anger twisted his face as he spurred his horse forward with sword raised high. Ander lifted his staff to block the blow, and the wood splintered as it absorbed the full force of the stroke. Before the leader could raise his blade a second time, Ander reached up and pulled him from the saddle. The man crashed to the ground and lay there stunned.

The final horseman looked on with wide eyes. Clearly neither he nor his companions had been at all prepared to deal with a man like Ander. Guessing what he might try to do next, Ander called to him, "If you run I'll come for you, and it won't end well."

The horseman hesitated.

"Tie them up," Ander ordered him. The man looked at the big soldier uncertainly for a moment, then he dismounted and approached his fallen comrades.

After ensuring that the men had been properly trussed, Ander tied the hands of his helper and hoisted him back into the saddle. Then he secured the other three men across the backs of their horses.

A well traveled road lay near at hand. "Is there a town along there?" he asked.

The other man nodded. "Blackmere," he said dispiritedly. "Don't go there—the headman is a fool."

Ander ignored him and led the party along the road toward Blackmere. Less than an hour passed before a large town came into view.

As Ander led in his unusual procession, people stopped in the streets to stare at them.

A man ran toward them. "Those are the men who robbed me!" he shouted.

Other townspeople gathered around as well, many of them calling out accusations.

Eventually the locals stepped aside as an official—presumably the headman—strode through the crowd importantly. "What is happening here?" he demanded.

Many voices called out at once, and he raised his hands for silence, a scowl on his face.

He turned to Ander. "Who are you?"

"I am a traveler, and I was set upon by these men. I overpowered them and brought them to you for justice."

The man sneered. "You're one of them more likely," he said. "I've seen before what happens when your kind fall out."

"He's not one of us!" spat the fourth member of the gang. "Everything was going good until he showed up!"

The headman stared at the gang member but offered no response. He turned back to Ander, clearly still suspicious. "You say you're a traveler. Where are you going?"

"I'm heading for the monks who used to have a monastery near here," he replied.

"Why?"

"I want to join them."

Ander ignored the snorts of incredulity that greeted his statement.

The headman did not seem entirely convinced by Ander's story, but he shrugged dismissively. "You'll find them in that direction." He pointed away into the distance. "I'll be watching for you," he promised.

The headman issued orders, and men came and took the robbers away.

Ander turned his back on the town and rode off, more than happy to see the last of Blackmere. He remembered his captive's description of the headman, "He's a fool." Ander heartily agreed with the assessment.

HE HAD BEEN TRAVELING for no more than thirty minutes when he crested a low hill and spotted a monk in the distance. The robed figure was sitting beneath the spreading boughs of an ancient oak. At the sight of the monk, all of his mixed feelings about what he was doing rose up once again. He ignored the inner debate and guided his horse toward the man.

Seeing a rider drawing near, the monk rose to his feet, calmly awaiting his arrival.

Ander pulled his horse to a halt and dismounted. He was astonished to see that he had found his way to the very man he sought.

In spite of his long anticipation of this moment, he felt uncomfortable and tentative. He bowed awkwardly.

"Brother Elias," he said. "I have been looking for you."

A pair of intelligent eyes gazed calmly back at him. The monk did not immediately speak. Then he nodded. "I remember you," he said.

His tone was reflective rather than reproachful, but Ander felt himself redden.

The monk watched him silently, waiting for him to say more.

"My name is Ander. I have come here because I want to join your monastery."

Had one of Brother Elias's eyebrows twitched slightly? He couldn't be sure. The monk seemed rooted to the ground, like the oak tree above him. Ander found himself wondering what it would take to startle him.

"Why do you wish to join us?" the monk asked simply.

"I've always been a soldier. But that life no longer satisfies me. I want to be different."

"What brought about this change of heart?"

"Brother Vangellis."

This time the monk's eyebrows definitely lifted.

"Do you know what has become of him?" Brother Elias asked.

"He is dead." Ander hung his head. He was not normally given to displays of emotion, but Brother Vangellis's passing had hit him hard. The monk had saved his life, and Ander felt that he had never properly thanked him. He had foolishly assumed there would be many opportunities.

Brother Elias apparently misunderstood the gesture. "Did you have a hand in his death?"

Ander looked up again. "No. Although there was a time when I did not wish him well," he admitted. "I set out to harm him, and it almost brought about his death."

The monk gazed at him with his searching eyes. "Are you hoping to join a monastery to atone for your past?"

Ander shook his head. "I have no idea how to atone for my past."

"Sometimes people come to us to escape from the world. That is not the right reason to join a monastery. The only valid reason is out of a desire to follow God."

"All I know is that I need a different purpose for living. Arvenon will always need soldiers, but I want to be something more than that."

Was it possible to be free of that life? The war had ended months ago, but even today he'd resorted to violence.

He had to try. He swallowed and took a deep breath. "I want to learn to do what Brother Vangellis did," he said. "At least in a small way."

Brother Elias considered his visitor thoughtfully. Then he slowly sat down again, waving Ander an invitation to join him. The soldier settled himself under the oak across from the monk.

"So you want to be like him? That must mean that Brother Vangellis found a way to escape the snare into which he had fallen," the monk offered.

"Yes. It happened gradually, but he became a very different man from the one we took away from the monastery."

Brother Elias nodded to himself, but said nothing further.

"Thomas Stablehand—the young man who was traveling with us when we came here—spent many weeks with him and learned his whole history," Ander told him. "He was with him at the end. Brother Vangellis revealed to Thomas what had caused him to give up hope and become a drunk."

Ander looked at Brother Elias uncertainly. "Thomas told me the story. I hope he didn't do wrong."

Brother Elias shook his head. "I do not think that Brother Vangellis would have minded."

"Thomas said that Brother Vangellis was grateful to me." Ander shook his head. "Me! After what I did to him."

"Would you be willing to tell me what happened?"

"Gladly."

The sun rose slowly into the sky as Ander retraced their journeys. He related everything that had taken place, particularly the events involving Brother Vangellis.

It was a long tale, and Brother Elias was clearly moved by what he heard. Ander appreciated the monk's attentiveness.

"He saved my life," Ander said, "even though he knew I hated him. I didn't understand at all why he did it. I still don't understand." He shrugged.

"Since then I've led men into battle—the greatest battle of our time. I'd wanted to command soldiers ever since I was a boy, and I finally had my chance. I've been told that I led well. I got what I always wanted, but it didn't satisfy me. I wasn't expecting that.

"Brother Vangellis's life counted for something. I've found myself asking what I will leave behind when it's my time to die. Will I be remembered as nothing more than a soldier who was good at killing?"

Ander shrugged, then he shook his head.

The monk sat silent, patiently waiting for him to resume.

Ander stood up and began pacing around restlessly. "A lot of good men died in the fighting. I don't know why I've been spared, but it must be for a reason."

Brother Elias watched him for a while. He seemed to reach some kind of decision. "So you wish to become a postulant?" he asked.

"What's a postulant?"

"It's what you become when you want to enter a monastery."

Ander shrugged. "I know nothing about that."

"Postulants take vows—of poverty, chastity, and obedience. Then they learn what it means to live that way in practice. The whole process takes a few years. Eventually, if they wish to continue and they have shown that they intend to live by their vows, they become full members of the monastery. After that they remain monks for the rest of their lives."

He looked at Ander intently. "Is this what you want?"

Ander could only shrug again. "I know what I want to become, but I don't know how to get there. If this is the pathway, I'm willing to walk it."

"It won't be easy for you."

"Because I'm a soldier?"

"Perhaps. But I was thinking more about your age."

Ander frowned in puzzlement.

"Most postulants start much younger, as Brother Vangellis did. It's harder to change when you've established your own ways of doing things and responding to the world around you."

Ander's eyes narrowed as he stared at Brother Elias. The monk claimed he was too old, but surely the truth lay elsewhere. More likely he simply thought Ander wasn't good enough.

"Are you saying you won't accept me?" he asked, an old bitterness beginning to stir within him. He began wondering what had possessed him to imagine he could measure up in the eyes of these people.

Brother Elias shook his head firmly. "It isn't about accepting or rejecting you. If we had to be accepted on our own merits, none of us would meet the standard. I welcomed Brother Vangellis into our monastery, and you saw the state he was in."

The monk's reference to Brother Vangellis shook Ander loose from his simmering anger. It was true. Brother Vangellis had been a hopeless drunk. There was no way he could possibly have measured up to any kind of standard the monks might have set. Yet Ander himself had witnessed Brother Elias's attempt to prevent Will from dragging him away from the monastery.

Some religious people deserved contempt—Ander knew that from bitter experience. But his own experience had shown him that superficial impressions could be misleading. He had been wrong about Brother Vangellis. Eventually he had recognized that the monk was far from contemptible, in spite of initial appearances. He sensed that Brother Elias might deserve his respect too.

Ander forced himself to calm down.

Many times he had tried to imagine how it would play out when he tracked down the old monk. But he hadn't known what to actually expect. He'd sometimes wondered if Brother Elias might poke and prod to uncover his guilty secrets, leaving him exposed and vulnerable like a child caught with his finger in the baron's honey pot.

More than once he'd even wondered if a public shaming of some kind might be required of him, perhaps as a condition of joining the monastery. The truth was he had plenty to be ashamed about.

Brother Elias didn't seem particularly interested in a roll call of his past misdemeanors though. And Ander acknowledged that he didn't appear to have approached Brother Vangellis's wrongdoings that way either.

The old monk had been watching him closely as he wrestled with his reactions, and Ander had an uncomfortable feeling that he either knew or guessed much of what was going on in his head.

"I would never lightly dismiss anyone who felt called to a vocation as a monk," Brother Elias told him. "And you seem to have a clear sense of call, even if such language means little to you."

Brother Elias studied Ander quietly with his penetrating gaze. "You're an intriguing person, Ander," he said.

He took a deep breath and exhaled slowly. Then he spread his hands wide, his face softening into a smile that reached to his eyes. "Come and spend some time with us. There's no rush about deciding anything—we can discuss the future later.

"And please, don't be troubled about being accepted—no one is going to reject you. As for joining the monastery, I am sure that any final decision we reach will be reached together."

8

Three and a half years after the Battle of Torbury Scarp

King Agon of Rogand sat enthroned in state in the grand reception hall of his palace in the capital, Rog. Before him lay a gleaming mosaic of marble tiles, depicting horsemen with leveled spears charging across a field of green. Beyond the mosaic, at the opposite end of the vast hall, a pair of gigantic doors stood wide open.

Agon's throne, magnificent and imposing, overshadowed it all.

Sunlight flooded into the hall through huge windows, bathing the throne in dazzling brilliance. During the hours of daylight, no visitors, be they commoners or monarchs, could long gaze upon the king on his gilded throne without being obliged to avert their eyes.

Marble columns rose majestically on either side of the throne, and identical pairs of columns marched the entire length of the hall. Flanking the columns, a long line of tall armor clad guards stood an arm's distance apart, stretching from the entryway to the throne at the distant end of the expanse. Every guard wore a shining silver helmet plumed in black and carried a golden shield bearing the royal standard of Rogand: a winged eagle above a writhing snake.

Many petitioners and ambassadors entered the reception hall hoping for an audience with the king. Every one of them was sent on the long trek from the threshold to the distant splendor of the throne, enduring as best they could the endless lines of watchful guards.

The experience was overwhelming and intimidating. It was intended to be.

On that particular day, the person journeying the length of the hall was a foreigner of noble birth. This supplicant had not come to Rog on his own initiative—he was there by invitation, a chosen guest of King Agon.

Agon calmly inspected his progress toward the throne. Since he inherited the crown the king had observed many such approaches. He looked on as a coiled serpent coolly watches a scurrying rodent wander within reach. Some petitioners hurried forward, tripping over themselves in their urgency to get the journey over with. Others shuffled restlessly, as if searching for any possible way to postpone the inevitable.

Years of careful scrutiny had shown Agon that a bold approach with a confident stride was rare indeed. It warranted special attention, just as a serpent offers wary respect to a mongoose. Agon never wasted time when dealing with potential threats. Bold petitioners quickly found themselves firmly under the thumb of the king. Either that or their lives soon came to an end.

Agon looked on impassively as the foreigner approached.

His latest guest showed every sign of tension. An entire regiment of Agon's soldiers had escorted the nobleman to Rog. The men had been under instruction to treat him with courtesy and satisfy his every need, while never permitting him to relax. A sizable ceremonial guard detachment had ushered him to the throne room and dumped him at the entranceway, leaving him to travel the length of the hall alone.

Agon smirked to himself in satisfaction. The necessary tone had been set.

Arriving at the throne, the nobleman hesitated, clearly uncertain about what was expected of him next. Like every petitioner who preceded him, he had received no briefing on appropriate formalities and conventions. Agon made sure of that. He liked his guests to be wrong footed from the beginning.

The foreigner stopped short of the throne and made a low bow. Agon allowed a slight frown to play across his face, as if his visitor had caused offense by breaking protocol. The nobleman registered the king's reaction before the radiance of the throne forced him to look away.

After allowing the visitor to stew for a while, King Agon decided not to prolong the farce any further.

He addressed his guest directly. "Welcome to my humble hall, My Lord." He then added pointedly, "You are undoubtedly unfamiliar with our ways, but you are nevertheless welcome here."

The nobleman winced momentarily, then clearly decided to put a brave face on it.

"You are most gracious, Your Majesty," he replied. "I am honored to be in your presence."

"I understand that you have been driven from your home," said Agon, coming straight to the point, "though you did nothing worse than make an honest attempt to serve your king and country."

The nobleman bowed once more. "Your Majesty is most understanding."

"Perhaps we can find a way to aid one another," said King Agon. "You will join me for dinner tonight, and we will discuss it further."

The man smiled—a self-congratulating simper that filled Agon with disgust, though he was careful to mask his reaction.

The nobleman bowed again, and Agon dismissed him.

The king sat brooding on his throne, watching the visitor retrace his lonely steps along the hall.

. . .

As usual, the food served at Agon's table was magnificent. The cuisine was sumptuous and varied, the dishes were beautifully presented, and every selection tasted delectable. The wine had no peer.

"Drink up!" Agon bellowed. "I insist! You're my guest!"

The former nobleman had already imbibed much more of the intoxicating liquid than he should have—the servers made sure of that. Every sip of wine led to his cup being refilled. Few people had the presence of mind to keep track of how much they were drinking under such circumstances. The fool would have a very sore head in the morning. In the meantime, he was becoming increasingly unguarded and far too relaxed.

Agon leaned closer to the foreigner.

"I am willing to extend generous resources to you," he said. "As much money as you could reasonably need as well as a constant flow of useful intelligence."

The foreigner could not hide the satisfaction in his eyes. Agon's agents had informed him that the disgraced lord had grown up accustomed to great wealth. He had not been doing well at adjusting to life without it.

"I warn you, though," Agon growled. "I will expect a bountiful return on my investment."

"Of course," the nobleman said eagerly. "I promise that you will be sa...satisfied—entirely so—with the outcome."

He was already beginning to slur his speech. And he was far too eager.

He would learn that Agon gave nothing away. The king was not understating the truth when he spoke of his expectation of a bountiful return. This man would be discarded if he could not deliver it. Agon would eventually discard him anyway, of course. But the fool would not find that out until it was much too late. In the meantime, with Agon's active assistance he should be able to do significant damage to the enemies of Rogand.

Agon departed from the banquet hall, leaving him to his feasting.

Based on current indications, the man would be carried away senseless to his quarters before the night was out.

It was already obvious that the foreigner was an insufferable bore. But Agon would be seeing much more of him in the coming days. At least two weeks of intensive contact would be needed before he had come thoroughly under Agon's spell. Or, rather, under the spell of Agon's unique and formidable talisman. Once that had happened, the transformation would be complete, and he would become a loyal servant of the king of Rogand, in his presence or away from it.

The process was extremely tiresome, though. He shook his head in annoyance. Unfortunately there was no way to avoid it—the investment of time was essential.

HAVING STEPPED outside the palace into the cold night air, Agon surveyed a sky dotted with countless sparkling lights. It struck him that the same stars had dispassionately looked down on every schemer in history, royal or otherwise, and they would continue to do so when he was gone. Such thoughts diminished the gravity of his grand strategies, and he quickly banished them from his mind.

He turned his attention back to the harsh realities of the present.

His current tactics had been made necessary by the failure of Lord Drettroth. Three years had passed since the ruinous debacle at Torbury Scarp. No one dared mention that name in the king's presence, but Agon would never permit its lessons to fade from his memory. He daily nurtured a bitter hatred toward his enemies.

Agon had always desired dominion over the kingdoms around him. He had never been content with what he had—he always wanted more. Now, dominion over the neighboring kingdoms would not be enough. After the shame his enemies had dared to visit on him, nothing less than their abject humiliation would satisfy him.

He paused long enough to master his fury. Then he demanded his horse. A brisk gallop would help clear his thoughts.

When the animal arrived he mounted it and set off, flicking his fingers imperiously to indicate to his guards that they should maintain a respectful distance.

The wind whipped at his hair as he rode, and the cold bit into his ears and cheeks. He paid no regard to it.

Astride a galloping horse, his body blending with its movement, he experienced a welcome release from the clinging demands of his daily round. King as he was, he was subject to frustrating limitations. Chief among them was the burden of being surrounded by fools and incompetents.

The only effective solution was frequent personal intervention to ensure that his purposes were appropriately advanced. Such interference was needed all too often.

But it wasn't always possible. The search for the Stone of Knowing provided a perfect example. Progress had been extremely disappointing, and entirely replacing his agents twice had so far achieved nothing useful.

Good agents were becoming harder and harder to find. Executing everyone who disappointed him was not proving to be a sustainable long term policy.

His thoughts were drawn once more to the late Lord Drettroth. The nobleman had been gone for three years now. As much as Agon had always despised the man, the painful truth was that he was proving difficult to replace.

It had now fallen to Agon to complete Drettroth's unfinished business, and to arrange for the destruction of the kingdoms that had dared to defy his armies. There would be little need for soldiers this time, though. The damage would be done much more subtly. With the right encouragement, the foreigners would simply destroy themselves.

The fool currently drinking himself under Agon's banqueting table had a part to play in the looming conflict. With proper planning and the right level of assistance, he would strike a heavy blow against Rogand's enemies. It would only be the first.

In the private wing of King Agon's castle, a human statue stood on the balcony of the king's apartments. It was Ennawi, entirely alone and staring fixedly into the outside world.

When the sun set Nistinaa appeared quietly at his side. She spooned food into his mouth with practiced fingers before administering his deep blue potion. Then she took a candle and led him to a small room tucked out of the way in a far corner of the suites. The room contained nothing apart from the low bed upon which Ennawi whiled away the hours of darkness.

Nistinaa set the candle down on the floor and guided him to the bed. Once he was reclining she gently pulled a blanket over him. Then she knelt beside the bed, mouthing silently. He gave no indication that he heard what she was saying, but her words were not directed at him anyway.

With her work done, she kissed him lightly on the head, blew out the single candle, and departed.

Ennawi lay unmoving where she had left him, staring up at the ceiling. Many hours passed before his eyes closed and the last traces of Agon's world slid away. Then he slept.

9

Three and a half years after the Battle of Torbury Scarp

Brother Ander ambled beside Brother Gerome on a sheep path, heading for the town of Blackmere. Free medical treatment was available to all comers at the monastery every weekday morning, and the monks also offered treatment in the town twice each week. On this occasion the two men were walking into town to see if further help was needed.

The former soldier was now a part of the monastery, having completed his novitiate and taken his simple vows. He would not be invited to take his solemn vows for another couple of years, so he had not yet committed himself to the monastery for life.

The afternoon sun warmed him pleasantly as he walked, and it occurred to him that he was actually feeling happy. He closed his eyes momentarily and let out a deep sigh.

Hearing it, Brother Gerome looked up at him with a smile. "That almost sounds like contentment, Brother Ander. Did you somehow manage to find enough food to fill your stomach for once?"

"Don't get me thinking about food," the big man grumbled. "It's already difficult enough to keep my eyes off those sheep over there." He waved his hand toward some particularly well fed specimens grazing just off the path.

Brother Gerome laughed. "I suppose when you were a soldier you took sheep whenever you were hungry."

"It wasn't that simple," Brother Ander replied. "Sheep always belong to someone, and farmers don't take kindly to soldiers walking off with their property. But we did enjoy some very tasty venison when the need arose." He rubbed his stomach wistfully.

Brother Gerome raised his bushy eyebrows. "Venison," he said. "I think I might have tried it once." He never seemed concerned about food.

Brother Ander shook his head in wonderment. The two of them were different in so many ways.

Many of the monks had responded with wariness when Brother Elias brought the big soldier into their midst. Some had even been openly hostile. Yet Brother Gerome had welcomed Ander from the moment he arrived, and had done everything he could to ease his initial adjustment. The resulting friendship came as no surprise—Ander saw no reason to dislike a person who so obviously enjoyed his company.

"I imagine your life here must seem strange at times," Brother Gerome continued, "even though you've been with us for almost three years now."

"There's plenty that's strange about living in a monastery," the former soldier replied.

"Like what?"

He glanced down at the other monk. "Like you. I've never known anyone who asked me so many questions!"

His friend laughed again. He did it a lot—it was one of the characteristics Brother Ander liked about him.

"As to what's strange, it isn't the obvious things," Brother Ander said. "I don't find the vow of poverty too difficult. Except for food, as you seem to have noticed—I could do with plenty more of it. I seem to be forever hungry, and I wouldn't complain about some variety." He stole another rueful glance at the sheep before shaking his head.

"I think I can live with the vow of chastity. Nothing ever prevented me from finding a wife and starting a family before I came here, but I never made it a priority. It probably sounds crazy to you, but I spent all my energy working on becoming a better fighter."

He shrugged. "Even the vow of obedience is probably less of an ordeal for me than for some. A soldier is forever doing what he's told."

"It sounds like you've had an easier adjustment than most of us," said Brother Gerome.

Brother Ander shook his head emphatically. "Absolutely not! A number of the brothers are still a bit suspicious about me. And life in the monastery drives me crazy at times. It's the peace and quiet that I struggle with most. My life never lacked action before. It wasn't so bad when we were rebuilding the monastery. These days I feel like I'm watching my fingernails grow."

He gazed down at his friend. "I'm not patient like you. I haven't mastered the art of sitting silently and contemplating. Most of the time meditation feels like punishment. I'm slowly starting to make sense of why we do it, but that doesn't make it any less monotonous."

His friend gave him a grin that suggested this information came as no great surprise to him.

The big monk-in-training decided to ask a question that had been on his mind for a long time. He turned to Brother Gerome. "Why did you join the monastery?" he asked bluntly. "I know why I came, but what brought you here?"

Brother Gerome looked up at him calmly. "Are you wondering if I joined because there was nothing else I was capable of doing?"

Brother Ander shook his head immediately. "Not at all. I can't see you as a soldier, and you wouldn't make much of a blacksmith. But I can think of plenty of other things you'd be good at."

In some ways his friend fit the image of a monk perfectly. He was calm and compassionate and slight of build. Physical strength was certainly not one of his assets. His robes always seemed baggy over his thin frame, and he wasn't tall—Brother Ander towered a full head above him.

But there was a wiry strength about him. He was very intelligent, and he demonstrated more persistence and determination than many men who boasted far greater physical stature. His capabilities could easily have been applied to a range of callings in life.

"Thank you, Brother Ander. It's generous of you to say so."

He paused, then a serious look came over his face. "There is a reason why I became a monk. When I was young I witnessed terrible injustices. The Rogandans were not responsible—this was long before they invaded. Arvenians were callously oppressing other Arvenians, the strong robbing and defrauding the weak.

"The local baron didn't seem to care. It felt like there was nowhere to turn for justice. A young friend of mine decided to take it upon himself to right some of the wrongs. It wasn't long before we buried him.

"Only the monks were doing anything effective to help the needy. I came to the monastery because I wanted to do something about it, and I saw no better option. But when I arrived I got more than I expected. It was obvious to me that the strong do whatever they like, so I thought the Creator had abandoned us. But I came to see it differently. Somehow I always knew that I would be held accountable for my actions. Now I believe that everyone will eventually be called to account."

Brother Ander nodded. "Injustice is a problem everywhere," he said. "There was a time when I traveled with Will Prentis, the commander of the army. On one occasion we came upon a situation of great cruelty, and the commander decided to do something about it. It was in a remote Arvenian village. I know Brother Elias teaches us that the Creator will hold a future reckoning, but we didn't wait for that. We fought the nobleman and his men. We called him to account ourselves and ended the oppression then and there."

"The commander has the right to act in that way," said Brother Gerome. "He represents the king, so it's his responsibility to do something about oppression."

"I was badly wounded in the fight and nearly died," Brother Ander continued. "I wouldn't be here today without Brother Vangellis and a girl called Elbruhe who'd run away from the Rogandans. They were there when I needed them. I think God might have had something to do with that.

"They went to great lengths to heal me, even though Brother Vangellis in particular had no reason to save me. We'd only met Elbruhe by accident, too—if you believe such things are accidental."

"I believe less in luck with every passing year," said Brother Gerome. "I've come to the conclusion that it's actually God who's responsible for much of what we call luck."

They had almost arrived at their destination, and they fell silent.

Brother Ander could smell the town long before they entered it, and he wrinkled his nose in disgust. Brother Elias made sure the monks worked hard every day to keep the monastery clean and tidy. At first Ander saw little point to it; he was well accustomed to dirty hovels in foul smelling towns and villages. But he must have gradually adjusted, because now he was finding it hard to put up with the filth and stench that always greeted him in this place.

He had never seen a town like this one. Garbage and human excrement were simply thrown into the streets, and dead animals were left to rot wherever they happened to expire. The only agency that ever attempted to clean the streets was the weather. A heavy downpour usually removed at least some of the refuse, but even then the rain left behind deep puddles filled with fetid water.

Brother Elias believed the rotting waste was partly responsible for the unusually high incidence of sickness and disease in the town. He had raised the matter with the headman more than once, but his warnings had been ignored. Brother Ander had not forgotten the first time he met the headman. The obstinacy shown by the official on that occasion had proven to be entirely characteristic.

The two monks walked through the streets of the town, stepping carefully to avoid the rubbish strewn across their path and keeping an eye out to dodge anything thrown from upper story windows. As they turned a corner near the building used to treat the sick and injured, they came upon a tense confrontation.

The town headman was glaring angrily at Brother Elias.

"As you know," Brother Elias said calmly, "I am greatly concerned about the state of the streets. I believe disease is breeding freely here. The foul air is a warning sign."

"So you do nothing to heal my son," shouted the headman, jabbing his forefinger into the old monk's chest, "and then you blame me for his illness?" The man's face was red with fury. Spittle flew from his mouth as he yelled.

When Brother Elias failed to respond, the man leaned forward and yelled in his face, "Are you deaf?" Then he planted both hands on the monk's chest and shoved. Brother Elias fell backward to the ground.

Brother Ander didn't pause to think. He strode forward and positioned himself between the two men, thrusting out his chest belligerently toward the headman.

His action made the headman even angrier. He quickly reached down and pulled a knife from his belt. Before he could attempt to use it, the big monk grabbed his knife hand by the wrist and slowly squeezed. The man cried out in pain and dropped his weapon.

The intervention of Brother Ander snapped the headman out of his fury. He glanced around him, his eyes narrowing. Many bystanders had been watching the conflict open mouthed, but not one of them met his glance. Several backed away, their heads bent low.

Finding no source of support, the headman took a slow breath and stepped back himself. Then he aimed a poisonous look up at the big monk. "You will pay for that!" he said, targeting Brother Ander with a single stab of his finger. Then he spun on his heel and left.

The crowd quickly dispersed as well.

Brother Gerome helped a shaky Brother Elias to his feet, and ushered him into the building, followed by Brother Ander.

"What was that all about?" asked Brother Ander.

"The man's son is very sick with fever and diarrhea," replied

Brother Elias. "Anything he drinks is vomited up immediately. We have been treating him without success. The boy is unlikely to recover, and the headman is worried and upset."

He pointed to a small bed inside the room. Two other monks stood beside it, and they looked up dejectedly as the three men appeared. A woman stood behind them, fear twisting her tear streaked face.

Brother Ander went to the bed and stared down at the pale figure lying there. The boy might have been ten years old. His breathing was shallow, and his face wore an ominous pallor.

"The headman will follow through on his threat," said Brother Elias. "He will feel shamed by what happened." He glanced across at the woman, who stared back at him for a moment, then nodded once.

Brother Ander frowned unrepentantly. "He can't be allowed to push you around like that just because he's the headman!"

"We are not soldiers," replied Brother Elias. "We do not respond to violence with violence."

"So I should have stood there and let him knife me?"

The old monk sighed. "I know you meant well, but he didn't intend to do me any real harm. There was no need to defend me."

Brother Ander shook his head in frustration.

The old monk turned sadly to the woman. "We have done everything for this poor lad that we know to do. I am truly sorry that our best efforts have failed. We will not leave you alone, of course, but I fear we can do little more now than pray for his soul."

She began to sob silently at his words.

Brother Ander looked down at the pale figure once again. It was obvious that the boy was close to death. As he gazed at the child something rose up within him. He, too, had once been written off as a hopeless case. He was alive only because a stubborn monk had refused to admit defeat.

He set his jaw. "I'm not ready to give up," he said. "I will stay with him."

"I will stay, too," said Brother Gerome.

Brother Elias looked at them quietly for a moment. Then he

nodded. “You will find a supply of herbs over there,” he said, pointing to a large jar near the head of the bed. “May God guide your hands.”

He led the other monks from the building. As he was leaving he paused in the doorway and looked back toward his big disciple. “The headman will come to the monastery. He will expect to take you. I will try to reason with him,” he said. Then he was gone.

The woman approached the big monk tentatively. “Thank you,” she said, tears glistening in her eyes. “Thank you for trying.”

Brother Ander nodded, then he turned his full attention to the patient. He felt the boy’s forehead. He was burning up with fever.

The monk cast about in his memories in a desperate attempt to find anything that might be useful in treating the boy’s fever. He had seen much sickness throughout the course of his life and observed many men suffering from fever during his years as a soldier. But had he ever witnessed a situation where a seemingly hopeless case had responded to treatment?

An incident came to mind where a number of soldiers had been laid low with fever. Unable to keep down treatments of any kind, their prospects had not been good. The only accessible water had been brackish. It had been too salty for Ander—he had spat it out when he tasted it. Nevertheless, with no alternative supply, the water had been given to the men. To the astonishment of everyone, they had slowly improved.

He called Brother Gerome to his side and told him the story.

His friend heard him out, then pondered silently for a few moments. “It’s worth a try,” he finally said with a shrug, although Brother Ander heard the doubt in his voice.

The big man turned to the boy’s mother. “Do you have any salt?”

“Yes,” she said. “I will get it.” She immediately left the building.

“What can I do?” asked Brother Gerome. “I feel useless.”

“You can pray,” Brother Ander replied. “You’re much better at that than I am.”

“Yes, of course,” said his friend, brightening. “Thank you!”

The mother returned with some salt, and Brother Ander mixed some of it with clean water. Then he began to spoon it into the boy's mouth. The lad took in very little of it, but the monk persisted.

"Can you prepare a broth with feverwort?" he asked Brother Gerome.

His friend nodded and set about the task. When he had finished, Brother Ander alternated between the water with salt and the feverwort broth.

True to his promise, Brother Gerome knelt and began to pray. Inspired by his example, Brother Ander himself began pleading silently for the boy's life.

The hours dragged slowly by. When the sun set, the boy's mother lit candles and brought them to the bed. Then she sat down. Before long she fell into an exhausted slumber.

As the night wore on, Brother Gerome began to visibly droop as well.

Brother Ander did not falter. His quest to save the boy's life had given him new purpose, and he pursued it with passionate intensity.

DARKNESS HAD YIELDED to daylight and the morning was well advanced when the headman again marched into the room. This time a squad of armed men filed in behind him. Noticing his arrival, his wife leaped at once to her feet and ran to him, a joyous smile covering her face. She reached up on tiptoes and whispered in his ear, pointing first to her son then to Brother Ander. He frowned at her, then glanced across at the bed.

Clearly nothing had prepared him for what he saw there. The boy lay unmoving on the bed as before, but his eyes were open, and his face had lost its deathly pallor. Brother Ander stood beside him, still mouthing silent prayers as he replaced the damp cloth on his brow.

Seeing his father, the boy managed a weak smile.

The leader of the squad pushed past the headman. "Is that him?" he asked, pointing to Brother Ander.

The headman turned to him in annoyance. "Stay out of the way," he snapped.

"But you wanted us to arrest him," the man protested.

"Are you blind?" the headman demanded, pointing to the boy on the bed. "Do you think I'm going to arrest the man who's just saved the life of my son?"

The squad leader frowned in confusion. When he did not move, the headman rounded on him. "Get out!" he snarled. "Now!"

The leader shook his head in bewilderment. Then he turned and left the building, his men trailing out behind him.

The headman came to the bedside and knelt down beside his son. His wife joined him there.

Judging it was safe to leave the boy untended for a while, Brother Ander stepped quietly away to give the family some time alone. Once outside, he stretched his aching limbs. He was basking in the sunshine when Brother Elias appeared around the corner.

"The headman hasn't come for you yet?" he asked.

"He's inside," Brother Ander replied.

Brother Elias raised his eyebrows in surprise. He disappeared into the building.

He did not reappear for many minutes. When he did, he was smiling. "The boy appears to be making a remarkable recovery!" he said. "You have done well, Brother Ander."

He studied the big monk for a moment. "I am pleased to say that the boy's father no longer feels a need to take action against you." He paused before adding, "Now would be a good moment to go to him and apologize."

Brother Ander was stunned. "Apologize? For what?"

"For using force against him."

"Has he apologized for pushing you to the ground?"

"No," Brother Elias replied. "Nor is he likely to."

"*Should* he apologize?" the big man demanded.

The old monk sighed. "Of course. But the choices he makes are not our responsibility."

"And you think I need to apologize to him?" The very idea left Brother Ander cold.

"We are not here in any official capacity," Brother Elias said. "We have no rights that we can insist upon."

Brother Ander shook his head. Then he shrugged. "Very well then." He took a deep breath and walked into the building, Brother Elias hurrying along behind him.

The big monk went straight to the headman. Seeing him coming, the man drew back defensively.

Brother Ander ignored it. "I wish to apologize for the way I behaved yesterday," he said roughly.

The man's face was unreadable. He said nothing for a long moment. Then he said, "I am willing to overlook it this time. Only because of your services to my son." Then his face hardened. "Don't expect me to be so forgiving another time."

Brother Ander opened his mouth to speak. Just as he was about to say something he would later have regretted, he caught sight of Brother Elias. The old monk's head was cocked and his eyebrow raised. Brother Ander closed his mouth abruptly. He gritted his teeth and contented himself with a nod.

The headman turned and left the building without another word.

Brother Elias came to Brother Ander with a smile. "Well done," he said softly.

Brother Ander shook his head again. Then he returned to the bedside of his patient.

"How are you feeling?" he asked the boy.

"A bit better, thank you," the child replied. He was visibly brighter, cheered by his father's visit.

Brother Gerome had taken over the role of tending to the boy's needs when Brother Ander stepped outside. He now looked up at the big monk. "Go and get some rest," he said. "I slept for a few hours last night, and I will stay with him."

Brother Elias nodded his approval. "I will send someone to relieve you as soon as I get back," he told Brother Gerome.

The old monk placed a hand on Brother Ander's shoulder. "Walk with me to the monastery," he said.

They left the building together and walked in silence for a time.

Finally Brother Elias turned to him. “I believe you might have found your calling,” he said.

Brother Ander returned a questioning look.

“I’d lost hope for the child,” Brother Elias said frankly. “You did not. Fierce as you appear to be on the outside, you have a gift for compassion, and you show considerable promise at leechcraft. I believe your calling is as a healer.”

The big man’s eyes went wide. Could his mentor be right? He had spent so many years gaining mastery at ending lives. Could he now become adept at giving life back?

He drew his eyebrows together. “I was only doing for him what Brother Vangellis did for me,” he said.

Brother Elias offered no further comment, and the big monk fell silent, musing.

Before long the monastery appeared before them. Seeing it, Brother Elias abruptly came to a halt. Brother Ander stopped as well, and the old monk gazed up into his face. “You showed great restraint when you spoke with the headman,” he said.

“I apologized. He should have done the same!” Brother Ander growled. “He had at least as much to apologize for.”

His mentor was silent for a moment. “You asked for forgiveness,” he finally replied. “Perhaps what you really wanted was justice.”

Brother Ander frowned. “What’s wrong with that? Isn’t God interested in justice?”

“He is,” Brother Elias confirmed, “although he doesn’t always seem to be in a hurry to provide it.”

“Am I supposed to be happy about that?” he grumbled.

Brother Elias didn’t answer, contenting himself instead with an inscrutable smile.

When Brother Gerome returned to the monastery he brought news from the town. “The headman has not been idle since you left,” he told Brother Elias. “He has gathered many men and set them to work cleaning up the streets.”

10

Four years after the Battle of Torbury Scarp

King Steffan of Arvenon sat restlessly in his audience chamber. One final matter needed to be dealt with today, but it couldn't be completed until the Varasan ambassador arrived.

He glanced across at Queen Essanda, sitting patiently beside him. She must surely find these sessions supremely dull. Yet she had never complained. And she didn't fail to offer useful insights later when they debriefed together.

She was no longer the girl he had first met in Castel Citadel more than four years ago. Her features and her figure had filled out. More importantly, her character had further blossomed and matured. She had developed into a truly arresting young woman—in body, mind, and spirit.

Apparently sensing his gaze, she turned to him and flashed him a smile. Her face was always beautiful, but when she smiled it lit up the room. He returned a happy smile of his own, then turned away, unwilling to allow himself the luxury of distraction. They were here for a reason.

It was especially fitting that she attend this particular session, since she had contributed significantly to finding a solution to the issue that had first been presented to him three months earlier.

Eventually the arrival of the ambassador was announced, and Steffan called for the merchants to be brought in.

The king turned his attention to the spokesman for the Arvenian merchants. “Some time ago you asked for permission to bring a complaint against two merchants from Varas,” he said. “Your request has not been forgotten, in spite of the delay in granting you an audience.”

The merchant bowed. “We are grateful for your consideration, Your Majesty.”

“Since that time,” King Steffan continued, “I understand that the Varasan merchants have discussed with their ambassador bringing a complaint of their own against you.”

“Some of our number may have been a little vigorous in expressing their displeasure, Your Majesty. But I believe they did so with good reason.”

“Your complaint is that Varasan merchants are being allowed to operate stalls in the main market of Arnost. Is that correct?”

The man bowed again. “Yes, Your Majesty. The complaint may sound trivial. But Arvenian merchants are barred from setting up stalls in the markets of Varacellan. When trading in Varas we are forced to sell our wares from outside the capital walls. We simply wish to see the same rules applied to foreign merchants here in Arvenon.”

Steffan entirely understood their frustration. Since any change in the policy of the Varasans seemed highly unlikely, his initial inclination had been to agree to the request of the local merchants, and to bar their Varasan counterparts from selling in the markets in Arnost. It seemed the simplest and most even-handed solution.

In the end the simple solution had been discarded, though. And that change had come about solely due to Essanda's persistence.

King Steffan addressed the merchant. "I believe that we have found a fair and equitable solution to the problem," he said. "The Varasan ambassador, Lord Haldenset, wishes to make an announcement."

He nodded to Lord Haldenset. The ambassador bowed to King Steffan, then stepped forward and unrolled a scroll. "The following proclamation is being read today in the Varasan capital of Varacellan," he said formally.

"His Royal Highness King Delmar of Varas, after consultation with his friend and ally, His Royal Highness King Steffan of Arvenon, is pleased to announce that Varas has concluded a trade agreement with Arvenon. From this day forth, merchants from Arvenon will enjoy the same access as local merchants to markets throughout Varas. In return, King Steffan has agreed to extend the same rights to Varasan merchants throughout the markets of Arvenon. Both Varas and Arvenon are today enacting laws to implement this agreement throughout the two kingdoms."

The wide-eyed surprise of the merchant gave way to an animated buzz as he discussed the implications with his fellow merchants. He soon looked up with a satisfied smile, bowing to Lord Haldenset.

"My Lord, I trust that you will convey to the Varasan merchants our regret at any...ah...inconvenience they might have experienced in the recent past. We look forward to welcoming them into the market at Arnost, and we will eagerly anticipate the same welcome in return when next we visit Varacellan."

Lord Haldenset responded with a brief nod.

"You have Queen Essanda to thank for this agreement," the king told the merchants as he dismissed them. "Her Majesty was responsible for the initiative that made it possible."

The merchants bowed deeply to their queen, who acknowledged them with a warm smile. Then they departed.

King Steffan conversed briefly with Lord Haldenset before the ambassador left the audience chamber. The two of them had seen a great deal of each other in recent weeks, and Steffan had developed a healthy respect for the nobleman.

As Steffan and Essanda left the chamber, she asked him, "Why did you give me the credit for this agreement, Steffan? You and Delmar carried out all of the negotiations."

"It would never have happened without you!" he replied. "I was ready to bar the Varasan merchants from the market in Arnost."

Steffan was not exaggerating—Essanda was entirely responsible for this outcome.

His thoughts went back to the day when she had sought Steffan out after hearing about the issue with the merchants.

"MAYBE THERE'S a way to resolve this problem," she had said. "Have you thought about discussing it with the Varasan ambassador?"

"Why would the ambassador be interested? Or King Delmar for that matter. I'd just be wasting my time."

"Would you have any objection if I spoke to the ambassador?"

Gazing down at her, he had seen hopefulness sparkling in her lovely eyes. She was young, and the world was full of promise. He felt sure any initiative would be a waste of time, but how could he refuse her? There was surely no real harm in it.

"Of course I don't object. Contact Lord Haldenset if you like. I will be happy to support you."

He knew she would be disappointed if nothing came of it, but disappointments were part of life. He would be there to comfort her.

Before many days had passed Steffan received a formal invitation to a royal lunch at the palace, hosted by the queen in honor of the Varasan ambassador. He had become aware that Essanda was doing a lot of preparation for the event. When he asked her what she was up to, though, she had simply beamed him a mysterious smile and sweetly requested that he wait and see. Steffan was intrigued rather than apprehensive, and more than a little curious to find out how she might be planning to handle the situation.

When the day finally arrived, Lord Haldenset had been admitted to the palace. Approaching the queen with a broad smile, he had bowed deeply to her. "I am greatly honored by your invitation, Your Majesty," he said.

Steffan could see that the ambassador was equally curious about the invitation. The Varasan was also quite obviously flattered to have been singled out.

During the meal the queen had drawn Lord Haldenset out, encouraging him to talk of his family and reflect on his childhood memories. She had also deftly introduced Steffan into the conversation. The two men were soon engaged in an animated and friendly interaction. No matters of any great significance were discussed.

After the meal the queen nodded to the attendants, and a special plate was brought out and placed with some ceremony before the ambassador. His eyes had immediately gone wide in surprise.

He closely examined the food on the plate before leaning forward to sniff it. "Your Majesty!" he said, barely able to contain his excitement as he turned to the queen, "this appears to be cheese from Rillen Dale."

She confirmed his guess with a smile and a nod.

"I am overwhelmed!" He turned to Steffan. "This is a rare variety of Varasan cheese," he explained, "a local delicacy in the east of Varas where I grew up. It's my favorite treat! I haven't had an opportunity to taste it for...for longer than I care to remember."

"Please!" said Steffan, pointing to the food and inviting the ambassador to enjoy it at once.

All conversation abruptly ceased as Lord Haldenset turned his full attention to the cheese. No words were necessary to report his assessment of the delicacy as he sampled it. The enraptured look on his face said it all.

Several minutes passed before he leaned back in his chair with an audible sigh of contentment.

Essanda had said very little during the meal, but she now addressed the ambassador directly. "My Lord, I know that all of us celebrate the strong bonds that exist between our two kingdoms. Those bonds were greatly strengthened as we stood together against a common foe and shared a great victory.

"The cooperation between our armies has never been stronger, and our foreign policies are closely aligned. Is it time, perhaps, to consider strengthening ties in other areas as well?"

She pointed to the cheese with a warm smile. "This cheese is truly delicious—I have tasted it myself, and I am now able to understand why you appreciate it so much. I don't doubt that it could become popular here in Arvenon, if only it wasn't so dreadfully difficult to purchase."

Steffan listened to her in amazement. He had no idea how Essanda had learned of Lord Haldenset's fondness for this particular delicacy, nor how she had managed to procure it.

"I have been wondering if a trade agreement between Varas and Arvenon might benefit us all," she continued. "I know your merchants wish to see our markets opened up to them. Going one step further and opening up the markets of both kingdoms would undoubtedly satisfy all of our merchants, and it could also lead to greater prosperity for everyone."

Lord Haldenset shook his head in wonder. He looked at Steffan with a smile and a bow. "I trust you will pardon my boldness in saying it, Your Majesty, but I can see that a shrewd mind lies behind the gentle manner of your estimable queen. I am well aware of the current dispute between our merchants, and I confess that she has won me over entirely to her point of view. Do you share the same mind on the subject?"

"I do," Steffan told him with a smile. "The perspective presented by Her Majesty enjoys my wholehearted support."

The ambassador rose to his feet and turned to Essanda, bowing deeply. "I am very grateful for your hospitality, Your Majesty, and more touched than I can say by your thoughtfulness toward me personally.

"I can make no promises on behalf of King Delmar, of course. But I can and will promise to contact His Majesty promptly with a proposal to explore the possibility of a trade agreement between Varas and Arvenon."

. . .

THE AMBASSADOR HAD BEEN as good as his word. Before long, Delmar had made contact with Steffan, and the two sovereigns were eventually able to broker an agreement. It had taken a number of weeks to settle on the details, but all parties agreed that it represented a further positive step forward in friendly relations between the two allies.

Since then Steffan and Delmar had jointly initiated negotiations with King Istel with the goal of establishing a tripartite trade agreement that included Castel as well.

Essanda's careful research and skillful diplomacy had set this entire process in motion. Steffan knew that she sought no acclaim for her efforts, but he had readily taken every opportunity since then to freely and widely acknowledge her role. She was already held in high regard within the three kingdoms. Her efforts toward the trade agreement had only enhanced that standing.

Delmar had wryly asked Steffan more than once if Essanda had any cousins. Steffan knew that he was only half joking.

11

As they left the audience with Lord Haldenset and the merchants, Steffan turned to Essanda and shook his head. "One of your rare shortcomings is that you're entirely too modest! You need to start recognizing how valuable you are to this kingdom!"

She took his arm affectionately as they walked together through the labyrinthine corridors of the castle. "One of your rare shortcomings is that you're altogether too serious," she said, favoring him with one of her dazzling smiles.

"I haven't had much time for amusements," he told her earnestly. "I've been wanting to go hunting with Torbury and Bottren and a few of the others, but all of us have been far too busy."

"Hmm," she said thoughtfully. "So you've been unable to chase down your quarry in the woods." She paused, releasing his arm. "I don't think you'll do any better in the castle."

So saying, she sprang away from him. "Catch me if you can!" she called back over her shoulder with a teasing laugh.

Steffan's competitive streak needed an outlet, and a challenge from his young wife was more than he could ignore. She flew before him on nimble feet, her hair streaming behind her as she ran. He immediately took off after her in hot pursuit. The shapeliness of her lithe form was not lost on him, and he grinned with delight as he urged his legs to greater efforts.

He was fast, but she was wily. Seeing him drawing close, she quickly abandoned the corridor, pulling open the door to a storeroom and disappearing inside. The door slammed shut in his face as he arrived. Steffan swung it open and raced inside, brim full of eager determination.

He found himself in the darkness of a large room with barrels stacked everywhere. Two other openings led into adjoining rooms. He selected one of the rooms at random and sprang inside. She was nowhere to be seen.

"There's no use hiding," he called. "I'll find you!"

A merry laugh sounded behind him as the door to the corridor slammed shut once again. Spinning around, he groped his way back through the storeroom and out into the corridor. He arrived in time to see her shapely form disappearing around a corner. When he reached the corner she was sprinting away, well ahead of him. She threw a glance back over her shoulder, laughing when she saw how far behind he was.

He took up the chase in earnest, gaining steadily with every moment that passed. A startled servant stared open mouthed as his king flew past, the comical look on the man's face drawing a strangled laugh from Steffan.

Essanda had barely reached her apartments and flung open the door when Steffan finally caught up with her. Hurtling into her bedchamber, she threw herself squealing onto the bed. She lay there, sprawled across the covers, disheveled and panting. Little peals of laughter punctuated her breaths.

Steffan came to a sudden halt and bent low with his hands on his knees, grinning stupidly as he sucked in great gulps of air.

Eventually they had both recovered enough to breathe more normally. She went quiet and stared up at him, a shy smile on her face.

For Steffan, the exhilaration of the chase gave way to a tide of passion that rose up within him, threatening to sweep him away. He gazed down at her, breathless once more and with his heart pounding. Everything in him wanted to reach out and scoop her into his arms, to shower her lovely face with kisses. And unless he was entirely deluding himself, she wanted it too. He leaned forward, bending over her slowly until their faces were almost touching.

Then abruptly he drew back, pushing down his eagerness and forcing himself to stand upright again. He knew beyond doubt that if once he started, he would never be able to stop.

It was maddening. But he had promised her on their wedding night that he would give her time to mature. "I won't ask you to take on the full responsibilities of a wife yet. That must wait until you are older," he had said. "They told me you were nineteen, and I give you my word I will wait until you are."

More and more often of late he'd found himself staring at her with helpless admiration. Her innocent way of embracing the world, her cheerful optimism, the little smiles she bestowed only on him, the carefree way she tossed the hair from her face—everything about her was hopelessly endearing.

Increasingly he'd been forced to consciously restrain himself when she was near. Sometimes his hand brushed against her when they passed each other, setting his whole arm tingling. He would have given anything to be able to run his fingers through her hair and hold her tightly in his arms. But he couldn't trust himself.

He found himself agonizing over the promise he had made. It had seemed only right when she was a child. But now? His wife had become an extremely attractive and eminently desirable young woman. But he still couldn't touch her. Not yet.

Meanwhile, the strain of waiting was taking its toll. She haunted his nightly dreams and invaded his every daydream. Outwardly he carried on as normal. He wondered if she had any inkling of his secret struggles.

Seeking a distraction from his inner turmoil, he gazed around her bedchamber. It only made matters worse. A small bunch of wildflowers stood in an earthen jar on a table right beside her bed. He had gathered them on the spur of the moment and handed them to her only two days previously. He could still picture the flush of pleasure that had rewarded his gesture.

Being alone with her in the intimacy of her bedchamber was more than he could bear.

"It was a wonderful race," he told her, trying to cover his awkwardness with a weak smile. "Even if you beat me!"

Then he turned and hurried from the room, trying not to think about the look of surprise in her eyes.

STEFFAN WENT to his bed that night determined for once not to think about Essanda. There was certainly plenty else to occupy his mind. The trade agreement with Varas had been concluded successfully, but many other matters of state remained to be resolved. Steffan tossed sleeplessly in his bed, his mind in a whirl as he attempted to bring order to the chaos of his competing priorities. The common people—and even some of the nobles—expected a king to have unlimited capacity to do whatever needed to be done. The reality was very different, and Steffan was keenly aware of his limitations. He had surrounded himself with wise and capable advisors. But it simply wasn't possible to delegate everything.

Something was niggling away at the back of his mind as he tossed and turned. He eventually identified it and dragged it out into the open. Troubling rumors had begun to emerge from Erestor, and even occasional reports of unrest and disturbance.

He suspected that his own needs and demands had contributed to the problem. At his insistence, Lord Burtelen, the most capable of the Erestorian noblemen, had been located almost permanently in Arnost, the Arvenian capital. He had come to lean so much on the nobleman's wisdom and judgment. Burtelen was not merely wise. He was a rare example of that most valuable of commodities—a nobleman actually capable of getting things done.

Lord Burtelen wasn't his only option for investigating the situation in Erestor, of course. There was always Lord Torbury. He lay there for some time trying to think of plausible reasons why he couldn't afford to send Torbury. He knew that he needed to do it, though. Finally, with a sigh of resignation, he gave in. The following morning he would instruct Lord Torbury to make an extended visit to Erestor.

He could ill afford to lose the services of Torbury. But someone needed to get to the bottom of what was happening in Erestor. Someone he could trust.

Lord Torbury was the newest of his nobles. Once known simply as Will Prentis, he had distinguished himself as commander of the armies of Arvenon and Castel. As an expression of his gratitude King Steffan had elevated him to the Arvenian peerage, christening him Lord Torbury in honor of his decisive victory over the Rogandans at the crucial Battle of Torbury Scarp. The new Lord Torbury had been granted the lands in Erestor formerly held by the Earl of Pisander, the man exposed as a traitor during the siege of Arnost.

More than four years had passed since the appointment, and in all that time Steffan had only once found it possible to release Lord Torbury to spend time at his new holdings. The nobleman was long overdue for another visit.

Steffan's attempt at sleep was fruitless, and he eventually gave up trying. Having propped himself up in bed with pillows, he was sitting there brooding when his door opened. A dark figure, visible only in outline in the firelight, slipped inside and approached his bed.

How had the intruder made it past his guards? Fully alert, he reached for his knife and prepared to defend himself.

A soft voice broke the silence. "It's me, Steffan."

"Essanda! You startled me!"

His thoughts went back to the last time she had entered his bedchamber. It had been at Castel Citadel on their wedding night, and it was the first time he had actually seen her face to face. He was expecting a young woman aged nineteen; he soon discovered that he had been deceived. Little more than a child, she had arrived exposed and vulnerable. She told him that she had celebrated her fourteenth birthday the previous day.

In that moment he had glimpsed the extent of her pluck and determination. It must have taken enormous courage to surrender her childhood and allow herself—for the sake of her kingdom—to be wedded to a foreigner who was a complete stranger.

At the time the situation had left him with a challenge of his own. Should he seek to have the marriage annulled?

One of his most compelling reasons for seeking a wife had been to provide his kingdom with an heir. If he abandoned the marriage the day after the wedding, he would be no closer to achieving that goal.

But if he continued with the marriage, any possibility of producing an heir would be long delayed, because he would not even consider consummating their marriage until she was much older. No other course could satisfy his honor and respect her dignity.

He had quickly decided to allow the marriage to stand. The decision had come with its own set of difficulties and frustrations. But he had stayed the course.

Now she had appeared in his bedchamber once more. But why?

"What are you doing here?" he asked softly.

"Well I am your wife," she retorted, not hiding the amusement in her voice.

"But we decided to wait. Until you were nineteen."

"You decided," she corrected him. "Don't you think I should be allowed a say in such an important decision?"

Her reply startled him. Frustrating as the waiting had been, his head had told him she needed time to mature, and his heart said it would be unfair to rush her simply to satisfy his own desires. It had never occurred to him that she might have strong opinions of her own about the timing. And he had never dared imagine that she might also be chafing at the delay.

With no response forthcoming from him, she continued. "I'm certainly old enough now. Many young women are already mothers by the time they reach the age of eighteen and a half.

"It's been well over four years since the day we married. During those years we've walked together through life. I've observed you closely and been guided by you, and I've watched as you faced difficulties and challenges. Never once have you sacrificed your integrity in favor of taking the easy way. And never once have you treated me with anything less than consideration and respect. I've learned to honor and esteem you more with each passing year."

She drew closer. "And I've grown to love you, too."

Her perfume filled his nostrils, and his heart began to race. She leaned in for a kiss—their first kiss, delicate and lingering. He wanted it never to end.

She drew back slowly and gazed at him with a tender smile. "You're a patient man, Steffan of Arvenon," she said. Then she lowered her voice to a whisper. "But I say we've waited long enough."

THE CROWDS PARTED RESPECTFULLY and people stood craning their necks as the royal carriage came to a stop right in the middle of the main marketplace at Arnost.

The young queen stepped out of the carriage and approached some of the merchants, who bowed deeply. She had chosen a location where the stall of a Varasan merchant stood beside that of a local merchant. The queen engaged both men in polite conversation before bidding them farewell with a smile and climbing back into the royal carriage.

The crowds closed in behind the carriage as it pulled away. Soon the noise and hubbub of the market had resumed at full strength, and people bumped and jostled each other good-naturedly as they bustled among the stalls, admiring the wares.

"Don't she look happy!" a young mother remarked to an older woman beside her. The queen, known for her serenity, had appeared to be carrying a special glow about her.

The older woman nodded, a sly smile on her lips. "No wonder, either. She's been visiting the king's bedchamber by all accounts." She reinforced this news with a big wink.

"How do you know that?" demanded the young mother's husband.

"Everybody knows! You can't keep such matters secret. It's all over the palace!"

The husband rolled his eyes. "Who'd be king?" he asked pityingly, directing his question to no one in particular.

"She'll be in her confinement soon," the older woman asserted with a knowing nod.

"Why? What'd she do wrong?" asked a grubby urchin, the son of the young mother and her husband. The boy had temporarily suspended his entertainment—poking his little sister in the ribs—while waiting for the answer to his question.

"She didn't do nothing wrong, you silly," chuckled the woman. "She's in the family way, that's all."

"What does that mean?" demanded the boy, giving his sister another poke.

"She's going to have a baby," his father told him.

"A baby?" the boy exclaimed, screwing up his face. "Why would anyone want a baby?"

This time he didn't wait for an answer. His whole attention had shifted to his little sister, who was scurrying hastily away after kicking him in the shins.

"Why indeed?" asked the father dryly. He raised his eyes heavenward and shook his head as he watched the retreating backs of his two children, both squawking at the top of their voices.

He turned to his wife. "Why *would* anyone want a baby?" he asked.

She came over and put her arm around his waist. "I only want them because they remind me so much of you," she told him with a wink.

12

Four years after the Battle of Torbury Scarp

King Agon of Rogand stormed about his private chambers, shouting at the top of his voice and lashing out violently at any fragile object within his reach. He didn't stop until nothing remained to be broken.

Agon's wild eyes chanced upon the untroubled figure of his slave standing motionless beside the entrance to the balcony. Ennawi seemed rooted to the floor like a statue carved from white marble. The slave's face was dispassionate as always. Nothing stirred in his eyes. If he perceived Agon's behavior as unusual—if he even registered that a human tornado had just been unleashed upon the room—he gave no sign of it. The king stared at him for a long moment before shaking his head in disgust and turning away.

Thrusting from his mind the frustrations that had led to his sudden eruption, Agon stepped calmly into the audience chamber that adjoined his apartments. The servants who cowered there aimed terrified glances in his direction before hastily lowering their eyes. He ignored them. "Bring in the foreign maggots," he said evenly, addressing himself to no one in particular. Two underlings immediately scurried to the door and disappeared outside.

A small throne dominated the room. Agon ascended the steps to its cushioned seat and made himself comfortable. The king was well aware that he could lay claim only to average height, although every detail of his surroundings served to divert attention away from such trivialities.

To Agon such things were indeed trivial. He cared not a whit about his physical stature—he cared only about power.

Two of his servants shuffled forward, offering drinks and delicacies. He waved them away with an impatient flick of the wrist.

The throne had been positioned between two large windows. Strategically placed mirrors directed light from each window onto a cluster of small ornate chairs that faced the throne. The effect was to dazzle anyone fortunate enough to secure an audience with the king. He could read every expression on the faces of his supplicants; they were barely able to see him at all.

The underlings soon returned, escorting three foreign noblemen.

"Sit," Agon commanded the visitors, jabbing a bejeweled finger toward the chairs before his throne.

The foreigners sat.

They squinted uncomfortably up at him, unable to meet his stare. The nobles were as different in appearance and temperament as three men could be, but they had in common the insatiable craving that comes with overwhelming ambition. And of late they shared another important trait—an unhesitating willingness to serve the interests of King Agon of Rogand.

Agon had spent sufficient time with each of them to ensure they were thoroughly under the spell of the Stone of Authority. The first two had been stubborn. It took two tiresome weeks to ensure their full compliance. The third had proven satisfyingly malleable from the beginning—Agon suspected the man would cheerfully run naked through the streets of Rog if he believed it would benefit his new master. Having the opportunity to cut short the necessary period of contact to just one week in his case had been a welcome relief.

All of them were now within his grasp, of that he was certain. If it were not the case, their usefulness—and with it their pitiful lives—would have come to an end. From the beginning their submission had never been in doubt, of course. No one could long resist the Stone of Authority.

Agon frowned down at the men. "Are your plans finalized?"

All of them looked flustered for a moment. Then the compliant nobleman stirred into life. "Our plans are well advanced, Your Serene Majesty, and lack nothing apart from your seal of approval. We carry a continual burden of anxiety while we await your coveted affirmation."

This particular fool might be the most pliable of the three, but his fawning was becoming unbearable. Agon couldn't wait to get the man out of his sight.

Nevertheless, he needed to act the part. "I am gratified to hear that your plans are well advanced," Agon told them, forcing himself to ignore the coarseness of their manners, "and I am eager to hear the details."

The men all began talking at once, interrupting each other constantly in their eagerness to impress him. Through the chaos he somehow managed to glean enough information to satisfy him. The men had not been idle, and their plans actually did offer considerable promise.

"You have done well," he told them, to their evident relief. "I release you to carry out your plans. I will not be meeting with you again. You will, however, find that I have arranged access for you to every resource you could need. My agents will supply you with a more than generous supply of finances and intelligence."

He paused to make sure they were paying full attention. "I trust I have made it very clear what I expect in return," he told them coldly. "Do not dare to disappoint me."

The noblemen bowed very low, and he dismissed them. They

scurried from the audience room, trembling in their haste to be gone from his presence.

AGON PUSHED through the adjoining door and reentered his chambers. No visible evidence remained of his earlier outburst—order had been fully restored during his interview.

Ennawi appeared not to have moved. Agon made his way past the slave, emerging into the sunshine and open air of his balcony. He observed the three men as they rode away, escorted by an imposing detachment of the royal guard.

The king glanced back over his shoulder at Ennawi. "Life has an irritating way of frustrating and disappointing me," he snarled. "I wield absolute power, and yet I am forced to rely upon creatures such as these foreigners."

He stepped back inside the room. "Am I not a god?" he demanded. "My devoted subjects insist that it is so—they scream it aloud whenever I appear before them in my glory."

Agon examined his slave closely. "Do you believe it to be true, Ennawi?"

The human statue didn't move.

Agon nodded sagely. "Your wisdom is greatly underrated," he told the slave. "I find I cannot argue with your response, nor can I dispute the logic that lies behind it." A peal of mocking laughter issued from his throat.

As his laughter died away, the king's expression became a scowl. "Deity or not, I am surrounded by mortal fools." He shook his head in disgust.

"Consider these foreigners," he added, waving a hand toward the road they had taken. "They are little better than worms." He spat over the balcony. "It physically pains me to be in the same room as such slithering vermin. I am compelled to waste precious hours in their company—feigning interest when I am almost swooning from the tedium. But I cannot delegate this particular task to anyone else," he added more calmly. "There is no one I could trust."

He turned to Ennawi, lowering his voice. “It’s the fault of my stone. This mindless little rock doesn’t take immediate effect—it requires TIME!” he said with a scowl. “What I need is the Stone of Knowing. That would allow me to see exactly when the Stone of Authority has taken full effect. It would no longer be necessary to waste even a minute with imbeciles like the men who’ve just ridden away.”

He opened his hand, and the Stone of Authority flashed in the sunlight. He studied it for a moment. “How have I become so dependent on a tiny lump of earth?” he asked, staring quizzically at Ennawi. “Surely a god has no need of trinkets.”

He smiled ironically. “The truth is that I am entirely reliant on this particular trinket—I might as well be addicted to it. So it seems I am not a god after all, whatever my people tell me.”

His hand closed over the stone once more, and he fell silent.

After many months with the stone, he still couldn’t claim to fully understand the way it worked.

The scroll had outlined the limits of the stone. Two limitations were especially galling: the stone could be used to target only one person at a time; and no subject could be forced to behave in a way that was inconsistent with their character or deeply held convictions.

The pronouncements of the scroll hadn’t deterred Agon from testing the second limitation. He had wasted two entire weeks trying to induce one of his minor nobles to kill himself. The man had gone away confused, but very much alive.

Agon was aware that the stone did not entirely wipe away the will of a person. The effect seemed more akin to training the will to see things the way the holder of the stone saw them. The subject still had the ability to make their own choices. They simply found themselves determined to strive for the same outcome as the stone wielder.

The stone had no impact on the effectiveness of those it influenced—its subjects did not become any more or less capable than they already were. A blunt instrument cut no more finely than it did before, and a sharp instrument lost none of its subtlety and precision.

After a few moments the king turned to Ennawi again. “Of course none of these little maneuvers with the foreigners would have been necessary if only Drettroth had delivered on his promise," he told him bitterly. "He was my childhood companion, and I expected better of him. No one ever equaled him in ruthlessness and effectiveness." He shook his head regretfully. "Those qualities are the only things I truly admire in another human," he added.

His brows furrowed. "None of it matters now. Drettroth is gone. He failed."

The slave showed no sign that he registered Agon's words at all.

Ennawi had been with Agon for so long that it was difficult to remember life without him, yet after all this time he remained an enigma. The slave had been little more than a foreign child when he was first presented to Agon as a food and wine taster. Agon was not told and had never asked how or where his servants had acquired him. He knew only that his new slave was unusually placid.

The other notable thing about Ennawi was that his tongue and both of his hands had been removed by his previous owner. Agon had never inquired as to the reason.

Without hands the slave could not feed himself, and Agon had soon demanded an able-bodied food taster. But he kept Ennawi around, mostly because as king he appreciated the rare freedom to speak freely in front of a safe audience. Agon had long recognized that he could best solidify his thoughts by verbalizing them. But in the murky cesspool of intrigue that was the Rogandan court, he could trust no one with his private thoughts and royal secrets.

No one except Ennawi.

Ennawi was unusually safe. Being unable to speak or write, the slave could not communicate at all—he was in a class of his own. Even if Ennawi had a mind to act on something he heard, he had no way of doing so. The king knew he had nothing to fear from this particular slave.

It had been suggested to Agon that Ennawi was deaf. He didn't know if it was true, but it seemed likely. Apart from rare and fleeting flashes of what might have been conscious awareness, the slave showed no sign whatsoever of understanding a single word that Agon said.

There was, of course, another possible explanation for his non-responsiveness. He was after all a foreigner. Perhaps his hearing was intact, but he had never learned to understand Rogandan.

The king approached him closely and peered into his eyes. “What goes on in that head of yours?” he asked, tapping Ennawi’s forehead determinedly.

The slave did not as much as blink.

Agon shrugged. “I’ll know once I get my hands on the Stone of Knowing,” he said.

The slave’s face appeared to twitch momentarily. Then he was still again, his face blank as always.

Agon frowned in bemusement. Had he glimpsed a spark of awareness in those eyes? He stared intently into Ennawi’s face, but could see no evidence of cognition.

He shook his head slowly. He must have been mistaken.

THE ARVENIAN FORMERLY KNOWN AS the Earl of Pisander was delighted to be gone from the presence of the unpredictable Rogandan monarch. It gave him no little satisfaction that he had managed to depart from Rog with his head still attached to his shoulders. He glanced across at his fellow conspirators. They appeared to be equally relieved.

Pleased as he was to be gone, he was far from content as the leagues rolled away under the hooves of their horses. King Agon’s detachment of guards did not afford their three charges a single moment to relax on their journey across Rogand. The harried former noblemen certainly found no opportunity to speak privately.

The situation did not change until they had almost reached the border with Arvenon. At that point Agon’s guards unceremoniously abandoned the three men and pointed their horses toward home.

Left finally to their own devices, the men turned aside from the main road and picked their way slowly through a heavily wooded area. They continued until they were certain they had crossed the border.

By unspoken mutual agreement, they rode until Rogand was well behind them. Then they dismounted and lit a fire. For a long time they sat quietly, none of them saying a word.

The former Arvenian lord finally broke the silence. “We will need to stay in close contact,” he said, “although I see no value in remaining together now. It would probably be dangerous to do so. We know where and when to next meet.”

There was no response, so he continued. “All of us know how to find Agon’s agents, and our saddlebags are stuffed full with enough coin to last us for a considerable time. I, for one, have associates I urgently need to make contact with.”

“It’s easy for you, Pisander,” said the Varasan. “You’re in your own country now.”

“Don’t call it ‘my country’,” snapped the Arvenian. “My country threw me onto the scrap heap. I was scheduled for execution, and I’d have been dead long ago if I hadn’t bribed my way out of a dungeon.” He spat into the fire. “This won’t be my country again until some radical changes take place.”

“You’re not the only one who was cast aside,” the Varasan replied. “When I was Lord Tarestel I did everything I could to spare my country the ravages of war. My king rewarded me with exile.”

Pisander gazed narrowly at Tarestel. He felt nothing but contempt for the Varasan and his relentless self pity. How had he come to be allied with such a whiner?

Both men turned to the Castelan, who sat staring into the fire, brooding. Perhaps feeling their eyes upon him, the former Lord Eisgold looked up. He stared pointedly at Tarestel. “What did you expect?” he asked derisively. “You set yourself up as ruler in place of your king. You’re lucky he did nothing worse than exile you.”

A bitter tone came to Eisgold’s voice. “My only crime was to ignore the orders of an upstart commoner—a foreign upstart at that.”

Pisander had more sympathy for Eisgold, if only because he had reasons of his own to passionately hate the commoner who had brought about the Castelan's downfall. He had little respect for Eisgold's intelligence, though—the man seemed to think himself a lot smarter than he actually was.

All of them fell silent again.

Pisander eventually broke the silence. "What are the two of you planning to do next?" he asked.

The others stared back at him. "Surely we've established that already," said Tarestel with a puzzled frown. "Our role is to further King Agon's purposes."

Eisgold appeared equally baffled by the question.

The former Earl of Pisander simply nodded, and all three of them resumed staring into the fire.

So it was true. Agon had somehow turned them into marionettes. He would pull the strings, and all three of them would dance to his tune.

Pisander tried to make sense of what had happened in Rog. He knew that the others had spent two full weeks in the company of Agon. He had found the man insufferable, and done everything he could to shorten the exposure. He had bowed and scraped, fawned shamelessly, and made a pretense of slavish devotion. The Rogandan king had apparently bought his little act, because he satisfied himself with just one week of constant contact.

Was that the reason Pisander seemed to have retained a greater measure of independent thought? He, too, found himself fully supportive of Agon's goals, even though he couldn't make sense of his own reasons for thinking that way. But he also had significant twists of his own that he intended to pursue. The other two didn't seem to have retained any desire whatsoever for independent thought and action.

How could two weeks in the company of Agon cause a man to be so thoroughly bent to his will?

His mind wandered back, as it often did, to the fateful council meeting where he had been exposed as a traitor. His eyes narrowed as he called to mind the young commoner who attended the meeting at Will Prentis's invitation. He ground his teeth involuntarily at the memory of the hated army commander. He shook his head, forcing himself to focus.

The boy seemed to have something in his pouch. At the time, it had prompted him to think about Lord Drettroth's deceptively innocent inquiry after a stolen heirloom—a tiny stone—and his promise of a rich reward if it was returned to him.

How had the youth managed to expose him? Pisander could only wonder if he had access to an object of power, perhaps in the form of a small stone. An object that gave him knowledge of other people's business. Ordinarily he would have scoffed at any such notion. But he had no better explanation for the manner in which he had been undone.

If it was true, how could an unkempt youth have gained possession of such a prize? And why hadn't Prentis simply taken it from him, by force if necessary? Surely Prentis must have known that the youth had it—why else invite him to the council meeting?

He frowned in puzzlement. There were mysteries to unravel here.

None of this explained what had happened with Agon though. Was it possible that the Rogandan king had access to a powerful object of his own? Had he discovered a means of reshaping the wills of those exposed to this power, with the result that they became determined to willingly further his purposes?

He stared into the fire. He would do Agon's bidding—somehow he could not even conceive of doing anything less. But he would also further some plans of his own. He would direct some of his new resources into hunting down the youth who had appeared at the fateful council meeting. And he would initiate some discreet investigations into Agon's remarkable persuasiveness.

There was something incredibly satisfying about the notion of using Agon's own coin for such purposes.

13

A few days after the Battle of Torbury Scarp

With the Rogandan army decisively defeated at Torbury Scarp, the invasion of Arvenon and the occupation of Varas were destined soon to become memories of the past. The allied armies pitched their tents not far from the battlefield, and wild celebrations were underway even before all the burials were over.

Rellan, still reeling from the death of his twin, Kuper, could muster no enthusiasm for celebrating. He instead focused his energy on arranging the burial of his brother. A few of his friends, in particular Will, Rufe, Ander, and Nestor, gathered around him to offer support.

Even Lord Burtelen found time to attend the committal ceremony to pay his respects. After it was over the nobleman sought Rellan out.

"The loss of your brother is very grievous, Rellan," he had said quietly. "It is hard to overstate the significance of your influence at Torbury Scarp. Without the intervention of you and Kuper the army of Erestor would have played no part in the battle. And Will Prentis has described the impact of your three hundred men on packhorses. The timing of your arrival was little short of miraculous. All of us owe both of you an immense debt of gratitude."

Words had failed Rellan in response, but he bowed low to acknowledge the nobleman's tribute.

Having laid Kuper to rest, Rellan rode at once for Erestor. Resolutely pushing the battle and its aftermath from his mind, he set his entire focus on reaching Anneka. His response was instinctive, just as a wounded animal drags itself past other accessible hiding places in an attempt to reach the comfort and security of its own hole.

Only a few days had elapsed since the battle when he reached the forest clearing on the borders of Erestor. He had been riding hard, his mind numb.

Seeing him arrive, a crowd of men, women, and children quickly gathered, eagerly calling out questions.

"Has a battle been fought?"

"Where's the army from Erestor?"

"Did the king defeat the Rogandans?"

Rellan waited for the din to die down. "We won a great victory, with the help of our allies from Castel and Varas," he told them, struggling to maintain his composure. "The war is over."

At his words an excited clamor arose, everyone talking at once.

Desolate and afflicted in spirit, Rellan had nothing further to say.

"Are you injured?" a voice asked suddenly. The hubbub quickly died away.

He shook his head slowly.

"Where's Kuper?" someone asked.

Everything went quiet.

Rellan's chin sank to his chest. He couldn't find a way to answer—the power of speech had deserted him.

The crowd stood silent, staring up at him.

Anneka appeared, stepping in front of his horse protectively. When the people didn't desist with their stares, she called out in exasperation, "Please! Leave him be for a while."

She didn't wait for the crowd to disperse. Taking the reins of his horse, she led him swiftly out of the clearing to a quiet place among the trees. Then she came to his side and stood gazing up at him.

The compassion in her eyes undid him completely. Tears began rolling freely down his cheeks. He slid from the saddle and clung to her desperately.

After what seemed an age, she gently detached herself from his embrace. She guided him back to the clearing, to a small hut set apart from most of the other dwellings. Then she called for Scar. "Make sure that no one disturbs him."

Scar had simply nodded.

Rellan entered the hut and lay down on a straw mattress. He was so exhausted that he went to sleep almost immediately.

As he slept, he dreamed.

In his dream he rode beside Kuper. Since infancy they had been inseparable—as close as twins could possibly be. On this afternoon they were relaxing in one another's company, joking and laughing together. There was no hint of battles or fighting—they were simply enjoying the opportunity to exercise their horses in the sunshine.

"When am I going to become an uncle?" Kuper had asked him.

"Not until I marry and have children, I suppose," Rellan had replied with a laugh.

"Well you'd better get started on it," Kuper had told him. Then he paused and added softly, "When it happens, make sure you tell your children about me."

Rellan had blinked in puzzlement at his brother's remark. Then, in the fraction of a moment it took for his eyes to flick open again, his twin had vanished. Bewildered, he halted his horse and peered around him in every direction. Kuper and his mount were nowhere to be seen.

He woke with a start to find himself lying alone in the hut. Everything was shrouded in darkness—it was clearly still the middle of the night. It took him a long time before he was able once more to fall asleep.

The sun was riding high in the sky when he finally awoke. Even so, he didn't emerge from the hut for another hour. He didn't know how to face people or what to say to them.

The first person he spotted outside was Scar. After acknowledging Rellan with a nod, the bowman ignored him.

It was immediately obvious that the people had taken Anneka's request very seriously. Rellan was met with curious stares, but no one spoke to him. Only the children stared and pointed, persisting until their parents came to shoo them away.

That afternoon Anneka took him aside, and they wandered together beside the small stream near the clearing.

"Tell me what happened," she said.

Rellan wasn't normally one to hoard his feelings, and he knew that hiding himself away was not an option. He needed to get it out.

He drew in a deep breath and released a long sigh.

"It took an age to get everyone through the quagmire below Steffan's Citadel," he told her. "We could easily have missed the battle. As it was, we barely arrived in time. Our mounted men reached the battlefield first. Kuper and I weren't far behind them. We were leading a few hundred men on packhorses."

"And you arrived while the battle was still being fought?"

Rellan began pacing back and forth restlessly. "We arrived at a critical moment. Kuper led us straight in. The Rogandan commander had broken through Will's lines with his bodyguard, and we arrived in time—barely—to push them back.

"I spotted their commander and went for him. It was stupid—I had no one to support me. It would have been the end of me very quickly if it hadn't been for my brother. He saw that I was in trouble and raced in to help me. It was Kuper who killed their commander.

"But then his bodyguard rallied, and Kuper was brought down himself." He raised his arms in a gesture of despair. "It was all over in a matter of moments. There was nothing I could do."

She stood silently for a couple of minutes, pondering his words. "Did you blame yourself?" she finally asked.

"Yes, I did. For a while. Will found me moping the next day and told me to snap out of it. He said that people die in battles, and that Kuper had made his own choices.

"It was obvious that the death of their commander had a big impact on the morale of the Rogandans. It helped change the outcome of the battle. And the credit for that belonged entirely to Kuper. Will said that by taking the blame I was diverting attention from his achievement. I was making it about me."

He winced as he remembered the interaction. "Will didn't pull any punches. He wasn't easy on me. But I knew he was right."

Rellan ceased his pacing. He sat down abruptly on a log and released a heavy sigh that came out more as a groan.

"I don't blame myself anymore, but that doesn't take away the emptiness. All my life Kuper's been beside me—he's been as much a part of me as my two arms. Nothing feels right anymore."

Apart from her occasional questions, Anneka had said nothing. Now she quietly came and positioned herself nearer to him. He found her presence reassuring, even though she remained silent.

After some time she spoke. "When I left our home—with Scar and all the others—I'd just lost my husband and my infant son. I thought life could never be the same again. I found a way to keep my head down and plod through each day, doing whatever had to be done to get all of us through. It went on that way for years."

She swung around to face him. Then she patiently waited until he turned his head and looked her in the eye. "Then you arrived. You're the only reason my situation changed." She spoke calmly, but he sensed the intensity behind her words.

She turned away for a moment and stared off into the distance. "You won't find it easy to adjust. It will take time. Perhaps a long time," she said calmly.

Then she looked at him again, gazing intently into his face once more. "But don't stumble around alone in the dark like I did. I'm willing to help you through it, Rellan. If you'll let me."

. . .

Not long after he returned Rellan was asked to repair a roof. As he climbed the ladder he realized that it was the same roof that Kuper had repaired on their first visit to the community. Feeling suddenly lightheaded, he quickly decided to climb down before he fell down. Anneka found him sitting on the ground with his head in his hands.

"Painful memories?" she asked quietly.

He felt his face redden with embarrassment. "Just ignore me! I'll be fine. I need to focus on getting the roof finished."

"No, you're wrong."

The change in her tone of voice startled him, and he looked up at her at once. Her normally unruffled face was pale and strained. He sensed that his current struggles had triggered distressing memories of her own experiences.

"I tried to keep busy, too," she said. "I didn't give myself permission to grieve for the ones I'd lost. So I never actually let them go." Her eyes filled with tears. "I didn't understand the damage it was doing to me."

Only once had he witnessed such a display of emotion in Anneka. Last time it had taken a catastrophic landslide to wring tears from her.

She turned her full attention to him, her eyes still brimming. "Don't you dare drag yourself through life!" she said fiercely. "Give yourself the chance to properly mourn the loss of Kuper. Remember him, think about him, talk about him, miss him—all of those things are important. Even if you can only do it with strong emotion."

He gazed wide-eyed at her for a few moments. Then he slowly nodded.

She wiped her eyes and smiled self-consciously. Then she left him.

Her words made a big impression on him. But her vulnerability had the greatest impact. He thought about the interaction many times in the following days.

And he promised himself he would stop pushing his grief away.

. . .

Rellan had been attracted to Anneka from the moment they met. Nevertheless the barriers that separated them had seemed insurmountable. Rellan could not imagine wooing a noblewoman, even one who had cast aside her life of privilege. And he came to see that Anneka was so adept at suppressing her emotions she couldn't find a way past her own defenses.

All of these obstructions had been swept away in the aftermath of the disaster at the lake. Their suppressed longings found sudden release and love flamed into life—effortlessly, and almost without conscious intent.

After his return from Torbury Scarp, though, everything had changed. She offered unstinting support as she had promised, but she did so as a caring friend and nothing more. Rellan understood why she was keeping her distance—she was trying to be respectful of his loss. She was giving him room to grieve. But he longed for the closeness they'd enjoyed previously.

The separation felt like a major step backward to him. It meant they needed to start all over again, and in spite of his boldness and bluster, he felt unexpectedly shy.

14

After a couple of weeks of growing awkwardness in his interactions with Anneka, Rellan decided to put aside his hesitation and attempt a romantic gesture. He hoped it might trigger a return to more carefree days.

Making his way to the wildflower meadow he'd found months earlier, he was delighted to find a few flowers in bloom. He picked a small bunch of blossoms, then he rode to the clearing and waited for a moment when Anneka was alone. Approaching her with a tentative smile, he pulled the flowers from behind his back and offered them to her.

She frowned uncertainly. "Are you trying to tell me I've been grumpy lately?"

"Whatever do you mean?" he asked.

"Last time you gave me flowers you told me it was because I was grumpy."

He grinned at the memory. "At the time I seem to remember also saying that you'd been working very hard and deserved a little beauty to lighten your day."

She tilted her head and cocked an eyebrow, which made him chuckle.

Putting mirth aside, he gazed at her seriously. "There's no sting to the message," he said. "I simply wanted to thank you for your support since I lost Kuper. You offered to help me through it, and you've been doing that. I truly appreciate it. It would have been very different without you."

He was entirely sincere, and he felt confident she was aware of that. She accepted the flowers graciously, but her answering smile didn't reach her eyes.

He walked away discouraged. She had apparently received his gesture as an expression of appreciation, not as a romantic initiative.

Anneka's mood over the following days only served to confirm his suspicions. If anything, he'd succeeded in increasing the distance between them.

The incident further shook his confidence. He wished he could have asked Kuper what he was doing wrong. His twin had a knack of stating the obvious, which invariably meant pointing out things that were obvious to everyone except Rellan.

He was none the wiser as the days went by. He slept poorly, and his old insecurities resurfaced. From the moment he first discovered that Anneka had been a noblewoman, he'd felt she was above him. For a time he'd allowed himself to forget the class divide, but the reality of it now came crashing in on him again. How could he have imagined that the chasm between them would simply disappear?

Weeks had now passed since Rellan's return. A day came when he found himself working with Scar repairing the roof of another dwelling, a task that had taken all morning and much of the afternoon. It hadn't gone at all smoothly, and Rellan's annoyance had grown steadily with each setback.

Late in the day Anneka came to check on progress. She arrived at the moment his frustration reached boiling point.

Leaning forward to secure a beam, he lost his footing. He crashed through the structure, wood splintering around him as a large section of the roof collapsed. Thankfully he was able to break his fall by clutching at a crossbeam as he fell, and he landed on a soft pile of hay. Remarkably, he was not injured.

Nevertheless he surveyed the destruction in total exasperation. "What a complete waste of time! I've squandered an entire day. This certainly isn't what I was hoping for."

Anneka fixed him in a stare. "What *are* you hoping for, Rellan?" she asked, clearly irritated. "Do you even know?" Then she spun on her heel and marched off.

Rellan turned to Scar, who was standing nearby. "What was that all about?" he asked, a frown of bafflement covering his brow.

"Her question deserves to be answered," Scar returned, a frosty look on his face.

Rellan looked at him in surprise. "Why is everyone so testy?" he asked.

"I don't exactly know what your intentions are with Anneka," Scar replied bluntly, "but whatever they are, I hope you're well aware that the two of you won't be the only people affected."

"What on earth are you talking about?" Rellan was completely mystified.

"This community has been led by Anneka for a long time," Scar replied. "What's going to happen if she marries you? Are you expecting to become the leader? All of us deserve to know."

Scar turned his back and departed without waiting for a response, leaving Rellan to gape after him.

A number of things instantly became clear. First, it was obvious that Scar had assumed they would marry. He almost certainly wasn't alone in that. Second, Rellan's relationship with Anneka had huge implications for the community, and he had failed spectacularly to grasp that.

More importantly for him, though, what was Anneka thinking? Did she have the same expectations as everyone else? Had she been waiting—perhaps daily—for him to conquer his self doubt and make his intentions clear? If so, his failure to act must have become increasingly painful for her, as well as confusing and unsettling for others. As he finally grasped what had clearly long been obvious to everyone else, his own mortification became unbearable.

Desperately needing time alone to think, he saddled his horse and rode away. He resolved not to return without a complete set of answers—for himself, for Anneka, and for the community.

Having been forced at last to do some honest reflecting, he saw that there was no excuse for his dithering. The loss of Kuper had been very unsettling, but it had never been a reason to leave his relationship with Anneka unresolved.

He had no doubt about his own desires—he wanted to be with her as much as ever. But he realized that deep down he'd never fully believed he could measure up to her. He was a commoner. He suspected that sooner or later she would see him for what he was, and when she did she was sure to reject him.

Everything had seemed so straightforward after the landslide. Now he needed to start again on his own, and his courage had abandoned him.

Why such timidity? He had charged into battle and attacked the Rogandan commander with less hesitancy. Why should the fear of Anneka's rejection be so crippling? He couldn't even pretend to be without hope. She'd told him plainly that his arrival had changed her life.

The situation had to change. His current position was beyond embarrassing, and the longer he left it the worse it would become.

Kuper's appeal finally sealed it. He remembered his brother's words in his dream—*You'd better get started...Make sure you tell your children about me.* He could ignore his own self-interest, but he'd never been able to deny his brother anything.

The time had come, and having put it off for so long, he was now unwilling to wait another minute. He mounted his horse and urged it toward the clearing.

To his relief he found Anneka alone. Best of all, she didn't appear to be distracted by anything pressing.

He took a deep breath to steady himself before approaching her boldly. "Would you take a ride with me please?" he asked.

Anneka's eyes narrowed, but she agreed. She retrieved her horse and accompanied him out of the clearing.

He led her among the trees for several minutes without speaking.

Finally he reined in his horse beside a pleasant meadow and slid off its back. Anneka dismounted as well.

As he turned to her, Rellan's heart began to pound. Her face was an impassive mask.

He shook his head. "I can't go on like this any longer. There are things I need to tell you, Anneka." He took another deep breath, trying to steady his nerves. "My whole world has been shaken since I met you. I never expected to give my heart to a noblewoman."

That earned him a disgusted look. "I told you before," she shot back, "I stopped being Lady Neave a long time ago! That isn't who I am."

"I know you said it, but it still hasn't been easy for me to fully accept it. But noblewoman or not, I can't let things continue the way they've been." He swallowed. "I'm sure you can't stand it any longer either."

The look on her face plainly confirmed it.

He bent down and plucked a wildflower. "You're the most amazing woman I have ever met. I know there's no possibility I could ever deserve you, but I can't bear the thought of going through life without you." He swallowed again. "Would you do me the great honor of becoming my wife?"

As he asked he stretched out his hand and offered her the flower, a delicate and beautiful bloom with large white petals.

She stood looking at him for a long lingering moment. Then she reached out slowly and took the flower from his hand.

"Yes, Rellan, I will marry you," she said. "I would be honored to be your wife."

His joy and his relief knew no bounds. He felt like leaping around the meadow like a young deer. Instead, he stood there staring at her with a stupid grin on his face.

She was magnificent. Reaching out almost instinctively, he swept her into his arms. She gazed up into his eyes, and his heart beat even faster. His eyes dropped to her lips, full and inviting. He bent his head toward her, and a thrill ran throughout his entire body as their lips met for the first time. His eyes closed, and he abandoned himself to the wonder of loving and being loved.

When they finally drew back from each other, he stood there silently, drinking her in, amazed at the tenderness he saw in her eyes. He'd scarcely allowed himself to dream of such a moment.

"I didn't know what to expect when I brought you here," he told her honestly. "I thought you were as likely to punch me as accept me."

She raised an eyebrow. "You're lucky I didn't punch you. I knew you needed to make up your own mind, but waiting for you to do it has certainly tested my patience!"

He took her hands, and gazed happily into her eyes until she began to blush.

Not wanting to embarrass her, he said contritely, "I'm sorry that I'm so annoying at times."

"At times?" she echoed, raising an eyebrow again.

He smiled at the irony in her voice. "I'll try to work on it, I promise."

She rolled her eyes. "And I'll try to restrain my expectations," she said.

He sighed contentedly. "I can honestly say that I've loved you from the moment I laid eyes on you." A cheeky grin came to his face. "Well, perhaps more accurately I've loved you from the moment you stole our horses and tried to trick us into working for you."

"And it would be accurate for me to say," she shot back, "that I've been intensely irritated by you from the first time you tried to flirt with me, which was the instant you met me."

"And yet you love me anyway," he said with a happy smile, reaching for her once more.

"I do," she said, resting her head on his shoulder. "Even though you're so masterful at exasperating me."

A flippant rejoinder came to his mind, but he decided it wasn't the time.

They stood there in silence for a while. Then she pulled away a little so she could gaze into his eyes. "From the beginning I tried desperately not to fall for you. I've never met anyone who drives me so crazy!" Her face softened. "Your brother listed your qualities, though, and he was right. You're kind and generous. And you're also loyal and courageous." She shrugged helplessly. "I gave up fighting it a long time ago."

"Are you sure this is me you're talking about?" he asked with a grin.

She gave him a mock frown before adding seriously, "I'm sorry I snapped at you earlier."

"It's a good thing you did," he replied. "It helped wake me up. That, along with some comments Scar made about whether I would be expecting to lead the community if we marry."

She shot him a glance. Then she drew back a pace, withdrawing her hands from his grasp. "That's an important issue. I'm not sure how some of them are going to feel about it."

"They needn't worry. You're the leader, and that doesn't need to change just because we get married."

She frowned at him. "So you're telling me you'd be willing to be led by your wife? It's hard to imagine how that would work."

"Are you worried that I'll feel less like a man if I'm not the leader?"

She hesitated for a moment, then she nodded.

He shook his head. "You've been my leader the whole time I've been in the community. I don't see why that needs to change, and I don't see why it has to become a problem once we're married. I'm not going to feel inferior if I'm not the leader."

Her skepticism showed clearly on her face.

"Perhaps we have different views about leadership," he said. "I see leadership as an ability—one of many abilities. Kuper was a better leader than me, and I was a better bowman. But neither of us felt superior or inferior because of that. We were twins, and we felt just as valuable as each other."

She offered no immediate response.

"Abilities are useful when deciding who to appoint to do a particular job," he continued. "Take Will, for example. King Steffan and

King Istel appointed him to lead the combined army of Arvenon and Castel because he was the best leader they had. It was the right decision—there's no way we would have won the Battle of Torbury Scarp with anyone else in command. But none of Will's soldiers felt inferior because he was the commander and they weren't. In fact they felt stronger and more capable themselves with an effective leader in command."

"That all makes sense," she replied, "but it isn't how the nobles see it. Believe me—I know from personal experience! To the nobility, a person's value comes from their bloodline. Not from anything else, and certainly not from their abilities. They see leadership the same way. You have no right to exercise authority unless you're born into the nobility."

Rellan nodded his agreement. "I'm sure that's why some of the nobles actively resisted Will's leadership."

"Exactly," she said. "They're nobles and he isn't, so in their eyes that makes him inferior, however capable he is. They wouldn't have been at all happy about coming under the authority of anyone they see as inferior."

She began to look uncomfortable. "You're saying that ability is what qualifies you to lead. If you're right, then I shouldn't be leading the community. The only reason I became the leader was because I was a noblewoman."

He shook his head in denial. "That may have been true in the beginning. But not now. You said yourself that you're not a noblewoman anymore. And yet the others still want you to lead them. It's because they know you're the best leader the community has. I've heard them say so.

"You're the right person to lead. And it isn't going to bother me. I've never seen myself as inferior because you lead the community and I don't, and becoming your husband isn't going to change that."

She looked at him thoughtfully. "I understand what you're saying," she said. "My former husband was always a leader—among the lords and on our estate as well as in our marriage. But he never treated me as inferior, and I never felt inferior. I always felt respected and honored by him."

She raised both eyebrows. "You're an unusual man, Rellan, and you certainly have some unusual ideas. But I believe that you mean what you say." She smiled. "I'm willing to see if we can make it work."

"That sounds good to me," he replied. "I should warn you, though —I'll be leading when it's just us."

So saying, he pulled her firmly into his arms once more. She lifted her face toward him, and he eagerly accepted the invitation, giving full expression to his yearning as he pressed his lips to hers.

The kiss seemed impossibly brief, but he comforted himself with the anticipation that more would follow it. He sighed with wonder as he gazed into her eyes. Why had he ever hesitated?

She smiled up at him, and he smiled back.

"Enough of all this talk about leadership and inferiority," he said. "Let's go tell everyone the news!"

15

Four years after the Battle of Torbury Scarp

In the four years since she married Rellan, the demands on Anneka's time had continued to increase. The community she led, now referred to as Newhaven by its inhabitants, was firmly established and thriving. But growth had brought its share of challenges as children were added, livestock numbers swelled, and cultivated strips expanded ever outward.

Anneka had been enjoying a rare opportunity to relax for a few minutes when Scar burst in. He appeared deeply troubled; it was obvious that he hadn't come with good news.

"Hender and Gunnar have been attacked," he told her. "Near our old dwellings in the clearing. Hender escaped, but Gunnar was killed."

Anneka's eyes went wide with shock. This was not the first time that her people had been attacked and killed—she had witnessed the savagery with her own eyes—but it was just a memory now. The community had long since escaped from those in Erestor who wanted them dead.

Since the day they retreated to the wilderness, no one had died as a result of violent attack. Not even in the days of the Rogandan invasion. She had thought such troubles were behind them.

Her heart sank as she pictured Gunnar. He was a good man, and he would be greatly missed. His wife had long since passed on, but his three children and his steadily expanding group of grandchildren would be shattered when they learned of his loss.

She turned her attention back to Scar. He looked weary, and his face was grim. She could hardly remember seeing him so concerned —certainly not since the Rogandan incursions that had forced them out of their dwellings in the clearing, their first refuge after they fled.

They were secure now in an even more remote location, one with better soil for farming as well as good hunting. But they had never entirely abandoned their former domain, and the awareness that her people were being attacked in their own forest was alarming.

"Do we know anything about the attackers?" she asked.

Scar shook his head. "Nothing at all. But Hender says it was a large party. They were long gone by the time we arrived."

Anneka frowned, completely mystified. She was not aware of enemies in the region, and bandits had been few and scattered. At least until now.

"Was Rellan with you?"

"Yes."

"Where is he now?"

"He stayed behind to do some scouting."

"On his own?"

"Hender is with him, and Petar as well." Scar gave her a knowing look. "Don't worry," he said. "He'll be careful."

She furrowed her brows, annoyed that her private anxieties should be so obvious.

"With your permission," Scar proposed, "I'll take a larger party, and we'll do some more serious scouting. I want to know whether it's a random attack by bandits, or if something else is going on."

Her brows furrowed. "What else do you think might be going on?"

Scar's face clouded. "I'm not sure. But our presence here hasn't been a secret since you and Rellan destroyed the Rogandan army camped outside Steffan's Citadel. Word has undoubtedly spread in Erestor that we're still alive and hiding away somewhere nearby. There might be people who haven't forgotten about us."

"Pisander was thrown into prison. He must surely have been executed long ago. Who else would care?"

"I don't know."

Scar looked very uncomfortable. And she'd learned to trust his instincts.

She nodded decisively. "You're right—we're much too ignorant about what's going on in the world around us. Take as many people as you need, and do a thorough investigation.

"You're right to be concerned, too. We were safe while our existence wasn't known. Now that it's been exposed, we can't be certain about the risks we might face.

"It's time we became more cautious. From now on, no one comes here by the direct route. No exceptions. I don't care about the wasted time. Every one of us needs to take extra precautions to ensure we're not followed."

Scar nodded. "I'll pass on your instructions immediately." He set off without delay.

Alone once more, Anneka allowed Scar's concerns to occupy her attention for a time. He had raised questions that needed to be answered. Uncomfortable questions.

Before long, though, she found her thoughts pulled irresistibly in a different direction—back to Rellan. She sighed, as much frustrated by her own fretfulness as by any reckless streak she could see in Rellan.

Was he reckless, or was she just too afraid of losing him?

Her memory took her back more than four years, to the eve of the decisive battle with the Rogandans at Torbury Scarp. She had watched with dark foreboding as Rellan rode east with Kuper and the host of Erestor. When Lord Burtelen's army had disappeared from all sight and knowledge, her fear told her she would never see Rellan again.

Her heart had dared to hope for a different outcome, and she had never entirely yielded to despair.

Rellan had been the irritant that prodded her back into life. At first she had blocked and resisted him.

Then together they had precipitated the landslide. Yosef and Jon had been lost, and she had almost lost her own life as well. She survived only because Rellan had saved her.

The surging waters had swept away the Rogandans laying siege to Steffan's Citadel—the entire army had simply vanished. Were it not for the endless piles of bodies downstream, there would have been no evidence that the army ever existed. Hundreds of workers had been deployed in the cleanup, and it had taken days to bury the bodies. The landscape had been left radically altered.

But the terrain wasn't the only thing that had changed. Her own carefully constructed emotional defenses had been swept away in the upheaval. Years of pent up feelings were released, threatening to utterly undo her.

To her lasting astonishment, in the days that immediately followed the landslide Rellan had been a rock, a still point in the maelstrom of her inner turmoil. He had been fully present—not his usual brash self, but a caring and considerate Rellan. She had never glimpsed this person. Had his existence been entirely hidden from her since she first met him? Or had she been unable to see it? Perhaps she would never know for certain.

When he had ridden away to war a part of her had died. She was all too familiar with separation, and this latest rending felt no less bitter than the first. Outwardly she carried on with life as before, but all the while her insides had been roiling.

Then, finally, came the day when Rellan returned. He had clung to her, as a drowning man might clutch at a log. There had been no words, only the emptiness in his eyes. He had no need to tell her what had happened.

She had known what to do—she saw at once that it was her turn now. He needed her to provide a place of refuge. Saying very little, she had willingly laid aside for a time the mantle of a leader and clothed herself instead with the compassion of a healer and the empathy of a woman.

Anneka and Rellan had in turn been compelled to part from the ones they loved the most. Each of them had helped the other in their journey through the shadow of the grief and the pain and into the light of day.

She sighed. The challenges of the past might be behind them, but Scar's report had shaken her. What lay ahead?

She got up, the restlessness of her thoughts demanding physical expression. Wandering about the room, her gaze fell on the remains of a bouquet resting on a shelf. Its blooms, once bright and colorful, had long since dried out and faded, but she smiled as she allowed her thoughts to drift back to the day she had been wed.

Fully grasping Rellan's sensitivities about her origins, Anneka had shunned fancy gowns and flashy ornaments. Instead she chose a simple but elegant frock of white embroidered linen. The young women had gathered around and pinned up her long dark hair before adorning it with wildflowers to honor Rellan's first gift early in their relationship.

She recalled the secret gratification of seeing his eyes go wide with wonder as she swept into view. She relived the delight of standing radiant before him as they exchanged their vows.

The reactions of the community had been mixed. They wanted her to be happy, but change is unsettling. Scar in particular had taken a long time to reconcile himself to her new status. But Rellan had spoken truly—he was more than content for her to lead, and he soon directed all of his considerable energy toward bettering the lives of her people.

The community wanted Anneka as their leader, but Rellan was well liked. He was capable, he was kind, and he made people laugh. More than once he had called upon his impish sense of humor to reduce the heat in a tense confrontation.

Rellan loved to poke fun at Anneka, especially in public. Occasionally she found it extremely irritating, but for the most part she took it in good spirit. Whenever it became annoying, she tried to remind herself that by far the most frequent target of his humor was himself.

The merry sound of little voices dragged her back to the present. Moving to the doorway, she gazed out on their twins, playing happily together in the sunshine.

Her life had undergone a total transformation, and she was more than content with the changes.

RELLAN STOOD IN THE OPEN, silent and angry as he surveyed the smoking ruins of the buildings that had once fringed the clearing. Hender and Petar picked among the debris. Neither of them had offered comment, but Rellan could guess how they must be feeling. This place had once been their home. Their home had been violated.

It held memories for him, too, memories that were no less significant. He had met Anneka here.

Rellan had no idea who had caused the destruction, or why. But in destroying the original refuge of Anneka and her people, the unknown marauders had achieved something that not even the Rogandans had managed to do.

He glanced around him, suddenly uneasy. They were too exposed here. He called to Hender and Petar, and they slipped away through the trees to retrieve their horses. They mounted and set off, wary and alert for any sign of trouble.

In the last couple of days they had scouted far and wide and seen no one. But the surrounding forest offered plenty of cover for anyone wanting to remain hidden.

Rellan was grateful to have Hender and Petar with him. Hender was the community's best archer, and Petar was not far behind him. Both men were also outstanding hunters and trackers. He couldn't wish for more capable companions. Nevertheless the surrounding forest felt surprisingly menacing. It was a disconcerting feeling—this had always been their domain.

He wondered what Anneka was thinking about the developments. He had no doubt that Scar had updated her by now. She would be worried about him. He peered out through the trees, a grim smile on his face. Perhaps she had good reason to worry.

After a time they came to a place he knew well. Wildflowers grew beside a tinkling stream that bubbled across a small meadow. He had picked flowers from this meadow and given them to Anneka. And he had come here again after he returned, alone and diminished from the loss of his brother at Torbury Scarp.

He closed his eyes for a moment and allowed the memories to drift through his awareness. Then he turned away from the meadow and the flowers and rode on.

"Rellan!"

The soft call reached him through the trees. If Hender was keeping his voice low it must have been for a reason. Rellan moved quickly to his side.

The bowman pointed away to the east. A group of horsemen could be seen riding toward them, not far away. They were traveling in single file along the forest path and didn't appear to be in a hurry.

"It's a large group," said Rellan, "and they're well armed. We'll observe them, that's all. Let Petar know."

Hender nodded and set off to inform Petar. Rellan tied his horse well back from the path. Then, finding a tree that offered an unimpeded view, he climbed it, carrying his bow and arrows with him. In spite of his close proximity to the trail, he was confident that the leafy foliage would hide him from sight.

He located a forked branch that pointed away from the path, allowing him to remain hidden behind the trunk of the tree. He set his feet cautiously on the branch to ensure that it would readily support his weight and enable him to stand with his legs slightly apart. His perch was perfect—sufficiently stable that he could use his bow effectively if the need arose.

Then he settled himself to wait.

Soon men began passing below him, unaware of his presence. He was not able to get any clear sense of who they were or what their purpose was.

As he continued to peer down at them he started, almost losing his footing in his surprise.

"Will!" he called excitedly. "Rufe! It's me! Rellan!"

The column of men halted abruptly, and every head swung in his direction. The riders appeared more curious than alarmed—they were clearly not on alert.

He scrambled down out of the tree and strode forward onto the path.

"Rellan!" cried Will. He dismounted and embraced the bowman warmly. Then he stood back, surveying him with a grin. "You look much too contented with your lot in life. We'll have to find something that offers you more of a challenge."

"No, thanks!" Rellan replied with energy. "I have a wife and children. They offer more than enough challenge for me!"

Rufe dismounted and pushed his way forward too. "Rellan!" he said, his face beaming his delight. "It's good to see you! I hardly dared hope we'd find a friendly face in this wilderness."

"It's good to see you both," Rellan returned. "What brings you all the way to Erestor?"

Will deflected the question. "We were almost ready to camp for the night. Would you like to join us?"

"Gladly," said Rellan. He turned aside and whistled, releasing a sound that rose slowly in both pitch and volume. Hender and Petar soon appeared from among the trees, and Rellan introduced them to his old friends.

Then Rellan took Will and Rufe aside, beckoning to Hender and Petar to join them.

"You'll need to set guards tonight," Rellan told Will. "I'm sorry to say that this stretch of forest is no longer as safe as it once was."

Will frowned. "What's happening in Erestor? We've heard rumors—rumors of trouble."

"We have no more answers than you," Rellan told him frankly.

"Our community used to live near here, but we've since moved to a more remote location. Some of us still visit from time to time, though."

He pointed to Hender. "A few days ago Hender was here with another of our men. They were attacked by bowmen, and his companion was killed. Since then the three of us have been scouting in the area. We've seen no sign of the attackers, but we've discovered that our old dwellings have been burned to the ground."

He shook his head in puzzlement. "The killing makes no sense. And the destruction seems pointless. We have no idea who is responsible."

Will's brow furrowed. "The king has become aware of trouble in this region. There have been persistent reports of unrest—rumors, mostly. Nothing that's easy to identify. But something strange is going on, and I have no doubt there's purpose behind it. We just don't know what it is yet."

"He must be concerned if he's sent the two of you," said Rellan.

"There are other reasons as well, but he does want us to find out what's behind it," Will replied.

One of the men approached, waiting respectfully for Will to notice him.

"Yes, Jonas?" he asked.

"Would you like us to make camp here, My Lord?" the man asked.

Will turned to Rellan. "Is this a suitable location?" he asked, ignoring Rellan's raised eyebrows.

"Here's as good as anywhere," Rellan confirmed.

Will turned back to Jonas. "Yes, we'll camp here."

Jonas bowed, then withdrew.

"Please accept my apologies, My Lord, for not addressing you appropriately earlier," Rellan exclaimed, a merry twinkle in his eye.

Will looked pained. "King Steffan insisted on elevating me to the peerage. I'm Lord Torbury now. It's another reason I'm heading for Erestor. I'm overdue for a visit to my new estates. They were previously held by Lord Dunnridge, who later became the Earl of

Pisander. His lands were declared forfeit when his treachery was exposed."

He lowered his voice. "Rufe still calls me Will when we're alone. I expect you to do the same."

"Whatever you command, My Lord," Rellan replied with a wink.

Will rolled his eyes.

Rufe had been observing the interaction with barely concealed amusement. Now he turned to Will, his face becoming serious. "We haven't even needed to enter Erestor to find evidence of problems. It's time the men became much more alert. We're not in Arnost now. I'll make sure guards are posted." He got up and moved away, calling for Jonas.

Fires were lit, and the men gathered around them to eat a simple meal. Then they settled down to sleep. Guards were assigned, four at a time, with each group due for relief every four hours.

Will and Rufe had shared some food with Rellan around a crackling blaze in a small clearing. As the air grew colder, Rellan banked the fire, then laid out his blanket. Will stretched out beside him. It brought back memories of nights by a campfire before Torbury Scarp with Will and his companions. They were good memories.

As he lay down, Rellan finally allowed himself to relax. Surrounded by a large group of alert soldiers, his former uneasiness dissipated like an early mist before the morning sun.

Rellan was startled out of deep sleep by the sound of an arrow whizzing past his head. It buried itself into the ground between him and Will. He leaped to his feet, sounding the alarm. The quiet scene immediately descended into chaos as men got up and armed themselves.

"To me, men!" Rufe shouted, and a group quickly gathered around him. He issued rapid instructions before sending them out scouting in pairs.

Within minutes cries could be heard further west along the path.

Rufe and two others leaped onto their horses and spurred them toward the commotion.

Rellan grabbed his bow and arrows and made to join them, but Will placed a hand quietly on his arm and shook his head. Then he swiftly drew Rellan back into the shadows among the trees, well away from the fire.

Rellan looked at him curiously. "What is it, Will?" he asked, keeping his voice low.

Will peered back at him in the gloom. "Was that arrow aimed at you, or was it aimed at me?" he asked calmly.

Rellan frowned, struggling to absorb the implications of Will's question. Then a movement on the other side of the fire caught his attention. He squinted into the dark. Black clad figures were moving among the trees on the other side of the clearing. He could not see faces—their heads appeared to be shrouded with dark hoods.

None of the men with him or with Will were clad in such garb. Then a glint caught his eye—firelight reflected off a naked sword.

Rellan reacted instinctively. He strung and released an arrow almost without conscious thought. A grunt was followed by the thud of a body collapsing to the ground. A couple of figures ran toward him. He put an arrow into the arm of one of them, then Will stepped forward with a drawn sword to engage the other one.

The attacker abruptly changed his mind and turned tail. Rellan sent an arrow chasing after him. A yelp of pain suggested it had found its mark somewhere.

All went quiet. After a couple of minutes Will cautiously made his way around the clearing, sword at the ready. Rellan retrieved his own blade and followed closely.

They found no sign of the attackers. The two wounded men were gone, and it appeared that others had removed the body of Rellan's first victim.

"It will be dawn in a couple of hours," said Will, glancing first at the embers of the fire and then up at the sky. "There's little point attempting anything before then."

Rufe returned a moment later. "They got away," he said. "But not before killing the two scouts I sent west along the path." His tone conveyed outrage. "They didn't have it all their own way, though. A couple of them will do well to survive their wounds."

"Rellan killed another of the attackers and wounded two others," Will replied.

He sheathed his sword, but remained among the trees away from the clearing.

"Who were they, and what was their purpose?" Will asked. "This was no casual raid by local bandits. It was well planned and carefully executed, and we're fortunate indeed if we only sustained two losses." He paused, staring away into the darkness. Then he returned his attention to the clearing, gazing over at the embers of the fire. "I thought the king was overly cautious sending this many men with me. Now I'm beginning to wish I'd brought more."

A dull gray light heralded the imminent arrival of the dawn. As soon as the sun rose, Rufe sent men scouting in every direction, after first instructing them to be doubly cautious. They departed in groups of four.

Once the light had grown sufficiently in intensity, Will and Rellan carefully examined the clearing.

"There's a lot of blood lying around," said Will. "Thanks to you."

Rellan shrugged. "What did they expect?"

"Not you, I'm sure. Very few archers can reliably hit invisible targets in the dark."

Rellan smiled mirthlessly. "It looks like they dragged a body in that direction." He pointed west through the trees.

"So several of them are wounded, and they're carrying a body with them. It won't make it easy for them to move quickly."

"What will you do?" Rellan asked.

"Once the scouts return we'll track them. I want to know who's behind this." He gazed at Rellan. "What about you?"

"I'm going back to the community with Hender and Petar. We need to warn them. I don't understand the purpose behind this attack, but it might have been targeting us. Especially given what happened earlier."

Will nodded. “I understand. We’ll be sorry to lose you. We won’t only miss your skills, either—it’s been good to see you again.”

“I feel the same way. It’s been too many years since I last saw you both. I hope we’ll meet again soon, and in more relaxed circumstances next time.”

Rellan called to his two companions, and they mounted and rode away.

“It’s a good thing it wasn’t just the three of us last night,” said Petar.

“I had the same thought,” said Hender. “There might be no one riding back to warn the community.”

Rellan grunted. “If it had just been the three of us, we wouldn’t have been sitting openly around a fire.”

“And I would have grumbled about that, even if not out loud,” Hender admitted. “It’s a reminder of why we need you, Rellan. You’re the only one of us with experience that counts.”

Rellan didn’t acknowledge the remark. His mind was on Anneka and on their children.

He clicked his tongue, and the horse moved forward. They would follow a roundabout route, and they would make doubly sure they were not followed. But they were going home.

16

Jonas glanced up at the sun, now riding high in the sky. It was time he reported back to Will.

Having fought under Will at Torbury Scarp, Jonas still thought of the commander as just Will, even though he was now a member of the nobility. Noblemen needed to be addressed appropriately, and Jonas felt certain he would get caught out sooner or later.

He chuckled to himself. He wasn't complaining. The only reason that addressing the commander had become an issue was that Will—or Lord Torbury or whoever he was—had been giving him more responsibility of late. A lot more responsibility.

That suited him just fine. He was ambitious and willing to do whatever it took to improve his lot in life. Having grown up in grinding poverty, he had no interest in ending his days that way. Direct access to Will must surely bring new opportunities. If it helped him get what he wanted, so much the better.

He soon joined Will's main group. They had been moving swiftly—they weren't far behind the scouts.

Will nodded a welcome as Jonas swung his horse alongside.

"They're still ahead of us, My Lord. By the time we got going this morning they had three or four hours head start. But we're gaining on them."

"Where are they heading?" asked Will.

"I'm not sure," Jonas answered frankly. "I'm not familiar with this region."

"Don't lose their trail," Will told him. "I need answers."

Jonas dipped his head, then pulled his horse clear and raced away. He rode hard until the column was out of sight.

After another hour had passed, he noticed a sudden change—the riders he was pursuing had altered their course, moving into open ground. The result was that the tracks ahead of him had become much easier to follow. He pressed forward eagerly. They couldn't be too far ahead.

He soon discovered the reason for the change. He wasted no time in returning to the main group.

"They've changed direction, My Lord," he said. "They must have realized we were getting close. They've joined the main road, which means their tracks are no longer recognizable. There's been so much traffic on the road that all the signs are confused."

Will frowned in annoyance. "Can we catch them before they reach Steffan's Citadel?" he asked.

Jonas shook his head. "I caught a glimpse of the citadel in the distance. They've probably passed through already." He hung his head. "I'm sorry, My Lord."

"It isn't your fault, Jonas—we were forced to wait for daylight to begin our chase. They've been far too canny from the beginning."

STEFFAN'S CITADEL loomed larger as the road climbed to meet it. Soon the fortress towered above Jonas, tall and immensely strong, straddling the only accessible pass through the mountains into Erestor. Its battlements looked down across the plains of Erestor to the west and the forests of Arvenon to the east. He knew that no enemy had captured it in the one hundred and fifty years since it was built by Steffan the First, the predecessor and namesake of the current king. Whoever commanded the citadel controlled access between Erestor and the rest of Arvenon.

Once they had passed through the gates, Will brought them all to a halt.

"I'm going to pay a brief courtesy call on the commander of the citadel," he said. "We need to question his guards at the gate."

He disappeared inside, returning in a few minutes. Jonas followed him to the gates, accompanied by Rufe.

"Did a large party of men pass through here?" Will asked. "It would have been no more than two hours ago."

"No, My Lord," one of the guards replied. "Several small groups of men passed through, but they didn't appear to be connected."

"Was there anything unusual about them?"

The guard paused, frowning. "One group was carrying a body. For burial, they said. A man who had died away from home. They were taking him back to his aged mother, so she could see him off."

"Were any of them wounded?"

"Not obviously," he replied.

One of the other guards spoke up. "One of the groups had a few men who looked like they were ready to fall from the saddle. The person who appeared to be leading the group said they were eager to get to Maranelle as soon as possible, so they'd been riding all night. He said they were very tired."

"Did any of their accents seem different?"

"No, My Lord, although most of them didn't speak. Those who did sounded like locals."

Rufe walked to the middle of the road and bent down, examining it closely. After a few moments he got to his feet, holding up a finger smeared with red. "Blood," he said. He turned to the guards. "These men were a lot more than just tired. They attacked us last night, and some of them were wounded during the fight."

The guards shrugged helplessly. Jonas understood their reaction —the kingdom was supposedly at peace. They would have seen no reason to be especially wary.

"Which direction did they go in?" Will asked.

"They just followed the road to Maranelle," they replied.

Will signaled to Jonas and the other scouts to rejoin the main group. All of them mounted up and passed quickly into Erestor. They rode swiftly, following the road for several hours. They saw no sign of the men they were pursuing.

The sun was sinking low in the sky when they paused to rest the horses. Will called over Rufe and Jonas. "They appear to have eluded us," he said.

Rufe nodded. "They must have found a place where they could leave the road without leaving a trail."

"What do you think, Jonas?" Will asked.

"I think Rufe is right, My Lord. We should have seen some sign of them by now." He shook his head, bemused by what had happened.

Will frowned. "There's no point in continuing to push the horses," he said. "We'll ride on until we find a suitable location to camp. There'll be no sitting around open campfires this time, though. From now on we're on full alert—we will ride and camp as we did during the war."

As soon as he arrived in Maranelle, Will sought out Lord Burtelen. The nobleman usually spent far more time in Arnost than in his native Erestor, but Will had become aware that he was currently in the Erestorian capital to settle some personal business. Will valued Lord Burtelen's effectiveness and reliability as highly as the king did. The nobleman was also well connected in Erestor, and Will hoped he might be able to offer insights into the disturbances.

"It's good to see you, Will. Or rather, Lord Torbury," Lord Burtelen said with a smile. "What brings you to Erestor? Are you paying another visit to your holdings at last?"

"That's certainly one of the main reasons why I'm here, My Lord," Will replied. "But the king is also concerned about rumors of unrest in Erestor, and he wants me to get to the bottom of it."

Lord Burtelen appeared unmoved. "I've heard similar rumors," he replied. "I'm sure we all have. But I don't believe there's any real reason for alarm. I've seen no evidence of unrest."

"Our party was attacked on our way here, and two of my men were killed," Will told him.

The nobleman was clearly shocked. "Were you able to establish who did it?"

"No. They attacked us at night. We pursued them as soon as there was enough light for tracking, but they joined the main road and passed through the citadel before we could catch them. They disappeared somewhere on this side of the pass."

Lord Burtelen's brows furrowed. "It seems incredible. I haven't heard of anything like this. Not since the Rogandan invasion. Could it have been bandits?"

Will shook his head. "Both the attack and their escape were too well planned and executed to have been carried out by bandits. There was purpose behind it, although I am at a loss to understand what it was." He frowned.

"I brought twenty men with me," he continued, "and I only did so at the insistence of the king. I will say, though, that traveling with a large group of men-at-arms no longer seems excessive to me. I would strongly urge you to go nowhere without a strong escort, My Lord."

The nobleman's brows furrowed again in puzzlement. "I don't understand it at all. But I appreciate your advice. And I will take it seriously."

Before they parted, Lord Burtelen had sent word to his holdings with orders for a squad of armed retainers to set out immediately for Maranelle. Will was able to extract a promise from him that he would not leave the capital until they arrived.

WILL ALSO ARRANGED to meet with the king's uncle, the Duke of Erestor.

The king's uncle had acted as regent while the king was absent in Castel seeking out a bride, and he had operated decisively and effectively on the king's behalf, successfully defending the capital during the Rogandan invasion. When the king returned to Arnost after the Battle of Torbury Scarp, the duke had asked the sovereign for permission to return home. Eighteen months passed before King Steffan relented and released his uncle.

The king greatly valued the duke's wisdom and support, and he had only granted permission reluctantly. But he also saw that the regency had wearied his uncle. The duke was no longer a young man, and he had neither the desire nor the energy to continue bearing heavy burdens of state.

All of this was known to Will. In fact he had personally interceded with the king on the duke's behalf. The duke was grateful for his support, and he only left Arnost after extracting a promise from Will to visit his castle when he was next in Maranelle.

Now that Will had arrived in Maranelle, he was looking forward to seeing the former regent. They had worked together closely in Arnost during the dangerous period following the Rogandan invasion, and Will had developed great respect for the duke.

Maranelle Citadel was the duke's ancestral home. It had been built on a rocky promontory above the city, and Will was grateful that his horse was doing the climbing as they traveled up the road to the castle.

When he reached the gates, Will paused to give his horse a rest. He looked down on the city below and beyond to the bay. Fishing boats were drawn up onto the beaches, at this distance little more than dark smudges on the white sand. Others floated in the bay, their sails visible as bright dots on the turquoise water.

He paused for a few moments longer to appreciate the peaceful scene, then he turned and guided his mount through the gates of the castle. One of the duke's retainers took the reins of his horse, and another led him to a terrace that overlooked the bay. He had been admiring the view for several minutes before the duke appeared.

"Lord Torbury! What a pleasure!"

Will bowed low. "My Lord Duke, the pleasure is mine!" Will had never seen the duke so relaxed and content. He waved a hand over the scene before them. "I can see why you were so eager to return to Maranelle."

His host smiled. "It is beautiful, is it not? And it's good to fill my old lungs with fresh sea air," he said. "Will you be in Maranelle for long?"

"Probably not. I need to visit my holdings, but I'll pass through Maranelle again before returning to Arnost."

"You should attend the Council of Lords while you're here. You have a seat on it, of course. In fact the size of your holdings makes you a senior member. The next meeting will be held in a few days."

"I presume you will lead it, My Lord." Will said.

The duke sighed. "I should, although I avoid it if I can these days. The truth is I find myself less and less patient with the petty power plays that occupy far too much of the time at these council meetings. Burtelen is a good man, and there are others, but many of them behave more like unruly children than noblemen. They could use a bit of your common sense."

Will had other things on his mind at that moment, and councils held very little interest for him. He decided to voice his concerns.

"There appear to be signs of unrest in Erestor, My Lord."

The duke glanced at him for a moment, then he redirected his gaze out across the boats on the bay. He didn't speak.

The silence soon weighed on Will, and he began to feel restless. Was the duke aware of the world beyond his walls? He glanced around him. His recent fight in the forest was surely worlds apart from this peaceful environment.

"I have one lasting regret," said the duke. "I had the opportunity to execute Pisander, and I didn't do it."

Will looked at him in surprise. He could not imagine what had prompted the duke's remark. "Surely Pisander is no threat. He was under sentence of death when he fled. He wouldn't be foolish enough to come anywhere near Erestor. Would he?"

The duke redirected his gaze to Will. "Pisander is a subtle and dangerous man," he replied. "Don't make the mistake of underestimating him."

Will shook his head, puzzled. “I don’t understand, My Lord. Are you mentioning him because you believe he might be somehow connected with the unrest?”

“I can’t tell you for certain who’s behind it, Will. But I do keep my ears open. I’m not entirely ignorant of what’s going on around me. And if you’ll take my advice, you won’t ignore any possible threat, however unlikely it might seem.”

WILL LEFT the castle with a great deal to think about. The duke had always been a shrewd observer. Could he be right? Was the trouble somehow connected with a traitor who had mysteriously decided to reappear, years after cheating death by bribing his way out of a dungeon?

And even if it were true, how was that information of any use to him? What could he possibly do about it?

17

Jonas had camped overnight with Will and his men almost within the boundaries of Will's holdings. By the time the sun had risen, they were in the saddle and on the move.

Before long they caught sight of an ancient pine tree standing alone at the top of a distant slope. "We're on my land now," Will announced.

They crested a hill, and he reined in his horse. Rufe and Jonas halted on either side of him.

A fertile valley lay before them, with a river winding through it. Will pointed toward a clump of trees far off in the distance. "The manor house is just beyond those trees," he said.

"It's good land," Rufe replied admiringly. "It must yield a worthwhile return."

Will nodded. "It'd been allowed to run down when I took it over. Most of the income for the first three years was consumed paying for repairs and refitting. There should finally be a good return this year."

He clicked his tongue, and they set off again, riding slowly down the slope into the valley.

"I appointed a reliable steward," Will continued, "a man named Timms. He isn't young anymore, but he still has plenty of energy, and he knows what he's about. I'm looking forward to meeting with him again—I haven't heard from him for a while."

Jonas raised his eyebrows in surprise. He couldn't believe that Will had been leaving subordinates to run his estates with so little personal supervision. If landowners expected issues to be dealt with quickly and effectively as they arose, they needed to keep in close contact with their retainers. Jonas had grown up on the land, and he had seen firsthand the consequences of leaving such things to chance. Even if Will was communicating regularly with Timms, Arnost was a long way from Erestor, and the delay between sending a message and receiving a reply must surely create the potential for a lot of problems.

If Will couldn't figure this out for himself he'd be in trouble. Perhaps he wasn't even aware of such basic necessities. He may have never gained personal experience of farming, much less running an estate.

Even if he did understand what was needed, though, it mightn't have helped. King Steffan placed continual demands upon his commander—Jonas had seen it for himself. Will simply didn't have the opportunity to visit his holdings in Erestor as often as he needed to.

Jonas was aware that other noblemen also spent much of their time in Arnost, but he also knew that most of them returned to their estates several times each year. Two visits annually had to be an absolute minimum. Will needed to put pressure on the king to release him more frequently—a lot more frequently. Even if the king was resistant.

Will probably wouldn't raise it with King Steffan unless someone prodded him. Rufe was the man. It wasn't in Jonas's interests to get involved.

As they drew nearer to the manor house Jonas started to become increasingly puzzled. It was gradually dawning on him that something wasn't right here. Where were the farm laborers? Rich land like this should be buzzing with activity. And where were the livestock? Sheep and cattle ought to be grazing everywhere.

Will had clearly noticed it too. He pulled ahead of the others in his haste.

They swung around the trees, and the manor house came into sight at last. Will pulled his horse to a sudden halt.

Jonas expected to see large barns near the main house, and dozens of sturdy little cottages spread out nearby to house the retainers and their families.

There was no sign of barns or cottages. Fire had swept through the area. Smoke still rose lazily from the charred remains of buildings. Apart from the manor house, nothing remained standing except blackened stumps and the remnants of stone chimneys.

Jonas and the others followed close behind Will as he spurred his horse toward the manor house. A few chickens scattered, squawking loudly. Nothing else disturbed the unnatural silence.

The manor house showed no obvious sign of damage until they rode up to the main door. Jonas saw then that the front doors had been torn off. He followed Will inside, trying to peer through the dust disturbed by their passage. He imagined that fine furniture and elegant settings had once graced the parlors and the sitting rooms. If so, all of it was gone. The rooms were largely empty.

An old woman emerged tentatively from within the house and peered fearfully toward them. When she saw Will, she bowed low and began to quietly weep.

"I remember you," said Will gently. "You're Timms's wife, aren't you?"

She nodded dully. "Yes, My Lord." Beckoning him to follow, she disappeared inside.

Will followed her into the building, Rufe and Jonas trailing behind. She soon came to a halt in a dimly lit room. An old man lay on a pallet on the floor.

Will knelt down beside the man. "Timms," he said softly. "What has been done to you? What has happened here?"

Recognizing his visitor, the man tried to get up.

"Stay where you are!" Will insisted firmly.

Timms collapsed back down, panting. "I am sorry, My Lord," he said feebly. "I was not able to prevent them."

"Are you injured?" Will asked.

The man nodded. "They beat me severely, but I think they wanted me to survive. Even if only barely." He grimaced—perhaps intending a smile—then he coughed weakly.

"Who did this?" Will asked.

The man shook his head slowly. "I don't know, My Lord. But I think they were working for...for him." He lowered his voice as he said "him".

If Will had any idea who Timms was referring to, he gave no indication.

"They told me to give you a message," the steward went on. He winced a little, clearly not eager to pass it on.

"Speak freely," Will told him. "I won't hold you responsible for whatever they said."

Timms nodded. "They said to tell you that you have no right to be here. They called you a common usurper and an upstart. They promised they will tear down anything you try to build, and kill anyone who tries to help you." He paused. "That was the message." The effort of speaking had clearly exhausted him.

"Thank you, Timms," said Will. "You need to rest now."

Will got up and left the room, Timms's wife trailing behind him. When they emerged from the house, he turned back to her, looking down into her pleading eyes.

"Can you help him, My Lord?"

Will nodded. "One of my men has some skill with healing. He will remain with you, and I will instruct him to help you in any way he can."

Tears of gratitude came to her eyes. She didn't immediately speak.

He lowered his voice. "The people and the livestock are all gone. Do you know where they went?"

She pointed vaguely toward the north. "The men drove everyone away after they burned the barns and the houses. They took the animals with them. Some of them stayed behind though, to beat my husband," she said.

She was wringing her hands, although she seemed unaware of it. A surge of anger washed over Jonas. What was the purpose of this suffering?

"When did this happen?" Will asked gently.

"The day before yesterday, My Lord," she replied.

"Thank you," said Will.

She bowed and hurried back inside.

Will called for one of his men and sent him in after her. Then he turned to Rufe and Jonas.

"Who did this?" Rufe asked, a baffled look on his face.

"I can't be certain," Will replied, "but I suspect that Pisander was behind it."

"Pisander? How could he have done this?" Rufe was clearly struggling to take such a notion seriously.

"It sounds unlikely, I know. But some recent hints have made me suspect it might be true."

"Are we going after them?" Jonas asked.

"That's certainly what they're expecting us to do," Will replied.

This remark took Jonas by surprise, although it shouldn't have. It was exactly the kind of thing Will was given to say. His ability to outguess his enemies was what made him such an effective commander—and such a dangerous opponent.

Will gazed at Jonas and Rufe expressionlessly. "We wouldn't want to disappoint them, would we?" he asked.

After Will had instructed his healer to remain behind to care for Timms and his wife, he and the rest of his party left the manor house without delay.

Since then they had been riding hard for several hours.

Jonas rode near Will. "No need for a tracker," he called. "I've never seen a more obvious trail. There's no way they could hide these tracks."

It was hardly surprising. A large group of people driving all their livestock left a trail that a child could recognize.

"They have no interest in hiding their tracks," said Will.

There it was again. The commander might have managed to make sense of all this, but Jonas certainly hadn't.

The afternoon was well advanced when they finally caught sight of a large body of people, accompanied by cattle, sheep, and goats. They appeared to be milling around aimlessly.

Will called to Jonas. "Scout out the immediate area. I don't expect to find any armed men nearby, but we need to check anyway."

Jonas called to a couple of men, and the three of them rode away in different directions.

Will's instinct proved to be correct. None of them could detect any sign of enemies in the vicinity.

As soon as he gave his assessment of the situation to Will, the commander approached the people.

It was obvious that they were greatly distressed.

"Have you been harmed?" Will asked them.

One of the older retainers stepped forward, bowing. "Most of us are well, My Lord," he replied. "But some of our men have been killed, and all of us are grieving."

"How many men attacked you?"

"There must have been thirty of them at least," the man replied. "They came upon us suddenly, and we had no time to arm ourselves. A number of our men resisted—they were killed without mercy." Tears came to his eyes, and he shook his head. "I don't understand it. I have never heard of anything like this happening before."

"I am as surprised as you are," said Will. "If there had been any history of such happenings in Erestor I would have made sure you were well protected. I am sorry for your losses, and for the way that all of you have been treated. Rest here tonight. You can return to the manor house tomorrow. I will leave behind two of my men to assist you. You will need to set up temporary shelters when you arrive. But while that is being done, the older folk and any women with small children should shelter in the house."

"You won't be coming back with us, My Lord?" The old man was clearly dismayed.

"Not yet. We must ride on. We won't stop until we deal with the men who did this."

The man bowed and turned away.

"Two men won't be able to do much to help them," Rufe observed.

"No, they won't," Will agreed. "But we can't spare any more."

Rufe selected two of the men and gave them instructions.

Jonas was puzzled. These people would never settle while they weren't properly protected. As long as they remained fearful, they wouldn't give themselves wholeheartedly to rebuilding.

What was the point in chasing their attackers? They would most likely escape as they had done previously, in which case it would prove to be a futile waste of time. He shook his head helplessly. The decision didn't belong to him.

Will selected two other men and sent them off to find the trail of the attackers.

"Move out!" Will's ringing call spurred the remaining men into action, and they swung in behind him.

"Rufe! I need you to take half the men. Follow us, but stay completely out of sight. We'll make sure our path is obvious. Jonas, you're with me."

Will's purpose in splitting the group wasn't obvious to Jonas, but he didn't voice his questions. Rufe didn't query the order, either. He selected a group of men and halted them. They were soon out of sight.

The men they were chasing had made no initial attempt to hide their tracks, and Will and his group at first were able to follow swiftly. After a couple of hours the tracks veered off toward a hilly region dotted with rocky outcrops. Will drew the men to a halt.

Jonas surveyed the terrain with narrowed eyes. Then he turned to Will. "If I were looking for a good location for an ambush, My Lord, I wouldn't look any further," he said, pointing ahead.

Will nodded. He waved toward the hills ahead. "If you were setting the ambush, where would you lie in wait?" he asked.

Jonas puckered his brows. "I'd look for a place where the path narrows, and passes between two rocky outcrops. And I'd make sure the trail is easy to follow."

Will gave him a lopsided grin. "It sounds like a perfect plan. I only have one question. Will they think we're stupid enough to fall for it?"

"They'll undoubtedly be hoping we're that stupid."

"What would you do in my position?" Will asked.

"I'd try to do something unexpected," Jonas replied.

"Precisely," said Will with a nod. He turned to another of his men and spoke quietly to him. The man quickly rode away, heading back toward Rufe and his group.

Will turned to Jonas. "I need you to ride ahead. When you find the ideal location for an ambush, come back and let me know. Make sure you stay out of range of their arrows."

Jonas nodded. "What then?" he asked.

"It will be time for us to do something they're not expecting."

"What did you have in mind?"

Will simply smiled back at him.

Jonas shrugged. Then he kicked his heels into his horse's flanks and rode forward.

18

"Keep the noise down!" Gareth growled, glaring at the men spread out around him. The persistent murmur of voices, punctuated by bursts of laughter, slowly died away.

These idiots would betray their position if he didn't keep a close check on them. He frowned. A big bag of money was waiting at the end of this job, and nothing would distract him from that. The others shouldn't need reminding—they were mercenaries, too.

He shook his head. Maybe it was time he considered a different line of work. No one lived forever, and mercenaries typically had shorter life spans than most. It was a high risk occupation, even if it did have the potential to deliver big rewards.

The problem was that a mercenary too often found himself doing dangerous jobs for very dangerous people. The man who had organized this expedition was a perfect example. Gareth had the feeling he would do anything—anything at all—if he thought it might advantage him. He wasn't the kind of person you wanted as an enemy.

Gareth's employer called himself Dunnridge, although it almost certainly wasn't his real name. He had known Will Prentis would be traveling to Erestor, and he had hired Gareth because of his reputation for stealth and reliability.

Gareth had concocted the plan to kill Prentis in the forest. He hadn't been dismayed when the attack failed. It had always been possible that the commander would bring a large group of soldiers with him. So he had devised a backup plan. His new plan was designed to reduce Prentis's force, and thereby to tilt the odds in his own favor.

After burying the dead mercenary and sending away those who were wounded, he had led the remainder of his men to Prentis's holdings. As soon as they arrived he had personally supervised the destruction.

Sparing most of the retainers was no act of mercy—he cared nothing for them. He spared them only because Prentis would be forced to offer them protection. That would compel him to divide his force. Once that was done, all that remained was to lure him to his death.

All these schemes might have seemed unnecessarily complicated to some of Gareth's men. But if you were in charge you got to call the shots. And his employer had accurately predicted that it wouldn't be a straightforward task to kill Prentis. Everyone said that the commander lived a charmed life. Gareth intended to put an end to that reputation.

Gareth wondered why Dunnridge wanted Will Prentis dead. He'd presented it as a simple case of revenge, but Gareth wasn't convinced. It didn't smell right. A deeper game was being played here. He was sure of it.

He was smart enough not to inquire too closely, though. Dunnridge had promised a payout that was more than generous, and that was all that mattered in the end.

Gareth gazed off into the distance, allowing his mind to wander. It was definitely time to consider a change. Sometimes he found himself thinking about buying an inn. Something seedy, filled with rough customers with a liking for ale, and plenty of it. And customers who were willing to pay well for other amusements. There would still be risks, but that was true of every profession. And compared to the risks faced by a mercenary, these would be very manageable.

"I see a rider!" The muffled call came from one of the lookouts he had positioned above the other men hidden among the rocks.

Gareth peered out cautiously. The rider halted his horse well before he reached their position and looked ahead warily. The path wound its way upward with rocky outcrops on either side of it. The rocks offered protection throughout the length of the path, so Gareth had positioned his mercenaries near the base of the outcrops. He wanted to keep Prentis's men out in the open, away from the shelter of the rocks where the mercenaries were concealed.

"Stay out of sight," Gareth hissed. "And don't fire at him! We don't want to alert them."

The rider peered ahead for a few moments, then calmly turned his horse around and rode away.

"It doesn't look like he spotted us," said the lookout.

Gareth's lip curled up in a lopsided smirk. "Remember why we're here," he growled. He kept his voice low, but made it loud enough that all of them could hear. "There's only one man we care about—getting the full payment depends on taking him down. The others don't matter."

As the minutes dragged by he could sense the tension slowly building. Something needed to happen, and soon.

"They're coming!"

"Is Prentis among them?"

"Yes. He's riding near the front of the group."

"Are you certain?" Gareth asked. Nothing could be left to chance.

"Yes. I've seen him plenty of times."

"So he's taken the bait. How many did he bring?"

"There's only about ten of them."

Gareth grunted in satisfaction. "So the fool left half of his men with the rabble as I expected. You know what to do."

Their targets disappeared for a moment as a distant boulder hid them from view. Once they emerged from the other side they would almost be within bowshot range. Gareth's men nocked arrows and bent their bows.

No one appeared. Gareth narrowed his eyes, searching for any sign of their quarry. Where were they? His gut began to twist as the moments passed. He peered about uneasily.

He pointed to two of his men. "You and you! Get down there, and find out what's going on." His finger stabbed toward the area where the men had disappeared, then swung wide to either side to indicate that they should approach from the flanks rather than directly. The men nodded, quickly slipping away among the rocks. They were soon lost to sight.

More minutes passed with nothing but silence. The knot in Gareth's gut began to tighten.

A sudden scream of agony behind him shattered the stillness. Gareth spun around to see archers on the rocks above, shooting down at his men. His eyes went wide as a shaft whizzed past his head.

He began scrambling up the rocks to reach the archers. "Follow me!" he shouted. The men around him responded immediately, emerging from their cover and clambering upward.

An arrow whistled past him from behind and bounced off a rock. He stole a glance back over his shoulder. Bowmen had appeared below, releasing a constant stream of arrows toward him and his men. They were caught in crossfire. Shocked speechless, his mind spun as he tried to dream up a way to regain the initiative. Another shriek beside him shattered his concentration. He glanced to one side in time to see two more men go down with arrows in their backs. It was difficult to think straight.

Abandoning any attempt at reason, he threw back his head and bellowed his fury, other voices joining him to swell the sound. He thrust everything from his mind except the need to visit ruin on his enemies. The archers above him were almost in reach. He leaped over the last rock that stood in his way and drew his sword. With a howl of rage he charged at the bowmen.

They drew their own swords and sprang toward him. He thrust his sword forward, penetrating his opponent's guard. The man went down, and he straightened, ready to find another.

Then an arrow took him in the square of the back, and he pitched forward onto the rocks. Pain overwhelmed his senses. His mind barely had time to register the futility of life before all awareness was snatched away.

"You did well, Rufe," said Will.

Rufe shrugged. "It took longer than I expected for us to find a way around that outcrop. Then we had to climb to a position above them. But your plan was good, and it played out as you expected."

"You guessed what they would do, My Lord?" asked Jonas.

Will nodded. "It wasn't difficult."

Jonas raised an eyebrow, glancing in the direction of Rufe, who wasn't looking any wiser than he felt.

"What were they trying to achieve?" asked Will. "That's always been the key question." He gazed off into the distance. "The attack in the forest was carefully planned. It appeared to be targeting either me or Rellan. When I saw what had been done to my estate, it became obvious to me that I was the target of both attacks. The attack in the forest failed. Apparently they had another plan ready just in case."

Jonas nodded. That made sense.

"After they came here and destroyed the buildings and forced the people to leave," Will continued, "I had no choice but to pursue them. Once we caught up with the people and the livestock I had some decisions to make. There weren't too many options."

"And none of them particularly good ones," Jonas agreed.

Will nodded. "The first option was to take the people back and stay with them to provide protection. It wasn't a solution, because I can't stay here forever. Before long I would have needed to return to Arnost. If I took all of you with me, it would have left the people without protection, and these men could come back and finish the job."

"And they probably knew you would figure that out," said Rufe.

Will nodded again. "I could prevent that by leaving most of you here. That would have left me largely unguarded, though. They could have attacked me again on my way back to Arnost, and with much better odds than last time."

It all sounded so obvious.

"The other option was to leave the people and go after the attackers. I've never been one to put things off, especially things that need to be dealt with immediately. They undoubtedly concluded I'd choose that option, because it offered me the only chance of finishing this once and for all."

"With your reputation, they would never have doubted it was going to end in a fight," said Jonas.

"So they pressed on until they found a suitable place for an ambush," added Rufe.

"Right," Will agreed. "But they wanted to find a way to tilt the odds in their favor. So they needed to give me some compelling reasons to divide my force before I set off after them. A prudent leader would leave a few men behind to protect the manor house, and a few more to protect the people. Chasing after them with a reduced force would have been hazardous, but I'm known as a man who's willing to take risks."

"But you took almost everyone," said Jonas. "And you divided our force to let them think you'd taken the high risk option and left a lot of your men behind."

Will nodded. "It was still a risk," he said. "But I am a risk taker."

"And you knowingly walked right into their ambush," said Rufe. "Or pretended to."

Will shrugged. "It seems to have worked out," he said.

Jonas stared at the commander. His reputation was well deserved.

"Whoever's behind this will eventually find out that they failed," said Rufe. "Will they try again?"

Will looked thoughtful. "The more important question," he said, "is why they wanted to kill me at all. They went to a lot of effort and a lot of expense. What was the reason behind it?"

"Some nobleman who doesn't like a commoner joining the nobility?" asked Rufe.

It was what Jonas was thinking, but he was glad that Rufe had been the one to say it. It sounded a bit blunt. "That was the reason given in the message passed on by Timms," he offered.

Will didn't look convinced.

"You said earlier you thought it might be Pisander," Rufe said.

Will nodded. "Timms clearly thought so," he said.

"Is that what he meant when he said these men were working for *him*?" Jonas asked.

Will nodded again. "I believe so. He was only guessing of course. But if Pisander was the one behind it, the question is why."

"You were responsible for his arrest," said Rufe. "Now you've taken over his lands. Someone like Pisander would want revenge."

Will didn't appear to be so easily satisfied. "It would seem to be reason enough. But is it the real reason, or just what I'm supposed to think?"

Jonas frowned. Rufe had already offered a perfectly good explanation. Why look further?

Will was clever, but no one could be right all the time. Jonas couldn't help wondering if he was trying to be too clever on this occasion. Why search for another motive?

Will looked troubled. "Where is he getting the money to pay for all these men?"

"Perhaps he had money hidden away," said Jonas.

Will gave no response.

He glanced back in the direction of the manor house. "I'll need to send men to my estate," he said. "They can provide protection and help with the rebuilding. It will have to be a lot of men. Otherwise the same thing might happen again."

"That's going to mean a few more years without a return from your estate," said Jonas.

"It can't be helped," Will replied. "Rufe, send ten men back to the manor house to help the people. Tell them I'll send others from Maranelle."

Rufe nodded and set off to select the men.

"Do you think we'll be attacked again?" asked Jonas.

"I don't think we're in immediate danger," Will replied.

Rufe returned as his ten men were riding away. "What next?" he asked.

"We'll return to Arnost," said Will. "But first we'll head for Maranelle. I have some pressing business to attend to."

THE FORMER EARL OF PISANDER had adopted his original name of Dunnridge, although he no longer used the honorific of "Lord". Being reduced to the status of a commoner might have been a bitter slap in the face, but he welcomed it. It helped ensure that his anger continued to burn hot. He never wanted to allow it to merely smolder.

He eventually learned of the demise of Gareth and the other men he had sent after Will Prentis. One of his informants overheard Prentis's soldiers boasting about it in an inn.

He wasn't at all disappointed to hear that none of his mercenaries had survived. There would be no need to pay them. He had, of course, advanced them an initial sum, but the bulk of the money was due only after the job had been completed successfully.

The mercenaries had never been aware of his true agenda, so they couldn't know that they had already largely achieved their purpose. The fact that they had generously done it almost for nothing only made it more satisfying.

They had failed in one important respect, though. Will Prentis was still alive. It was intensely annoying to discover that.

Dunnridge's own downfall had been at the hands of Prentis, an upstart commoner who had since received the title of Lord Torbury. And this Torbury had the effrontery to accept from the king the ancestral holdings of the Dunnridge family. The only thing he deserved was a painful death.

It made little difference, though. Prentis could celebrate his survival as much as he liked. The fool of a commander might think himself so very clever, but he had no idea what was coming. No idea at all.

19

Will had only been in Maranelle for a few hours before he once again stood with the duke on his terrace overlooking the bay.

"Did you find everything in order at your holdings?" the duke asked him.

"Far from it, My Lord," he replied. "A group of mercenaries destroyed almost everything, and carried away my retainers. I've just spent the morning hiring men to help with the rebuilding and to protect my retainers."

The duke frowned. "So it is worse than I feared." He glanced at Will sympathetically. "I am sorry that this misfortune has fallen on you," he said. "Although I suspect that you will be able to bear it better than most."

He gazed out over the bay and sighed. "I have received reports that Lord Burtelen was attacked on his way to Arnost. Fortunately he was accompanied by a sizable escort." He glanced back at Will. "Was that your doing?"

Will nodded. "Yes, My Lord. I made him aware of the attack in the forest on my way to Erestor and advised him not to travel without an escort."

"Then you saved his life. He is returning to Maranelle, and I expect him to arrive in the next couple of days." His eyes narrowed. "It has not escaped me that the attacks have been directed at the most capable of our leaders."

"Are you taking measures for your own protection, My Lord?" asked Will. "You are the most capable of us all. But you are much more than that—you are also an important figurehead."

"I cannot accept your generous assessment of my capabilities, Will. But please don't be concerned on my behalf. I can look after myself."

Will frowned. He sincerely hoped that the duke was treating the situation seriously enough. The kingdom could ill afford to lose him.

"The council meets tomorrow, and I want you to be there," said the duke. "I have my suspicions about some of the minor nobles."

"Do you suspect them of involvement?"

"Not directly. But some of them are opportunists, and a situation like this provides an unusual opportunity for their loyalty to be tested."

"How do you propose to do that?" Will asked.

"There might be a way," the duke replied. "I'm giving it some thought. In the meantime I need your opinion about the other members of the council."

He went on to share his suspicions in some detail.

It was difficult for Will to know how to respond. Some of the duke's suspicions seemed to him a bit unusual. But Will was also aware that he knew little about the local nobility beyond their reputations. The cost of having spent nearly all of his time in Arnost was that he had been almost entirely insulated from the politics of Erestor.

Nevertheless he heard the duke out, and promised to help in any way he could.

As he left, he made a final plea to the duke. "Please don't go anywhere unless you're well protected, My Lord."

"Thank you for your concern, Will," the duke replied. "I'm sure that nothing unpleasant will happen to me."

There was nothing further Will could say. But he left feeling uneasy, unable to shake off a sense of foreboding.

WHEN WILL ARRIVED in the council room the next day he was welcomed by one of the local noblemen and directed to an empty seat at a huge wooden table. A number of other nobles had already arrived. Some of them eyed him curiously. A few faces wore open hostility.

Will was not particularly concerned by their responses. Since being invested as Lord Torbury, he had been on the receiving end of the full range of possible reactions from the existing nobility in Arnost, and he had learned to take it lightly. His elevation to the peerage had been guaranteed to upset the most conservative of the nobility, especially those who had no personal connection with him. Most of the nobles in Arnost had eventually come around. There were some who would never accept it, though, and he knew there was little he could do about that. He had long since decided he wouldn't let it bother him.

The meeting showed no signs of starting, and the steady murmur of background conversation gradually became more pronounced. Noticing his bemusement, one of the nobles who had displayed a neutral face eventually leaned toward Will. "We're waiting for the duke," he whispered. "He's often late."

Will nodded his thanks. If the duke was merely late, Will didn't mind at all.

Then a servant burst into the room, an expression of alarm on his face. He hurried to one of the noblemen and bent low to speak to him.

The buzz of conversation ceased abruptly.

The nobleman rose to his feet unsteadily. "I have just received terrible news!" he said. "The duke has been murdered!"

This announcement resulted in instant uproar. Men sprang to their feet, and many began talking at once. Will sat dazed. He had tried to warn the duke. But to no avail.

Then one of the noblemen turned to Will. "HE is responsible!" he shouted, pointing an accusing finger at the army commander. Will did not recognize the man, but the venom in his look was not new to him. He had endured worse since his elevation first to command of the army and later to the nobility.

His thoughts flew to his conversation with the duke the previous day. The former regent had clearly anticipated something like this, although Will hadn't taken it seriously enough at the time.

His accuser hadn't finished. "The duke himself warned me about this man. He told me that he feared for his own life. He was aware that this would-be nobleman wanted him out of the way—that he would never rest until he had seen it done."

The assertion was ridiculous—surely no one on the council would believe it. But as Will looked around the room he saw uncertainty on many faces. These men did not know him. By contrast, what possible reason could they have to doubt the word of one of their own?

A second nobleman leaped to his feet. "I can confirm Lord Orkan's account," he said. "I was also present when the duke said these things. He warned us not to trust this pretender."

This second accusation was met with silence. All eyes turned to Will.

Another nobleman rose slowly, raising his hands in an appeal for order. "No lord can be condemned without a trial. Even on the evidence of two witnesses."

"This man is no lord, Rutledge," spat Lord Orkan. "He is not entitled to our privileges."

Lord Rutledge's brows bristled. "He was appointed by the king himself," he protested.

"The king will quickly rescind his decision when he is made aware of the truth."

"There must be a trial," Lord Rutledge insisted.

"We will try him, Rutledge, and we will do it promptly. Then he will hang."

The situation was becoming dangerous. Will began to rapidly consider his options.

A third nobleman, Lord Ryde, rose slowly to his feet. The man was known to Will. In their brief interactions he had treated the new Lord Torbury with exaggerated respect. But there was something slippery about him.

All eyes turned to Lord Ryde, and he waited until he had their full attention. "This is not a time for hasty actions," he said calmly. "Lord Rutledge is right, of course. We must follow an orderly process." Will saw a number of heads nodding in agreement.

"However," he continued, "I must warn you that I, too, have been party to similar declarations from the late duke. This Lord Torbury is a dangerous man, and he must be placed into custody immediately. Indeed it is only right to secure him for his own protection. When our countrymen become aware of what he has done, some of them may well be tempted to respond out of anger."

He tilted his head back and contemplated Will haughtily. Then he sniffed. "A man like this is also unpredictable. He is not one of us. He was not raised to an awareness of the weighty responsibilities that come with privilege. We cannot know what other schemes he has been hatching. Restraining him is also a necessary measure for the protection of others."

Will scanned the room with narrowed eyes, his hands clenching and unclenching restlessly. No good options remained to him now.

It was conceivable that he could break free of the council room using force—he was almost certainly the most capable fighter present, and no guards were in evidence. But any such action would be perceived as an admission of guilt. And some of the noblemen around him might be injured if it came to fighting. That would not be a good outcome.

How could he allow these men to deprive him of liberty, though? With the duke assassinated and Lord Burtelen still on his way back to Maranelle, he had nowhere to turn for support.

His enemies had cleverly seized upon the opportunity presented by the duke's demise to maneuver him into a corner.

But were they merely opportunistic? It occurred to him that they might have arranged for the duke's assassination themselves.

Desperate as his own situation had become, his mind rapidly assessed the broader implications. Why was he a target? Some of the possible explanations were obvious. Conservative elements in the nobility had always struggled to accept a commoner among their ranks. Revenge must also be a consideration as long as Pisander remained alive. None of these reasons satisfied him though. In his mind they did not account for the singleminded persistence of the attacks he had endured.

No, something bigger was at stake. But he couldn't immediately grasp what it was, and unless he could quickly find a way out of his current predicament, it wouldn't matter anyway.

Silence filled the room. Will was still sitting at the table. He had not uttered a word, and every person present appeared to be waiting to see what he would do.

Before he could do anything, a commotion was heard outside the council room. Every eye turned toward the door. A collective gasp arose as a new arrival strode through the door. It was the Duke of Erestor. Rufe Sarjant followed closely behind him with ten of Will's men.

Lord Rutledge sat down abruptly. Only Will's accusers remained on their feet, stunned looks on their faces.

The duke studied them silently for a moment. "You have made some bold accusations on my behalf," he said. "Never fear—I heard every word."

His face set hard. "You claim that I feared for my life, that I accused Lord Torbury of evil intent. You are liars. And I will not tolerate your vicious deceptions."

The duke pointed to the three noblemen. "Arrest them!" he ordered.

Rufe barked an order, and his men moved to seize them.

The third accuser—only minutes before so cool and composed—underwent a sudden transformation. His face twisted with fury. "Perhaps you think you have won," he snarled. "You will live to see otherwise!"

"Perhaps we will," the duke replied. "But you certainly will not. I have learned from my past mistakes, and you will suffer the consequences. The three of you will hang at dawn."

The other two conspirators showed no fight at all. Both of them were dragged from the room pleading for mercy.

The duke ignored them.

When the three men had been removed, the duke turned to Will. "My sincere apologies for subjecting you to this farce, My Lord," he said. "I knew we harbored traitors in our midst and could not ignore an ideal opportunity to flush them out."

He stood silently before the remaining noblemen, coolly assessing their reaction. "Many of you are shocked," he said. "A few of you are angry. You have more reason to be angry than you realize. The actions of a few traitors have brought the entire council into disrepute."

Some muttering arose at his words.

"Perhaps you are tempted to think that these men were acting out of spite, grasping an opportunity to bring down a man elevated beyond his station. You might even think that I have over reacted. Make no mistake. What you have witnessed today was treason, and carefully planned treason. Lord Torbury was targeted only because he has repeatedly proven his value to the king. This little drama has been the third attempt on his life since he came to Erestor. His holding has also been almost completely destroyed."

They listened silently, some of them eyeing Will narrowly. He had the feeling they were not entirely convinced.

"I intentionally misled you in allowing you to believe that I had been assassinated. However, it was not entirely fiction. I barely survived a serious attempt on my life today. It should now be obvious to you who was responsible."

The duke had finally managed to convince them. Many of them gaped at him open mouthed.

"And that is not all. I learned yesterday that Lord Burtelen was also attacked as he tried to return to Arnost."

This final piece of news was met with consternation, and he had to pound the table for silence before he could continue.

"Lord Burtelen and I escaped without injury," he told them. "But only because Lord Torbury warned us both not to travel without a large escort. I now offer you the same advice. From now on, go nowhere without the protection of armed men."

His words caused a sensation, and he was eventually forced to shout them down before he could regain their attention. He waited patiently until they fell silent.

"The men I arrested today are merely dupes," he said. "Traitorous dupes deserving of death, but dupes nonetheless. Erestor will not be safe until we have caught and executed the ringleaders."

He dismissed them, and they scurried away like ants seeking the safety of their nests.

When the room had been cleared, the duke sat down with Will and Rufe.

"I am alarmed to hear that you were attacked, My Lord Duke," said Will. "But I am greatly relieved that you escaped harm. And not just for my own sake, although your intervention today was certainly timely."

The duke smiled grimly. "Perhaps you thought me dismissive of your warnings when we met yesterday. I was paying full attention. And I am grateful to you." He shook his head. "We have become relaxed and comfortable in these years of peace and security, and it has made us careless."

"You hinted at a hidden purpose behind these attacks," said Will. "That is also my belief. I have been wondering for some time if the attempts on my life and the attacks on my holdings were intended as a diversion. Someone wants me dead, and if not dead then at least fully occupied and distracted. But distracted from what? I am now impatient to return to Arnost. I am beginning to fear that Erestor was never the target."

"I know nothing with certainty," replied the duke. "But I suspect you might be right. And Lord Ryde's parting comments could be seen as supporting that view."

"We will leave immediately," said Will. "May I request that you take steps to thoroughly secure Steffan's Citadel? And that you instruct the commander there to be ready to close the border between Erestor and the rest of the kingdom at a moment's notice should the need arise?"

"Such requests must surely be based on dark forebodings, Will. I hope you are wrong. Nevertheless I have long since learned to trust your instincts. I will arrange for it to be done. And I will send one hundred Erestorian soldiers with you—men who can fight with both the bow and the sword. I will also instruct them to take with them an abundant supply of arrows. You may have need of both the men and the arrows."

Will bowed a grateful acknowledgment.

The duke had not finished. "You may rest assured that this time the traitors will not escape. Your own men are guarding them now, and I realize you will need them when you depart. I will arrange for them to be relieved by some of my own men—reliable men that I trust. Tonight I will personally interrogate your false accusers. They will hang at dawn as I have promised."

Confident that Erestor was in firm hands, Will left Maranelle a few hours later.

The duke was as good as his word. Will was accompanied not only by his own men, but by a detachment of one hundred soldiers. Their leaders had been personally selected by the duke, and they in turn had been instructed to choose their best men.

Every rider carried a longbow as well as a sword. Each horse bore a plentiful supply of arrows—bundles of arrows had been secured to the saddlebag on one side of the horse, and an easily accessible quiver with a dozen arrows rested against the saddlebag on the other side. Six spare horses with halters also accompanied the riders. Each of them bore specially designed saddlebags that bristled with many bundles of arrows.

The duke was clearly expecting trouble.

Another strong contingent of the duke's men were also accompanying Will as far as Steffan's Citadel. The men destined for the citadel would be posted there for the foreseeable future. They carried specific instructions to close the border between Erestor and the rest of the kingdom.

The gates would be opened for one hour only twice a day—once in the morning and once in the afternoon. Armed men were to be turned away. If any body of soldiers approached, the gates would be closed immediately and would remain closed until the duke ordered otherwise.

Exceptions would apply only to Lord Burtelen and Will.

WILL and his men did not pause when they reached the citadel. They rode for Arnost without delay.

Will heard the gates clang shut behind them as they emerged from the pass. There was something portentous about the sound.

Sealing shut the gates of the citadel provided a tangible reminder of the Rogandan invasion. Once more Erestor stood isolated from the rest of the kingdom.

VOLUME 2—THE STORM BREAKS

20

"Dadda! Come see!"

Thomas, hard at work in the garden, glanced up with a smile. His daughter had apparently found an egg. A steady supply of eggs was just one of the benefits that flowed from the hens pecking around the cabins hidden in the forest. Chickens had been Elena's idea, and once established they had reliably delivered both eggs and fertilizer for the garden.

Elena appeared and knelt down to admire the two-year-old's discovery. "It's beautiful, Tammi," she said, kissing her on the cheek.

Thomas joined them, and hoisted Tamara into his arms, careful not to dislodge the prize in her little hands. After examining it for a moment, he set her down again. "Go and show Papa," he suggested. She ran inside the cabin, calling for her grandfather.

Thomas's hands were covered with dirt from digging. With a cheeky grin he grabbed Elena by the waist and drew her close. She squealed and pulled away, glaring at him through narrowed eyes. She nevertheless blew him a kiss as he returned to work in the garden.

Thomas had worked without interruption for a couple more hours when he heard Elena call his name. She sounded tense.

Curious, he stood up and brushed off his hands. He caught a glimpse of a man on horseback talking to his wife.

"Well, ain't you a perty little thing," the stranger was saying.

Thomas struggled with the tie on the pouch at his belt and reached in for the stone. Then he headed toward the horseman.

Seeing him coming, the man spun his horse around and rode swiftly away through the trees.

Elena's face was pale. "We never see strangers," she said anxiously. "And I'm glad we don't. Something about this one made me shudder."

"Get Tamara and your father!" Thomas replied, his heart pounding. "We need to leave. Immediately! We can grab a few supplies, but there's no time for anything else. Only take what you can carry on horseback."

She stared back at him, stunned into silence.

He lowered his voice. "I was holding the stone," he said. "I saw why he's here."

He ran off toward the stream. "I'll find Haldek! Hurry!" he called back over his shoulder.

He returned with Haldek to a scene of confusion. Tamara was crying, Rubin was trying to comfort her, and Elena was hurrying back and forth between the cabin and her horse, putting items into a large sack. She had saddled her horse, but Rubin appeared to have done nothing to prepare to leave.

"What's going on?" he asked Thomas.

"I'm sorry," Thomas replied. "But we need to leave urgently. We won't be coming back."

"Whatever do you mean?" asked Rubin. Haldek simply looked confused.

"A group of men have been searching for us," Thomas replied. "They just found us. We need to leave now. If we don't, all of us will die."

"But how can you be sure?" Rubin protested. "This is our home. We can't just leave!"

"You must listen to him, Father." Elena's voice was firm. Thomas had rarely seen her so determined. "For now you will just have to trust him," she said.

Thomas gave her a grim smile of appreciation. "We need to be gone within the next few minutes," he said.

"I am not leaving here," said Haldek.

"You must!" said Thomas.

"How many men?" he asked.

"One. But he will soon return with others."

"Maybe not," Haldek replied stubbornly.

Thomas paused for a moment, his mind racing. "Very well," he said. "Let me suggest a compromise. You stay here, Haldek. The rest of us will ride toward Tallesford. We won't attempt to hide our tracks. After the road crosses the river the trail runs across stony ground for many leagues, and hoof prints will not be visible. We will not cross the ford. The river is shallow for a short distance, and we will instead head downstream in the direction of Arnost. We will find a suitable place where we can leave the river, and we will wait for you there."

"For how long?" Haldek asked.

"The men will be here very soon," Thomas predicted confidently. "But if you haven't reached us by morning, we will return to the cabins," he promised.

"It is good," said Haldek, nodding with satisfaction.

"You must stay out of sight," Thomas insisted. "Don't let them see you!"

Thomas could tell that Rubin was still not convinced. But he agreed to the arrangement, and having done so he actively helped Thomas and Elena prepare to leave.

It took much longer than Thomas expected, and he was extremely fretful by the time they eventually mounted up. Tamara sat in front of him, and he had never been more grateful that all four adults had horses of their own.

"Be careful, Haldek!" he called as they rode out.

Haldek frowned back at him. "I am a soldier!" he declared, pounding his chest.

. . .

HALDEK CAUGHT up with them as the sun was setting, his face red with anger.

"They burn our cabins. Destroy our garden. Even kill our chickens!" he said. "I want to fight them. But they are five, and Haldek only one."

"Were they Rogandans?" asked Rubin.

"No," replied Haldek. "They are speaking your language."

"Did they follow our trail?" Thomas asked.

"Yes. I ride behind them. Their leader say you all go to Tallesford. Just like you want him to think. They cross ford, and they go." Haldek flicked his fingers in the direction of Tallesford. "Then I ride here, along this river."

Rubin shook his head in bafflement. "What possible reason could they have for doing this?"

Thomas shrugged. "Perhaps we are known to be friends of Will. And also of the queen," he said. "I don't doubt that all of them have enemies."

His father-in-law shook his head again. "We have no choice but to leave now," he said. "There's nothing left for us to go back to."

Thomas suspected that neither Rubin nor Haldek would be at all satisfied with what he had told them so far. They must surely be wondering how he could have known so much based on so little evidence.

He moved his horse closer to Elena's. "Do you think the time has come to tell them about the stone?" he asked, keeping his voice low.

"I've been asking myself the same question," she said. "The stone is what's putting them in danger, so maybe it's fair that they know."

They rode in silence for a while. "Perhaps there's another way," she said finally. "Could you tell them what you're able to do, but not explain how exactly you're able to do it?"

"You mean tell them I can see into people's thoughts, but not tell them it's a stone that lets me do it?"

"Yes, I suppose so."

"Maybe. I can try."

Thomas was not sure how quickly the men pursuing them would discover their mistake. So he suggested they ride on into the evening and stop only when night was well advanced.

They were all weary when they finally made camp. Little Tamara had spent some of the journey sleeping fitfully in Thomas's arms. Back on solid ground again she was soon soundly asleep.

Their location was well hidden, so they decided to risk a small fire. They had brought food, and they sat down together around the fire and shared it.

Thomas glanced at Elena, and she smiled encouragingly at him. He swallowed nervously, then he broke the silence. "I imagine you're wondering how I knew that our visitor would come back. And why these men were searching for us in the first place."

His comment was met with silence, but it was obvious to him that he had hit the mark.

He glanced at Elena. "I've been hiding a secret," he said. "I haven't told you because it's a dangerous secret, and I thought you would be much safer if you didn't know." They looked puzzled, but there was no immediate response. "Hiding it from you hasn't been helping to keep you safe anymore, though."

"I'm wondering if I really want to know," said Rubin. "But I think you should tell us."

Thomas nodded. "It's very likely that the men chasing us know little more than you," he said. "They almost certainly haven't been told the real reason why they were sent to find us."

He took a deep breath. "I have the ability to see what other people are thinking," he said.

Haldek looked doubtful. Rubin simply frowned.

"I won't try to prove it to you," Thomas said. "I long ago decided never to use this ability to pry into the thoughts of anyone close to me. So you are safe from me.

"The visitor who arrived today was different—I examined his thoughts because I needed to know if he was a threat. He turned out to be far more dangerous than I could have imagined. He knows nothing of my gift, but he was looking for me. He was also looking for you, Haldek, although he doesn't know why. He knows all of us have been seen together."

He paused to assess their reaction. Both of them were frowning now.

"They are mercenaries. Their instructions were to kill us all and to bring our bodies back to the man who hired them. Our visitor knew that, but not a lot else."

"Who hired them?" asked Rubin.

"He doesn't know. He was hired by the leader of these men. I doubt that even the leader knows who the real employer is."

"Where did your gift come from?" asked Rubin. He still appeared to be skeptical.

Thomas sighed. "That knowledge is very dangerous. For all of us. Would you be willing to trust me with it?"

Rubin looked at Elena. "Are you aware of this?"

She nodded, blushing as she did. "I'm sorry, Father. I never wanted to have secrets from you."

"I trust you, Elena," he said without hesitation. He turned to Thomas and gazed thoughtfully at him. Then his face softened. "I trust you, too, Thomas. We need speak no more about it."

Thomas glanced across at Haldek, raising his eyebrows questioningly.

Haldek spread his hands. "I know nothing," he said. "So it is easy."

"Where will we go now?" Rubin asked.

"I think we should go to Arnost," Thomas replied. "Briefly, anyway. It isn't a good place to remain hidden for any length of time. But I would like to consult with Will. And my parents would want to meet Tamara."

Elena nodded eagerly. "And I want her to meet them too."

Rubin pondered for a moment, then he also nodded. "And after that?" he asked.

"I don't know," Thomas replied. "I traveled with a soldier—his name is Rellan—who lives in a small community somewhere near

Erestor. They are in a remote location, hidden from the world. The people went there fleeing from trouble. They keep to themselves, and I think we would be safe there. Will might know how to find them."

Conversation soon dried up, and they lay down and tried to sleep.

Thomas had a restless night. He'd spent plenty of time on the run, but it felt like long ago. He'd been foolish enough to believe it was all behind him.

They rose before dawn, setting out as soon as they had broken their fast.

They continued their journey toward Arnost without incident for three more days, avoiding roads and any signs of habitation. Twice they came within the vicinity of a village. Each time they gave it a wide berth.

Late on the morning of the fourth day their progress came to a sudden halt.

A fox bolted across the path of Thomas's horse, spooking it. The horse reared up, whinnying shrilly. Tamara had been perched in front of her father, and she was flung from the saddle before he could prevent it. Thomas launched himself toward her, managing to catch and cradle her as they both hit the ground. He landed hard on his back, knocking the wind from him. His head connected heavily with a rock, and his vision filled with stars.

Elena swung down out of the saddle and raced to Thomas and Tamara.

Thanks to Thomas's efforts, their daughter appeared to be unhurt. The toddler stared wide-eyed at her mother for a moment. Then she opened her mouth, filled her lungs, and began to scream. Elena picked her up and tried to examine her injured husband while comforting her.

"Take her somewhere else!" said Rubin, rushing out his words when Tamara paused for breath. "We can tend to him," he said, waving her away.

Reluctantly she followed his advice.

The moment her daughter had calmed down, Elena returned anxiously to Thomas. His eyes were open, but he looked dazed. He hadn't moved.

Rubin took her aside. "Haldek says he's seen similar injuries on the battlefield," he said grimly.

Elena struggled to remain calm. "What is he expecting will happen?" she asked.

"It's possible that Thomas might lose consciousness," her father replied.

"And after that?"

"It's difficult to be certain," said Rubin.

She had the definite impression he knew more than he was willing to say.

"We have to get help," said Elena desperately.

"Where from?" her father asked. "Who could we ask that will be safe? We've been trying to keep away from people."

"I know. But we can't just leave him like this," she said, tears welling up in her eyes. She continued to agonize uselessly, unable to think of anything worthwhile to do and unable to accept the situation as it was.

Her father moved back and forth restlessly for a few minutes. Then he seemed to reach a decision. "I'm going to find help," he said.

"Where?" she asked.

"I don't know," he replied frankly. "There must be other people nearby. Surely one of them can do something for us."

She looked at him uncertainly for a moment. Then she nodded. They had to try.

Once Rubin had gone, Elena returned to Thomas's side. "How are you feeling?" she asked him softly.

He didn't answer immediately. He appeared distracted. Finally he said, "My head hurts."

Her agitation slowly began to grow. Tamara, apparently sensing her distress, became fretful and demanding. Haldek took it upon himself to distract her, and his antics soon had her giggling uncontrollably. Elena shooed them away to give Thomas some peace and quiet.

The wait felt interminable, but in reality no more than thirty minutes had passed before Rubin reappeared, accompanied by another rider.

Elena saw that the new arrival was a woman, small in stature and clad in bright garments. Large gold earrings flashed brightly beside her dark curls. She was attractive—she might almost have been beautiful were it not for the hardness on her face.

Her mouth curled into a smile. To Elena the gesture appeared forced.

"We don't often see travelers in these parts," she said. "Rubin here tells me that one of your number is injured." She peered down at Thomas lying on the ground. "What happened?"

"His horse threw him when he was riding with our daughter," Elena replied, her voice trembling. "He managed to protect her, but he hit his head."

The woman turned to Elena, scrutinizing her for a long moment. Then she put on a cheerful voice. "I live in a small community," she said, "and one or two among us have some skill with healing. You must bring him to us."

"We can't move him," said Rubin.

"No, he will need to be carried." She paused to think. "I will get help. Wait here until I return."

She wheeled her horse around and rode off.

"I do not like this woman," said Haldek.

"She looks rough. But she seemed sincere," said Rubin hopefully.

Elena didn't reply. Something about the woman made her uneasy, and she didn't feel enthusiastic about her offer of help. But what choice did they have?

Her insides churned unrelentingly. It wasn't just her anxiety about Thomas. Her own responses to the stranger left her feeling extremely uncomfortable. Throughout her childhood she had managed to remain generous in her assessment of other people, even when they were unkind to her. She knew from bitter experience that people were capable of great evil, but she had learned to extend her generosity of spirit even to those who did her harm. Neither had her nature changed when she and her father began to emerge from their self-imposed isolation after meeting Thomas.

Now, desperately in need, she had received an offer of help. Yet she was filled with suspicion and mistrust. What was happening to her?

She was aware that her outlook had shifted when she became a wife and mother. Was she being reshaped by these new responsibilities? Or did the changes signal a more sinister process? Was she gradually becoming hard-hearted, just like so many others in the world around her?

Long after the rider had disappeared, Elena remained rooted to the spot, staring after her.

21

After leaving the injured man and his companions, the woman rode swiftly toward her home. She didn't slow her pace until she reached the outer ring of the camp where she lived.

Twenty five colored wagons stood before her in a field, drawn together into a rough circle. A familiar sense of belonging washed through her as she slid from her horse and stepped among the wagons. This was where her heart lived, among the Clan, among her people.

Her serenity was short-lived though, as it always was. A wave of bitterness surged over her as she glanced around, sweeping away any traces of contentment.

After standing motionless for a moment to settle herself, she strode over to the largest and most brightly painted of the wagons. The Clan's leader sat outside it, brooding over a blazing fire.

He glanced up, a surly look on his face when he saw who it was. "And what have you been doing?" he asked brusquely, spitting into the flames.

"I have been meeting new friends," she said.

"How many of them? Are they wealthy? Are they well armed?"

"There are three men, a woman, and a small child. They are not well armed. They appear to be poor, although they have four good horses. One of the men is injured."

He spat again. "Then we will pay them a visit. I'm sure they'll be delighted to make us a gift of anything of value they might have. At the very least we can find a new home for their horses."

She shook her head firmly, setting her dark curls swaying. "I have invited them to join us. I told them we have healers among us."

His face became red with fury in an instant. "How dare you invite them here? I gave you no such permission!"

Her jaw set stubbornly. "The leadership is not yours by right, Viggor—even if you were elected. So don't expect me to bow and scrape to you."

He pushed himself to his feet and towered over her menacingly. "One day you'll push me too far, Ronya."

She raised her chin defiantly. He might talk tough, but he would never dare to touch her. "I will need a litter. And two men—to carry back the one who is injured."

He made no response. The contempt on his face rendered any response unnecessary. He sat down again, ignoring her.

An angry retort rose to her lips. Somehow she managed to swallow it, inhaling slowly to steady herself.

Viggor's reaction was hardly surprising. She had extended an offer of hospitality to these strangers, a magnanimous gesture that was no more appropriate than it was sincere. It was foolish and empty for her to play at being leader of the Clan.

Without support from Viggor, she would have to find two litter bearers herself. They would need to be men willing to weather the displeasure of their leader. Perhaps Andri might be agreeable.

Could there be another way, though? She turned back to Viggor. "I get a feeling about these people," she murmured. "A lucky feeling." Then she added, "The woman—she is very beautiful."

He studied her with an unreadable expression. Abruptly he stood again and bowed expressively. "How could anyone dismiss a lucky feeling of yours, my lady? You may choose the litter bearers yourself. The Clan will be honored to host your new friends."

Viggor was a fool. And a predictable fool. "The woman is also married with a child. You will keep your wandering hands to yourself."

He snorted. "Or what?"

"Or I will make it my business to see that you regret it."

A scornful look flashed across his face. Then he threw back his head and burst into laughter. "The Clan's fierce little kitten has claws," he said. "I trust that your new friends will not get themselves scratched."

THE WAITING HAD BEGUN to feel unbearable. Much as she mistrusted the woman and her offer, Elena now found herself longing for the promised help to arrive.

Her heart pounded in her chest as she peered down at her husband's pale face. How badly hurt was he? Was it possible that he wouldn't recover? She pushed the thought from her mind, refusing even to consider such a possibility. She placed a hand on her heart and sent a fervent prayer into the heavens. Surely there must be something that could be done for him.

As she stared anxiously at him, Thomas's lips moved weakly, and he shifted his gaze to her. He groaned.

She bent low to caress his brow. "Thomas!" she whispered tenderly.

"Where am I?" he asked, his voice weak. "I can't see properly. Everything's blurry. What happened?"

"You hit your head when you fell. But you saved Tamara from harm."

He peered back at her. He seemed to be struggling to grasp what she was saying.

"Help is on the way," she added.

Something must have penetrated through the haze, because a

frown slowly came over his face. "The stone," he said, slurring his words. "Can you get it?"

His question startled her. He was right, of course. He couldn't be expected to protect it while he was incapacitated. And they couldn't allow the woman and her people to get their hands on it.

She fumbled at the drawstring of his pouch, eventually freeing it. Then she took out the stone.

"Take it," he breathed.

"I will keep it safe for you," she promised.

"No," he said slowly, wincing as he tried to shake his head. He went quiet for a moment. Then he murmured, "I want you to have it."

Her eyes grew wide with alarm. "No! I can't!" Keeping the stone safe for Thomas was one thing; receiving it as a gift was another matter entirely. She had no desire to bear the burden of its revelations.

The effort of speaking had come at a cost. His eyes rolled up, and his head lolled to one side.

Thoroughly alarmed, she put her ear to his mouth. To her profound relief he was breathing steadily.

After a few moments he stirred again, opening his eyes. She was still bending over him. "You must take it," he said with an effort. His eyes fluttered closed once more. "I give it to you," he breathed.

Her life changed forever in a single moment.

A flood of sensations swept over her, leaving her gasping in shock. Thomas's inner world lay exposed, his thoughts and memories naked to her gaze. Her entire body froze. Even as it did so, her mind was racing—probing, absorbing, analyzing. She did it instinctively and without conscious thought, unable at first to prevent herself.

Then Elena's self awareness forced its way past the overwhelming deluge of impressions, and her will reasserted itself. Registering too late what she had been doing, she shook herself free of her paralysis and spun away from Thomas.

She could immediately have prevented herself from staring at Thomas had she understood exactly what he was intending. But she had been caught entirely off guard, and her response had been involuntarily. Did that absolve her for not turning away more quickly though?

In her heart she felt that she had violated him, and a flush of shame flooded her face.

She knew that Thomas had managed to avoid doing this to her—she had seen it in his memories. Her own sense of betrayal distressed her beyond words.

Having first been weighed down by anxiety, she now found herself confronted by an ugly set of unfamiliar emotions—her suspicion of the woman, and now shame at her own behavior. The tranquility that had always defined her lay shattered. Her whole world had tilted, in just a few hours.

Once Elena had witnessed a small boat drifting unattended down a river. She felt as if her inner self had broken loose from its moorings.

She glanced at the stone, nestling in her palm. It appeared so innocent and attractive, so small and insignificant. But its potency appalled her. Thomas had made her aware of the stone's capabilities, but nothing could have prepared her for the reality. She hadn't gone close to guessing at the extent of its power, or imagining the impact it would have on her.

She closed her hand over it, extinguishing its gleam, and thrust it into a hidden pocket in her clothing.

It would remain there, untouched. Because she was never going to use it again, no matter what happened.

Ronya returned to find that the little group had not moved. They seemed relieved to see her, but at the same time she couldn't help noticing the wariness in their response. They had reason to be wary —more than they could know.

"My name is Ronya," she said brightly.

"I'm Elena," the young woman replied. "Thank you for your willingness to help us." Her tone was humble, and she was clearly worried about her husband. But Ronya nevertheless saw that she was very much in two minds about the offered assistance.

Elena pointed out each of the others in turn. "You've met my father, Rubin. This is our friend, Haldek. My daughter here is Tamara. And you've already seen my husband, Thomas."

Was it her imagination, or had Elena emphasized the word husband? Ronya ignored it, smiling an acknowledgment.

She introduced the two men who had ridden in with her. "This is Andri, and this is Olver."

Andri and Olver nodded to the others without speaking, their eyes lingering on the young woman.

Elena's beauty was impossible to ignore, and Ronya felt the sharp pangs of envy. She herself was not unattractive—she had seen the way men looked at her. But alongside this young woman? Could the moon outshine the sun?

The men dismounted and placed the now unconscious Thomas onto a litter they had brought with them. Elena supervised the process anxiously, her child perched on her hip.

Ronya studied her attentively, all the while pretending disinterest. When they had first met, Elena seemed anxious and on edge. Now she was restless as well, unable to remain still for more than a moment. Ronya noticed her sucking in sharp breaths and pushing them out slowly between clenched teeth. She gave every appearance of being deeply troubled. Ronya took careful note, wondering how she might make use of this information.

Andri and Olver set off for the camp, carrying the litter between them. Ronya took their horses in tow and rode behind them at a slow walk. The other strangers mounted and followed her.

The terrain became rough at times. At one point the men stumbled, almost tipping the patient off the litter. He stirred, mumbling incoherently, although his eyes didn't open.

"Be careful!" she snapped at the bearers. Then she frowned, unsettled by her own reaction. She had claimed she had a lucky feeling about these people, and she had told the truth. Why then was she so brittle? Perhaps it was her frustration over Viggor's leadership.

Or could it be the provocation of the young woman's beauty? Ronya chewed at her lip, annoyed at being so easily discomposed.

The bearers soon needed a break. Rubin and Haldek offered to share the burden, and the journey resumed. With the two pairs of men alternating, they were able to continue without interruption.

After a night in the open, they reached the camp late the following day.

Viggor came forward to greet them.

"Welcome, weary travelers!" he said. "Please, set your injured friend down over here. Our healers will examine him very soon. I am Viggor, and I lead these people. I will invite our good Ronya to introduce you all."

Viggor's false congeniality irritated Ronya more than ever, but she nevertheless obliged, naming each person in turn. As she had expected, Viggor's full attention was captured by Elena. Ronya's eyes narrowed as he flashed the young woman his oily smile and overflowed with his insincere benevolence.

"I do have one request," said Viggor regretfully. "We are unable to welcome visitors to our camp if they are carrying weapons. I am sure you will understand. I trust you will allow my men to examine you and your possessions. Any weapons will, of course, be returned to you when you leave us."

He nodded to Elena congenially. "Please do not be concerned. I would never permit any of my men to approach you," he said, beaming her a smile. "I am certain that Ronya can oblige."

None of the travelers looked at all happy, but they were smart enough to recognize that they had no choice but to submit. The men were searched first, very thoroughly. Few weapons were found, but every item of any possible value was promptly removed, "Purely for safe keeping," as Viggor explained apologetically.

Even the unconscious Thomas was meticulously searched. The pouch at his belt attracted special attention, but it proved to be empty.

If the travelers had been carrying items of value on their journey, they had clearly hidden them before Ronya returned. Such a possibility would certainly occur to Viggor. If they had secreted items of value, he would find an effective way to motivate them to reveal the location. She didn't doubt that he would quickly obtain their enthusiastic cooperation.

She thought it unlikely they had anything to hide. Apart from their steeds, they appeared to possess nothing of value.

The horses were a notable exception. They were fine animals, and all of them were in excellent condition. At least one of the travelers understood how to care for horses. She wondered how they had acquired them. Perhaps they were stolen. Something told her that was unlikely.

By the time the men had been searched, the true nature of Viggor's hospitality must have been obvious to them all.

Only Elena remained.

Ronya approached her. The young woman's face was expressionless, but she appeared to be struggling to keep it that way. A careful search at first revealed nothing at all of interest. Then Ronya felt a lump within her clothing. It was so small she had almost missed it. Could it be a precious gem? She immediately focused her entire attention on uncovering it.

The object had been secreted in a hidden pocket, and Elena's obvious alarm at its discovery only intensified Ronya's interest. As she removed it, Elena lunged forward and snatched it away from her. As she did so, her eyes went very wide. She glanced first at Ronya, then at Viggor, then down at her hand as Ronya grabbed her wrist, determined to wrest it from her grasp.

The young woman clearly had little experience of physical violence. It took only moments before she cried out in pain and released the object. It fell to the ground and disappeared in the dirt, buried by their scuffling feet.

Ronya got down on her hands and knees and poked around until she felt something small and hard. Standing up again, she dusted if off and held it up with great anticipation. She frowned in disappointment. It was only a small stone. Its coloring gave it an attractive appearance, but it was otherwise unremarkable. It was almost certainly worth nothing.

Was all the fuss about this small stone? A glance at Elena confirmed that it was. The young woman stood before her with a pitiful expression of dismay twisting her lovely face.

"What is it?" Ronya asked, unable to account for the misery caused by the loss of such an insignificant object.

"It's a family heirloom," Elena replied, grimacing as she rubbed her wrist.

Ronya stared at it, frowning. It wasn't hard to believe that the stone had no worth at all apart from sentimental value.

"It doesn't belong to you!" Elena exclaimed indignantly, glaring at Ronya.

Ronya looked up. "It does now," she said, staring coldly back at her.

Until that moment, Ronya had been considering returning it to her. Now she was determined to keep it, if only to spite her rival.

The young woman's face twisted with anger, or maybe fear. The emotion, whatever it was, looked entirely out of place on her.

The clanswoman glanced at her contemptuously. Clearly Elena had lived an untroubled life—she had never needed to face the hardships that Ronya had endured. Every benefit that came with great beauty was hers to enjoy, and she could probably make a reasonable claim to virtue as well, questionable though its benefits might be. But she was weak. And from now on she would have to do without her little heirloom.

22

Elena stood behind a small wagon, pacing back and forth restlessly as she gazed up into the night sky. It had become clear to her that the responsibility for finding a way out of their current predicament rested on her shoulders, and hers alone. And she knew she would never find a solution if she wasn't able to take control of her own emotions and reactions.

All was silent in the camp. At that moment the world around her was at peace. Her own sense of inner peace had deserted her. She had been in turmoil even before they arrived at the camp of the Clan.

It was time for that to change. She had faced trouble before, and she had never allowed it to define her. Her troubles might have multiplied from the moment Thomas was thrown from his horse, but the same choices were still available to her.

The wagon beside her had become a temporary home for the little group. It was adequate, if a bit crowded, and it was at least providing shelter for Thomas. The previous occupant—an elderly man well past his prime—had vacated it to make way for them, moving in with the family of his daughter instead. The elderly man and his daughter were not at all satisfied with the arrangement, but Viggor had not offered them a choice.

True to Ronya's promise, healers from the camp had tended to Thomas soon after their arrival. Elena quickly warmed to them. The healers were a married couple with no children of their own, and they seemed genuinely caring. They had not been alarmed by Thomas's condition, and they had every expectation that he would fully recover in a few days if he continued to enjoy quiet and rest.

Thomas had regained consciousness soon after they reached the camp. He had spent much of the day sleeping, but he was lucid when he was awake. Thankfully he had accepted without question the need to rest. He reported that his head was pounding much of the time, and the discomfort was undoubtedly contributing to his meek acceptance of being confined to bed.

Elena had not told him about the stone. She knew he would have wanted to do something to retrieve it. Any such attempt would likely prove dangerous, and it would certainly do nothing to promote his recovery.

Rubin had quietly taken responsibility for his granddaughter. Throughout their first full day in the camp Tamara played happily with the other children, watched over by Rubin. Elena was grateful for his help—she had far too many things on her mind.

They had little contact with members of the Clan. Ronya had sauntered by a couple of times. After what had happened with the stone, Elena found it difficult even to be civil with her. She knew, though, that her attitude and approach to Ronya was the first thing that needed to change.

Even if she was struggling to feel sympathy toward the clanswoman, Elena did at least understand her. In the moments before the stone had been forced from her grasp, Elena had been able to rapidly scrutinize the thoughts of both Ronya and Viggor. Although further investigation was now impossible, she had come away with an abundance of insights to draw upon. She was under no illusions about Viggor's true intentions and motivation, and she fully comprehended the reasons why Ronya was behaving as she did.

After her mistake with Thomas, she had vowed never to use the stone again. She was now seriously considering the unhappy possibility that the stone might offer the only way she could extricate them from this situation.

ELENA RETURNED with Tamara from a walk across the fields to find Thomas out of bed and sitting up eating some food.

Tammi ran to him, a happy cry on her lips. “Dadda!”

Elena watched on with a smile as the little girl reached up and kissed him on the cheek. Then she ran off to find the other children.

“How are you feeling?” Elena asked.

“Much improved,” he said brightly. “I expect I’ll be able to ride again soon. We should be able to leave before long—maybe even tomorrow.”

Elena had said nothing to Thomas about the reality of their situation there, and clearly her father and Haldek hadn’t either. She had especially avoided any hint about the loss of the stone, out of fear of threatening his recovery.

She’d never been good at hiding her emotions, though.

“What’s wrong?” he asked, a frown of concern appearing on his face.

Her stomach twisted as she stared at him. What should she say? Was it fair to hide the truth from him? She sighed in resignation, simply unable to do it.

It all came out in a rush. “They searched us when we arrived here. They took everything of value, especially the horses. We’re little more than prisoners.” She paused, trying to steady herself. “And Ronya found the stone. She’s taken it.”

Tears had begun to well up in her eyes as she was speaking, and now she began to sob quietly. Thomas had entrusted the stone to her care, and she hadn’t been able to keep it safe even for two days.

Thomas came and held her close. “I will get it back,” he said fiercely.

She pulled away from him. “No, no! You mustn’t!” she cried. She had seen into their minds, and she knew what they were like. Especially Viggor. Thomas must never find out what Viggor had in mind for her.

"Please," she said, "you have to let me do it."

"But how?" he asked, holding his head and slowly shaking it.

"See!" she said. "You'll hurt yourself."

She took a deep breath to calm herself. "I was able to look into the minds of both Ronya and Viggor," she told him. "I believe there's something I might be able to do."

"What?" he asked, frowning doubtfully. He didn't look well. These problems were more than he could reasonably be expected to cope with at that moment.

"I need you to trust me, Thomas. Can you do that?" she asked plaintively.

He had never been able to resist her when she pleaded with him.

He sighed deeply, then nodded slowly in resignation and lay back down on his bed. The fact that he had given in so easily said a great deal about how far he still needed to go before he could say he'd recovered.

She had told him there was something she might be able to do. As soon as she rose the next morning she would attempt it.

VIGGOR HAD RIDDEN out of the camp at dawn with two youths, and Elena had overheard someone saying that he wasn't expected back before nightfall. Elena had been waiting for much of the morning for the right opportunity to talk with Ronya. When she noticed the clanswoman striding alone through the field not far from their wagon, she felt sure that her moment had finally arrived.

Elena hurried toward the brightly clad woman.

"Ronya, may I please speak with you?" She was trying hard not to tremble.

The clanswoman paused, looking Elena up and down with casual disinterest. Finally she shrugged. "If you have something worth saying," she said, "then say it." Her tone suggested she had no expectation whatever of hearing anything of value.

"You hate Viggor," Elena began tentatively, trying not to notice the suspicious glare that came immediately to the eye of the other woman. "You hate him because by rights he should not be Clan leader. The succession should have passed to you."

"Who told you this?" Ronya demanded angrily.

"No one told me. I had no need to be told," Elena replied, somehow succeeding in her efforts to keep her voice calm.

The clanswoman snorted. "So you are claiming you have the Sight?" she said, curling her lip sarcastically.

"Viggor got you out of the way. For long enough for him to be appointed instead. And now that an appointment has been made, nothing can be done about it."

Ronya scowled. She clearly was not impressed. Elena could have learned this information from anyone in the little community with a loose tongue. More would be needed.

"And you are interested in Andri," she continued. "You believe he is interested in you, too, and you're upset and disappointed by his failure to take any initiative." She paused. "Would you like me to continue?"

At first Ronya had been shocked at the mention of Andri's name, but her surprise rapidly transformed into fury. Before Elena could blink, Ronya had a knife at her throat. "Who have you been speaking to?" she hissed. "Have you dared to spread these lies?"

"I have spoken to no one," said Elena, trying desperately to remain calm. "I have no desire to embarrass you. I only wanted to get your attention." She strained her eyes downward toward the knife without daring to move her head even slightly. "I appear to have succeeded," she said uncomfortably.

The clanswoman held her position for a moment longer, then she lowered the knife and stepped back a pace. "Very well, you have my attention," she said. "Why do you want it?" Her voice was steady, but it held a tone of menace.

"I can help you, Ronya," Elena said. "If you will let me."

"You? Help me? How?" Ronya spat dismissively onto the ground.

"Before I tell you, I have two conditions." The words tumbled out, in spite of Elena's attempts to settle herself.

Ronya's eyes narrowed. "I could just slit your throat right now."

Elena shook her head. Why did Ronya have to be so stubborn? "You would be the loser," she retorted.

"What are your conditions?" the clanswoman asked.

Elena found that she had regained her courage. "First, when I have helped you, you will freely allow us to leave with our horses and all of our possessions."

"And the second condition?"

"You return my heirloom to me, right now." Her voice held steady, and her gaze didn't waver. It was her turn to be stubborn.

A calculating glint came into Ronya's eye. "You seem very interested in this heirloom," she said suspiciously. "Could it be that your second sight is granted by this little stone?"

"You should be able to answer that question yourself," returned Elena boldly. "You're the one who has it." She placed her hands on her hips. "Has it made you any the wiser since you stole it from me?"

The clanswoman frowned. After a moment's hesitation, she reached down and lifted a finely wrought chain from beneath her clothing. A clasp hung from the chain. She had mounted the stone on it and fastened the chain around her neck. The clasp had been fashioned from a thin sheet of gold with four tiny arms to hold the stone in position.

The clasp spun lazily on the chain, the glitter of the stone alternating with golden flashes from the clasp.

Elena held out her hand for it, a frown of determination on her face.

Ronya hastily tucked it away again. "I'm not going to give it to you," she said mockingly. "You've done some clever guessing, but you've done nothing to benefit me. Why should I do anything at all for you?"

"Look, Ronya," said Elena, frustration rising in her voice. "Your healers have cared for my husband, and we're grateful for that. But that doesn't excuse what you've done. You came to us when we were vulnerable and in need, and you lured us here with offers of help. All you ever intended was to rob us! You and your people have taken everything we had. Everything! And don't imagine I'm ignorant about Viggor's intentions toward me!" An involuntary shudder shook Elena's body. She closed her eyes for a moment, trying to push the memory of Viggor's thoughts from her mind.

She opened her eyes again and frowned at Ronya. "I've already proven to you that I have second sight. And I'm willing to use that ability to help you, even though most people would call me crazy for even considering it. But you seem determined not to give me a single reason why I should."

Elena set her jaw. "You might have been defrauded of your birthright, but no one forced you to spend your energy preying on the helpless and unwary. I thought I glimpsed something more than that in you. But if you want my help, you're going to have to show me I wasn't just imagining it."

Ronya was silent.

Elena threw her hands into the air. "What have you got to lose?" she asked. "My heirloom is of no use to you. And any dealer in gems would tell you that your gold clasp is worth more than the stone you've mounted onto it."

Ronya lifted out the stone once more and stared at her for a long moment. Then she shrugged. Removing the chain from her neck, she handed it to Elena.

"Take it," she said. "I'm giving you what you wanted—now it's your turn. I'll be watching you. And I'll be very eager to see what you do for me in return. It better be good." Her face went hard. "Don't imagine I'm giving it to you permanently, though. You'll return it to me when the sun sets tonight. Or..."

Elena looked Ronya in the eye as her hand closed over the stone. "Or you will take Tammi away from me until I give it back," she said with a sigh, placing the chain around her neck and hiding the stone beneath her own clothing. "I know what you're thinking, Ronya. It isn't necessary for you to tell me."

Ronya's startled eyes stared back at her. The clanswoman was impressed, and it showed on her face.

Elena no longer needed visual clues to guess at her reactions, though. With the stone in her possession, she knew exactly what was going on in the other woman's mind.

She turned on her heel and headed back to the wagon.

Thomas was waiting for her. "I stayed out of sight," he said, "but I overheard that entire conversation." His eyes shone with admiration as he drew her close. "You were incredible, Elena!"

She smiled gratefully at him. After the blows she had sustained over the last few days, his support came as a welcome relief. He held her tightly, and she allowed her anxiety and weariness to fall away as she relaxed into the familiar security of his love.

And his encouragement was timely too, because she knew that a challenging day lay ahead of her.

ELENA WAS EXHAUSTED by the time she finally returned to the wagon that night. Only Thomas had waited up for her—the others were already asleep. He embraced her, his eyes full of concern, then he encouraged her to lie down and sleep. Thankfully he seemed to understand that she had no energy left to talk about what she had been doing.

She had spent the afternoon moving from wagon to wagon, studying people as she spoke to them, men as well as women. By the time she had finished the entire camp was buzzing.

Her actions had been motivated by a single purpose. The stone's brief insights into both Viggor and Ronya had exposed an injustice, and also revealed a possible way of making it right. And she had told Ronya the truth—she had seen that there was more to the clanswoman than her actions had so far suggested. That insight had prompted Elena to do what she could to right the wrong, in spite of the way that Ronya had behaved toward her and her family.

Before returning the stone to Ronya, her final visit had been to

Andri. He glanced up when she arrived at his wagon, then nodded her to a seat beside his small fire.

"Why haven't you told her how you feel?" Elena asked him gently.

His brows drew together, but he had nothing to say.

It was immediately clear to him that his intimate feelings were no secret to her, but he wasn't offended by her directness. She knew, because she had the stone.

Elena decided to steer in a different direction. "Her situation offends your sense of justice," she said.

He shrugged. "What can anyone do?"

"There is something that could be done," she said. "Let me make you aware of it."

She began to speak quietly, her words weaving a tapestry that portrayed what was and what still might be. A faraway look came to his eyes as he listened, and he leaned back, the tension in his body slowly easing.

When finally she halted, weary and depleted, he removed his cap and got to his feet, his face glowing with a new light. He bowed respectfully to her, then stood silently as she hurried away to meet Ronya.

It quickly became apparent that Ronya was well aware of what had been happening around her. Her eyes were wide with awe when Elena approached her. The clanswoman would not have refused if Elena had insisted on keeping the stone, but they had made an agreement, and that was enough for Elena.

The stone had done everything she asked of it. But it had also done much more than she expected. As she spent time with each of the Clan members, its revelations had aroused her compassion as never before. She was beginning to see that it held almost limitless potential to bring about changes for good in people's lives.

She handed it over to Ronya with mixed feelings. A large part of her was relieved to be rid of it. At the same time, she had gradually become attuned to it, learning to hold her ground against the deluge of impressions, to sift through the emotions and memories to find what she needed. Never could she have imagined the depth and complexity of the mind of another person—the accumulated years of experiences, good and ill, and the far-reaching consequences of the ways each person had chosen to respond to those experiences.

It was completely overwhelming. How could she possibly manage to disengage from it all?

Elena crawled into her bed utterly spent. Never before had she talked to so many people in a single day. Given her reserved nature, it was surely one of the most difficult things she had ever done.

She wondered if she would sleep at all that night. Nevertheless sleep took her almost from the moment she climbed beneath the blankets.

23

The sun was shining brightly when Elena finally awoke the next morning. Thomas was already out of bed, and he greeted her with a happy smile and a warm and lingering embrace.

"I feel almost normal," he said. He looked it, too.

There was to be no chance to celebrate his recovery, though. At that moment Ronya appeared. "I need to speak with you, Elena," she said. She sounded tense.

Elena smiled at Thomas, then she stepped out of the wagon and followed Ronya a short distance into the field beside it.

"I've just learned something," said Ronya. "Something that might be of great importance to you." Her face was grim. "I've found out that one of the clansmen encountered some men a few weeks ago. They were searching for a small group of people, and they offered a reward for information about them. The group supposedly included a young married couple and two older men, one of the men Rogandan." She glanced significantly toward the wagon.

"Viggor has recently heard about this—that's why he left the camp yesterday. He didn't find the men, but he thinks he knows where they might be, and he's planning to send his sons to meet with them. He returned to the camp this morning to make sure none of you leave. He wants the reward!"

Elena's mouth hung open in dismay.

"I don't doubt that he also hopes to find a way to get the reward and keep you as well," she added darkly. "In the meantime, though, you need to come with me. You stirred up a hornet's nest yesterday. The people have been gathering, and trouble is brewing."

Elena called to Thomas, asking him to bring Rubin and Haldek. Then she followed Ronya, doing her best to push the alarming news to the back of her mind.

The entire Clan had gathered in the space between the wagons. As Elena appeared with Ronya, a murmur went up. Thomas came and stood beside her, followed by Rubin with Tamara and Haldek.

"Ronya is a fool," Viggor snarled. He stabbed an accusing finger at the new arrivals. "She brought these people here! They've done nothing but abuse our generosity. But I've learned the truth. They are fugitives, fleeing justice!" He turned to two of his men. "Seize them!"

The murmuring became loud calls of anger as the men stepped forward.

"She has the Sight!" called a voice.

"Do you dare to bring bad luck on us all?" cried another.

Viggor watched on with fury as his men backed away. "Are you cowards?" he shouted.

At that moment Andri stepped forward. "You are not the rightful leader of the Clan, Viggor," he said calmly.

Viggor scowled at him. "I was appointed by the gathering in the ancient way," he said.

"After you arranged for Ronya to be drugged so she couldn't participate," said Andri.

"That is a lie," spat Viggor. "And even if you could prove it, which you cannot, the decision of the gathering is binding."

"Yes, it is binding," Andri replied. "But our laws allow for the leader to be challenged."

"A ritual challenge, with knives?" Viggor laughed contemptuously. "Let Ronya challenge me if she dares."

"Our laws also provide for the challenger to be represented by a champion," said Andri.

Viggor's eyes narrowed. "Who told you this?"

Andri did not respond.

"Let the Law Keeper speak," someone said.

All eyes turned to an old woman, her face wizened with age. She rose slowly to her feet. "That condition has always been a part of our law," she called in a thin voice. "Perhaps it is not well known, but it has never been a secret." She sat down abruptly, shaking her head.

Viggor's eyes sought out Elena.

Others saw it too. "She knew," a voice called from among the gathered Clan. "She has the Sight."

Looking back at Viggor, Elena saw raw hatred in his face. In spite of his lustful intentions, he would have killed her then and there if he dared—that much was obvious to her, even without the stone. But the people of the Clan would never permit it. Not when they believed she had the Sight.

She had established her standing in just one afternoon, and with very little effort. She made no attempt to manipulate anyone. Nor had she tried to influence them to act in any particular way. She had done nothing more than show concern.

Sitting down with individual family members, she had probed their thoughts and memories as they conversed. As she had done with Andri, she quickly gained their respect by mentioning innocent secrets known to them alone, then proceeded to reveal things they were not aware of.

She had set out to reveal mysteries hidden deep within them that she believed they would benefit from knowing. She had done it in her own gentle way, choosing only to disclose insights that would encourage and restore them.

She hadn't lingered—she had soon moved on. Within a few hours she had bonded deeply with many of the adult members of the Clan. Word of mouth had done the rest. Glancing around at them now, she had no need of the stone to see that these people would never allow harm to come to her. Viggor was not without his supporters, but they were a small minority, and most of them also held her in awe.

If only Viggor knew, it was his own mind that had provided her with the crucial information about their laws. He was well aware of the right of a challenger to appoint a champion, and he had done everything he could to keep it quiet.

He had also persistently used his influence as leader to weaken Ronya—to isolate her and keep her wrong footed. He arranged for some of his supporters to whisper to Andri that Ronya secretly despised him. Others went to Ronya pretending that Andri had confided in them. They claimed that he had no interest in her.

Viggor intended to ensure that even if the relevant provisions of their law came to light, none of the Clan would ever consider championing Ronya.

His scheming could not be hidden from the stone, though. And it took little more than a few well placed words from Elena to quickly undo much of the damage done by the whispering.

"Ronya is the rightful leader of the Clan," said Andri loudly. "I challenge Viggor on her behalf."

He did not wait for a response. He slowly stripped to the waist, exposing his muscular physique. One or two of the older women whistled their appreciation. He ignored it.

Andri was powerfully built. He had the frame of a fighter, and his jaw was set with determination. After pounding his massive chest, he reached down for a pair of knives, carefully balancing one in each hand. Then he began to feint forward and back, stabbing and slashing in precise motions. His face was calm, but Elena could see that fierce anger bubbled not far beneath the surface. Andri had a point to prove.

Viggor went pale. He was a big man, but he had established himself by cunning rather than by physical prowess.

He also had the right to appoint a champion. But Elena already knew that the Clan boasted no fighter to compare with Andri. And she guessed that none of them—including Viggor's supporters—would risk their chances against Andri. Not for Viggor's sake.

There could only be one possible outcome from the looming fight. And in spite of Viggor's dishonor and deceit, Elena had no desire to see him or anyone else die that day.

She stepped forward. "There is no need for blood to be spilled," she called, trying to keep her voice steady. "Your law provides another way."

No one said a word.

"Viggor can yield to the claim. He can separate himself to establish a new camp. He must go far away—a journey of at least five days. But he need not go alone. He has supporters who can help him."

She turned slowly, facing each of his supporters in turn. Some of their faces colored quickly. Others glared back at her with angry expressions. But she continued until every one of them had been clearly identified.

Elena's action had been carefully considered. Viggor might accept her compromise while quietly instructing a few of his followers to remain with the larger group to undermine and spy on Ronya. Elena had preempted any such ploy by openly identifying every one of them. No one would doubt the accuracy of her insights. She knew where their loyalty lay. She had the Sight.

Her words hung in the air. Andri stood silent, waiting for a response from the leader.

After a long pause, Viggor turned and spat on the ground. "I will go," he said. "For years I have selflessly served the interests of this camp, and this is how I am to be repaid? Your disloyalty shames you. You are not worthy of my leadership."

Then he pointed at Elena. "You have torn our Clan apart. But your turn will come. You are being hunted, and every hour brings the hunters closer. I will make sure they know where to find you."

Her heart skipped a beat. She was careful not to show it.

He glared at her poisonously. Then he spat again, turned on his heel, and left. His supporters followed close behind him. All of them quickly began to prepare their wagons for departure.

Those who remained gathered around Ronya immediately to

anoint her as their leader. They drew Elena into their midst, and it was some time before she managed to steal away.

Noisy celebrations had begun, and as Elena left the revelers, she saw that gaps had appeared in the circle of wagons. Viggor and his supporters had already departed.

Spotting Rubin, she ran to him. "We need to leave!" she said urgently.

He nodded. "We've saddled our horses. We're ready to go right now," he assured her.

"There is one thing I need to do first," she said. He nodded as she ran back to find Ronya.

Andri stood at her side, her hand clasped firmly in his own. Their faces were glowing.

"Ronya, I must speak with you."

Ronya smiled at Andri, then left him and followed Elena away from the celebrations.

"We must leave," said Elena. "Viggor did not speak truly—we are not fleeing from justice. But the men pursuing us do not wish us well."

"You have used your gift to benefit us all, and I honor you for it," said Ronya, bowing her head. "It has also earned you a new set of enemies. We will help you in any way we can."

"If the men who are hunting us arrive here," said Elena, "perhaps you could send them in a different direction from the one we will take."

"Gladly," said Ronya with a smile.

The new Clan leader gazed upon Elena with respect in her eyes. "I thought you were weak," she said, "and I held you in contempt. I was jealous of your beauty, too. But you have shaken me."

She shook her head in wonder. "I was raised to lead the Clan, but the opportunity was stolen from me. You have given me a chance to fulfill my birthright. And thanks to you, the man I love is now standing beside me as well." She stole a glance across at Andri. He caught her glance and grinned back at her.

"All my life I have witnessed violence, scheming, and unscrupulous behavior from everyone around me. I believed there was no other way to accomplish anything worthwhile. Yet you have done all this without resorting to violence or deception. And when I treated you unjustly, you refused to sacrifice your honor in an attempt to get even." She shook her head once more. "I promise you that I will learn from what you have done."

She dipped her head respectfully. Then she smiled. "If there is anything I can do for you, Elena—anything at all—you need only ask."

"Thank you, Ronya. What you have said means a great deal to me. I truly need nothing from you though—apart from my heirloom, that is."

The smile vanished from Ronya's face in an instant. "I haven't told you!" she said. "So much has happened, and this matter was pushed entirely from my mind."

Dismay twisted the new leader's face, and she passed a hand across her eyes. Then she shook her head. "Viggor is a greedy man. You already know that he planned to take you for himself when he thought the time was right. He also witnessed me snatching away your heirloom when you first arrived, and he has been lusting after it ever since. It wasn't because he cared about it for its own sake—he didn't even know what it was. He simply couldn't bear for me to have something that he didn't have. When we met this morning he took it by force. I no longer have it!"

Elena felt the blood drain from her face.

"I am so sorry, Elena," said Ronya miserably. "Andri and I will gather some men and pursue him right now. We will do whatever it takes to get it back."

Elena shook her head firmly. "No. You have separated peacefully from Viggor, and you must not turn to violence now. We will pursue him."

Ronya opened her mouth to argue, but Elena cut her off. "Perhaps there is a way you can help us. Would you be willing to send us away with a few supplies? We must leave quickly, though."

Ronya agreed without hesitation. Then she hurried away, calling for Andri's help.

Thomas joined Elena. "We are ready to go," he said.

She took his hands and peered wretchedly up into his eyes. "Viggor has taken the stone," she whispered.

Thomas was thunderstruck. He shook his head in anger. Then he groaned, placing both hands over his face.

"Look at you, Thomas! You're not even fully recovered yet," she exclaimed. "I know what you'll want to do. But it's still my problem. I'm the one who lost the stone, and it's my responsibility to get it back."

"But how?" he asked.

"I'm not sure. But I'll find a way somehow."

He gazed into her eyes, then he shrugged helplessly. "You've already achieved more than I would have ever believed possible," he acknowledged.

Thomas turned to Rubin. "Viggor has taken something that belongs to us. We must retrieve it from him before we continue our journey."

Rubin raised his eyebrows, but he didn't argue.

While they were waiting for Ronya, Rubin brought out a simple sling he had fashioned during their time with the Clan. It was designed to hold Tamara while she was on horseback. His intention was to avoid any repetition of the incident that had led to Thomas's head injury.

Rubin now put on the sling, and Thomas handed Tamara up to him. She was soon perched snugly and securely in front of her grandfather, while he retained full use of both hands. Seeing how well it worked, all of them were enthusiastic in their praise of his innovation.

At that moment Ronya returned and pressed two bulging sacks into Thomas's hands. They thanked her warmly, and Elena embraced her.

As soon as they were all mounted they said their goodbyes and set off after Viggor.

. . .

THE WAGONS HAD LEFT A PLAINLY visible trail, and they followed it swiftly. They caught up with Viggor after little more than an hour had passed.

When he became aware of them he stopped his wagon. The other wagons quickly came to a halt as well. "So you have come to throw yourself upon my mercy," he said mockingly.

"You have something of mine," said Elena, her voice trembling. "An heirloom that you took from Ronya. I want it back."

So much had changed for her since Thomas's accident. She had turned Ronya from an enemy into a grateful friend. One at a time she had won the respect of most of the members of the Clan. And she had orchestrated a bloodless change of leadership. She had also made a bitter enemy.

All of it, the good as well as the bad, had come at considerable cost. The pressure within her had built up relentlessly until she was almost at breaking point. The tension from this latest crisis was finally more than she could bear. Her body began to tremble. She tried to master it, but failed miserably. Soon she was shaking uncontrollably.

The woman sitting beside Viggor on his wagon turned to him in alarm. "She is going into trance," she said. "Who knows what might happen? Give her what she wants! Now. Quickly, before she does something that ruins us all!"

Viggor stared at Elena with wide eyes. Then he pulled the chain with its golden clasp from a hidden pocket and threw it to the ground.

"Take it, then!" he said. "You've done enough to us already. Leave us in peace!"

He called to his horse, snapping the reins sharply. His wagon began to move away, the others soon following.

Thomas climbed down from his horse. He retrieved the chain, looking curiously at the stone held within it. Then he brought it to Elena and placed it into her shaking hand.

Viggor's face appeared from around the side of his wagon as it rumbled away. Her tension subsided at the sight of him leaving, and she finally managed to control her shaking.

The ease with which she had retrieved the stone astounded her, and the means by which it had happened was no less remarkable.

Back at the camp she had reached a crucial turning point. She had thrust aside the suspicion, fear, and shame that had assailed her since Thomas became incapacitated, choosing instead to return to what she knew best—a gentle manner that sought to encourage rather than to disapprove.

She remembered something she had heard many years earlier from Brother Vangellis, the monk who later become Thomas's mentor. He had told her, "God's grace is all you need—his power is strongest when you are weak."

It hadn't made sense to her at the time, but it did now. She hadn't outsmarted Viggor with her cleverness, nor had she come after him with overwhelming force—that simply wasn't her way. Strange as it might be, her weakness had been the means of resolving this latest crisis. Somehow that seemed fitting.

Slipping from her saddle, she handed the stone to Thomas. "It's yours!" she whispered spiritedly. "I'm giving it to you!"

He tore his gaze hastily away from her, looking instead toward Viggor's wagon. She followed his glance and caught a final glimpse of the deposed leader as his head disappeared behind the wagon.

She understood why Thomas had avoided looking at her once he regained possession of the stone. Gently taking his face in her hand, she turned it back toward her. His eyes went wide as the stone showed him the reason for her action. A fleeting look of disappointment crossed his face, but it was quickly replaced by awe and amazement as he perceived everything she had achieved while he was laid low.

He closed his eyes and looked away again.

She gazed earnestly up at him. "I know you never wanted to see into my mind. But I needed you to understand."

"I do understand," he said, "and I don't blame you. It wasn't your fault that you saw into my mind when I gave you the stone."

He slipped the stone into his pouch along with the chain and the clasp.

"Let's not do it again," he said.

She nodded her agreement, leaning forward and kissing him gently on the lips.

"We need to go!" he said. "I caught a glimpse of Viggor after you gave me back the stone. He's very angry, and he'll make us pay if he can find a way to do it."

She looked at him in surprise. "I saw him, too—as I was handing it over," she said. "All I could see was his pain. His parents never praised him—not ever—and he's been trying his whole life to prove he's worthwhile. Now he sees himself as more of a failure than ever."

They stared at each other in confusion for a lingering moment.

Then they remounted. Thomas retrieved Tamara and the sling from Rubin, and the little party set off.

THEY RODE until well after dark, aided by the light of a moon that was almost at its full. When they eventually made camp, they didn't risk lighting a fire.

Tamara soon fell asleep. The others sat quietly with not much to say.

"These men that chase us," said Haldek finally. "They want your little heirloom?"

Thomas groaned inside. So many eyes were now upon the stone. Keeping it unknown and out of sight was becoming almost impossible. He looked at Haldek then across at Rubin.

"Haldek and I have been talking," Rubin confirmed.

Thomas sighed. "The man who found us doesn't know exactly why they're chasing us," he said. "I can't speak for the others riding with him. But I won't try to pretend that the heirloom has nothing to do with it."

Rubin turned to Elena. "I don't understand what happened back at that camp," he said, "and I'm not sure I want to know. But I have a bad feeling that you're now mixed up in it as well."

Elena glanced at Thomas. "The heirloom belongs to Thomas," she replied. "He gave it to me so I could keep it safe while he was injured. As you know, Ronya stole it from me, but we got it back in the end. More could be said, but those are the important parts."

Neither Rubin nor Haldek looked satisfied, but Rubin did make a final promise. "Haldek and I will keep this to ourselves. And we will do anything we can to protect you both."

Both Thomas and Elena quietly expressed their gratitude for the support and the discretion shown by the older men. Then Rubin and Haldek lay down with their blankets and were soon asleep.

Elena and Thomas settled beside each other.

"You said that the stone belongs to me," whispered Thomas. "That's not completely true anymore."

"What do you mean?" she whispered back, alarm in her voice. "It's yours! I don't want it!"

"You let me into your mind," he replied, "so I saw what you did when you were with those people. None of that would even have occurred to me. I just don't think the same way you do. And even now that I've seen what you did, I still don't think I could do it."

He paused, trying to find a way to properly express his thoughts. "When I have the stone I can see what people are thinking and planning, and I see their motives. I see what they're feeling, too, but it never occurs to me to dig down to understand why they feel that way. That doesn't particularly appeal to me."

"There's a lot I don't see either," she said. "I've learned to overlook the mean and unpleasant side of people and to find reasons to excuse them. Like my final glimpse of Viggor when he was leaving. Even with the stone in my hand I think I completely missed a lot of what was going on in people's minds."

"And that turned out to be a good thing. You probably wouldn't have wanted to help Ronya if you'd only seen her ugly side. But you looked past that, and now their whole Clan has changed as a result.

The truth is, Elena, that you're a much more generous person than I am."

Seeing that she was about to protest, he hastily added, "I'm glad you think I have some good qualities, too. Especially now that you've seen into my mind!"

He paused again. "What I'm trying to say is that even though the stone gives both of us complete access to another person's mind, we see different things. There's far too much there for one person to grasp anyway, and we can only sift through a tiny part of it. So we find our way to whatever makes most sense to us."

Her head nodded in the dark. "You're probably right."

"So...I see part of the picture, and you see a different part of the picture. Together we see a lot more."

"What are you suggesting?" she asked.

"That it's time we shared it," he said. "We can pass it back and forth between us as the need arises."

She appeared too nonplussed to respond.

"As far as I'm concerned it's settled," he concluded. "If you still need convincing in the morning, we can talk about it then."

He leaned forward and kissed her delicately on the lips. "You are the most gracious and generous person I have ever met," he said, "and I still can't believe that I was the one fortunate enough to marry you."

All conversation ceased as she leaned in to kiss him back.

24

The little group of travelers paused in sight of Arnost, standing just off the main road as they discussed their plans.

Thomas had donned his usual broad rimmed hat to hide his face, but an unfamiliar cloak covered his frame. Ronya had sent them away with ample provisions, thoughtfully including cloaks for each of them along with the food. The fabric of Thomas's new garment was more colorful than anything he had worn previously, and he decided that it suited his purposes perfectly for that very reason.

Not wishing to stand out more than was necessary, Elena had clad herself in her usual black hooded cloak rather than the much more attractive one sent for her by Ronya. She had long since abandoned her old hunchback disguise—a hunchback crone with a young child was sure to attract attention.

Although they had seen no sign of their pursuers, Thomas felt sure that the approaches to Arnost would be watched. They therefore decided to split up before they joined the main road.

Rubin and Haldek had no plans to enter the city at all, and Thomas intended to separate himself from Elena and Tamara before they reached the gates. As they stood together discussing it near the main road, they noticed a wagon filled with produce approaching. Elena hurried to the road and spoke to the man and woman driving the wagon. After confirming that the farmer and his wife were heading for the market in Arnost, she asked if she could ride with her daughter in the back. They readily agreed, and she clambered aboard with Tamara in her arms.

With Elena's horse in tow, Rubin set off with Haldek for the place where they had agreed to meet after Thomas and Elena eventually left the city.

Thomas directed his horse out onto the main road and followed along behind the wagon, careful to keep his distance. He had arranged to rejoin Elena and Tamara inside the city walls, far enough from the gates to avoid attracting the attention of anyone keeping watch for them.

The stone hung from the chain around his neck beneath his clothing, his close fitting tunic holding it firmly in position. Many times already he had silently breathed his thanks to Ronya for her innovation. The stone's insights were available to him for as long as the clasp held it against his skin.

The flow of revelations became a relentless onslaught whenever other people were constantly in view. Thankfully, though, it was easy for him to take a break. He only needed to briefly lift his tunic away from his skin and rotate the clasp, bringing the thin layer of gold instead of the stone into contact with his skin. With a little practice he was able to do it relatively unobtrusively.

DUSK HAD FALLEN by the time he eventually reached the city walls, still trailing behind the wagon.

Thomas led his horse through the gates of Arnost, keeping his head down and avoiding eye contact with anyone. The stone was not idle though, and what he saw disturbed him greatly.

The walls had fallen away behind him when he heard Elena's voice calling to him softly. She appeared from the shadows as he was slipping from the horse's back. Lifting Tamara from her arms, he held his daughter close. She snuggled into him, too tired for chatter.

All traces of light had faded from the sky by the time they arrived at the little cottage beside the stables. Thomas quietly opened the wooden gates, and they hurried inside. He took Elena aside to the stables and handed Tammi back to her. Then he groped his way in the dark to the cottage and tapped lightly on the door.

After a long delay, Axel Stablehand opened the door a crack and peered out suspiciously. His eyes went wide when he realized who it was. He didn't invite Thomas inside. "Wait there," he whispered. Then he closed the door.

Moments later Thomas heard a muffled cry. The door swung open again, and Thomas saw that the candles inside the cottage had been extinguished. The only light came from the flicker of the fire. Then his mother appeared and flung herself into his arms.

"Thomas!" she whispered excitedly. "Is Elena with you?"

"Yes," he whispered back, immediately leading her toward the stables.

His father quickly closed the cottage door and hurried after them. Arriving first, Axel steered them to one of the smaller stable buildings. A dark figure soon joined them. "I'm here," said Elena quietly.

Axel ushered them all inside and closed the door firmly. Then he lit a candle.

Thomas's mother could barely contain her excitement when she found herself face to face not just with Elena, but with a granddaughter. "This is Tamara," whispered Elena with a smile.

Tears of joy flowed freely down Marya's face as she embraced Elena and gazed down at the child sleeping peacefully in her arms.

"You came!" she said. She turned to her husband. "I told you we needed to wait."

The stable master raised his hands helplessly. "I've been telling her she needs to leave. I wanted to send her south to her brother's farm again—where she stayed during the Rogandan invasion. But she wouldn't go. She insisted that the two of you would come, and she refused to leave before she'd seen you."

"And I clearly did the right thing," said Marya with evident satisfaction.

"Why do you need to send Mother away?" Thomas asked his father. "Are either of you in any danger?"

"We haven't personally been threatened," the stable master replied. "But Arnost has become a dangerous place. Even more so than during the invasion." He shook his head. "I never thought I'd live to see such a day."

"Where is the king?"

"The king and the queen both left to confer with the kings of Castel and Varas. They set out a couple of weeks ago, and nothing has been heard of them since."

"What about Will?"

"He's gone to Erestor. He left before they did. He took Rufe Sarjant with him."

"Who did the king leave in charge?"

"Lord Bottren. Supposedly he is still in authority in Arnost. Everything is done in his name. But I can't find anyone who has seen him —not for more than a week. The man who is actually in control now calls himself Lord Lygell. I have no idea where he comes from, but the men who answer to him are no good."

Marya looked at Thomas and Elena with worry on her face. "Everything has changed so quickly. I wouldn't have believed it was possible. And men have been snooping around here. Asking after you, Thomas, and your Rogandan friend. We knew you were off living in a forest somewhere, but we had no idea exactly where, of course, so we couldn't tell them anything."

"Have you been harmed in any way?" Thomas asked her in alarm.

"Nothing's happened so far," his father replied. "But I've been worried about when that might change. I'll feel much better when your mother is safely away from here."

"Enough of our troubles!" said Marya. "Tell us about you! And your beautiful little daughter!"

"I've been longing to share it all with you," said Elena eagerly.

"I've so much wanted you to meet Tammi! But how will we make it work? It sounds like it isn't safe here anymore. Not for any of us."

Thomas nodded. "We clearly won't be able to relax and talk freely until we're somewhere else. Perhaps we could all leave the city for a while."

"Leaving the city quietly won't be easy," said his father. "Our absence would certainly be noticed. You need to be aware that your mother and I are being watched. It's been obvious to me for some time. Did anyone see you when you came here?"

Thomas shook his head. "I don't think so. We were very careful. We split up before entering the city, and we only came here after dark."

"What prompted you to take precautions?" asked his father. "Were you aware of our situation?"

"No," Thomas replied. "A group of men have been hunting us. We were living in a very isolated location, but they somehow found us anyway. They destroyed our home."

"You could come with me!" said his mother excitedly. "To your uncle's farm. We'd all be safe there!"

"Before I go anywhere else," said Thomas, "I need to pay a visit to the castle."

Marya's face showed her apprehension. "Why would you want to do that, Thomas? It's too dangerous. You know that people are looking for you."

"I owe it to my friends—to Will and the others—to find out what's going on here."

Seeing that Thomas's mother was opening her mouth to say more, Elena drew her aside and began eagerly sharing the details of Tamara's birth. Marya was immediately captivated, and the two of them moved off to one side and settled themselves on bales of hay.

"You'll be taking a big risk if you go into the castle, Thomas," his father warned. "You won't find too many friendly faces—almost everyone you knew before has gone."

"There aren't many horses in the stables," said Thomas. "Where are all the soldiers?"

"As you know, most of the army was made up of farmers or tradesmen during the invasion," his father replied. "They simply returned to their homes after Torbury Scarp. The king still has a lot of permanent soldiers of course, and a good few of them went with the king and queen to protect them. Another large contingent just left for Erestor. We've heard rumors of a rebellion there, supposedly led by none other than your friend Will Prentis—Lord Torbury."

"That's ridiculous!" Thomas exclaimed. "Will would never rebel against the king."

"Of course he wouldn't," said Axel. "No one who knows him at all would ever believe it. What reason does Erestor have to rebel anyway? The old duke is still in charge there, and he's the king's uncle. He was the regent during the Rogandan invasion while the king was away from Arvenon, and always fiercely loyal. But that isn't all. Another force was sent to the borders of Castel. Supposedly the Castelans have threatened to invade Arvenon."

Thomas stared at him in disbelief.

Axel shook his head in disgust. "All of it is complete nonsense. Why would Castel attack us? They're our allies! They fought at our side against the Rogandans. And our own queen came from there." He raised his hands helplessly. "None of it makes any sense."

Thomas frowned. Something very odd was going on. And he couldn't ignore a pressing burden of responsibility to learn more. Tempting as it might be to simply slip away from Arnost with his family in search of an even more isolated place to hide, he knew he couldn't do it. He had the stone, and that gave him a better chance than anyone of getting to the bottom of whatever was happening.

Such considerations could wait until the morning, though. For that moment, he was glad to be with his parents again. Having a child had given him greater appreciation for his own parents—even his father—and he had been looking forward to them meeting his daughter. Tammi was fast asleep, but they still wanted to see her and to hear every little detail about her. Tammi already had a loving and involved grandparent in Rubin, but sharing the experience with his own parents, and witnessing their enthusiasm, proved to be just as rewarding as Thomas had hoped.

They could have talked all night, but eventually his mother brought blankets for the new arrivals, and they slept among the hay.

Thomas and Elena stole away from the stables before dawn had begun to lighten the sky. Tamara was still asleep, cradled in Elena's arms.

Marya came with them. She brought with her a large sack into which she had placed a few essential belongings. She was not intending to return to the cottage—Axel had finally convinced her to join her brother on his farm away to the south.

Thomas knew that his mother entertained hopes that he and his little family would accompany her. He had no intention of joining her, though. There was no doubt in his mind that sooner or later he would be pursued, and he would never knowingly place either her or her brother's family at risk.

At the very least it should be possible for them to enjoy some time together before they parted. The first priority was to depart from the city without being observed.

The little party arrived at the city gates as the first hint of daylight appeared in the sky. A number of wagons were lined up within the city walls, waiting to leave Arnost as soon as the gates opened. Once again Elena found a friendly farmer willing to allow her and Tamara to hitch a ride. She also carried his mother's sack of belongings into the wagon with her.

Thomas watched carefully as the wagon rolled through the gates, making sure to keep the stone in contact with his skin. No one that he could see showed any interest in the wagon or its passengers. Marya soon followed them on foot, and once again he saw no sign that she was under observation.

Axel was intending to slip out of the city just before the gates were closed that evening. He would return the next morning as soon as the gates opened. If they were fortunate his absence would not be noticed. All of them planned to spend the night in a secluded location not far from the city—they would brave the cold and sleep under the stars. Marya at least would be able to spend an entire day with Tammi before they parted.

Having seen his family safely through the gates, Thomas turned away from the wall and began to retrace his steps. He would not be leaving the city until he had paid a visit to the castle.

The sun had risen by the time he arrived at a little used side entrance to the castle. He knew that countless people would be stirring within its walls—from the kitchens, where cooks and their helpers stoked the kitchen ovens, to the reception hall, where servants scurried about piling logs onto the great fireplaces. Thomas planned to move purposefully—just another underling eager to perform his tasks without attracting attention.

Pulling his hat down low over his face, he pushed through the side entrance into the castle. Finding himself in a familiar passage, he hurried along it, turning in different directions as the mood took him. All the while he allowed his eyes to roam freely, absorbing information greedily whenever his gaze happened upon another person.

It took no more than a few minutes for Thomas to establish that most of the people scurrying about the castle were anxious and unhappy. The only exceptions were the mercenaries. He encountered far too many of them, and they were sauntering about as though they owned the place.

Before an hour had passed it was clear to Thomas that the kingdom was in serious trouble. Lord Bottren was leader in name only—he and his most trusted retainers had taken up residence in the dungeon with the rats. Lord Lygell was now firmly in charge. The stone soon laid bare abundant evidence of both the ruthlessness and the effectiveness of the new leader. But it also revealed that he was little more than a pawn. Thomas had not been able to uncover any details about Lygell's agenda, but he knew that the man was acting on behalf of another.

Thomas now faced a difficult decision. Should he remain in the castle until he caught a glimpse of Lygell? Or should he leave now, before trouble found him?

While he was pondering his next move, a harsh voice snapped him out of his reverie.

"You! Who gave you permission to be here? Come here. NOW!"

Thomas's head jerked involuntarily toward the speaker. He was alarmed to see that the man was pointing directly at him.

His eyes saw a mercenary. The stone showed him a man with a reputation for brutality—a reputation that the hired soldier carefully cultivated. The man enjoyed throwing his weight around. And his full attention was now focused on the intruder.

Thomas didn't pause to consider his options—he turned and fled.

"Stop or die!"

Thomas sprinted away, pursued by increasingly strident threats.

A growing commotion behind him told Thomas that others were also joining the chase. The hunt was on.

He had been in the castle many times during his childhood but had never explored it fully. The majority of its labyrinthine ways were unfamiliar to him. He dashed into the first side passage that presented itself, throwing himself forward heedlessly with no idea where he was heading. He twisted and turned through passages, at one point emerging in a corridor behind his pursuers, having somehow managed to come full circle. Someone noticed him, and the chase resumed.

A door appeared before him. Thrusting it open, he cast himself forward into a medium sized meeting room. At the same moment, a lavishly dressed nobleman in early middle age entered the room through another door off to the side. Thomas caught a quick glimpse of sharp eyes peering out at him from a narrow chiseled face. The man calmly regarded the fugitive, an expression of casual malice on his face. His robe was even more arresting than his countenance. Thomas's eyes were drawn irresistibly to the dazzle of shimmering silk that flowed in a rich red cascade around the lord.

No more than a glance had been necessary to assure Thomas that he had stumbled upon Lord Lygell himself. In the brief seconds that his eyes lighted upon the nobleman he learned all he needed to know and more.

Several of Lygell's retainers trailed in behind him, even as Thomas's pursuers burst into the room. Thomas's eyes darted around wildly as he sought a way of escape. Two other doors faced him. He selected one at random and flung himself through it before anyone could utter a word.

Fear lent him tremendous speed. Lygell's face haunted him. The nobleman had the eyes of a killer—death would overtake Thomas swiftly if he was caught. Such an outcome had to be prevented at all costs. And not just for his own sake. The stone must never be allowed to fall into the hands of such a man. Or, even worse, into the hands of the traitor who had employed him.

Thomas unexpectedly found himself in a familiar passage. He raced along it before pushing through a narrow entrance and dashing toward the winding stone stairway that lay beyond it.

Bounding up the stairs two at a time, he emerged breathlessly into a small tower room. He glanced around him. Once again he stood in the private retreat where he had whiled away many happy hours with Will and Rufe. There was no opportunity to savor it though.

He shut and bolted the door. Someone had almost certainly seen him enter the passage that led to the stairs, and pursuers were undoubtedly close behind him. But he didn't care. Kneeling down, he pushed aside the large rug that covered the floor to expose a round piece of wood with a metal handle set into it. He tugged at the handle, lifting the wooden cover to reveal a small opening in the floor. A flight of stone steps was dimly visible below it. He lit a candle before carefully positioning the rug over the wooden cover. He knew from experience that as soon as he closed the cover, the rug would slide back into place to completely hide the opening.

Climbing down the steps, he carefully lowered the wooden cover into place, sealing the hole above him. The cover settled with a satisfying thud as it dropped into position. Holding the candle in front of him, he made his way carefully down the stone steps into a small chamber that lay below the main stairway.

It had been Rufe who revealed the chamber to him. On occasion the three friends had climbed down into it, and they had sometimes joked about hiding in it to baffle unwelcome intruders.

Only Thomas, though, had ever ventured out of the chamber's small window onto the flying buttress that lay below it. Such forays were beyond foolhardy, and having dared it once he saw no need to prove a point by doing it again. The buttress stretched upward over his head, but a larger horizontal buttress lay below it. On the far side of this lower buttress another small window beckoned to him.

He could see no way of climbing safely down onto the lower buttress. If he could somehow find a way to do it, though, clambering across it and climbing into the far window should be relatively straightforward. He had once searched out the room to which the other window belonged, and he knew that another stairway led down from it into a lightly trafficked section of the castle.

A bird could fly from one window to the other in little more than a heartbeat. Thomas was no bird, but at that moment other options were not available. And he could ill afford to delay. He needed to make good his escape before the entire castle had been roused against him.

Taking a deep breath, he climbed out of the window onto the buttress, willing himself not to look down.

25

Perched high above the ground, Thomas took a deep breath and tried to calm his jangled nerves.

The horizontal buttress below him was no wider than the one on which he stood, so there was no way to step down onto it. He knew he would not even be able to see the lower buttress if he looked straight down. Without a rope there was no simple means of descending safely.

No alternative presented itself that seemed better than dangling his legs over the side of the higher buttress and planting his feet on the lower one. The challenge would be to get the rest of his body down without toppling over the edge.

Thomas had once witnessed a cat successfully complete the journey from one window to the other. Somehow the cat had made it onto the lower buttress, but try as he might he could not recall how.

Muffled voices called in the tower room above him. The mercenaries must have broken down the door. He couldn't delay any longer. Placing both arms across the upper buttress, he lowered himself over the edge. At this point, near to the tower, the lower buttress was not far below him, and he was able to get his feet onto it. He tried to find a handhold that would allow him to lower himself in safety. He could see nothing vaguely suitable anywhere within reach.

Thomas was not left searching for long. He abruptly discovered he was not alone. Disturbed by his clumsy maneuvering, a pigeon leaped into the air, wildly flapping its wings right in his face. Startled out of his wits, he lost his grip. As he fell, he reached desperately for the lower buttress, somehow managing to get both hands onto it. He clung precariously to it, far above the ground, panting with fear.

The buttress was almost as tall as he was, and a childhood memory came to him of scaling stone walls in the stable. He stood head and shoulders above the stable walls now, but they had seemed tall at the time. Partly from memory and partly by instinct, he bent his knees and planted both feet lightly onto the stonework below him. Then he carefully hooked his right leg up until his heel caught the top of the buttress beside his hands. With three points of purchase, he strained upward until he had positioned his body atop the buttress. He sat transfixed, wide-eyed and quivering with shock. Forcing himself not to think, he crawled across the buttress until he arrived at the far window. Then he clambered through it and cast himself down trembling onto the floor.

After a few minutes he picked himself up and plodded unsteadily down the stairs. He had no idea what he would do if he met another person, but somehow he made it outside the castle without even catching sight of anyone.

Finding a place where he could remain hidden, Thomas considered his options. He had now become frantic to leave the city. Horses were available in plenty in the stables, but he knew that the stables were being watched.

Before he could reach any conclusion, hoofbeats sounded. Slipping deeper into the shadows, he looked on in silence as a dispatch rider appeared. The rider brought his horse to a halt not far from Thomas and swung himself down from the saddle, immediately disappearing into the castle.

Thomas didn't pause to consider the risks. He strode boldly to the horse, whispering soothingly to it as he approached. Then he climbed into the saddle and rode swiftly away from the castle, heading in the direction of the city gates.

As the walls of Arnost appeared before him it occurred to Thomas that the alarm might have been raised and the gates closed against him. To his relief, though, the gates stood wide open, and the guards were no more vigilant than usual. He rode through, keeping his head down and trying not to hurry.

Once clear of the city, he headed toward the agreed meeting place in search of Elena and his mother.

THOMAS PARTED with the horse soon after leaving the city, pointing it in the direction of the city gates and slapping it on the rump. It was not impossible that the animal might somehow manage to find its way back to where its rider had left it. If it did, no trace would remain of Thomas's escape.

He hurried to the agreed meeting location, half walking half running. As soon as he arrived Tamara stretched out her little arms to him. He lifted her up and held her tight, finally able to master his agitation after the tension of the stone's revelations at the castle and his narrow escape. Turning to Elena and his mother, he managed with an effort to speak to them calmly. He was, however, unable to prevent himself from pacing restlessly back and forth while he waited for his father to arrive.

All the while his mind was churning over everything that had taken place in the city. So much about the experience was disturbing, but Thomas at least had the satisfaction of knowing he had left Lord Lygell and his lackeys with a puzzle. He was confident that he had not been recognized—the stone hadn't shown him anything that suggested otherwise—so it was likely that Lygell's men would be reduced to guessing who he was and why he was wandering around the castle.

From their perspective it must seem that he had somehow

contrived to vanish completely. Even if they found the hidden trapdoor in the tower room—which seemed unlikely—it would leave them none the wiser about where he had gone. They would almost certainly believe he was still hiding in the castle somewhere. As far as he was concerned, they could search for him there as long as they chose.

It was quickly obvious to Thomas that his mother had become anxious by the time he arrived. Elena, by contrast, had never doubted that he would find a way to safely extricate himself from the city. He guessed that she was trusting in the stone to help him find a way through. If so she was setting too much store by it. Thanks to the stone he was aware of what other people were thinking. Such insights were extremely useful, but they offered no guarantee of keeping him out of trouble.

It was now Thomas's turn to become restive. His father should already have arrived. If the stable master had been detained for some reason, Thomas would have no alternative but to return to the city. That prospect filled him with apprehension.

The sun had set by the time Axel finally appeared. Nevertheless, Thomas would not hear of any of them resting until they had relocated to a safe location much further from the city. They finally found a place where Thomas was willing to light a fire and sit down around it to talk.

"What's wrong with you, Thomas?" his father asked, traces of his old irritability creeping into his voice.

"I met Lord Lygell," said Thomas, unable to suppress a shudder. "Now I know what he's planning. I have to find the king and warn him."

His father stared at him curiously in the firelight. "What is he planning?" he asked.

"It's safer if you don't know," Thomas replied. "It's easier to behave normally if you have nothing to hide." He spoke in a tone that did not invite disagreement.

Axel frowned. "I need to know what I'm going back to," he insisted.

"You can't go back!" Thomas said in alarm. "You need to join Mother. You'll both be safe at my uncle's place. Stay there until all of this is over."

"I can't just abandon the stables!"

"Other people will care for the horses," Thomas told him. "They have no choice—they need them."

He peered at his father anxiously. "Did you bring any coin with you?"

His father snorted. "I have no lack of money—I brought all of it. My savings are no longer safe at our house." He shook his head in disgust.

Thomas brightened immediately. "Wonderful! Then there's no reason at all for you to go back. You can leave at once."

The stable master frowned. He opened his mouth to speak, but then he closed it again.

"Is the situation really as bad as that?" asked Thomas's mother.

"It's worse," Thomas told her. "Much worse. Until the king returns to restore order, Arnost isn't safe. Not for any of us."

Thomas didn't say it, but the king would never get an opportunity to restore order in his kingdom if Lygell and his employer had their way. He had enough sense to keep that knowledge to himself. His mother looked alarmed enough already.

Axel was choosing not to argue, which surprised Thomas—it was something to be grateful for. Nevertheless it was obvious to him that his father had by no means made up his mind to leave Arnost.

Only Elena appeared to be entirely peaceful, no trace of any shadow darkening her lovely features. Reflecting on all that had been demanded of her in the brief period of time since they left their refuge, Thomas could only marvel at her calm demeanor. She was a remarkable person. And for some mysterious reason she had chosen to bind herself to him. He shook his head once more at the wonder of it, a surge of joy momentarily easing the crushing burden of the challenges that confronted him.

The night was well advanced before any of them even attempted to sleep. Only little Tammi had slept uninterrupted through the hours of darkness, and apart from her no one could muster much enthusiasm for the new day.

Tamara greeted the dawn with seemingly boundless energy. When Thomas groaned aloud at her noisy exuberance, his father responded by taking her little hand and leading her to a nearby meadow. After a few minutes Thomas followed them to ensure that she wasn't wearing out her grandpa. He discovered his father patiently pointing out the wildflowers and the worker bees attracted to the pollen in their blooms.

Elena later retrieved Tammi to offer her some food. After she had eaten she loudly called for "Gampa". Grandpa was by no means displeased, and the two of them happily spent a busy hour in one another's company.

Thomas had the feeling that if Elena and Tammi had been going with his mother to her brother's farm, his father would agree to accompany them without hesitation. He needed to find the king, though, and he was unwilling to part from his wife and daughter, even if he might be leading them into danger. It was clear to him that the stone's capabilities could be used much more effectively if he shared it with his wife.

Once Elena had settled Tammi for an afternoon nap, Thomas's father surprised them all with a sudden pronouncement. "I can afford to leave the stables for a while. It's not essential for me to be there—not with the king away. I have a couple of capable assistants who come in each day. They're more than able to provide basic care for the horses."

Thomas stared at him wide-eyed.

"I will leave Arnost and go with your mother, Thomas," said the stable master. "On one condition."

"What's your condition?" asked Thomas. His father's face was an unreadable mask, and Thomas was left guessing whether he should be pleased or suspicious.

"It's obvious that you'll need to settle again soon—if only for the sake of your daughter. When you do, I would like you to allow us to visit you." He paused, before adding roughly, "I know your mother would like that."

Elena was overjoyed at the suggestion, and wasted no time in letting him know.

"I agree to your condition with pleasure," Thomas assured him. He was working hard to conceal his utter astonishment at any such initiative from his father. "You will be welcome to stay with us, of course—for as long as you like."

His mother said nothing, although she brushed tears from her eyes. His father contented himself with a grunt by way of acknowledgment. But he looked pleased. Thomas had the feeling that the credit for his sudden change of heart belonged entirely to Tammi.

His father hadn't quite finished. A look of concern came to his face. "I don't pretend to understand how you've become caught up in the affairs of the king again, Thomas," he said, studying his son thoughtfully, "but be careful. The king is a good man, and we owe him our loyalty. But you have a wife and daughter to consider now."

Unsure of how to respond, Thomas said nothing.

"My father and Haldek will be wondering what has become of us," said Elena, deftly changing the subject.

"You're right," Thomas replied. He turned to his parents. "Come with us," he suggested. "They will be pleased to see you."

Rubin and Haldek were indeed pleased to see Axel and Marya again, and greatly relieved at the safe return of Thomas and Elena and little Tamara. They enjoyed an evening and most of a day together before Thomas informed them of his intention to leave. Keenly aware of his responsibility to find and warn the king, he was becoming more restless with each passing hour.

Axel and Marya were also ready to depart at once. They had managed to secure a ride with a farmer who was heading south in the general direction of Marya's brother's farm. The farmer couldn't take them all the way, but they were confident they would find another ride when they were closer to their destination.

Although Thomas's parents had invited Rubin and Haldek to

accompany them, the two men had no hesitation in deciding to remain with Thomas and Elena. Rubin knew how much they appreciated his help with Tammi, and Haldek felt as protective as ever toward Elena and her little daughter.

All of them promised to meet up again as soon as they could.

Tammi cried when her grandpa and grandma said their goodbyes and left the little company. Axel had been holding her, and she parted from him unwillingly and with many tears. Marya wept openly, and even Axel appeared to be trying a bit too hard to look normal. Thomas could only marvel at the difference a grandchild had made, especially to the attitude of his father.

As his parents were about to climb into the farmer's wagon, Axel approached Thomas. He nodded toward Elena and Tamara. "Look after them, son," he said, before adding, "And you be careful too." Then he pulled Thomas into a quick embrace, slapped him once on the back, and released him. Thomas was too astonished to do more than nod.

As the wagon rolled away Elena came to Thomas and nestled her head into his shoulder. They waved his parents off together.

"Well that was unexpected," he murmured, glancing down at Elena. She simply smiled at him.

Once his parents had left, they all mounted their horses and set off together on their search for the king. Their journey would take them north, but they initially headed southwest, since Thomas wanted to skirt around Arnost to stay well clear of any mercenaries in the area who might be searching for him.

Their efforts to avoid the main road slowed them down at first, but once they were well clear of the city they swung north. Crossing the main road, they headed into the rolling hills and fertile valleys to the north.

Travelers were not unusual in these parts. Their horses set them apart from the common folk, but to a casual observer they might have appeared to be a small group of merchants or wealthy farmers going about their business.

A considerable period of time had now elapsed since their last sighting of the men who destroyed their home in the forest. If those men were still continuing their pursuit, there was no indication of it. Thomas dared to hope that they had made good their escape.

He was mounted on a fresh horse with a blue sky above him. His little family was at his side, and he had the surprise of his father's farewell to savor. Thomas finally allowed himself to relax.

26

In the wide world the sun was shining brightly. Inside the cabin the time of day might as well have been twilight. Alfic squinted about him. The scattered rays of sunlight that filtered through the single narrow window of the room succeeded in picking out the specks of dust in the air, but did little to penetrate the gloom.

Alfic peered testily into the darkness across the room. The man who was hiring him had positioned himself behind an elaborate chair in the corner. He was visible only in outline. It was obvious that he had planned it that way.

The man's eyes glittered with an unwavering intensity. "Do you understand what's required of you?" he asked.

"I know what you want," Alfic growled. "Trying to achieve it with forty men is absurd."

The dim figure shrugged. "Hire one hundred, then. The payment will be the same either way. You can share it with as many men as you want."

Alfic scowled, although the other man probably couldn't see it.

"You're not going to need an army." The voice was beginning to sound impatient. "There's no reason to panic—this entire exercise has been meticulously planned."

"No one's panicking," grumbled Alfic, furrowing his brows even more deeply.

"Good. Then carry out your role exactly as you've been instructed, and everything will go smoothly. If you try to get creative you'll fail and end up with nothing."

He paused as if waiting for a response.

Alfic offered none. The patronizing attitude of the other man was beginning to irritate him. Having never been told the name of his employer, Alfic silently dubbed him Count Nothing. He had the feeling that it would give the plotter considerable satisfaction if he could somehow find a way of paying nothing.

The voice continued as if sensing his thoughts, "You'll be well paid—when the job is done."

A bag sailed through the air in his direction. "Here's the first installment."

Startled, Alfic reached out instinctively. Catching the bag cleanly in the dark proved impossible, though, and it crashed to the floor. Filled to overflowing with coins, the bag burst open as it landed, spilling its contents freely.

Alfic bent down, cursing loudly. The coins had scattered far and wide, and retrieving them in the dark was a slow and frustrating task. He was reduced to scrabbling around on his hands and knees.

Eventually he stood to his feet and straightened, clutching the bag possessively. He knew he hadn't managed to retrieve every coin.

Count Nothing observed him silently. His face was hidden, but Alfic didn't doubt that he was gloating. Furious and humiliated, Alfic left the room without a word, pushing his way out of the cabin into the bright sunlight.

He had no idea of the identity of his employer, but a bitter hatred of the man welled up within him. There was nothing he could do about it, though—the bulging bag of coins held him in thrall. In that moment he hated his own greed as well.

He made his way to his horse, muttering angrily to himself. After stuffing the coins into a saddlebag, he climbed into the saddle.

As he rode away he reflected on the interaction. Reluctant as he was to admit it, his shadowy employer was right. Even two hundred men wouldn't be enough if the rest of the plan wasn't carried out properly.

If he trusted in the plan, though, it also meant that he wouldn't even need forty men. His lip curled upward in a sneer. He would hire thirty, and he would pocket the coins intended for the other ten.

Now it was his turn to gloat. That didn't mean Alfic had forgiven Count Nothing for humbling him. He never forgot an insult, and he would never pardon any person foolish enough to deliver one.

IN THE CABIN two other men emerged from the shadows. "Will he get the job done?" one of them asked gruffly.

"He might not be happy about the terms," the first man replied, "but he'll do it. And based on his reputation, he'll do it well."

The third man said nothing. Spotting something on the floor, he bent down and picked it up. Silver glinted in the dim light as he held it up to inspect it. He slipped it quietly into a fold in his cloak before returning his attention once more to the floor.

The first man turned away, shaking his head.

"WE'RE ALMOST THERE, YOUR MAJESTY!"

The coach driver's news came like a much longed for tonic, and Queen Essanda drank it in gratefully. Leaning forward, she peered out of the carriage window, bracing herself against the constant jolting and lurching.

The coach was following a track that could barely be called a road, and it seemed to catch every possible rut. Not far ahead, though, located in the heart of a lush valley, stood a large manor house, surrounded on three sides by barns and other dwellings.

The site had been chosen primarily for its location. It lay within

Arvenon, but it was much closer to the Castelan and Varasan borders than to Arnost.

A river flowed lazily on the far side of the buildings. The scene was breathtakingly beautiful. If her situation had been different she might even have thought of it as idyllic.

Columns of soldiers formed an escort that stretched out before and behind her. A few of those riding ahead had almost reached the house.

The maid traveling with her in the carriage poked her head briefly out of the window. "Not exactly royal apartments," she muttered under her breath.

The queen laughed. "This isn't Arnost, Ava. Count Lonnigen has been very generous in offering his mansion for the gathering."

"Did you say 'mansion', Your Majesty?" The maid raised her eyes heavenward. "I actually heard someone claiming this place is called Paradise Valley," she added with a disdainful grunt.

Her reaction drew another laugh from Essanda.

Ava was the perfect companion—sensitive, levelheaded, and even-tempered. She did, however, have a way of taking instant offense when anything less than absolute perfection was offered up to her mistress. Her expectations were impossibly unrealistic, but Essanda found her concern endearing.

With the destination now in sight, Essanda allowed herself to indulge in the anticipation of lying down at last—on a motionless feather bed. Everything possible had been done to ease the journey for the heavily pregnant queen, but the bumping and shaking had steadily worn her down. It was no one's fault except her own, of course—she was attending this gathering at her insistence.

More than once she had asked herself why she was so determined to travel all this way to meet with the three kings. She knew it was partly because she had become so invested in Arvenon and everything that affected it. Arvenon had been nothing more than a neighboring kingdom for the first years of her life. From the moment she was crowned queen, though, it held a claim on her loyalty. And Arvenon had become far more than that to Essanda—in yielding up her heart to its king she had also transferred her allegiance to his kingdom. Arvenon's future was her future now. And the future of her unborn child as well.

It occurred to her there were probably other motivations as well. She wanted to see her father one more time before she gave birth. And perhaps it had a lot to do with her stubborn determination not to be parted from Steffan, especially at this point in her pregnancy.

She gave up trying to understand herself and sank back into her seat.

No more than a few minutes passed before the coach finally rolled to a stop. Count Lonnigen was on hand to greet Queen Essanda, and he himself helped her down from the carriage.

"Welcome to Paradise Valley, Your Majesty," he said with a bow. "You honor us with your presence at my humble home. A suite has been prepared for you—it is available right now if you would like to rest after your journey. I can arrange for refreshments to be sent up to you."

"Thank you, My Lord, you are most gracious. The prospect of resting is very welcome indeed."

A small but impressive staircase faced her as she entered the count's mansion. Her host had thoughtfully assigned her a suite at ground level, though, and he directed her to it. She found King Steffan resting inside it.

He leaped to his feet with great delight when he saw her, embracing her tenderly. "It's such a relief to see you, Essanda! I was very concerned for you once I saw the condition of the road."

"You told me exactly what the journey would be like, and you're generous not to remind me of it," she replied with a weary smile. "I'll admit that I did have second thoughts, especially once we left Arnost behind and the roads started to deteriorate. But it was a bit late by then."

She took Steffan's arm and eased herself onto a bed with a sigh. "None of it matters now, because I've arrived, and with no harm done. I'm not even going to think about the journey home—that can wait until it happens."

Resting her hands atop her ample belly, she closed her eyes and exhaled noisily. It wasn't very elegant, but her current condition didn't exactly lend itself to elegance.

COUNT LONNIGEN HAD FREELY OFFERED his own retainers to serve the monarchs during their stay at his estate. Nevertheless the task was beyond the capabilities of his own people, so he had soon sought additional resources from elsewhere. One of his nephews had joined the monastery led by Brother Elias, and the count had established a connection with the abbot. Hoping to enlist the aid of the monks, he sent a message to Brother Elias with a request for assistance.

The abbot had readily agreed. In his reply he noted that he understood the challenges that came with the exercise of authority, and he saw it as a privilege and an honor to serve those who bore the heaviest leadership burden of all. He also felt confident that a change of environment would prove worthwhile for his monks.

Brother Elias had duly arrived with twenty white-clad monks. He set them to work without delay.

BROTHER ANDER and his fellow monks would have gladly released Brother Elias from physical work. The old abbot was not content simply to organize his brothers, though—he insisted on working alongside them. Any attempt to limit him would have been a waste of time.

The truth was that in spite of his age and apparent frailty, Brother Elias was entirely capable. His energy had not been noticeably diminished by the passage of the years, and his desire to serve had never been stronger.

And he somehow managed to do whatever was needed without complaining. His cheerfulness set the tone for all of the brothers.

Once the kings and their retinues arrived, the monks became increasingly busy. Count Lonnigen's mansion was able to accommodate the three monarchs in comfort, but it had never been designed to host entertainment on such a scale. However a large barn stood adjacent to the main house, and the count had arranged for it to be cleaned out and decorated and equipped with tables and elegant chairs. Daylight flooded into the barn through a pair of large doors at one end, and the overall atmosphere was pleasant and cheerful.

A makeshift but well supplied kitchen had been established at the far end of the barn, with clusters of candles for lighting and access through a side door. The monks were soon working alongside the local cooks.

Brother Ander was approached by his mentor one afternoon.

"I'm sure you must recognize some of these kings and their noblemen," said Brother Elias. "Does it bring back uncomfortable memories for you?"

Brother Ander shook his head. "No, I've left that life behind. It's been more than four years since I joined the monastery, and my days as a soldier seem..."

"Abhorrent?" the old monk asked.

He puckered his eyebrows in response. "I'm not even sure what that word means," he replied. "What I wanted to say was that becoming a healer has changed everything for me. I have no desire to be a soldier anymore. I can't even imagine what it would be like to go back to it."

Brother Elias smiled. "I have no doubt you were very effective when you were a soldier. But you've certainly been developing into an extremely capable healer."

King Steffan sat with Queen Essanda in the barn, enjoying the opportunity to relax before the other kings joined them. His wife had slept well after her long journey and appeared somewhat refreshed.

Count Ranauld stood at their side, and Steffan waved him to a seat.

Steffan glanced around the barn, impressed at how much Count

Lonnigen had achieved in a short period of time. The count had confessed to him that a few weeks earlier it had been just another dusty outbuilding. The nobleman had nothing to be ashamed of. Now it was a pleasant and well appointed living area. Comfortable seating surrounded tables covered with clean white cloths and adorned with flowers. Large benches at the far end of the barn held a variety of food and drinks.

After admiring the setting, he found his eyes drawn to the monks, and one of them in particular. "That monk over there," he said, leaning toward Ranauld and nodding in the direction of the white-robed figure in question. "There's something familiar about him."

The man towered above most of the other monks, and something about the way he moved set him apart from his brothers.

"He used to be a soldier, Your Majesty," Ranauld replied, speaking quietly. "He commanded a large group of men at Torbury Scarp, and he fought well. His name is Ander."

Steffan shook his head. "What's he doing here dressed like that?"

Ranauld shrugged. "I'm not sure," he replied. "But I know that Lord Torbury agreed to release him from the army."

Essanda had been listening to their interaction. "It wouldn't be the first time a soldier decided to renounce fighting and became a monk," she said thoughtfully.

Their conversation was interrupted by the arrival of King Delmar, accompanied by several nobles who had traveled with him from Varas.

Steffan rose from his chair, dipping his head. "Your Majesty," he said, greeting his fellow sovereign warmly.

Count Ranauld had also stood, and he brightened as he saw Lord Karevis enter the barn behind his king.

Steffan singled out the Varasan army commander for a special greeting. "My Lord Karevis."

Karevis smiled before bowing low in response. "Your Majesty."

Essanda shared his respect for the Varasan nobleman, and she was clearly pleased to see him too. "We are honored to have you with us, My Lord," she said with a warm smile.

"The honor is mine, Your Majesty," he replied respectfully.

Karevis headed for Ranauld, and the two of them were soon engaged in animated conversation.

Last to arrive was King Istel, followed by several Castelan nobles. The old king had a disheveled look about him, and his hair was in disarray.

"My apologies for being late," he said, addressing no one in particular. "These days I like to take a brief nap after my midday meal." He raised his hands helplessly. "Unfortunately I don't always wake exactly when I intend to." He shuffled over to Essanda and kissed her on the head. "You look radiant, my dear," he said fondly.

"I confess that I don't feel especially radiant," she replied. "But thank you all the same, Father." She smiled up at him affectionately.

Steffan was impatient to begin, so the moment King Istel had seated himself, the Arvenian king turned to his father-in-law.

"You called this meeting, Your Majesty," he said, "and I for one have been very curious to understand the reason. Please tell us what has been concerning you."

Istel's face took on a grave look. "I don't doubt that all of us have appreciated the peace and stability enjoyed by our kingdoms after our victory at Torbury Scarp. None of us wish to see that tranquility threatened. However I have become aware that such a threat exists, and the information I have to share will be of grave concern to us all." He paused to scan their faces.

Steffan's brows furrowed. Castel might be a small kingdom, but in recent years it had boasted a formidable network of foreign agents.

He had witnessed their effectiveness himself. His mind flew back to his first visit to Castel. Istel had warned him about a traitor among the Arvenian nobility, right at the time of the Rogandan invasion. Steffan had been dismissive at first, but the information proved accurate. Will Prentis had later unmasked the Earl of Pisander as the renegade.

The Arvenian capital of Arnost would have fallen if the traitor had not been identified at a crucial moment. Will had credited

Thomas, the stable master's son, with exposing Pisander, although it wasn't at all clear to Steffan how he had managed it.

The traitor had later bribed his way out of prison and escaped. Steffan still harbored frustration that his uncle, acting as regent at the time, had not decisively dealt with Pisander while he had the chance. His uncle, the Duke of Erestor, had otherwise shown himself to be very effective as regent, and Steffan didn't want to dwell on one blemish. Pushing the matter from his mind, he returned his attention to his father-in-law.

"I have learned that certain men—none that I can identify, unfortunately—have been hiring mercenaries with a view to creating unrest. The initial target is apparently Erestor."

Steffan frowned. This information could explain the reports he had been receiving from Erestor. Sending Will to investigate was now looking like an astute decision—he could hardly imagine anyone better suited to ferret out whatever might be going on.

"Varas was also mentioned," Istel continued. "And I don't doubt for a moment that my own kingdom is also a target."

Delmar had offered no comment, but it was obvious to Steffan that the Varasan king was deep in thought.

"There were no details on offer," Istel continued, "but since all three kingdoms appear to be affected, it seemed important to pass on the information and coordinate our responses."

Steffan nodded his thanks. "I certainly appreciate your initiative."

"There's more," Istel said grimly. "This most recent information didn't reach me until after I set out for this meeting. My agents believe that the purpose goes far beyond unrest. It seems that the ultimate goal is assassination." He poked a finger first in the direction of Steffan, then at Delmar. "Removal of the monarchs. I don't doubt that I am also on the list."

No one spoke.

"One last piece of information," said King Istel. "I am told that the plotters have access to almost limitless financial resources."

"Agon," said Steffan bitterly. "Who else has vast financial resources, and who else would be eager to see us all brought down?"

Delmar locked eyes with him for a moment. Then he nodded slowly.

"Strangest of all," Istel added, "my agent almost had the feeling that the original information about the mercenaries had been leaked intentionally."

Steffan frowned skeptically. "Why would they want to do that?"

"Perhaps they were looking for a way to bring all three kings together," said Lord Karevis. "They might reasonably expect Your Majesties to meet in a central location. Of necessity, any central location is going to be remote, and therefore less secure than the capitals." Karevis became increasingly restless as he spoke.

"But each of us brought at least two hundred soldiers," Steffan protested, "and they're stationed in the fields around us. It would require a small army to deal with a force that size, and I've had no reports of armies on the move."

The kings went quiet. The noblemen found nothing to say either.

King Delmar eventually broke the silence. He turned to Lord Karevis. "Am I right in thinking that the perimeter guard duty is currently assigned to our men?"

"Yes, Your Majesty," the Varasan commander replied.

"Double the guards," Delmar ordered, "and make sure that all of them are on high alert."

Lord Karevis nodded and left the barn immediately, slipping out through the side entrance.

Delmar turned back to his fellow sovereigns. "Hunting down and dealing with these plotters is clearly a pressing priority," he said. "In the meantime we find ourselves here together, whether by our own design or that of another. That offers us an opportunity to combine our resources. We need to make the most of that opportunity."

27

Alfic and his band of mercenaries had been watching the barn all day from the cover of a thick stand of trees some distance away.

They had watched the kings emerge from the mansion and enter the adjacent barn to be served their evening meal. A number of nobles had accompanied them, but few soldiers joined them inside the barn. The only other people in the vicinity were a group of monks who had apparently been brought in to serve the meal.

Careful observation throughout the daylight hours had shown that each king had no more than a dozen members of their royal guard stationed at the mansion where they were staying. However Alfic knew that the surrounding fields hosted busy encampments, each of which housed a substantial contingent of soldiers.

Three army camps had been established—one for each kingdom. The encampments were sited so that they were completely independent of each other, and they had been situated far enough away from the mansion to ensure that a hostile force coming from any direction could be challenged well before it came anywhere near the kings.

Between them the kings had brought several hundred soldiers—more than enough to heavily guard all approaches to the mansion.

Alfic had not been deterred. His men had avoided roads and trails and slipped through the trees in ones and twos under cover of darkness. The guards had not presented any difficulties. They had been well positioned, but they'd been far too relaxed. They clearly weren't expecting trouble.

The role of observing had quickly become tiresome. None of Alfic's thirty hired men showed any aptitude for waiting patiently. He had repeatedly been forced to warn them to keep quiet and stay out of sight—every one of them was now ready to erupt at the slightest provocation. They needed action, and the sooner it started the better.

As for him, he was focused entirely on the payout waiting for him at the end of this job. It was unlikely he'd ever need to work again once this exercise was behind him. The anticipation of the reward made him willing to put up with a lot.

Others had been tasked with dealing with the encamped soldiers. He didn't know the details—his employer insisted that Alfic already had plenty to focus on—but the other pieces had better be in place. He and his men would do what they had come here to do, but none of them would be alive for long if the rest of the plan fell apart. He pushed such considerations from his mind. His employer was right—he had more than enough of his own business to worry about.

As soon as the light began to fade he gathered his men. All of them were armed with bows, and each of them was a capable marksman. Their first task would be to deal with the soldiers outside the barn. They'd have no further need for the bows after that. Inside the barn it would be a matter of swordplay.

"You two. Stick close to me once we're inside." He jabbed a finger at his key Castelan and Varasan contacts. He needed them to identify King Istel of Castel and King Delmar of Varas. He had no need of assistance in identifying King Steffan—he had seen the Arvenian king often enough himself.

He pointed to four others. "Once we've dealt with the soldiers, torch the mansion. And make it quick! We need as much confusion as we can get. Then join us in the barn."

He pointed to two of the men. "There's a side entrance near the back of the barn. Find a way to block it, then join the rest of us."

He pointed to another two men. "Once all of us are inside, you two will close the main doors at the front and guard them. No one gets in or out. No exceptions."

He turned a stern face on his men. "Kill everyone you find in there—women as well as men."

He eyed them critically. "Do all of you get it?"

They grunted in response.

"Good. When we've dealt with them all, we'll burn the barn as well. Then we get out of here. Fast. The only thing left to do after that will be to collect our reward."

IN THE HALF light of dusk, an old horse plodded across the fields, pulling a wagon behind it. A gray haired crone trudged along in front of the horse, guiding it forward. She headed toward the encampment housing the Arvenian soldiers that had accompanied King Steffan to the gathering.

A sentry challenged her as she approached.

"A luv'ly evening to you, good sir," she gushed. "It's only old Gretchen, here with a tiny treat from the king. Something wet to grease the insides of his loyal soldiers on a cold night." She waved at the barrels in the back of the wagon.

The sentry brightened, and called to some of his comrades. "Let's have some help over here! Unload those barrels!"

"Now, now!" scolded the crone. "Don't you be greedy! Just four of them barrels, and no more. There are other soldiers camped out as well, you know."

"Only the Castelans and Varasans. None of them would be thirsty," insisted the sentry.

"Don't you be playing your silly tricks on old Gretchen!" she cried, wagging a finger at him. "I know what's what. You keep your grubby little mitts off them other barrels!"

"All right, old woman. No need for a fuss." The sentry turned to his fellows. "Just take four of 'em," he instructed.

Ale was already being drawn from the barrels, and someone handed the sentry a large mug, delivering it with a hearty slap on the back.

Tilting back his head, the sentry took a swig. He screwed up his face. "I've tasted better!" he exclaimed.

"It's a fresh barrel," said Gretchen soothingly. "The first sip always tastes a bit off." She winked at him. "The next mouthful will slide down better."

The sentry took another swallow. He grimaced slightly, but kept drinking.

"I'll be on me way, then," said old Gretchen. "Others might be thirsty too!"

She tugged at the horse. It pulled obediently at the load, and the wagon lurched into motion, its wheels squeaking in protest.

She smiled toothlessly to herself as she left the encampment behind. "Enjoy your evening, boys," she mumbled. "It'll be your last."

Before long she reached the Castelan encampment. The soldiers there were no less thirsty, and she departed after leaving them four barrels of their own.

Everything was going perfectly.

The final encampment belonged to the Varasans. As soon as she had delivered the final four barrels, her job would be done.

Once again she was challenged. "Who are you, and what are you doing here?" the sentry demanded.

"I've brought a nice little surprise for you all, courtesy of the king," she replied.

"What surprise?"

"Some tasty ale. Just the thing to warm your insides."

"Which king?" asked the sentry.

"Eh?" asked the crone, bewildered.

"Courtesy of which king?" the sentry repeated, rudely this time.

"Your king, of course. King Istel, bless him."

"Istel isn't our king." The sentry looked her up and down suspiciously.

"I meant King Steffan, of course," Gretchen replied. She berated herself for her sloppiness, and the attention it was drawing to her.

"Go find Lord Karevis!" the sentry called to another soldier. The soldier disappeared immediately.

Gretchen's heart began to race. She felt like turning and running, but she knew she wouldn't get very far. Besides, the situation might still be retrievable. She tried to calm her ruffled nerves.

A nobleman appeared, presumably Lord Karevis.

"What's your business here?" he asked her. He wasn't rude, but she had the impression that not much got past him. All at once she found herself feeling very uneasy indeed.

"I'm just delivering some ale to you and to your men, Your Worshipfulness," she said.

"Who arranged this?"

"King Delmar," she said with a deep bow, finally getting the name right.

"She told me King Istel sent it, My Lord!" the sentry said indignantly. "Then she said it was King Steffan!"

Lord Karevis looked at her searchingly for a long moment. "Detain her," he told the sentry. "Don't allow her to go anywhere. I will return soon."

He called for his aides and his horse, and left immediately.

Lord Karevis dismounted beside the barn and followed a servant through the side entrance.

An industrious group of monks were serving food, and the tables were laden. The kings were relaxing together in comfortable chairs, surrounded by members of the nobility who had accompanied them.

Karevis approached King Delmar discreetly. "Could I please steal you away briefly, Your Majesty?"

Delmar rose without hesitation and followed his friend. Karevis retraced his steps through the side entrance and paused once they were outside the barn.

"Did you arrange for ale to be sent to the men?" Karevis asked him.

"No," the king replied with a smile. "But I wish I had. It's an excellent idea."

Karevis shook his head. "Something very suspicious is going on," he said. "An old woman has appeared at our encampment with barrels of ale—supposedly sent by you. I've had her detained."

The king's smile faded.

"Do you have any idea who might be behind this?" Karevis asked. "It could be innocent, but something tells me otherwise."

King Delmar frowned. "Let's find out. I want to be present when you interview this woman."

He called for a horse, and the two men quickly mounted and rode away, followed closely by members of the king's guard.

NOT LONG AFTER Lord Karevis left with King Delmar, Alfic's men at last sprang into action.

Two men ran to the side entrance of the barn to block it.

Four others sprinted to the mansion bearing flaming torches. All of them carried rocks, and they smashed the windows of the mansion, thrusting forward their torches until the heavy drapes were alight. Then they threw the torches inside.

One of the men also carried a small cask of oil. Unstopping it, he splashed oil liberally inside the entrance way of the mansion. Then he smashed it and threw the pieces inside, followed by his torch. A roaring blaze now commanded the entrance to the building.

The four men positioned themselves around other doorways. Fugitives were soon flying from the building in mindless terror. Alfic's men ignored the servants, allowing them to flee in confusion into the gathering darkness. They struck down every other person who escaped the building. Nobles and soldiers alike met the same fate.

Smoke now billowed throughout the mansion and flames licked at the roof.

As the trickle of fugitives came to an end, the men ran to the barn to join the others.

ALFIC SPOTTED King Steffan as soon as he entered the barn. The king was positioned across the other side of the open space, laughing with a small group of noblemen. Alfic pointed to the Arvenian king, and six of his men ran across the barn toward him.

Alfic turned to his Castelan confederate. The man pointed out King Istel, who was sitting very close to the barn entrance. With a wave of his hand, Alfic directed several men to the Castelan king. They reached him in a few strides, putting him to the sword even before he understood what was happening. The men around the king drew their weapons and frantically began to defend themselves.

When Alfic turned to his Varasan accomplice, the man was frowning.

"Delmar isn't here," he said.

"Are you sure?" Alfic asked.

"I'm certain!"

Alfic spotted Queen Essanda sitting apart from her husband, with members of the Arvenian royal guard around her. Alfic pointed to them, and the Varasan set off with several others.

Small knots of fighting men had spread out around the barn, and Alfic now directed his remaining men to throw their weight behind those attacking King Steffan and Queen Essanda.

Two of his men had closed the doors of the barn and now stood guard just inside them. The four who had torched the mansion arrived and were quickly admitted to the barn after supplying an agreed signal.

A group of monks had apparently been serving food, and they had huddled together at one end of the barn. Alfic sent the new arrivals to kill them.

In the chaos it was difficult to determine with certainty what was happening. The location of King Delmar of Varas was a mystery. But the Castelan king was dead, and Alfic was confident that nothing could save the Arvenian royals.

DURING HER CHILDHOOD, Gretchen had seen her beloved father defrauded and mistreated by a noble family. Her father was a gentle man, and the action taken against him had left him in desperate circumstances. He had quickly declined as a result, to the point where he was unable to work.

With the breadwinner transformed into a burden, the entire family had been plunged into grinding poverty. From that time Gretchen had nursed a bitter hatred of every member of the upper classes, along with all those who willingly served them.

Now she stood beside her horse and wagon with growing anxiety. She had organized the horrific deaths of many unsuspecting men that night, but her grisly handiwork was not the reason for her distress.

While she was bolder than most, she was by no means fearless. Now she had been caught, and she greatly feared the consequences.

She soon began to weep. "What is to become of me? And all I've done is bring ale to some thirsty soldiers." Her tears were only partially faked.

A few other soldiers happened to be within earshot. "What's this about ale?" one of them asked.

"Lord Karevis said not to touch it," the sentry replied, lifting his chin officiously.

"He said no such thing!" Gretchen retorted. "He made no mention of my ale." She began to weep again.

"What are you doing to this poor woman?" another of the soldiers demanded.

The sentry scowled at him. "I'm detaining her. By order of Lord Karevis!"

"And what about the ale?" The soldier pointed to the wagon.

Other soldiers had arrived, and a small crowd now awaited his answer with keen interest.

"She claims it's a gift from the king. Lord Karevis wasn't convinced. And I'd suggest you move along if you don't want to get in trouble with him."

"Who gave you the right to speak on his behalf?" the first soldier asked. "If the king sent us ale, what business is it of yours?" Growls of assent rose in a rough chorus.

The men didn't wait for an answer. Eager hands reached for the barrels, and they were quickly pulled from the wagon.

"You'll answer to Lord Karevis for this!" yelled the sentry.

Some of the men held back uncertainly, but others broached the barrels and began passing around mugs of ale. New arrivals soon appeared, and before long they were pushing and shoving to get their share. The scene quickly descended into chaos. When the sentry tried to intervene he was shoved to the ground.

Gretchen took her opportunity and slipped away. She was forced to leave the horse and wagon behind, but she didn't care. She would be paid handsomely for her efforts.

She chuckled to herself as she waddled away. She would be out of sight before the fool of a sentry noticed she was missing. And by then he would have plenty else to think about.

KING DELMAR and Lord Karevis arrived at the encampment to a scene of unimaginable horror. Many of the men were thrashing around in agony on the ground, and more succumbed even as they watched. The remaining soldiers looked on in helpless dismay.

Karevis had no doubt that the men were in their death throes. He quickly located the sentry. "What happened here?" he demanded.

"I tried to prevent them from touching the barrels, My Lord," he replied miserably. "But they wouldn't listen. They pushed me to the ground."

"Where is the woman?"

The sentry hung his head. "When I got up she was gone."

Karevis turned to the king. "The ale was clearly poisoned," he said, grimacing as he surveyed the devastation.

He drew the king aside. "This was a carefully planned attack, Your Majesty," he said. "I fear we would find a similar scene if we visited the Arvenian and Castelan encampments."

He furrowed his brows. "We need to get you to safety. And I need to warn the other kings!"

Delmar opened his mouth to protest, but Karevis shook his head determinedly. "Can you imagine what's going to happen to Varas if we lose you? Preserving your life has just become our most pressing priority!"

He called to the sentry. "Find six men who didn't drink any of the ale and get them mounted. Then bring them to me. And hurry, man!"

The captain of the king's guards and a detachment of his men had followed Karevis and the king from the barn. Karevis turned to the captain. "Round up anyone else who hasn't touched the ale, and tell them I'm placing them under your command. Get King Delmar away from here, as quickly as possible. Escort him somewhere safe, somewhere defensible. As soon as you're confident you have the situation under control, send someone to find me. I'll be with the other kings in the barn."

The captain nodded and immediately sent several of his men to gather survivors.

The sentry arrived with six mounted men.

"You!" Karevis pointed to one of them. "Go to the Arvenian encampment. Tell any soldiers who are still alive to ride to the barn immediately and protect their king and queen!" He pointed to another soldier. "Do the same at the Castelan encampment. Get moving!"

The two soldiers rode off in great haste.

Karevis faced the five remaining soldiers. "The rest of you follow me," he said. He galloped away without a backward glance.

28

Lord Karevis drove his horse forward as fast as he dared. Nevertheless, his unease increased as he began to imagine what might be happening in the barn. He tried not to think about the possible consequences should any of the kingdoms be stripped of their leaders.

Someone was behind this, but the mystery of who it was would have to wait. He could afford no distractions.

A glow in the night sky heightened his alarm. Drawing closer he saw that the mansion was ablaze. He urged his horse to a last burst of speed.

Bodies lay scattered around the flaming building, and he forced himself to ignore the feeble cries and moans that reached his ears. He sent his horse sprinting instead for the barn.

As the huge structure came into sight, sounds of fighting reached him. Karevis drew his sword and leaped from the saddle. He spared no attention for the men who had followed him. They shouldn't need to be told what to do.

The main barn doors were shut, and he burst through them, crashing into two men on the inside who had been standing in front of them. The first was knocked to the ground; the second immediately attacked him. Dancing away from a slashing sword, Karevis took his opponent in the side with a precise thrust of his own weapon. Without waiting for the outcome, he skewered the other man before he could regain his feet.

His five soldiers ran into the barn, and clustered behind him. He paused then, glancing rapidly around him.

King Steffan of Arvenon stood at bay across the barn with Count Ranauld, fighting off four opponents. They were barely holding their own. Karevis could see no sign of the Castelan king, Istel. He spun around to face his men. "Help him!" he commanded, pointing to Steffan. They immediately raced over to join the fight.

Then he noticed Queen Essanda huddled in a corner of the barn, defended by just one soldier. Even as he watched, the defender went down. Karevis didn't pause for thought—he immediately sprinted toward her.

One of the men stepped toward the queen, raising his sword high. But his blow never fell. A sword point emerged briefly from his back before disappearing again. He stood rigid for a moment, then slowly crumpled to the ground.

Underestimating the heavily pregnant young queen had cost the attacker his life.

Four remained, and the queen faced them alone, a determined expression on her pale face. Before any of them could move, Karevis smashed into them from behind. He ran one of them through with his sword as he burst past them.

He came to a halt beside the youthful queen, panting from the exertion. They raised their swords and confronted their enemies together.

Having served the food, the white robed monks were clearing tables when the attack in the barn began. Seeing they were trapped, they scurried to Brother Elias and thronged around him fearfully.

Unperturbed, the old monk was surveying the scene as if trying to assess where he might best be of use.

Brother Ander stood silently beside his mentor. Such a situation could not have been fashioned more precisely to challenge the transformation that had taken place within him. What kind of a man could remain detached while witnessing cold blooded murder? And he was a seasoned warrior—how could he stand by and do nothing? He looked on with growing alarm as King Istel was struck down and King Steffan beset. His hands began to twitch involuntarily.

Everything within him demanded a response. He knew what to do, and it was obvious that his skills were sorely needed. But he had chosen a different path. He had vowed to follow the way of peace.

His mind wrestled mightily with his instincts. God was not dependent on him to save these people. The destiny of every person was in his hands. And if the Almighty chose not to send others to help, he must have his reasons.

But was there a reason why he found himself there at such a time? Was he the one that God had sent?

It couldn't be. He knew from experience that violence only gave rise to more violence, and he had turned his back once and for all on resolving conflict by the sword. He shook his head in a vain attempt to dispel his inner turmoil.

"Get rid of those monks," a harsh voice called. "Leave no witnesses!"

His alarm turned to anger as four men with drawn swords stepped toward his brothers. His eyes narrowed. What kind of men would slaughter defenseless monks?

He turned to Brother Elias. How could his mentor remain so calm?

The old abbot caught his eye. "You must allow God to direct your ways," he said quietly.

What did Brother Elias mean? Ander looked from him to the advancing killers and back again. The four men had almost reached them.

Brother Ander himself was not afraid to die. But how could he stand idly by and allow these butchers to snuff out the lives of his brothers?

The attackers must have realized that Brother Elias was the leader of the monks, because two of them headed straight for him. Brother Ander saw the death of the abbot in their eyes.

He could not permit it—he *would* not permit it. The twitching in his hands became uncontrollable.

The killers raised their swords to strike the abbot down. They had no way of knowing it, but they had just pronounced their own death sentences.

Brother Ander's inner debate ceased abruptly as his anger hit boiling point. Completely overcome with indignation, he stretched down for a wooden bench. The two men reached Brother Elias just as he hefted it into the air. He brought it smashing down on their heads.

The attackers collapsed to the floor and lay unmoving. Their companions came to a sudden halt, staring at him open mouthed.

The big monk waded into the attack, wielding the bench as a club. His opponents ducked and weaved frantically as he swept his makeshift weapon back and forth like a scythe. They were not nimble enough to completely avoid his blows.

No one could long survive such bludgeoning. A heavy blow to the side of the head sent one of them crashing to the floor. The full force of the former warrior's fury was now turned on the remaining attacker. The man made the mistake of turning to flee. The entire weight of the wooden bench slammed into the back of his skull, breaking his neck. He slumped lifeless to the floor.

The monks were now safe, at least for the moment. Brother Ander was just getting started.

Quickly scanning the chaos in the barn, he chose another target. Then, roaring a challenge, he sprinted toward the men who had dared to bring death and destruction into the peaceful barn.

Lord Karevis accepted that he could not himself survive, but he was determined to keep Queen Essanda alive for as long as he could. Unwilling to allow her to remain at his side facing their attackers, he tried to push her behind him.

She refused to budge. And in spite of her condition, she was by no means proving to be an easy kill.

At first their enemies targeted her, two of them coming at her at once. With their attention diverted, Karevis saw an opportunity. Deflecting a blow from the remaining attacker, he leaned forward and punched him in the face. As the man staggered back, Karevis attacked the other two from the side. He thrust his sword into the nearest man, shoving him against the other as he collapsed.

The queen did not waste her chance. While the other attacker was unbalanced, she stabbed forward with her blade and took him in the neck.

One opponent remained. Having recovered from the blow to the head, he renewed his attack on Karevis, a nasty look on his face. Off balance himself, Karevis did well to survive the first frantic moments of this new onslaught.

And even before he had settled into a rhythm, he saw from the corners of his eye two new attackers heading in their direction.

Brother Ander threw the heavy wooden bench at two more attackers. Snatching up a discarded sword, he stabbed down at them while they lay stunned on the ground. Then he ran on, grabbing hold of a large earthenware jug in his other hand as he ran past a table.

He became aware of Queen Essanda's plight just as two additional men joined the assault on her and her defender. Recognizing the Varasan nobleman at her side, Brother Ander raced to his support.

Having vented his initial rage, he found that his head had cleared. Rather than roaring a new challenge, he chose subtlety. Running up behind the men, he smashed the heavy jug over the head of one, then plunged his sword into the back of the other. The third attacker glanced behind him in alarm, and paid for his distraction as Lord Karevis ran him through.

"Get her out of here, My Lord!" Brother Ander cried, pointing to the now unguarded doors. "I'll cover you."

They hurried outside, the nobleman taking the queen's elbow and helping her forward. The queen's maid, Ava, who had been cowering behind them in the barn, scurried out after her mistress. The big monk followed them watchfully.

With no immediate need to defend herself, Queen Essanda began to look increasingly distressed. Brother Ander marveled at her pluck in facing what must have seemed like certain death. With limited support, she had somehow outlasted her attackers. It occurred to him that the unborn baby might well have been put at risk by the almost superhuman efforts she had been called upon to make. He sent up a fervent prayer for the safety of them both.

Arriving outside, they met a dozen soldiers in Arvenian livery belatedly approaching on horseback. Their faces wore haunted looks, and the men appeared dazed and disoriented.

They came to their senses when the monk bellowed at them to protect their queen.

Brother Ander pointed to Lord Karevis. "This man is the commander of the Varasan army. I fought beside him at Torbury Scarp. Do whatever he tells you to do!" he ordered. "I'll need some of you to come with me."

He jabbed a finger at four of them, and they dismounted. Drawing their swords, they followed him back into the barn.

FROM THE MOMENT the attack began, King Steffan's only thought was for the safety of his wife. Determined to protect her, he set out at once to move to her side. He quickly found his path blocked completely by attackers. Their relentless onslaught offered him no chance to go anywhere, and little opportunity to think of anything beyond his own survival.

Of the nobles who surrounded him, only Count Ranauld had fought in a battle. Most noblemen routinely carried a sword, though, if only for symbolic reasons, and all of them were trained from an early age to use it. As a result, every one of his companions mounted a vigorous defense.

Nevertheless they were outnumbered and outmatched. Their host, Count Lonnigen, was the first to fall. Before long just Steffan and Ranauld remained. Between them the others had accounted for only two of their attackers.

The king and Ranauld now fought side by side, with the barn wall at their backs.

Steffan barely found time even to glance elsewhere. But he was aware that his father-in-law was dead. He saw Lord Karevis arrive, and realized that his pregnant wife was alive only thanks to the help of the Varasan nobleman. Unable himself to reach Essanda, he saw that he had no choice but to rely on others to protect her.

Other Varasan soldiers had arrived with Lord Karevis, and five of them now ran to his aid. For a time the odds tilted in Steffan's favor, but more enemies came against them, and the attackers gradually regained the initiative.

Steffan caught a glimpse of Brother Ander when he joined the fight, and saw to his relief that his wife had been rescued and ushered to safety.

There was no opportunity to enjoy the moment, though. One by one his new defenders were overwhelmed. Once again he fought side by side with Ranauld against superior numbers.

Another attacker joined the fight—one who appeared to be the leader of his enemies. He wondered who the man was, and what had motivated him. But his thoughts were forced back to the basic necessities of block, thrust, twist, turn.

He felt so weary. Where were his soldiers? Why couldn't Will Prentis have been here, and Rufe Sarjant?

Brother Ander reentered the barn followed by four Arvenian soldiers. Perhaps help was arriving at last. Some of the new arrivals must surely have gathered around Essanda to protect her. He felt as if a huge weight had been lifted from his shoulders.

ALFIC GROUND his teeth in frustration. After a very promising start, the attack had become completely bogged down. If only he had a few more men. A flush of anger washed over him. He would have brought forty if his employer's barbs hadn't stung him into hiring thirty.

The only victory—and it was increasingly feeling like a minor one—had been killing Istel. Delmar had somehow contrived to vanish before the fighting started, and Steffan was proving unexpectedly difficult to kill. Every time the resistance of the Arvenian king appeared to be ending, more soldiers arrived to defend him.

You always needed to expect the unexpected. But there had been far too many unforeseen developments. Where had the Varasan nobleman come from? He had killed the men guarding the door, sent his soldiers to rescue Steffan, and still somehow managed to save the Arvenian queen.

The most ruinous surprise had been the monk's intervention. Monks weren't supposed to be fighters. How could he have anticipated that one of them would turn out to be such an efficient killer? The big monk must have killed more of Alfic's men than any other person.

When the monk disappeared outside with the queen, Alfic saw his opportunity. He would finish off Steffan, then get out of there fast. He waded into the attack.

"The monk! He's back!"

The warning held a tone of panic. If Alfic wasn't careful, his few remaining men would turn and run. He pressed forward with renewed urgency.

He lunged at the Arvenian king with his sword. The king twisted aside, blocking the blow with his own blade. Instead of drawing back, in one smooth motion Alfic pulled a knife from his belt and thrust forward with his other hand.

King Steffan had no time to avoid the blow and no armor to protect him. The knife took him in the side, and he went down with a cry of pain.

Alfic heard a roar behind him, and spun instinctively to the side, barely avoiding the monk's sweeping sword. The moment he regained his balance, he sprinted for the doors of the barn, dodging fallen tables and leaping over chairs and wooden benches.

More soldiers were running into the barn. He crashed through them, knocking two of them to the ground, and ran off into the night. He didn't pause until he was well hidden among the trees. No one appeared to be pursuing him.

He finally came to a halt, doubling over with his hands on his knees and gasping in air.

The monk had nearly ruined everything. As it was Alfic could claim only one confirmed kill and one probable kill. The third king had avoided his trap, and the Arvenian queen had apparently escaped entirely.

He should still receive half of his reward. And there wouldn't be too many of his hired men left to share it with. He doubted that more than two or three of them had escaped. A smile of satisfaction crossed his face.

He would find his horse and ride to the agreed meeting point. Then he would wait for other survivors.

But not for long.

29

Queen Essanda stood outside the barn with her maid, Ava. A small group of soldiers surrounded them. Most of them were glancing around nervously, as if expecting to be attacked at any moment.

Only Lord Karevis projected calm. He stood beside the queen, shooting frequent glances at her face and her bulging stomach. He was clearly concerned for her.

"Don't worry about me," she said, forcing the words between clenched teeth. "The king needs our help!" She took a deep breath, willing herself to ignore the painful tightenings of her abdomen.

"Ander—Brother Ander—will do whatever is necessary," he replied. "We need to get you somewhere safe, and somewhere comfortable." He paused. "Then I must see to my own king," he added apologetically.

"Of course, you should go! Do what you need to do," she told him.

"I'm not going anywhere until you're safe," he insisted.

She was too exhausted and too distressed to argue with him. Her father's life had ended that night, and she had been permitted no opportunity to mourn his passing. Grieving would have to wait.

Outside in the open, the roar of the flames filled her ears, and even at a safe distance the heat from the fire beat upon her. Glowing embers billowed up into the night sky with the smoke from the burning mansion. It was a terrible and imposing sight. She tried not to notice the bodies strewn around the building.

The angry red glow of the fire filled her vision, but her heart was with her husband. Essanda could think of nothing else. As she was helped from the barn she had caught a glimpse of him. He looked weary and vulnerable, but he had risked a glance in her direction. She knew it would comfort him to know she was safe.

She knew a queen should be thinking of her subjects at such a time, but she was fearful and burdened and had nothing to give.

A man ran from the barn and disappeared into the trees. Two more men followed him. Then Brother Ander emerged with Count Ranauld, carrying King Steffan.

Her pain and weariness forgotten, she ran to him, crying out his name.

"He's unconscious," Brother Ander told her. "But he's alive. He took a knife in the side."

A group of monks emerged from the barn, the oldest of them hurrying over to join them. He knelt with Brother Ander beside the king, examining him.

"He's badly wounded. He's lost a lot of blood, and he needs immediate attention," the monk said gravely.

Brother Ander responded at once. "Tell me how I can best help, Brother Elias!"

"You can begin by praying," Brother Elias said simply.

Brother Ander bowed his head. But he appeared shamed rather than prayerful.

Brother Elias saw his response. "I don't want you to limit yourself to praying," he said. "God uses our hands as well as our prayers. And you were made to be a healer—I have never seen anyone learn so quickly or apply that learning so effectively."

Brother Ander remained silent, but he joined his mentor at the side of the king. The two of them worked swiftly to expose the wound. An anguished sob shook Essanda's frame when she saw the damage, and she tore her eyes away, blinking back her tears.

Unable to watch, she fixed her gaze on the two healers. There was something incongruous about them. One was old and wizened and slight of frame. The other had the build of a burly warrior in the prime of life. Yet both were clad simply in the robes of monks, and both had eyes only for their patient. Both of them were clearly competent, although the big monk deferred to the older man.

Brother Elias was surprisingly deft, the nimbleness of his fingers belying his age. He did not seem dismayed by the task before him, and her trembling gradually subsided as she allowed his calm demeanor to wash over her anxieties. She closed her eyes and slowly released a long shuddering sigh.

A Varasan soldier galloped up, leaping from the saddle the moment he spotted Lord Karevis. He bowed, then leaned in and spoke to the Varasan commander in low tones.

Karevis nodded, and turned to Essanda. "Our men have located a farmhouse not far from here. They have set up defenses around it, and King Delmar is using it as a temporary base. He is not aware of what has happened here, but he requested me to invite his fellow monarchs to join him. Everyone here will be welcome."

Of the Castelan lords who had accompanied King Istel, just one —a pompous nobleman called Lord Eravitt—appeared to have survived the attack. "Will you join us?" Karevis asked him.

A look of disdain came across the noble's face. "I have just located four Castelan soldiers who survived," he said. "We leave immediately for Castel." He frowned darkly as he glanced around him. "This is not a time for playing at alliances. No outsiders need expect a warm welcome in our kingdom. I will be instructing our soldiers to seal off Deadman's Pass immediately."

Essanda glared back at him. "What are you saying, My Lord?" she demanded.

The nobleman winced. "As a native of our land, you will of course always be welcome, Your Majesty." He bowed stiffly. "I must go. Your brother is now the king, and the Council of Lords will need to appoint a regent."

Her heart went out to her brother. Prince Rupert—King Rupert, she corrected herself—was all that remained of her family now. The youth was barely seventeen. She had seen him just once since leaving Castel, and then only briefly. "Please convey my love and best wishes to my brother. Our prayers will be with him in these difficult times."

She took a breath to steady herself. "What of my father?" she asked.

The nobleman bowed. "With your permission, we will take his body with us," he said. "I regret that we will not be able to transport him with the dignity that is his due. But he will be buried in state in his capital."

She nodded, unable to find words to speak.

Eravitt bowed again, then hurried away, calling to his men. She turned her back as they brought out the body of her beloved father and tied it to a horse. She could not bear the thought of it, and could not allow such a sight to become her final memory of him. The Castelans rode quickly away into the night.

Tears of grief rolled down Essanda's face as they left. Better men than Eravitt had died tonight, her own father chief among them, but there was nothing she could do to help Castel at that moment.

She returned her attention to the pressing matter of her husband.

Lord Karevis was kneeling beside Brother Elias. "Can King Steffan be moved?" he asked.

The abbot shook his head unequivocally. "Not by horse," he replied.

"My carriage!" cried Essanda. "Is it still intact?"

"Yes, Your Majesty," a soldier replied. "I saw it earlier. It was moved away from the house, and the flames have not reached it."

Brother Elias pondered for a moment, then he nodded. "He would certainly be better off in proper shelter. We must move him slowly and carefully, though."

"Fetch the carriage, and quickly!" Count Ranauld ordered.

As a number of his men scurried away to do his bidding, another monk drew near. Beyond him, a group of monks huddled together. Their eyes wore a haunted look. Some of them were staring openly at Brother Ander.

The new arrival first addressed the big monk. "Thank you," he said simply. When Brother Ander did not respond, he turned instead to Brother Elias. "How can we help?" he asked.

"I must go with the king," the old monk replied. "I am leaving you in charge of your brothers, Brother Gerome. Please tend to any wounded who might benefit from your help. I will send for you all later."

Brother Gerome nodded and returned to the other monks, speaking quietly to them. They quickly dispersed.

After what felt like an eternity, a group of men returned with the carriage. King Steffan was gently lifted into it, both Brother Elias and Brother Ander climbing in beside him.

Ava appeared at the side of the queen, pale but determined. "You, too, Your Majesty," she insisted.

Lord Karevis nodded his agreement and offered Essanda his hand. Then he helped Ava up as well. "Pay close attention to her," he murmured.

After closing the carriage door, Karevis briefly conferred with Count Ranauld. Then the Varasan commander climbed up beside the driver.

Count Ranauld stepped forward and called to the men around him. "I need five volunteers! The rest of you can follow the carriage to King Delmar's new base."

No one moved at first, but five men eventually stepped forward. Count Ranauld nodded his thanks to them. "We must find mounts and ride to each of the encampments," he said. "Others may have survived. We will gather the survivors and bring them here. Be alert —we don't know if any enemies are still in the area."

"We will send a guide and instruct him to wait for you here," Karevis told him. "We will also return the carriage for the other wounded."

Count Ranauld nodded, and led his men away.

Karevis called to the Varasan soldier, "Lead on!"

The carriage rumbled slowly forward, and the rest of the men followed it, some on horseback, others on foot.

Essanda winced at every jolt. Could the ride have been this bumpy when she traveled from Arnost? Ava found her a cushion and insisted she take it.

Brother Elias turned away from his patient to address the queen. "When we arrive, you must leave the king with us for a time," he said gently, indicating himself and Brother Ander. "You need to care for yourself too." He glanced briefly down at her belly before directing a significant look toward her maid.

Ava nodded an acknowledgment.

Essanda gazed back at him for a moment, then gave a single nod. She knew she wouldn't find it easy to leave Steffan's side, but she recognized the wisdom in the monk's words. It was impossible to know how much the baby had been affected by the upheaval. She sent a fervent prayer into the heavens for her unborn child.

Brother Ander had nothing to say, so Essanda leaned over and placed her hand on his arm. "I owe you my life," she said. "For that you have my heartfelt thanks!"

He bowed his head, but offered no other response.

Sudden insight came to her as she gazed across at him. "Perhaps you have paid a price of your own in fighting to save me and others. Was it possible to help us only by laying aside your principles?" she asked. "If so, I am truly sorry that our situation demanded that of you."

His head sank lower still. It was obvious to her that she had hit the mark.

"I have survived," she said, "in spite of the best efforts of the murderers who attacked us tonight. I am praying that my baby is unharmed too. Perhaps we are still here because that is what God intended."

Brother Ander's head came up slowly, and his eyes met hers. Then he stole a glance at Brother Elias.

The old monk gazed back at him quietly. "I have firmly taught you to renounce violence," he said. "But I cannot presume to understand God's purposes. It is difficult to imagine that your presence in the barn tonight was an accident. God brought you to us by a winding path, and that same path led you to the barn. You were in the right place at the right time—of that I have no doubt. Be at peace, my young friend."

Essanda's delicate fingers still rested on Brother Ander's arm, and the old monk covered them with his own worn hand. A gentle smile softened his wrinkled visage. "The queen has spoken wisely," he said.

She smiled back at him, even though she felt more perplexed than wise.

She stared at the prone figure of Steffan. Who had done this, and why? She could make no sense of the blood crazed savagery that lay behind them.

Tearing her eyes away from her husband, she stared out of the carriage window into the night sky. Thin wisps of cloud draped themselves across the face of the moon, and a dazzling array of stars winked down at her.

Brother Elias followed her gaze for a moment. Then he turned to her. Glancing across at him she saw the deep contours of his face twisted with sorrow. "It is strange, is it not?" he asked. "How is it that such beauty can coexist with the madness we have witnessed?"

He might have been reading her mind.

He peered back out into the starlit night, and slowly his face became calm again. "It is as beautiful as it is unwavering," he said. "Everything above us in the heavens continues its stately procession. Day follows night, night follows day, and seasons give way to seasons, just as they always have. The whole of nature dances and sways in time to a divinely ordered rhythm."

He shook his head sadly. "Humankind alone resists it."

She gazed absently out of the window, a single tear welling up in her eye and rolling down her cheek.

. . .

THEY HAD JOURNEYED for no more than thirty minutes when the carriage at last rolled to a stop.

Men with torches appeared, and Lord Karevis issued a rapid set of instructions. A litter was found, and King Steffan was carried into the farmhouse, the two monks remaining at his side.

Essanda heeded Brother Elias's words, and stayed away from the room where her husband had been placed.

Instead she dismissed Ava with a tight smile and wandered aimlessly outside in the dark, passing among the soldiers settling in around the farmhouse. Most of the men who weren't on duty had positioned themselves before one of a number of roaring fires. They stared into the flames, silent and brooding. They could almost have been struck dumb.

With her uncertainties about the future weighing heavily on her, the oppressive atmosphere only served to heighten her fears and doubts.

Physical exertion had also taken a heavy toll on her body. Her abdomen was becoming increasingly uncomfortable, and her head had started to throb. When she also found herself shivering uncontrollably with the cold, she hurried indoors.

Ava had been waiting anxiously for her return, and the maid ushered her to a rough bed that she had prepared.

COUNT RANAULD eventually reached the farmhouse. The queen had been resting when she was told of his arrival, and she felt strong enough to get up and seek him out.

She discovered that he had brought twenty men with him. Three of them were Castelan, and he was in the act of excusing them to follow Lord Eravitt when she joined him. She greeted her former countrymen solemnly and wished them well on their journey. They managed to thank her politely, but they seemed barely able to focus. It was obvious they were traumatized by the things they had witnessed. The men rode away the minute they were released.

Essanda mustered up a smile for Ranauld. "It's pleasing to see that you found more men, My Lord," she said. "Are others following behind you?"

He bowed formally. "As far as we can tell, Your Majesty," he said, "there are no other survivors."

Her face fell. "You visited all three encampments?" she asked in dismay. "And you found no one else?"

He shook his head without speaking. The tension on his face hinted at the horrors he had seen.

"Lord Karevis has told me that the men were deliberately poisoned," she said. "I must go to our encampment tomorrow to pay my respects to the fallen."

He responded with immediate alarm. "You must not, Your Majesty!" he insisted. "Not in your condition—it would be much too distressing!" He hesitated, then added, "Their...their end was not a pleasant one."

She contained her emotions with an effort. "How are they to be laid to rest?" she asked.

He shrugged unhappily. "I do not know," he said. "There are so many of them and so few of us. Defending our monarchs must be the priority for the moment. But I have sent to Arnost for reinforcements."

"If only Will had been here," she murmured.

Ranauld nodded slowly. "The same thought has come to me more than once. I can't help thinking that the outcome would have been different if Lord Torbury and Rufe had been here." He passed a hand across his eyes. "I'm not at all sure how I survived."

"I saw you in there. You're alive because of your skill and your determination," Essanda told him. "And the king is still living only thanks to you."

"Each of us did what we could, Your Majesty," said Ranauld. "I would not be here without His Majesty's skill and determination."

She found nothing further to say.

Ranauld eventually broke the silence. "Where is Brother Ander?" he asked.

She took a deep breath to steady her voice. "He is inside. Caring for the king."

Ranauld nodded. "If it hadn't been for him," he said, "none of us would still be alive."

None of the men guarding the approaches to the mansion had been affected by the poison, since they were not in their encampment when the ale was handed out. By agreement between the kings, the perimeter guard duty was shared on rotation among the three contingents. The Varasans had been taking their turn at the time, and King Delmar had ordered the guard to be doubled not long before the ale was delivered.

As a result, King Delmar's contingent had been least affected by the attack. Even so, three Varasan noblemen had died in the barn, as well as a high proportion of the soldiers present in the Varasan encampment.

King Delmar was eager to return to his capital of Varacellan as soon as possible. It seemed likely that the assault in the barn was part of a larger strategy, and Delmar was eager to assess the state of his kingdom and put in place a range of security measures.

He also intended to seal tight his border with Arvenon. The Rogandan invasion a few years previously had taught him the consequences of half measures.

He was keenly aware, though, that most of the surviving soldiers belonged to him, and that the small number of Castelans had already returned to Castel. If he departed now, he would leave the remaining Arvenians vulnerable. Doubly so since King Steffan could not be safely moved, and the queen could not ride a horse in view of her pregnancy.

Out of consideration for his friend and ally, Delmar decided to delay his departure until reinforcements arrived from Arnost.

Varasan reinforcements finally appeared after four days, led by Lord Nilsean, one of Lord Karevis's senior commanders. With no sign of the Arvenians, even though Arnost was relatively close at hand, Count Ranauld reluctantly concluded that his messenger had met with an accident. Although he could ill afford to do so, he now sent two more men, with instructions for them to return promptly with medical help as well as soldiers.

The following day King Delmar called a meeting with Queen Essanda and Count Ranauld. He also invited Lord Karevis.

"I must be direct with you," he said to the queen. "I have delayed my departure as much for your sake as for my own. But I cannot afford to delay any longer."

Queen Essanda nodded, her face unreadable.

"All of us came to this location for the sake of our security. Now that my reinforcements have reached us I no longer feel quite so vulnerable as I did previously. I am confident we now have more than enough men to ensure our safety during our return to Varas. Lord Karevis agrees with me." He nodded to his commander, who bowed in response.

"I am therefore willing to leave fifty of my soldiers here under Lord Nilsean. I will instruct Lord Nilsean to report to Count Ranauld. I will leave them with instructions to return to Varas as soon as your own reinforcements have arrived."

"We are exceedingly grateful, Your Majesty," said the queen.

"Please, there is no need to thank me! I have not forgotten that King Steffan lent me more than one thousand of his own soldiers to help me take back Varas from the Rogandans. This tiny gesture in no way erases that debt."

Queen Essanda nevertheless thanked them sincerely, expressing her profound appreciation for their help and friendship at a time of great need. She assured them too that she would never forget her own personal debt to Lord Karevis for his life-saving intervention during the attack in the barn.

King Delmar and Lord Karevis rode away in no doubt of Queen

Essanda's staunch support should they ever find themselves in need of it.

"What do you make of the Arvenian situation, Karevis?" the king asked his friend. "It seems surprising that reinforcements have not arrived."

"I admit to being greatly concerned about it, Your Majesty. And not just for the sake of King Steffan and Queen Essanda, who are friends as well as allies. We share our most accessible border with Arvenon. If Arvenon stumbles, we are certain to be affected."

Delmar offered no response, and they fell silent for a time.

"What do you expect us to find when we reach our own kingdom?" asked the king.

"The reinforcements reported no hint of trouble at the time they left, Your Majesty. But I'm not sure if that means a great deal. Even if there is no obvious trouble, we would be wise to keep our forces on high alert."

The king drew his horse closer to Karevis. "And what of our foreign agents?"

Karevis lowered his voice. "We've worked very hard to strengthen and broaden our agent network. I think it's time we put them to work."

30

Alfic stood once again in the darkened cabin with the man he thought of as Count Nothing.

"Have you completed the job?" he was asked.

"I kept my part of the agreement," he replied. "To the degree it was possible."

"What does that mean?" asked the Count.

"Istel is dead. Steffan is as good as dead—I knifed him myself."

"What about Steffan's woman?"

"She's still alive."

"What? You had clear instructions to kill everyone. That included her!"

"She had unexpected help."

"What help?"

"From a monk."

"A monk? A large group of mercenaries couldn't handle a monk?!"

"This was no ordinary monk. And I've already told you—we dealt with the king."

"She's pregnant with his heir, you fool. You didn't even get half of the job done. And what about Delmar? You made no mention of him."

"He wasn't there."

"What do you mean he wasn't there?"

"He was there for most of the day, but he disappeared just before we moved in."

"So even by your own account, you only dealt with one king. You were supposed to deal with three kings, a queen, and an unborn heir."

"I told you, Steffan is as good as dead."

"One king means one fifth of the pay. And you won't get that until we confirm your story."

"You call me a fool, but you're the fool if you think you can cheat me and my men," growled Alfic.

"You surely can't expect to be paid for work you didn't do," was the retort. "I would never have hired you if I'd realized you were so incompetent."

Alfic's eyes narrowed. All his life he had taken the risks, while men like this sat back and criticized from their couches. Fury began to slowly build inside him.

"Anyway, you'll still be very well off," the voice continued, "even with a fifth of the payment. It doesn't look like you have too many men left to claim a share."

A bag of coins flew through the air. Alfic was ready this time and caught it cleanly.

"That's a down payment. You'll get the rest when Castel announces the death of Istel. And there'll be more if Steffan does die."

Alfic left with the money. But he was furious.

The contract had always been to kill everyone present. But payment was only ever about the three kings. There had never been any suggestion that the amount depended on the queen and her unborn child.

Count Nothing had claimed that Alfic was better off because fewer men would share the money. But Alfic had never expected to share the payment with all of them. No one in this line of business would imagine for a moment that an entire group of mercenaries would survive such an operation.

Some of Count Nothing's money would be used against him. Alfic would begin making discreet inquiries about him. And he would have him constantly watched, starting immediately.

No one cheated Alfic and got away with it.

King Agon glared down at his agent. "Get up and tell me what's been going on!" he commanded irritably.

The man abandoned his bow and scrambled to his feet, standing awkwardly at attention. He was Agon's best agent—more accurately the best of those who hadn't yet lost their heads—and the deep lines under his eyes suggested he hadn't managed to sleep for some time. He had probably been riding all night. Most likely he hadn't eaten in a while either.

That awareness did nothing to diminish Agon's impatience. His subjects existed solely to do his bidding.

"Have my pet foreigners delivered on their promise?" he demanded.

"They have been successful at least in part, Your Majesty. The kings of Arvenon, Castel, and Varas were successfully drawn into meeting in a remote location," the agent told him. "One of our agents planted the idea in King Istel's mind, and he took the bait. The kings were attacked after most of their soldiers were disposed of."

"Well? What was the outcome?" Agon's heart began to hammer with annoyance. Why couldn't the idiot get to the point?

"At least one of the kings is dead, Your Majesty. Another is believed to be close to death. The foreign noblemen were vague about specifics of how he managed to survive."

Agon felt the blood rising to his head. "I give you every agent you ask for!" he howled. "And you're relying on foreign dupes for information?"

"No, no, Your Majesty!" said his agent, cringing. "The foreigners made bold claims about what they had achieved. But every fact that is known for certain about the kings comes from our own sources!"

Agon's eyes bulged as he tried to master his fury. "I gave them unlimited resources," he shouted. "And this is the best they can do?"

After all the bold plans and confident expectations of the foreign noblemen, the fools had somehow managed to bungle it.

"What is being done about the survivors?" the king demanded, seething in anger.

"The foreigners are very confident they will be able to finish the job, Your Majesty."

Agon felt like his eyes were about to pop out of their sockets, and his head had begun to throb painfully. He realized he needed to act quickly, before he did something he would later regret—he knew he could never replace this particular agent.

"Get back out there!" he shouted. "Deal with this situation!"

Agon noted with satisfaction the panicked look in his eyes. All of his servants needed frequent reminders that the king could not be trifled with.

The agent fled from the room without risking a backward glance.

Agon's head was pounding now, and he headed immediately for his rooms. He needed to get there before his vision began to blur.

As soon as he reached his suite he stretched out on a couch. As always, Ennawi stood close at hand.

"I am surrounded by fools," Agon moaned. "I have the power to make my servants want what I want. But what use is it if they are incompetent idiots?"

He covered his face with his hands, trying to shut out the light.

"I expected by now I would be entering Arvenon as its new overlord. But my highly paid assassins have failed to kill the king. Or his wife. And the woman is pregnant with his heir!"

He closed his eyes and groaned.

"And they're still no closer to bringing me the boy with the other stone—the Stone of Knowing. They're chasing him all over Arvenon, and they haven't caught him."

He groaned again. The pain was becoming unbearable.

It was infuriating. He could not afford to leave his servants unsupervised. But there was nothing for it now—he had no choice but to lie down in the quiet and the dark and try to sleep.

Queen Essanda entered the small room that had been hastily erected for her convenience on the side of the farmhouse. Count Ranauld and Brother Elias had already arrived in response to her invitation. She eased herself into the rough wooden chair—the best the farmhouse had to offer—and squirmed awkwardly, trying without success to make herself comfortable. This was not at all a good time to be so far advanced in a pregnancy.

"Thank you both for joining me," she said. "Our situation has been weighing on my mind, and I would value your counsel."

Ranauld's face showed no obvious emotion, but the stiffness of his posture betrayed a hint of the underlying tension that she knew he must be feeling. Brother Elias appeared unmoved, no more affected by their current circumstances than the mountains distantly visible to the north.

She first directed her attention to Ranauld. "What is your assessment, My Lord?"

Ranauld bowed his head briefly. When he lifted it his face was grim. "We are confronted by unknown enemies, Your Majesty, and the king has been gravely wounded. We find ourselves in a barely defensible location with only twenty five of our own men and the fifty Varasans that King Delmar left behind with Lord Nilsean. We have sent two separate requests for reinforcements to Lord Bottren in Arnost, and have received no response."

He waved his hand around the room. "And this is the best we can offer you, Your Majesty. In your condition. In short, I am deeply concerned!"

"What do you suggest?" she asked calmly.

"It appears that Varas is the only place where the king's safety can be assured. I would recommend that we set out for the border at once. If it is safe to move His Majesty, of course."

She shook her head firmly. "I understand your concerns, My Lord, but I have no doubt that the king would not countenance such an action. The assassins who attacked us apparently intended to destabilize all three kingdoms in a single blow by removing their monarchs. It was a bold strategy, and it appears to have been carefully planned. But the attackers were few in number. We have no information to suggest that an army has invaded Arvenon, or that Arnost has been attacked."

Ranauld frowned, but he offered no response.

"Our attackers didn't manage to kill us," she continued. "But if we flee the kingdom in a panic, that must surely be almost as good from their perspective." She shook her head once more. "If the king needs to be moved, it will be to Arnost."

"But we've heard nothing from Bottren," Ranauld replied.

"The attackers may have been lying in wait for any messengers," said the queen. "They may not find it quite so easy to deal with seventy five soldiers."

Ranauld bowed his head, but he was clearly troubled.

The abbot had been watching the exchange impassively. "What are your thoughts, Brother Elias?" the queen asked.

He dipped his head. "I would not presume to offer anything other than medical advice, Your Majesty."

When she nodded, he immediately continued.

"As you are aware, the king has been gravely ill. A couple of days after the attack his wound became red and swollen and he became feverish. We applied poultices to the wound, and we fed him broth laced with feverwort. Thankfully his fever shows signs of abating, and his wound no longer looks quite as angry. Nevertheless he cannot be moved without risk."

He sighed and shook his head. "And yet he is at great risk here, too—perhaps at greater risk. We only expected to serve food when we came here. Our supplies of herbs are severely limited, and we carried no medical texts with us. The resources available to the king in Arnost—or in Varacellan—would be vastly superior."

Noticing the queen opening her mouth to protest, he added, "Varacellan is much further away, of course. A journey to Arnost would be much less taxing for His Majesty." He glanced at Ranauld. "Assuming that such a journey could be completed safely."

The queen sat silently, trying to ignore her own discomfort.

Brother Elias looked at her thoughtfully. "If you do decide to move the king to Arnost, Your Majesty, I think it would be wisest if my monks do not accompany you. We would only get in the way. However I will not leave either His Majesty or yourself untended. Two of our number at least will accompany you."

Her face lit up in a grateful smile. She knew that her husband was alive only thanks to the efforts of Brother Elias and Brother Ander.

THE FOLLOWING morning they broke camp. The queen sincerely thanked the farmer and his wife for their hospitality, presenting them with a generous payment to cover their costs. The couple bowed deeply in response. They had been attentive and respectful hosts, but Essanda didn't doubt that they would be relieved to finally have their farm to themselves again.

Soldiers had been busy preparing the royal carriage. As soon as they had driven it to the front of the farmhouse, several monks brought out the king, still weak and unconscious, and laid him carefully within it. With the help of her maid, Ava, the queen clambered up after him. Ava followed her into the carriage.

Brother Elias came to speak with the queen. "Brother Ander has agreed to accompany you, Your Majesty. He is the best healer we have."

"We are very grateful," Essanda replied.

"He particularly asked me to convey to Your Majesty that he is not willing to fight again. Under any circumstances." The abbot paused before adding, "This is his own decision. I have not tried to influence him."

"His skills as a healer will be more than adequate," she assured the old monk.

"Brother Gerome has also agreed to travel with you," said Brother Elias. "I believe that Brother Ander will welcome his support, both spiritually and medically. But he has also assisted in the delivery of babies whenever need has arisen." He glanced down at her swollen abdomen.

"Thank you, Brother Elias," she replied gratefully.

"Brother Ander is a capable rider," he concluded. "But Brother Gerome is not. Would you be willing for him to ride with you in the carriage? That will also allow him to attend to the king while you travel."

"Brother Gerome will be most welcome," she assured him.

The monk climbed into the carriage and positioned himself beside the king.

Count Ranauld placed his twenty five soldiers ahead of the carriage, while Lord Nilsean and his men brought up the rear. At Ranauld's command, the column moved forward, heading in the direction of Arnost.

Looking back, the queen saw Brother Elias standing in the road behind them. His head was bowed in prayer. He wasn't looking in their direction.

She redirected her eyes back into the carriage, acknowledging to herself that they were going to need all the help they could get.

THOMAS and his little group of travelers had not long crossed the main road west to Erestor. They were heading north.

"See that hill," said Haldek, pointing to a high point not far to the east. "I am going up it to look around."

Thomas nodded. "We'll wait for you over there." He pointed to a thick stand of pines not far north of their current position.

Checking to see if they were being followed was a sensible precaution, and Thomas realized he should have thought of it himself. He'd never been more grateful to have a former soldier traveling with them, even one who'd fought with the Rogandans.

The others followed him to the shelter of the pines. They dismounted while they were waiting.

Haldek was away longer than Thomas expected. When Thomas eventually spotted him, he was heading toward them and riding swiftly.

The moment he arrived, Haldek gabbled out something urgently in Rogandan. Thomas frowned, struggling to make sense of it. Elena had made considerably better progress in learning Rogandan, and she turned to her husband at once with a frown of concern.

"Haldek says that a large group of armed men—maybe as many as two hundred—is heading this way. They're coming from the direction of Arnost. If they leave the road where we did and follow us, they'll reach us in less than half an hour."

Haldek spoke rapidly again.

"Another group of armed men is approaching from the other direction—from Erestor. They're half the size of the first group. They're not using the main road. And they'll be here even sooner."

"What should we do?" Thomas asked Haldek anxiously.

"Not run," he replied. "No time. We hide here."

They led their horses in further among the trees. Then Thomas signaled to Haldek, and they ran back to the outskirts of the wooded area.

After ensuring that he was out of sight and the stone was in contact with his skin, Thomas settled down to wait.

He didn't have long to wait.

Only a few minutes had passed before a rider appeared from the west, most likely a scout from the smaller group. He didn't approach their position—instead he headed for the same hill that Haldek had used.

As he passed, Thomas got a good look at him. He grabbed Haldek's arm in great excitement, and ran back to the others.

"Mount up!" he told them. "That was one of Will's men!"

They reappeared in the open at the same moment the scout left the hill. The man was clearly in great haste and probably wouldn't have noticed them. But Thomas urged his horse forward, calling out at the top of his voice.

"Wait! Can you take us to Will Prentis? It is very urgent!"

Surprise showed on the face of the man. Slowing his horse, he glanced rapidly toward their little party before nodding once.

"Follow me if you can. I can't wait for you though. Armed men are heading toward us, and I think they spotted me."

Without further comment he spurred his horse back the way he had come. It sprang away with Thomas and the others racing after it.

The scout was a competent rider, and the horse he rode was swift. He had soon opened up a substantial lead on them. Thomas could have kept pace, but Elena was riding with Tamara perched in front of her in the sling, and he wasn't willing to leave them.

At one point the scout disappeared entirely. Haldek had seen the group from the hilltop, and he didn't pause even for a moment. They followed Haldek over a small rise and suddenly found themselves in the middle of a group of riders. Will and Rufe were among them.

"Well met, Thomas," said Will with a tight smile, nodding briefly to the others as well. "We don't have time for pleasantries. Are you up for some hard riding?"

They all nodded. Thomas came alongside Elena and retrieved both Tamara and the sling. The moment his daughter sat securely in front of him, the entire group raced to the west, away from Arnost.

They rode until they came to a river. Splashing across it, they swung around, dismounting and taking cover among some trees that lined the bank. The men lifted arrows from their quivers and thrust them point first into the ground before them. Then they unslung their bows from their backs and tested the strings.

"I need all of you to stay out of sight," Will instructed Thomas.

They responded immediately, hiding themselves among the trees. Elena took Tammi again, speaking to her quietly.

Before long a number of riders came into view. They rode toward the river, slowing as soon as they saw the line of bowmen waiting for them on the opposite bank.

"Why are you pursuing us?" called Will. "Who are you, and what do you want?"

One of the riders came forward. "We mean you no harm," he said. "We're searching for a youth and a young woman with a small child. Two older men are traveling with them. They're wanted for questioning. Have you seen them?"

"We've just ridden in from the west," Will replied. "We haven't seen anyone heading that way who matched that description."

"Why aren't you riding on the main road?" the other man asked. He managed not to sound imperious, but he couldn't keep a hard edge from his tone.

"There's been unrest where we came from," Will replied evenly. "We're simply being cautious."

The other man considered them carefully. "Where are you headed?" he asked.

"Arnost," Will replied.

His interrogator seemed satisfied. "If you see them, report it when you arrive in Arnost," he said.

Will nodded. "You can count on it," he lied.

The other man called out a command, and the whole group turned about and headed back to the main road. When they reached it, a couple of riders split off from the main group and headed back toward Arnost. The others continued riding west in the direction of Erestor.

"There'll be more riders heading our way before long," Will predicted confidently. "Most likely a lot more."

He turned to Thomas. "What brings you all out here?"

"Can we talk in private?" Thomas asked, moving his head to indicate Will and Rufe.

Will nodded, and the three of them moved out of earshot of the main group. "I'm sure I don't need to tell you to keep it brief," said Will.

Thomas came immediately to the point. "Lord Bottren is nominally in charge in Arnost, but he and any other loyal leaders are in the dungeons. The person who's really in charge is a man known as

Lord Lygell." Thomas shuddered. "He's an evil and devious man. He has many plans, and none of them are good."

Then it occurred to Thomas to add, "The men you just spoke to are working for him."

"In that case we can definitely expect to see a large number of riders heading in our direction," said Will grimly. "I'm fairly confident that some of those men recognized me."

"How do you know all this, Thomas?" asked Rufe in amazement.

Will gave him a warning frown, and Rufe subsided, clearly still baffled.

Thomas ignored the question. "It's much worse than that," he continued. "The king and the queen have gone to a remote location that's near both Varas and Castel to meet with King Istel and King Delmar. The idea of the meeting was planted by the people who are paying Lygell. A group of assassins is planning to go there to kill them all."

"The king would have taken soldiers for his protection," Will said. "Plenty of them, I expect. The other kings would have done the same."

"There was some kind of a plan to poison the soldiers," Thomas replied.

Rufe was listening with his jaw agape.

Thomas quickly added, "None of the others know all this. They know we're trying to find the king to warn him, but I haven't told them any details."

Will simply nodded. He didn't seem especially surprised. The look on his face suggested that a lot of things had finally become clear to him.

"How long do we have?" asked Will.

"I don't know," Thomas replied.

"When did the king and queen leave for the meeting?"

"More than two weeks ago. Nothing's been heard from them since."

"In that case the attack has already happened," said Will. "It's possible that Arvenon, Castel, and Varas are all without leaders right now."

Thomas saw his own shock mirrored on the face of Rufe.

Will simply looked grim. "Do you know the location?"

"I think it was somewhere called Paradise Valley," said Thomas.

Will nodded. "Count Lonnigen's holdings. I know roughly where it is." He turned to Rufe. "Mount up the men. We need to get there, and get there quickly. It might be too late, but it's possible that someone has survived."

Rufe hurried away, calling to the men.

Will gazed off into the distance for a moment. Then he shifted his attention back to Thomas. "If we arrive in time to save anyone, Thomas, the kingdom will have you to thank."

31

Will kept his men in the river for as long as he possibly could, then they splashed out onto firm ground and headed north. The little diversion wouldn't delay a determined tracker for long, but it should give them a head start.

Since that time they had barely paused. Will could not afford to slow the pace, but he occasionally managed to spare a thought for Elena. Whenever she caught him glancing at her, she simply smiled, and he gradually permitted himself to believe that she was coping with the pace. He acknowledged to himself that she was more resilient than he'd given her credit for.

Will had scouts ranging ahead, although they were hard pressed to stay far in advance of the main body. Rufe had a couple of men following behind. They were doing whatever they could to confuse the trail as well as keeping an eye on their pursuers.

As far as Rufe's scouts had been able to estimate, at least three hundred men were now in pursuit of them. It was now almost certain that someone had recognized Will. Lygell had wasted no time in sending a strong force to intercept him. The pursuers were a few hours behind, but that was nowhere near enough of a gap to be comfortable.

Will never doubted that Lygell would be sending men to Paradise Valley as well. He could only hope either that the assassins had failed entirely in their mission, or that any survivors had fled from Count Lonnigen's lands before Lygell's men arrived.

As soon as they paused to rest the horses, Will called Rufe, Jonas, and Thomas aside. "We have to suppose that some people have survived the attack. But it wouldn't be wise to assume that we will find them at Paradise Valley. If they're unaware of what's been happening at Arnost, they will try to go there. So we will need to send scouts to watch for anyone heading in that direction."

"What of the men pursuing us?" asked Rufe. "It won't help to have them breathing down our necks when we join forces with any fugitives."

"It's time we arranged a little surprise for them," replied Will. "The duke told me he'd selected a hundred of his best men to accompany us. Erestorians pride themselves on their ability with the bow. It's time we gave them an opportunity to demonstrate their skills."

RUFE WAITED with fifteen bowmen behind a hastily erected barricade. Will's scouts had found the perfect location for an ambush. The terrain narrowed to a pass between two low cliff faces that resembled a long and slender neck. The only way to avoid the pass would be to journey far to the east or to the west to divert around the area entirely. Any such diversion would waste the better part of a day.

A few trees had been felled to form a barricade halfway along the pass. Twists and turns in the neck of the pass meant that the barricade would not be visible until the riders were almost upon it. Unfortunately the twists and turns also meant that Rufe's bowmen could not get a clear view along the full length of the pass. For that reason, men under the command of Jonas scrambled up the low cliffs on each side. As well as the fifteen bowmen waiting at the end of the pass, another twenty were now spread out on each side of it as well.

When the pursuers approached, a signal was passed from the

men on the cliff to Rufe and his bowmen. Riders soon filled the pass, milling around aimlessly when they reached the barrier.

Rufe barked a command, and archers appeared at the top of the barrier, pouring a steady stream of arrows down upon the men in the pass. Those at the front tried to push back the way they had come, but downed horses and men hampered their efforts. Almost fifty mercenaries fell in the first few minutes. Then the rain of arrows came to an abrupt end.

The panicked men in the pass discovered that their attackers had abandoned the barrier and simply melted away. They quickly began working to dismantle the barrier, soon discovering that its construction made it easy to clear a pathway wide enough for a horse, and difficult to dismantle it entirely. They chose the easy solution.

As soon as a solid mass of men had filed through the opening, they charged together along the pass, hungry for revenge. Instead of bursting free into open terrain, though, they found another barrier waiting for them at the end of the pass. They immediately turned back, frantic to escape the latest trap. The original barricade halfway through the pass had not been entirely removed though, and there was no quick way for the men to escape. To their horror, they soon found themselves beset from above on each side as well, arrows raining down on them from the cliffs along the entire length of the pass.

Fifty five bowmen poured a continuous stream of arrows into the confused ranks. Another hundred riders fell in the next few frenzied minutes. Soon no rider was left alive in the pass. The only survivors were those able to retreat well out of bowshot range.

Once again Rufe's and Jonas's bowmen melted away. They left behind them a demoralized mob. In the space of a few minutes their pursuers had been reduced from three hundred men to a force half that size. The battle had not cost Will a single soldier.

The men pursuing Will's force now hunted with new caution. Scouts were sent out to probe ahead of the main body of mercenaries. Jonas responded by setting ambushes for the scouts. After several of them failed to return, the scouts too learned to be extremely wary.

Will's men were no longer closely pursued, and Will took the opportunity to hasten his advance. His men traveled into the night as well as all day.

The pursuers were glad to put the pass behind them. They left their dead unburied. The carrion birds had barely gathered when three of Rufe's men appeared in the pass and sent them flapping to safety.

The duke might have provided an abundant supply of arrows, but Will was conscious that the stockpile was by no means unlimited. Rufe accordingly left behind three of his men with instructions to gather spent arrows and rejoin the column whenever it was safe to do so.

Having collected a large pile of reusable shafts, they tied them together in bundles. Then they remounted their horses and rode away.

THE PACE soon began to wear on Tamara. She somehow learned to sleep in the sling while bumping along on horseback, but she never slept for long enough or frequently enough. Whenever she was hungry or thirsty she began to wail. "Dadda! Hungy!"

"What's a kid doing here?" spat one of the soldiers rudely. When it became clear that no one was going to back him openly, he went to great efforts to ensure he never traveled anywhere near her. He wasn't the only one.

Others responded very differently. "Come on, Dadda! Where's the food? The poor little mite's fading away!" Before long Thomas faced a continual stream of good-natured wisecracks if he failed to deliver food or water to the toddler quickly enough.

Whenever they stopped for breaks, men would gather round Tammi and engage her in childish banter. She warmed to the smiles and the attention, and her endearing ways soon made her a great favorite with most of the men. Hardbitten soldiers as they were, before long they had adopted her as their mascot.

Thomas was just as concerned about Elena, and not only because of the punishing pace of travel. It was impractical for her to constantly cover herself entirely, and she reluctantly accepted the necessity of having her face openly exposed to a large group of men. Never in her life had she been so directly confronted with the reactions of so many men. The soldiers gradually became accustomed to her presence, but it was a rare moment when one of them wasn't staring directly at her.

Once again she showed her resilience, but Thomas could see that it was far from easy for her. He hovered nearby as much as he possibly could, and neither Rubin nor Haldek ever left her side for more than a few minutes at a time.

Nevertheless, there was bound to be trouble sooner or later. On the second night when Will finally called a halt so they could sleep, Elena briefly moved away from the others to find a quiet place to relieve herself. As she was returning to the camp, one of the soldiers confronted her.

"How about a little kiss, darlin'?" he demanded.

Thomas stepped out of the darkness. "Leave her alone," he said calmly but firmly.

"Or what, little boy?" the soldier retorted scornfully. Reaching out, he shoved Thomas in the chest. Thomas landed hard on his back. The soldier stood over him, drawing back his foot to kick him in the head.

Before Thomas could respond in any way, the soldier let out a howl of pain and hopped backward on one foot.

Elena stood glaring at him, fully prepared to repeat the treatment by stamping down hard on his other foot.

"So the little vixen has a bite, has she?" the man snarled, reaching out to grab her by the arm.

At that moment the giant form of Rufe appeared from out of the gloom. The big guardsman grabbed the soldier by the collar and lifted him bodily off the ground. The man was left with his feet dangling in mid air.

Rufe pulled the soldier toward him until their faces were almost touching. "Go near her again, or her husband," he snarled, "and I'll separate you from the source of your trouble." He shook the man hard. "Do you take my meaning?"

The soldier hesitated, then he attempted a nod.

"I didn't hear that," said Rufe loudly.

"Yes," the soldier croaked, unable to breathe properly.

Rufe responded by dropping him. The man picked himself up, then turned to glare first at Rufe, then at Thomas, and Elena.

Rufe stepped toward him with menace in his eyes. That was too much for the soldier. He turned tail and fled.

Others had witnessed the confrontation, and Thomas knew that word would spread quickly.

Rufe left nothing to chance, though. From that moment, he made sure that he always rode and camped within easy reach of Thomas and Elena.

THOMAS WAS RIDING BESIDE WILL, answering a range of questions about what he'd learned in Arnost. Their conversation ceased abruptly when a scout appeared, riding in from the northeast. As soon as the scout spotted Will he headed for him, pulling his mount alongside.

"I've just seen a group of soldiers," he reported breathlessly, "fewer than a hundred men, traveling slowly toward Arnost. They have a carriage in the middle of their column. From the markings on it, it's the royal carriage."

Will called for Rufe and Jonas, and they quickly joined him. Then he turned back to the scout.

"Go on," he said.

"There's a larger group, well over two hundred men, coming from the direction of Arnost. The two groups are likely to meet."

"When?" demanded Rufe.

"A few hours at the most," the scout replied. "They're not much further away than we are."

Will nodded. "Lygell will have sent them from Arnost. Can we get there first?"

The scout didn't hesitate. "Yes, if we hurry."

"Is there a vantage point that allows all of these groups to be seen at one time?" Will asked.

The scout shook his head. "No, the terrain isn't well suited to visibility over long distances. I only know about the second group because I've just met with one of our other scouts."

Will nodded in satisfaction. He quickly halted the column. Then he stood up in his stirrups, and called out, "The king and queen are ahead of us. More of our enemies are heading right for them! Ride as if the hounds of hell are chasing you!"

So saying he spurred his horse forward. The troop followed hard behind him.

Elena rode as fast as she could, but she couldn't match the pace of the soldiers. Thomas, Rubin, and Haldek remained with her, and before long all of them were bringing up the rear. When the soldiers galloped over a ridge a short distance ahead of them, Thomas lost sight of them entirely.

At that moment a soldier reappeared over the ridge, riding purposefully toward them with a drawn sword. Quickly bringing the stone into contact with his skin, Thomas recognized the man as Elena's attacker, and saw exactly what he was intending to do. He signaled to the others to halt and swung his horse protectively in front of his wife.

Haldek drew his sword and rode past them to engage the soldier.

The soldier spat. "Ha! So the filthy Rogandan thinks he can fight, does he?" He spurred his horse forward, raising his sword to strike Haldek. Ducking under the swipe, the Rogandan raised his own sword, managing to nick the soldier's arm as it flew past. Cursing with fury, the man swung his horse around wildly and crashed it into Haldek's mount.

Haldek's horse reared up with a scream, thrashing its forelegs in the air. Haldek was thrown from the saddle. Unhurt, he scrambled to his feet and cast about for his sword. As he reached out to grasp it, the soldier swept his horse around and prepared to ride him down. Thomas looked on helplessly, berating himself fiercely for his ineptitude with weapons.

As the soldier rode toward Haldek with his sword raised, he suddenly threw his arms into the air and slumped forward, tumbling from the saddle. Thomas stared down at him in amazement. He lay unmoving on the ground, an arrow protruding from between his shoulder blades.

Jonas rode up, his bow still in his hand. "Rufe sent me back to keep an eye out for you," he said. Glancing down at the dead soldier, he shook his head. "What a senseless idiot!"

Thomas stared at him with relief. "Thank you!" The words felt woefully inadequate.

Jonas nodded curtly. "There's no time to bury him—the buzzards can have him. We've got some hard riding to do!"

Haldek remounted, and all of them raced toward the ridge with the riderless horse trailing behind them.

32

Hazor narrowed his eyes as he gazed across the rolling hills ahead of them. Paradise Valley wasn't far off, and they'd seen no sign of fugitives.

He spat in annoyance. They should have set out days earlier.

Hazor had personally squeezed every last scrap of information from Ranauld's messenger before he died. He knew that the few soldiers who'd survived the poisoning were spooked and distracted, and that the royals who'd evaded the assassins were unprotected as never before. King Steffan was badly wounded—if he was still alive—and his queen was heavily pregnant. They wouldn't be going anywhere in a hurry—riding a horse was not an option in their condition.

A hundred men could have finished it off at that point if they'd moved quickly.

But Hazor had been ordered to wait. Lygell wanted to assemble an overwhelming force, whatever that meant, and he didn't want any of the king's soldiers included in it. He wanted men he could rely on, which meant mercenaries.

So here they were. It was laughable—two hundred and fifty men hardly constituted an overwhelming force. By now the wounded king and his pregnant queen were probably on their way to Varas. It was even possible they were already sheltering behind a Varasan army. Lygell might be a dangerous man to cross, but he wasn't the smartest person Hazor had worked with.

Hazor's thoughts were interrupted by the arrival of one of the scouts.

"I've caught sight of a body of soldiers ahead. There aren't many of them. Barely a quarter of our number. They must have decided Arnost isn't safe—they're heading away from us in the direction of Varas. They have a carriage with them. We've finally found the royals!"

"Stick to the facts," Hazor snarled. "I'll draw the conclusions."

"They had scouts trailing behind them," the rider added.

Hazor frowned. "Did they see you?"

The scout nodded.

"You idiot!" snapped Hazor. "Now they'll run."

He swung around to face his men. "Move!" he shouted. "The chase is on!"

Hazor charged forward with his men close behind. He'd already caught one distant glimpse of his quarry, and he knew the carriage must be slowing them down significantly.

A small stand of trees stood in their path, and Hazor raced around them, his men close behind him. As they passed the trees an arrow whizzed past his face, barely missing him. The whistle of flying arrows soon filled the air. Glancing behind, he saw several of his men tumble from the saddle.

His men were already swinging around to confront the bowmen.

"Keep riding!" he shouted.

The men swung back into line and urged their horses forward. As they raced past the last of the trees, Hazor glanced back once more. Judging by the number of riderless horses, he must have lost thirty men. He cursed in exasperation.

It wasn't entirely bad though. Their attackers had already been left far behind. That meant fewer men to protect the carriage.

A river appeared before them, and Hazor spotted a suitable ford without even slowing. Reaching the ford, his mount splashed across it and scrambled up the opposite bank. His men were soon strung out in a line leading to the ford.

Barely three quarters of his force had crossed the river when a new hail of arrows rained down from a ridge on the opposite bank. Hazor looked on in fury as arrows found their targets. The ford was soon littered with bodies, staining the river red.

Hazor ground his teeth. His enemies were deploying a simple but effective strategy. If he stopped to fight, a small number of attackers would succeed in bogging down his entire force. If he left behind enough men to deal with the bowmen, they would have succeeded in splitting his group.

He wasn't taking the bait. Let his enemies be the ones to diminish their numbers.

"Ride on," he shouted again, and his men galloped away from the ford, leaving their dead and wounded behind them.

The trail left by Hazor's enemies was broad and impossible to miss. He had no need of scouts. Rolling hills lay before him with no obstructions and no obvious locations for further ambushes. Furious after his losses at the ford and impatient for revenge, he charged forward at the head of his men.

Before another hour had passed, Hazor crested a high ridge. The position commanded a view of the entire area, and he quickly brought his horse to a halt. His scouts guided their horses onto the ridge beside him as he peered out across the terrain.

Below him lay a broad plain, stretching out many leagues into the distance. Far ahead a small cluster of horsemen rode swiftly away from him, heading for Varas. He could see no sign of a carriage.

Hazor cursed again. They must have hidden the carriage somewhere along the way. In his eagerness he'd led his men right past it.

"Find that carriage!" he ordered his scouts.

The scouts turned their horses immediately and rode back the way they had come. Hazor and the rest of the troop followed behind them.

One of Lord Nilsean's riders drew his mount alongside the nobleman and pointed back the way they had come. "They've made it to the ridge, My Lord."

The nobleman stared over his shoulder, slowing his horse without completely stopping. A row of tiny figures could be seen silhouetted against the horizon.

"Do you think they'll follow us?" the rider asked.

Lord Nilsean shook his head. "No, they're not interested in us. They'll be looking for the carriage. It's the king and queen they want."

"What do we do now?"

"We keep going. We've done what Will Prentis—Lord Torbury, that is—asked us to do. It's up to him now."

"Will the king survive?"

The nobleman shrugged. "The king is vulnerable in his condition," he said. "The queen too, since she can't ride. But Torbury's with them now, so they're in good hands. He did the impossible at Torbury Scarp, and I'd never place a bet against him."

Lord Nilsean turned away from the ridge and focused his attention on the distant mountains on the horizon ahead. They would come to a broad river before they reached those mountains—the border of Varas.

They were going home.

Hazor's search for the carriage had so far been a miserable failure, and his frustration and rage grew steadily as the sun slowly made its way toward the horizon.

Four of his scouts had now failed to report in. The horses of the missing men eventually led to two of the scouts. The horses were found grazing peacefully, with the bodies of their riders lying nearby.

Both men had been felled with arrows. Hazor gave the other two up as lost.

The phantom bowmen were attacking his riders with impunity. His entire force had been ambushed as they rode beneath a steep hill. Hazor sent men scrabbling up the slope in pursuit of the archers. Not many of them made it to the top alive. Those who did reported that the bowmen had already ridden away.

Night fell without any sign of the carriage. Hazor called a halt, and his men began to set up camp. They were soon building campfires and preparing food.

Before they could relax, arrows came streaking out of the dark, picking off men sitting beside their campfires. Hazor set off after the attackers personally with a large group of his men. They eventually returned weary and empty handed.

Conscious that he couldn't risk losing even more of his mercenaries, Hazor ordered them to put out the fires. They went to sleep cold and hungry.

The tension steadily escalated as the next day progressed. By the time a scout brought him the news he had been waiting for, Hazor was almost ready to erupt.

"I found the carriage," the scout reported.

"Where?" demanded Hazor.

"West of here. It was empty."

Hazor ground his teeth in fury.

"It is the one they were using, though. I searched the surrounding area and found a blood soaked bandage. And there were fresh tracks nearby—wagon wheel tracks."

Hazor forced himself to remain calm. "Which direction were they heading?"

"Southwest."

"So they're not heading for Arnost."

The scout shook his head. "No, they're heading in the direction of Erestor. I followed the tracks until they disappeared across stony ground."

"They'll be forced to travel slowly. We can still catch them."

With his other scouts either missing or out searching, Hazor selected several more men. "Forget the royal carriage," he told them. "You're looking for a body of soldiers protecting a wagon. Get going!"

His scouts rode away.

Hazor faced the rest of his men. "No more distractions. If we're attacked again, we ignore it. Whatever happens we keep riding."

JONAS PEERED over the tip of the rise, watching his enemies ride past below him. They were heading in the wrong direction, and he would make sure that his next ambush pointed them even further away from their intended target.

His nighttime raid had forced the mercenaries to forego their hot meal and bed down in the cold, and he knew that they would be weary and disgruntled. But such successes also came at a cost to him and his men. They couldn't afford to use fires either, and he couldn't remember when they'd last enjoyed an uninterrupted sleep.

Will had given him more authority, which was what he wanted. But the role also came with more responsibility, and no shortage of risk.

Will would surely look after him when everything returned to normal—at least Jonas was counting on him to do so. But who could say when that might happen? And there was always a chance that one or other of them wouldn't survive. War was an uncertain business, and no one was invincible. They'd done well to stay alive as long as they had.

His biggest concern was for his aging parents. He did everything he could to support them, and he didn't like to think about their chances if anything happened to him.

His mind went back, as it so often did, to his big sister. She'd been his best friend from the earliest time he could remember—the two of them had been inseparable. Her future looked bright. Everyone agreed she was the most beautiful young woman they'd ever seen.

She could have taken her pick from among the young men in the village.

Then she became sick.

His parents couldn't afford a healer. They'd barely been able to feed their family even before the baron seized their milking cow for his latest feast. Jonas had watched on helplessly as his beloved sister slowly wasted away.

It was no use dwelling on the past though.

Jonas sighed as he turned away and remounted his horse. Life was unpredictable. And it certainly wasn't fair.

QUEEN ESSANDA SIGHED with relief when Will called a short break. The cart carrying her and Steffan rolled slowly to a stop, and Ava hurried to help her down from it. All around them men quickly dismounted, gratefully accepting the opportunity to stretch. Brother Ander remained in the cart with Steffan, attentive as always at his side.

The occupants of the royal carriage had been transferred to a farmer's cart as soon as Will and his men connected with the royal party and its largely Varasan escort. The empty carriage became nothing more than a decoy, and Lord Nilsean had agreed to take charge of it. His squad of Varasan soldiers changed course and headed in the direction of Varas, intending to hide the carriage somewhere suitable along the way. Count Ranauld and his small squad of Arvenian soldiers parted from their Varasan friends and attached themselves to Will's force.

On the journey to Paradise Valley Essanda had thought of the royal carriage as uncomfortable. Now she remembered its cushioned seats and sheltered interior ruefully. By comparison with the wagon, the carriage was impossibly luxurious.

Noticing Brother Gerome approaching, Queen Essanda managed a weak smile of greeting.

"I am truly sorry that we cannot offer you more appropriate traveling conditions, Your Majesty," he said regretfully.

"It isn't your fault, Brother Gerome," she replied.

He glanced forthrightly at her distended belly. "Would you be willing to discuss your condition with me?" he asked.

Essanda turned to Ava and gave her a significant nod. The maid raised an eyebrow, but she bowed respectfully and left them without comment.

"Do you know when you are due, Your Majesty?"

"At the time I left Arnost my best guess was another six weeks," she replied.

His eyes went wide.

"I know," she said with a sigh. "You don't need to say it." She glanced across at the prone figure of her husband in the wagon. "It was my choice to accompany the king, and I'm not sorry that I did."

Brother Gerome noticed Elena nearby. "May I invite Elena to join us? She has personal experience with the birth process, and her insights might prove helpful."

"By all means," Essanda replied.

Brother Gerome called to Elena, and she quickly joined them.

"Have you noticed anything different or unusual, Your Majesty?" asked the monk.

Essanda hesitated momentarily before deciding to be direct. "I've been experiencing sharp pains at times. I've wondered if they were contractions."

"How often?" asked Brother Gerome.

"Infrequently. Sometimes two or three times in a hour, then nothing for long periods."

The monk nodded. "You are most likely experiencing false labor."

"I had similar pains," Elena confirmed, "especially in the weeks leading up to Tamara's birth."

"Has the baby been moving?" asked Brother Gerome.

"Yes. I felt some kicking just a few minutes ago."

"Any bleeding?"

She shook her head.

Brother Gerome had many more questions, but he seemed satisfied with her answers when he left. Essanda was grateful for their concern, and told them so frankly.

She saw now that her need for reassurance had been more pressing than she'd realized. Since the horrors of the fight in the barn at Paradise Valley and the death of her father, Essanda had endured the constant stress of fleeing under rough conditions with a gravely wounded husband. She now acknowledged her growing concerns about how these experiences might have affected her baby.

Having confronted her own anxieties, Essanda bent her thoughts once more to Steffan. She returned to the wagon and stood beside it gazing helplessly at the prone figure of her husband.

Brother Ander looked up, and their eyes met. The compassion in his eyes still astounded her. She couldn't forget his fury in the barn as he single-handedly wrested control away from the attackers. Difficult as it had been to comprehend his transformation from fierce warrior to gentle healer, she readily acknowledged that Steffan was in capable hands.

"He's improving, Your Majesty," Brother Ander told her, answering the unspoken question in her eyes. "I am hopeful."

"Thank you, Brother Ander," she said, her voice trembling. She brushed away the tears welling in her eyes, and turned aside to compose herself.

Will called the men to horse, and the wagon rumbled forward again. Essanda sucked in a sharp breath as another contraction compressed her abdomen. She gritted her teeth against the pain and tried to think of anything except the desperate state of their circumstances.

WHEN THE RIDERS next stopped for a break Essanda clambered down out of the cart to stretch her aching muscles. Glancing up, she saw Elena coming to her. Tamara arrived as well, pausing for a few moments to stare wide-eyed at the queen's distended belly before running off to play. Essanda paid no attention to her undignified appearance—she was beyond caring about how she looked.

The queen greeted her friend warmly, a wry smile covering her face. "I seem to remember us talking about what it would be like to have babies of our own, back when we were chatting in the castle at Arnost," she said. "The idea seemed so exciting at the time. In practice it hasn't been working out quite the way I imagined." She sighed deeply.

Elena's concerned eyes peered back at her. "Can I do anything to help, Your Majesty?" she asked.

"Yes, you can," Essanda replied without hesitation. "Stay and talk to me for a few minutes. It's been far too long, and I've missed you!"

As the soldiers saw to their horses, the queen and the commoner wandered together arm in arm among the scattered trees of a forgotten valley. For a time the bouncing of the wagon, the condition of the king, and the uncertainties of the future slipped away, as Essanda laid aside her burdens to share her self with a true friend.

When the order came to move out, Elena helped the queen back into the wagon. Essanda squeezed her hand, allowing the moisture in her eyes to express without words the overflow of her heart.

Awareness returned slowly to Steffan, with dim hints of a blue sky above and a shaking and jolting below. The only certainty was unbearable pain.

A face swam into view as a monk bent low over him. The monk attended to him silently. The face seemed somehow familiar, but Steffan slipped into oblivion before understanding why.

When next he awoke he sensed through a haze of pain that Essanda was sitting nearby. She seemed peaceful and well, and the knowledge comforted him for reasons he couldn't recall. When the blackness came for him once more, he surrendered to it calmly.

. . .

THE SKY WAS dark when Steffan woke again. The bouncing had stopped, and he lay peacefully beneath a starlit expanse. His side throbbed incessantly, but he decided he could bear it. His beloved Essanda came to him, her face flickering in the firelight. Tears glistened in her eyes, but she smiled tenderly down at him, whispering words of comfort and hope. He tried to smile back, but his mouth wouldn't cooperate, twisting awkwardly as a wave of pain washed over him.

He reached up a hand, and she took it, squeezing it gently.

Memories came to him then, dull memories of fighting and of fear. More than anything, he remembered his weariness.

He decided to close his eyes, just for a moment, and everything slid away again.

THOMAS RODE alongside Rubin to retrieve his daughter, then he steered his horse closer to the royal wagon so Tammi could catch another sight of the queen's bulging belly. The toddler was fascinated by the idea that a baby was hidden inside the bump, almost ready to come out.

Humble as the farmer's cart was, Thomas couldn't help thinking of it as the royal wagon. In reality, there was nothing regal about it beyond its passengers. Brother Ander sat beside the king, wincing every time the cart bounced across an especially rough patch of ground. The monk had packed straw beneath King Steffan's prone body in an attempt to cushion the king against the jolting, but the effectiveness of the makeshift mattress was questionable.

The only other passenger was the queen. She appeared pale and preoccupied. This rough mode of transport was surely doing nothing useful for her unborn child.

Seeing him riding behind the wagon, Elena guided her horse toward him. Thomas knew that her gentle heart had been deeply stirred by the plight of the king and queen. Whenever the wagon bounced and shook its passengers, she saw more than just the reigning monarchs. She also saw a gravely wounded man and his heavily pregnant wife. More than that, since Elena's first visit to Arnost the queen had been her friend. Their current helplessness tugged at her compassion.

"How are you feeling, Your Majesty?" she asked the queen.

"A little better, thank you Elena," the queen replied. She sighed. "If circumstances were different, I'd very quickly be exchanging places with Ava."

Both women glanced briefly back at the queen's maid, riding serenely behind the wagon.

Ava had taken Thomas by surprise—she was proving to be much tougher than she appeared. The maid had surprised everyone by announcing that she did not require a seat in the farmer's cart. She promptly climbed into the saddle of a spare horse, explaining breezily that she had grown up around the animals.

The other passenger displaced from the royal carriage was Brother Gerome. Since then, he had spent the daylight hours perched uncomfortably on a horse, trying desperately to absorb everything Thomas was teaching him about riding. The former horse master was encouraged by the monk's progress—Brother Gerome was doing much better than he himself realized.

Brother Gerome rode closer to the wagon. "How is the king?" he asked his fellow monk.

"He's slipping in and out of consciousness," Brother Ander replied. He frowned. "This jolting isn't helping his recovery."

"It's time for me to take a turn," Brother Gerome told him. "You need to stretch your legs."

For a moment Brother Ander looked as if he might argue, but then he nodded once and leaped nimbly from the moving wagon. Brother Gerome rode to him and stopped his horse. After climbing awkwardly from its back, he ran alongside the wagon and clambered in. He turned first to the queen, speaking quietly to her, then he moved to the side of the king.

The big monk swung himself into the saddle and immediately

rode away at a trot, clearly relishing the opportunity to be on horseback again.

Thomas still hadn't fully adjusted to the changes in Brother Ander. He had last seen his old traveling companion when he visited the army camp at Hazelwood Ford after the Battle of Torbury Scarp. The big soldier had announced his intention to become a monk at the time, but it still felt strange seeing him in his white robe. Hearing him referred to as "Brother Ander" was even stranger.

Strangest of all were the stories floating around about Brother Ander at Paradise Valley. It was said that he had destroyed the enemies of the king and queen almost single-handedly, rising up like an avenging angel. Thomas couldn't get his head around it all.

The big monk might be taking a brief break now, but it was apparent that his attention was focused almost entirely on his patient. On one occasion when Thomas had been openly staring at the former soldier, Brother Gerome hastened to assure him that Brother Ander was the best healer he had ever seen. Thomas had no reason to doubt it. He had simply been struck by a memory from the past. In his mind's eye he could still picture Brother Ander as the patient hovering on the brink of death.

Tamara laid her head back and went to sleep. Thomas decided to use the opportunity to speak to Will.

Clicking his tongue, he directed his horse forward to where Will was riding. Will glanced across at him without speaking, and they rode together in silence for a time.

Thomas felt tense and uneasy. Something had been weighing on his mind, and he wasn't sure how to approach it.

"I wanted to ask you something," he began. Then he shrugged. There was no easy way to say it. "I've learned to use the stone sparingly—I try very hard not to abuse it. It still occasionally reveals things by accident though. The last time that happened I was with Jonas."

Will looked at him with a raised eyebrow.

"I don't want to give the wrong impression," Thomas added

hastily. "I'm very grateful to Jonas—he rescued us when one of the men tried to assault Elena."

"I heard about that," growled Will. "The fool got what he deserved."

"Do you completely trust him?" Thomas asked bluntly. "Jonas, I mean. I only had a brief glimpse, but his motives are...complicated. He isn't just fighting because it's the right thing to do—he's hoping to benefit personally."

Will's lip curled up in an ironic grin. "How many of us could truthfully claim that our motives are never mixed?"

"Of course. But..." Thomas shrugged helplessly. He didn't know what else to say.

"I realize that you're trying to help, Thomas, and I do appreciate it. But there's no need for concern in this case. Jonas isn't going to betray us."

Both of them fell silent again.

After several minutes of awkwardness, Thomas asked a question to change the subject. "Where are we heading?"

Will's eyes flicked in his direction. "We're going to try to find Rellan."

Thomas couldn't hide his surprise. "Isn't he living somewhere inaccessible? I thought I heard he was in the wilderness near Erestor."

Will nodded. "Inaccessible sounds very attractive right now."

Thomas stole a glance back at the king. "How long will it take us to get there?"

Will shrugged. "The speed of the wagon is entirely dependent on the terrain. Our arrival time also depends on the people pursuing us. If they manage to track us down, we probably won't get there at all."

33

Hazor spurred his horse to the top of a rise and peered in the direction his scout was pointing. A moderately sized group of men was riding away from him, clustered around a wagon. They were moving slowly.

He rode back down the slope and faced his men. “We’ll finally get our revenge!” he shouted. Then he spun his horse around, and charged over the hill. Eager for blood, his mercenaries raced after him.

As they drew closer to the group ahead a hail of arrows flew toward them. Men went down around him, but Hazor ignored it. He wouldn’t be denied. Drawing his sword, he shouted his fury.

The riders had spun around to face him now. But they were greatly outnumbered. When Hazor’s men crashed into their line, they turned and scattered.

The wagon had been pulled aside into a small wooded area. “To me, men!” Hazor shouted, and led his men into the wood. More arrows flew their way, but Hazor had caught sight of the wagon now. He charged up to it with sword raised.

Then he bellowed in frustrated rage. The wagon was empty, just like the carriage.

Once more his enemies had offered him a decoy, and once more he had fallen for it. He had lost more men, and he was no better off. The handful of enemy dead behind him were cold comfort for Hazor.

How many more decoys would there be?

His only consolation was the knowledge that the king and queen must surely be in a wagon somewhere, and they couldn't be too far away.

HAZOR SCOWLED when he looked up and noticed another of his scouts riding toward him. He turned his head away and spat onto the ground. It hadn't been a good day, and his scouts weren't known for bringing good news.

"What is it?" he snapped.

"I just ran into a scout from another group sent out by Lord Lygell. They were following Will Prentis, but they lost him."

"Prentis! He's around here?" A number of mysteries were suddenly being resolved for Hazor. Will Prentis's reputation was legendary.

"How many men are with this other group?" Hazor asked.

"Fewer than two hundred. They started out with three hundred."

Hazor scowled. He must have lost at least ninety men himself. He had no idea how many were riding with Prentis, but whether it was few or many, he'd been using them very effectively to tilt the odds in his own favor.

"Who's leading our other group?"

The scout shrugged. "Apparently the leader appointed by Lord Lygell has been killed. A man named Jobin is leading them now. He doesn't seem to have much of a clue."

"Take me to this Jobin. Now!"

Hazor was actually smiling as they rode out. He'd just found a way to more than make good his losses. For once his day might actually end well.

. . .

"WILL Prentis and his bowmen make it impossible," said Jobin despondently.

Hazor couldn't argue with that. Arrows had been buzzing around like angry hornets for days. And apart from one small skirmish over a decoy wagon, he'd barely managed to catch a glimpse of his opponents, much less draw them into open battle.

He wasn't about to give up though. Prentis appeared to have sucked the life out of Jobin, but Hazor wasn't so easily intimidated.

Sooner or later Prentis would make a mistake—no one was infallible. And Hazor was more than happy to be the one to end his run. With over three hundred men under his command, it was time to take the fight to Prentis.

His first step would be to divide his force into three. It would allow them to cover more ground, and three groups would be harder to ambush than one. The main goal hadn't changed—find the king and queen and finish them off. If he could do away with Prentis at the same time, so much the better.

HAVING SEARCHED out a quiet location to confer with Rufe and Jonas, Will withdrew with Count Ranauld and his two senior leaders to discuss his plans. Rufe and Jonas had recently arrived in response to his messages requesting them to ride in to meet him as soon as possible.

"It's time for a change of strategy," he told them. "But first I want to acknowledge the excellent work you've both done to keep the mercenaries away from the king and queen. Fortunately for us the real wagon hasn't been exposed yet. We have you to thank for that."

"Your strategy has been working brilliantly," Rufe told him. "My men have been ambushing them from every possible location. The ambushes haven't cost us a single man, either. Our only losses were when they caught up to the small group with the decoy wagon."

"They still haven't found our decoy wagon," said Jonas, "and we haven't lost anyone either. We've been harassing them day and night." He grinned. "They're too frightened to light fires at night now."

Will grunted in satisfaction. "So small mobile groups have been working well."

Rufe nodded. "We're very fortunate that the duke sent those archers along with us. They've made all the difference. We've been able to constantly harry the mercenaries without needing to fight them directly."

"Are you running low on arrows?" asked Will.

"Yes!" Jonas replied. "We've followed your suggestion to retrieve arrows whenever we could, but even so we're running dangerously low."

"We don't have many left either," said Rufe, "but I'm not too concerned. One of the duke's commanders has told me about a large stockpile of arrows. Apparently the duke ordered fresh arrows to be hidden securely on both sides of Steffan's Citadel."

"Does the commander know where they are hidden?" asked Will.

Rufe nodded. "Yes, and I've sent him with a couple of men to retrieve them. They've probably already returned."

Will nodded in satisfaction. "We have a lot to thank the duke for. We wouldn't have made it this far without his foresight. I knew we would have to fight, but the extent of it has been beyond anything I imagined."

Jonas grunted his agreement. "Even with more arrows, we have a big task ahead of us," he said. "We've whittled down their numbers significantly, but they still have a much larger combined force than us."

"And they're finally getting smarter," added Rufe. "I've just learned that they've split into three smaller groups. That will make our task more difficult."

"We've almost reached our destination, so it's time for us to combine our forces," Will told them. "Sooner or later they'll probably merge again as well."

"Are we going through Steffan's Citadel into Erestor?" Rufe asked.

Will shook his head. "It's more important to remain hidden, at least until the king recovers and the queen delivers her baby—I've been confronted with a few too many traitors in the recent past."

"Have you made contact with Rellan?" asked Rufe eagerly.

"Yes, we have," said Will, his delight showing on his face. "They've had people watching for intruders, and it wasn't long before they spotted our scouts. He's agreed to lead us to Newhaven, his community. It should be a secure place for the king to recover in peace and quiet."

"Won't the mercenaries simply follow us in?" Jonas asked.

"Getting there is not at all straightforward," Will assured him. "You need to know exactly where you're going."

"If we don't go to Erestor, our medical resources will be limited," said Jonas. "Is Brother Ander good enough as a healer?"

Will nodded. "He knows what he's doing. He's been treating the king while we've been traveling, and he expects the king to recover as soon as we can stop shaking him around."

"Is the king conscious yet?" asked Rufe.

"He's conscious for at least some of the time now," said Will. "Brother Ander says he isn't out of danger though. It's a key reason why we need to get to somewhere quiet and safe."

He bent down and drew in the dirt. "This is where we are now. And here's where Rellan will be leading us. Tomorrow you need to bring in your men. All of us can go with Rellan together. We'll be much less likely to be followed if we disappear at the same time."

HAZOR THREW up his hands in frustration. "What's Prentis doing? Our scouts have been watching every approach to Steffan's Citadel, and there's been no sign of him or any of his men."

"The army Lord Lygell sent to Erestor is camped outside the citadel," Jobin replied. "Prentis isn't likely to go anywhere near them—it would be too risky. He's supposedly leading a rebellion against the king."

Hazor smiled ironically. "People are incredibly gullible if they believe Prentis would turn rebel. He's probably the only friend the king has right now."

Jobin shrugged. "People will believe anything. If a lie is outrageous enough, they're even more likely to buy it."

Hazor waved a hand dismissively. "Forget all that. I want to know what Prentis is up to. Spread the word—there'll be a reward for anyone who gets me answers."

ONE OF HAZOR'S scouts appeared. He looked excited. "I've heard there's a reward for information about Prentis. We've captured one of his men!" He pointed to a man who was being pulled from his horse.

Hazor wasn't impressed. "How do you know he's one of Prentis's men? He could be anybody."

The scout looked smug. "He's one of Prentis's commanders. One of the men who fought at Torbury Scarp recognized him and even remembers his name—he's called Jonas."

Hazor narrowed his eyes. "Bring him here. I want to question him."

The man was dragged over.

"Who are you?" asked Hazor.

"I'm a local farmer," the man replied. "I was just going about my business when your men grabbed me. I have no idea why they're interested in me."

Hazor sneered at him. "You're heavily armed for a farmer."

The man shrugged. "These are dangerous times."

"You have two options," Hazor told him. "Help us, or die. Which will it be?"

The man looked pained. "There has to be a third option, surely."

"Prentis isn't going to care if you live or die," said Hazor. "He's Lord Torbury. Who are you? You take the risks, but who gets the rewards? Are you any wealthier since you started fighting for him?"

The man appeared to flush slightly, but he quickly hid it behind a bored expression.

Hazor smiled to himself. He'd clearly found an open wound.

"Be smart, Jonas," he said reasonably.

The man started.

"Yes, I know who you are," Hazor added calmly. "Look, my employers reward all of us handsomely for our efforts. If you're smart you can have your own share in the spoils."

Jonas was pretending boredom again. It wasn't entirely convincing.

"I know you think you're supposed to be loyal to Prentis. But what about the people you care for, the people who've depended on you? Have the wealthy and powerful shown any loyalty to them?"

This time Jonas wasn't able to fully mask his reaction. Hazor would have been willing to bet that Jonas had watched someone suffer cruelly from poverty or injustice. Someone he cared about.

"If you have it in your power to act, and you stand back and wait for a lord or a king to make it right, you're as bad as they are."

He paused to let his words sink in.

"I'm willing to be reasonable," said Hazor. "I won't ask you to slip a knife into anyone. All I want is information. I want to know where Prentis is heading. Before long we'll find out for ourselves anyway, so it isn't as if you'd be compromising anyone."

Jonas's face was expressionless. But he wasn't looking bored.

Hazor was careful not to appear smug. "Here's what will earn you a share of the reward..."

THOMAS AND TAMARA stood with Elena, Rubin and Haldek, watching a crowd of soldiers milling around on the path behind them.

The royal party had been positioned ahead of them. The king lay on a stretcher that was currently resting on the ground, with Brother Ander hovering protectively near him. The queen stood beside them, with Brother Gerome and Ava flanking her on either side. A stretcher lay on the ground ready for her use as well. Ten guards commanded by Count Ranauld stood around the little party.

Thomas watched in admiration as Will walked among the soldiers, turning chaos into order.

While Will was forming up the soldiers into disciplined lines, Rellan approached Thomas, slapping him heartily on the back.

"Look at you, Thomas—you're all grown up! And you're a father!"

"This is Elena, my wife," said Thomas, smiling warmly back at him. "Elena, this is Rellan—you've heard me talk about him."

Her beautiful face lit up. "It's a great honor to meet you, Rellan!"

"The honor is all mine," he replied, offering her a sweeping bow. He surveyed Thomas with raised eyebrows. "I must say I'm in awe of the transformation you've performed on our Thomas," he added with a wink.

"I am sure he must have changed a great deal since you saw him last, but none of the credit belongs to me," she protested with a merry laugh.

Then he turned his attention to Tammi, perched wide-eyed in her father's arms and gazing at him coyly.

"This is Tamara," said Thomas proudly.

Rellan pulled a face and rolled his eyes at Tammi, and the toddler rewarded his antics with giggles of delight.

Will arrived before Thomas could introduce Rellan to his father-in-law and Haldek.

"Are you ready, Rellan?" Will asked.

Rellan nodded. "I'll join you right now." As he departed he called back over his shoulder to Thomas and Elena, "I'll look forward to introducing you to my own lovely wife and children."

Thomas reached out his arm and drew Elena in. As she nestled into his shoulder, he briefly closed his eyes, savoring the moment alone with his own little family. Then they headed over to join Rubin and Haldek.

While they waited for the column to move out, Thomas spotted Jonas among the soldiers, making his way to the rear. He immediately reached down and twisted the clasp on the chain suspended around his neck. As the stone came into contact with his skin, he caught a fleeting glimpse of Jonas before he disappeared out of sight. The little he saw filled Thomas with alarm.

Excusing himself from his family, he hurried toward Will. Finding the commander was easy; getting a quiet moment with him was another matter entirely.

Will eventually glanced in his direction. Noticing Thomas, he paused what he was doing and came over to speak to him.

Will gave him a wry smile. "I know that look, Thomas—something's bothering you." Before Thomas could respond, he added, "You're still worried about Jonas, aren't you? You have no reason to be."

Someone called loudly for Lord Torbury, and the commander hurried away without giving Thomas an opportunity to say a word.

The contact with Jonas had been too brief to allow Thomas to build a complete picture, so perhaps there was more to it than he had seen.

Thomas shook his head helplessly. What more could he do? Will had understood his concern before he even voiced it. Thomas could only hope that Will's insight into Jonas was equally uncanny.

Will ordered Count Ranauld to move out, and the royal party set off with their escorts around them. Both the king and queen were carried on stretchers. Thomas and his little group followed close behind them. Will didn't order Rufe to follow with the soldiers until the royal party was long gone.

The path twisted and turned from the very beginning of the journey, with the result that Thomas rarely caught a glimpse of the soldiers behind them. At one point when the soldiers were out of sight, Rellan led the party down from the main path through some thick bushes. A faint animal trail soon appeared before them, and they hurried along it. At first the animal trail must have run alongside the main path, because Thomas occasionally heard the sounds of soldiers tramping along above them. In time the trail turned away, though, and they descended until they reached the banks of a swiftly flowing river.

Rellan left them at that point and headed back along the animal trail.

A large raft had been pulled up onto the near bank, and Ranauld led the group aboard. The raft was soon floating down the river. As the landing place slipped away behind them, Thomas peered back for any sign of Rellan or the soldiers. He saw nothing, and a bend in the river soon hid the scene entirely from view.

The river carried them for more than an hour, then the raftsmen pulled in to the opposite bank, and they continued the journey on foot. Cultivated fields eventually came into sight, and a large cluster of huts appeared before them, smoke rising lazily from many roofs.

Men and women hurried out to greet them, led by a woman of noble bearing.

"My name is Anneka," she said. "We are honored to welcome the king and the queen to our midst, and we bid all of you welcome to Newhaven. We established this community as a place of peace and security where all could prosper without interference. We trust that your needs will be met and your hurts will be healed here."

"Thank you on behalf of us all, Anneka," Queen Essanda replied. "We are grateful for your willingness to offer us sanctuary at a time of great need."

The king and the queen were brought into a large and well appointed hut, and every effort was made to make them comfortable.

Thomas kept watch for many hours, his uneasiness growing as he waited for Will and Rellan to arrive with the soldiers. The sun slipped below the horizon, and stars began to twinkle in the sky. Still he saw no sign of them.

34

One of Hazor's scouts called the mercenary over and pointed beneath a bush. Hazor bent low, noting with satisfaction the small piece of scarlet cloth lying there. Jonas might have kept them waiting for a few days, but he was keeping his end of the bargain.

"Keep moving!" he shouted.

Hazor's men had been following a path dotted with such markers for a couple of hours. The surrounding trees were closely set, and thick undergrowth covered the ground between them. Only the path was easily accessible. It had been a necessary decision to leave their mounts behind when they entered the deep forest.

Based on what Jonas had said, Hazor expected them to break free of the dense canopy soon. Before long the prize would be in reach.

It wouldn't be easy to kill the king and queen—Prentis would make certain of that. But surprise would give them a huge advantage. No one was expecting them to reach the hidden community.

The men were much too spread out, and Hazor moved to the rear to bunch them closer together. He was still at the back when he heard cries and shouts break out far ahead. The bends and turns of the path made it impossible to get a clear line of sight, so he hurried forward, impatient to discover the cause of the commotion. As he ran, arrows whistled over his head from behind. His men were under attack from the rear.

Shoving aside anyone who stood in his way, Hazor rounded a bend and came to a long section of path that ran along the base of a steep hill. An appalling sight awaited him. Huge rocks bounded recklessly down the slope, crushing men before his eyes. Even worse, the slope was clearly unstable. Rocks and loose soil began to flow down as he watched, covering the path and burying alive anyone unable to flee in time.

The only possible direction in which to flee was down, away from the slope. His men leaped from the path, forcing their way through the undergrowth among the trees below it. Hazor followed them in.

He was soon panting from the effort. As he sucked air into his lungs his nostrils tingled. A steady breeze was blowing along the path from behind him, and it carried with it a strong smell of smoke. He paused for a moment with his nose to the air, and a white-tailed deer bounded past him, springing nimbly away between the trees. A large buck followed close behind it. The behavior of these creatures told him that a forest fire was coming his way, and coming fast.

Panicked cries sounded behind Hazor now, and he resumed his headlong flight downhill. A large boulder struck a tree nearby, bringing it crashing to the ground. The tree narrowly missed him, and he ran faster, with heart pounding and ragged breath. After what seemed an age he pushed through the last of the trees, emerging onto the banks of a river. The river was narrow at this point, and it ran swiftly down to a series of rapids not far below him. The roar of the water was almost deafening.

Other men had arrived before him, and they stood unmoving, staring nervously back toward the forest. Already wisps of smoke were appearing among the trees. Men continued to spill out of the forest onto the riverbank, many of them coughing and hacking from the smoke. Hazor bent double, panting from his exertion.

At that moment arrows began to fly across the river from the opposite bank. Missiles soon filled the air.

He could hear the crackle of flames now, and thick smoke billowed from the trees. With a fire behind and death raining from the sky above, a few men panicked and cast themselves into the river. Hazor watched wide-eyed as they were swept into the rapids.

"Follow me!" he yelled above the din. Some of the men heard him and hurried to his side. He began weaving a path among the trees at the edge of the river, working his way upwind and upriver. The ranks of his companions thinned as arrows found their marks, but the trees offered some protection, and shafts began to fall uselessly to the ground as they moved beyond the range of the bowmen.

In time the smoke ahead cleared as well, and Hazor guessed that the fire was almost behind him.

Sounds of fighting began to reach him, and he belatedly realized that it had been very fortunate that his men had not all bunched together. Some of them at least had been able to avoid the rocks and the fire.

He drew his sword and crashed through the trees.

Men fought desperately all around him. Archers had perched themselves in the trees, and he watched them calmly picking off any of his men who strayed too close.

He cursed the almost total absence of archers among his own ranks. He was not himself an archer, and he had recruited men like himself who were good with the sword. It had proven to be a colossal mistake. Capable archers invariably came from Erestor—he would make sure he recruited heavily from Erestor next time.

As small knots of men fought back and forth among the trees it became increasingly clear to Hazor that his men were not giving a good account of themselves. He cursed Will Prentis—the very name of the man was enough to weaken the hands of the fainthearted. He was beginning to wonder if his men dared to believe they could defeat Prentis.

Hazor was beginning to doubt it himself. He had brought a huge advantage of numbers into this fight, and once more Prentis had found a way to even the odds.

The more he pondered it, the more Hazor began to realize that the chances of his men breaking through to the king and queen were fast diminishing. Seen in that light, it became clear that his responsibility had changed. He now had a rough idea of the location of the community sheltering the king and queen, even if the specifics of the route were far from certain. That information needed to be brought to Arnost. Lord Lygell could assemble a real army, one big enough to brush Prentis aside and finish the job.

He began edging around the battle lines, avoiding the fighting whenever he could and killing anyone who got in his way. Eventually the conflict lay behind him. He crept through the trees, desperate to stay out of sight of any bowmen watching from the branches above.

To his intense annoyance he noticed other men slinking away from the fighting. He had a good reason for leaving; their motivation could be nothing more than cowardice. He cursed them silently before completely ignoring them.

Slipping from tree to tree made for slow progress—the return journey took him more than twice as long as following the path. Nevertheless he finally came within sight of the place where his men had left their horses. He peered about him in surprise. There was no sign of the animals.

Drawing closer he noticed several bodies lying on the ground. It quickly became clear that the men he had left to guard the horses had been killed and the animals scattered.

Hazor cursed silently. His task had just become much more challenging.

The trees thinned out ahead of him, offering little cover. The only sensible option was to settle down and wait for darkness.

The day was almost spent when Hazor noticed a horse wandering nearby. Unwilling to miss such an opportunity, he leaped to his feet and sprinted toward it. He had covered half the distance when he saw that the horse was not alone. A dismounted rider stood behind it. It made little difference to him—he was more than happy to dispose of the horseman. He drew his sword and ran on.

The rider came out from behind the horse, and Hazor caught a glimpse of his face. Before him stood Jonas. The man had treated Hazor's bargain with contempt. Jonas had ruined any hope of finding and killing the king and queen and had brought about the destruction of Hazor's entire army.

Infuriated with the monstrous repercussions of his own blindness, Hazor bellowed a challenge and charged.

A WRY SMILE came to Jonas's face when he realized that the man running at him was Hazor. Quickly unslinging the bow from his shoulder, he nocked an arrow and waited calmly until his enemy was almost upon him. Then he put the arrow into Hazor's chest. The mercenary crashed to the ground.

Jonas gazed thoughtfully down at Hazor's body for a long moment, reliving their interaction. Measuring Jonas by his own standard, the mercenary had managed to convince himself that the lure of riches would be enough to win the loyalty of his captive.

Jonas shook his head scornfully. Then he spun on his heel, mounted his horse, and rode away.

WILL and Rellan stood together surveying the destruction from a high vantage point. A vast pall of smoke still covered the entire area.

"The fighting is over," Will told his friend, "but we'll need to guard the approaches for many days. Any mercenaries who survived are hiding in the forest. They've been trying to creep away, and they've kept my men busy."

"I'll leave you to organize the guard duty if you're willing," Rellan replied. "Our people have been fully occupied ferrying the wounded to Newhaven and setting up shelters for your men."

Will nodded. "We can handle it." He glanced at Rellan. "Newhaven isn't hidden now. How does Anneka feel about that?"

"It's a big adjustment—for her and for everyone. But we couldn't remain cut off from the world forever. And it's not as if Newhaven has suddenly become easy to find. We only found it by accident in the first place. Even if the mercenaries had made it to the end of that path we lured them onto, they'd have discovered it doesn't lead anywhere. It's hard to imagine any strays appearing on our doorstep."

"No," agreed Will. "But my men know how to get there now. We can ask them to keep it quiet, but word will leak out eventually."

Rellan shrugged. "We couldn't turn away the king and queen, and that meant we needed to welcome your soldiers as well. If it all leads to dire consequences, then so be it. There's no point in worrying about the future before it comes."

Will grunted his assent. "In the meantime, we'll make sure that no one else gets in or out of here."

THOMAS AND ELENA stood together at Newhaven, watching Tammi play with some of the other children. Their daughter had settled in almost immediately. Both Rubin and Haldek longed for the solitude of their old home in the forest, but they were doing as well as could be expected.

Thomas was feeling foolish and discouraged. Earlier that day Jonas had arrived at Newhaven, escorting a group of wounded soldiers. Thomas noticed his arrival and quickly used the stone to find out if his earlier concerns had been well founded. He soon discovered that he had completely misread Jonas. It was becoming apparent to him that superficial attitudes, thoughts, and desires weren't always a reliable indicator of how someone would behave when tested.

Thomas was relieved at the outcome, and equally dismayed about getting it so wrong. It was especially embarrassing that Will had assessed Jonas so much more accurately than Thomas, and he had done so without recourse to an all-seeing stone.

When Jonas next came into view, Thomas retrieved the stone from around his neck and handed it to Elena. "Could you please take a look at Jonas?" he whispered.

Elena frowned at him.

"It's important to me!" he insisted.

Somewhat reluctantly, she took the stone and turned her gaze upon Jonas. After a while she returned the stone to Thomas, who quickly slipped it back over his neck.

Jonas noticed them looking his way and came to join them.

Elena greeted him warmly. "Hello, Jonas. It's wonderful to see that you made it through safely!"

Thomas mumbled a welcome as well.

Jonas returned a friendly greeting of his own, but he appeared distracted.

Elena considered him for a moment. "I remind you of your sister, don't I?" she asked.

He gazed back at her in surprise. "How did you know?"

Elena smiled. "A lucky guess?"

Jonas shook his head in puzzlement.

"Tell me about her," Elena suggested gently.

Jonas stared at Elena for a moment. Then his head went down, and he shrugged. "She was the best person I ever knew. We were very close."

"And she became sick?"

He nodded without speaking.

Elena gazed at him compassionately. "You're a good man, Jonas. She would have been very proud of you."

Jonas looked up and met her eyes. Then he released a long shuddering sigh.

"Perhaps you couldn't save her," Elena said, "but you've been doing whatever you can for the helpless ever since, haven't you? I've benefited personally from that." Reaching out for his hand, she squeezed it briefly before releasing it.

Finding a way to master his emotions, Jonas returned a lopsided smile. "You're like her in more than just looks, Elena," he said. "Thank you."

The soldier's attention was captured by the arrival of a new group of men. "I'd better return to my duties," he said apologetically. Then he hurried away.

As he left Thomas raised his hands helplessly. "You're so much better at this than I am!" he told Elena.

She smiled and put her arm around his waist. "Not better, just different. We don't seem to notice the same things when we look at people with the stone."

He sighed. "If I've learned anything at all today, it's that I need to dig a lot deeper than initial impressions."

THE NEWHAVEN COMMUNITY boasted a modestly sized hut for the sick, but the number of men wounded in the recent battle far exceeded its capacity. A large hall had been built for community activities in cold weather, and the hall quickly became the main accommodation for the wounded.

Every available healer was needed to treat the men, and Anneka, Brother Ander, and Brother Gerome rarely left the building.

King Steffan was well on the way to recovery, but Brother Ander insisted on complete rest while his patient rebuilt his strength. Accordingly, the monk had relocated the king to the healing hall. Having all of his patients in easy reach allowed him to closely monitor the king's progress while also responding to the more pressing needs of the many wounded.

The queen had no objection whatever, and she soon spent a good proportion of her time there. She didn't limit herself to visiting her husband.

The men were curious about the king's wounds, and word gradually spread about the attack in the barn and his bravery in fighting off so many attackers. His willingness to convalesce among them lifted their spirits.

Once Essanda's exploits became known, men never tired of hearing of the heavily pregnant queen's courage in taking up a sword and vigorously defending herself and her unborn child. In the recovery hall, though, they saw only her gentleness. Many of the wounded were in pain, and the visits of the queen cheered them enormously. They waited patiently for their turn as she made her way slowly among them, resting her hands on her belly as she paused at each bed to speak a quiet word with the patient.

Reports of Brother Ander's intervention also circulated among the men, and the tales quickly grew in the telling. His deeds eventually achieved legendary status without him ever knowing it. Men followed with their eyes as the big monk walked among them, quietly going about his business.

The queen did not limit herself to visiting the wounded. In the evenings she spent time among the able-bodied soldiers and community members, expressing appreciation for their help and listening to their stories and concerns. With Brother Ander's permission, the king often joined her for brief periods.

The royals had been distant figures to those without personal contact with them. As the men basked in the attention of the recuperating king and the pregnant queen, their reverence slowly ripened into an ardent devotion.

The day soon came when the queen did not appear in the recovery hall. The men quickly noticed that the king had become tense and distracted, and the news was whispered abroad excitedly that the time for the queen's confinement had arrived.

KING STEFFAN HAD BEEN ASSURED by Anneka that the queen would be well cared for when the time came to deliver her baby. Newhaven might have been isolated from the rest of the world, but the community was not entirely unprepared for such an event. As chief healer,

Anneka could lay claim to a wealth of experience as a midwife. And the king knew she would also call upon Brother Gerome if the need arose.

As soon as Essanda's labor began, Anneka whisked the queen away to a specially prepared birthing room, ejecting everyone except two of her trusted helpers.

Several hours passed without news of any kind. Steffan waited anxiously in the recovery hall, conscious that all eyes were on him and trying hard to remain calm. Finally a woman bustled in and hurried to his side. Every head turned as the woman bowed, then leaned forward to whisper in his ear.

"It's a boy!" he cried jubilantly, and the room erupted around him.

Steffan threw an eager glance in the direction of Brother Ander.

"Go, Your Majesty," the monk exclaimed with a smile, waving an arm toward the door.

The king left the hall and hastened to his wife's side. Arriving to see her pale and tired, he stared at her in concern.

Anneka noticed his reaction. "Her Majesty has done extremely well," she assured him briskly. "You should be very proud of her!"

Steffan broke into a pleased smile, and he was relieved to see an answering smile appear on Essanda's face. Anneka brought his baby to him, and he held the infant awkwardly, staring down wide-eyed at the wrinkled little face. As he watched, his son opened his mouth, filled his tiny lungs, and let out a mighty squawk. The baby's lower lip trembled pitifully as he wailed.

Anneka retrieved him with a matter-of-fact air and returned him to his mother's breast. "You won't get your milk for a couple of days, Your Majesty," she told her. "But this will comfort him in the meantime."

She turned back to the king. "Her Majesty needs rest," she advised him gently.

He left reluctantly, but the contented smile on Essanda's face eased his mind as he went.

A wave of joy flooded over Steffan as he returned to the recovery hall. His beloved wife had presented him with a son. He had become a father.

Whatever storms the future might bring, they would weather them together.

The little prince's naming ceremony was not marked with the pomp that would have accompanied it in Arnost, but the king and queen were at least spared the insincere flattery that would have been served up by some noblemen and courtiers. They instead found themselves surrounded by simple men and women who truly wished them well.

Brother Gerome conducted the ceremony, managing to provide a dignified sense of occasion while showing no sign of being overawed by the responsibility.

King Steffan and Queen Essanda proclaimed together, "We name our son Aiden!"

The crowd broke into loud cheers for Prince Aiden, and a procession of people filed past the royal family, presenting modest gifts and hearty congratulations. Steffan and Essanda thanked the most humble of the well wishers with the same sincerity they offered to Will, Rufe, and their other friends.

The recovery hall was empty—even the few remaining convalescent soldiers had been brought outside for the occasion—and the whole community made their way to a huge bonfire where freshly cooked venison and other treats awaited them.

Before the feasting was fully over, Thomas and Elena were summoned by King Steffan to a conference. They arrived to find the king and queen already there with the baby prince, along with Will, Rufe, Jonas, Count Ranauld, Anneka, and Rellan.

Thomas and Elena had brought little Tammi with them, and late as the hour was, she was soon playing happily with Anneka and Rellan's two-year-old son, Kuper, and his twin sister, Bella.

"Will tells me that the duke has sealed off Erestor," began the king. "Apart from that, the rest of Arvenon is now controlled by the mercenaries. Thomas, I hear from Will that you can provide more information about who the mercenaries answer to."

Thomas bowed deeply. "Yes, Your Majesty. I made some discoveries while I was in Arnost a number of days ago. Lord Bottren has been imprisoned, and a man known as Lord Lygell is in charge of the capital. He commands the mercenaries, but he is not the real leader. He was placed there by the Earl of Pisander."

The king scowled. "I'll have that traitor's head!" he exclaimed.

"Pisander seems to have access to a lot of resources," said the queen. "Those resources must have come from somewhere."

Thomas nodded. "Your Majesty is right. His money and most of his spies have been provided by King Agon of Rogand. I understand that King Agon wants to take over Arvenon, and Castel and Varas as well."

Steffan slowly shook his head. "Drettroth so nearly succeeded in annexing the three kingdoms. It was too much to expect that Agon would simply walk away from that failure."

A puzzled look came to Essanda's face. "Surely our soldiers won't simply follow the orders of these usurpers!"

King Steffan shrugged. "So far our own men haven't been called upon—mercenaries seem to have done all the fighting."

Thomas nodded. "My father told me that the soldiers have been sent away from Arnost, Your Majesty," he said. "Some were sent to Erestor. A story has been put out that Will...Lord Torbury, I mean," he added awkwardly, "has stirred up a rebellion against the king in Erestor."

Will simply raised his eyebrows. "Pisander won't want us to make contact with those men. If he realizes that we're anywhere nearby, he'll undoubtedly arrange for them to be sent somewhere else."

"The rest of the soldiers have been sent to the border with

Castel," Thomas continued. "They were told that the Castelans are planning to invade Arvenon."

The queen shook her head in anger. "Surely no one believes this nonsense!" She turned to her husband. "Can't you simply reappear and tell people the truth?"

"The king needs to be careful, Your Majesty," said Will. "His life will be at risk the moment his whereabouts become known. Pisander has done his preparation well—he appears to have far too many highly placed traitors in his pocket. And right now he has more fighting men available than we do. He will be eager to finish the job one way or another."

"I'm sure our soldiers are loyal at heart," said the queen.

"Soldiers do what they're told," the king replied grimly. "If Pisander—and ultimately Agon—can find a way to control the leaders, he'll control the army too."

"Either that, or Pisander will disband the army," said Ranauld. "It would be safer for him to rely on men who answer only to money."

Thomas said nothing, but his thoughts were churning. He knew from the scroll that the Stone of Authority was somewhere at large in the world, and he had seen hints at Arnost that Pisander might not simply be acting on his own behalf.

Thomas was beginning to suspect that Agon had indeed found a way to control people. But how could he voice his suspicions without exposing his own secret?

He decided that for the moment he would do nothing. He would discuss it later with Elena.

Will knew about his stone as well of course. If it seemed important enough, Thomas could always choose a suitable moment and pass on his suspicions to Will.

THE COOKING FIRES had long since died down to glowing embers, and the feasters had scattered. Steffan and Essanda stood alone together beneath the stars, cradling little Aiden.

"It appears that I no longer have much of a kingdom to pass on to my son and heir," Steffan said gloomily.

Essanda frowned up at him. "We can't let these people win. It isn't just about Aiden's inheritance—we've already seen what they do to anyone who gets in their way. The common people will suffer most."

Steffan nodded. "I don't know how we can turn the tide, but we will find a way."

He glanced down at the prince, then out into the night. "Whatever else happens, I'm not going to sit here hiding for the rest of my life," he vowed. "I will win the kingdom back, or I'll die trying."

EPILOGUE

Agon's best agent stood before him, trembling with fear. The man had delivered a full report, and Agon was not at all satisfied with what he'd heard.

"So this boy you've been tracking has slipped through your fingers—you have no idea where he's gone?"

The agent could only nod mutely.

"And you sent a small army after Will Prentis—hundreds of men—and not one of them has returned?"

The agent winced, but he nodded again.

"I'm plagued by fools and incompetents!" the king shouted. "Is nothing ever done properly unless I do it myself?"

The man didn't dare to look at him.

"Get out of my sight!" Agon bellowed.

The agent scurried away.

The king shook his head in fury.

He'd poured in so much money, and what did he have to show for it? His search for the Stone of Knowing had stalled, and he still couldn't claim full control even over one of the three kingdoms.

Closer to home, he'd made no progress at all on uncovering the priests' secrets around extending life. It was true that one or two unlucky priests had fallen into the hands of his men, but either they knew nothing, or they were tight lipped fools.

He ground his teeth.

Perhaps he would execute all of his agents and start again fresh. The thought almost calmed him.

"ENNAWI, THERE YOU ARE!"

The slave barely seemed to have moved since Agon had last seen him.

"I'm planning a little trip—to Arnost, the capital of Arvenon. You can come too. You'd like that, wouldn't you?"

As usual, the slave offered no response.

Agon ignored Ennawi's apparent lack of interest. "I'm going to base myself in Arvenon for a while. It seems I must be there in person if things are to be done properly."

He patted a hidden pocket in his cloak. "I'll take my little prize with me of course."

He'd arranged for a cloak to be specially designed with a pocket to hold the Stone of Authority securely. Now he could simply slip his hand into the pocket whenever he needed to put the stone to use.

Agon felt almost cheerful. He saw no reason to be entirely dissatisfied with his efforts so far. He had recently recruited a new agent—a tracker without peer. His new tracker would find the Stone of Knowing, and the fool who had dared to take possession of the stone would be dragged before Agon.

Much as Agon liked to rail at his agents, his plans hadn't ended in complete failure. Castel had closed its borders, but it was now ruled by a child. Although Varas had withdrawn into its shell, isolation had done nothing to guarantee its security last time.

Neither country mattered, though. Controlling Arvenon had always been the key to controlling the region, and his pet Arvenian nobleman had largely done as he promised. The former Earl of Pisander now controlled the entire country apart from Erestor, and Pisander was ready to welcome Agon into the capital.

Once he was in Arnost, Agon would spend time with key Arvenian noblemen and the leaders of the army—enough time to bring them thoroughly under the control of the Stone of Authority.

Then he would deal with Erestor. Best of all, he would use Arvenon's own armies to do it. Castel would come next, and then Varas.

The Stone of Knowing would have nowhere to hide.

He turned back to Ennawi with a self-satisfied smirk. "I hear it's very pleasant in Arnost at this time of the year," he said.

The End

The saga continues in
The Struggle for Authority

PART II

THE STRUGGLE FOR AUTHORITY

THE STONE CYCLE BOOK 4

VOLUME 1—THE SWELL BEGINS TO BUILD

PROLOGUE

Heaving up a final sack of turnips, Carnwill clambered onto the cart.

"Move!" he growled. The crack of a whip sounded, and the horse took up the strain, rolling its burden slowly forward.

To outward observation, Carnwill and his two companions were traders, selling vegetables to the army camped outside Steffan's Citadel on the border of Erestor. A shrewd observer might have called them an unlikely group of produce merchants.

For a man of Carnwill's talents, his current occupation was incongruous. Competent and accomplished, he was an Arvenian native who spoke Rogandan fluently. From early beginnings as a farmer and a trader, he had made his mark as a sailor and a soldier.

Carnwill was dangerous and relentless. As a tracker he was second to none, and his skill had led to a covert role in the employ of King Agon of Rogand. Agon trusted him implicitly, which made Carnwill the rarest of the rare.

He now had a single purpose—to find Thomas Stablehand. He would have been willing to drag him before King Agon as well, but his employer made it clear he intended to use other resources for that purpose. Carnwill's brief was to hunt him down and inform the king of his whereabouts.

His quarry had been traced to Carnwill's current location, and the tracker needed a way to explore the region without attracting attention. Trading vegetables provided a perfect cover.

The work was boring—mind-numbingly so—but Carnwill was a patient man.

1

Six days after Hazor's mercenary force was destroyed in Will's ambush

The sun had disappeared below the tree line, and darkness was creeping slowly in to take its place, settling over the forest like a heavy mantle. Breysen knew he should be grateful for the protective cover of night, but the forest felt alien and hostile to him in the gloom. Each night his discomfort had grown as the hours stretched away beneath the somber boughs. At times he imagined the low hanging branches were reaching down to strangle him. His head told him sternly that any such notion was ridiculous, but his heart wasn't convinced.

Campfires burned brightly just beyond the edge of the forest, and delicious smells often wafted toward him when the wind shifted in the right direction. There was no welcome for him there. Will Prentis's men were vigilant, and every fugitive who emerged from the forest had been dealt with ruthlessly.

He wondered once more what had possessed him to sign on as a mercenary. Hazor, his recruiter, had sought Breysen out, somehow aware that he had fought at Torbury Scarp and that he needed coin. The mercenary leader insisted he was not looking for paid killers; he had been commissioned to rapidly build a force of irregular soldiers with the sole purpose of maintaining order throughout the kingdom.

The wages on offer should have given sufficient warning, but Breysen chose to ignore the signs, lured by the size of the promised payout. A bag bulging with coins had been dangled before him as a reward for signing on, and he had hesitated for barely a moment before taking hold of it. He saw now that he had been a fool, and a credulous fool at that.

At first Hazor's group had done little more than canter about the countryside. Everything had changed when they set off in pursuit of a group of armed men. Hazor's hunters enjoyed an overwhelming advantage in numbers and most of them were hungry for a fight, but their apparent superiority proved illusory.

The ferocity of their quarry beggared belief—Breysen had once hunted a wounded bear that seemed genial by comparison. The hunters were never allowed to rest. Arrows descended from the sky at any time of the day or night, and always when least expected. The size of Hazor's band rapidly diminished; the deadly rain eventually accounted for hundreds of the mercenaries. The men had fallen with barely a glimpse of their enemies.

Rumors began to surface. A few of the mercenaries whispered that their targets were the king and his pregnant queen. The idea hadn't troubled most of them, but Breysen had been appalled. He hadn't signed on for treason, and he wasted no time in confronting Hazor directly with the rumors. The mercenary leader reacted with fury, and Breysen had hastily withdrawn without answers and in fear for his life.

Then came the rumor that their invisible enemies were being led by Will Prentis.

A veil had finally been lifted from Breysen's eyes the moment this latest rumor reached his ears. Everything suddenly made sense. He had served under Will and his deputy Rufe, and it no longer came as any surprise that the fighting had been so one-sided.

From that moment he had abandoned hope. Hazor was doomed, and all of his men with him.

The mercenary leader apparently couldn't see it coming. Hazor could reasonably boast his share of animal cunning, but he clearly lacked the wit to grasp what lay in store for him and his men.

The unequal struggle continued until Will finally lured Hazor into the forest. The mercenary's entire force had been wiped out in the disastrous battle that followed. Breysen had been one of the few who survived.

Almost a week had passed since the battle. The forest still smoldered from the fire that raged through it during the fighting, and bodies lay scattered among the charred undergrowth, many of them burned beyond recognition. The stench had become almost unbearable. Bird song echoed through any normal forest; the trees here were as silent as the grave.

Breysen knew how to survive on his own in the wild, but he could find precious little that was safe to eat in this scorched wasteland. Streams still flowed freely, and he was largely reduced to satisfying himself with fresh water.

Other mercenaries had survived, although none so far had matched Breysen's patience. One by one the ragged fugitives had appeared at the forest's edge, hungry and miserable as they waited for nightfall. He had watched as they abandoned the cover of the trees, willing to risk discovery in their desperation. Not one had survived.

Every night the bright moonlight had conspired with the sentries against the fugitives. Nature itself seemed set on bringing the mercenaries to final ruin.

On that particular night, Breysen's luck appeared to have turned. Thick clouds covered the moon completely. His moment had arrived.

Making his way carefully to the very edge of the forest, he positioned himself behind a large tree and peered out at the sentries. As usual, very few of them were sitting around the campfires. Most of them were out patrolling in the darkness.

His reserves of stamina had long since been depleted, but he wasn't planning a desperate sprint to freedom. He was willing to content himself with an undignified crawl on his belly.

As he steeled himself to go, a branch cracked behind him in the forest. Spinning around, he dimly saw another man creeping stealthily toward him. He drew his sword frantically, his heart racing, dismayed at having been exposed at last. When the other man made no move to attack him, Breysen belatedly realized he was facing another fugitive like himself. As the figure drew closer it became obvious that he was in an equally miserable condition.

Breysen sheathed his sword, frowning at the intruder. His chances of survival were poor enough as it was. He hadn't planned on being burdened down with another helpless runaway.

The wiry newcomer drew alongside, contenting himself with a nod in the direction of Breysen. His face was drawn, and his arm had been bandaged crudely. From the stains on the bandage he had been losing blood, although he seemed unperturbed by the injury.

Breysen didn't mince his words. "Don't expect me to look out for you," he whispered roughly. "I won't be expecting help from you, and I have nothing to offer myself."

The other shrugged in the darkness. "No quarrel with me," he replied. "Our chances are better on our own."

With that the stranger touched his forehead in a simple salute, then slipped away from the shelter of the trees and disappeared into the darkness.

Breysen forced down his annoyance. He didn't need distractions. Now he had to choose whether to set off immediately or to wait until the other man was long gone. The sentries were undoubtedly on high alert given the moonless night. If the other man was caught, they would be doubly cautious.

He quickly decided that his best option was to leave immediately. If one of the two fugitives was detected, the other might have a better chance of slipping away in the confusion. He took a breath, then headed out into the open.

Dark as it was, Breysen knew where he was heading. He had not entirely wasted the days of enforced inaction that lay behind him.

Climbing repeatedly into a tall tree during daylight hours to assess the topography of the area, he had plotted his escape route carefully. A broad stretch of undulating land lay before him, and he intended to avoid exposed ridges and take full advantage of every available depression. His journey would proceed in four stages, with a pause as soon as he reached each landmark. He hoped that the dense cloud cover would reduce the likelihood of him being spotted.

Breysen scurried forward in a low crouch until he reached a natural hollow in the ground. The first and easiest part of his journey was now behind him.

The next stage was the most dangerous. A long stretch of exposed ground lay ahead with no natural protection. Every other fugitive had been run to ground in this area. Most of them had tried to run as quickly as possible across the open space. Now that he was there himself, the temptation to run like a rabbit was almost overwhelming. He thrust such urges aside. He had a plan, and he intended to stick to it. He would crawl.

Lowering himself onto his belly, Breysen squirmed out into the open.

Progress felt painfully slow, and he forced down the panic that threatened to overwhelm him, concentrating instead on the patch of ground immediately before him. He had plenty of time. Night had barely begun, and he expected to be long gone when daylight dawned.

After a few nervous minutes Breysen had made slow but steady progress. Then he came to a sudden halt—his surroundings were slowly becoming visible. His heart began to pound, even as his eyes widened with alarm. A quick glance into the heavens confirmed that the clouds covering the face of the moon were beginning to dissipate.

Acting instinctively, Breysen dropped to the ground to conceal himself. As he did so, a dark figure rose up behind him, closer to the forest. Breysen had passed his fellow fugitive in the dark. Apparently spooked by the sudden change in the conditions, the other man decided to run for it. It was a poor decision, because it exposed him to one of the patrolling soldiers. The sentry spurred his horse toward the fleeing figure.

From his prone position on the ground, Breysen saw that the speeding horse was heading directly toward him.

There wasn't time to think. As the rider approached, Breysen leaped to his feet, directly in front of the animal. The horse reared up, squealing in fright. Its rider was thrown to the ground. Before the man could get up, Breysen threw himself forward and punched him hard in the face. The sentry went down and didn't move.

Shouts sounded from the direction of the campfires. Other sentries must have become aware of the disturbance—he had very little time. Hurrying to the horse, Breysen grabbed its reins and swung himself into the saddle. His feet had barely settled into the stirrups when the horse reared up again. The other mercenary had reappeared.

Breysen struggled to calm the animal. Then he turned to his fellow fugitive. "Quickly! Get up behind me!"

The other man ignored him at first, pulling a knife as he turned away. Bending low, he plunged his blade several times into the unconscious sentry before turning away and clambering onto the horse's back. The knife disappeared again into his clothing. He hadn't bothered to wipe the blade clean.

Breysen sat frozen in the saddle, shocked at the cold-blooded execution of a defenseless man. "Go!" the other man demanded. Snapping out of his daze, Breysen urged the horse forward.

Their attempt at escape might have been short-lived, except that heavy cloud cover once more blanketed the moon, plunging their surroundings into total darkness. Breysen steered the horse away from the forest, trying to roughly follow the path he had planned. Voices called out behind them, but the darkness shielded them as they raced toward freedom.

They continued to ride with only short breaks until the sky began to lighten with the coming of the dawn.

By then the horse was almost spent. Neither of the riders were in any better condition. Breysen was barely able to stay in the saddle.

For much of the night they had ridden across grasslands and rolling hills. The open ground had disappeared just before dawn, and the trees of a vast forest again surrounded them. To hide their tracks they sought out a suitable stream and rode along it for the best part of an hour. Finally they guided the horse out of the water onto rocky ground where its hoof prints would not be visible. Then they sought out a quiet clearing hidden among the towering trees.

Both of them were utterly exhausted. Breysen managed to find some strips of dried meat and some stale bread in a saddlebag. He shared it with his companion, who chewed it unthinkingly before lying down. He was asleep almost immediately.

In defiance of his depleted state, Breysen somehow found the energy to remove the saddle and bridle from the horse before slumping to the ground. Rich green grass flourished in the clearing, and the last thing he remembered before falling asleep was the sight of the animal quietly cropping the grass.

It was the cold that eventually woke him. Daylight had almost faded away. The cloud cover had disappeared entirely, and stars were already winking in the open sky above the clearing.

The other fugitive was still sleeping, and Breysen grasped the opportunity to take a searching look at his companion. The mercenary looked emaciated—hardly surprising given the circumstances of the last few days—and his face was drawn and haggard. He had a hard face.

Breysen got up and stretched, wincing at the tightness in his muscles. Every part of him ached.

Glancing across at his companion, he noticed that he had woken.

"I'm Breysen," he said with a cautious nod.

"Kantor," the other replied. He peered around him in the gloom. There was no sign of pursuit or any kind of threat. "Looks like we've beaten the odds," he grunted. "We're probably the only ones who managed to escape that death trap."

"We're not out of this yet," said Breysen. "They'll track us. They seemed determined to keep the king's location secret."

Kantor snorted. "You think that's their reason for killing every person who tried to escape?" He shook his head dismissively. "They're butchers. No other explanation is necessary."

"Is that why you killed the sentry?"

"Did I need a reason?" snarled Kantor, glowering at him. "He would have killed me without blinking. Or you, for that matter."

Breysen shrugged. "He was helpless," he said. "He had no way of harming us."

"And if I'd been lying helpless? Do you think that would have saved me?" Kantor looked at him in scorn. "Have you gone soft in the head? It's us or them. It's that simple."

Kantor was right, of course—the sentry would have killed them without a second thought. Somehow it seemed different to Breysen though. Was it because he saw himself as a traitor, and therefore deserving of death? Either way, Kantor clearly wasn't interested in discussing the rights and wrongs of it. Breysen said nothing further.

His companion got up, stretching as uncomfortably as Breysen had. He placed a hand gingerly on his neck, screwing up his face as he briefly massaged the muscles on his shoulders. Then he turned his attention to his injured arm. He unwrapped the bandages, wincing with pain as he pulled the cloth away from the wound.

Even in the gathering dark the wound looked ugly. "That needs to be stitched," Breysen told him. "Would you like me to do it?"

The mercenary looked doubtful, but he didn't refuse.

Breysen led him to a nearby stream and did his best to clean the wound. It was becoming increasingly difficult to see what he was doing, but he managed to retrieve a small cloth bundle from the pouch at his belt and unfolded it. Within it was a tiny piece of wood, roughly the thickness of his little finger but only two thirds the length. He tugged at the wood with both hands, and it fell apart into two pieces, revealing a long piece of thread and a thin needle.

Kantor eyed it curiously. "Where did you get that?"

"I made it," Breysen replied. "It's been useful on occasion," he added simply.

He had fashioned the needle himself from the bone of a bird, carefully sharpening one end and boring an eye into the other.

Constructing the little wooden box to house it had taken many hours.

It took him many attempts before he succeeded in threading the needle. Deciding to act quickly before the light faded entirely, he pulled Kantor's arm closer and began pushing the needle through his skin as if mending a garment. The mercenary grimaced but said nothing.

Breysen sewed the flesh together quickly and efficiently. When he had finished, he squinted down at the arm before nodding once in satisfaction. Then he cleaned the needle and wiped it dry on his tunic before returning it to its wooden box. Finally he instructed Kantor to lower his arm into the water to wash it clean.

The light had faded away completely by the time they had finished.

"It's time we were gone," Kantor grunted.

Breysen nodded in the dark. They couldn't afford to wait for the dawn. "Where to?"

"West, toward Erestor," grunted Kantor. "I've heard there's an army camped outside Steffan's Citadel. It isn't far from here. We know roughly where the king is hiding out, and that information will be worth a lot of money to the right people."

Rejoining an army didn't appeal to Breysen at all. All he wanted was to slink away, as far from here as possible. Somehow he had survived where so many others had died, and he had no interest in tempting fate any further.

Beyond that, selling out the king didn't sit right with him at all. He'd lost interest in being a mercenary from the moment he realized that Hazor's orders were to kill the royals.

It was obvious to him that his reservations would make no sense to Kantor. What could he say?

He decided to say nothing. He would bide his time.

Breysen bent down briefly and drank from the stream. Doing so made him realize how hungry he was. It was time to divide up any food remaining in the saddlebags and refill the water skin.

"Where did you leave the horse?" asked Kantor.

"I don't remember exactly," Breysen replied.

Kantor gave a low growl in response, then he ignored Breysen, whistling for the horse as he crossed the clearing.

After many minutes of increasingly frantic searching, it became clear that the horse was nowhere in the area.

Kantor came to Breysen. "You took off the saddle and bridle," he spat. "Did you think to put a halter on it?" Even in the dark Breysen felt his fury.

"I can't be certain," he grunted.

"You incompetent idiot!" roared Kantor. He grabbed Breysen's clothing with his good arm. "This will be the death of both of us! You understand that, don't you?"

"And what did you do to secure the horse?" Breysen asked, struggling to stay calm.

Kantor shook with anger for a moment, then he seemed to master himself. He released Breysen and stepped back, spitting on the ground. "I should just knife you and be done with it. I'd do it right now if you hadn't sewn up my arm. If you cause me trouble again I won't hesitate. You've been warned."

With that he stepped into the stream and began wading along it.

Breysen stood undecided, staring after Kantor in the dark. Finally he shook his head and stepped into the stream after him.

2

Will frowned in exasperation at the two sentries brought to him by Rufe. "A mercenary escaped? After all this time? And stole one of our horses? How is that possible?"

The men stared at the ground. "There was heavy cloud cover last night, My Lord," one of them replied. "The mercenary took advantage of it. One of our men still spotted him and ran him down. There was a fight, and the guard was killed. The mercenary took his horse."

"How did a fugitive manage to kill a soldier on horseback?"

"The tracks indicate there were two of them," the other sentry replied, his face downcast. "That's the only reason they managed to overwhelm the guard."

"Are they being followed?" demanded Will.

Rufe nodded. "I've sent ten men after them, including our best trackers."

"We can't afford to have any of these men on the loose," said Will. "If they report our whereabouts, the king and queen will be exposed. The next time we see mercenaries here, they'll have brought a real army."

He shook his head grimly. "Gather the men," he told Rufe. "All of them. I want a sweep done through the forest. Today. If anyone's still alive in there it's time they were hunted down."

LATE THAT AFTERNOON Thomas and Elena were summoned by Will to a conference. Having been directed to a large hut where the meeting was to be held, they hurried there to discover they were the first arrivals.

Ten seats had been positioned around a huge wooden table in the center of the hut. The table dominated the space. It had been constructed from a solid slab of wood hewn from a single tree of great girth, with striking knots and swirls in the grain highlighting its smooth polished surface.

Thomas gazed at it in awe, admiring its rugged beauty. Being both sturdy and refined at the same time, the table somehow captured the spirit of Newhaven.

The next arrival was Will, soon followed by Anneka and Rellan, Rufe, Jonas, Count Ranauld, and finally the king and queen. Thomas noticed immediately that no other children had been brought to the conference, and he shot a wide-eyed glance at Elena, relieved that she had arranged at short notice to leave their little daughter Tammi with Elena's father, Rubin.

As soon as the king and queen were seated, the others took their seats as well. Only Will remained on his feet, his face somber.

"Your Majesties," he began, bowing to the king and queen. "Yesterday our men carefully searched the forest where the battle took place. It was harrowing work—the battleground is not a pleasant place to visit right now." His expression showed his distaste. "We were looking for survivors. We found none."

"That's encouraging news," offered the king.

"I wish it were so, Your Majesty," Will replied grimly. "Unfortunately, our search was prompted by an incident." He nodded to Rufe.

Rufe got to his feet, bowing to the king and queen before speaking. "Since the battle, Your Majesty," he said, addressing the king, "our men have been patrolling the fringes of the forest, alert for any sign of survivors. The conditions have favored us, with a full moon making our task much easier. A small number of mercenaries tried to escape during that time, and our men successfully intercepted them all. Until last night."

Rufe's face appeared flushed. "Two men managed to escape after killing one of our guards and taking his horse." He bowed to the king. "There is no appropriate way to apologize, Your Majesty. We have failed you."

The king shook his head firmly. "Preventing every surviving mercenary from escaping was never going to be easy. I know how hard your men have been working to secure the area, and from what you've said they did intercept these men last night, even though they were unable to stop them.

"I fully understand the likely implications. But I haven't lost sight of the bigger picture, Rufe. We are here today only because of the extraordinary efforts you and others made to bring us to safety. We could never have survived without you. I will not allow you to berate yourself."

Rufe bowed low again.

"Have men been sent after these mercenaries?" asked the king.

"Yes, Your Majesty," Rufe replied. "And they were ordered not to return until they find them."

The king nodded, and Rufe sat down.

The king directed his attention to Anneka and Rellan. "If word of our location leaks out, we will not be the only ones affected. The community at Newhaven will be at risk as well if another army is sent against us." He turned to Will. "We must take that into account in whatever we decide to do."

Will acknowledged the king's statement with a bow. "As you are all aware," Will said, addressing the entire assembled group, "we have been conferring with the king for some time, considering a range of options. The potential consequences of this escape now force us to act immediately.

"We have not been entirely idle during our time here at

Newhaven. Our scouts have traveled widely throughout Arvenon, and all of them have now returned. We know that Pisander has assigned a number of smaller mercenary forces to patrol the countryside. A couple of those groups pursued us when we left Paradise Valley after the assassination attempt. We ambushed and destroyed them not far from here. The two mercenaries who just escaped appear to be the last remnant of that combined force.

"When Pisander took control of Arnost, he arranged for Arvenon's standing army to be split into two forces. Both are now commanded by unknown mercenaries appointed by him. Other mercenaries loyal to Pisander have undoubtedly infiltrated their ranks. We need to regain control of those two armies."

"What do you propose?" asked the king.

"We have limited resources, Your Majesty," Will replied. "We will need to stretch them as far as we can." His face became grave. "We have four immediate problems to address. First, Pisander has sent one of the two armies westward to blockade Erestor, after spreading the story that I have been fomenting a revolt against Your Majesty." Snorts sounded around the table, and Will waited for the noise to die down before he continued. "That western army is currently camped outside Steffan's Citadel, at the gateway to Erestor. Your uncle, the duke, closed the border with Erestor at the time Pisander took over. We know that the duke remains loyal to you as always, and he will be able to assemble a formidable army on our behalf from within Erestor. We need to contact the duke and let him know that the king and queen are alive and well. We need his army."

"I might be able to help with that," said Rellan. All eyes turned to him. "I know how to get through to Erestor without going through the pass at Steffan's Citadel—I've done it before. And Lord Burtelen knows me. He will get me access to the duke." He looked at his wife. "I can imagine what you're thinking, Anneka," he said, acknowledging the alarm on her face. "No one else can do this," he said gently. "I'll be careful."

Anneka didn't look at all happy. But she said nothing.

Will glanced at the king, who dipped his head silently in approval.

"Thank you for your offer, Rellan," said Will. "I wish I could promise that no one will suffer loss in the days that lie ahead. But all of you understand the realities as well as I do."

Rellan simply nodded.

Will addressed Anneka. "If Rellan were to go, would you be willing to oversee the defenses of Newhaven on your own until he returns?"

"I bore that responsibility on my own for many years," she replied grimly. "I can do it again."

Will thanked her before continuing. "Contacting the duke is only part of the solution," he said. "The duke's forces can't move out of Erestor while Pisander's western army is blockading the citadel and the pass that runs through it. Pisander's appointees might command that army today, but most of the soldiers in it are likely to still be loyal to the king. Their original leaders know me, and I need to find a way to communicate with them. If we can regain control of that army, we can assign some of the men to protect the approaches to Newhaven. The rest can be deployed along with the duke's army from Erestor. Lord Burtelen will be able to help provide leadership."

"You can't just show up there, Will," growled the king. "You're supposed to be a rebel. The mercenary commander will have you killed before any questions can be asked. I'm not going to throw away your life on a risky adventure."

"I don't deny that there will be risks, Your Majesty," Will replied calmly. "But what other options are available to us? I assure you that I have no desire to throw my life away. I will take Rufe and Jonas with me, and we will do nothing rash."

The king was clearly not satisfied with this answer. "We will speak more about this," he warned.

"I understand," Will acknowledged, moving immediately to the next topic. "The second problem is the remainder of Arvenon's standing army. It is also currently commanded by mercenaries that are not known to us. Pisander sent it north to the borders of Castel, supposedly to forestall a Castelan attack on Arvenon. I expect this northern army to be stationed outside Deadman's Pass. We need to make contact with the loyal soldiers in that army. We also need to find a way to make direct contact with the Castelans. Queen Essanda's young brother, King Rupert, is reigning in Castel now, and he needs to know that King Steffan and Queen Essanda are still alive, and that they have a son and heir. He also needs to know that the army threatening his borders was not sent there by King Steffan."

"These are tasks for me to attempt," Count Ranauld said, rising from his seat. "I know many of the original leaders of the army—I worked closely with them after the Battle of Torbury Scarp. I don't doubt they would have been demoted when Pisander's mercenaries took control, but hopefully they are still with the army. I can also try to make contact with the Castelans. I have connections with some of King Rupert's senior noblemen."

The king assented with a grateful nod to the count.

"Thank you, Ranauld," Will replied. "I can think of no one better suited. Unfortunately we cannot send a force with you. You will need to rely entirely on diplomacy."

"I understand," said Count Ranauld with a nod, sitting down once more.

"The third problem presents us with a more difficult challenge," said Will. "It won't be easy to find an effective way to deal with Pisander and his lackeys in Arnost."

No one immediately commented or offered to help. Thomas had been the one who brought back information from Arnost about Pisander. Was it possible that Will and the king might expect him to volunteer? Surely not. He simply couldn't imagine anything useful he could do to unseat the traitor. Nevertheless he kept his eyes down, sweating uncomfortably.

Thankfully it quickly became apparent that Will had ideas of his own on the topic. "The key to resolving this problem is regaining control of the western army on the border with Erestor, and the northern army on the border with Castel," he said. "If we are able to do that, those armies, along with the duke's army from Erestor, will readily be able to block any attempt Pisander might make to deploy more men throughout Arvenon. Retaking Arnost will follow, sooner or later."

He glanced around the table. When no one offered comment, he continued. "The final problem is the most difficult of all," he said. "Thomas discovered previously that Pisander's maneuvering has been funded by King Agon of Rogand, and that Agon has been scheming to annex Arvenon, Castel, and Varas. Some of you might not be aware that Thomas also learned that Pisander intends to invite King Agon to Arnost."

"That's madness! Why would Pisander do that?" asked Rellan in consternation. "Surely it wouldn't be in his own interests to allow Agon anywhere near Arnost."

Will shrugged. "Perhaps he had no choice. Agon might have made it a condition of helping him."

Rellan slowly shook his head, his brows creased.

Thomas felt sure there was a different explanation. If Agon had the Stone of Authority, Pisander might be acting under some kind of compulsion. Thomas had no way of knowing for certain, though, and he could hardly speak openly about the stones. He needed to keep his guesses to himself. He could discuss his suspicions with Will later if the need arose.

"Is Agon planning a short visit, or does he intend to base himself in Arnost while he attempts to subdue the kingdom completely?" Will wondered. "We can only guess. But he won't leave Rog until he is confident that his own kingdom will remain secure in his absence. Either way, he will want to arrive before winter sets in. So we don't have a lot of time."

As Will paused to scan the faces around him, Thomas glanced around the table himself. Everyone was looking grim. He had no need of the Stone of Knowing to tell him what people were thinking.

Will's expression was grave, yet he somehow managed to project a calm confidence. Thomas could only admire his composure. He had no idea how Will did it.

"We cannot afford to let Agon get established in Arnost," Will said. "He'll undoubtedly bring an army of his own with him from Rogand, and it won't be easy to displace them. We know ourselves that Arnost is well able to withstand both an assault and a siege."

"How can we stop him?" asked the king.

"I propose that we send a force to secure our border with Rogand," Will replied.

"We'd need a big force to do that," said the king, "and we don't have one available."

"You're right, Your Majesty," said Will. "Right now we cannot spare even one hundred men. We will need the western army currently camped outside Steffan's Citadel, combined with the duke's army from Erestor."

"If these men are sent to the border, how can we bottle up Pisander? And how can we retake Arnost?" asked the king.

"I am hoping that Count Ranauld will also eventually be able to bring us the northern army camped outside Castel," Will replied. "It's all a question of timing. Denying Agon access to Arvenon is the crucial first step. The other steps will need to follow at an appropriate time."

The king hesitated for a moment, but he soon nodded his agreement. "What you're proposing makes sense, Will. All of it. Implement it as you see fit."

Will bowed his thanks to the king. Then he turned to the others. "Each of us knows what we need to do," he said. "Those of us leaving Newhaven will set out at dawn the day after tomorrow."

"There's no point in delaying the journey to Maranelle to meet with the duke," Rellan said abruptly. "I'll be ready to leave at dawn tomorrow."

Anneka glared at him, but his face was set stubbornly.

"You need to come to a conclusion together," Will told them.

Neither commented, but they both nodded tightly. Thomas found himself thinking that the discussion was likely to be animated.

Anneka and Rellan rose first and left the building. Rufe, Jonas, and Count Ranauld followed closely behind them. As they did so, the king moved closer to Will and began conversing quietly with him. The queen joined them, listening attentively.

Thomas and Elena were about to leave the hut when Thomas noticed Will's hand go up to forestall them. Having caught their attention, Will waved them over to join the conversation.

As they approached, the king nodded a welcome, and Queen Essanda beamed them a friendly smile.

"Thomas has an unusual ability to ferret out information from people, Your Majesties," said Will. Thomas felt his face redden. Will was clearly referring to the stone, although it seemed apparent that he had not told the king or queen about it.

Not for the first time, Thomas wondered what the king might say if he learned of the stone and its powers. Would he demand that Thomas hand it over to him? Kings could issue whatever commands they chose, and their subjects were expected to obey. If anyone refused, a king had ways of forcing them to comply.

A jumble of thoughts went through Thomas's mind as he settled himself after the king waved them both to their seats. Uppermost in his thoughts was the awareness that he had no interest in giving up the stone. It was curious that Will had never suggested that Thomas needed to surrender it to the king. Nor had he ever asked for the stone for himself, even though there must surely have been times when he would have found it invaluable. Will had instead consistently protected Thomas's secret, accepting from the beginning that Thomas was the custodian of the stone. Thomas had no idea what Will's reasons were.

Thomas didn't fully understand his own unwillingness to give it up either—it was one of many mysteries surrounding the stone. It had certainly brought him far more than his share of trouble. And the ripples had since spread to encompass his family.

He told himself that he felt responsible for the stone. Was it as simple as that though? He set aside his musings to focus on what Will was saying.

"I am going to need your help when I go to the army outside Steffan's Citadel, Thomas. I'll need to know where the leaders stand."

Thomas suppressed a shudder. Will's request—and it clearly wasn't a request—showed how far out of reach a normal life had become for him. He nodded, not trusting himself to speak.

"If Thomas is going, I will go too," said Elena abruptly.

All eyes turned in her direction. Will and the king both began speaking at the same time, expressing alarm at any such idea.

Elena simply stared back, her beautiful face unyielding.

The king raised a hand, and Will fell silent.

"I greatly admire your pluck, Elena," said the king. "But I would never forgive myself if I allowed you to put yourself at risk in such a manner."

Elena's expression did not waver, although Thomas saw her lips trembling.

Finding the boldness to speak up in such exalted company was no easier for Thomas than it was for Elena, and even the idea of challenging the king unnerved him. But he could not allow his wife to stand alone. "Elena has proven herself many times," he said quietly, "and in situations that would overwhelm most people. I would not be alive today without her resourcefulness."

The queen smiled at his words. "I might add that I too was sternly discouraged from joining my husband when he traveled to Paradise Valley," she said. "Yet when all of us were put to the test, I like to think that I gave a good account of myself. Even though I am a woman, and even though I was well advanced in my pregnancy. I don't think we should deny Thomas and Elena the final say in deciding whether she should go."

"My comments were intended only to spare Elena whatever trouble might lie ahead," the king replied. "I had no desire to call her capabilities into question." He gazed at his wife. "No one could question the significance of your contribution on behalf of the kingdom. Your influence has been decisive on more than one occasion."

Essanda smiled, grasping Steffan's hand and squeezing it. The king smiled back at her affectionately.

Then he turned to Elena. "I don't claim to know you well, Elena, but all of us have caught glimpses of your determination. I don't doubt that you might have a part to play that I cannot foresee. Nevertheless, I am still not convinced about the wisdom of you accompanying Will and Thomas."

"I have a proposal," said Will. "It would strengthen the resolve of the soldiers greatly if they could catch a glimpse of their king and queen. It would be even better if they have an opportunity to see the baby prince with their own eyes. I know that sounds extremely risky," he added quickly, "but I am not proposing that Your Majesties join us when we make initial contact. Only when we are absolutely certain that we have won over the soldiers and their leaders, and dealt with any traitors among them. If you are waiting nearby we can send for you to join us. If you hear nothing from us by an agreed time, you can withdraw to safety."

He turned to Elena. "I would like to suggest you wait with the king and queen, and join Thomas when they meet us."

She looked uncertain.

Will looked at her frankly. "May I be direct, Elena? If you're with us when we meet with the soldiers, none of them will pay attention to a single word we say!" The king stifled a laugh, and the queen put a hand to her mouth to hide a smile.

Elena blushed deeply. But she looked at Will and nodded her head to indicate her acquiescence.

Thomas expelled a breath, discovering in the process how tense he had been feeling. He reached out and took Elena's delicate hand in his own.

"Does my proposal meet with your approval, Your Majesty?" Will asked the king.

"It does," King Steffan replied. "Your plans are bold given our slender resources. But I cannot offer better options, and you always seem to find a way through."

"We will do our best," said Will in response. "It hardly needs to be said that you will be left largely unprotected if we fail."

"We will not speak of failure," declared the king firmly.

3

Ashar drew his horse to a halt beneath the spreading boughs of a huge tree. The canopy above offered limited protection from the incessant rain, but any respite was welcome.

He studied his surroundings carefully. He could reasonably claim to be widely traveled, but this part of Lestanor was entirely unknown to him.

The sun had almost touched the horizon, and the cold had begun to gnaw at his bones. Shivering in his sodden garments, he reminded himself of the size of the payout once he'd delivered the package.

If he didn't reach a village soon he'd need to find a place to camp. The thought held no appeal, and he decided to ride on for a few more minutes.

Ashar had almost given up hope when he caught a distant glimpse of a cluster of dwellings. Peering through the driving rain in the fading light he couldn't be certain of the size of the village, but it might be large enough to boast an inn. He urged his horse forward in eager anticipation of hot food and a bed.

No one was abroad in the village by the time Ashar reached the first of the low huts. Even without a glimpse of the inhabitants, though, the appearance of the dwellings in the gathering gloom told him everything he needed to know about this place.

Fully alert, Ashar took careful note of his surroundings. He did it effortlessly and almost without conscious thought. He knew how to take care of himself. His employers had chosen well, but he didn't waste energy congratulating himself with the knowledge.

When a modestly sized inn appeared before him, he dismounted and tied his horse to a post. Then he pushed open the door and stepped inside. He removed his dripping cloak and hat and hung them on hooks on the wall, scanning the room as he did so.

He found himself in a large room filled with a number of small tables. Upwards of twenty men sat around the tables holding mugs of ale. The low rumble of conversation had ceased abruptly at his appearance. Every person in the room was now eyeing him warily.

Ignoring their stares, Ashar made his way to the serving counter. The innkeeper nodded a guarded greeting.

"Do you have hot food and a room?" Ashar asked, slipping easily into the local language. "And can you stable my horse?" His fluency in the language of Lestanor had already proven invaluable.

The innkeeper looked his visitor up and down, his eyes lingering on Ashar's sword and knives. "If you have the coin," the man finally returned.

Ashar pushed a few silver pieces onto the counter, and the innkeeper nodded once more. "Find yourself a table," he said. "I'll bring the food over. My boy will see to your animal."

Ashar located a table off to one side of the room and took a seat. Conversation had resumed in the room, but many eyes remained fixed on him.

The innkeeper arrived with a mug brimming with ale and a bowl filled with steaming meat and a few scrawny vegetables. He put it down and left without a word.

Ashar paused long enough to place a long-bladed knife within easy reach on the table. Then he wasted no time getting into the food.

A small group of men at a nearby table watched him closely. After a few moments one of them swung his chair deliberately around to face him. He aimed a scowl first at the new arrival, then at his knife.

Ashar spared the man a glance between mouthfuls, noting the way the firelight picked out the prominent scars on his face.

"What brings scum like you to our village?" demanded Scarface.

Ashar paused in the action of chewing and looked up, his eyes narrowing. If this fool wanted to die, Ashar would be happy to oblige him.

He hadn't come looking for trouble though. All he wanted was a meal and a good night's rest.

"Just passing through," he replied evenly, ignoring the provocation.

He added a question of his own. "I'm looking for someone—perhaps you know him."

Scarface glowered at him. "Who?"

"A man by the name of Jace."

The room went instantly silent. Nobody moved except Ashar, who resumed his assault on the food.

Scarface laughed—a harsh and grating sound. "You have no idea who you're dealing with," he said contemptuously.

Ashar stared back at him. "The same could be said of you," he observed casually.

Scarface's eyes hardened. But he turned away and moved to a different table.

Conversation in the room was still muted when Ashar decided to turn in for the night. The innkeeper led him up a flight of stairs to a room above the public room. Ashar poked his head in and looked around, then returned to the passage and examined the approaches to the room.

The innkeeper watched him for a minute before stating adamantly, "I don't allow trouble in my inn. Keep to yourself, and others will do the same."

Ashar shrugged. There would be trouble. If not in the inn, then after he left it.

He had no reason to doubt the innkeeper. Nevertheless he slept lightly, as he always did.

Ashar appeared in the public room at sunrise to find the proprietor already hard at work. "Food is cooking if you want some," the innkeeper told him.

Ashar shook his head. He never broke his fast until later in the day. "I'll be on my way."

He handed over more silver pieces to pay for his stay. His host was clearly more than satisfied. "Are you still determined to continue your search?" he asked.

Ashar nodded. He couldn't fail to notice the innkeeper's unwillingness to speak the name of the man he was seeking.

The man shrugged. "It's your funeral then. Follow the road out of the village. In a couple of leagues it forks. Take the left fork. It heads southeast. He'll find you before you find him."

Ashar dug into his pouch for another silver coin and handed it to the innkeeper.

Glancing at the pouch, the proprietor added, "You might find some company waiting for you down the road."

The warning wasn't necessary, but the innkeeper couldn't know that. Ashar palmed him a final coin, then headed outside for his horse.

He emerged into the open to find that the rain had cleared. As he mounted, a rider galloped away on the road ahead of him. No doubt the rider was a sentry charged with warning the ambushers that Ashar was about to set out.

Ashar took the road out of the village, remaining on it until the buildings were out of sight. Then he turned aside into the trees. When the road lay two bowshots behind him, he resumed his journey.

As he picked his way through the undergrowth he pondered the likely motives of his ambushers. Scarface was undoubtedly blinded by his wounded pride. And his friends would have noticed the silver coins Ashar handed to the innkeeper. Perhaps they'd guessed—correctly in this case—that he had plenty more.

Whatever their reasons, they were fools if they thought he would simply blunder into their trap.

After a while he heard the soft nickering of horses. Dismounting, he tied his horse to a branch and crept forward. Four horses stood in a huddle, tied up with halters.

Ashar snorted to himself. Scarface and his friends had a lofty opinion of themselves if they thought four of them were enough to bring him down. He considered turning aside to kill them all. It would bring a satisfying end to the foolishness. But there wouldn't be a payout, so it wasn't worth the time or the effort.

He untied the horses instead and led them to his own animal. Remounting, he set off with the four horses in tow.

As soon as he was well clear of the area he rejoined the road, urging his horse into a trot. After two hours of steady riding, he spotted a small stream near the road and brought the animals to a halt. Removing the halters from the other horses, he released them. They soon moved away from the road and began cropping the plentiful grass beside the stream.

If the horses were stupid enough, they might eventually find their way back to their owners. Ashar was content to let them decide for themselves. Either way, he didn't expect he'd ever see Scarface or his friends again.

When the sun set he found a place to camp for the night. Having chosen a sheltered location well away from the road, he saw no reason not to build a small fire. He retrieved some dried meat and stale bread from his saddlebags and sat down to warm himself by the fire while he ate it.

He had barely finished his meager meal when a sharp object stabbed into the back of his neck.

"Get up. Slowly," said a cold voice.

He complied, berating himself for his carelessness.

"Remove your sword and knives. Put them on the ground, then step away from them."

He did as he was told, slowly and deliberately.

"The knife in your boot as well."

This man didn't miss much.

"Now stand with your back to that tree, facing the fire."

He eased back to the tree and stood unmoving with a sword at his throat.

He finally had an opportunity to observe his captor. The man's face was turned away from the fire, but the captive could see cold eyes glinting dimly in his face. They were remorseless eyes—the eyes of a killer. A cold chill ran up Ashar's spine.

"I am Jace. You've been looking for me. You found me." The killer's voice was as cold as his eyes.

Someone had sent Jace a warning. The innkeeper?

"I was hired to bring you a package," said Ashar, succeeding at keeping his voice steady.

"Where is it?"

Ashar reached for his chest.

"Careful," warned Jace.

Ashar reached carefully into his clothing and withdrew a small parcel. He held it out.

Jace took it and unwrapped it with one hand, his eyes never leaving his captive.

A sheet of parchment appeared in his hand, and a bright object fell to the ground. Ashar shifted his eyes downward to look at it. It was a golden dagger, its hilt encrusted with jewels. He'd been carrying around a small fortune inside his vest.

Jace glanced briefly down at it, letting it lie where it had fallen.

The killer scanned the parchment, his eyes flicking up frequently to ensure his captive hadn't moved.

Ashar forced himself to relax. He was nothing more than a messenger. Jace had no quarrel with him.

"Did you open this package?" the killer demanded.

"No," Ashar replied truthfully.

"Have you read the message?"

"No." Ashar paused for a moment before adding, "I can't read."

Jace nodded. "That must be why you weren't worried about the final instruction."

Ashar had no idea what Jace meant. He wasn't granted an opportunity to find out.

JACE MOMENTARILY CONSIDERED TOSSING the parchment into the fire started by his victim and letting the flames reduce it to ash. Then, deciding abruptly to keep it instead, he tucked it into his clothing.

The message was from Lord Drettroth. The nobleman had been the highest profile casualty of the disastrous Rogandan invasion of Arvenon, and Jace was well aware that he was dead. Receiving a message from beyond the grave was therefore unexpected and disconcerting.

When he first heard of Drettroth's death, the assassin had felt something akin to regret. The Rogandan nobleman was a rare individual—one of the few men Jace respected as a peer. As a result, Jace was more than willing to undertake an assignment on his behalf, whether or not he was still alive.

It seemed that before his death Lord Drettroth had left a package with a trusted retainer. In the event of Drettroth's demise, the retainer had been instructed to wait for five years, then to arrange for the package to be delivered to Jace.

The five years had now elapsed. Following his late master's instructions, the retainer had engaged a messenger to deliver the package.

The commission described in the parchment was for an assassination on the usual terms: payment in full in advance, buried in a secure location; freedom for Jace to choose his own means and his own timing; and no suggestion of returning the payment if the target was no longer alive when the commission was delivered. The message even used a secret code devised by Jace to describe the location where the payment had been hidden.

The Rogandan nobleman, as always, had done his preparation thoroughly.

Jace threw a casual glance down at the body lying in the dirt before the fire. Drettroth had never liked loose ends, and it came as no surprise to Jace that the parchment ended by instructing him to dispose of the messenger.

He located the ornate dagger and retrieved it from the dirt, dusting it off before turning it over in his hand. The weapon itself was worth almost as much as the promised reward.

Beyond its intrinsic value, the dagger was a signature that clearly identified the author of the parchment. It further confirmed Drettroth's seal. Jace recognized the dagger, because years earlier Drettroth had given him its twin, part of the reward for a similar assignment he had carried out on behalf of the nobleman.

Jace ignored the body of the messenger. Sooner or later someone would find it, and as far as he was concerned they were welcome to loot it. However he did thoughtfully remove the saddle and the bridle from the messenger's horse before setting it free.

His next move would be to retrieve Drettroth's payment. Not that he needed it—he was already wealthy beyond imagining. But a workman was worthy of his hire.

After that he would begin his planning. It would need to be careful planning indeed. Assassinating a king involved the highest level of risk and danger.

He was not deterred. As usual, Drettroth had not stinted on the payment. But Jace had another more compelling reason for accepting the commission. He had always risen to a challenge, and he had been lacking a worthy challenge for far too long.

4

King Agon of Rogand sat sullenly on his throne in the audience chamber adjoining his private apartments, waiting for Pisander's envoy to arrive. The king was not in a good mood. His body ached all over, and the padded cushion beneath him felt hard and lumpy. The discomfort did little to improve his temper.

Agon had slept badly. His head had been pounding before he rose for the day; he felt certain he was coming down with some kind of illness. After examining him carefully, his doctors had assured him nervously that it was nothing worse than a cold. One of the imbeciles had almost referred to it as a common cold—from the look on the fool's face he had barely caught himself in time. It would have been a fatal mistake, and Agon could only scowl at the leech's lucky escape. Whatever name might be attached to his malady, the doctors apparently also expected to find the ailment lurking among the most wretched of his subjects. The king could only rail at a universe with the audacity to behave so indiscriminately.

A goblet of wine on a table beside him caught his eye, and an entirely different thought came abruptly into his mind. Would anyone be stupid enough to risk poisoning him?

Chaotic thoughts tumbled about in his head, and for one delicious moment it occurred to him to execute his current food and wine taster. He shrugged off the idea indolently.

A servant entered and bowed low, waiting to be acknowledged before daring to stand upright in Agon's presence. As he stood bent in an awkward posture, the king studied him casually, much as a spider might study a fly struggling feebly in its web.

After a while Agon tired of the amusement. "Well?" he asked imperiously.

The servant attempted to conceal a wince of pain as he straightened. Agon was not sympathetic. If the king wasn't well, it was only right that others should suffer too.

"The envoy has arrived from Arnost, Your Majesty."

"Show him in," growled the king.

The envoy also bowed low as he entered, although he did not wait for permission before standing upright again. Agon reminded himself with difficulty that he needed to exercise restraint.

"Speak," the king commanded.

"I bring greetings from your loyal servant, the Earl of Pisander, Your Majesty. He eagerly awaits the pleasure of your arrival in Arnost."

The envoy had a great deal more to say on Pisander's behalf, although the words danced around all of the issues that most interested Agon.

"What of the former king and queen?" the king asked bluntly.

"His lordship has been reliably informed that they are dead, Your Majesty. He is daily expecting final confirmation."

"And what of Erestor?"

"The old duke is still hiding there, trapped by one of his lordship's armies. He can be dealt with at any time."

Agon scowled with annoyance. This latest message from his pet noble in Arvenon gave no more answers than the one that preceded it. As usual, if Agon wanted things finished off properly, he would be forced to do it himself. The pace would change considerably once he arrived in Arnost.

Tiring of words and needing to get the man out of his sight before he lost control of himself, Agon decided to call the audience to a close. “Scurry back to your master,” he told the envoy dismissively, “and tell him I demand to see the heads of Steffan and Essanda. I’ve given Pisander enough money to buy two kingdoms, and I’m tired of promises and excuses.”

In fact the entire exercise had barely troubled Agon’s coffers. But the king wasn’t about to acknowledge that to Pisander or anyone else.

The Arvenian hurried away, and Agon grasped the opportunity to swallow a potion prescribed by his doctors. He’d used it before at such times, and it had helped with his aches and pains.

He had no opportunity for a real break before his next visitor arrived. His servant introduced a person very familiar to Agon. She entered with little ceremony.

Since the demise of Drettroth, Ona had gradually emerged as the most effective of his subjects. She had somehow wormed her way into this status almost before he was aware it was happening. Once he saw what she was capable of, though, he offered her unstinting encouragement. He had already promoted her to more than one formal role, and he would continue to expand her responsibilities for as long as she proved loyal and reliable. Officially she had administrative responsibility for trade, both local and foreign, and for tax collection. Unofficially he had recently given her oversight of his network of foreign agents. Perhaps most usefully of all, she kept an eye on his nobles for him.

Agon never failed to make time for Ona whenever she wanted to see him. She had never yet wasted his time.

He eyed her hungrily as she entered the room. Seeing his reaction, she leered provocatively at him. She had never made a secret of the fact that she dressed and presented herself specifically to provoke such a reaction. No other woman had ever dared to flaunt herself in his presence in this way.

The truth was that she fascinated him. The woman was commanding, beautiful, sophisticated, and utterly ruthless. In short, Agon found her positively delectable.

Mouthwatering though she might be, he had never been seriously tempted to make her his plaything. She wasn't a person to be toyed with, and unlike so many of her victims, he saw from the beginning that he could never afford to let his guard down with her. King or not, she wouldn't hesitate to find a way to take advantage of him if he offered her half a chance.

That didn't mean he couldn't appreciate from a distance the assets she flaunted with such self-assurance.

Ona was far beneath him, of course, as every other mortal creature must inevitably be. She was noble born—she would never have been able to make her way so effortlessly among his nobility if she was not—but she also had the common touch. She knew how to dress and carry herself like a peasant, and she could move among them as if she were one of their own.

Possibly Ona's most striking quality was her single-mindedness. And she was almost as callous as he was—he admired that in a person.

"Your Majesty," she simpered, offering him a mock curtsy.

"My Lady Ona. What havoc have you been wreaking in my kingdom?" he wondered idly.

"I've been poking around here and there," she replied. Her face turned suddenly serious. "You have problems in your outlying provinces, Your Majesty."

His smirk instantly became a scowl. "What problems?"

She waved her hands vaguely. "Grumbling about taxes. And about your continuing fascination with foreign adventures."

A frown furrowed his face. She needn't think that her impertinence was guaranteed to amuse him. Perhaps he should remove her pretty head after all.

"I found I was able to...divert the energies of some of them," she continued pertly. "Once I had captured their full attention, I offered very sweetly to bring their concerns to the direct attention of their sovereign." Her lip curled. "For some reason, none of them seemed enraptured at the prospect," she added with her usual flair for understatement.

He nodded with satisfaction. Lady Ona was good. And she'd wasted no time in reminding him why he valued her so highly.

"Krasmir?" he asked.

A delicate frown flitted across her bewitching features, as a cloud might briefly shroud the sun. "Lord Krasmir is a man who's never been frightened to state his opinions. It's been suggested in some quarters that he has more reason than most for discontent. But he seems surprisingly untroubled by these issues."

She raised her hands heavenward. "I can't make him out," she acknowledged helplessly.

Agon grunted. Krasmir's unlikely compliance came as no surprise to him, thanks to the small stone concealed on his person. He had chosen Krasmir as the first important test of the Stone of Authority, and the results had far exceeded his expectations.

"I want names, and every detail of their mutterings," he growled, moving quickly to change the subject away from Krasmir.

She smiled indulgently back at him. "I have no doubt that Your Majesty will use the information...carefully," she offered.

"You will not be exposed as the source," he assured her in a bored tone.

He gazed at her steadily for a moment. "Keep me informed of your whereabouts," he said. "I might have need of you again very soon."

She bowed briefly and delivered an immodest curtsy before sweeping elegantly from the audience chamber.

He'd never used the stone on her. In recent times he'd considered it more than once. But there was something raw and unpredictable about her. As long as she continued to serve his interests, he saw no reason to risk dulling her razor edge.

Agon's servant made another appearance almost the moment she had left the room.

"No more audiences!" snapped Agon.

The servant fled while attempting to execute a hasty bow.

Agon got up slowly and headed into his private apartments. Without the distraction of Lady Ona his symptoms were quickly reasserting themselves, and he suppressed a moan, determined to pay no attention to the discomfort. If he didn't improve soon, he might find it necessary to distribute some pain among his doctors.

Ennawi, Agon's mute slave with no hands, was occupying his usual position by the balcony. Approaching the slave casually, the king peered into his habitually unresponsive face. "I wonder if Lady Ona might be able to get a reaction out of you," he said thoughtfully.

Ennawi's face didn't twitch.

Agon shrugged. "My plans have progressed well in Arvenon," he said. "Pisander has almost outlived his usefulness, but not quite. Once I'm properly established in Arnost I'll find a less willful local to rule in my name. Someone without expectations should be appropriately grateful for the opportunity."

His expression turned to a scowl. "And yet the moment an opportunity arises to cross the border, new obstacles appear in my path. My barons have the effrontery to whine about me. Behind my back! The fools will learn there is a price to pay for saying what they think.

"And that isn't the worst of my difficulties. Who can I leave in charge of Rogand when I am gone? I have no heir, and none of my aides are suitable."

The uncomfortable truth was that Agon never retained competent administrators for long. Before long he always found a reason to thrust them aside.

At least he was no longer executing every administrator or agent who disappointed him. Not usually, anyway. He had been working hard on exercising restraint. Summary execution might have offered a satisfying resolution for his disappointment, but it had proven counterproductive as a long term policy. It completely unnerved whoever he tried to bring in as a replacement.

Now he once more found himself needing someone competent—more so than ever before.

"None of my barons can be trusted," he grumbled.

His conversation with Lady Ona about Lord Krasmir came suddenly to mind. "I wonder..." he said, musing aloud. "Is it possible that Krasmir could do the job? He certainly wouldn't be frightened to apply a heavy hand when it's called for."

Could Krasmir be trusted to act on Agon's behalf? Lady Ona had confirmed that he remained compliant. Perhaps the Stone of Authority had provided an unlikely ally.

"Krasmir," murmured the king thoughtfully.

There was no way he could just announce such an appointment of course. It would be necessary to acquaint the nobleman with any responsibilities that couldn't be deferred during the king's absence. The handover would take time—at least a month. That period would give him further opportunity to focus the stone on Krasmir. It would also allow him to decide whether the arrangement might work.

He stood before his slave and examined his face. "What do you think about Lord Krasmir as regent, Ennawi? Any concerns with the notion?" He paused for a few moments. "From your silence I take it that you approve. You are very wise."

Agon snorted. He was never backward in enjoying his own cleverness.

"I like this idea of a regent," he continued more seriously. "I can see the benefit of allowing someone else to take the heat for a while."

Even if Krasmir solved Agon's problem of appointing a regent, the king would still be faced with an irritating delay before he could follow through on Pisander's invitation. Moving into Arvenon would not be possible anytime soon.

As he turned the issue over in his mind an intriguing possibility occurred to him.

"I promised you a trip to Arnost, Ennawi," he told the slave. "I'm sorry to say I need to delay it further. But there's no reason I can't send a representative ahead of me. It has to be someone I trust implicitly—I need an accurate assessment of what's really going on there. So much the better if it's someone capable of unsettling the Arvenian rabble who call themselves nobility."

He smirked at the slave. "I've just realized that I have the ideal person—Lady Ona."

The idea was delicious. He would be sending a fox among lambs.

After she'd finished with them, they'd welcome Agon as a deliverer when he arrived. They'd find out too late that the fox had been replaced by a wolf.

"What do you think, Ennawi? I know she speaks Arvenian." The king's lips peeled back in a smile of satisfaction.

No response was forthcoming, exactly as Agon expected. He nodded solemnly. "I'll order her to set out as soon as she can make herself ready."

The king knew he could not delay lying down for much longer. He'd still done nothing about his recalcitrant nobles, but that would have to wait. Deferring his response didn't mean he'd decided to tolerate their sedition. He was simply allowing himself time to dream up a truly gratifying way of abasing them.

5

The unusual isolation of Newhaven had ensured that Anneka's community had remained small. Nevertheless, Brother Ander had been searching for his fellow monk for some time before he located him beyond the cultivated fields that surrounded the settlement. His friend was sitting quietly on a log, peering into the gathering dusk.

"There you are, Brother Gerome. You're a hard man to track down."

"Newhaven offers a number of perfect scenic outlooks," the monk replied contentedly. "I've been relaxing here enjoying the sunset."

"The sunset?" replied Brother Ander, glancing belatedly up at the sky. "I hadn't noticed it."

Brother Gerome sighed. "Perhaps you see things the same way as Brother Kaylis. His view is that nothing in nature matters if it doesn't have a clear purpose. For the most part it is obvious how natural elements and living creatures are useful. For example, a mighty river and a lowly dung beetle each fulfill a role. However Brother Kaylis sees no possible benefit from sunsets, so he ignores them."

"Do Brother Kaylis's ideas have a useful purpose?" asked Brother

Ander with a shrug. "I never paid much attention to him. His head is in the clouds."

"Very apt, since we're discussing sunsets," said Brother Gerome dryly.

Brother Ander groaned. He opened his mouth to change the subject, but his friend got in first.

"Sunsets are remarkable," said Brother Gerome. "They're never the same from day to day. And I'm told that the same sunset looks different from different locations."

"And that tells you what?" asked Brother Ander. He knew his friend would get to the point sooner if he humored him, but it didn't stop him feeling restless.

"It tells me that the Creator is incredibly extravagant," said Brother Gerome. "He isn't solely interested in utility, whatever Brother Kaylis says. I have the feeling that sunsets are designed mostly to delight us."

He looked up at Brother Ander with a knowing smile. "But you didn't come here to talk about the wonders of nature. Something is bothering you," he said.

Brother Ander nodded impatiently. "Will...Lord Torbury I mean...wants me to leave. He says that the king and queen will be going somewhere with their baby son, and he thinks they might benefit from having me with them." He shook his head.

"And why is that a problem?"

He looked at Brother Gerome in surprise. "I was just getting settled here. For the first time I'm starting to understand how my calling as a monk and as a healer might work in practice. That's only been possible because I came to this community."

"And why can't you exercise your calling with the king and queen?"

"You've seen what life is like around them. Their lives are a never-ending drama of intrigue and battles. Fighting was my life once, but all I want now is to escape from it. I've put all of that behind me. The king needs warriors, not monks."

"You saved the king's life. It isn't hard to understand why they might want a healer on hand."

"That wasn't just me. And anyway, I didn't become a monk so I could spend my days as medic to the royal family." He shot a glance around them before adding, "I mean no disrespect to Their Majesties."

Brother Gerome offered no immediate response, and both of them gazed for a time out into the gathering gloom.

"What about you? What will you do?" Brother Ander eventually asked.

"I have been giving that question much thought and prayer," Brother Gerome replied. "Anneka and Rellan have told me how much they've appreciated having us both here at Newhaven. Anneka remembers fondly the priest from her estate in Erestor—Father Bryan I believe he was called. She said the Newhaven community had nowhere to turn for spiritual guidance before we arrived."

He gazed up at Brother Ander. "I've been thinking that I will stay here. Brother Elias spoke with me at Paradise Valley, before he sent us off with the king and queen. He told me then that the future was uncertain, and that I should be willing to follow God's leading, wherever it might take me."

"He had a similar conversation with me," replied Brother Ander. "I think he suspected at the time that we might not return."

"So what are you going to do?" Brother Gerome asked.

Brother Ander shrugged. "I will go with the king and queen. I'm not sure that refusing them is an option, even if I wanted to."

Brother Gerome nodded. "You could ask God to show you a way to wiggle out of it, but I'm not sure it would do any good. I have a feeling it's what he wants you to do."

As Thomas was leaving the conference, Will had asked Thomas to meet him later that day. The commander had suggested a quiet location overlooking Newhaven. Thomas arrived early to gather wood and light a fire. He now sat watching the flickering glow while he waited for Will to arrive.

The light was slowly fading from the sky as Will hobbled toward him and took his place before the fire. Thomas peered curiously at his friend in the semidarkness, wondering what he wanted to talk about.

The commander wasted no time in getting to the point. "Why is Elena so set on joining you, Thomas? I can understand that she doesn't want to be parted from you, but this assignment will be dangerous."

"There's a lot I haven't told you, Will," Thomas replied awkwardly. "Everything was frantic when we first saw you again after we'd left Arnost to search for the king. Then we were all on the run for so long, and you've been busy since we arrived here."

"I understand," Will told him. "I don't have a lot of time right now, either, but I'm listening."

"After we fled our home in the forest, I was badly injured, and Elena needed to use the stone to get us out of a dangerous situation. The way she handled it was astonishing. And we discovered that the stone reveals different things to her. Or rather she discovers different things from what it reveals. Since then we've been handing it back and forth between us as the need arises."

Will looked surprised. "I would never have guessed that sharing the stone was even a possibility," he said.

Thomas shrugged. "There's so much we still don't understand about it. But I have to admit that Elena's insights are sometimes more useful than mine."

Will raised an eyebrow. "Jonas?"

Thomas winced. "That's a particularly embarrassing example," he said. "I can't believe that I ever thought him capable of treachery. I never managed to get a good enough look at him at the time. It was only ever fleeting glimpses. After it was all over I asked Elena to do a check of her own. She saw right through to the heart of it. As always."

Will laughed. "Don't worry, Thomas. You don't have anything to be ashamed about. Without you the kingdom would have been in big trouble on more than one occasion."

"Thanks, Will. The reason I'm telling you this is that Elena is much more resourceful than people think, and unusually insightful as well."

"There is a great deal more to Elena than meets the eye," said Will with a wry smile. "And the stone can be shared..." He fell to musing for a while.

Thomas began to feel uneasy. What was Will thinking?

Will studied Thomas's face knowingly. "I'm sure you're wondering about the possible consequences of having told me that. Let me assure you that I've never wanted your stone, and knowing that it can be shared doesn't change that."

He stared into the fire. "You've chosen to be open with me about the stone, Thomas, and I appreciate that. I've never had designs on it, though. My life is complicated enough already." He laughed, although there was no humor in it.

"I'm very grateful that you've always protected my secret," Thomas told him.

"I haven't always protected it as well as I should have. That council of lords meeting in Arnost during the siege comes to mind. I haven't hesitated to drag you into some dangerous situations so you could use it to help me out. So I owe you something."

"You don't owe me anything, Will," Thomas replied. "The debt lies much more heavily on my side."

They both went silent for a time. Thomas had known for some time that he needed to share his suspicions with Will. Now that a perfect opportunity had presented itself, he didn't quite know how to begin. After a few moments of fruitless rumination, he shook his head, frustrated at his own hesitancy. He decided he just needed to speak.

"There's something else I need to tell you, Will."

Will's face turned serious. "Why do I get a bad feeling about this?" he murmured.

"You know that after Elbruhe died, Brother Vangellis and I went to a monastery," Thomas said.

"Up in the mountains?"

"Yes. They have a huge library there, with a lot of old scrolls. We asked the monk who was their librarian if he'd ever heard of anything like the stone. He did a search and found an old scroll."

"You've never mentioned this," said Will.

"I did set out to tell you on one occasion," Thomas replied. "When we were at Hazelwood Ford, after the battle. You were too busy. You couldn't spare the time, so I decided not to bother you with it."

"I'm sorry I shut you out, Thomas. I was completely overwhelmed. Even after the fighting was over there was so much to think about. The kingdom was devastated after the Rogandan invasion, and we needed to shift our energies to rebuilding. It was hard to know where to start."

"I could see the pressure you were under," Thomas said, "and my news didn't seem pressing. The scroll raised as many questions as it answered. But I've started to wonder if some of it might be important now, even though it didn't seem especially relevant at the time."

"Tell me," said Will.

"The writer of the scroll knew about the stone I have—he called it the Stone of Knowing. What he said about the stone was accurate, so it seemed to me he must have known what he was talking about. But I was surprised to learn that there are two other stones. One of them apparently grants long life. He called that the Stone of Vitality. The other one he referred to as the Stone of Authority."

"What did the scroll say about this Stone of Authority?" asked Will, listening intently.

"It was only a brief mention, because the scroll had been torn and maybe half of it was missing. But it said that the stone granted power and influence. Only the Stone of Knowing was described in any detail in the fragment the librarian found."

Will's brows were furrowed, but he said nothing.

"There were times when I wondered if you had the Stone of

Authority," Thomas said with a self-conscious laugh. "You're such an effective leader."

Will shook his head. "I know nothing of any other stones," he said.

"I'm not actually serious," said Thomas. "But I did find myself thinking about the scroll again when I discovered that Pisander was planning to invite Agon to Arnost. I can't imagine Pisander wanting to share power, much less hand power to anyone else. It seems so out of character. If Agon has the Stone of Authority though, he might have been able to use it to influence Pisander. Could that be why Pisander agreed to something he wouldn't normally consider?"

Will frowned. "Very possibly. This information raises questions about the attack at Paradise Valley. One person was almost certainly behind the attacks. The obvious candidate is Agon, but I haven't been able to see how he could make it happen. Someone needed to get Pisander working effectively with people from Castel and Varas on a goal that's bigger than any of their own personal agendas."

As always, Will's mind quickly led him to the broader implications.

"I haven't been able to understand why Pisander would plan such an attack," Will continued. "Why would he try to kill all three kings at once? It would increase the risk significantly. And even if he succeeded, he wouldn't be in a position to receive any direct benefit. But if Agon has found a way to impose his will on individuals from all three kingdoms..." He shook his head. "That would make him very dangerous indeed."

An important question was weighing on Thomas. "Are you going to tell the king about this?" he asked. He wasn't able to keep the anxiety from his voice.

Will smiled grimly at Thomas for a moment before shaking his head. "Your suggestion about this Stone of Authority would sound preposterous to anyone who hadn't already seen you in action with your Stone of Knowing. And I'm not eager to expose your stone more widely."

Thomas tried not to let his relief appear too obvious, but Will looked at him shrewdly. "I'm sure you must have wondered why I've been so willing to keep quiet about it," Will suggested.

Thomas hesitated for a moment before deciding there was nothing to be gained by pretending. "Yes, I have," he said frankly. "Many times."

"You once promised that you would never use the stone on me," Will reminded him. "Have you kept that promise?"

The question sounded casual, but Thomas was not deceived for a moment. He could never forget the day on the riverbank, and the fury in Will's eyes as he slapped the stone from Thomas's hand.

"I've kept the promise," Thomas assured him. "I long ago decided not to use the stone on anyone I have regular contact with. Elena can confirm that I have followed through on that decision."

Will simply nodded. "And that's a key reason why I've been content to leave the stone with you, hidden from the world. There's more to it than that, of course, and I'm happy to explain if you like. I'm sure that the subject is of considerable interest to you." He gave Thomas a knowing look.

Thomas nodded. He quietly took a deep breath, then released it slowly in an effort to calm himself.

"A leader faces many challenges," Will began. "There are so many things to consider. Leaders must represent the interests of whoever appointed them. They also need to anticipate the likely ways that powerful people might react to whatever they do. It doesn't end there, either—in my view no leader is worthy of respect unless they also consider the interests of the powerless."

"I have no idea how you balance all these things," Thomas said, shaking his head.

Will sighed. "It isn't easy," he said. "I'm surrounded by intrigue, and there are times when I would be very pleased to have a way of finding out what others are thinking. If I tried to base my decisions on what other people think, though, I'd invariably end up confused and frustrated."

"I can believe that," Thomas replied. "I'm sure it's impossible to please everyone."

"Completely impossible," Will agreed. "Always knowing what others think would become a distraction. That isn't a distraction I need."

Will creased his forehead, adding new lines to his scarred visage. "And that isn't the only complication. What if you knew the secret thoughts of everyone around you, and you also had the power to prevent them from ever acting on the worst of those thoughts? It would become very tempting to deal with possible threats before they could be carried out. When you knew that someone had become a potential threat, you wouldn't give them the benefit of the doubt, because there wouldn't be any doubt—not about what they were thinking, anyway. The more powerful you were, the more dangerous such an ability would become."

Thomas understood completely. Drettroth had lusted after this power, and there was no doubt in Thomas's mind about how the Rogandan commander would have used it.

"People don't always put their thoughts into action though," said Will. "Sometimes fear of the consequences holds them back. Sometimes they simply change their minds. None of that would matter—they could be condemned before they ever had a chance to exercise restraint. Normally people are punished for what they do. Now they'd be punished for what they think."

As always, Will had seen the bigger picture clearly and completely.

A grim smile came over Will's face. "Who can be trusted with this kind of knowledge? I'm not confident that I can be trusted with it. It's safer in your hands, Thomas."

Was it truly safe to entrust the stone into his hands? Thomas had misused it terribly when he first found it, with dire consequences for him and for others. But so much had changed since then. And now Elena bore it with him—both its revelations and its burden. Thomas was only beginning to understand how much of a relief that was for him.

Fortunately, Thomas's status limited his ability to act on the stone's revelations. That was also a very good thing.

"I think I understand what you mean," Thomas replied. "Whenever I've discovered anything truly alarming, I've come to you, because you have the power to do something about it. I don't have that power myself, and it's safer that way."

"Exactly," said Will. "Jonas is a perfect example. You shared your concerns with me, then left it to me to decide how to respond."

"And it would have been a terrible mistake if you'd taken me too seriously," said Thomas, shamefacedly.

"No harm was done," Will replied. "Both of us did what we needed to do."

Will clapped him on the back. "This has been a very enlightening conversation, Thomas," he said.

"For me as well," agreed Thomas.

"I'm happy for Elena to join the king and queen," Will said. "You'll need to make arrangements for your daughter."

Thomas raised his eyebrows in surprise. "It sounds like you're expecting we'll be gone for some time. Would it be possible for Rubin to come—to help with Tammi? That means that Haldek will want to come as well, of course."

Will pondered a moment before nodding. "If they're willing to take the risks, I'm willing to let them come too. In fact it might prove useful at some point to have Haldek along," he added thoughtfully.

"We have some preparation to do," said Thomas, suddenly anxious to be gone.

"We leave at dawn," Will reminded him as they parted. "Don't be late!"

6

The morning after the conference Will rose early to see Rellan off. Anneka and Rellan had already arrived with their two children, and they stood huddled together. A small party that included the king, Rufe, and Brother Gerome joined Will just before dawn.

The king approached Anneka and Rellan and gravely expressed his thanks to them both, offering his best wishes to Rellan for his journey. They bowed in response, and he moved away to allow Rellan to say his goodbyes.

Anneka held their two-year old daughter, Bella, in her arms. Rellan stood beside her, stomping his feet restlessly as he cradled Bella's twin brother, Kuper. Neither of the twins were awake. Brother Gerome stood beside them.

Rellan was poised like an arrow ready for release. He was waiting only for the first glimmer of sunrise, determined to set off for Erestor as soon as the light allowed it. He would not be traveling alone. Petar, an exceptional hunter and tracker from Newhaven who was also an unusually capable archer, had agreed to accompany him. Petar waited patiently nearby, holding their horses.

Rellan handed little Kuper to Brother Gerome before briefly

embracing Anneka. He then took the reins of his horse from Petar and mounted, turning back once to wave farewell as he rode away.

Anneka, her face a mask, stared after him until long after he had vanished from sight.

SOON AFTER RELLAN and Petar had left, Rellan noticed his companion guiding his horse closer. Petar's face held a question. Rellan could guess what was coming.

"Are we heading where I think we're heading?" asked Petar.

"There's no other option," Rellan replied. "The journey will take long enough even going the quick way."

Petar grimaced. "The 'quick way', as you put it, won't help anyone if we end up floating face down in the lake. You know better than anyone how unstable that slope can be."

"What's the alternative?"

Petar pointed behind them. "We could head south, around the mountains."

Rellan shook his head. "That would take weeks. We don't have that kind of time."

"Did Anneka know you were going to risk the lake?"

"We didn't discuss details—we didn't need to. She understands the situation."

Rellan slowed his horse and turned to his companion. "It isn't too late to change your mind, Petar. You don't have to come with me. You didn't volunteer for this, and there'll be no shame if you decide to head back."

Petar shook his head firmly. "Forget it," he replied. "I'm not going to let you do this on your own, Rellan." With that he clicked his tongue and moved his horse forward again.

Rellan accepted Petar's response at face value and put the matter from his mind. He knew that they wouldn't reach the lake until the following day at least. Once they had crossed into Erestor, an even longer journey lay ahead of them before they reached Maranelle.

Everything would depend on finding a way past the lake.

A SMALL GROUP had already gathered on the outskirts of the Newhaven community when Thomas arrived with his little party the following morning. They stood shivering in the cold air as they watched the sky for any sign of the coming dawn.

Will stood off to one side talking quietly with Count Ranauld. Rufe and Jonas waited nearby with their horses, longbows slung across their backs and quivers bristling with arrows.

The king and queen arrived just as the first hint of the sun brightened the sky. Ava, the queen's handmaid, hurried along with them, holding the baby prince. Brother Ander followed close behind. Brother Gerome had also accompanied them, Anneka at his side.

Will ended his conversation with Ranauld and turned to face the group. "Everyone ready?" he called. Without waiting for an answer he added, "Time to go."

Count Ranauld set off first with two soldiers, heading north. Thomas knew that Will had offered him more men, but Ranauld felt that a small party was less likely to attract unwanted attention.

Thomas had been holding Tammi. As Will mounted his own horse, Thomas handed the toddler to Elena, kissing his wife lightly on the lips.

"Be careful," she whispered to him.

Thomas nodded to Rubin and Haldek, then mounted up. Clicking his tongue, he guided his horse over to Will, who waited with Rufe and Jonas.

Thomas's stomach had begun to clench uncomfortably—it was hard to leave Elena and Tammi. As he rode away, he looked back in time to see the rising sun light up the scene behind him. Elena clutched Tammi almost defiantly, her attention fixed unwaveringly on her departing husband. Rubin had wrapped his arm around her shoulder. Anneka stood to one side of them, her expression unreadable. Brother Gerome's head tilted upward to the heavens. His eyes were lightly closed, and he seemed to be mouthing a prayer of blessing over the departing men. Brother Ander towered beside him, his head bowed. The king's face wore a stern look. Only the queen seemed calm.

The future held no guarantees for any of them. Only danger and uncertainty lay ahead, and each of them would need to face it as best they could.

Long after the scene had disappeared behind him, it remained etched in Thomas's memory.

A SENSE of foreboding descended over Elena as she watched Thomas ride away. Their brief period of peace at Newhaven had ended so abruptly. When would they enjoy such tranquility again?

The Stone of Knowing had gone with Thomas, and she experienced nothing but relief to know it was so far from her reach.

She was not free of it, though. It had been the stone, and only the stone, that made Thomas so necessary to Will. Thanks to the tiny object her beloved was heading into danger. As long as Thomas retained the stone, it could upend her world at any time.

Would they ever be free from its unsettling influence? She could not pretend herself ignorant of the stone's potential for good, though the power of its insights held no lasting allure for her. She would cheerfully cast it off the edge of the world if she could be certain it would never be found again. But she knew of no effective way to conceal it. As long as the stone remained accessible, it would forever be at risk of discovery by the unscrupulous.

Like Thomas before her, she had acquired a sense of responsibility for the stone. She sighed and shook her head.

With an effort, she put the subject from her mind.

WILL'S small group had long disappeared from sight, and Elena saw that the king and queen were about to mount their steeds. Rubin had offered to make a sling for Prince Aiden—a smaller version of the one he had fashioned to allow Tamara to be carried safely and comfortably while on horseback. The sling had been positioned around the queen's neck, and the little prince was now nestled snugly within it.

Before the queen could climb into the saddle, Ava ran to her, wringing her hands. "Please let me come with you, Your Majesty," she pleaded. "I don't want to leave you. Who will serve you?"

"You've been a wonderful and a faithful companion, Ava," the queen replied quietly, "and I'll miss you very much. I can't know what the coming days might bring. I only know that there will be danger and uncertainty. I want you to stay here—to make a life for yourself in Newhaven. I release you from my service."

At her words Ava began to weep inconsolably, covering her face with her hands. Clearly moved by her former handmaid's distress, the queen drew her into a lingering embrace. She caught Brother Gerome's eye and nodded to him, and the monk moved quickly to Ava's side to comfort her.

Tears glinting in her own eyes, the queen turned away and mounted her horse, guiding it alongside the king's animal. The monarchs moved forward, surrounded by a dozen guards hand selected by Rufe.

Elena and Tamara, along with Rubin and Haldek, intended to accompany the royals and their guards, and they also mounted. Brother Ander completed the party, and he stood ready nearby with his horse.

All of them would ride toward Steffan's Citadel and position themselves near the western army camped outside the citadel without getting close enough for their presence to be detected. They would not see Will again until he called for them. That request would not come until Will was certain it was safe for them to rejoin him. What might happen after that, Elena had no idea.

When the soldiers began to move out, the king and the queen among them, Elena nudged her horse forward to join the column. Rubin guided his horse alongside her. Tammi rode with him, settled into her sling and still sleepy from the early start. Haldek swung in behind them.

Brother Ander brought up the rear, his face somber. He appeared lost in thought. Elena had no way of knowing what he might be thinking, but his mood matched her own if his expression offered any indication.

RELLAN AND PETAR rose at dawn and set out immediately. They rode hard throughout the day, with the result that they reached the lake that afternoon. Roughly three hours remained before the sun would reach the western horizon. The question facing them was whether to risk the slope immediately or wait for the following morning.

They stood beside each other, scanning the landscape before them apprehensively.

"How many times have you crossed that slope?" Petar asked.

"Twice," Rellan replied. "Once in each direction. I also partially crossed it with Anneka the day of the landslide."

He fell silent as the memories flooded through his mind. He relived his horror as the slope slid away before his eyes, carrying Anneka with it. Somehow he'd reached her in time. Never would he forget clinging to her as they dangled on the end of a rope, watching wide-eyed as the tidal wave swept inexorably toward them.

He returned to the present with an effort. "What about you?" he asked.

Petar stared into the distance. "Only once. When we first came here with Anneka. Somehow we all made it across from Erestor. The men hunting us were another matter. They deserved everything they got and more, but watching them sliding helplessly into the lake with their horses…it wasn't pretty." He gazed into the lake with obvious distaste.

Rellan nodded, his head down. "Anneka has told me about it. You did well to defeat those men."

The lake stretched out before them, no breeze ruffling its surface.

The scene was one of complete tranquility, although both Rellan and Petar knew how deceptive appearances could be.

"Should we attempt it before sunset?" Rellan asked. "A good night's sleep would be welcome. But time is against us, and I'm not sure that the crossing will seem any easier after a whole night thinking about it."

Petar looked down at the slope before glancing across to the trees on the far side of the lake. "We might as well do it now," he said.

Rellan gave a sharp nod. "I agree. Let's not carry anything we don't need. Just in case." He dismounted, removing his sword, his bow, and his cloak, and securing them to the saddle. Petar did the same. Both men had brought ropes with them, and they placed them within easy reach, loosely attached to their saddles.

Rellan led his horse out onto the slope above the lake. Petar followed a couple of horse lengths behind.

The slope beside the lake seemed stable enough; Rellan knew from experience that the most dangerous section lay ahead of them. He moved carefully forward, the horse between him and the lake. The animal seemed jittery, perhaps sensing his mood, and he spoke to it quietly to calm it.

An hour had passed by the time Rellan finally reached the part of the slope that he knew to be most unstable. This was the spot where Yosef and Jon had set out to trigger a landslide, succeeding beyond their wildest imaginings and losing their own lives in the process.

He paused and peered forward intently. Several years had gone by since the fateful day when a thick layer of soil had flowed down into the lake, but the slope appeared little altered. If anything, it looked steeper and more treacherous.

Rellan glanced back at Petar. His companion's face was pale but determined. Taking a deep breath, Rellan led his horse slowly onto the slope. His feet slid downhill with every step, making forward progress extremely hazardous. His horse plodded slowly beside him, snorting nervously.

A part of Rellan wanted to abandon caution and common sense, and sprint across the slope until the unstable section lay safely behind him. He knew such an approach would end badly, so he paused for a moment to allow his heart to stop racing.

Rellan began to breathe more freely once he caught his first glimpse of more stable ground, only a few horse lengths away. Anxious not to make a mistake with safety so close at hand, he stepped out more warily than ever.

A sharp cry sounded behind him, and he swung his head around to see that Petar had lost his footing and was sliding under his horse's legs. He was clutching desperately to the reins, but before Rellan could react he lost his grip and began sliding down toward the lake.

Rellan responded instantly, reaching for his rope and quickly tying one end of it to his saddle. He turned to throw the other end of the rope to Petar, but the hapless rider was already out of reach. Keeping hold of his own rope, Rellan moved as quickly as he dared to Petar's horse and grabbed the other rope, tying one end of it to his own rope. Making a loop in the other end of the rope, he placed it over his shoulders, tightening it under his arms.

Then he allowed himself to slide downward, playing out the rope as he went. He tried to tell himself that he had done this before, but it wasn't the same. This time everything depended on his horse remaining in position at the top of the slope and supporting his weight.

Rellan looked down and saw Petar at the edge of the lake, trying to pull himself out of the water and onto the bank. At every attempt the edge of the bank simply crumbled away.

"Swim to me," Rellan called.

Petar saw him coming. Abandoning his attempts to climb out of the lake, he swam awkwardly to where Rellan was heading. Petar's condition was rapidly becoming critical. He was shivering uncontrollably in the icy cold water.

As soon as Rellan reached the edge of the lake he allowed the rope to tighten, hoping desperately that his horse would not lose its footing. The animal whinnied, but seemed to take up the strain.

Rellan reached down just as Petar strained an arm up to him. Grabbing hold of Petar's arm, Rellan dragged him bodily from the water. The rope stayed taut, but there was no telling how much the horse could take.

They needed to get back up the slope. With a mighty effort Rellan took a step upward, dragging Petar with him. It was obvious immediately that this approach was doomed to failure. The slope was simply too long and too slippery, and the effort was beyond them both. Even if the horse was somehow able to keep supporting their weight, Rellan would never manage to climb all that distance with Petar hanging on as little more than a dead weight.

Rellan planted his feet and held his current position, his mind whirling. He needed to find an alternative, and find it quickly.

The hint of an idea came to him. Whistling to the horse, Rellan urged it forward. The horse didn't respond, so he whistled again, louder this time. The animal took a step forward, then another. Keeping the rope taut, Rellan began to shuffle along the slope, barely above the waterline, dragging Petar along behind him. Once or twice the horse almost lost its footing, slipping down a short distance, but it recovered, and Rellan took up the slack on the rope, hanging on grimly. He called out a continual stream of encouragement as the horse continued to struggle forward.

Refusing to dwell on the odds of success or failure, Rellan narrowed his entire world to the next step before him. Slowly, laboriously, they moved across the slope.

It felt as though an eternity had passed by the time they finally reached more stable ground, although it surely must have only been a few minutes. The slope around them now consisted of firm soil interspersed with rocks. It showed little sign of giving way beneath them.

Rellan allowed the rope to go slack, and encouraged Petar to sit. Then he carefully climbed up to the horse and untied the rope. Petar's horse had trailed along behind his mount and he went to it and retrieved Petar's cloak. Then he climbed back down to Petar.

His companion was trembling violently. The first priority was to get him dry and warm.

"We need to get you to your horse, Petar," he said. "Come on, I'll help you."

On many occasions throughout his eventful life, Rellan had faced physical challenges. The final climb back up the slope with Petar surely ranked as his greatest feat of endurance. By the time they reached the horses, both men were utterly spent. But Rellan could not afford to rest.

Somehow he got Petar onto his horse, then he remounted as well and led them both forward until the lake lay behind them. The light was fading quickly. The moment he found a sheltered location under some trees, Rellan retrieved every available blanket and left Petar to struggle out of his wet clothes. Then he set about building a fire. Once it was crackling heartily, he positioned some branches near it and spread Petar's sodden clothes across them. Then at last, weary beyond words, he slumped down himself before the fire.

A couple of hours after the sun had set, Rellan felt able to bestir himself. He prepared food and managed to get Petar to eat some of it.

Petar, too, was showing tentative signs of recovery. He was no longer shivering violently, he had hot food in him, and some of his clothes were almost dry.

After seeing to the horses and gathering an impressive pile of wood to keep the fire burning throughout the night, Rellan finally allowed himself to relax. He sat down before the fire and released a heavy sigh.

"Why did you do it?" asked Petar.

"Do what?" asked Rellan, puzzled by the question.

"Come down for me. It was madness! I'm not sorry you saved me, of course. I'll forever be in your debt. But it's a miracle that either one of us survived. What were you thinking?"

Rellan glanced briefly at him. "I remembered you saying what it had been like to watch the men and their horses sliding helplessly into the lake. The memory was clearly horrific, even though they were your enemies."

Rellan stared back into the fire. "You risked the slope anyway. I couldn't leave you in the lake when it happened to you."

He fell silent, and Petar found nothing further to say either.

Before another hour had passed, Petar's clothes were almost dry. Rellan woke him from his doze, and he dressed again and returned Rellan's blankets. Rellan banked the fire, and both men settled down to sleep.

When the sun rose once more, Petar felt able to continue their journey. They saddled their horses, mounted up, and headed for Maranelle.

Nothing now prevented them from reaching the duke. They would let him know that the king and queen were alive and well and on the move. And they would convey how urgently the monarchs needed the army he commanded in Erestor.

Before long the lake was lost to sight. Rellan prayed fervently that he would never clap eyes on it again.

7

Thomas stood huddled with Will, Rufe, and Jonas as the sun rose on a new day. Two days ago they had left Newhaven. It had taken much of the day to travel upriver and trek through the ruined forest. They had camped in the forest beyond the battleground, and ridden northwest for much of another day. They halted as soon as the western army, camped outside Steffan's Citadel, lay within reach. They spent the rest of the afternoon watching it from a safe distance. When the sun set, they tried to sleep, knowing that the following day would decide their future, one way or another.

When the sun rose Will called them together. "Are you all clear about what you need to do?" he asked.

They nodded in unison.

Jonas needed to leave immediately, and he accordingly mounted his horse, preparing to ride away.

Will preempted him, hobbling over and reaching up to clasp Jonas's forearm in a salute. "We're indebted to you once more, Jonas," said Will soberly.

Jonas shrugged. "All of us are doing what we can."

Will nodded, releasing his arm.

"I have no way of knowing when I'll be back," Jonas told them, "but it might be sooner than you expect."

"We'll be ready," Rufe promised.

Jonas called to his horse, and it sprang away.

Thomas watched him leave with trepidation. His own turn would be coming soon, very soon.

Will's plan was bold and risky. Thomas tried to assure himself that Will knew what he was doing—no one was better equipped than Will to successfully navigate a situation like this. But cheering on the commander from the sidelines was very different from playing a part as an active participant.

Thomas thought of Elena. She wouldn't be as terrified as he felt—he was certain of it. He could almost see her smile of encouragement, assuring him that he could do it.

He sighed, trying not to sweat too much while he waited for Rufe to say it was time to go.

"Who are you, and what's your purpose here?"

The tone of the sentry was rude and aggressive, but Jonas ignored it. "I'm here to speak with your commander. Hazor sent me."

The sentry grunted, clearly unimpressed, but he nevertheless sent another soldier to pass on the request.

"What have you all been doing?" Jonas asked, keeping his tone light.

The sentry paused, considering whether to reply. "Sitting. Always sitting," he finally replied, spitting on the ground beside him to underscore his frustration. He eyed Jonas narrowly for a while before his curiosity apparently overcame his brusqueness. "What's going on in the rest of the kingdom?" he ventured.

Jonas gazed down at him casually. "The usual kinds of things," he said.

The sentry frowned up at him, clearly annoyed at the evasive reply. Then he turned away, ignoring Jonas entirely.

At least thirty minutes passed before the soldier reappeared. "Come with me," he said curtly.

Jonas dismounted, leaving his horse with the sentry. He smiled to himself as he followed the soldier. From his perspective it was as promising a beginning as he could reasonably have hoped for.

As they made their way through the camp, Jonas took careful note of the mood of the soldiers he passed. The men seemed restless and disaffected. He wasn't surprised. Soldiers never coped well with idleness. By now they were undoubtedly spoiling for some action. He dared to hope that some of them might also be disillusioned with their current leaders.

Yes, the tone of the camp was definitely encouraging.

Jonas found himself ushered into a hut. Three men were sitting behind a table, apparently waiting for him. They didn't offer him a chair.

"You claim that Hazor sent you." So they knew who he was. Perhaps the various mercenary leaders were known to each other.

The scowl on the speaker's face and the way he spoke Hazor's name made it clear that Jonas need not expect a warm welcome. Jonas was not daunted by their cold reaction.

"Describe Hazor," the man demanded.

Jonas raised his eyebrows in mild surprise at the request. Nevertheless he was not alarmed. He might have only clapped eyes on the mercenary leader once—apart from when he killed him—but he remembered him well enough.

He described Hazor as requested.

The grunt from his inquisitor offered little indication of his reaction, but Jonas could see that he was satisfied.

"Who are you?" the man demanded.

"My name is Jonas. Hazor recruited me because I fought under Prentis, and I know how he thinks."

The commander eyed him silently.

Jonas stared back at him. "And who are you?" he asked bluntly. It wouldn't serve his purpose if they thought he was soft.

The commander's eyes narrowed for a moment, then his expression cleared. “I’m Lord Redfass,” he said silkily. “These are my senior commanders—Kernon, and Namor,” he added, stabbing a finger toward the men beside him.

Jonas bowed deeply. “My Lord,” he said respectfully.

He had never heard of any of them, and he didn’t doubt for a minute that ‘Lord Redfass’ was no more a nobleman than he was. He wondered where Pisander and Lygell and their cronies managed to dredge up such trash. Now these men had the temerity to command one of the king’s armies. This was not just any army, either—it was part of the renowned force that had crushed the Rogandan invasion. Redfass dared to pretend he was acting in the king’s interests, supposedly to quash a rebellion stirred up by none other than Will Prentis, the former commander of this same army. The effrontery of it made him sick to his stomach.

“So Hazor sent you, did he? What does that ambitious mongrel want?” growled Lord Redfass.

“Hazor would wish to return your compliments, I’m sure, My Lord,” said Jonas dryly.

“If you have something to say, then say it,” said Kernon.

“Hazor needs your help,” began Jonas.

“Why am I not surprised?” said Lord Redfass, turning to his companions and raising his hands heavenward. “He should have come here himself if he wanted to beg for help.”

“He couldn’t risk it,” returned Jonas. “He has the king and queen trapped, and he isn’t going to let them out of his sight.”

“I thought the king was dead,” said Namor suspiciously.

“I never believe anyone’s dead until someone I trust has seen the body,” replied Jonas.

“If he has them trapped, why doesn’t he go in and finish them off?” asked Lord Redfass contemptuously.

“Because the king and queen are defended by Prentis,” said Jonas.

All three of the mercenaries raised their eyebrows at that.

“How many men does Prentis have?” asked Kernon.

“No more than a hundred,” Jonas told him.

“And how many does Hazor have?”

"Three times that," Jonas replied.

"What's he waiting for then?" sneered Lord Redfass. "I've always known he was a coward."

"This is Prentis we're talking about," said Jonas seriously. "I'm sure you know his reputation as well as I do. No one in their right mind makes a move against him unless they have overwhelming force to back them up."

"Three to one isn't overwhelming?" sneered Kernon.

"Not with Prentis," returned Jonas stubbornly.

"So why should we trust you?" Kernon persisted.

Jonas shrugged. "It's your choice. The royals won't be going anywhere—Hazor will make sure of that. If you're not interested I'll head for Arnost. I imagine Lord Lygell might show a bit more interest than you have." He raised an eyebrow. "He might also be curious to know why you turned the opportunity down."

Kernon sneered in response, but his silence was telling.

"The king, the queen...and Prentis," mused Lord Redfass. "Taking them down is an attractive idea. It could be very rewarding indeed."

Jonas nodded. "Hazor is willing to share the spoils as well as the glory. Half to him, half to you."

Guffaws of scoffing laughter immediately sounded from all three of them. "So he wants us to do the dirty work while he gets the glory?"

"He's the one who has the royals bottled up," Jonas pointed out.

"I presume you know the location yourself," Lord Redfass said smoothly. "We can make it worth your while if you tell us where it is. Or, if you prefer, we could just squeeze the information out of you right now at no cost to ourselves."

"I do know where they are," said Jonas calmly. "But I also know something Hazor doesn't know. While I was on the way here I caught sight of Prentis. I saw him at the edge of a forest, alone and a long way from his main group."

"Why should we care?" asked Kernon.

"He didn't see me, and I can lead you to him."

"It'd be a waste of time," said Kernon dismissively. "He'll be long gone by the time we get there."

Jonas shook his head. "I don't think so. I watched him for a while. He was examining the hoof and front leg of his horse. It showed all the signs of being lame. After he finished with the horse Prentis sat down, apparently to wait. If he's expecting someone to join him, he'll be stuck there until they arrive. If we leave now, we can deal with him before moving on to the royals. They'll be a lot easier to manage without him."

The men still looked doubtful.

Jonas shook his head in frustration. "What do you have to lose? It's on the way to Hazor anyway. If Prentis is gone, we'll simply continue on and help Hazor finish off the royals."

"And share the spoils with Hazor?" scoffed Namor.

"I'm sure you'll find a way to satisfy him."

He made no comment about the smug smiles that appeared on the faces of the three men.

"Namor, go get a couple hundred men," said Lord Redfass.

"Wait!" said Jonas. "We haven't agreed on terms." He paused before coolly offering them a proposal. "Why not split the spoils four ways? I'm not greedy—I'm willing to settle for a quarter share."

"Done," said Lord Redfass.

Out of the corner of his eye Jonas saw Kernon and Namor exchanging smirks. He pretended not to have noticed.

Jonas addressed Lord Redfass. "I don't know who you're planning to take with us, My Lord, but I hope it's not the regulars."

"Why not?" Redfass demanded.

"They've fought for Prentis and for the royals. The outcome is going to be very unpredictable if you give them an assignment like this. Take men you're sure you can rely on."

"He's got a point," Namor conceded.

Lord Redfass nodded. "Bring our own people."

"What about the regulars?" asked Kernon.

"What about them?" Redfass waved a hand dismissively. "They

can stay here. They won't be going anywhere." He turned to Kernon. "Make sure our insiders stay with the rabble to keep an eye on them."

So the mercenaries had planted their own people among the soldiers. That was no surprise. Leaving them with the soldiers wasn't what Jonas had been hoping for, but there was nothing he could do about it.

He followed Lord Redfass to the edge of the camp and retrieved his horse. Then he waited, becoming increasingly impatient as he watched the mercenaries assemble. He couldn't afford to reach Will too quickly, but he'd expected to be long gone from the camp by now.

Jonas counted almost three hundred by the time the force was finally ready to depart. He led the men out.

"Where are we heading?" Lord Redfass asked him.

"We're taking a roundabout path, My Lord," Jonas replied. "Prentis is positioned at the edge of a forest. If we approach head on, he'll see us coming long before we arrive, and he'll try to disappear into the forest. I'm going to lead us in from a different direction—we'll approach him from the side. He won't know we're there until we're on top of him."

Redfass nodded. "Lead on, then. But you'd better be aware that we'll be watching you."

AFTER THEY HAD BEEN RIDING for two hours, Lord Redfass pulled his horse alongside Jonas's mount, his face twisted in a scowl. "How much further?"

"Another hour or two I expect, My Lord," replied Jonas. "It's frustrating, but there's no way to get there more quickly."

A perverse desire came over him to take a poke at the so-called nobleman.

"Do you ever find yourself envying the endurance of lesser creatures?" he asked innocently. "Just the other day I saw a spider sitting on its web for hours, waiting for an insect to happen by."

Redfass glowered at Jonas. "So who's the spider, and who's the fly?" he growled. "Get your head out of the clouds, and concentrate on getting us there!"

Jonas made no further comment, but he smiled to himself. Redfass hadn't entirely missed his meaning, and he had responded with a telling question.

Four hours eventually passed before Jonas slowed his horse to a halt, holding up a hand. The column came to a stop behind him.

Lord Redfass rode up, Kernon and Namor beside him.

"We've arrived," said Jonas. "If all is going to plan, we should spot him as soon as we round those trees ahead."

"Well get on with it," snapped Redfass.

Jonas kicked his horse in the flanks, and it sprang away. He rounded the trees at speed, the other horsemen following hard behind him. Once he was in the open he halted his horse again, facing the forest. Lord Redfass's mercenaries flowed around him, spreading out on either side.

Ahead of him, no more than a furlong away, stood Will Prentis. He was standing among the trees on the outskirts of the forest. He was entirely alone. He slowly mounted his horse, seemingly untroubled by the sight of the large body of soldiers swinging around to take up positions around Jonas.

Will Prentis made no attempt to flee. Silent and unmoving, the solitary figure faced Redfass's hundreds.

BREYSEN HAD HIDDEN in the forest for days, overwhelmed by the stench of decay and stumbling over the detritus of battle before risking everything on a desperate escape in the dark. Since then he had been trudging on foot for several days through an unfamiliar landscape, without food, and accompanied only by a dangerous and highly strung killer. Life had not been easy for him, but never had he faced a more grueling experience.

Quiet despair washed over him as he considered his situation. What would become of him? And what of his wife and little ones back home? He thought of the two children they hadn't so far needed to bury. Even if he survived and made it back to his family, he had no idea how he could provide for them.

The only thing he knew for certain was that he would never again sign up as a mercenary.

He couldn't be sure if anyone was still tracking the two fugitives, but a considerable amount of time had now elapsed since their escape from the forest, and every hour surely made it less likely that they would be found.

For much of the day he had been wondering if he should continue to follow Kantor or head off on his own. Neither of them would ever have selected the other as a companion—they had been thrown together. He didn't trust Kantor even slightly, and the idea of parting company with him was extremely appealing.

The only reason he hadn't done it already was in response to a strange sense of duty. The more he thought about it, the greater his misgivings about having helped Kantor to escape. A sense of impending doom hovered about the man. Breysen hoped his premonitions were wrong, but he decided to stick around, at least for a while.

His musing was interrupted by the sight of Kantor's hand raised in warning. His companion moved quickly to conceal himself behind a tree. After creeping closer, Breysen did the same.

Voices sounded ahead, not far away. Were they about to be discovered at last?

As Breysen peered around the tree, listening intently, he was reassured to hear the voice of a woman. He couldn't imagine a woman among their pursuers.

She laughed, and the simple sound was almost enough to undo him. It evoked memories of home, of family, of companionship. Memories of joy and of laughter.

He had given it up. And for what?

He had become a mercenary for the promise of money. Poor as he was, he saw now that what he left behind was worth much more than any payout offered by Hazor. He swallowed against a lump in his throat.

The woman's voice pulled him back to his current situation. "No need to worry about me," she was calling. "I won't be gone for long."

It wasn't difficult to guess why she might need a few moments' privacy, and she had no reason to suppose that stepping away from her companions might place her in danger.

Her voice was drawing closer, and Breysen's heart began to race when he realized that she was heading directly toward Kantor.

Kantor waited until the woman had almost reached his tree. Then he drew his knife in one fluid motion and leaped forward. Grabbing her, he spun her around before him, one hand smothering her mouth and the other holding a knife to her throat.

"Easy now!" he said quietly to the woman. Seeing Breysen hurrying toward him, he scowled. "You have no part in this. This woman is my free pass out of here. I'm getting me a horse, and she's coming as a hostage. Do whatever you like, but stay well away if you value your skin."

Anger rose up in Breysen as he glared at Kantor, his unease about his companion hardening into an unshakable determination to resist him at any cost. He'd seen for himself the mercenary's casual cruelty, and he was ready to do whatever it took to prevent him from harming an innocent victim.

Then he glanced at the woman and stopped in his tracks. Something about her seemed familiar, and his mind raced as he tried to figure it out.

All of a sudden it came to him, and the blood drained from his face. Kantor had made a hostage of the queen.

8

"Are you ready, Thomas?" asked Rufe.

The two men waited on their horses. The camp of the western army was in sight, but no one appeared to have spotted them yet.

"I'm ready," Thomas replied, trying to hide his nerves. "I'll let you know whenever I spot someone I don't think we can trust. And I'll also keep an eye out for anyone likely to be especially sympathetic to our cause."

Rufe looked at him strangely, but he nodded. "Let's go," he said, setting off toward the camp.

Thomas followed him in, twisting the clasp suspended beneath his vest to bring the stone into contact with his skin. He wondered if his friend truly believed he could do as he'd promised. If so, what did he make of it?

More soldiers were coming into sight now, and a tidal wave of impressions began to sweep over him, pushing Rufe from his mind. Thomas tried to narrow his focus, to sift out anything irrelevant to their situation.

One man stood out at once. He needed to warn Rufe.

Thomas urged his horse alongside the big soldier. "Rufe! Over there." He nodded toward the man, realizing at once there was little chance that Rufe knew who he meant.

The man headed away from them, hurrying back into the camp. Rufe did appear to have noticed him, but he seemed unconcerned. Other men were hurrying forward, some with weapons drawn. Open shock showed on many faces when they saw who was approaching.

Rufe drew his horse to a halt, Thomas pulling up beside him. The milling soldiers also came to a standstill immediately before them.

"It's Rufe!" a number of voices called. Men crowded closer. Thomas had no idea what might be about to happen.

"Who's that with him? Is it Thomas, the horse master?"

Startled, Thomas cast his eyes to identify the speaker. One of his former students must have recognized him. Thomas had been in hiding for years. He was surprised—and gratified too if he was honest—to discover that he hadn't been entirely forgotten.

His musings came to an abrupt end with the arrival of a group of mounted men. The soldiers had drawn their weapons, and their faces showed they meant business. They were led by the man Thomas had singled out previously. The stone showed him exactly what they had in mind, and the weight of their malice took his breath away.

Thomas turned to Rufe in alarm. The big soldier caught his eye as Thomas nodded urgently toward the group of men. Rufe followed his glance, but he didn't react at all. To Thomas's bemusement, he seemed neither surprised nor concerned.

What should he do? Thomas's misguided warnings to Will about Jonas came abruptly into his mind, and a flush of embarrassment washed over him. This was surely different though—a further glance at the approaching horsemen left no doubt about their intentions.

Had Will told Rufe about Thomas's mistake with Jonas? Surely not—Will had promised not to expose his secret. Perhaps Rufe was simply unconvinced that Thomas could help in a situation like this.

His consternation grew as the men drew closer.

Not all of the mercenaries had ridden away with Lord Redfass from the camp of the western army. The commander had intentionally left behind a few of the men he had placed in the ranks to inform on the regular soldiers.

The most senior of the informers was Belac, and he watched with narrowed eyes as the two men rode in. One of them didn't appear to be armed, and he immediately dismissed him as any kind of threat. The other rider was imposing and vaguely recognizable. Belac identified Prentis's right hand man before anyone else seemed to. Rufe Sarjant meant trouble, and Belac hurried away to get support.

As he ran, he cursed Redfass for disappearing with most of the reliable people. None of them could have known that Rufe Sarjant would show up the minute they'd gone of course, but it was spectacularly bad timing. Now it was up to Belac to retrieve the situation. He comforted himself with the knowledge that Redfass would make it worth his while when he returned. The mercenary commander had always come through in the past.

After locating another of the men Redfass had inserted into the ranks, Belac sent him off to help gather the others. In an impressively short time a group had assembled. All of them were mounted and fully armed. Belac led them back to the outskirts of the camp to deal with the big interloper.

Sarjant's unarmed companion saw them coming, and he was clearly terrified. He had reason to be. Sarjant also spotted them, but he seemed content to ignore them. Belac chuckled to himself. By the time he learned his mistake it would be too late.

Sarjant was standing up in the saddle. "Will Prentis needs your help," he called. "The king and queen are nearby too, and they're counting on you to help them deal with these mercenaries."

"Move aside!" Belac roared as his men tried to push through the press of soldiers. "Don't listen to these men—they're traitors to the king!"

Normally horses could be relied upon to force their way through any crowd, but soldiers were not the common rabble. They weren't intimidated by the animals, and their densely packed ranks made forward progress almost impossible.

Sarjant sat on his mount watching them calmly. "The real traitors are here before you," he called to the men. "Take a good look at them so you know who they are."

Belac's face twisted into a scowl as all eyes turned on him and his men.

"He's a snake!" someone shouted, pointing at Belac. "He goes slithering to Lord Ratface—I've seen him!"

Another soldier pointed at one of Belac's companions. "He had my friend arrested for no reason!"

Angry voices began to be heard until a voice bellowed above them all. "It's their turn!"

Loud cries sprang up all around, and Belac and his men were set upon from every side. Horses reared in the confusion, throwing some of Belac's men. Others were dragged from their saddles.

After a few minutes of chaos, the mercenaries were all disarmed. Several of them were dead.

Belac was dragged before Sarjant.

"What's your name?" the burly soldier asked him harshly.

He said nothing, but someone called, "His name is Belac."

"Well, Belac, this is your lucky day. I'm going to let you and your fellow reptiles slither away. You can keep your horses, but you won't be taking weapons or provisions. If you're anywhere near this camp in the next few minutes, consider yourself fair game."

The men around him stripped Belac of his weapons and pushed him to his horse. Only four others were able to mount up behind him. They rode out accompanied by loud jeering from the soldiers. A few of the men pelted them with rocks as they left.

As soon as they were clear of the camp, they reined in their horses.

"What are we going to do?" asked one of the men. "We need to find Redfass. Where did he go?"

"I have no idea," Belac replied, "but it makes no difference. Joining him is pointless. Sarjant has the whole army licking his boots now, and Lord Redfass doesn't have anything like enough men to bring them back into line. We'll head for Arnost. Like as not Lord Redfass will be following us before long."

He squinted off into the east. "Someone needs to get to Lord Lygell and tell him what happened here. When he finds out, he'll sort out this rabble for good."

He clicked his tongue and pointed his horse in the direction of Arnost.

THOMAS SAT on his mount watching the frenzied preparations as soldiers collected their weapons and saddled their horses. He had no idea why he was there. The stone had been almost useless in such a vast crowd, and although he had managed to focus his attention on one bad apple in the barrel, it had made no difference to the outcome. His efforts to warn Rufe about Belac were neither effective nor necessary.

He had been hunting an unknown number of adversaries among a multitude. Rufe had employed the simplest of strategies to flush out the lot of them.

Thomas had never felt more useless.

After dismissing Belac and his companions, Rufe ordered the men to prepare urgently to ride to the aid of Will. Word spread quickly—"Will needs our help!"—and the soldiers sprang immediately into action.

Now Rufe was waiting quietly, watching the men assemble. From the look on Rufe's face, they were taking far too long.

"Why did you let Belac go?" Thomas asked. "He'll take the news back to Pisander and Lygell in Arnost."

"It was Will's idea," Rufe replied. "Pisander and Lygell have had it all their own way so far, and he wanted them to know we've taken control of their army. It's about time they took a turn at guessing and worrying. People make mistakes when they're anxious."

As he was speaking, Rufe's attention was drawn to a soldier he knew. He called the man over. “Where are the other leaders, Timo?” he asked. “And why aren’t you with your men?”

“All of us were either dismissed or demoted,” Timo replied. “You can thank Lord Ratface for that,” he added, spitting contemptuously into the dirt.

It wasn’t the first time Thomas had heard the nickname. The soldiers delivered the title like an obscenity, invariably spitting whenever they used it. Ratface wasn’t his real name of course—one of the soldiers had told them that the western army was commanded by Lord Redfass. He spat twice after speaking the name.

“Ratface appointed new leaders from his own people,” Timo continued. “They called themselves leaders, anyway—most of them were useless. They all went off with him earlier.”

“How many of the original leaders are still here?” Rufe asked.

“A reasonable number,” came the reply.

Rufe nodded. “Round them up! I need to speak with them.”

Timo hurried away.

No more than two or three minutes passed before men began to present themselves to Rufe. He greeted several by name. He waited impatiently until a sizable group had gathered.

“How can we help, Rufe?” one of them asked.

“All of you have your old responsibilities back,” Rufe told them. “If any of the soldiers argue, send them to me. Round everyone up! We can’t wait any longer.”

While they were gone, Rufe moved among the soldiers who had already gathered. He pointed to about a dozen men that he seemed to recognize and drew them aside. “I’ve seen all of you in action,” he told them. “We’re missing too many of our leaders, so consider yourself appointed.” He pointed off to one side. “Go over there and spread yourselves out,” he ordered.

Some of the men looked startled, others looked delighted. All of them moved immediately to the place he indicated.

Rufe faced the soldiers already gathered. “If you don’t have a captain, go attach yourselves to one of these men,” he said, pointing to his new appointees. "They're your new captains. No more than fifty men to each. Move!"

Soldiers who had already reconnected with a captain remained where they were, but others surged across to the new appointees.

Ignoring the chaos of jostling men and horses, Rufe called Timo aside. When he had finished speaking, Timo nodded once and positioned his horse beside Rufe's.

Even before order had entirely emerged, Rufe decided it was time to go.

"We can't wait any longer," he bellowed, "we're moving out. New captains can follow Timo. The rest can follow me."

Thomas didn't stay with Rufe. He had nothing to offer in the fighting that lay ahead. Feeling like useless baggage, he allowed the men to ride by, drifting to the rear of the column.

As the soldiers surged past, Thomas tried to estimate the size of the troop. It was impossible to be certain, but he suspected more than eight hundred were following Rufe.

The thunder of hooves shook the ground as the soldiers rode away in a seemingly endless stream.

Carnwill and his vegetable traders watched the men ride out with considerable interest.

The person trailing behind the giant leader had especially captured Carnwill's attention. He closely fit the description of Thomas Stablehand.

There was a simple way to be certain. Carnwill had learned from King Agon that Thomas's wife was reported to be unusually beautiful. If this was Thomas, his wife wouldn't be far away.

"I'm going to find out where they're headed," Carnwill told his men. "You stay here."

He raced away in pursuit of the soldiers, staying close enough to remain in touch, and far enough away not to be noticed.

Something was happening at last.

THE SENTRIES on the walls of Steffan's Citadel watched curiously as the camp below them slowly emptied. The citadel commander arrived on the battlements as the last of the men disappeared from sight.

"A smaller group—maybe two or three hundred—left earlier, Commander," he was told. "The camp seems empty now, although they haven't packed it up."

The commander looked on silently. "Where are they going?" he wondered aloud. "They've left for a reason, and they're expecting to return."

He turned to an aide. "Get an errand rider. Something's happening, and the duke needs to know."

9

"Let her go!" demanded Breysen.

Kantor sneered at him. "Go find your own hostage."

Something snapped in Breysen. He stepped in front of Kantor menacingly, pulling his knife and bending low in a fighting crouch.

"Get out of my way," growled Kantor.

"Or what?" asked Breysen. "If you slit her throat, your only free pass will be to your grave." He moved closer. "And you'll have to deal with me before you try anything with her."

"That's easily done," snorted Kantor. He hurled his hostage roughly to the ground and lunged at his challenger, his flashing knife almost finishing the fight before it had begun.

Breysen barely managed to lurch out of the way. He'd been in good condition once. But the deprivations of recent days had weakened him, and his reactions had slowed considerably. As Breysen slowly circled, his opponent lunged again. Kantor was weaker himself, though. Breysen swayed out of danger, stretching out with his own knife and nicking Kantor's arm as he withdrew it, drawing blood.

Overcome with fury, Kantor slid forward, sweeping Breysen's feet out from under him. Breysen fell heavily, landing hard on his back. Kantor was astride him in a moment, his knife raised high for a killing thrust.

Before the knife could descend, Breysen grabbed Kantor's arm, desperate to keep the blade away. Kantor drove the knife downward with all his might, bringing it ever closer to his enemy's chest. Breysen's eyes bulged as he struggled to prevent it. He couldn't keep it up for much longer.

Kantor tumbled suddenly forward, a startled look on his face. He collapsed on Breysen, his knife barely missing Breysen on its way down.

Heaving his attacker aside, Breysen stumbled to his feet. Bemused and panting heavily, he peered around anxiously for the queen.

The queen was on her feet, shaken and dusty, but apparently unhurt. Her would-be abductor lay unmoving in the dirt, a knife protruding from his back.

"He isn't the first mercenary to die by my hand," she said shakily, glancing down at her victim with a haunted look in her eyes. "It doesn't get any easier." Her face was pale, and she was trembling.

Hurrying across to her, he offered his arm, and she took it gratefully, leaning heavily on him as she attempted to steady herself.

A robed monk appeared from among the trees. He moved quickly toward them, his eyes flicking from the queen to Breysen and finally to Kantor's body.

"Your Majesty?" he asked, a deep frown upon his face.

Breysen stepped away from the queen as the big man approached, surprisingly apprehensive. He'd never been anxious around monks before, but this man was no ordinary monk. His face might radiate calm, but there was something perilous about him.

The queen shook her head as the monk took her arm. "You needn't be concerned about him, Brother Ander," she said, nodding at Breysen. "He nearly lost his life defending me from the other one."

The monk turned briefly away. "Her Majesty needs help!" he called loudly. Then he returned his attention to the queen.

Soldiers raced toward them, a more lavishly dressed man not far behind. Breysen realized at once that he was looking at the king.

When King Steffan reached his wife, the monk also relinquished her arm and positioned himself beside Breysen.

The king took his wife by the shoulders and drew her into a quick embrace. Then he stood back, examining her carefully.

"Are you hurt?" he asked, his voice shaking with agitation.

"I'm fine," she assured him.

The king glanced at Breysen, then locked eyes with the monk, his eyebrows raised questioningly.

The monk seemed to understand the unspoken request. He bowed. "I will join you shortly, Your Majesty," he said.

The king nodded once. Then he turned back to his wife and ushered her quickly away.

A couple of soldiers moved to the body of Kantor. After removing the queen's knife, they turned him over to examine him. Others headed into the surrounding trees. No doubt those protecting the king and queen would be doubly alert after what had happened.

Ignoring the soldiers, the big monk placed a hand on Breysen's shoulder. Breysen started at the touch, but the monk's grip was surprisingly gentle as he steered him away.

"I'm Brother Ander," said the monk.

"My name is Breysen," he returned nervously.

"Where are you from, Breysen?" Brother Ander asked in a friendly tone.

"From a small village near Danford."

The monk nodded. He jerked his head toward Breysen's former companion. "Who was he?" he asked.

"His name was Kantor. I didn't really know him—we stumbled upon each other a couple of days ago." He passed a hand across his face. Had it really been only a couple of days?

"And what brings you here to the forest?" asked the monk.

Breysen's heart skipped a beat. What could he say that wouldn't betray his role as a mercenary? If these people discovered what he had been doing, he would be finished. His brain seemed frozen. He couldn't find an answer to the monk's question.

After an awkward silence, Brother Ander looked him up and down. "You look famished," he said cheerfully.

Breysen nodded dumbly. He hadn't answered the monk's question, and the possible consequences of that omission filled him with apprehension. Nevertheless, the thought of food drove all else from his mind.

The monk led him to a clearing occupied by the king and queen. They were accompanied by a woman of unusual beauty, a couple of men, and several soldiers. The beautiful woman had been holding a small baby, and she was in the act of handing it to the queen. An older man cuddled a small child. Beside him stood a man whose features suggested he was foreign, possibly even Rogandan.

A delicious smell drew Breysen's attention to a pot of hot food, apparently prepared over a fire by some of the soldiers. He tried to restrain his eagerness, but having spotted the food he couldn't keep his eyes off it.

Brother Ander introduced him around. He bowed to the king and queen and tried with limited success to pay attention to the other faces and the names that went with them.

The queen was the first to speak. "I haven't thanked you for defending me," she said, looking at Breysen earnestly.

He felt his face redden. "You were the one who saved me, Your Majesty," he managed, bowing low once more.

The queen waved off his comment. "You look hungry," she said. "Please, take as much food as you want."

He thanked her sincerely, and she rewarded him with a gentle smile that reached to her eyes.

A soldier handed him a plate laden with stew, and he accepted it wide-eyed. How long had it been since he last enjoyed a proper meal?

Sitting down, he directed his full attention to the food. It occurred to him that he shouldn't embarrass himself, but before long he abandoned all restraint, shoveling down the stew with a zeal that bordered on desperation. When the plate was empty, he sat back and closed his eyes. An involuntary sigh of deep contentment escaped his lips.

A stifled laugh startled him back to reality. He opened his eyes to discover every single person staring at him, many of them grinning broadly.

"You haven't eaten for a while," observed the king.

He blushed deeply again.

"I'm sure we all have things to do," said the king pointedly, and the clearing abruptly filled with bustle.

Another plate laden with food was offered to Breysen. He took it gratefully, trying not to feel too ashamed.

He managed to show a measure of restraint as he ate this time. As he methodically chewed and swallowed, he noticed the king conversing quietly with Brother Ander. The king was doing most of the talking, the monk mostly contributing an occasional nod.

His attention was drawn irresistibly back to the food though, and he soon ignored everything else as he focused on eating.

Before long Breysen was startled out of his absorption. Both men joined him, sitting on the ground before him. He froze, his mouth full of half chewed food.

"Thank you for defending the queen," began the king. "We owe you a debt of gratitude."

Breysen dipped his head awkwardly.

"You've stumbled upon us at a sensitive time," the king continued. "We cannot afford for our whereabouts to become known." He looked Breysen in the eye. "We're going to need you to remain with us for the moment. I hope you will understand."

Breysen nodded, not sure if a response was expected. He sincerely hoped not—he had no idea what to say, and he could hardly speak with his mouth stuffed full of food.

The king fell silent. Breysen glanced at Brother Ander, and the monk caught his eye.

He couldn't look away. His eyes grew wide, and his heart skipped a beat, a wave of panic threatening to overwhelm him. The monk could see right through him—he was certain of it. Those eyes seemed to penetrate his defenses, laying bare his every secret.

Breysen swallowed convulsively, grimacing as the partially chewed food made its slow and painful journey down his throat. His hand trembled as he put down the plate, his eyes flicking to the king as he did so. The monarch was studying him with a thoughtful expression on his face.

Breysen stole another glance at Brother Ander. The monk too was gazing intensely at him, although nothing now seemed unusual about his regard. Had Breysen just imagined his earlier impression?

He felt exposed and vulnerable. Surely these men must have pieced together where he'd come from. Someone might have told the king that a pair of mercenaries had slipped through the patrols at the edge of the forest. If so, he would also know that one of his guards had been butchered during the escape. Breysen felt the blood drain from his face.

And yet the king hadn't called for his immediate execution. Not yet, anyway. When Kantor had taken the queen, Breysen had leaped instinctively to her defense. Had that act saved him?

He managed to look more calmly at the two men again, lowering his head respectfully after little more than a glance at the king.

"You've clearly been through some difficult times," said the king. "I've asked Brother Ander to look after you. He will make sure you get whatever you need." He nodded to the monk. "Thank you, Brother Ander," he said. Then he got to his feet and moved away, leaving Breysen alone with the monk.

A couple of soldiers swung in behind him as he left. They had been hovering protectively nearby the whole time. Breysen hadn't noticed.

The moment the king had gone, Breysen discovered that his body had been almost rigid with tension. He abruptly went limp, feeling as though he had just emerged from a physical pummeling. A long, shuddering sigh escaped from his lungs.

Brother Ander looked at him calmly. He gave Breysen a few moments to settle himself, then he asked, "How do you earn your living?" His tone was friendly rather than accusatory, but Breysen guessed that a great deal might be riding on his answers.

"I'm a blacksmith," Breysen replied without conscious thought. He was relieved to note that it hadn't even occurred to him to say he was a mercenary.

"At least I've been a blacksmith since I married. I was a sailor before that."

The monk raised his eyebrows in curiosity. "A sailor? Did you grow up in Maranelle?"

"No, although I've been there many times. My mother was Arvenian, but my father was originally from Varas. I was born in Varacellan, the capital of Varas. It's a major seaport—ships of all sizes go there. I grew up around ships, and I went to sea with my father from the time I was a child. I expected to become a sailor myself. Then he was badly injured and couldn't sail anymore. We moved to Danford."

"And you became a blacksmith?"

"Not at first. The mouth of the River Dan is at Varacellan, but the river flows all the way from Danford to the sea. When we arrived in Danford I spent my time on river boats at first. I only became a blacksmith after I married and moved to my wife's village."

Brother Ander pondered this information silently. After a couple of minutes he pointed off into the trees. "One of the horses seems to have a problem with its shoe," he said. "Would you be willing to take a look?"

"Certainly," Breysen replied. He guessed that the monk was testing his story, but he didn't care. He was desperate to do anything that might make him useful to these people.

He followed Brother Ander to where the horses were tethered. For a brief moment he was almost overwhelmed by a wild urge to jump on a horse and flee, but he mastered the impulse. Quite apart from the soldier guarding the horses, something told him that the monk might not stand by and watch him gallop away.

He allowed himself to be led to a horse that was clearly favoring one leg. The animal seemed uncomfortable whenever the leg touched the ground.

Lifting the leg, he thoroughly examined the hoof. His attention was immediately drawn to a telltale white spot on the hoof. Both the monk and the soldier came closer and watched over his shoulder.

"It appears to be an abscess," he said, looking up at them. "It doesn't look too serious. Do you have any cloth I can use to wrap the hoof?"

"I'll get some," the soldier replied, and hurried off to the main campsite.

"Can you please soak it in water?" Breysen called after him.

The soldier soon returned and handed Breysen a large piece of cloth, dripping wet.

Breysen tore off a long strip of the cloth, intending to use it to secure the cloth to the horse's leg.

Pulling out his knife, he carefully exposed the pus. "It will drain away when the horse lowers its foot," he explained. Then he folded the moist cloth several times and placed it over the hoof, tying it into position with the long strip.

"This will act as a poultice to encourage the pus to drain," he said. "It will also prevent dirt or other material from getting into the hole while it's healing. The horse shouldn't be ridden for a few days."

Brother Ander thanked him and led him away from the horses. When they came to a quiet place they both sat down.

"You appear to know what you're doing," said the monk.

The comment came with a smile of encouragement, but Breysen shrugged uncomfortably. "I enjoy my work," he said. "I just wish I could still do it."

Brother Ander looked puzzled. "What do you mean?"

He sighed. "My wife comes from a small village. It's big enough to support a blacksmith, but only barely. I was able to support my wife and children. We never had any coin to spare, but we got by. Then the Rogandans invaded. Our local baron came to our village to collect men to join the king's army. He told me the army needed blacksmiths. He didn't offer me a choice of course—I had to go with him." He shook his head. "I soon discovered that the army already had plenty of blacksmiths."

Brother Ander nodded. "We had more skilled people than we needed. Those who weren't needed ended up as soldiers."

Breysen looked at him with raised eyebrows. "You were in the army?" He wasn't entirely surprised at the thought. He'd sensed from the beginning that there was more to this monk than met the eye.

"Yes," confirmed Brother Ander with a nod. "I haven't been a monk all my life. How did your family manage while you were away?"

The question poked at painful memories, and Breysen closed his eyes for a moment in an attempt to control his emotions. "Without me there to provide for them, they struggled to survive. When I returned, after the fighting was over, my wife was so thin it scared me. She'd almost wasted away. She looked like she'd aged ten years. There was nowhere near enough food for the children either. In the time I was gone, two of them had weakened and died." Tears welled up in his eyes, and he dashed them away with his arm.

"Did you return to your blacksmithing?"

"I intended to, but while I was gone a young man had started out on his own. He'd been my apprentice when the Rogandans came. He'd injured his leg, so the baron didn't take him as a soldier. As soon as his leg recovered he married, so he had a wife to support as well. There wasn't enough work for both of us."

"Why didn't one of you move?" asked the monk. "Surely other villages could have used a blacksmith."

Breysen looked at him blankly. "How could we do that? My wife's family has lived in that village for generations. Where would I take her? And who'd want strangers moving into their village anyway?"

Brother Ander nodded slowly. "I understand. It was like that where I grew up too. People thought that moving to the next village was migrating to a foreign country. I left to become a soldier when I was still young, and my father was completely baffled when I left. He could never understand why I stayed away." He shrugged, then redirected his attention to Breysen. "What did you do?" he asked.

"Both my wife and I turned our hands to anything that came along. None of it was enough though."

"So you agreed to become a mercenary?"

The abrupt question shocked Breysen, and he stiffened, staring back at the monk out of startled eyes. So the monk really could see right through him. His shoulders slumped in defeat. There was no use pretending. He was exposed now, and he had nowhere to go.

"Yes, it's true. Hazor sent out scouts around the countryside. Once he heard I'd fought at Torbury Scarp he wanted to recruit me. He offered money—a lot of it. He told me our role would be to keep the peace, nothing more, and I believed him." He paused for a moment, stealing a glance at the monk. "I suppose it would be more honest to say I chose to believe him." Breysen shook his head. "It did start out innocently enough."

He sighed deeply. "I gave my wife the initial payment before I left. She'd never seen that much money before. For the first time in years I saw a glimmer of hope in her eyes again, and it convinced me I was doing the right thing. I told her there would be a lot more when I got back. There won't be any more now of course—maybe there never would have been." He ran a shaky hand through his hair. "She won't have used it all yet—she's incredibly thrifty—but when it does run out she'll be destitute again. It will be worse than ever."

He buried his face in his hands.

"You said it started out innocently," said Brother Ander. "What went wrong?"

"After we'd been out on patrol a while we started pursuing a group of armed men. It went very badly for us. After a while I heard a rumor that our real targets were the king and the queen." He nodded in the direction of the campfire.

"I confronted Hazor with the rumor. He was furious with me, but he didn't deny it. I lost all interest in fighting for him then, but what could I do? I couldn't just ride away. Or maybe I didn't have the courage to do it." He hung his head.

He fell silent. As the moments dragged slowly by he discovered, somewhat to his own surprise, that he didn't care about being exposed as much as he'd expected. He was sick to his stomach of feeling conflicted. His unease had grown stronger the longer he worked for Hazor, and he was bone weary of it.

A minor commotion at the campsite distracted his attention. One of the soldiers seemed to have brought in a couple of men to speak with the king. They conversed in low voices for a couple of minutes, then all eyes turned in his direction. The interaction continued for a while longer, before the king appeared to dismiss them. The soldier led them away.

As soon as they were gone, the king headed over to Breysen and the monk, flanked by two of his soldiers.

He faced Breysen, his countenance stern and unyielding. "It seems that you've had trackers on your trail, Breysen. Why are you here?" he asked bluntly. "And why were you traveling with a man who took the queen hostage and threatened her life?"

Breysen's heart sank. He opened his mouth to speak, but nothing came out.

"He originally came here with a group of mercenaries, Your Majesty, led by a man named Hazor," said Brother Ander calmly.

"I am now aware of that," the king replied. "You need to explain yourself," he said to Breysen. He spoke severely, but he appeared willing to listen.

Breysen swallowed. "I was a mercenary, Your Majesty, and I won't pretend otherwise," he said miserably. "I'm only here by accident. Several days ago we were led into battle not far from here. There were plenty of rumors flying, and they said we'd be fighting men led by Will Prentis. We'd been told he was a traitor, but I never believed it. I fought under him at Torbury Scarp, and there was no way I was going to fight him or kill any of his men. I didn't know when I joined that we would ever be asked to fight our own people. As soon as the battle started I concealed myself. I knew it would be seen as the act of a coward, but I didn't care.

"Almost all of Hazor's men were killed. The only reason I survived was because I avoided the fighting. I hid in the forest and waited a few days until the moon was covered with clouds. Kantor, the man who attacked the queen, showed up as I was about to leave. I'd never met him before. Both of us got away on a sentry's horse. Kantor knifed the sentry as we were leaving. There was no need to kill him—I'd knocked the man unconscious."

He stared off in the direction of the campfire. "Kantor would have killed the queen as well if he thought it would benefit him. I think he enjoyed killing. He was never my friend, and I regret having played any part in helping him escape."

The king made no immediate response, and Breysen lowered his head in despair.

Of all the people he could have stumbled upon, why did it have to be the royal party?

10

Lady Ona sat calmly on the windowsill of her suite, gazing down across the rooftops of Arnost. She liked almost everything she had seen of this city.

The day she arrived she had dressed as a commoner and hidden her face, then she had wandered among the markets and mingled with the people. Two things were immediately obvious to her. First, the grinding poverty so prevalent in Rog was much less evident in the capital of Arvenon. Second, a mantle of fear had settled over the city. She was used to that in Rog, but somehow it felt out of place in Arnost.

Her inquiries indicated that the mood of the city had changed the moment Pisander and his minions took control. The new masters intended to stamp their authority from the very beginning, and enough people had been hanged for one reason or another to ensure that the populace got the point.

Pisander had based himself in the castle, and it came as no surprise that the biggest changes had taken place there. Many of the former castle servants had quickly abandoned their posts, and by all accounts the people brought in to replace them left much to be desired. The kitchens had clearly been affected—thus far the quality of her food had been disappointing. Cold seemed to ooze out of the walls of any castle, and she'd needed to get angry before fires were lit and properly maintained in her suite.

Even so, she had noticed a cheerful straightforwardness about the people in the markets that hadn't been entirely stifled by the city's new masters. She wondered whether such buoyancy could long survive the arrival of Agon.

Standing up, she stretched luxuriously, delighted at the prospect of an extended period out of the saddle. Her second morning in Arnost had dawned, and it was time she began to stir the pot. An impressive wardrobe had accompanied her on the long journey from Rogand, and she picked her way through the finery, selecting garments in her usual calculated way. On this occasion she wanted to strike a balance between intimidating and provocative. Having arrived with a clear strategy, she intended to waste no time implementing it.

A large mirror had been provided for her use, and she positioned herself before it while her maid fussed around her.

When finally she was satisfied, she sent her maid to fetch a servant who could lead her to Pisander.

The former earl was occupied with one of his soldiers when she arrived. He nevertheless waved her to a chair.

"Where was this disturbance?" he demanded of the soldier.

"In the markets, My Lord," the man replied. "Two of the merchants were complaining loudly about the policies of the current administration."

"Hang them both," Pisander said coldly. "Leave their bodies dangling on the edge of the market square for a few days. The other merchants will benefit from the example."

He dismissed the soldier curtly, and the man departed after a quick bow.

Lady Ona observed the interaction with interest. The punishment might have been excessive considering the offense, but it was consistent with what she knew of Pisander's approach. She couldn't help wondering if the extreme response was partly for her benefit.

The former earl turned to her. "Lady Ona, this is Lord Lygell," he said, nodding toward the official who stood beside him. "I have entrusted him with oversight of Arvenon."

Lygell nodded stiffly. He appeared restless.

Pisander stared at her dispassionately for a moment. "You seem to have made yourself comfortable, My Lady," he observed dryly. He pointed at a parchment that had traveled with her from Rog. "I see that King Agon has requested me to grant you extraordinary powers during your stay in Arnost."

She smiled to herself. Agon wasn't the kind of man who 'requested' anything, and she had no doubt that Pisander understood that as well as she did. "I am sure you and your aides will support me wholeheartedly in my endeavors," she said, fixing both men with a steely gaze.

Pisander seemed bored. "Of course," he replied languidly. "Lygell will provide you with anything you need."

She nodded slowly, redirecting her attention to Lygell. "Tomorrow I will confer with the official responsible for collecting taxes, and also the person who manages the central market. But today I want to meet whoever oversees garbage collection in Arnost. The entire city stinks!" she declared, screwing up her nose in disgust.

Before her comment, Lygell had already been looking uncomfortable. His face now colored red, whether from anger or embarrassment she couldn't tell.

She stared back at him. "You will attend of course," she informed him. "We will meet as soon as I have broken my fast."

With that she gave both men a curt nod, and left the room.

Having established herself in a meeting room provided for her personal use, Lady Ona waited impatiently for Lygell and his underling to arrive.

King Agon had granted her sweeping powers, but she was well aware that respect could not be granted by decree—she needed to build respect herself. She would establish her authority by her actions. She wasn't concerned. She was an ambitious and capable leader with no compunction about manipulating people whenever the need arose.

She needed to start somewhere, and the issue she had seized upon would serve her purposes as well as any. It would give her insight into how administration was handled in the city. And observing how Pisander's people reacted to her intervention would also be very revealing.

Lygell marched into the room, annoyance showing plainly on his face. Having become expert at reading the signs, she could see that he was strongly attracted to her. He was probably irritated by his own response, which would undoubtedly contribute to his frustration. She suppressed a smile. She had no doubt she would win his enthusiastic cooperation before long, one way or another.

The minor official ushered into her presence by Lygell appeared terrified. He had no need to be. Not yet, anyway.

"I am told you are responsible for keeping the streets clean," she told him, keeping her tone neutral.

He shot a glance in the direction of Lygell before nodding once.

"How many people work for you?"

"Fifty," he replied.

She raised her eyebrows. "How many of them actually do their job?"

"Maybe five or six," he replied bitterly.

"And what have you done about it?" she asked patiently.

He looked baffled. "I've threatened to dismiss them. But it hasn't helped."

She nodded. The man was clearly incompetent. The only question that remained was whether he was capable of improvement.

"Here's what you're going to do..." she told him.

Two hours later Lady Ona looked on as the official stood before a small crowd of scruffy men and women in the courtyard.

"Everything is about to change," he told them importantly.

"Beginning right now. I pay you to clean the streets, and you will spend the rest of the day doing it. Then I will assess your work. We will meet here again tomorrow at the same time. If you're not here, you will be hunted down and punished. You are dismissed! Get to work!"

Once they had gone he looked toward Lady Ona expectantly. She nodded her approval.

The following day the official once again met his workers in the courtyard. A count was carried out, and two of them were missing.

A group of guards waited nearby. The official called four of them aside and gave them names and descriptions of the malingerers. "Search for them," he instructed the guards loudly. "When you find them, hang them. They're lazy incompetents, and I've given them too many chances already."

The guards glanced at Lygell. He nodded once, and they hurried away.

Lady Ona rolled her eyes at the garbage official's response. She had no real complaint though—he'd grasped the general idea even if he was a little enthusiastic.

The other workers now watched wide-eyed as the official turned to them. He called one of them forward. It was a woman, and she was trembling uncontrollably as she came to him.

"You've done your job well," he told her. "Your section was the cleanest in the city. Here's your reward." He pressed a couple of coins into her hands. She returned to her place with a look of delighted astonishment on her face.

He called ten other names, and the men and women he had named stepped forward eagerly, all with greed written across their faces. The official glared at them. "Good-for-nothing layabouts!" he yelled. He turned to the remaining guards. "Throw them into the dungeons!" he ordered. "Don't release them until this time tomorrow."

The ten were dragged away screaming and pleading. When they were gone, the official turned to the remaining workers. He had their undivided attention. "You've all seen how things are going to work from now on. You will be paid if you do your jobs properly. Anyone who is lazy will receive a more appropriate reward. Now go and do what you were hired to do!"

When he dismissed them they scurried away, eager to be gone.

Lady Ona was impressed. She approached the official and ruffled his hair indulgently. "Well done," she told him with a little smile. He beamed back at her happily.

Lord Lygell had watched the process silently. As soon as the official had gone, Lygell approached her boldly. Executing a sweeping bow, he invited her to join him for dinner.

The man was pitifully transparent. She kept him hanging for a few moments before accepting his invitation.

She walked away shaking her head. These people weren't going to know what hit them when Agon arrived.

Lady Ona's initiative with the garbage collection official was just the beginning. Not all of the officials proved to be equally cooperative or teachable, and her efforts yielded mixed outcomes. A few had conspicuously failed to produce results, and she made sure that Lygell threw the worst of them into the dungeons. She didn't offer him a choice. He had appointed the officials, and she suspected that many were personal friends or even relatives. If so, he had no one to blame but himself.

Lygell had exclusively appointed men to positions of authority. Capable women were surely available, and he was the loser by overlooking them.

Ona was a woman with many talents, and she had never limited herself to administration. From the moment of her arrival in Arnost she had begun preparing for more interesting pursuits, and it suited her just fine that Lygell's officials were all men. It made her task that much easier.

Her restless energies had soon been directed along a familiar path. As usual, her endeavors were rewarded with success. As a conspicuously attractive and blatantly available woman, she received attention from a long line of hopefuls among the officials below Pisander. She made no attempt to discourage them.

A few days had now passed since her arrival, and she had set the whole castle buzzing. She had every intention of ensuring it stayed that way.

On that particular afternoon, she followed her usual practice after a meeting, returning to her apartments to change her garments.

As the special envoy of King Agon, Lady Ona had been assigned a lavishly appointed suite in the castle. In the days since her arrival in Arnost she had already added to the imposing array of fine clothing that traveled with her from Rog. Her wardrobe could only be described as formidable. Having selected a dazzling outfit, she occupied her usual position in front of the mirror while her maid prepared her to return to the fray.

Satisfied with her appearance at last, she stepped into the passageway and made her stately way down to the lower levels of the castle.

Having reached ground level, she stepped out into the courtyard to find herself confronted with a heated argument between two men. They abruptly fell silent the moment she appeared, the flush on their faces making it obvious that she had been the subject of their disagreement.

Someone abruptly took her arm, and she looked up into the smiling and handsome features of another of Lygell's self-appointed noblemen. As he led her away from the quarrelers, she aimed a wink in their direction. She couldn't tell if they noticed or not—they were too busy glaring at their supplanter.

Lady Ona shook her head as she turned away. Men could be such babies.

The upheaval was entirely her doing of course. Since her arrival she had been stoking the flames tirelessly. Arnost had provided her with a marvelous new stage on which to strut. None of Pisander's men had any inkling of her existence, and they greeted her arrival with the same open mouthed wonder that a simple shepherd boy might afford a meteor as it flashed across the evening sky.

She boldly flaunted both herself and the authority she enjoyed as Agon's representative. Physical allure and raw power made for a heady mixture, and it was hardly surprising that few could resist.

She never hesitated to take the initiative, although her actions were always understated and indirect.

In Arvenon no less than in Rogand, men and women used subtle hints to communicate availability and degree of interest. Such communication transcended language and custom, and Lady Ona had attained unrivaled mastery at the delicate dance.

The man now at her side had first approached her at a banquet the previous night. They had exchanged a series of charged glances that spoke more eloquently than words. Ona had been anticipating the outcome with considerable interest ever since.

Not everyone succumbed to her glittering intensity. As she glided along beside her new admirer she caught sight of one of the few men who had chosen to ignore her charms. His eyes slid across her as they passed, and she gazed thoughtfully at his retreating back.

She had glimpsed him with a woman of his own hanging on his arm. The woman could not have been called a beauty. Nevertheless it seemed apparent that he had made promises to her, and it was even possible he intended to keep them.

While Lady Ona respected the man's self-restraint, she had no more interest in him than he had in her. People like him bored her.

She returned her attention to her latest paramour. Before they managed to leave the castle grounds their progress was interrupted by the arrival of Lord Lygell. Moving at once to intercept the couple, he approached with chin held high, not deigning even to spare her companion a glance.

"My Lady Ona," he sniffed, thrusting out an arm possessively.

"My Lord Lygell," she replied coldly. "Perhaps you hadn't noticed that my attentions are otherwise engaged at the moment."

Lygell stared back at her dumbfounded. She deftly steered her companion around him.

She didn't bother to glance back to see Lygell's reaction. After her arrival she had allowed the puppet ruler of Arvenon to wine and dine her. He hoped to lure her to his bedchamber as well, but she had declined haughtily. She nevertheless kept him dangling, allowing him to parade about with her on his arm. As a result Lygell dared to imagine he had made a conquest. The fool was about to make the painful discovery that she wasn't the one conquered.

Lady Ona leaned closer to the man at her side. "I trust you are willing to brave the displeasure of your master," she ventured.

His reply was a dismissive snort, and she patted his arm approvingly.

A FEW DAYS later Lady Ona retired to her apartments to review her progress. She had made considerable inroads in her efforts to understand the fledgling power structures of the new Arvenon. Pisander had dredged up officials who were eager to lead, and given them the appearance of credibility by allowing many of them to call themselves nobles. All of them excelled at infighting. Beyond that, the vast majority had little or no idea about effective administration. She had poked and prodded them into action, managing to spearhead a few worthwhile changes in the process, but her view was that many officials were beyond help, from her or anyone else.

The former earl was an obvious exception. To begin with, he was a capable and effective leader much of the time, unlike the majority of his underlings. He was, of course, twisted and unscrupulous, and his methods were frequently inhuman. She could see why Agon had recruited him.

He also seemed immune to her charms. She couldn't quite put her finger on the reason, but if she was reading him correctly it had nothing to do with his proclivities.

His disinterest in her was by no means the strangest thing about him though. There were ways in which he seemed completely vacant, as if portions of his thinking process had gone missing entirely.

For the most part Pisander had reasons for everything he did, and he was both willing and able to articulate those reasons clearly.

When it had anything to do with Agon though, Pisander planned and took action without ever articulating reasons for his behavior.

She shook her head. That wasn't quite right. It wasn't just that Pisander never articulated his reasons—he behaved as if he didn't have reasons. That made no sense.

It brought to mind an experience on a recent visit to the coast near Rog. As a child she had stayed in a pretty cottage perched at the top of a cliff. Finding herself in the area she had sought out the location, eager to savor again the fresh sea air and spectacular views.

Upon arrival she was baffled to find no sign of the cottage. The sea still sparkled and the cliff still towered above it, but something wasn't right. After inquiring of the locals, she was astonished to learn that a large section of cliff had crumbled into the sea, carrying the house with it.

In the same way, some parts of Pisander's thinking processes had seemingly disappeared. Curiously, she'd noticed very similar behavior from Lord Krasmir in Rogand the last time she met with him.

Something strange was going on. Was it possible that Agon had a hand in it? She decided to make an extra effort to keep her eyes and ears open.

Her attention had by no means been focused entirely on Pisander of course. She had cut a swath through the new nobility of Arvenon, most of them proving powerless in the face of her beguilement.

Privately she held her starry eyed admirers in contempt. Bedding them held no interest for her and hadn't proven necessary even once; most of her admirers would have been astonished if they knew how disinclined she had been in that regard. She had been amused to discover that a number of the hopefuls believed they alone had missed out. Perhaps over time they would learn, as she had, that reputation should never be confused with reality.

Her most important conquest had been Lord Lygell, the vain peacock placed in authority over the kingdom by Pisander. She had used him shamelessly to rapidly expand both her influence and her notoriety.

Lygell was a devious man with grand ideas. The real question was whether he could follow through successfully. She had been singularly unimpressed by most of what she had witnessed.

The man had a vicious streak and had taken prodigious advantage of it. After sufficient exposure to him she concluded that he was unwittingly compensating for a deeply rooted lack of confidence. Once or twice she'd been tempted to croon in his ear, "There, there. Didn't daddy take you seriously?"

She smiled wryly to herself, trying to imagine how he might react to such behavior. Violently, if she knew anything. She'd have been forced to kill him, and that might have led to misunderstandings.

No, she was better off humoring him. She'd be doing it from a distance in future. Sooner or later he'd get over the humiliation of being dumped by her.

A servant appeared at her doorway. "The Earl of Pisander requests that you join him," he said with a bow.

Her curiosity aroused, she left her apartments and followed the man to the upper reaches of the castle. On the way they passed Lord Lygell. Peering at her inquisitively, he swung in behind her and followed tentatively in her wake.

She soon arrived at a small meeting room to find Pisander standing beside the window waiting for her. The servant bowed and excused himself.

Lygell had followed her to the entrance of the room, and he stood peering in with a look of mingled envy and annoyance. Adopting a prim smile, she moved serenely to the door and closed it in his startled face.

She turned back to Pisander. "My Lord Earl, I believe you requested to see me. What is your pleasure?" she asked boldly.

He stared at her for a moment, an unreadable expression on his face.

"I have found you to be...accomplished," he said. "You get things done. You have a way of drawing the best from people, even as you manipulate them. And you don't hesitate to fully use your... formidable assets."

The unexpected compliments brought a pert smile to her face. She offered him a slight bow.

Pisander continued. “I have a task I wish to offer you, one that requires unusual delicacy. A successful outcome would lead to further opportunities. I am sure I don’t need to state that the inducements would be considerable.”

She stared back at him coolly. “You have people of your own. Assign the task to one of them.”

His brows drew together in a deep frown. “Far too many of my subordinates disappoint me,” he said. He shook his head. He mumbled, almost to himself, “I have need of a Will Prentis, or someone very like him.”

Her eyebrows rose at once. “There’s that name again,” she said thoughtfully. “I would very much like to meet this Will Prentis. I have heard a great deal about him, and he sounds uncommonly promising.” She twirled a finger around a loose strand of her dangling hair, lost in her imaginings.

Pisander glowered at her. “Are you refusing my offer?”

“I am,” she told him bluntly. “King Agon didn’t send me here to become one of your paid lackeys. You have been appointed by the king to act on his behalf, and I am here to report on your effectiveness. I plan to do just that. No more, and no less.”

She turned on her heel and glided from the room without bothering to wait for Pisander’s reaction.

Lygell was skulking in the corridor, and he reached out hesitantly to her as she approached. Lady Ona ignored him, sweeping past without a backward glance.

11

Pleasant as Arnost might be, Lady Ona soon decided she was ready to leave. She quickly wearied of the men who fawned incessantly upon her. Some of them boasted openly to anyone who would listen about their supposed exploits with the foreign beauty. She shook her head in disdain. They were equally pathetic. It would be refreshing just for once to meet a real man in this former kingdom.

Pisander was the only reasonably capable leader among them, even if she couldn't entirely figure him out. As for Lygell, although he wielded significant authority, he was heavily reliant on his underlings to make him look good, and most of them were not delivering.

Agon had reason to be gravely concerned.

Pisander's attempt to recruit her had also made her curious. What were the crucial tasks he needed her to carry out? She immediately began digging. The results were revealing.

Pisander controlled Arnost and the surrounding countryside. She was not aware of any organized resistance. She had briefly visited the dungeons to observe Lord Bottren, the man placed in charge of Arnost by King Steffan when he left for Paradise Valley. She didn't understand the reasons why Pisander kept him alive, but whatever they might be it was clear that Bottren offered no threat. He was a shell of the man he must once have been.

Two Arvenian armies still existed, both under the control of men appointed by Pisander. One was camped to the west outside Erestor, and the other to the north on the border with Castel. She had learned that these armies largely consisted of veterans of the war with Rogand, which suggested they were formidable fighting units. However, since they had been given no recent tasks to perform, it was impossible to form any assessment of their new leadership or their current effectiveness.

One very serious concern had emerged. The attempt to assassinate the rulers of Arvenon, Castel, and Varas had met with limited success, with the king of Castel the only confirmed kill. No one could state with certainty that either King Steffan or Queen Essanda was dead.

In view of that, Lygell had sent two large squads to Paradise Valley with orders to finish off the Arvenian king and queen. Neither squad had reported back.

Unconfirmed reports suggested that a large body of men had been seen riding in the opposite direction, away from Paradise Valley. No reports of any kind had been received since then. Lygell's men had apparently vanished from the face of the earth.

If Lady Ona had been placed in charge of Arvenon, she would have found this information very disturbing indeed. She would have placed the highest priority on getting to the bottom of it.

Decisive action was clearly needed in a number of crucial areas. Lygell held the reins of power, but the man was paralyzed. He seemed more concerned about Lady Ona's indifference toward him than about fulfilling his responsibilities.

Pisander clearly harbored many frustrations about his underlings, and with good reason. It wasn't difficult to see why he had tried to recruit her.

In spite of the challenges faced by Pisander, Lady Ona could only marvel at how much the disgraced exile had achieved. It was true that King Steffan and Queen Essanda had not yet been accounted for, but

Pisander's accomplishments were nevertheless remarkable. He had wrested control of Arvenon, or at least Arnost and most of Arvenon, from the ruling monarchs. The assassination attempt had been accompanied by a smooth and rapid takeover of the capital. The entire Arvenian army had quickly been placed under the command of men loyal to Pisander. The magnitude of these achievements should not be understated.

At the same time, it was equally obvious that after seizing power so effectively, Pisander was finding the task of wielding power considerably more challenging.

To function well, a kingdom required more than just willing leaders. An endless list of routine but essential roles needed to be carried out by competent people. The garbage disposal system in Arnost offered a perfect example. Until her intervention, it had been heading for collapse. Sooner or later the result would have been disease and death, with the rich and powerful suffering along with the poor.

There was a limit to how much she could achieve, and it had become obvious to Lady Ona that little could be gained by remaining in Arnost. She accordingly began making preparations to return to Rog. Pisander offered no response of any kind when she notified him of her plans. She didn't bother even to inform Lygell.

King Agon had sent her to review the overall strategic situation in Arvenon, and to get the measure of Pisander and his henchmen. She had done what she came to do.

The king wasn't going to be at all happy when he heard her report.

KING AGON STARED WILDLY at Ennawi, his eyes almost popping out of his head. Agon's heart was pounding, and he could feel his veins standing out. He ground his teeth noisily before tilting his head back and shouting at the top of his voice.

The king turned away without bothering to see if his mute

servant had registered a reaction. A response of any kind was so unlikely it wasn't worth checking for.

A small figurine lay on a side table in his apartments. Reaching down for it, the king hurled it across the room. The sight of the ornament hitting the wall and shattering into pieces felt intensely satisfying. His breathing began to slow, and his heart gradually stopped racing.

When he was almost feeling normal again he turned back to his servant. "Did you know who summoned Krasmir to Rog?" he asked calmly. "It was me! I wanted to brief him on the practicalities of ruling. I can't hand over power without some kind of preparation."

He threw up his hands. "I even thought I might pass on some of the subtleties. What made me think it was going to be straightforward?"

Agon drew closer to Ennawi and peered into his eyes. "Krasmir's a complete idiot. Why didn't any of my servants warn me?" He jabbed a finger into Ennawi's chest. "Why didn't *you* warn me?"

The king released a huge sigh. "I'm meeting with the fool again in the morning. Did you know I've been avoiding my sword, Ennawi?" he asked. "Sometimes I feel my hand twitching for it." He reached out a trembling hand and examined it.

"I can't trust myself with a sword. It wouldn't matter if I decapitated one of my servants—you, for instance. No one would care. But I'd end up lopping off Krasmir's head, and that would make the last three weeks a complete waste of my time. Worse, I'd be leaving for Arnost without a regent."

He clenched and unclenched his fists. Then he closed his eyes and took another deep breath. Finally he left his apartments, still struggling to keep his composure.

Two agents were brought to the king as soon as he had settled himself into the small reception chamber adjoining his private apartments. The king came immediately to the point. "Well? What have you learned about Krasmir?" he asked bluntly.

"He has a reputation for brutality, Your Majesty," one of them said.

"I know that," snapped the king.

The agent hesitated. "It seems that the reputation is not well founded," he finally added.

Agon frowned. "What? Impossible! What are you talking about?"

"Our sources suggest that Lord Krasmir has encouraged false rumors to reinforce his reputation for barbarity. One of his servants claims he even intentionally dresses like a brute to support the idea."

"Why would he do that?" demanded Agon.

"Apparently to discourage people from daring to challenge his authority, Your Majesty."

The king shook his head dismissively. His own opinion of Krasmir was nothing new—he had believed for many years that Krasmir was little better than a beast. Other members of the Rogandan nobility saw it the same way. His agents had more than once reported comments to that effect. It was impossible to believe that Krasmir had been putting on an act all along.

"What of his wife and children?"

"None of them have ever uttered a word on the subject, Your Majesty. But we secretly observed him with his family. He appears to treat them with great gentleness. And he has an old mother. All of his servants claim that the two of them dote on each other."

The king fell silent.

"Not one of his household servants has ever been heard whispering about the way their lord treats them. We learned that positions among his household servants are greatly coveted. Once he appoints a servant, they never want to leave."

The king's brows were furrowed. "What about his intelligence?"

"He is regarded as sharp-witted and shrewd, Your Majesty. Those who know him best all agree on that."

"And his estates?"

"Well managed by all accounts."

The king dismissed his agents, struggling to fully grasp the implications of all they had said.

Their reports had shaken him. Was it actually possible that Krasmir's reputation was nothing more than a clever pretense? Had the nobleman truly succeeded in deceiving everyone, including the king?

The most important question was whether Krasmir could be trusted. Was he a danger to Agon or his interests? He quickly dismissed any such notion—without the Stone of Authority he might have considerable cause for concern. Having subjected Krasmir to the stone, he had no doubt that the nobleman could be trusted to act in the royal interest.

As he pondered it further, he reminded himself that the nobleman had never been known to act in either an aggressive or a duplicitous manner. He was wealthy and powerful, but he had not attained that status at the expense of his peers among the nobility. His deception—assuming that's what it truly was—seemed primarily defensive in nature. He apparently wanted to make others think twice before moving against him.

It did give the king pause. He had spent a lot of time with Krasmir in recent weeks, and he had witnessed the stupidity of the nobleman for himself. It now occurred to him that other explanations could also be offered.

Was it possible that he had misjudged Krasmir? He instantly discarded the thought. No king worthy of the name doubted himself.

"I HAVE ALREADY EXPLAINED THAT, My Lord," snapped Agon, eyeing Krasmir closely as he said it.

Krasmir gazed back at him, his eyes glazed.

There was no fight at all in the nobleman, and Agon knew he could thank the Stone of Authority for that. But Krasmir appeared obtuse and uncomprehending, and if the reports of Agon's agents were to be believed, the man was anything but dull-witted. The stone was surely not to blame either. According to the scroll, the stone neither diminished nor enhanced the intelligence of the people it influenced.

Was Krasmir putting on another act?

Agon groaned. Whether Krasmir was dull-witted or not, the king had little choice but to persevere with these briefings in the hope that the nobleman would finally begin to make sense of it all.

"I will explain it again," said the king irritably. "Pay attention this time!"

LORD KRASMIR WALKED beside the king, working hard to conceal his boredom. The last few weeks had felt like the longest of his life. The king intended to bring Arvenon finally to heel, and he expected it to involve a long absence from Rogand. With that in mind he had approached Krasmir to explore the possibility of appointing the nobleman as regent.

Krasmir supposed he should have felt honored, but it increasingly felt like a bad dream. The regency itself wasn't the problem. It was the time preparing for it with the king.

"As my representative, you will be expected to attend the solstice festivals at the temple," the king was saying.

Krasmir was familiar with the solstice festivals, but on the rare occasions he attended he had paid no attention at all to the role of the king. He therefore found himself wondering what he would be expected to say, what symbolic acts he might need to perform, when he should arrive, and how long he would need to stay at the festival.

If only he dared ask.

Krasmir knew that the king believed he was providing a detailed briefing. As far as the nobleman was concerned, Agon did little more than ramble on endlessly, usually without addressing the most important questions. His long-winded explanations were rarely useful, yet he apparently felt the need to repeat himself over and over again. More often than not, Krasmir found it almost impossible to make sense of any of it. Worse, any request for the tiniest clarification inevitably led to Agon rolling his eyes and repeating everything again with exaggerated patience, each time without making it any clearer.

The king wasn't stupid. He just wasn't naturally gifted as a tutor.

And having always done whatever he pleased without question, he'd never developed the skill of explaining himself.

Even when Krasmir did understand the king's ways of doing things, they didn't always make sense to him. Every one of Krasmir's peers on the Great Council had recognized for years that the king was often his own worst enemy. No one was more practiced than Agon at working against his own best interests.

Not one of the nobles was foolish enough to say so. The king derived far too much delight from ordering executions.

It was frustrating, because Krasmir intended well. He didn't at all understand why he had the king's best interests at heart, especially in light of their shared history, but the truth was that the king could trust him completely.

Krasmir could only carry on in the hope that it would all work out somehow.

12

Kernon peered toward the lone figure of Will Prentis standing on the outskirts of the forest. "That's him all right," he said.

Lord Redfass looked at Jonas. "So you were on the level," he said.

"We had our doubts," Namor added coolly.

Jonas shrugged.

Kernon ignored them. He had eyes only for Will Prentis. "He's making no attempt to flee," he observed, shaking his head.

"That makes no sense," said Namor, frowning. "If he's entirely alone, why is he so calm?" He began peering around uneasily.

"I have no idea," Kernon replied. "But we need to take him down before he decides to make a run for it."

Jonas pulled his sword. "Who said he's entirely alone?" he asked fiercely. Kernon looked at him blankly.

Swinging his horse around, Jonas dug in his heels and charged at Redfass. The expression of the mercenary leader changed in an instant from puzzlement to fury. He raised his sword defensively, but Jonas drove furiously through his guard and sent him crashing from the saddle. Both Kernon and Namor watched open-mouthed. Before they could react, Jonas turned away and galloped toward the lone figure among the trees.

With a cry of rage, Kernon rose in his stirrups, calling the men forward. A shout arose, and the entire line of horsemen charged after Jonas.

As Kernon galloped forward, he noticed something happening along the line of trees. His eyes went wide as horsemen streamed out from between the trees, surging past both Jonas and Will Prentis.

A huge soldier rode at their head, and Kernon's heart abruptly missed a beat when he realized who it was. Rufe Sarjant was leading the charge. Where had he come from?

A hunting horn sounded from somewhere behind them, then another. They were surrounded. Kernon saw then that they had been outwitted and deceived.

It made no difference. Victory or death, there was no backing out now.

Kernon galloped forward, screaming his defiance.

The lines crashed together, and Kernon's world descended into a confusion of shouting men and screaming horses. He had fought before, but the fury of the men before him was unlike anything he had encountered. His attackers were literally howling for blood. And there were so many of them.

Assaulted from two sides, Kernon cast his eyes around frantically, searching for support. No help would be coming. All of the mercenaries were equally beset, and men went down even as his glance fell on them.

Taking advantage of his distraction, his attackers broke through his defenses. He toppled to the ground, agonizing pain overwhelming him. Before everything went dark a face he recognized flashed briefly into view. His fading thought was the realization that he had been brought low by his own soldiers—the men he had left waiting in the camp below Steffan's Citadel.

THOMAS REMAINED among the trees when the fighting started. He had never witnessed a battle on this scale before, and even as a distant observer he found the experience confronting. The chaos bewildered him—how could any commander make sense of what was happening?—and the harrowing cries of men and horses oppressed him.

To his untrained eye there was little to distinguish between the two sides, and when the fighting eventually ended he wasn't at first certain who had won. It was with enormous relief that he eventually spotted Will. The commander stood on a low mound surveying the scene, Rufe and Jonas beside him. All of them appeared unharmed and in control of the situation.

Thomas eventually mustered the courage to approach them, although he stayed out of the way, both to avoid distracting them and because he felt completely out of place.

After the battle, soldiers collapsed to the ground in exhaustion. Others tended to the wounded. No one seemed to notice his arrival, and he was happy to remain inconspicuous.

Thomas's attention was soon drawn to Will. The commander mounted his horse and rode slowly among the men, greeting them and thanking them for their efforts. A murmur of voices rose in anticipation as he drew near. Hands reached out to touch his horse as he passed. Even the faces of gravely wounded men lit up when he turned their way, his regard somehow dulling their pain for a time.

Was it always like this after a battle? Thomas had heard about Will's reputation, but he'd always assumed it arose from his uncanny strategic abilities. He saw now that there was more to the commander than he'd ever imagined.

"They claimed you were a traitor," one of the soldiers called to Will, shaking his head.

"Yeah. Supposedly you'd run off to Varas!" scoffed another. "Rufe too."

"None of us believed it. Not for a minute," said a soldier. Loud grunts of assent accompanied the remark.

"I am grateful to you all," Will told them. "After the lies you'd been told, we didn't know what to expect," he said frankly.

Many of the soldiers looked baffled at the idea there could be any uncertainty about their response. "'Will needs your help,'" one of them said simply. "That's what Rufe told us." He said it as if no further explanation was necessary.

The men around him grunted their affirmation.

Will nodded gravely, and moved on.

Thomas looked on in astonishment. How could any leader inspire such devotion from battle-hardened warriors? He felt like he was seeing Will properly for the first time.

These men called him 'Will', not Lord Torbury, and Will made no move to correct them. Thomas guessed that many of the soldiers had served under him at Torbury Scarp. Will was the kind of man to value the bond he shared with his men far above any formal title.

After spending time moving among the soldiers, Will made his way to a large group of men off to one side. The survivors from Lord Redfass's mercenary force—perhaps eighty men—had been herded together and stripped of their weapons. They gave him a very different kind of response. Most of them had been sprawling listlessly on the ground. They sat up at once when they saw who was approaching. Some faces showed defiance. Others simply showed fear.

Will sat on his horse for a considerable time, regarding them silently. "What's that symbol tattooed onto your right arms?" he finally asked.

At first no one responded, but eventually one of the men said, "It's Lord Redfass's mark. He required every man who signed on with him to have it."

The commander studied the men thoughtfully. "It would be simplest just to kill you all. You deserve it after your treason."

Many faces paled at his remark. But he had more to say.

"I'm going to give you a second chance. You can leave and go wherever you want. You'll be going without your weapons and without your horses. Take a water skin and food from your saddle-bags—nothing more. Every one of you can be identified by your tattoo. If you ever sign on as mercenaries again, you won't receive mercy a second time."

The men were led to their horses to collect a few provisions, then they were escorted away. Thomas noticed a few of them scowling, but most seemed grateful to have escaped with their lives.

The men had been gone for only a few minutes when Thomas noticed a commotion off in the distance. Most of the mercenaries were still striding away, shadowed by a mounted escort. But about twenty men had broken away from the main group and stopped entirely. Two of the soldiers escorting the group had remained with them, and a third was riding back toward Will.

"What's the holdup?" Will asked when the soldier arrived.

"Some of the men insist they want to join your army, Will," he replied. "What do you want us to do with them?"

Will turned to Rufe and raised his eyebrows.

Rufe nodded. "I'll check them out," he said. "Where's Thomas?" he asked.

Thomas rode forward. "Over here, Rufe," he called.

The two of them rode together to the smaller group. Thomas tried to look casual, but it brightened him enormously to know that Rufe thought he might have something to offer.

"Tell me if you see anything unusual," Rufe said as they approached the men.

Bringing the stone into contact with his skin, Thomas scanned the men. In most of them he saw regret and a desire to set things right. Two of the men were concealing a very different set of motives.

Rufe glanced in his direction, and without saying a word Thomas pointed the two men out.

Seeing that the game was up, both of them immediately turned and sprinted off after the main group.

"The others?" asked Rufe.

Thomas furrowed his brows for a moment, then nodded slowly.

"Come with us," Rufe told them. "The final decision lies with Will."

Thomas quietly exhaled a sigh of relief as they rode back to the commander. He'd finally been able to make a contribution of his own. Until that moment he'd felt completely useless.

When they reached Will, the commander turned a questioning look on the men.

"We didn't sign up to fight you or the king, Will," one of them told him. "I was with you at Torbury Scarp!"

Will eyed him for a moment, then cast his eyes across the whole group. "I'm willing to give you a chance," he told them. "Don't make me regret it."

Unable to contain their delight, they all began talking at once, their faces glowing.

"Shall I spread them throughout the ranks?" asked Rufe.

Will shook his head. "No. The other men will give them a hard time. Find them a captain of their own. They'll do better if they stay together."

Rufe nodded and headed off with Timo to find someone suitable to lead them.

They returned with a grizzled veteran who looked as if he wouldn't take any nonsense. But he spoke to the men reasonably enough as he led them away.

Will never seemed able to relax. He called Timo to his side. "Rufe told me you were leading half of the men today," he said. "You did well."

"Thanks, Will," Timo replied. "It was an honor."

"I'm going to need to ask much more of you," Will told him. "I want you to lead this army."

His request clearly took Timo by surprise. "What about you? And Rufe?"

"We're needed elsewhere. We can talk more about it later. Are you willing to lead?"

Timo nodded.

"Then you can make a start almost immediately. I'm expecting a couple of visitors soon. When they arrive I'll need you to call the men together."

Timo nodded once more. "I'll be ready."

Thomas could readily guess who the visitors might be, and he was not surprised when the king and queen rode in, escorted by Jonas and a sizable group of soldiers.

Timo gathered the troops together, and a ripple of anticipation passed through them when they realized who stood before them.

Will led the king to a mound, and he climbed upon it and faced the troops.

Every head was turned to him as he addressed them in a loud voice. "You have been reunited with your commander today." Loud whoops of jubilation broke out across the throng. "You have fought at his side once more, and you have won!" The king had to wait for some time before the cheering subsided.

"You have cast aside the traitors who claimed to be acting in my name. The kingdom is not yet safe, though. The traitors are led by the former Earl of Pisander, the man who plotted to turn Arnost over to the Rogandan commander during the invasion. At the time your commander exposed him and prevented him from carrying out his plan. Then you crushed the Rogandan army at Torbury Scarp!" Deafening cheers broke out.

The king continued when the din subsided a little. "We thought that the war was over. But King Agon of Rogand paid Pisander to hire assassins. They tried to kill me and the queen, along with our allies, King Istel of Castel and King Delmar of Varas. It grieves me to say that King Istel, my father-in-law, was killed. I was gravely wounded, but your queen fought back vigorously, and with the help of others the assassins were driven off."

More cheering broke out. The queen waved to them, and the men roared in response.

The king continued as soon as the noise abated. "I wish I could tell you that the kingdom is now secure. But it is not. Pisander has taken control of Arnost, and he intends to repay his debt to King Agon of Rogand by inviting him to Arnost. The king of Rogand expects to take control of Arvenon."

The king's news was initially met by stunned silence, but a howl of anger quickly went up at the suggestion of a Rogandan king taking control of Arnost. Only a few years had passed since these men and their comrades had suffered and died to prevent exactly that outcome.

The king waited until the clamor died down. “We will need you to secure our border with Rogand. Agon must be prevented from entering Arvenon.” A growl of affirmation rose at this statement.

“There is a great deal at stake still, and I must borrow your commander for a while longer. I promise that you will be capably led by trustworthy men, though.” Without waiting for the grunts of dismay to die down, the king called out more loudly than ever, “But I can leave you with some exceedingly good news!” At this, Queen Essanda stepped up beside him, holding a bundle in her arms. “Your queen has given birth to our son and heir! I present to you Prince Aiden!”

The king took the baby from his wrappings and thrust him into the air above the multitude.

His news was greeted with a thunderous roar of acclamation. Thomas joined in at the top of his lungs. The cheering continued until the king gave a final wave and stepped down with the queen and baby prince.

Will quickly took their place, holding up his hands for silence. The din gradually died away.

“As you have heard, I need to accompany the king and queen for a while longer. In the meantime, you will be led by one of your own—Timo.” As he was speaking, he waved Timo up beside him.

The appointment was greeted by more muted applause, but Thomas noticed many heads nodding in silent approval. It appeared that Timo would begin with the cautious support of his men. Whether or not the support matured into enthusiasm would be up to him.

Thomas had little doubt about the outcome. Will would never have appointed Timo if he didn’t already hold him in high regard, and Thomas had witnessed Will’s ability as a judge of character. He also knew from personal experience that Will had a way of drawing out the potential in a person.

Spotting Elena among the royal party, Thomas eagerly set out to join her.

HIDDEN AMONG THE TREES, Carnwill watched with fascination as the ascendancy of Redfass and his cronies came to a sudden and decisive end.

The appearance of the king and queen of Arvenon ought to have been enough to capture Carnwill's full attention, but his eyes were drawn only to a young woman of rare beauty. He was not at all surprised when the companion of the big soldier sought her out after the battle. The way they embraced settled once and for all the question of their identity.

Carnwill was looking at Thomas Stablehand and his wife, and a gloating smile came over his face as he eyed his prize. King Agon would be very pleased indeed.

Wresting Thomas away from the soldiers would present a worthy challenge, but it was someone else's problem.

13

The commander of Steffan's Citadel stood on the battlements gazing down at the camp below him. Soldiers had returned to it the previous day, but tents were now being taken down and the men showed every sign of preparing to leave. Something significant had clearly happened down there. He wanted answers, but he was not willing to risk sending any of his men.

He was about to turn away when he noticed a small group of men riding up from the camp toward the citadel. He peered down curiously at them until they disappeared from sight as they reached the gates.

A soldier soon climbed to the battlements and approached him. "A visitor has arrived at the gates of the citadel, Commander," he said. "He claims he has permission to enter."

The commander frowned. "Who is it?" he demanded. He had been commanded to close the border between Erestor and the rest of Arvenon, and to deny access to all comers, with just two exceptions: Lord Burtelen, who had already passed through the gates, and Lord Torbury, better known as Will Prentis.

"It's Will Prentis."

The commander glanced at the soldier in amazement. "You mean Lord Torbury. How do you know for certain it's him?"

"A number of the men recognized him."

"Well don't just stand there, man! Let him in!"

THE FOLLOWING morning the commander sat in his private quarters pondering the events of the last couple of days. The brief contact with Lord Torbury the previous day had raised many questions while providing few answers. A conference had been arranged, though, and it was due to begin in a little over two hours. To the commander's astonishment, Lord Torbury had announced that the king and queen would be attending.

Since then the citadel had been buzzing with activity. The commander's men were scurrying about the citadel, scrubbing, tidying, and preparing refreshments. Now, with most of the work done, the commander finally felt able to relax. He was anticipating the meeting with considerable interest.

His musing was interrupted by one of his aides. "The duke has arrived and wishes to see you, Commander."

"The duke? Already?" The commander raised his eyebrows. "It's surely only a couple of days since we sent him a message. Show him to our best guest chambers and make sure he is comfortable. I will come down directly."

The aide hurried away to do his bidding.

The citadel had never been in better condition for a surprise visit by the duke. The timing of Lord Torbury's meeting was fortuitous indeed. The commander put on his best uniform and headed down the stairs.

He entered the guest chambers to find the duke sipping on a goblet of wine. "My Lord Duke—this is an unexpected pleasure! I sent a message to alert you to some changes, but I didn't expect you would even receive it before today."

The duke smiled. "Yes, I encountered the messenger on my way here. It seems to have been excellent timing on my part."

“To what do we owe the honor of your visit?” the commander asked.

“Two men—one of whom is known to me—arrived with a message from Lord Torbury,” the duke replied. “I rode here with the messengers,” he concluded with a smile.

The commander’s eyebrows rose in surprise. How had these messengers reached Maranelle if they came from Lord Torbury? The only way into Erestor was through the citadel, and no one at all had been admitted in recent days.

The commander thrust aside his own questions. “As it happens I will be meeting with Lord Torbury in little over an hour. He is planning to bring the king and queen with him. Perhaps you would be willing to join us?”

“It would be my pleasure, Commander. Perhaps you would be kind enough to send the king and queen to my quarters when they first arrive.”

“As you wish, My Lord Duke.”

The commander bowed and departed.

THE DUKE RELEASED a deep sigh of satisfaction. It was good to relax for a moment before Will Prentis arrived with the king and queen.

He had been taking his ease in a comfortable armchair in the private chamber set aside by the commander for his use whenever he visited the citadel. The journey from Maranelle to the citadel took longer than he’d remembered, and his old bones had felt thoroughly shaken up by the time he arrived. It had become obvious to him on the first day of riding that he should have taken the advice of his aides and used a carriage. Riding was so much faster than a carriage, though, and the information provided by Rellan convinced him that timing was important. The imminent meeting with Will, and especially with the king and queen, provided an ample demonstration of the benefits of moving quickly.

“Uncle! What an unexpected pleasure!” King Steffan beamed a smile as he burst through the door.

The duke rose to his feet. "Your Majesty!" he replied with a smile of delight. "I hadn't expected to see you when I came here. I've been hearing such alarming rumors about you in recent weeks."

"Probably most of them are true," the king replied grimly.

"And Queen Essanda!" said the duke as she appeared in the doorway. "Just look at you!"

He favored Essanda with a wink, and she flew across the room into his open arms. As he embraced her warmly, he peered at the king from over her head. "You're fortunate I'm not forty years younger, Steffan," he said, "or you might have had some serious competition for the hand of this beautiful young woman."

Steffan laughed. "You're far too late," he said. "She's all mine!"

Essanda pulled back from the duke and tossed the hair from her face. "We have a surprise for you, Uncle," she said with a twinkle in her eye. She turned away and hurried from the room.

He shook his head in admiration as he gazed at her retreating back. His quips to his nephew might have been flippant, but she truly was captivating.

He locked eyes with Steffan, raising an eyebrow as he nodded in the direction she had gone. "She's quite something, isn't she?" he asked with a wink.

Steffan grinned back at him.

She soon returned with a bundle in her arms. "I would like to present to you Crown Prince Aiden," she said, lifting her chin proudly.

The duke's eyes widened. "This is wonderful news!" he said with a beaming smile. "Congratulations to you both!"

The baby let out a lusty squawk as Essanda handed him to her uncle. The old duke held him awkwardly for a moment, then hastily handed him back, exhaling with relief as Essanda took the baby in her arms. She jigged the little prince up and down for a few moments until he settled.

The duke shook his head. "There's a reason why such delights are entrusted to the young," he said, pointing at the infant.

"He does bring us great delight," said the king. "And he arrived hard on the heels of the most difficult time of our lives." His face grew serious. "There's a lot we have to tell you, Uncle. But it can wait a while longer. We are planning to discuss the future with Will. I can't tell you how pleased I am that we'll be able to include you in the conversation."

"Well let's get to it," said the duke, clapping the king on the shoulder and heading out the door. One of the soldiers stationed outside his private room led them all to the reception hall.

As they walked the duke leaned over to the king. "It's only fair to let you know that none of your news came as a complete surprise," he said. "Rellan reached me a couple of days ago with his friend Petar and briefed me fully. You have him to thank for my presence at the citadel. The three of us traveled here together."

They entered the hall to find Rellan talking energetically with Will, Rufe, and Jonas. The commander of the citadel sat nearby, although he wasn't participating in the conversation. Brother Ander sat off to one side, looking as if he felt a little out of place.

When the king and queen entered with the duke, everyone immediately pushed back their chairs and rose to their feet.

"Please, there's no need to get up," protested the queen.

All of them sat down again except the citadel commander, who made to leave. The king waved him to a seat. "Please stay, Commander. You are most welcome to join us." he said graciously.

"We face some difficult challenges," the king began. "Arnost is under the control of the former Earl of Pisander. I'm sure you are all aware of his history. It isn't good news for anyone in the kingdom, especially the long-suffering people of Arnost."

The duke hung his head. It had been his responsibility to execute Pisander, and he would never forgive himself for having allowed the traitor to slip through his fingers.

"We have regained control of the western army stationed here at Steffan's Citadel," the king continued. "And with reinforcements from Erestor we will have a sizable force available to us."

"Several thousand soldiers under arms are stationed nearby," the duke told him. "I expected that you would need them sooner or later."

"Thank you," the king replied. "Even with your soldiers, our task will be far from easy. We know that Pisander has invited Agon of Rogand to join him in Arnost. If Agon is allowed to establish himself there, it will not be easy to remove him. We must make every effort to prevent that from happening. Closing our border with Rogand is the first step."

"Based on what the duke has told us, we should have enough men to do that once the army from Erestor joins us," said Will.

The king nodded. "Retaking Arnost from Pisander is also a key priority. We don't have enough men to do both though." He nodded to the duke. "My uncle did an excellent job of repairing Arnost's defenses only a few years ago. That is not going to work in our favor on this occasion."

"You are right, Your Majesty," agreed Will. "A great deal will also hinge on whether Count Ranauld is able to regain control of the northern army camped outside Castel at Deadman's Pass."

"Yes. If the number of men camped outside the citadel offers any indication, I imagine that the army on the Castelan border must be considerably larger than the one here," said the king. "Even with those men we won't have the strength both to secure the border and retake Arnost. Without them, we will struggle simply to maintain our position."

"Perhaps it's time to consider other options," offered the duke.

All heads turned in his direction.

"I imagine that King Delmar would believe himself to be in your debt," he said. "And Varas seems to be the one kingdom that has largely been spared upheaval. Perhaps he would be willing to help."

"That has occurred to me," the king replied cautiously.

"Would you approach King Delmar yourself, or send a representative?" asked the duke.

King Steffan did not hesitate before responding. "What we need from Delmar is an army. He can't send an army into Arvenon without my direct involvement—it would be an act of aggression." The king shook his head decisively. "No, I need to be there in person."

"The major challenge, Your Majesty," said Will, "would be getting you to Varacellan safely. It's a grueling ride that would take more time than we can easily afford—it's a very long journey. We know because we've already ridden much of the way not long ago.

"It's likely to be dangerous too. We can't predict when we might encounter mercenaries from the northern army camped outside Castel or other men controlled by Pisander. To properly protect you and the queen we would need to divide our available force, weakening the army we send to the border."

"That isn't the only way to get to Varacellan," said the duke.

Everyone looked at him questioningly.

"Varacellan is a seaport," he reminded them. "You could board a ship from Maranelle with a small escort and be in the Varasan capital in just a few days."

The duke could not resist smiling at their faces. From their reaction, he might have been suggesting they all take poison.

"Shortening the journey is an attractive idea, My Lord Duke," said Will evenly. "But we mustn't overlook the risks."

"Sea monsters?" asked the duke innocently.

Will did not respond, but he was clearly not excited by the duke's proposal.

Only the commander of the citadel seemed to take the suggestion seriously. "I have taken more than one sea voyage," he said, "and I found it less difficult than I expected."

"I can certainly echo the sentiments of the good commander," the duke offered with a smile.

"Have any of the rest of you been on a ship?" asked the king, looking around the group. "I've traveled on small river craft on occasion, but I've never been to sea."

Every one of the others shook their heads, a few of them emphatically.

"We have one person among us with extensive experience at sea," said Brother Ander.

All eyes turned to the monk.

"Who is that, Brother Ander?" asked the king.

"Breysen," he replied.

The king's immediate response was a disdainful grunt.

The queen was not satisfied to leave it at that. "I don't think we should be so quick to dismiss him," she said.

"I believe Your Majesty is wise as well as gracious," said Brother Ander, dipping his head respectfully in the direction of the queen. "Listening to Breysen's story gave me a new perspective on his actions."

"How can we trust him?" asked the king. Seeing the look on his wife's face, he added placatingly, "I haven't forgotten that he risked his life to defend you. That is worth a great deal to me."

"I am willing to do some further investigations," said Rufe. "I'll take Thomas with me," he added, with a glance at Will.

Will's face was unreadable, but he added, "A good idea, Rufe. Take Elena too."

The duke looked curiously at Will. The mention of Thomas abruptly reminded him of the momentous meeting in Arnost during the Rogandan invasion—the council of lords meeting where Pisander had been exposed. Thomas had been no more than a tousle haired youth. He had been brought to the meeting by Will, and the duke remembered him standing awkwardly off to one side.

Will had never explained why he had invited Thomas or exactly what role he had played in identifying the traitor. Thomas had been fingering something in his pouch—what was it? The duke wasn't the only person present at the meeting who had asked such questions.

Thomas had gone with Will when he left Arnost, and the chatter had gradually died away.

Now there was talk of an Elena. Who was she?

"All of us need time to consider these matters further before we make any decision," the king was saying. "Please stay within the citadel, at least for the rest of the day. I might need to consult with you again."

With that the king called the meeting to a close.

Before anyone could leave, the commander stood up. "May I speak, Your Majesty?" he asked.

The king nodded. "Of course."

"I'm sure you are all hungry," the commander suggested. "Food will be served in the adjacent room in thirty minutes."

The duke slipped away quietly and headed for his private chamber, determined to take a few minutes to relax in peace.

Breysen had been standing beside Brother Ander when the king addressed the soldiers. It would have seemed like a good speech if it had been directed at him. But he couldn't claim to be one of the king's loyal soldiers. Not anymore.

Based on what he had seen of the king, both at the campsite and before the soldiers, he could only admire him. He hadn't seemed lofty and distant—not at all like Breysen might have expected. And the queen had treated him almost like a friend. He wished he'd never set eyes upon them though, not under these circumstances. The king had left him alive, at least for now, but that said nothing about the future. Breysen's wife and children were so vulnerable. How could they ever hope to survive without him?

Will had released the surviving mercenaries, even allowing some of them to join his army. But it wasn't Will who would decide about him. His future would be settled by the king, and he didn't have the slightest idea of the king's intentions.

Brother Ander had barely left his side—perhaps at the king's request. He didn't mind at all. He had grown to appreciate the monk's calm demeanor, and he had the feeling the monk felt a degree of sympathy for him. That couldn't hurt.

Then the king and Will left for the citadel, taking Brother Ander with them. Breysen was left in the charge of two soldiers. They didn't treat him harshly—they basically ignored him—so he couldn't complain. But he missed the easy companionship of the monk.

One of the people he'd briefly met at the king's campsite was

Elena, and before long he discovered that she hadn't forgotten about him. Not long after the monk had gone, she came to visit him, bringing her husband Thomas with her as well. At first they had each looked at him a little strangely, but they soon seemed to relax. The soldiers left in charge of him didn't seem to object to their presence, and spending time with them and their little daughter Tammi lifted his spirits enormously. He was sorry to see them go when they eventually excused themselves and slipped away.

At least there was no shortage of food anymore. The soldiers ate simply, but every meal still seemed like an unexpected feast to him. He gradually felt his strength returning.

14

Thomas and Elena at last found the opportunity to enjoy some relaxed time with Tammi.

Elena had been darting strange looks at Thomas for some time. "What's on your mind, Thomas?" she eventually asked him.

Thomas put Tammi down and watched her as she ambled off to look at the horses. Did he really want to speak his thoughts? Some part of him worried that his fears might gain strength if he brought them into the open and named them. Glancing at the calm and untroubled face of Elena, he knew at once that such thinking was foolishness.

"I'm wondering what will happen to us," he told her. "Since we joined the king and queen, it's as if we have no control over our own future."

Elena nodded. She didn't seem surprised. "What would you like to do—if you had a choice?" she asked.

"I'd go and live somewhere far away," he said. "Like we were doing before. I miss our old life. I'm a simple person—I don't want the constant challenges Will and the king have to face."

She gazed at him knowingly. "And you're afraid that the stone will prevent that from ever happening."

He nodded unhappily. "Will and Rufe and the others are valuable to the king because of their skills and abilities. I'm only useful because of the stone. If I didn't have it, he would have released us long ago."

"Do you ever think about giving it up?"

"I used to. I often wondered if I was only keeping it out of selfishness. I thought that handing it to someone like Will or the king would be the most responsible thing to do. Then I had that conversation with Will—the one I told you about. I realized that it wouldn't be doing either of them a favor."

She nodded.

"According to the scroll," he continued, "the first person who had the stone, or the rock as it was then, gave it to his king. It didn't end well."

"So you've decided you're stuck with it."

"We're stuck with it," he reminded her.

She came to him, putting her hands on his waist and looking up into his eyes. "I know that heavy burdens have been placed on your shoulders ever since we were forced to leave our home—I've experienced it with you. I'd also be happy if we could leave it all behind and disappear into the wilderness again. Maybe that can't happen anymore. Maybe for as long as the stone is with us it won't be possible to take responsibility only for ourselves. But whatever happens, I want you to know that I'm willing to share the burden. We'll manage. We'll do it together."

He gazed down into her beautiful face. He felt bad about having dragged Elena into his troubles, but he acknowledged to himself that being able to share the stone with her was a huge relief.

She put her arm around him and nestled into his shoulder. "I admire the king and queen very much, and I think Will is amazing. But I'd leave all of them behind in a heartbeat. You and Tammi, my father, your parents, and Haldek. You're all I need."

He bent down and kissed her on the forehead. "What would I do without you?" he murmured.

Putting kings and conferences out of his mind, he turned his attention back to Tammi. A few minutes in her company helped settle him. He had discovered that his little daughter drew something out of him that found no other expression. He wasn't sure if he was entertaining her or she was entertaining him, but she was soon giggling uncontrollably as he tipped her upside down and waved her through the air.

Elena watched them for a while, a smile playing across her face. Finally she reminded him that Tammi was overdue for a nap, and he reluctantly redirected his efforts toward calming her down. Their little toddler soon fell fast asleep, completely exhausted.

Almost at the same moment, Rufe appeared.

"I've just been spending time with the former mercenary, Breysen," Rufe told them. "I'd like to know what both of you think of him. I believe you've already met him, Elena."

"We spent some time with him earlier today," Thomas told him, wondering what lay behind Rufe's request. It seemed ironic that Rufe should appear so soon after Thomas had been wishing he wasn't an ongoing part of Will's world.

"Do you think he's what he seems to be?" Rufe asked.

"Yes, I do," Thomas replied. "I have no doubt about it."

Rufe turned to Elena, an eyebrow raised questioningly.

"I believe he's genuine too," she said seriously. "He's very worried about his wife and children, and he joined the mercenaries mainly out of a desire to provide for them. It breaks my heart to see what's happened to him as a result."

"Now that he's spent time as a mercenary, do you think there's any doubt about his loyalty to the king and queen if things get difficult?" Rufe asked.

"I don't think he's ever intentionally done anything disloyal to the king and queen," Elena replied.

Thomas nodded. "I agree," he said without hesitation. "As soon as he realized who the mercenaries were fighting, he avoided fighting himself."

"Thank you," Rufe said. And without further comment he mounted his horse and returned to the citadel.

When they received an invitation to meet with the king early the following morning, Elena gazed at Thomas with a resigned smile on her face. It was obvious to him that she felt no more desire to belong to the king's inner circle than he did. He shrugged.

It seemed likely that their immediate future would be decided for them. He found it overwhelming even to imagine what it would be like to determine the futures of so many people. Who would ever want to be king?

And who would want to bear the burden of advising and protecting him? King Steffan had almost been killed when his enemies tried to wrench his kingdom away from him, and the task of preventing them from succeeding had fallen to people like Will and Rufe and Jonas. Not to mention the queen and Brother Ander. He shook his head.

The stone had also played its part. A small part, to be sure, but he knew it had made a difference. If he and Elena had remained hidden away in the forest, he wouldn't have met Will on his return from Erestor. He wouldn't have been able to alert Will to what was happening with the king at Paradise Valley.

He couldn't ignore the responsibility that came with the stone. Would a normal life ever be possible for Thomas and his family again?

He shrugged off such gloomy thoughts, deciding instead to spend some time with his father-in-law and Haldek.

THOMAS AND ELENA rose at dawn the next day and once again left Tammi with Rubin. They found themselves riding to the citadel with Brother Ander and Breysen. The former mercenary looked nervous, but he managed a weak smile when they greeted him.

The four of them made their way to the reception hall together.

They arrived to find Will, Rufe, Jonas, and Rellan already there and engaged in a quiet but animated discussion.

The king, the queen, and the duke arrived immediately after them, and all conversation ceased at once. Every eye turned to the king.

"Agon plans to establish himself in Arnost, with the intention of annexing Arvenon, then Castel and Varas. The Rogandan invasion made it clear what we can expect if he succeeds."

He glanced around the group. "You are here because each of you will be affected by the decisions I have made. I am going to need your full support to have any hope of thwarting the plans of Agon and his henchmen."

Thomas couldn't guess what was coming next, but it didn't sound promising.

"I have decided to travel to Varas to seek the support of King Delmar," the king continued. "We defeated the Rogandans at the time of the invasion because the three kingdoms stood firmly together. We will need to do so again."

From the look on the king's face, he was about to say something that even he found distasteful. Thomas held his breath involuntarily.

"I have decided to travel by ship from Maranelle to Varacellan. And I need all of you to join me on the voyage."

Thomas was too stunned to do more than stare wide-eyed at the king. A quick glance around the room showed him that he, Elena, and Breysen were the only people surprised by this announcement.

The king nodded to the duke. "There will be two exceptions. The first is Rellan, who will help lead the army stationed below us and the reinforcements from Erestor. The second will be my good uncle, who has graciously agreed to remain here to act as regent once more in my absence."

King Steffan turned to Breysen. The former mercenary was staring at him open mouthed, apparently relieved and alarmed in equal measure. "I imagine you might not have been expecting this, Breysen," said the king. "Do you have any questions?"

Breysen managed to close his mouth. "I am grateful to Your

Majesty," he said. "I am just..." Then he hesitated, seemingly unable to find the courage to continue.

"Concerned about what it might mean for your wife and children if you disappear off on a sea voyage," Brother Ander finished for him.

The haunted look Thomas could see in Breysen's eyes confirmed the monk's assessment.

"There are ways we can help," Brother Ander told him. "I have just made contact with a traveling monk who comes to this region from time to time. I asked him if he would be willing to go to your village near Danford, and to do whatever he can to assist your family. The monk agreed, and the king has entrusted to him a gift of money for your wife. You can provide the monk with directions before we leave."

Hope and relief flashed across Breysen's face before being displaced by a look of such pathetic gratitude that Thomas turned away feeling awkward.

The king's attention had already turned elsewhere. "Brother Ander and Breysen will set out for Maranelle as soon as Breysen has spoken to the monk, accompanying the duke and Rufe. The rest of us will leave later today. Thank you all."

The people around Thomas stood up and moved to the door. He was in the act of pushing back his own chair when the king addressed him and Elena directly. "Please stay a moment longer."

Thomas and Elena obediently resumed their seats. Soon only the king and the queen remained in the room with them.

"Perhaps you are wondering why I have asked you to join us on this voyage," he told them frankly. "I felt that you would provide useful companionship to the queen, Elena—she holds you in high regard." Seeing the look on the queen's face, he quickly added, "I must make it clear that Queen Essanda had no desire to see you caught up in our troubles."

"I would very much appreciate your company, Elena," added the queen. "But I tried very hard to talk the king out of involving you. Being dragged around the world with us would not be your first choice I'm sure, especially with a small child in your care."

The king didn't wait for Elena to respond. "Will was insistent, Thomas. He pointed out that you have a way of ferreting out information. He told me you took the risk of visiting the castle in Arnost, and you were almost caught by Lygell's men as a result. You did much more than escape though. You managed to get wind of Lygell and Pisander's plans. And Will has told me that this is not the first time you've provided him with information that proved significant. Rufe supported him strongly."

Rufe's involvement surprised Thomas. A long forgotten interaction came abruptly to his mind. When Rogandan soldiers had appeared at the gates of Arnost, the stone had exposed their intent. After Thomas had alerted Will, his friend had immediately called for Rufe and given him urgent instructions to kill the men at the gates identified by Thomas. *"Can Thomas really be certain who deserves to be put to death?"* Rufe had asked Will. *"He can,"* Will had replied. *"There's no time to explain now. Don't fail me in this, Rufe!"*

Rufe had never spoken about it after the fight at the gates, although Thomas had sometimes wondered what he must have thought. Since then the big soldier had seen for himself, more than once, that Thomas knew things—things that no one should rightly be able to know. Was Rufe beginning at last to guess at Thomas's secret?

"How you manage it is a mystery to me," the king was saying. "But all of us would value your insights."

The king didn't realize it of course, but it wasn't Thomas's insights he needed. It was the revelations from the stone.

Thomas bowed his head in acceptance of the king's decision. It wasn't as if he had a choice.

"We would be happy to help however we can, Your Majesties," he replied evenly. "I hope it will be possible for Rubin and Haldek to come with us."

"Yes, of course," said the king. "Will also felt that it might prove useful for Haldek in particular to join us."

As soon as the king released them they returned to their horses.

"I'm so sorry, Elena," Thomas said as they rode back to their campsite. "This is all because of the stone. Where will it end?"

"I don't know," Elena replied with a gentle smile. "But nothing happens without a reason. If it weren't for the stone I would never have met you."

She was right. The stone had brought so much trouble into his life. But gazing into her lovely eyes he had to acknowledge that it had brought him a great deal of good as well.

Rubin and Haldek accepted the news about the upcoming sea voyage calmly. The two men exchanged a look that indicated they understood perfectly how this had come about. Rubin directed a searching look at both Thomas and Elena, but he didn't comment.

Thomas felt uncomfortable. He sensed that something more was needed, but he wasn't sure whether to apologize or to attempt a more complete explanation. He needn't have worried, because Elena knew exactly what to do. Moving to her father, she embraced him, nestling comfortably into his shoulder. He held her tightly for a long moment, then he placed his hands on her shoulders and held her at arm's-length, gazing steadily into her face.

No shadow troubled her smile, and he seemed to relax as he recognized the peace and contentment that so readily defined her. A tender smile came to Rubin's lips and reached to his eyes. After a while he released his daughter and busied himself gathering up their meager possessions.

Bundling Tammi up once more, the four of them mounted up and rode to the citadel to join the party traveling to Maranelle with the king.

EVERY MOVEMENT of Thomas had been observed closely by Carnwill. When Thomas disappeared into Steffan's Citadel with his daughter as well as his wife and failed to return before nightfall, it became apparent that they intended to remain in Erestor. Most likely they were heading for Maranelle.

Carnwill took a parchment and penned a brief note to the Rogandan king. It simply read,

'Fugitive located near Erestor, but now on the move.
In pursuit.
C.'

He arranged for it to be delivered to a trusted courier who would take it to King Agon in Rog.

No longer needing a cover, he paid and dismissed his two associates. They could do whatever they pleased with the cartloads of vegetables they had accumulated.

The next challenge was to gain admittance to Erestor. Deciding on a bold and simple approach, he rode up to Steffan's Citadel and demanded to speak with the commander.

Two hours passed before the commander arrived. "Well?" he demanded, looking Carnwill up and down with indifference.

Carnwill handed him a parchment. He did not offer comment.

"This is the Duke of Erestor's seal," said the commander in surprise. He opened it and scanned its contents before looking uncertainly at Carnwill. Then he dismissed the guards.

The tracker waited until they were alone. "I need to enter Erestor," he said.

"The border is closed," the commander replied flatly. "It will remain closed until the king orders otherwise."

"You've seen the document," Carnwill replied calmly.

The commander hesitated. "The duke only left a while ago. You could have appealed to him in person if you'd come earlier."

"You mean *you* could have appealed to him in person," growled Carnwill. He pointed at the parchment. "The duke's instructions are clear and unambiguous. If that's not good enough for you, send a messenger after him. Be ready to explain why you ignored his orders and hindered one of his agents."

"What is your purpose in Erestor?" asked the commander stiffly, trying to sound like he was still in command of the situation.

Carnwill bristled. "You said yourself the duke has been here at the citadel. If he chose not to tell you, then it isn't your concern. He won't thank you for prying into his business."

The commander frowned. Two options lay before him, and he was clearly comfortable with neither of them. Carnwill folded his arms, silent while he waited for the inevitable conclusion.

"The guards will let you through," the commander finally said, returning the parchment to him. "If you hurry you might catch the duke before he reaches Maranelle. Now get out of my sight before I change my mind."

EMERGING IN ERESTOR, Carnwill rode away from the citadel without a backward glance. In the duke's absence, the parchment had been unanswerable. Things would have ended very differently if he had called on the commander while the duke was still present at the citadel.

When the tracker had left Rog after two bizarre weeks in the presence of Agon, the king had given him a number of valuable gifts. The parchment was chief among them. Carnwill had no idea how King Agon had acquired the parchment, but the gift highlighted the significance of the mission the king had entrusted to him.

The message on the parchment was simple and clear. It read, "The Duke of Erestor commands that every requested assistance be provided to the bearer."

Whether the seal was genuine, Carnwill couldn't say. But the citadel commander had been convinced, and he must surely have seen the seal many times before.

Carnwill turned his mind to his reason for entering Erestor. Locating Thomas had been a major achievement, but his quarry was on the move. King Agon had known that Thomas was in hiding, and expected to be able to send in men to retrieve him as soon as the location had been identified. All that had now changed. Carnwill's efforts would have been completely wasted if he failed to keep Thomas in sight.

Based on his observations, a number of key people were heading for Maranelle, including the king and queen, Will Prentis, his deputy Rufe, and Thomas Stablehand with his family. They could be taking refuge with the duke in Maranelle, but it seemed unlikely.

The king had just taken control of an army, and his key commander was not staying behind to lead it. That must surely mean the king had something more important in mind.

Carnwill nodded with satisfaction. The king must be planning to travel by sea, almost certainly to Varas, and he was taking the most important of his subjects with him. The heirloom stolen by Thomas was clearly of great significance if he had been able to use it to gain the attention and favor of King Steffan.

Carnwill urged his horse forward. If Thomas was sailing to Varas with the king, Carnwill intended to make sure he sailed with them.

15

The sun cleared the treetops, flooding the grounds of Agon's palace with misty light. The king stood sullenly on his balcony peering out across the vista before him. Some might have called the scenery spectacular, but he wasn't in the mood.

Life would have felt a lot less frustrating for him if he'd managed to choose a regent who showed more aptitude as a student. Yet the grindingly slow progress with Krasmir was not the only thing that kept him awake at night.

Since the death of Lord Drettroth, Agon had become aware that two goals consumed much of the attention of his late army commander. The first was his quest to find and take possession of the Stone of Knowing. The second was his mission to attain unending life by sealing a bargain with the dark gods. His planned conquest of Arvenon, Varas, and Castel had been devised primarily in support of these purposes.

Once he fully understood what Drettroth had intended, Agon did not hesitate to adopt these goals as his own. And he was determined to succeed where his commander had failed. To his intense annoyance, both matters were yet to be resolved.

Agon spotted movement in the corner of his eye and turned to see a servant hovering fearfully near the door. Seeing that the king had spotted him, the man bowed deeply. "Great King, may you live forever..."

Agon eyed him impatiently. "Well?" he snarled.

"Your visit, Your Majesty."

The king glared back at him, trying to guess what visit he might be referring to.

"You wished to see the mystic..."

Agon flew into an instant rage. "Do you think I need to be told? Am I stupid?"

The man bowed and fled, almost tripping over himself in his haste to be gone from the king's presence.

The king left his private chambers immediately, heading for his horse. A guide was waiting for him, and he led the king out of Rog after explaining that the mystic lived about two hours' ride away.

The extended period in the saddle gave Agon an opportunity to reflect on his situation. After learning of Drettroth's plans he had at first decided to focus on finding the Stone of Knowing, both because it promised immediate benefits and because organizing a search seemed relatively straightforward.

As time went by, though, his attention had increasingly shifted to Drettroth's search for unending life. The lifespan allotted to him would come to an end sooner or later, however much his subjects might intone, "Great King, may you live forever." Without an effective bargain with the dark gods, none of the stones would be able to deliver lasting value to him. With such a bargain in place, his prospects would change dramatically. Perhaps he could even find patience for the time it was taking to add the Stone of Knowing to his arsenal.

Agon had found a scroll among Drettroth's effects that spoke of his plans to forge a deal with the dark gods. The problem had been to find a compliant priest who might be willing to shed light on the scroll and its vague references to the practical considerations involved in striking a suitable deal. No progress whatever had been made in finding such a person.

Rumors had long persisted that Drettroth once trained secretly to become a priest. The king dismissed such rumors, if only because he was certain Drettroth could never have found the time. Even so, Agon had wondered at times if he might be forced to undertake such training himself. He knew the idea was preposterous of course. Apart from the fact that he would find it abhorrent, he knew it would be no more realistic for him than it had been for Drettroth.

None of it would matter if only he could have made sense of the ramblings in Drettroth's scroll. With no hope of understanding it on his own, Agon's only other resort was to find someone who could.

He needed to make a copy of the scroll before letting another person anywhere near it. Given the supreme importance of protecting it from other eyes, Agon briefly considered doing the copy himself. Knowing he lacked the necessary patience, he took a more realistic approach and commissioned a scribe to do it on his behalf.

The moment the task had been completed, Agon snatched the duplicate from the scribe and examined it eagerly. The king had promised a handsome reward if the job was properly done, and he was as good as his word. The scholar had applied an exacting standard to the task, and the payment was thoroughly deserved.

The scribe left delighted, naively unaware that he would be executed the moment he left the king's presence. Disposing of the workman seemed to Agon an obvious necessity given the pressing need to keep the contents of the scroll secret. A side benefit was that the copy would cost him nothing once he retrieved his payment to the scribe.

With an exact duplicate now available, the king immediately secured the original scroll in a safe place. Agon would allow the mystic to peruse the copy. He was eagerly awaiting the assessment.

The dwelling occupied by the mystic was located deep within the forest, far from any other human habitation. When Agon first caught sight of it, he spat onto the ground in disgust, gesturing with his right hand to ward away evil. He hadn't expected a palace, but the hovel before him seemed scarcely fit for swine.

Before he could ride away, a grizzled figure in a dirty robe appeared in the entranceway. Although the man appeared old, he bent over in a surprisingly fluid bow. "Welcome to my humble dwelling, Great King," he said calmly, his bright eyes staring up at the king. "My name is Chalno."

Agon was taken by surprise. He realized he'd half expected the man to be completely insane. The mystic was merely disgusting. His teeth were rotten, and pus oozed from an open ulcer on his leg.

The king reluctantly decided he could tolerate disgusting, at least for a short time. The only question that mattered was whether this Chalno could shed light on Drettroth's scroll.

Two of Agon's guards checked the man for weapons before nodding to the king.

Agon had previously instructed his men to position themselves near at hand while remaining out of hearing range. He now waved them back.

Dismounting, he approached the mystic. "Read this," he commanded. "I want to know if you can make any sense of it."

The man studied the king quietly for a moment, his face a blank mask. Then he nodded once. Reaching for the scroll, he received it from the king's hand.

Chalno read the document slowly from start to end. "It is a scholarly text," he observed respectfully. He read it again thoroughly before finally gazing at the king.

"You wish to extend your life, Your Majesty. You wish to extend it indefinitely."

Since the mystic had not asked a question, the king did not bother to respond.

"The writer anticipates a heavy price. Are you able to pay it?"

"The payment is my business," the king replied testily. "What of the scroll? What sense do you make of it?"

Chalno again regarded him silently for a moment. "The author is a madman. Else a genius."

"Which is it?" demanded the king.

The mystic shrugged. "Either. Or both." He gazed into the heavens, and his eyes glazed over. The silence seemed to stretch out endlessly before he spoke again, his voice solemn. "The ravening she-wolf—is she a dangerous monster, or a nurturing mother?" he droned. "Her prey squeals one answer; her pups howl a different tune. What is the truth?"

Agon frowned. He had no interest in riddles. "Does the scroll offer a way of extending life indefinitely?"

"It does," purred the mystic, nodding wisely. "As it must."

"How is it to be done?"

"Slowly, and with great caution. How else can one make a captive of the wind?"

Agon clenched and unclenched his fists, working hard at containing his anger.

"What...do I need to do...to make it happen?" he demanded through gritted teeth.

"The stars of heaven shout an explanation, and the scroll echoes a reply: the spirit must grovel so the body can soar."

The king's patience ran out. "Don't dare to play word games with me," he roared. "Disappoint me and I'll have your heart ripped out! Once you find yourself in the clutches of Malzakh you can try your riddles on him!"

Chalno showed no concern whatever at the threat. He stared at the king thoughtfully. "I myself was a priest of the dark gods. It was long ago. But I have the knowledge still. Everything I once learned is in here." He tapped his skull. "The dark gods wanted everything." He slowly tapped his chest. "I fought for independence. The path was bitter—there is no easy road."

Agon scowled at him. He had no idea what the mystic was raving about. He opened his mouth to renew his threats, but Chalno got in first.

"You invoke the dread name of Malzakh, King Agon," said the mystic, apparently deciding to speak plainly at last. "But what do you really know of the Destroyer? And what do you know of Nehrvina, his Awful Sister?"

Agon shuddered involuntarily. He made no reply.

"I see you know no more than I guessed. These are not the right questions to ask you then," Chalno concluded with a shake of his head.

The mystic stood silently, peering at Agon with his penetrating eyes. The man seemed oblivious to the certain demise of anyone who dared talk down to the king. Finally he nodded to himself. "Here are the questions I must ask the king of Rogand."

He pointed at his chest. "What am I? Madman? Or genius?" He jabbed a finger at Agon. "And what are you? Wolf? Or prey?"

He nodded slyly. "You offer to separate my heart from my body. You suggest that the Destroyer will feast endlessly on my soul." He paused. "Perhaps you are wrong. Perhaps Nehrvina will take me."

Eyeing the king conspiratorially, he lowered his voice almost to a whisper. "Or perhaps neither destiny awaits me. Perhaps I have already made different arrangements of my own."

Agon stared wide-eyed at Chalno, completely bemused. What did the mystic mean? Was he suggesting he had some kind of leverage of his own with the dark gods?

The king ground his teeth in frustration. What could he do? He had threatened the mystic, and it had made no impact. Where could he go next? He saw that he had lost the initiative. Having done so, he found he had no idea how to regain it.

The king couldn't rule out the possibility that the fool knew something. He might even have the knowledge that Agon needed. Much as it galled him, he knew his only option for now was to exercise restraint.

"Four weeks," said the mystic abruptly, handing the scroll back to Agon.

Agon stared at him blankly.

"Come back in four weeks," the man repeated. Then he disappeared into his dwelling.

The king stood dazed for a moment. He had been dismissed. Turning meekly away, he headed for his horse.

Agon couldn't decide what to think of Chalno and his strange behavior. The mystic made no promises, but he had hinted he would have something further to say to the king in another four weeks.

A future meeting with Chalno would delay Agon's planned move to Arnost. It would also force him to extend his time in the company of Krasmir. Neither outcome was acceptable to him, and it was galling to find himself in such a position. As the king, Agon was the one who called the tune and settled the dates.

Nevertheless, he intended to do as he had been told.

As he rode back to Rog, he could not shake from his mind the mystic's question. What am I? Madman? Or genius? It would be so easy to conclude that Chalno was mad. But the mystic had taken the scroll seriously. And he was a former priest.

Agon had always been the one in command. Was he being played for a fool? He shook his head grimly. He would return in four weeks, and when he did all of the questions would be answered.

Chalno had asked another question. What are you? Wolf? Or prey?

If Agon didn't like the mystic's answers, Chalno would swiftly discover the answer to his question.

LONG BEFORE HE arrived back at the palace, Agon's mind had veered in a different direction. Drettroth's scroll had long baffled him. Now that he nurtured at least a faint hope of its mysteries being unraveled, his thoughts turned once more to the quest for the Stone of Knowing.

Drettroth had come tantalizingly close to achieving the goal. The Stone of Knowing had been almost within his grasp, and only his murder had denied him the prize. Agon had initiated his own search for the elusive stone as soon as he learned of Drettroth's actions. By then the trail had gone cold. After many months and more than one group of investigators, he was only now beginning to see progress.

Carnwill was the best of the best among trackers, and luring him to Rog was something Agon should have done much sooner. Two weeks under the influence of the Stone of Authority had been enough to ensure Carnwill's loyalty. Agon passed on every piece of information his previous agents had uncovered, then sent out his new tracker to resume the search.

Walking into his private suite in the palace, Agon found Ennawi standing near the balcony.

"It isn't all bad news," the king told the slave. "I've just heard from my newest agent. He's a tracker, and he's been searching for Thomas, the person who dared to take possession of the Stone of Knowing. He has him in sight at last."

Accustomed to a total lack of response from his slave, the king continued. "I'm sure you're asking where this Thomas has been hiding. It's an astute question, Ennawi, and no less than I've come to expect from you."

He nodded wisely at his slave. "All will be revealed before long. In the meantime, Ennawi, don't give in to impatience. No fugitive can hide forever, and the time is fast approaching when we'll run this one to ground."

16

The morning was not entirely spent when Breysen arrived at Maranelle with Brother Ander and Rufe, accompanied by the duke and his escort. A series of foothills overlooked the seaport, and he had stared down with astonishment at the panorama that opened before him as his weary horse crested the final ridge. A citadel built from white stone crowned the gleaming city that lay below him, and pennants of every color fluttered from the tall towers that climbed boldly into the blue sky. White sands shone on the broad beach that fringed the bay below the city, and fishing boats bobbed peacefully in the bay or sat proudly up on the sands. The scene could only be described as idyllic. And if that hadn't been enough, the smell of sea air filled his nostrils.

Noticing his expression, the duke had regarded him with amusement. "It's beautiful, isn't it?" the duke had asked.

"I never imagined that Maranelle could be described as beautiful," Breysen had replied. "I visited the port many times in my youth, but I don't recognize anything I'm seeing down there at all."

"You probably never left the port when you were here before," the duke suggested.

The duke was right.

The port at Maranelle was seedy and squalid, just like the ports in every city he had ever sailed to. No one could have described it as idyllic. And on his previous visits, Breysen had never found occasion to leave the dockside.

The duke pointed to a headland that jutted into the sea at one end of the wide bay below the city. "The port was built on the far side of Maranelle Head," he explained. "Fishing boats are always working the bay and the waters beyond it, so oceangoing ships are prohibited from sailing across the fishing grounds when they approach Maranelle. Ships heading for the port approach from the far side of Maranelle Head, and always from well out at sea. So you probably never even caught a glimpse of the city from the seaward side."

Breysen could only nod in wonder. As a lowly sailor, he'd never shown interest in such subtleties. He suddenly wondered how many other cities he'd visited without ever seeing them.

The duke led them to the citadel. After giving them an opportunity to wash off the dust of the road, he offered them refreshments. Breysen had surveyed the feast laid out by the duke's servants for no more than a moment before setting upon the food energetically. He noticed the duke eyeing him with a grin, but decided he didn't care. He'd never eaten this well. Who could guess how long it might last?

Even before all of them had eaten their fill, Rufe had become impatient. "We are grateful for your hospitality, My Lord Duke," he said. "Our pressing need now is to find a suitable ship."

"It isn't safe for you to wander around the docks on your own," the duke told him. "One of my men will escort you there." He called at once for one of his retainers, then added, "Speak to me before you make a final decision on a ship. I know something of most of the captains."

They thanked the duke gratefully.

The duke's man arrived and spent several minutes in quiet conversation with the duke.

Breysen watched them curiously. The duke's choice of a guide seemed eminently appropriate. The man's hard-bitten appearance and well worn clothing appeared more in keeping with a dockhand than a duke's retainer.

"This is Jaxin," the duke told them. "He will help you find what you're looking for."

Jaxin nodded to them sternly, then led them away without a word.

As they headed for the docks, Breysen noticed that Rufe seemed even more reserved than usual.

"Have either of you ever been to a port before?" he asked.

Both Rufe and Brother Ander shook their heads.

"Don't wander off anywhere," Breysen warned them. "The dockside district is controlled by a person known as the Peerless Mariner; there's one in every port I've ever visited. His men keep an eye out for strangers. Sailors are left alone if they mind their own business. But if you have no business in the docks you'll very quickly find yourself in trouble."

"Will they leave you alone?" asked the monk.

Breysen shrugged. "Maybe. Maybe not. If they decide any one of us is here without a good reason, we'll probably end up floating face down in the harbor before long."

Rufe raised his eyebrows. Brother Ander seemed unconcerned.

Many years had passed since Breysen last visited the docks of Maranelle. He quickly saw that very little had changed.

Jaxin clearly knew his way around. He led them to a large tavern with a narrow door. A couple of burly men stood just inside the entranceway. The sounds of loud conversation punctuated by raucous laughter issued from within.

Jaxin eyed them all closely, then nodded to Breysen. "You're with me."

He turned to Rufe and Brother Ander. "Wait here," he instructed them. "Don't follow us in. And stay out of trouble."

The men at the door admitted Jaxin without comment. They eyed Breysen briefly before stepping aside to let him in as well.

Breysen followed Jaxin into a large and dimly lit room dotted with tables. A haze of smoke filled the air, and sailors slouched on large stools around most of the tables. Many of the customers were loud and boisterous, and most of them were clearly tipsy.

Jaxin went to the bar and exchanged a few words with the bartender, who poked a finger at a couple of tables across the room. Many eyes turned in their direction as Jaxin headed for the first of the tables, Breysen close behind him.

A grizzled sailor with a long silver beard sat alone at the table, a large tankard of ale before him. He was chewing on the stem of a well worn pipe.

"Captain Yordin of the Nomad Lady?"

"Aye, that's my name and that's my ship. I know your face," he told Jaxin. He turned to Breysen. "Who might you be?"

"This is Breysen," said Jaxin, jabbing a thumb in Breysen's direction. "And in case you've forgotten, I'm Jaxin, and I work for the Duke of Erestor."

"The duke is known to me," the captain said noncommittally. He waved them to stools opposite him.

"The duke is looking for someone reliable to deliver some cargo for him," Jaxin said.

Captain Yordin grunted. "What's the nature of this cargo?"

"Passengers mostly. Thirty or so."

The captain's bushy eyebrows raised in mild surprise. "Where do they want to go?"

"Varacellan."

The captain grunted again. "The Lady is fast—she's a two master, a proper oceangoing ship—and she carries a bigger cargo than most vessels. What about the fee?"

Jaxin frowned. "Has the duke ever defaulted on payment?"

"He's reliable enough, and he knows the rate," the captain acknowledged with a nod. "When are these passengers wanting to depart?"

"As soon as you're ready to sail."

"My crew is short two or three men, but the mate should be able to find replacements today," the captain said. "We can sail with the tide tomorrow."

"The duke will want a say in any final decision," Jaxin told him. "If you don't hear otherwise by nightfall, you can assume that he has engaged your services."

The captain nodded. "Make sure your passengers are ready to board the Lady at sunrise," he said.

Jaxin shook his head. "Discretion is required in this particular case," he said. "You'll need to stand to as soon as the Nomad Lady has cleared the harbor. The passengers will be delivered to you by fishing boat."

Captain Yordin showed no sign of surprise. "Discretion costs more," he told them bluntly.

"You'll get your gold," growled Jaxin.

The captain pulled tobacco from a pouch and carefully began packing it into the bowl of his pipe. He appeared to have lost interest in them entirely.

Jaxin and Breysen stood up together and headed for the door. The noise level dropped momentarily, and Breysen noticed many pairs of eyes darting between them and Captain Yordin as they left.

Brother Ander glanced around him. No more than a few minutes had elapsed since Jaxin and Breysen disappeared inside the tavern. In that time a small group of men had gathered. They were staring at Rufe and the monk with undisguised disdain.

"We seem to have attracted some attention," Brother Ander observed.

Rufe didn't respond.

A wizened man stepped out from the group, looking them up and down contemptuously. "I don't like you," he said, jabbing a finger at the monk. "You don't belong here."

Brother Ander gazed back at him. "You and I have something important in common," he said calmly.

"Do we now?" snarled the wizened man, his fingers twitching around a knife that had appeared suddenly in his hand. "I live in the devil's backyard, and you live in a monastery. What could the likes of you possibly have in common with me?"

"We both draw breath from the same Creator," said the monk. He swept his arm around the group that had gathered. "It's true of all of us."

The knife man spat into the dirt. "Is that so?" he sneered. "I might just cut out your lungs. Then we can see for ourselves where your breath comes from."

The attacker lunged at the big monk with his knife extended. Brother Ander twisted easily aside, grabbing the man's wrist before he could withdraw it and squeezing hard. His assailant cried out with pain and dropped the knife.

Other men stepped forward, all of them armed with knives or clubs.

Rufe positioned himself beside the monk. He had picked up a large lump of wood, and he thumped it rhythmically into his other hand. The attackers drew back warily, sensing that the two strangers might not be the easy pickings they had first imagined.

At that moment Jaxin reappeared from inside the tavern, taking in the scene at a glance. He frowned at the semicircle of armed men hovering just out of reach. "Mess with them," he growled, jerking his head toward his companions, "and you'll have the duke down on you."

The monk's attacker stood cradling his crushed hand and wincing uncomfortably. "You don't rule here, Jaxin," he sneered, "and neither does your precious duke."

"Really?" asked Jaxin, raising his eyebrows. "Are you speaking on behalf of the Peerless Mariner or on behalf of yourself? Because I have a feeling that the duke would find that remark very interesting."

Another voice broke in. "We don't want no trouble." In little more than a heartbeat the other men had melted away. Brother Ander's attacker stood entirely alone.

"Perhaps we should continue this conversation in the city lock-up," Jaxin suggested.

"No harm done," mumbled the man sulkily before he too turned and scurried away.

"It's time we were gone," said Jaxin.

BREYSEN HURRIED AFTER JAXIN. Having witnessed a few too many dockside brawls in his past life, he had no desire to participate in one. Rufe and Brother Ander followed hard on his heels. They needed no urging either.

As they left the docks Breysen pondered the scene he had just glimpsed. The monk had faced down a hostile crowd, apparently without fear. Breysen had never met a monk quite like him. Rufe had seemed equally calm and untroubled—he was a good person to have around in a crisis.

All that aside, it was abundantly clear that they would have achieved nothing useful without Jaxin.

He thought about Captain Yordin. Breysen had served under many captains, and he knew how to read the signs. His instincts told him this man could be trusted, provided he was paid fairly and his ship wasn't put at risk.

Breysen was no untrained novice when it came to the sea though. Even with a reliable captain and a seaworthy vessel, nothing was ever certain the moment you stepped across the gangplank and said goodbye to solid ground.

CAPTAIN YORDIN'S interaction in the tavern with Jaxin had attracted the interest of one sailor in particular. Carnwill sat quietly sipping his ale and listening intently to all that was said.

As soon as Jaxin left, Carnwill sought out the mate of the Nomad Lady. Before the day was out he had boarded the ship as a new hand. He was soon hard at work with the other sailors preparing for departure the following morning.

He had no doubt that Thomas would be boarding the following day. The king and queen and a number of others would be sailing as well. Carnwill would need to be careful.

Caution was needed for another reason. King Agon had given him a very specific instruction before sending him away from Rog. *This Thomas must never be allowed to see you—not even to glimpse you,* the king had said. *Do you understand?*

Baffling as the instruction had been, the king must have said it for a reason, and Carnwill had taken careful note.

How he would manage to complete a voyage on the same ship without being noticed by Thomas he had yet to figure out. But he would find a way.

RANAULD HAD LAIN HIDDEN on a ridge with his two companions for several hours, peering down at the Arvenian army encamped below. It would be dark in little more than an hour. They would need to find a sheltered place to camp soon. He would use the hours of darkness to rest before he made his move.

It had taken several days of steady riding to reach this region and three more days to find the place where the northern army had camped. Army patrols seemed to be everywhere, and they had been forced to move cautiously to avoid being discovered. Eventually they had found an ideal location where they could observe the campsite undetected.

Ranauld had set out before Will made his attempt to regain control of the western army outside Steffan's Citadel. Even without knowing whether Will had been successful, though, Ranauld was confident that the vast majority of the regular soldiers in both locations were loyal to the king.

Ranauld's intent was to find a soldier he could trust, and ask that person to put him in touch with one of the original leaders of the army. Ranauld would have connected personally with many of them at one time or another.

The task shouldn't be difficult; in his role as a senior commander he had rubbed shoulders with a considerable number of soldiers after the Battle of Torbury Scarp. This army camp was vast, which made his job more challenging, but he only needed one person to start the process.

Sounds of restlessness from their tethered horses put Ranauld on sudden alert. He spun around to find that five mounted men had come between them and their horses. All of the riders held drawn weapons.

Ranauld's mind raced. The furtive nature of his behavior must have made it obvious that he was not connected with the army below. He and his men had been distracted with their observations, and therefore unusually vulnerable, yet the five men had not raised the alarm or moved against them while they held the advantage. The new arrivals had not even challenged them.

The most likely conclusion was that the newcomers were no more connected to the army below than Ranauld and his men were.

He stood up slowly and carefully, keeping his hands well away from his sword. "Who might you be?" he asked.

Several of the newcomers flicked a glance at one of their number, a wiry man with a confident demeanor. He was clearly the leader. "We could ask you the same question," he said. "What are you doing spying on the army?"

These men must surely be Castelan soldiers. Ranauld decided to take a risk. "You're Castelans, aren't you?"

The wiry leader offered no immediate response. But he didn't deny it. Then he spoke abruptly. "I know you," he said. "You were with Will Prentis at Torbury Scarp."

Ranauld gave a slight bow. "Count Ranauld at your service," he confirmed. "Did you fight there?"

"I did," the wiry man told him. After a pause, he added, "You're right. We are Castelans."

Ranauld nodded. "You asked why we are here. Enemies of King Steffan have taken control of the capital, Arnost, and placed mercenaries in charge of the king's armies. The army below has come here on their orders. Most of the regular soldiers are loyal to the king. Our goal is to make contact with them, and regain control of the army on behalf of the king."

He peered at the Castelan leader. "Why are you here?"

"I can tell you that we're not in any way associated with your mercenaries," the stranger returned. After a moment's consideration, he added decisively, "You need to come with us. Details can wait until we're back at our base."

Should he go with them? If he did it would almost certainly prevent him from making contact with the army anytime soon.

However, Ranauld's other key purpose was to communicate directly with the Castelans on King Steffan's behalf. It appeared he was being offered an unusual opportunity to do just that. Having just left the king he was in a unique position to explain to the Castelans that his monarch had no hostile intentions toward them.

Peaceful intentions made little difference, of course, while King Steffan was not in control of the Arvenian forces. But Ranauld could also make the Castelans aware of the king's fierce determination to do whatever was necessary to regain control of his country and his armies.

He would have preferred not to be faced with achieving only one of his two goals. Nevertheless he soon reached his decision. "We'll come with you," he said.

The wiry man shook his head. "Just you, Count Ranauld. Your friends can do as they please."

Ranauld hesitated, frowning. Then he nodded reluctantly. He turned to his companions. "You know why we're here. Do anything you can," he told them.

The men looked bewildered, but he had no real choice but to leave them to take their own initiative. They were reliable men, but he knew they had little chance of achieving anything useful without him.

He walked to his horse and mounted, then with a wave to his companions he rode away with the Castelans.

The men carefully worked their way around the encamped

northern army until they came to open ground, then they rode swiftly in a northerly direction.

Even before they reached their destination, it became obvious to Ranauld that they were heading for Deadman's Pass, the only accessible pass through the mountains that marked the border between Arvenon and Castel. His guides were clearly Castelan scouts, sent to observe the Arvenian army.

When they arrived at the entrance to Deadman's Pass, the leader gave a password, and a path was opened wide enough to admit one horse at a time. The barrier was replaced as soon as the last of the men had ridden through.

The leader of the scouts disappeared for a few minutes. The moment he returned he approached Ranauld.

"Please come with me, Count Ranauld," he said. "Our commander has requested that you leave your weapons with us." He nodded toward one of his men. "Purely in view of the current uncertainties between our armies. I hope you understand. We will take good care of them until they can be returned to you."

Ranauld hesitated only briefly. Quickly deciding that he would probably make the same request if the roles were reversed, he removed his sword belt and his knife and handed them over.

The scout led him to a tent. The guards standing outside nodded to the scout, and he ushered Ranauld inside. A thick set man sat in an elaborate chair. His face appeared neutral at best.

"Count Ranauld, this is Lord Kaebon. He commands the Castelan army here."

Ranauld bowed, and the commander nodded stiffly in return before waving him to a seat.

"Why are you here?" Lord Kaebon asked him bluntly.

"Your men insisted I return with them to your base," Ranauld replied evenly. "Fighting Castelan soldiers was never on my agenda, so I agreed to join them."

Lord Kaebon made no response.

Ranauld decided to be more direct. "I have recently come from

King Steffan. It occurred to me that there might be an unexpected opportunity for dialogue between our two kingdoms."

The commander grunted. "I will send to Castel Citadel for instructions," he said. "In the meantime I will arrange for you to be offered refreshments and somewhere to sleep. I will also assign two soldiers to you for security."

When Ranauld raised his eyebrows, Lord Kaebon added, "Purely for your own protection, of course. Given recent provocations, I'm sure you will understand that not all of our men are inclined to view Arvenians in a favorable light."

The commander nodded stiffly once more, and Ranauld was ushered from the tent.

17

Thomas and Elena had gathered with the other members of the party heading for Varacellan.

"Yordin's boat, the 'Nomad Lady', is eminently seaworthy. And the man himself is dependable, Your Majesty," the duke was saying. "He's as solid as any of the captains out there."

"None of that sounds like a ringing endorsement," the king told him. His brows drew together. "I hope we're doing the right thing."

The duke didn't seem at all concerned. "It will all turn out well in the end," he said with a smile. "I have a very good feeling about it."

"I hope you're right, Uncle," the king replied. He raised his arms in a gesture of resignation. "We're in your hands. When do we need to head for the port?"

"Yes...," said the duke, looking a little uneasy. "About that..." Glancing first at Jaxin, then at Breysen, he squared his shoulders. "You won't be boarding from the port," he announced.

The king stared at him blankly.

The duke looked the king squarely in the eye. "If you appear on the docks with your retinue, Your Majesty," he said, "you might as well proclaim your intentions from the rooftops. Within twenty-four hours the entire world will know that the king has fled Arvenon for Varas."

The king threw up his arms again. "So how do we board?"

"We'll wait until the ship has left port, then we'll board you from fishing boats."

"From fishing boats? In the middle of the ocean? How do you expect to get a baby on board? And what about the queen?"

"It won't be entirely straightforward," admitted the duke. "But the captain and his crew are resourceful people, and none of you are in any way disabled. The queen has proven herself capable of managing in much more challenging circumstances."

"No one so much as hinted at any such necessity when I was considering the options," grumbled the king.

The duke winced a little, but he said nothing further.

"What do you think about this, Breysen?" the king asked.

"The transfer won't be straightforward, Your Majesty," Breysen told him frankly. "But I'm sure we will manage it." He hesitated for a moment, then he added, "Provided the seas aren't too rough of course." He glanced at the duke before quickly adding, "I believe that My Lord Duke is right about what will happen if you board at the port."

The king ran a hand across his face. Then he shook his head. "I suppose we're committed now," he said. "Somehow we'll have to find a way to make it work."

Breysen stood on the pitching deck of the Nomad Lady, peering down at Rufe as he steadily climbed the rope net to the deck. Little Tamara was carried along as well, secured to him in her riding sling.

After a few minutes of nervous deliberation, Elena and Thomas had agreed to entrust their little daughter to Rufe. Now they stood beside Breysen on the deck, looking on anxiously as the ship swung erratically back and forth, threatening to pitch the burly soldier and his little passenger into the rolling seas. They were visibly relieved when he safely completed the climb.

King Steffan had been one of the first to clamber aboard, and he monitored Rufe's progress closely. Seeing that the journey had proceeded without incident, the king waved his permission for little Prince Aiden to be transported in the same way, secured to Brother Ander. The queen watched from a fishing boat below as the monk took his turn on the rope net, her face noticeably pale even from a distance.

The prince reached the deck safely and without incident as well.

With the exception of the queen and two final soldiers, the rest of the party had already braved the hazardous climb. Although the swell was by no means mountainous, the boat rocked back and forth constantly, occasionally lurching violently as it rolled after cresting a wave. The unpredictable movement made the climb up the ship's side extremely challenging, and Breysen was both amazed and relieved to see person after person complete the journey without incident.

The time had now come for the queen to take her turn. The fishing boat that had brought her to the ship was also pitching and rolling in the swell, and like those who had preceded her she had to wait for the right moment to launch herself forward onto the coarse rope netting.

The king gasped audibly as his wife leaped from the fishing boat and grasped hold of the net. She began to climb steadily upward, pausing whenever the ship's movement made it unsafe to continue. She appeared to be in no danger of falling, and the king began to relax a little as she crossed the halfway mark.

Below her the first of the remaining two soldiers made the leap and began scaling the rope net. He had barely begun his upward journey when a larger than usual wave caused the ship to roll viciously. The netting swung outward before crashing back into the side of the ship. The queen, higher up the net and less affected by its movement, managed to cling on. The soldier was not so fortunate. After swinging far away from the ship, he came smashing back into its side as the Lady rolled the other way. The force of the shock dislodged his grip on the rope, and he fell backward toward the sea. As he fell, one of his legs caught in the netting. Breysen heard a sickening crack as the force of his fall snapped his leg. The soldier cried out in agony.

Every watcher on board gasped. Without a moment's hesitation, the queen climbed back down to him. A moment later, one of the sailors on the fishing boat grabbed a hatchet and jumped for the netting.

"Can you lift him, Your Majesty?" the sailor cried over the loud groans of the injured man.

"He's too heavy for me," she called back. "Give me the hatchet!"

The sailor hesitated at first, but seeing no alternative, he yielded to her demand and handed it over.

"Don't let him go!" she called as she began hacking away at the rope around his leg.

Whenever she hesitated, the sailor offered directions. "That piece next!"

She continued chopping with all her might.

As the last piece of rope parted, the sailor grasped the injured man tightly as he fell free. Another cry of agony came from the soldier, causing Breysen to wince again.

Other sailors on the fishing boat had retrieved a piece of fishing net, and they prepared to throw it across to their fellow crewman.

"Support him, Your Majesty!" the sailor called as the net was thrown across to him.

The queen took hold of the man while the sailor wrapped the net around him.

Lengths of rope stretched from each end of the new net back to the fishing boat, and the sailors took in the slack. Another of the sailors jumped into the water holding a large wooden plank and swam it across to the ship, drawing as close as he dared to the pitching vessel. Assisted by the queen, the sailor beside her lowered the injured man onto the wood as carefully as they could manage in the rolling seas, the sailor in the water holding him steady.

The first sailor retrieved his hatchet from the queen and slipped into the water on the other side of the wooden plank. The queen watched from her position on the rope netting as the men on the fishing boat steadily pulled on the ropes, drawing in the sailors with the soldier floating between them. When they reached the side of the boat, the net was lifted on board, bringing its human cargo with it.

The two swimmers were pulled from the water.

The first sailor waved to the queen. "We'll get him back to shore," he called.

She waved back, then once again began climbing upward, soon followed by the final soldier.

The king began to pace restlessly along the deck, almost frantic with worry whenever the ship rolled more vigorously than usual. When the queen finally appeared over the side of the deck, he ran to her and embraced her fiercely, completely oblivious to the stares of everyone on board.

The queen quickly detached herself and hurried to her infant son. Only once she had satisfied herself that he was well did she allow herself to relax. Heaving a slow sigh of relief, she beamed a smile at the people around her.

Thirty handpicked soldiers from the army of Erestor had accompanied the king and his party, every one of them expert with both the bow and the sword. They had long since climbed aboard. Another fishing boat had transported their supplies, and swords, bows, thick bundles of arrows, and additional food supplies were now hauled up to the deck.

Captain Yordin had insisted on giving up his own cabin to the king and queen, and Breysen noticed him showing them to their quarters. He was not absent for long. The ship was now under sail, and the captain soon hurried back to the helm, shouting orders as he went.

With the drama of the boarding behind them, Breysen was soon busy helping the soldiers and the other members of the king's party find hammocks below decks. Few of them had ever sailed before, and it was obvious to Breysen that many of them would be emptying their stomachs before long. He was determined to return to the deck as soon as he possibly could. Experience had taught him the wisdom of staying well clear of first time passengers when things started to get messy.

THE WIND HAD PICKED up noticeably, and the crew of the Lady were reefing the sails. Spotting Will leaning over the railing, Breysen hurried to his side.

"Careful you don't fall in," he said, speaking loudly enough to be heard over the wind and the creaking of the timbers. He was only half joking.

Will glanced at him with heavy lidded eyes. Seeing the look on his face, Breysen's first instinct was to burst out laughing. But he quickly choked it back. He hadn't forgotten how kindly he had been treated when he was at his lowest point.

"You look a little green about the gills there," he said.

"Do you...enjoy this?" Will managed, waving a hand vaguely about him.

Breysen took hold of the rails and tilted back his head, closing his eyes as he filled his lungs with the cold salty air. "Yes!" he replied with feeling. "It's been far too long."

Will risked a glance over the railing. "Even in these mountainous seas?"

Breysen's eyebrows went up in surprise. "These seas are by no means mountainous. Wait until you experience a real storm!"

Seeing the look on Will's face, he hastily added, "You needn't worry. Unless I've completely lost my weather sense, the wind is much more likely to ease off."

Will turned away to retch helplessly once more over the side. Then he pushed himself back from the rail and headed unsteadily for the hatch and the ladder that led below.

As he left, the king and queen appeared on deck. Swaying in an effort to compensate for the motion of the deck, they wended their way to Breysen's side. The queen held her baby firmly in one arm.

With the other she had locked arms with the king to steady herself against the constant rolling of the ship. Neither of them seemed at all troubled by seasickness.

The three of them watched together as Will stumbled down the steps on his way below.

"Poor Will," said the queen. "He doesn't look at all well."

"No, he doesn't," said the king. "It seems we've finally found something that doesn't come naturally to our worthy commander," he added with a wry smile.

"He has the first stage of seasickness, Your Majesty," Breysen noted dryly.

"What's that?" asked the king.

"It's when someone feels so ill they're afraid they're going to die," Breysen replied.

"Is there a second stage?" asked the queen.

Breysen nodded. "The second stage is when they're afraid they're going to live," he told her.

The queen burst out laughing.

Noticing that the king's only response was a raised eyebrow, Breysen turned quickly to the queen to change the subject. "How is the baby coping, Your Majesty?" he asked.

"Surprisingly well," she replied, gazing down tenderly at the infant. "He's mostly been asleep since he came on board."

Seeing the way she responded to her son brought to mind his own wife and children, and Breysen shifted his attention to his feet in an attempt to recover himself.

Queen Essanda must have guessed what was on his mind. "Brother Ander tells me that the monk is very reliable. I mean the one you spoke to, who's planning to search out your wife and children."

"Thank you, Your Majesty," he replied. He managed to master himself again, but the silence still felt awkward.

"Do you know these waters, Breysen?" asked the king briskly.

Breysen nodded. "I have traveled them many times before, Your Majesty. We're currently sailing north along the coast of Arvenon.

Depending on the winds, we should cross into Castelan waters sometime tomorrow. We'll continue north until we sight Point Turtan. Captain Yordin will then have a choice. He can steer a northeasterly course through Savage Strait, between the mainland and Baron Island. Or he could head north for a while longer and sail right around the island. The strait is quicker to navigate, but it has many shoals. Traveling around Baron Island would allow us to avoid the shoals entirely. It's a longer journey, though, and it would take us into open sea, well away from coastal waters."

"Savage Strait doesn't sound promising," the king observed.

"It can certainly be true to its name if the weather is bad," Breysen told him. "But the passage isn't usually difficult provided the weather is good. And the scenery is quite unique."

"And will we reach Varacellan once we navigate the strait?"

"Not quite. There will be more small islands to sail past and more shoals to avoid. But those waters are more protected. As long as we navigate those seas during daylight hours there should be little risk. If the captain decides to use Savage Strait, he'll try to enter it soon after dawn. If the winds are fair, we should be able to reach Varacellan by nightfall."

"Have you ever been shipwrecked, Breysen?" asked the queen.

"Yes, once. If you are interested I would be happy to tell you about it sometime, Your Majesty. Perhaps after our voyage is over," he said with a smile.

A particularly large wave loomed ahead, seeming to tower above them. The ship rose high on the wave before plunging down again as it rolled past.

"I don't want to hear anything about shipwrecks until I'm back on solid ground," said the king emphatically.

18

Pisander wandered along the battlements of Arnost castle, head down and with his hands clasped behind his back. He avoided eye contact with the soldiers on the walls; they took the hint and ignored him.

He needed the fresh air—it cleared his senses. These days he spent far too long in his office trying to administer Arvenon. Even his own private schemes had largely been pushed into the background.

Lady Ona had ridden out the previous day, and he was glad to see the last of her. There was no denying the woman had stirred a few of Lygell's people into action, but she'd also exposed the incompetence of many among his new nobility.

She'd even forced Lygell to send some of his officials to the dungeons. Pisander supposed he should be grateful to her—sooner or later he would have needed to execute some of them himself, and she'd helpfully identified the most likely contenders for the hangman's noose.

She'd become a problem only when she refused to let him recruit her. He wasn't lying when he told her he needed her skills, but putting her to work wasn't his sole motivation. She was going to report back to Agon, and he'd counted on having her in his employ when that happened. She would have been much more likely to deliver a sympathetic report if he'd been lining her pockets.

There was no use worrying about it. He would figure out how to handle Agon when he arrived.

He was still waiting for clear information about the date. The Rogandan king had deferred his trip more than once already, and Pisander couldn't help wondering why.

There were benefits to the delay—it gave him more time to get his own house in order.

The robed figure of Lygell was trudging in his direction, and Pisander paused from his pacing to observe his progress. His deputy was joining him on the battlements in response to Pisander's summons. Lygell didn't look happy. This meeting wasn't going to improve his mood.

Pisander waited until Lygell reached him. "You've got work ahead of you," he said bluntly. "Lady Ona hasn't made either of us look good. Fixing that is your problem, because you appointed the incompetent idiots she flushed out."

Lygell made no immediate reply, but his face darkened at the mention of Lady Ona.

Pisander saw his reaction and was not impressed by it. "Wake up to yourself, Lygell!" he snapped. "You were a fool to let her get to you. She never had any interest in you—she was only ever using you from the beginning."

Seeing Lygell's brow darkening with anger, Pisander reached out and slapped him hard on the face.

Before his deputy could react, Pisander leaned in and jabbed a finger painfully into his shoulder. "Don't think you can behave like a child around me, Lygell! I'm not here to coddle you. You'd better sharpen up! Agon is coming, and Lady Ona will have delivered her report before he gets here. If you haven't turned things around dramatically by the time he arrives, he'll separate your head from your shoulders in a heartbeat."

Lygell stared at Pisander with startled eyes.

Pisander glared back at him. "You wanted power, didn't you? Is that what you thought this position was about? Getting a chance to throw your weight around? If that's what you thought, you'd better think again. I've given you plenty of chances, and this will be the last. I want a plan on my desk by sunset tomorrow. You're going to show me how and when you're planning to fix everything that's broken. You'll hand me a list of every one of your people who hasn't been performing. I don't care if you send them to the dungeons or the gallows, but a lot of your precious friends won't be here next week. It'll be them or you. Your choice."

Lygell's cheeks were flushed, and he couldn't meet Pisander's eyes.

"Get out of here!" growled the former earl.

He shook his head in disgust as Lygell retreated in disarray from the battlements. It remained to be seen whether Lygell would be able to extricate himself from his predicament. If not, Pisander would be finding himself a new deputy.

He cursed under his breath. Good people weren't easy to find. If they were, he wouldn't be in this position.

He largely had himself to blame though, and he knew it. Appointing Lygell was shaping up as a major blunder.

He thought he'd recognized something of himself in his deputy. Lygell had the same hunger for power, the same ruthlessness, the same ability to focus, and the same ability to strike fear into both subordinates and enemies.

He seemed to have begun well. However it was becoming clear that he lacked the ability to see the bigger picture. Since he seemed unable to focus on the overarching goals, his failures were hardly surprising. He hadn't acted to achieve his goals, nor had he identified likely barriers to his success. If Lygell couldn't do it himself, he had no hope of effectively mobilizing the people below him.

Pisander headed back down to his office. He had troubles of his own to attend to.

One of his aides intercepted him. "Jarah has arrived and wishes to speak with you, My Lord."

Pisander nodded. "Send him to my office."

As he returned to his office, it occurred to Pisander that Jarah's arrival might be timely. If things turned ugly, Pisander was going to need a few reliable people on hand who weren't frightened to knock heads together.

He'd worked with some good people over the years, and he wished he could still call on some of them. During his early years in Erestor—when he was still known as Lord Dunnridge and before he became the Earl of Pisander—he'd employed an enforcer named Fowkes. Of all his past associates, he missed Fowkes the most. The man had been reliable, dedicated, effective, and utterly ruthless.

No one had unlimited luck though. Having sent Fowkes to finish off a noblewoman called Lady Neave, there had been no further word from him. It later became apparent that Fowkes and his men hadn't succeeded in finishing the job, since Lady Neave, or Anneka as she now called herself, had resurfaced during the Rogandan invasion.

It was long past time Pisander did something about her. He had never tolerated unfinished business. At the same time, he had never allowed his need for revenge to blind him to more important priorities. He would deal with Anneka when he had his house in order.

Jarah appeared at the door of his office not long after he arrived himself.

Pisander waved him to a seat. "Have you made any progress? I'm overdue for some good news."

Jarah had been gone a long time. The grim look on his face ruled out good news, but he didn't look entirely discomfited. That suggested he had at least something to report.

Before Jarah started, Pisander added, "You fed me a lot of information when you last reported, and I've had far too much on my mind since then. Give me a simple summary to refresh my memory."

"Certainly, My Lord," Jarah replied. "You might remember that after a considerable amount of effort we eventually identified the boy who showed up at your council of lords meeting. His name is Thomas. He wasn't easy to track down—he's moved around a lot, and he mostly kept well out of sight. He did come back to Arnost a few years ago to get married, and some very interesting people attended the wedding. Will Prentis was there. And the queen."

Pisander nodded. These details weren't easy to forget.

"After the wedding they disappeared. The young woman he married was unusually beautiful though, and that helped a lot in tracking them. It's much harder to hide someone who stands out. They hid themselves away in a remote location in a forest with two or three others. We eventually found the location, but it had been abandoned. Either they burned their own dwellings to the ground, or someone got there before us."

"Who else would go after them?" Pisander asked skeptically.

Jarah shrugged. "I don't know. Probably no one. The trail led back to Arnost. We found out that his parents had been living right next to the castle the whole time. His father, Axel, was the stable master. When we went to get the parents we discovered they'd fled as well. We only just missed them. That's a summary of my last report."

"So what have you been doing since?"

"It seemed likely that this Thomas and Elena had gone with his parents, so we set off after them. Then we received word that they had parted company and headed in the direction of Erestor. So we stopped trailing the parents and went after them instead.

"We didn't find them, but there were indications they'd joined up with Will Prentis. As I'm sure you know, Will Prentis vanished around that time. They apparently vanished along with him."

Pisander glowered at Jarah. He was not in the mood to be presented with the latest in a growing list of failures.

Jarah apparently decided it was time to change the subject. "There's more, My Lord," he added hastily. "As you know, Lord Redfass has been commanding the western army camped on the borders of Erestor, just outside Steffan's Citadel, with the support of a large number of mercenaries. On our way here we unexpectedly met some of Lord Redfass's men. They told us that Will Prentis has reappeared. With help from Rufe Sarjant, he's taken control of the army. Lord Redfass and almost all of the other mercenaries have been killed. Prentis let some of the survivors go, without horses or weapons, and they're on their way here now. A few of them even begged Prentis to let them join his army."

Pisander scowled.

"The Thomas and Elena we've been searching for are probably there as well, assuming they remained with Will Prentis. And that's not all. When the mercenaries were leaving, they saw someone ride up and address the soldiers. They were a long way off by then, but a few of them swear it was the king."

Pisander narrowed his eyes. The situation had deteriorated more than he could have imagined possible.

"Your search for Thomas is on hold, as of now," he told Jarah. "For the immediate future I'm going to have more pressing tasks for you to do. Get your men settled in at the castle, and make sure I know where to find you at all times."

Having dismissed Jarah, he located one of his aides. "Find Lygell, and bring him here. Now!"

The aide hurried away immediately.

Jarah's report had shaken Pisander from his lethargy. Having begun with real energy, the former earl saw now that he had allowed his focus to wander since taking control of Arnost. Apparently Will Prentis had not made the same mistake.

Everything was about to change. Pisander had clawed his way into a position of strength, and he wasn't about to give it up. The king might have an army now, but without control of Arnost, his options were limited.

Pisander did not waste a moment. He located a quill and a blank parchment and sat down to write a note to King Agon. He debated with himself for several minutes before deciding he needed to keep it brief and to the point. Eventually he simply urged the king to come to Arnost as soon as possible, and to bring an army with him. Agon would have come with an army anyway, but Pisander's request should cause him to be especially alert.

By the time Lygell arrived, Pisander's messenger was already on his way to Rog with the dispatch.

As Lygell entered the room, Pisander was pleased to see anger prominent in the mixture of emotions revealed on his deputy's face.

Now was not the time to search out a replacement for Lygell. Pisander needed to work with what he had.

"The king is back," he told Lygell bluntly. "And Will Prentis is with him. They have taken control of Redfass's army. Close the gates of Arnost immediately, and get men onto the city walls. From now on the gate will be opened briefly twice a day, and anyone entering or leaving will be questioned and searched. Send armed men into the surrounding countryside to requisition supplies. I want the city fully stocked in preparation for a siege. As of now we're effectively at war."

He stared grimly at his dumbfounded deputy. "Your opportunity to redeem yourself has just arrived."

Without waiting for a response, he added, "Send messengers to the northern army camped at the borders of Castel and find out who's commanding it. If it's our people, tell them to break camp and return to Arnost. We won't bring them into the city—they'll be needed to keep Prentis away from the border with Rogand. I don't want King Agon forced to fight his way into Arvenon. And tell them to find anyone in the ranks who used to be a captain under Prentis. Any leaders who served under the king should be executed immediately."

He shook his head. "Redfass was a fool. He demoted the original leaders to the ranks. Prentis probably has them all reinstated by now."

Lygell's mouth had been hanging open, but his eyes had narrowed and his face had set. His features now showed nothing but determination. "There's a lot I need to do. With your permission, I'll withdraw and get started."

Pisander nodded. He watched in satisfaction as Lygell strode from the room.

All of them, himself included, had been asleep at the helm. Lady Ona had attempted to shake them out of their stupor, but it had taken Will Prentis to fully wake them.

Now they were alert at last. Prentis had poked his stick into the viper's den, and the serpent was about to slither out, fully aroused. Will Prentis would have no one but himself to blame.

19

Thus far little Tammi was not coping at all well with life at sea, and neither Rubin nor Haldek was doing much better. Thomas and Elena found themselves tending to all three. Thomas insisted that Elena should take a break, and when she returned he made his way onto the deck for some fresh air.

Seeing Brother Ander standing alone by the rail, Thomas joined him.

The two of them stood in companionable silence for a time, watching a large pod of dolphins frolicking beside the ship. There was something captivating about the exuberance of the animals as they glided through the water, slicing effortlessly through the bow wave before diving and reappearing alongside.

Thomas stole occasional glances at his friend. The monk seemed relaxed and content, so different from the man Thomas had known before the fight in the village where Ander almost lost his life. So much had changed for all of them since then.

“Do you think about Brother Vangellis much?” Thomas asked.

The monk glanced briefly at him, then nodded. “Yes. Often.”

Thomas had once put a question to Brother Vangellis that his late friend had not been able to answer. The question related to Brother

Ander, and it struck Thomas that now might be the perfect opportunity to resolve a matter he had long wondered about.

"I know you came to respect Brother Vangellis as much as I did," said Thomas. "But why did you dislike him so much at first?"

The stone could readily have provided a detailed answer, of course, but Thomas refused to consider using it for such a purpose.

Brother Ander gazed out over the waves for some time without speaking.

The silence stretched out for long enough that Thomas felt uncomfortable. He began to wonder if his bluntness had been offensive. "Forgive me if I was too intrusive," he said awkwardly. "Just ignore the question."

After a further short silence Brother Ander turned to look at him. He didn't look upset. "I don't mind talking about it," he said. "It brings back painful memories, and that's the only reason I've been slow to answer."

The monk sighed. "I had a younger sister when I was growing up. We all agreed she was made of sunshine and laughter." He nodded toward the bow where the dolphins were still playing. "Those creatures make me think of her—they're all carefree energy and playfulness."

He stared off into the horizon. "Sickness came to our village from time to time. The very old and the very young were always vulnerable, but one of the contagions took my sister. She was her normal happy self in the morning, and by the time the sun had set she was dead.

"All of us were devastated. My parents went to the priest to arrange her burial. He was well known to be an evil man—it's obvious to me now that he didn't know God at all, in spite of his profession. He demanded money to do burials, and in my sister's case the amount was much more than my parents could afford. He said if they didn't pay he would bury her outside the graveyard with the murderers. We'd been told that anyone buried there was doomed to spend eternity in hell.

"My mother was horrified. The very thought of her precious

daughter being condemned for eternity was more than she could bear. She somehow came up with the money and paid the priest, against my father's wishes. My father knew our family was being plunged into poverty, and he told the priest exactly what he thought of him.

"The priest carried out the ceremony, then told the gravedigger to bury her outside the fence. It was his way of hitting back at my father. My mother never recovered—the horror of it sent her to an early grave herself."

Thomas was appalled.

"My father refused to have anything more to do with the priest," Brother Ander continued, "so my mother was buried outside the fence as well, beside my sister."

He shook his head. "My father was never the same. He became consumed with anger—he was difficult to be around. I came to hate the priest bitterly.

"The priest spent the money he extorted on wine, and one day I came upon him when he was drunk. I railed at him to his face. I would have killed him if I dared. He cursed me in return. He told me I was destined for an eternity in hell with my sister and mother.

"The moment I was old enough, I left the village to become a soldier. I had a deep well of anger inside me, and the army gave me an outlet for it.

"Eventually we all joined Will when he left Arnost, and he led us to the monastery to collect our new guide. I hated Brother Vangellis from the moment I clapped eyes on him. I was blinded by my bitterness—all I could see was the drunken priest from my village. If he'd died when I slashed his wineskins, I wouldn't have cared a bit."

Thomas listened wide-eyed, horrified at the chain of events that had brought Ander to such a state.

"As you know, I was soon on the brink of death myself after the battle with Baron Rudungen's men. I had no idea that Brother Vangellis was fighting for my life, refusing to rest for days on end. I could never have imagined any man doing that for a person who hated him so much." He shook his head.

Brother Ander looked Thomas in the eye. "I've never told anyone else about this, Thomas, but I had a vision while I was lying there wounded. I know it was a vision now, but it felt completely real to me at the time.

"I woke to find myself in hell. It was horror beyond description. I was absolutely terrified. And who should be there to greet me but the priest from my village? I knew he'd died since I joined the army. He was in torment himself, but he was delighted when he saw me arrive. He shouted at me, 'You finally got what you deserve!'

"I was in dread of him and turned away to look for my sister and my mother. When he saw what I was doing, he just laughed at me. 'They're not here, you fool! It makes no difference what side of the fence you're buried on!' He started gloating. 'I was the one who taught you to hate. Now you're condemned for all time! You'll spend eternity here, with *me*!'"

Brother Ander passed a hand across his face. "I know it wasn't real, but I've never forgotten the sound of him mocking me."

The look in the monk's eyes unnerved Thomas. "What happened?" he asked.

"I was completely without hope. Then Brother Vangellis called me. I can't really explain what happened—all I know is I woke up to find him tending me, along with Elbruhe."

"So your sister and mother didn't end up in hell?" Having blurted out the question, Thomas immediately berated himself for his insensitivity in asking.

Brother Ander didn't mind. "That isn't for me to say. God decides a person's destiny." He shrugged. "It might have felt real, but it was just a vision. It's true that the location of a person's grave makes no difference though."

"Was the vision the reason you became a monk?" asked Thomas.

Brother Ander shook his head. "No." A wry smile came to his face. "Some people probably think I became a monk out of guilt, or because I needed to repay a debt. They weren't the reasons.

"I hated Brother Vangellis, and I knew from experience that hate is more infectious than the plague. Yet he wasn't infected by it.

"In the end he did a lot more than dress my wounds when I was lying there. I wasn't in a good state, even before the fight in the village. My anger was never far from the surface—hatred oozed out of every pore. The weird thing was that Brother Vangellis might have had his own flaws, but grace oozed out of him.

"You asked why I decided to become a monk. When he pulled me out of hell—and I don't just mean in my vision—it undid me completely.

"All my life I'd wanted to lead men into battle. I finally got my chance at Torbury Scarp, and it didn't satisfy me at all. After a while I realized I wanted to do what he'd done." He raised his arms helplessly. "So I decided I needed to become a monk."

"And now you've become a healer as well." Thomas gazed at the monk in wonder. "I remember what you were like before," he said. "You're different. You seem more content."

Brother Ander said nothing in response, but he returned a smile.

Realizing that he needed to return to his duties, Thomas said a reluctant farewell to the monk and headed below deck again.

The impact of Brother Ander's words remained with him long after the conversation had ended.

A STIFF BREEZE pushed the hair from Breysen's eyes as he stood on the deck basking in the sunshine. No matter how many years he might have spent on dry land, the sea was in his blood.

The king stood beside him, gazing around in wonder and peering up at the squawking gulls that wheeled overhead. "It's stunning!" He pointed to a land mass rising out of the sea off to one side. "What's that ahead? Given the direction we're sailing, I suppose it must be an island, but if so it seems surprisingly big."

"That's Baron Island off the port bow," Breysen told him. "Captain Yordin must have decided to navigate the strait." He slowly turned full circle, staring at the horizon and glancing up at the sky. "There seems little likelihood of a storm right now. We're probably more at risk of losing the wind altogether."

"Why is that a risk?" asked the king.

"Any ship that's becalmed is at the mercy of the tide. When you're near land, you might drift onto some rocks."

"Why would the captain risk that happening?"

"Nothing is ever certain at sea," Breysen said with a shrug. "There's always risk, no matter where you steer the ship." He glanced again at the sky. "Sometimes when the weather looks calm, squalls blow up out of nowhere. At other times the sky looks threatening, but conditions turn out to be perfect. You have to trust your experience. And your instinct."

Breysen nodded toward the helm. "Captain Yordin has a good reputation. I'm willing to trust his judgment."

There was no sign of the queen. "How is the little prince coping with the conditions, Your Majesty?" asked Breysen.

The king's brows drew together. "He's managing, although I won't be sorry to get him back on land again. The queen had a restless night with him."

Other soldiers had been spilling onto the deck. Seeing Will emerge with Rufe and Jonas, the king waved them over.

"You look a little better, Will," the king offered. "Have you found your way to the galley?" he asked with a grin.

Will screwed up his face. "I'm not ready to eat just yet, Your Majesty," he replied. He adopted a more cheerful look. "I didn't get much sleep last night, but I'm feeling more normal now. Hammocks are surprisingly comfortable."

Will's attempt at brightness didn't fool Breysen.

Even in the current mild conditions the commander didn't seem entirely himself. He appeared to be adjusting to the rhythmic motion of the ship, but his stomach was still very unsettled if his face offered any indication.

"Keep your eye on the horizon," Breysen suggested. "That helps when the ground won't stop moving under your feet."

Will took his advice, returning a nod of thanks.

It did seem to help. Over the next few minutes the gaunt look gradually began to fade from the commander's face.

As the sun climbed slowly in the sky, the breeze became fitful, and the forward movement of the ship began to slow noticeably.

Thomas and Elena joined them. Elena looked concerned, and a glance at little Tamara was enough to explain the reason. The toddler was clearly not coping well at all.

Breysen had seen children sicken and die on longer journeys. Memories still haunted him of parents watching helplessly as the bodies of their little ones were committed to the deep.

He comforted himself with the knowledge that this particular voyage would be brief.

20

Breysen's musing was interrupted by an exclamation from Thomas. "What is that sailor doing?"

He followed Thomas's gaze to a sailor perched high in the riggings. The sailor appeared to be stuffing something into his clothing. The brief glimpse revealed nothing particularly unusual to Breysen about the man's behavior. He glanced back at Thomas, frowning in puzzlement at the alarm on his face.

At the same moment a voice rang out from the crow's nest above, "Sail ahead!"

"Another ship!" No ship sighting had been announced since the Nomad Lady left the harbor at Maranelle, and the soldiers ran to the railing, peering ahead curiously in hope of a sighting.

Thomas stared up at the sailor above, though, his brows drawn together in concern. He turned to Will and spoke quietly into his ear.

Will at once became alert, any queasiness thrust aside. "Breysen, go ask the captain what he knows about that sailor." He pointed aloft. "Hurry! And ask him if he's expecting trouble from that ship ahead."

Surprised by Will's request, Breysen opened his mouth to question him, but the look on the commander's face changed his mind. He turned and sprinted to the helm.

"Captain Yordin, how well do you know that sailor? Will Prentis sent me to ask you." He pointed to the man, who was now climbing down from the rigging.

The captain peered up at him. "I don't know him at all. He's one of the men we took on at Maranelle." He turned to the mate who stood beside him at the wheel. "He had the necessary experience," the mate said defensively. "He ain't no saint, I imagine, but how many of 'em are?" He waved his hand in the direction of the crew.

"And the ship ahead?" Breysen pointed to the distant sails, now noticeably closer.

The captain frowned at him. "What are you suggesting?"

He raised his hands helplessly. "I know nothing more than you."

"What is she?" Captain Yordin asked the mate.

The mate peered forward. "She's too far off to say anything for certain. But she appears to have three masts—isn't that a square-rigged foresail?" He added darkly, "Pirates like fast vessels."

The captain frowned, glancing up at the two lateen-rigged masts towering above his own ship.

Looking down at the deck below him, Breysen saw that Will had not waited for the captain's response. His men had seized the sailor the moment he reached the deck.

The captain had seen it as well. A look of thunder came to his face. "King's commander or not, this is my ship!" He stormed down onto the foredeck.

"What's the meaning of this?" he roared, approaching Will belligerently.

"The same question I was going to put to you," Will replied calmly. "Was this man signaling from the rigging on your orders?"

"Signaling? What are you talking about?" The captain glared at the sailor. "Well?"

The sailor squirmed uncomfortably. "It ain't true, Cap'n!" he said sulkily. "It's all lies."

Thomas whispered in Will's ear, and the commander reached out and in one smooth motion hoisted up the sailor's vest. Two pieces of brightly colored cloth fell to the deck.

The captain stared at him in disbelief. "Tie the cur to the mast!" he shouted.

Several sailors pinned him against the mast and tied him securely in place. A never ending stream of abuse and curses spewed from him until someone shoved a rag into his mouth and tied it in place.

"Never before has one of my men betrayed his own ship," the captain said gruffly, shaking his head.

"Are pirates common in these waters?" asked Will.

The captain shook his head. "Not at all. It's only twice I've been boarded. No one yet has taken my ship, and it won't happen today neither."

"The target might be the king and queen rather than your ship," Will told him.

"I don't care what the target is," replied the captain. "If they try to board us we'll slit their throats." He glanced ahead at the sails drawing ever closer. "They'll have to catch us first. I have the fastest ship in Arvenon. Even with only two masts."

He called to his men as he hurried back to the helm, "All hands! Prepare to defend the ship!"

The sailors scurried about the ship, arming themselves with swords, knives, and long gaffs tipped with vicious hooks.

"Will we be able to get past them?" Will asked Breysen, nodding toward the approaching ship. "And if we do get past, can we outrun them?"

The former sailor looked up at the sails of the Lady, flapping listlessly in the gentle breeze. "Perhaps. If we had wind." He shook his head. "Even with wind, they have three masts. More likely it will come to a fight."

Will's face turned grim. "Make sure the men are fully armed," he told Rufe. "We're told they're all capable with the bow and the sword. They're about to have an opportunity to demonstrate it."

The commander called to Jonas. "Get the king and queen below. And Thomas and Elena too. Make sure they're properly defended."

Rufe and Jonas left immediately to carry out his orders.

"What are these pirates likely to do?" Will asked Breysen.

"I've only been boarded once," he replied. "It turned ugly quicker than you could blink." He saw again in his mind's eye the deck slippery with blood. He pushed the memories aside. "They'll row over in longboats. Then they'll climb aboard any way they can. Pirates get creative—I've heard some tales."

"We need our archers to take them out before they get here then."

"That sounds easier than it's likely to be," Breysen murmured grimly.

Rufe hurried up, and the commander turned away to speak with him. Breysen took the chance to do some preparations of his own.

Noticing a sailor hurrying past, Breysen strode across to him. "Where do you keep your supplies of pitch?" he asked.

The sailor pointed vaguely down into the hold, then turned to hasten away.

Breysen grabbed his arm. "You need to show me. Now!"

The sailor scowled down at the hand restraining his arm, and Breysen hastily released him. "It's important," he added gruffly. "The safety of the Lady could depend on it."

The sailor glared at him for a moment, then seeing the confusion of people dashing in every direction, he shrugged. "Come with me."

The hatch was already guarded by Jonas and several soldiers. The sailor led Breysen past them, down the steps, and deep into the hold. After pointing to a few barrels in a corner, he left without comment.

Blocks of pitch had been stacked in the barrels, and Breysen hunted around for something to carry it in. Finding a sack, he upended its contents and began stuffing lumps of pitch into it. Once the sack was bulging, he headed for the galley.

The cook was nowhere to be seen. Glancing around, Breysen noticed a large metal pot filled with potatoes. Dumping the potatoes unceremoniously onto the floor, he filled the pot with pitch.

The galley boasted two metal ovens that saw constant use for cooking. Satisfying himself that the fires were still alight, Breysen set the pot on one of the ovens. While he was waiting for the pitch to melt, he hurried off to find a few torches and a flint.

Long before Breysen was satisfied that the pitch had liquefied sufficiently, he had begun pacing the floor restlessly. When he was finally convinced that the liquid was ready, he grabbed a bundle of rags and used it to protect his hands as he lifted the metal handle of the pot. He tucked the unlit torches into his belt, then he headed up to the deck, working hard to keep the pot upright as he carried it across a surface that was rolling unpredictably.

The ship was pitching much less than usual and he discovered the reason why as soon as he arrived on deck. The wind had died away almost completely, and the ship was rolling only in response to the gentle swell of the ocean.

Men lined the rails, many of them armed with bows. When he looked past the prow of the Lady his eyes opened wide in shock. He had expected to see three or four longboats heading toward them, but he counted eight, each of them crammed with armed men who were jeering and shouting as they watched the preparations on the Lady.

Even given the size of the other ship, it was difficult for Breysen to imagine how so many longboats had been safely secured and so many men accommodated. Clearly this was no ordinary pirate vessel.

Spotting Will near the bow, Breysen set down the pot of hot liquid in a safe location and made his way forward.

"Wait until they are much closer!" Rufe called to the archers. At the rate the longboats were moving, they would be in range very soon.

"Target the rowers in the leading boat," Breysen urged Will. "On the starboard side."

Both Will and Rufe turned to him, puzzled looks on their faces. "Which side is that?" Will asked. "And why?"

"Their right side. Our left," Breysen replied. "Try it—you'll see."

Will nodded to Rufe.

Rufe selected four of his men. "Target the rowers in the nearest boat," he told them. He pointed left. "Only the ones on our left side."

Firing arrows on land could not compare with firing from on deck, due to the movement of the boat. But the swell was gentle, and there was no wind to speak of. Arrows sliced into the water around the longboat, but some found their mark. Two of the rowers slumped over their oars unmoving, and a third cried out in pain, dropping his oar. With fewer men now rowing on one side of the boat, the bow of the longboat swung abruptly around. The boat was no longer drawing closer. It sat in the path of other boats, and shouts of annoyance came from the men forced to row around it.

Splashes sounded as lifeless bodies were dumped overboard, and other men took the place of the rowers. The boat slowly faced forward again and began to move.

"Keep at it!" Breysen urged.

Rufe nodded. "Don't stop!" he called to his four archers. "More of the same!"

Other boats were now well within bowshot, and Rufe selected other groups of four and ordered them to apply the same strategy to different boats. Loud curses could be heard from the longboats as a continuous treatment of arrows now flew through the air toward them.

Breysen hurried away and returned with his pot of pitch. Men in the longboats were becoming noticeably reluctant to take the place of rowers on the starboard side. Nevertheless, all of the boats had drawn slowly closer.

Putting down his pot, he took up the rags he had used to carry it and tore them into strips. Then he dipped them carefully into the hot pitch.

"Rufe!" he called. "Wrap these around some arrows. We'll light them before they're fired."

Rufe nodded. He decided to try it himself first. While he wound a strip onto an arrowhead, Breysen lit a torch. Rufe drew the bow, Breysen touched the torch to the arrowhead, and Rufe released the arrow. It landed in the closest longboat, and men frantically moved to smother the flames before they could spread. No damage was done, but the distraction added to the confusion.

Rufe's next arrow sank into the arm of a rower, setting his clothing alight. The man screamed and jumped overboard to douse the flames. Unable to swim with his injured arm, he clung onto the longboat with the other hand. With the extra drag of his body in the water, the forward progress of the boat was slowed further, and the wounded man cried out in pain and anger as others in the boat shoved him away from the boat with their oars.

Rufe quickly called aside several other archers, and a steady stream of flaming arrows soon filled the air.

All this time the other ship had slowly drifted nearer.

"Can any of your archers reach that ship?" Breysen asked Will.

The commander turned to him at once, clearly willing to receive any suggestion Breysen might offer. "Why?" he asked curiously.

"When we try to get away from here we need to make sure they can't follow us," Breysen replied. "If we can get some flaming arrows into their sails..."

Will nodded. "Jonas!" he called.

Jonas came running across the deck.

Will pointed to the other ship. "Can you put arrows into their sails? The arrowheads will have burning rags wrapped around them. That will reduce their range."

Jonas squinted across at the other ship. "Maybe. I can try."

"We'll only get one attempt," said Breysen, frowning. "They'll withdraw as soon as they see what we're up to."

Will nodded. "Wait until you can be certain, Jonas."

Jonas prepared several arrows, then waited.

The first longboats were almost upon the Lady. The archers had now abandoned their earlier strategy. Their only goal now was to reduce the number of attackers.

Breysen caught Will's eye. He pointed down at the longboats. "If we burn their sails, this lot will have even more reason to take our ship."

Will nodded grimly. "I understand. We'll do it anyway." He turned to Jonas. "Can you do it?"

Jonas took a calculating look at the other ship. Then he selected an arrow and drew back his bow. Breysen touched the torch to the tip of the arrow.

Jonas released the arrow. It flew truly and buried itself into the sail. But the flames had gone out before it struck.

Faint shouts could be heard from the other ship. Sailors began reefing the sails.

"Quickly!" urged Breysen.

Jonas chose another arrow with more rag on it. He dipped it once more into the pitch and Breysen lit it. This time the flame was still burning when it struck the lateen sail on the main-mast opposite. The canvas around it slowly began to ignite. Sailors climbed into the rigging in an attempt to smother the flames. They were too late. Both the square-rigged foresail and the sail on the mizzen-mast were quickly alight as Jonas continued his onslaught.

The only possible way of limiting the damage now seemed to be to reef the sails, and sailors were frantically attempting it. Burning debris was falling all around them though, and they were hard pressed to prevent the flames from spreading further on the deck.

Breysen's satisfaction was short-lived. Cries of warning around him alerted him to a new danger.

Longboats had reached the Lady.

21

One longboat had disappeared behind the stern, and two more had pulled in close under the prow of the Lady where it was difficult for the defenders to reach them. Ropes with grappling hooks had already been thrown onto the ship.

Other boats had come alongside the ship, and men were climbing up ropes toward the deck or attempting to smash their way into the ship through portholes.

Jonas had returned to the hatch to oversee the defense of the king and queen and little prince, and Rufe was fully occupied directing archers and preparing men for hand-to-hand fighting.

The unlit torches were still tucked into Breysen's belt. Thrusting the burning torch into Will's hand, he said to him urgently, "Come with me!"

The pot had cooled, but its contents were still liquid. Breysen picked it up and carried it to the side of the ship. He tipped it over the side, half of its contents spilling onto a longboat that had just pulled alongside. Grabbing an unlit torch from his belt, he touched it to the burning torch in Will's other hand and dropped it over the side. Seeing it coming, one of the men in the longboat swatted it aside, but Breysen had already sent two more torches after it, and he only managed to intercept one of them. The other landed squarely among the pitch, spreading flames across the boat. After a frantic attempt to smother the flames, men leaped into the sea, some of them with their clothing on fire.

Breysen didn't stay to watch. Calling for Will to follow him, he hurried to the other side of the ship in time for another longboat to arrive. Positioning himself above it, he upended the pot entirely, emptying the remainder of its contents directly onto the longboat. The men in the boat had not witnessed the earlier incident, and they were taken entirely by surprise. That longboat too was soon ablaze.

All of the pitch was now gone, and Will hurried away, no doubt seeing that he was needed elsewhere.

Breysen looked up to see the head and shoulders of an attacker emerging over the side of the ship. Swinging the empty pot wildly, Breysen raced toward him.

The heavy metal pot connected with the man's head just as he bent to step over the rails. Falling backward over the side of the ship, the invader dislodged another attacker from the rope he was climbing. Both men crashed heavily onto the near side of the longboat, causing it to capsize and pitching the other occupants into the water.

In spite of the best efforts of Breysen and the archers, men had scrambled onto the Lady, and vicious fighting had broken out across the deck. He glanced around, trying to decide what to do next.

Muffled cries from the hatchway suggested that a deadly struggle was underway below deck. Remembering his debt to the king and queen, Breysen made his choice.

Hurrying to the hatchway, he found it entirely unguarded. Jonas and his men must have been drawn away in defense of the royals. Even as he peered down the stairs, he heard the sound of running feet behind him. He spun around to face two attackers making directly for him.

Determined to deny them access below deck, he stood before the hatch and prepared to defend it.

His mind was quickly consumed with a frenzied struggle to stay alive. He knew he could not long defend himself against two determined opponents, but he fought with every ounce of determination he could muster.

Ducking under a furious sword swipe, Breysen stumbled into the entranceway of the hatch. Somehow he managed to plant his feet on the ladder, but he knew he had neither the strength nor the skill to force his way back onto the deck. And if he retreated further down the ladder, it would quickly become impossible to prevent his attackers from leaping down after him.

Abruptly he was seized from behind and pulled off the stairs. Before he could react in any way, the hatch cover was slammed shut above him and fastened with a beam of wood used to secure the hatch in heavy weather. The shouts of anger from the men above were instantly reduced to muffled yells. Feet began to stomp on the hatch cover above, but it had been made to withstand the elements, and it held firm.

Lying on the floor at the base of the stairs as the hatch was being sealed, Breysen saw that his rescuer was Brother Ander.

"Thank you," he said breathlessly.

The monk nodded. "That will hold them for a while."

Cries and the clash of weapons drew his attention from the hatch.

"You're needed below," the monk told him.

"Lead the way," Breysen said, scrambling to his feet.

The big monk hastened through narrow walkways and down another level before they burst into a large hold. A quick glance revealed Jonas and another soldier fending off four attackers. The king and queen, both armed with swords, faced two more together.

The attackers fought with their backs to Breysen. Heads turned as they belatedly registered his arrival, but they were too slow to prevent Breysen from stabbing forward, once, twice—killing one man and injuring another.

His arrival tilted the balance, completely changing the momentum of the struggle. In just a few moments, all of the attackers lay dead.

Both King Steffan and Queen Essanda turned to their baby son who lay in a basket behind them. He appeared to be unscathed.

The monk turned to Breysen. “I couldn’t…I couldn’t do it,” he said, raising his hands helplessly.

Breysen stared at him for a moment, uncomprehending. Then suddenly he understood. Unable to bring himself to fight, the monk had gone for help and found Breysen. What would he have done if Breysen hadn’t been there, and he had instead found himself facing two more attackers coming down the hatchway?

Brother Ander’s relieved face stared down at him. “Thank you,” he said.

Before Breysen could respond, Jonas joined the monk, echoing his thanks. The king and queen were not far behind him.

Their appreciation overwhelmed Breysen, and he could do no more than dip his head awkwardly in response. He wasn’t fighting for money now—he was defending people worthy of his respect. Everything had changed so rapidly.

“Get them somewhere safe,” Brother Ander was telling Jonas, “somewhere defensible.”

“I’ll see if Will can send reinforcements,” said Breysen.

Jonas nodded, and Breysen set off to retrace his steps.

He reached the hatch without encountering another soul. The hatch cover was still intact and the hatch sealed. He could hear no sound above him.

Should he risk opening the hatch? He stood silently for a couple of minutes, wrestling with the dilemma.

Eventually he climbed the steps. As silently as he could, he pulled away the beam securing the cover. Then he carefully lifted the cover a crack, ready to slam it back shut at a moment’s notice. He saw no sign of another person.

Opening the cover completely, he emerged onto the deck and looked around.

Bodies, both of attackers and defenders, lay strewn around, and several small knots of men were still fighting. But something else had changed. Breysen sensed it the moment he emerged on deck. The wind had picked up, filling the sails. The ship was moving.

A loud splash sounded. Looking in the direction of the noise, he saw a man disappear over the side of the ship. Another splash soon followed. The attackers had apparently decided to get out while they still could.

Others followed, and Breysen looked down to see several heads bobbing in the water as men swam for the remaining longboats. The Lady was gradually picking up speed, and the longboats had already fallen noticeably behind.

Spotting Will and Rufe with Captain Yordin at the helm, Breysen decided to join them.

"Rufe is going to do a sweep right through the ship," Will was saying. "We'll need a few of your sailors to guide us, to make sure we don't miss anything."

The captain called four sailors by name. "Go with this man, and show him through every corner of the Lady. We don't want a single one of those pirates left on board."

The men grunted their understanding. As they were about to go, Will said to Rufe, "Find the king and queen before you do anything else."

"I've just come from them," said Breysen. "Jonas is with them, Brother Ander too. Jonas was planning to hide them away somewhere safe."

Rufe nodded and set off with the sailors and six of his surviving soldiers.

Will nodded a salute to Breysen. "If you hadn't been here, the outcome might have been different. You evened the odds considerably."

Unable to decide how to respond, Breysen said nothing.

Will left the captain and headed to the railing, waving for Breysen to join him.

"I wasn't certain we could trust you," he told Breysen frankly. "I don't doubt you any longer."

Will gazed back toward the ship and its longboats, steadily falling further behind the Lady. "Who were those men? What was their purpose?"

Breysen raised his hands helplessly.

"The man lashed to the mast might give us some answers," said Will, heading for him.

Long before they reached the mast, it was obvious that the man was no longer there. The ropes that had restrained him lay severed at the foot of the mast.

"His friends must have cut him loose," said Will, a frown of annoyance covering his face.

The commander hurried back to the helm. "Did those men seem like pirates to you?" he asked the captain.

"I've had little enough experience with pirates," Captain Yordin replied. "And I can't say I'm sorry about it."

He turned to the mate, who shrugged. "That weren't no pirate ship," he said.

"Why not?" demanded the captain.

"She was flying a Castelan flag," he replied.

"I saw no Castelan flag," said Will, frowning.

"They took it down," the mate said indifferently. "I didn't see it until after they launched the longboats. Too little wind—I only saw it when they removed it."

"Are you certain?" asked Will, clearly unconvinced.

The mate shrugged noncommittally.

Rufe appeared in the hatchway followed by the king and queen, with Jonas close behind. Thomas and Elena emerged with Brother Ander soon after them.

Will hurried over to them with Breysen in his wake.

"We're fine, Will," the king said, preempting his commander's question.

"Thanks to Jonas. And Breysen," added the queen.

Feeling himself coloring, Breysen bent his head in a bow.

Multiple conversations broke out, giving vent to the general sense of relief now that the ordeal was behind them.

Breysen noticed Will drawing aside with Thomas. After a whispered conversation, Will approached the king and queen.

"I have surprising and disturbing news, Your Majesties," he said. "The ship that attacked us was flying the Castelan flag."

The king snorted in disbelief.

"I refuse to believe it, Will," said the queen defiantly. "What makes you even consider such an idea?"

Will looked at her steadily. "The mate saw them lowering the flag."

The interaction bemused Breysen. Will had seemed no more convinced than the queen after hearing the mate's account. Yet a brief conversation with Thomas had left him with no doubt at all. He stole a quick glance at Thomas.

He wasn't the only one whose curiosity had been aroused. Rufe was also observing Thomas keenly. And the big man didn't seem at all surprised by Will's assertion.

What did it all mean?

The conversation drifted on without clear resolution to the mysteries surrounding the attackers.

Baffling as their identity and purpose might be, one thing was clear to Breysen—no question remained about his own reliability. The degree to which his situation had turned around was nothing short of astonishing.

There could be no certainty about the final outcome of the king's efforts to regain his kingdom, but Breysen had at last found himself fighting for a cause he could believe in. The king could rightly demand his full allegiance, but in Breysen's eyes he was a man who also deserved it. Close exposure to Will, Rufe, and the others surrounding the king and queen had only reinforced the reputations of them all.

ONE SAILOR HAD FOUGHT with special vigor against the boarders. Apart from the fact that it wasn't in Carnwill's interests for Thomas to fall into anyone else's hands, he could barely remember when he last had a good fight. Once Thomas disappeared below decks, he saw no reason to hang back.

He hadn't realized how constrained he'd been feeling until he had a chance to take out his frustrations on someone else. He must have accounted for at least six of the attackers. It had been invigorating. And if no one had especially noticed his efforts, then so much the better. He needed to stay out of sight.

Before long they would arrive in Varacellan. Once they reached the port, he would notify King Agon of Thomas's new location.

The Rogandan king would have agents in the city, and an opportunity for them to abduct Thomas would present itself before long. And Thomas would be closer to Agon than ever—only a short voyage by sea separated Varacellan from Rog.

THE GRIM TASK of committing to the deep the bodies of the slain fell to Brother Ander. Captain Yordin's sailors, the king's soldiers, and fallen attackers alike had been sewn without distinction into canvas bags.

Putting aside his habitual reticence clearly cost the monk a lot, but he nevertheless stood calmly beside the long line of canvas-wrapped corpses.

"Some of these men were friends, and some were foes," he called. "They share one thing in common, besides the watery grave that awaits their earthly remains. Each must give account to their Maker for their choices while on earth."

His eyes scanned the gathered crowd. "All of us are accustomed to receiving services in return for goods or the use of our skills. Occasionally we might benefit from an unearned service too great to be repaid. That was my experience. My own life was saved by a man who owed me nothing and received nothing in return except my gratitude."

Breysen's curiosity was aroused. He wondered who might have saved the monk's life.

"I lay mortally wounded after a battle," Brother Ander continued, "and I neither earned nor deserved the help of the man who healed me. In the same way I will rely on the mercy of my Maker when I stand before him. I won't have earned or deserved mercy any more than I did my healing."

Bodies were released as he spoke, sliding one by one into the sea and sinking slowly into its depths.

Breysen had heard many words spoken over the dead, both on land and at sea, but the monk's words stirred his interest. Perhaps it was because he had so recently received mercy from the king, in spite of having thrown his lot in with a mercenary.

Perhaps it had to do with Brother Ander himself—Breysen had never met a monk like him. Whatever the reason, Breysen wanted to know more, and he resolved to engage the monk in further conversation when he found an opportunity.

The voyage continued without further incident, and at noon on the following day they entered the broad bay into which the River Dan emptied. A forest of masts crowned the tall ships at anchor in the sheltered harbor, and many buildings sprawled across the docks and beyond them.

Above the port lay the city of Varacellan with its many fair towers. The royal castle crowned the city, bright flags fluttering from its sturdy battlements in the gentle breeze.

A pilot met them and guided them to a place among the anchored vessels—single-masted, two-masted, or even three masted-caravels. Captain Yordin arranged for the king and his party to be transported to shore in a longboat. Finding himself sitting alongside Thomas when he climbed aboard, Breysen was unable to prevent himself from directing frequent curious glances at the young man.

Once they reached the shore, they were met by officials who arranged an escort to the castle. A messenger was sent ahead, and they were met part way by a squadron of King Delmar's personal guard who led them to guest quarters within the palace walls. Lord Karevis appeared and greeted them warmly, bringing an invitation for the king and queen to meet with him privately at their earliest convenience. King Steffan's entire party was invited to join King Delmar at a welcome banquet that evening.

They had safely reached the capital of Varas at last.

VOLUME 2—THE BREAKERS COME CRASHING IN

22

Ranauld's days in the Castelan camp crawled painfully by without a second invitation to meet with Lord Kaebon. The two soldiers assigned by the commander were dour men who rarely spoke, although they stuck to Ranauld like molasses.

His boredom and the enforced inaction allowed him unlimited opportunity to repent of his decision to go with the Castelan scouts. He had done nothing whatever to carry out one of the two key tasks assigned to him on behalf of the king. It seemed unlikely in the extreme that the two men he had left behind would achieve anything useful on their own.

He had followed the scouts here with hopes of engaging in a fruitful dialogue with the leadership of Castel. He decided ruefully that any such hope was no more substantial than the morning mist that blanketed the Castelan camp each morning, dissipating slowly as the sun rose.

After almost a week had passed, a small group of men rode into the camp. After disappearing briefly into Lord Kaebon's tent, one of the men approached Ranauld.

"I have been sent by King Rupert," he said crisply. "You will ride with us to Castel Citadel." It was not a request.

The man had not extended the courtesy of introducing himself. Ranauld did not intend to show the same disrespect.

"Count Ranauld at your service," he said with a small bow. "I do not recall having had the pleasure of meeting you before."

The other man winced slightly. "I am Lord Mardone," he announced hastily, delivering a small bow of his own.

So they had sent a nobleman to escort him to the capital. Ranauld supposed that counted for something.

The two men set out for Castel Citadel within the hour, accompanied by a dozen soldiers. Ranauld was allowed to take his horse, along with the spare clothing and basic supplies in his saddlebags. His weapons were not returned to him. He was a prisoner in all but name.

His situation could have been worse. Ranauld rode with Lord Mardone in the center of the column of soldiers, and having been nudged in the general direction of civility, Lord Mardone's attitude gradually thawed. After no more than a couple of hours in the Castelan nobleman's presence, Ranauld was convinced they would have become friends had circumstances allowed it.

"Have you visited Castel Citadel, Count Ranauld?"

"I'm sorry to say I've never had the opportunity," he replied. "Count Gordan promised me a tour if I was ever able to make the journey."

A shadow passed across the face of Lord Mardone at the mention of Count Gordan, and he quickly changed the subject. Ranauld had not failed to note his reaction, and it filled him with foreboding.

"I am expecting our journey to be comfortable," Mardone said brightly. "We typically see a lot of rain in the capital throughout the year, but the weather has been unseasonably mild of late."

Ranauld accepted the change of direction in the conversation. "I understand that Castel Citadel, like Arnost, is a long way from the ocean," he replied. "That apparently makes a difference to the weather."

"So I am told. Castel has no port of any significance—only a number of seaside towns, all quite modestly sized. Our coastline does not offer the advantages of Varacellan with its well protected harbor. I understand that your own kingdom also boasts a thriving port at Maranelle. Castel does have a navy, though," he added proudly. "We may have a limited number of ships, but all of them are well equipped. We have even commissioned a three-masted ship in recent times."

Count Ranauld was no expert in naval matters, but he was well versed enough to know that most vessels used either one or two masts, and he made an effort to sound suitably impressed.

Lord Mardone had arranged accommodation for them throughout their trip, and for Ranauld the journey proved to be unexpectedly relaxed, and as comfortable as his host had predicted.

As they rode through the countryside Ranauld was struck by the number and size of the orchards they passed. He also noticed the abundance of fruit in the meals served by the Castelans.

"I am impressed by the quality and variety of the fruit here in Castel," Ranauld told the nobleman.

Lord Mardone brightened. "Every Castelan, from the poorest to the most wealthy, enjoys a wide range of fruit in their diet," he said.

Apparently sensing that his visitor was interested to learn more, Lord Mardone warmed to his subject. "The cooler climate suits apples in particular, and from our earliest years we enjoy fresh apples in season, as well as stewed apples for dessert. Every farm also takes advantage of a frost proof root cellar, usually below ground, that is used to store apples for many months out of season, along with other fruit and a range of root vegetables and nuts."

It quickly became clear that on this topic the nobleman needed little encouragement. "We also use horse-powered crushing wheels to prepare a wide range of apple based beverages, including fermented cider, hot mulled cider, and sparkling cider. Some here even refer to Castel as the Apple Kingdom. Pears and stone fruit are also served fresh as well as preserved for consumption out of season."

Ranauld absorbed all of it with interest. The commoners they passed appeared healthy, and their bright clothing and attractively decorated dwellings seemed to suggest a general contentment with life. He liked everything he was seeing of Castel, and he could only wish he had found himself there in more genial circumstances.

The following day his curiosity was aroused when they rode past row upon row of what appeared to be bricks laid out on the ground. "Are those bricks? For building?" he asked Lord Mardone. "Wattle and daub is used in most of the dwellings through Arvenon, and country folk mostly thatch their roofs, but I haven't noticed buildings of that type in Castel."

The nobleman seemed pleased by his interest. "Yes, you're right. The clay in this region, and indeed throughout Castel, is ideal for brick making. The clay is ground into powder, then moistened and pressed into molds before being laid out in the sun to dry. Once the bricks have dried they are fired in a kiln.

"Every peasant is able to make bricks, and both rich and poor alike build their houses from them. Those who are wealthiest build from stone, but most other houses throughout Castel are made from clay bricks. We also use clay tiles on the roof. The dwellings are sturdy and weather proof, and not as flammable as houses made from some other materials."

"There is a great deal to admire about your country," said Ranauld, waving an arm about him. "That applies to its people too," he added. "Our queen—your former princess—is one of the most estimable people I have had the privilege of knowing."

"We have much to be grateful for," Lord Mardone replied with a nod. But Ranauld thought that the nobleman seemed troubled as he said it.

If the Castelan did indeed feel some degree of discomfort, he quickly shook it off, and the two men chatted amicably throughout the remainder of their journey.

Ranauld's first view of the capital of Castel took his breath away. The road had taken them over a ridge to reveal a broad and fertile valley below them. The sun had completed half of its journey to the western horizon, and gray clouds covered much of the sky. Afternoon light flooded through gaps in the clouds, illuminating the rich greens and blues and browns in the scene before him.

The citadel from which the capital took its name had been built upon the foothills that climbed above the plain. The fortress was built in light gray stone, and colorful flags waved from its tall battlements. The effect was both imposing and pleasing to the eye.

The city designers had taken good advantage of the topography. A huge outcrop of rock rose up behind the fortress and spread out on either side of it. The rock formed an impenetrable barrier denying access to the fortress from behind. A broad river swept in a wide arc around the outcrop, completing a natural barrier that enclosed an area large enough to host the citadel and the city spread out below it.

The natural defenses were strengthened by a city wall that stretched along the river, rising up from the opposite bank. The wall followed the line of the river, merging with the tall outcrop of rock on both sides.

The vista was stunning. Ranauld would have been able to appreciate it more had he felt hopeful about the likely outcome of his visit.

In recent times dwellings had spread across the river, and the two parts of the city were connected by a stone bridge of great size. Riding through the outer section of the city, they crossed the bridge. A huge pair of wooden gates stood open wide at the far end of the bridge at the point where it reached the city wall. The guards at the gate halted them briefly, then waved them through with a nod of acknowledgment to Lord Mardone.

The nobleman led Ranauld to a rough stone building and ushered him inside. The building was well guarded and at first glance it appeared to be a prison. However Lord Mardone led him up several flights of steps to a comfortable if simply appointed room with a small window onto the outside world. Glancing out of the window, Ranauld saw a panorama of the city. He also saw that the room was high above the ground, offering no opportunity to exit the building from the window.

"Please make yourself comfortable, Count Ranauld. Your horse will be cared for and the contents of your saddlebags brought to you. I will arrange for food to be served. I believe that the king is planning to meet with you, although he is a busy man, and I can't tell you when that might happen."

"Thank you, My Lord," Ranauld replied. "You have been most courteous. I hope we will meet again soon."

"I hope so too," Lord Mardone replied with a bow. He left the room, closing the door behind him.

As soon as the sound of his footsteps had faded away, Ranauld went to the window and gazed out at the view. He didn't bother to test the door, assuming it was locked.

The room was furnished with a bed, a comfortable armchair, and a small table that supported a pitcher filled with water and a wooden cup for drinking. A small adjoining room featured plumbing and a large jug of water for washing. Anyone occupying the room was clearly expected to be self-sufficient apart from food.

It seemed apparent that none of his usual ways of occupying himself would be available. Perhaps it was a good thing, since his most important priority was to prepare himself for his meeting with the king. He settled into an armchair, brooding.

A KNOCK at the door brought him leaping to his feet before he remembered that he had no way to unlock it. After a polite pause, the door opened. A soldier appeared in the doorway holding a tray with food and a goblet of wine.

The food looked good, and Ranauld eyed it hungrily. "Thank you," he said, before asking, "Will I be allowed to leave the room to stretch my legs?"

The soldier looked surprised at the question. He glanced behind him and saw that no key protruded from the inside of the door. "I wondered why you didn't unlock the door when I knocked," he said. "I will fetch you a key. You are welcome to lock the door whenever you choose for the sake of your own privacy."

He glanced at Ranauld strangely. "This is not a prison. We have been requested to ensure that you remain within the building at all times, so that you will be available whenever the king calls for you.

But you may wander freely throughout the building. An excellent view of the city is available from the roof."

"Thank you," said Ranauld again with a smile.

The soldier bowed and left the room, leaving the door ajar. He returned a few minutes later with a key, which he placed on the inside of the door. Then he bowed again and left without locking the door.

Ranauld allowed himself to relax. He brought the tray of food and the goblet of wine to the armchair and devoured it hungrily. After he'd finished he got up and tested the key. It did indeed lock the door.

The sunlight had almost gone by the time he climbed to the top of the roof of the building and looked out over the city. Little twinkling lights gave the place a magical feel. The thought of his friend Count Gordan and his offer of a tour prompted a sigh.

Lord Mardone's reaction to his mention of the count reminded him that a great deal had changed in Castel. The reception offered to him was a key example. In the past, a visiting senior nobleman from a key ally would have received a warm welcome and been treated as a dignitary. The soldier who brought his food had been polite and helpful, but he had not greeted Ranauld with the deference due a nobleman.

Ranauld might not exactly be a prisoner, and he hadn't been treated badly. But his hosts were keeping him on a very short leash. All of it was a reminder that he needed to remain on his guard and keep his wits about him.

Acutely aware that he was weary in both body and spirit, he headed back to his room and lay down to sleep.

23

As soon as Essanda and Steffan arrived at the royal castle, one of King Delmar's aides ushered them into a pleasant reception room. "King Delmar will be with you shortly," he told them.

Essanda glanced around her, struck by the contrast between her current situation and the drama that had surrounded them when last they had met.

King Delmar appeared in the doorway, his face beaming. "Your Majesties! I can't tell you how delighted I am to see you!" His eyes widened as he glanced at the baby in Essanda's arms. "And who is this?"

"This is Prince Aiden," she told him proudly.

"He shows no signs of having been adversely affected by all that his mother went through."

"Thankfully not," she assured him.

Delmar turned to King Steffan. "It's so good to see you, Steffan," he told him warmly. "I'm more relieved than I can say to see you on your feet and so obviously recovered," he added seriously. "It distressed me greatly to leave you in the condition you were in."

"You did what you needed to do," Steffan assured him. "Your first responsibility was to your kingdom. And I was well cared for."

"I was surprised and alarmed when Lord Nilsean rode in without you. But he assured me that he was playing a part assigned by your Lord Torbury."

Essanda nodded. "We were very grateful that you lent us Lord Nilsean and his men. And he spoke truly—he was very reluctant to leave us. But he carried out his role as a decoy perfectly. He bought time for Will to escort us well away from the area."

"I was much more hopeful once I knew that Will was with you. It seems that the monk—the one who was previously a soldier—did a good job of caring for you, Steffan."

"He did," Steffan agreed. "All of us have a great deal to thank him for."

"You must have quite a story to tell," said Delmar. "What happened after Will joined you?"

"The story is quickly told," Essanda replied. "Will outmaneuvered and outfought a much larger force, and got us to safety. We've been hiding away in a remote refuge near Erestor."

Delmar's face turned grim. "I imagine that the news is what brought you out into the open again."

"What news?" both of them asked at once.

"We thought the location of our hiding place had been compromised," Steffan told him. "That's the only reason we left."

"Then I'm sorry to be the bearer of bad tidings," said Delmar. "Is it true that your ship was attacked on the way here?" They nodded. "And by a Castelan vessel?"

Steffan frowned, but neither of them could confidently deny it.

"There was a reason for the attack," Delmar told them. "Castel has announced that, in view of Arvenian aggression, a state of war now exists between the two countries."

"Castel! At war with Arvenon? But that's ridiculous! It's all nothing more than a misunderstanding," cried Essanda in dismay.

Steffan's response was very different. "How can they dare to attack us?" he asked in anger. "After all we've done to support them!"

"Killing us does not appear to have been the only goal of the people who planned the assassination," Delmar told them. "That was just the beginning. Their failure to kill me set them back in Varas, but they seem to have made inroads in both Arvenon and Castel."

"Do you know who is influencing my brother in Castel?" Essanda asked him.

"Yes, I do," he said. "It's the former Lord Eisgold."

"Surely not!" she said, shaking her head in disbelief. "The man was completely discredited. Are you certain?"

Delmar returned a reluctant nod. "I trust my sources implicitly."

"So how did they come to attack us at sea?" asked Steffan. "How did they even know where we were?"

"As you know better than most, Castel has always enjoyed a well informed spy network," said King Delmar. "You were spotted in Maranelle. Castelan agents saw one of the duke's men engaging a captain in the port and arranged to place one of their own on board."

Steffan shook his head, a fierce look on his face. "Someone will pay for this!" he said.

Essanda looked at him in concern. "We mustn't forget who our real enemy is. Castel is just as much a victim as Arvenon."

"They're victims through no fault of their own, but no one forced them to become credulous fools!" he insisted.

"They're being misled," she replied. "They're like our soldiers outside Steffan's Citadel. Some might argue that they were credulous fools too. But they showed their true colors once they saw the truth."

Steffan grumbled, but he became silent.

"I must compliment you on your own spy network," Essanda said with a wry smile. "You seem to know a great deal about what's going on."

Delmar smiled, although there was no humor in it. "We certainly haven't been idle. I will be happy to make our findings available to you both."

"Thank you, Delmar," said Steffan. "We are very much in your debt."

Delmar waved his comment away. "Let us not speak of such

things. Should we ever decide to do an accounting, it will quickly become obvious that I am hopelessly in your debt." He sighed. "If it's any comfort to you, our enemies had plans for Varas as well as for Arvenon and Castel. The man planning the undoing of Varas was the same person who ruled as a Rogandan puppet during my imprisonment—the former Lord Tarestel. He was not as fortunate as his fellow conspirators. After my agents identified him, they were able to capture him while he was trying unsuccessfully to foment revolt in the provinces. They dragged him to Varacellan. He has been a guest in my dungeons for a short time."

"What have you learned from him?" growled Steffan.

"Very little, unfortunately. He has told us nothing useful. He almost appears tongue tied."

"So he is still alive?" asked Steffan.

Delmar nodded. "He is. But not for long. I made the mistake of banishing him before. This time I will leave nothing to doubt. He is under guard by men I trust completely. I haven't finally despaired of learning something useful from him. But one way or another, he will be hanged before the week is out."

THOMAS AND ELENA had been accommodated in a section of the castle maintained for royal guests. Tammi was sharing their room, while Rubin and Haldek each had smaller rooms of their own. Both the accommodations and the food were excellent, and all of them were thoroughly enjoying the unfamiliar luxury.

Will sought out Thomas on the morning of their second day in Varacellan. "I need your help, Thomas. King Delmar has a prisoner here. I suspect there's a lot we could learn from him, but he's refusing to talk." He looked at Thomas significantly.

Thomas nodded. "I'll come with you," he assured Will.

"Bring Elena too," suggested Will. "She might discover something useful."

Thomas couldn't help wondering if Will might be hinting that his insights from the stone were not always entirely accurate. If so, he could hardly complain—he had given Will good reason to question the accuracy of his perceptions. In any event, Elena had demonstrated her own facility with the stone, and the two of them complemented each other perfectly.

They were led to a circular staircase built from stone that wound its way into the bowels of the castle. A guard with a torch preceded them, and another followed behind.

"Not too many customers down here at the moment," the first guard said conversationally. "The king only sends the worst of the worst to his dungeons."

The stairs led down to an iron door. One of the guards unlocked it and swung it open. They stepped through to find themselves in a dank corridor dimly lit by torchlight, with many iron doors stretching away into the distance on either side. No sound could be heard except the occasional dripping of water.

The guard led them to the first of the cells and inserted a key into a huge padlock. He glanced at Elena as he shoved open the door. "No need to fear," he said roughly. "The prisoner is fully restrained."

Thomas stepped into the room behind Will, gagging involuntarily as the smell of the place assaulted him. Elena followed close behind. Until the guard made his way into the cell with a blazing torch, the scene before Thomas was illuminated faintly by the guttering light of a single candle.

He saw a prisoner chained to the wall, sitting on a low bed. A small table beside the bed held nothing except a jug of water and the candle. The prisoner looked up and gazed at them vacantly.

Will turned to the guard. "Thank you," he said.

The guard shrugged as he handed him the torch. "Take as long as you like," he said. He left the cell, leaving the door ajar.

Will moved to Thomas's side, glancing at him questioningly. In response Thomas fixed his gaze on the prisoner and reached for the clasp dangling from the chain around his neck. Spinning it around, he brought the stone into contact with his skin.

A wave of impressions immediately assaulted him as the stone granted him access to the mind of the former Lord Tarestel. He braced himself, working to sift the thoughts and memories, to follow the tendrils back to the secrets denied to Tarestel's inquisitors.

The effort of wading through the murky world of Tarestel quickly exhausted Thomas. The imprisoned man had lived a hard life. From his earliest childhood he had been subjected to systematic abuse of various kinds, and he had seen no reason to restrain himself when the opportunity arrived to inflict abuse of his own. It was beyond distasteful—Thomas felt as though he was wallowing in a sewer.

Eventually he navigated his way to the assassination plot. Pisander had been the prime mover; Tarestel had played a peripheral role. Nevertheless, a great deal of information was transferred to Thomas in just a few moments—he witnessed the interactions with Alfic and understood the role of Gretchen. Above all, he understood the master plan that lay behind it all. And he knew he would be able to call upon his own memory to revisit the information at a later time.

Determined to expose any possible role of the Stone of Authority, he chased the memories back—and hit a dead end. Baffled, he tried to find a way around the blockage. Every attempt failed. Something was preventing him from gaining access to Tarestel's memories. He could follow the disgraced nobleman to Rog, and back to Arvenon. But key sections of the time in Rog seemed covered with fog.

After a few minutes of complete frustration he gave up the attempt. Taking Elena to one side, he made her aware of what she would encounter in Tarestel's mind, then he outlined his difficulty. She looked as bemused as he felt, but she took the stone when he removed the chain from around his neck.

Thomas put his arm around her as she fixed her gaze on the prisoner. She started, staggering for a moment, and he held her more tightly. He could imagine what she was seeing. Then he waited, trying to be patient.

Eventually Elena snapped her eyes shut and looked away. After slipping the stone to Thomas, she lowered her gaze until he had replaced it once more around his neck. Then she turned troubled eyes to him. She had no need to express in words her urgent need to be gone from that place.

Thomas had to restrain a desire to run as they left the dungeons. It wasn't just the setting. There was something unnerving about Tarestel. The way men looked at Elena acted as a constant irritant to Thomas. Defensiveness on behalf of his wife had become a normal part of his world since they left the safety and isolation of their home in the forest. Yet when Tarestel first caught sight of Elena, he had looked right through her.

It had nothing to do with the man's sexuality. Thomas had been holding the stone at the time, and he saw that the prisoner simply didn't register her any more than he registered his other visitors. Part of Tarestel's being had completely shut down. Thomas had no idea what might have triggered it, but the effect was profoundly disturbing.

THOMAS AND ELENA hastened after Will, scurrying up the stone stairs that led out of the dungeon. Only when they had emerged into the open air did Thomas permit himself to relax.

A quick glance at his wife showed him she had found the visit to Tarestel equally oppressive. He put a supportive arm around her shoulder, and she leaned in and buried her face in his shoulder. He stroked her hair tenderly while she recovered herself.

Will examined their faces quietly for a few moments. He turned first to Thomas. "What did you learn?"

Thomas closed his eyes for a moment, shaking his head. "I haven't often glimpsed a mind so...so disturbing." He shuddered involuntarily. Then he steadied himself. "I learned a great deal about the plotters and how they set up the attempted assassination. Their planning was painstaking, and we're fortunate that they succeeded only in part. I also learned that assassination was merely the first step in their plans. As we already suspected, extending the power of King Agon is their real goal, even though they expect to benefit personally as well."

He outlined everything he had learned, and identified the key people hired to carry out the plans.

"You've done well, Thomas! We will track down their paid helpers, particularly Alfic and Gretchen. They must be held to account for their actions. The final goal of the plotters seems remarkably selfless. Did you discover any hint of the involvement of this other stone—the Stone of Authority?"

The final question was delivered casually, but Thomas guessed that Will was much more interested in the answer than he might appear.

"It was very strange," he replied. "Tarestel did go to Rog, but I could discover nothing at all about his time there. It was almost as if his thoughts and memories about it were blocked. I have never seen anything like it."

Will glanced at Elena, his eyebrows raised questioningly. "Did you have any success?"

She nodded cautiously. "Thomas briefly explained the situation when he gave me the stone. I knew he had explored the matter of the plotters, so I ignored that. I was also confronted by the barrier, and I couldn't find a way through it either." She closed her eyes, as if recalling the experience. "I decided to try to go around it. I went back to the young Cedric. That was his name before he became Lord Tarestel."

"Did that approach work?" asked Thomas eagerly.

"Partially. Cedric has struggled with authority figures throughout his entire life, mainly because of the influence of his father. He learned from an early age that authority figures were greatly to be feared. He could never afford the risk of trusting them. In his mind, the only guaranteed way to be safe was to gain power and exercise it himself. If he was the one holding the power, with no one else in authority over him, he had nothing to fear.

"Eventually he inherited the title of Lord Tarestel. He himself wasn't at all safe as an authority figure. All his life the young Cedric had seen what his father did, and he instinctively behaved the same way. He exercised power with little concern for the effect it might have on others. King Delmar is a very different person—he doesn't make a habit of abusing his power—but Lord Tarestel seemed unable to learn from that."

She paused in an attempt to collect herself. "I'm sorry," she said, "some of the things I saw..." She shook her head as if to clear it.

"I saw glimpses of King Agon's effect on Lord Tarestel. King Agon reminded him of his own father, only worse. It reawakened all his fears. His response was to lock himself away, deep inside, for protection."

She trembled, and Thomas moved to her side once more to offer support.

"That doesn't seem to explain why his mind is blocked, though. The cause of that might have been the Stone of Authority. It didn't seem to be anything natural."

She paused, frowning. "There's one other thing. Usually when people behave in a certain way, they're prompted by their hopes or fears, they're expressing their beliefs, or they're reacting to things that happened in their past. Some of Lord Tarestel's decisions didn't seem to come from any of those motivations. Especially decisions that involve helping King Agon. He decided to act, but he did so for no apparent reason."

Elena fell silent, and all of them stood pondering her words.

Will finally broke the silence. "There's only one way we can know for certain what Agon is planning, and whether he has the help of the Stone of Authority. We need to find a way to get access to him directly. If we can do that, the Stone of Knowing will be able to answer all of our questions."

With nothing further to say, the meeting ended. But Thomas could not get Will's parting words out of his mind. They continued to haunt him long after the conversation had ended.

STEFFAN WALKED the castle battlements with Delmar, squinting against the sun as it climbed over the horizon. Both men had clothed themselves warmly against the cool breeze from the sea.

He gazed up at the gulls as they wheeled above, shattering the stillness of the early morning with their cries.

Delmar turned to him. "I have just received confirmation that Tarestel was executed before dawn."

Steffan grunted his satisfaction.

He stared into the west in the growing light before shifting his gaze southward, almost expecting to glimpse his enemies if he strained hard enough.

Finally Steffan redirected his attention to his friend. "The challenge now is to arrange a similar fate for Pisander and Eisgold," he said.

"That is indeed the challenge," agreed Delmar.

24

"Count Ranauld. King Rupert commands your attendance—I am here to escort you to him."

Ranauld followed the royal aide out of the building that had become his home, conscious that he had been offered no opportunity to prepare himself. He had at least taken the precaution of abandoning his travel stained garments in favor of the most presentable of the clothing available in his saddlebags.

He had woken on his first morning in the capital of Castel with high hopes of an early audience with the king. That had been more than a week ago. In that time he had seen Lord Mardone once, and only briefly. He was bored beyond words, and ready to welcome change of any kind, be it good or bad.

A squad of royal guards fell in with them as they left the building, and they proceeded quickly to the castle. Once they had arrived, Ranauld was shown into a long reception room with a small throne at one end. With no other chairs in sight, he had no choice but to stand.

After waiting for almost an hour he heard voices, and a group of men entered the reception hall from a door off to one side. Ranauld had never met King Rupert, but it was immediately obvious who he was. More elaborately clad than all of his companions, he was also the only one younger than late middle age.

A surge of compassion rose up in Ranauld at the sight of the young king. What must it have been like, just a few short months ago, to have been thrust into the kingship at the age of seventeen after the violent murder of his father, King Istel? Ranauld knew that both Essanda and Rupert had loved and respected their father. Prince Rupert must have looked forward to many more years of observing and learning from him before his own turn came to ascend the throne. But every opportunity had been snatched away from him.

None of the men entering with the king were known to Ranauld, with one notable exception. When he saw who was whispering in the king's ear, his jaw dropped in utter astonishment. The king's confidante was none other than the disgraced former Lord Eisgold, exiled by King Rupert's father after the Battle of Torbury Scarp.

The young king's eyes sought Ranauld out and studied him evenly for a moment.

"Count Ranauld," he said. "I have granted you an audience—against the wishes of my advisors, I must say—only because I know my late father held you in high esteem."

Ranauld bowed deeply. "I am grateful, Your Majesty. This meeting may be unexpected for us all, but I know that Queen Essanda and King Steffan would wish me to pass on their warm greetings."

A frown crossed the face of the young king. "Are you loyal to King Steffan, Count Ranauld?" he asked.

"Yes, Your Majesty. Wholeheartedly."

"Then perhaps you can explain to me why my brother-in-law's forces are attacking my kingdom. That is not the action of someone who wishes me well."

"The army outside Deadman's Pass is not there on the orders of the king or queen, Your Majesty. After assassins attacked the kings in the barn at Paradise Valley, the man behind the attack took control of Arnost. The army camped at your border is acting on his orders."

"Then what were you doing there?"

"I was sent by King Steffan to attempt to take control of the army in his name. Your scouts came upon me before I had opportunity to make contact with soldiers loyal to the king."

"So one of Arvenon's most senior army commanders was present at Arvenon's largest army camp, yet he had no connection with that army?"

"Had I been commanding the army, Your Majesty, I would have been in the camp, not peering down at it from a ridge. Your scouts will confirm that they found me doing just that."

"My scouts returned immediately to the army to defend the pass, so it is pointless to appeal to them. But you should be aware, Count Ranauld, that I received a very different account of your movements."

Ranauld forced down a surge of frustration. He couldn't afford to let his anger bubble out. With Eisgold whispering in King Rupert's ear, it was hardly surprising that the king was hearing warped versions of the truth.

He decided to change tack. "King Steffan and Queen Essanda are victims like you, Your Majesty, not aggressors. King Steffan almost died of his wounds in the attack at Paradise Valley. Your sister was forced to fight for her life and for her unborn baby. I was present, and I witnessed it firsthand."

The king sighed. "I saw a great deal of Steffan during his time in Castel, and I cannot believe he would have wanted to see my father murdered," he said. "As for my sister, she is incapable even of imagining such an atrocity."

He fixed his gaze on Ranauld. "You say you were there. Where was King Delmar during this attack?"

"He was not in the barn. He had been called away briefly."

King Rupert nodded significantly. "Very convenient, I am sure."

Ranauld shook his head, struggling to remain calm. "It wasn't like that, Your Majesty. King Delmar was not involved in the attacks. His army commander, Lord Karevis, risked his life to defend Queen Essanda. She would tell you that she survived only because of his help."

The young king sighed again. "I may be young and inexperienced, but it is obvious to me that you believe what you are saying,

Count Ranauld. That does not mean that you are speaking the truth."

Ranauld bristled. "One of your own noblemen was also present, Your Majesty. Lord Eravitt if I remember correctly. He can confirm my account."

"Lord Eravitt has been much occupied on his estate in recent times. After the trauma he endured, I agreed to release him from his duties in the capital. But even if he has a similar perception—and most likely he does—the facts do allow for a very different interpretation. I have been assured that our agents have uncovered compelling evidence about the attack that resulted in the murder of my father. It was planned and carried out on the orders of King Delmar."

Count Ranauld was too astonished to respond.

"Was Will Prentis present during the attack?" asked the king.

"Sadly he was not, Your Majesty. If he had been, the kings would have been better defended."

"His absence was indeed significant, although not for the reason you seem to suppose," the king replied grimly. "We have reason to believe that Prentis colluded with King Delmar in the attack. He hoped to receive as his reward the kingdom of Castel."

Ranauld furrowed his brows in disbelief. He was unable to fathom what he was hearing.

The youthful king shook his head sadly. "It doesn't end there. I wonder if you know the whereabouts of your monarchs, Count Ranauld. They are currently in Varacellan, having thrown themselves upon the mercy of King Delmar of Varas, the very man whose scheming brought about the death of my father. We tried to make contact with them during their voyage by sea, but I am told that our overtures were violently rejected. In their minds, friends have apparently become foes, and foes are friends.

"Perhaps their vulnerability has blinded them to Delmar's true intentions. Or perhaps he has managed to persuade them he avoided the assassins himself only by good fortune. You said that Delmar's army commander, Lord Karevis, intervened to help my sister. Delmar may have used that to convince them he was not involved in the attack."

The young king shrugged. "Maybe Steffan and Essanda are simply too desperate to acknowledge to themselves that he is manipulating them. By whatever means it has come about, in making common cause with Delmar they have become a danger to every kingdom that desires only peace."

Ranauld's jaw dropped again. The king's assertions were monstrous. "Who is feeding you these...these distortions, Your Majesty?" He turned his eyes upon Eisgold, glaring openly at him.

Eisgold regarded him disdainfully before turning to the king. "I warned you of the futility of trying to reason with him, did I not, Your Majesty?" he sniffed.

He turned a cold gaze upon Ranauld. "I have no need to justify myself to you," he said. "Nevertheless you yourself are well aware of the charges leveled against me. Our beloved King Istel never once accused me of treason. My only crime was to have questioned the orders of Prentis, a commoner foisted on King Istel against his better judgment. Recent events have more than vindicated my suspicions about Prentis's character and integrity. As for his abilities, they were always overblown. The huge loss of life suffered by our forces at Torbury Scarp was entirely unnecessary. In his overweening pride Prentis fancied himself a commander. He refused to listen to my advice, and the army of Castel suffered terrible losses as a result.

"And yet we have seen that granting him the title of commander was only the beginning. Your king made a mockery of nobility everywhere by elevating him to the Arvenian peerage." Eisgold threw up his hands in disgust. "Recent events have shown that, even after all of this, Prentis's greedy ambition was still not satisfied."

Ranauld stared at Eisgold dumbfounded, wide-eyed with shock at the grotesque parody of the truth peddled by the conniving deceiver. He stood paralyzed, helpless to imagine how to begin responding. What could gainfully be said while the truth was being twisted so cynically?

Eisgold shifted his attention to the king. "This Count Ranauld heaped shame upon the nobility when he abased himself so abjectly before Prentis, a commoner. And there are serious questions around his behavior at the border. Nevertheless, Your Majesty has declared him ignorant of the truth rather than intentionally duplicitous, and in doing so I believe you have once again demonstrated wisdom beyond your years. He is a pawn and nothing more. Yet even pawns can be dangerous."

At that moment an aide came to Eisgold's side and whispered urgently in his ear.

"Other more important engagements await you, Your Majesty," Eisgold announced importantly. "Please accept my apologies for failing to alert you sooner."

When King Rupert offered no protest, Eisgold bustled him from the reception chamber. The entire party hurried away without as much as a backward glance.

Count Ranauld was escorted back to his quarters. The royal aide who accompanied the count made it clear that he was not at liberty to leave the building.

Two dreary days followed, with Ranauld in constant turmoil. What should he do? What could he do? He was no closer to an answer when a soldier appeared at his door early one evening and announced that he had a visitor. He followed the soldier to the uppermost level of the building. His guide came to a halt outside the door of a room at the far end of the passageway. The soldier ran his hands carefully over Ranauld, checking for hidden weapons, then after pointing him to the door, the soldier stepped back. Ranauld noticed several other soldiers positioned nearby, all of them armed and alert.

Was he about to meet with some kind of 'accident'? After a moment's hesitation, he shrugged and opened the door. A fire crackled in the hearth and clusters of candles attached to the wall were burning brightly. He saw at a glance that the room was empty apart from a cloaked figure standing beside the window opposite him. The unknown individual was facing away from the door, apparently gazing out over the city. As Ranauld stepped into the room a guard closed the door behind him.

The figure turned toward him, and he sucked in a breath of surprise. His unexpected visitor was King Rupert.

"Count Ranauld," said the young king with a nod. He sounded weary.

"Your Majesty," Ranauld replied with a deep bow.

"I am sorry to be the one to make you aware of this, but Castel has declared war on Arvenon."

Ranauld was aghast, but the king seemed not to notice.

"This outcome is not what I ever wanted. I hope you understand that. But the Arvenian aggression at Deadman's Pass has forced it upon me. If Steffan and Essanda had remained in control of Arvenon, it would never have come to this. But for all practical purposes my brother-in-law and sister no longer rule, and my advisors have convinced me that a statement is necessary. I cannot afford to allow Castel to appear weak."

Ranauld clenched his fists. He had no doubt that Eisgold was behind this, almost certainly with the goal of undermining King Rupert's position.

The king bowed his head, covering his face with his hands and groaning softly. A long moment passed before he recovered himself and looked up again.

When he did, Ranauld saw that his eyes appeared sunken.

A feeling of dread settled over the count. "Your Majesty! Are you well?"

The young king stifled another groan. "I don't know what's wrong with me, Ranauld. My head pounds and my gut clenches tightly. At times it's so bad I can scarcely bear it. It's happening most days now. My doctors have no answers."

Ranauld stared at him uneasily. "Is someone tasting your food and wine before you consume it?"

"I had a boy. But he proved to be a sickly lad, and I had to release him. I have a young woman now. Eisgold found her for me. He tells me she's reliable." The king gritted his teeth as another wave of pain seemed to pass over him. "She mostly seems interested in relieving me of my virtue." He shook his head. "Her brazenness is beginning to weary me."

"Dismiss her, Your Majesty!" urged Ranauld, thoroughly alarmed. "Go to someone you trust, and command them to find you a new food taster!"

"You're suggesting I can't trust Eisgold." The king gazed up at him quietly. Then he shrugged. "The others are all so...so insipid. Eisgold, at least, is willing to take the risk of expressing a point of view."

"What of Count Gordan?" asked Ranauld tentatively. "Your father trusted him."

King Rupert glared at him in sudden anger. "Don't mention that name in my presence!" he hissed. He straightened himself. "I shouldn't have come here," he said, muttering angrily to himself.

Then he abruptly seemed to reconsider. He took a slow breath, struggling to regain his composure. The harsh lines in his face gradually softened.

"You have become an enemy now, thanks to our declaration of war," he told Ranauld. "But you fought beside my father's soldiers at Torbury Scarp, and I believe you are a good man. I could not allow you to find out from someone else."

He reached out and grasped Ranauld's hand firmly. "I want you to know I bear you no ill will, Count Ranauld."

Before Ranauld could respond, the king turned away, opened the door, and was gone.

Alone in the room, Ranauld's thoughts tumbled over each other as he tried to make sense of the visit. The king had sought him out—had chosen to confide in him.

Mentioning Gordan's name had broken the spell, and Ranauld berated himself for his foolishness in doing so.

Ranauld lingered for a while in case the king decided to come back. By the time he eventually gave up and trudged back to his room, his own troubles had faded entirely from his mind. The king's vulnerability alarmed him. King Rupert might be the sovereign, but he clearly had nowhere to turn, no trustworthy shoulder to lean upon.

When Ranauld finally retired to his bed, he lay awake for many hours, burdened with an overwhelming sense of hopelessness. It was obvious to him that the young king was in grave danger. And there was nothing whatever he could do about it.

AS TWO MORE DAYS DRAGGED SLOWLY BY, Count Ranauld mastered his agitation. His frustration had not lessened a whit. Castel was steering a course that would yield benefit to no one except Eisgold. But what could he do about it? His helplessness galled him.

Soon after he had eaten in his room that evening, he heard a soft knock on the door. He hurried to open it, scarcely daring to hope that the king might be calling on him once more.

The person outside the door was hooded and cloaked. A hand reached up and removed the hood, revealing the drawn face of Lord Mardone.

"Come with me," Mardone whispered.

Ranauld followed him to the roof, and they sat together on the edge of the building in the fading light, gazing out over the city.

Lord Mardone did not long delay before speaking. "Your arrival has stirred up a hornets' nest, Count Ranauld."

The count glanced at him curiously.

"Castel is now at war with Arvenon," the Castelan continued. "And Eisgold has tightened his grip on power."

A rumble of anger burst forth from Ranauld's throat. "King Istel should never have shown mercy to that traitor!"

"Many here share your perspective. But none dare to speak it aloud."

"What happened with Count Gordan?" Ranauld couldn't restrain the question—it burst out of him.

Mardone sighed. "When Eisgold first appeared, Gordan opposed him openly, even when it became clear that the king was softening to him. Gordan spoke forcefully, but with great discretion—he has always been a diplomat by nature. When King Rupert announced that he was pardoning Eisgold, though, Gordan told the king to his face that he was dishonoring the memory of his father. He said it boldly and in public. All of the nobles and courtiers were present."

"What did the king do?"

"He flew into a rage. He was incensed at any suggestion he would dishonor his father. He was not dissembling, either—he truly did respect his father, and he reverences his memory. The king was beside himself. He shouted that Gordan would not live to see another dawn if he ever caught sight of his face again."

"What did Gordan do?"

"He didn't utter another word. He turned and left. No one has seen him since. Sadly, the incident only served to reinforce Eisgold's standing. His authority has increased since then. And he has moved swiftly to silence any who dare to speak against him. Most of the nobles are now too frightened to say a word against him, even in private."

"Did you know that the king came to see me?" asked Ranauld.

Mardone stared back at him in astonishment. He shook his head.

"I'm greatly concerned about him. From what he told me, it seems likely that he's slowly being poisoned. He can't see it, though."

"You're not the first person to raise that possibility with me," the Castelan told him grimly.

"Can't you get him a different food taster? The current incumbent was recommended by Eisgold. The king is irritated by her constant attempts to seduce him."

"Some of us are working on it," said Mardone. "I can't say more than that."

It came as a huge relief to Ranauld to hear that the Castelan nobility was neither unaware nor completely paralyzed. "I wish there was something I could do," he said.

"Perhaps there is."

Ranauld directed a sharp glance at his visitor. "What did you have in mind?"

Lord Mardone lowered his voice. "Suppose you were to find that the door to the building was left briefly unguarded? And that a horse was waiting for you just beyond the gates of the city?"

"How could I return to Arvenon with a Castelan army camped inside Deadman's Pass? And what could I do even if I could get past them? Unless something has changed dramatically, I will not be welcomed by the Arvenian army camped on the other side."

"There are other ways. There is a small fishing village called Pescadere on the coast. If you ride northeast, keeping the mountains on your right, you will eventually reach it. From there it's a short journey by sea to Varacellan. A fisherman named Carpis will take you. I can't pretend there is no risk."

"I'm willing to take my chances," said Ranauld without hesitation. "When can I leave?"

"Right now," said Lord Mardone.

Ranauld's eyes went wide. But he quickly nodded in satisfaction.

The Castelan looked relieved. "I can do nothing to guarantee your safety, but some of my men will tail you. They might be able to direct at least some trouble away from you. If you reach Varacellan, make sure that your king and queen and King Delmar understand the true situation here."

"I'll do whatever is in my power," Ranauld replied.

Lord Mardone clasped his hand firmly. "Thank you, Count Ranauld. I hope we have opportunity to meet again in more congenial circumstances."

He handed Ranauld a heavy cloak with a hood. "Put this on."

The two of them slipped out of the door and made their way quietly downstairs to the entrance of the building.

As Lord Mardone had indicated, no guards were anywhere in sight. Ranauld wondered what had become of them, and what the consequences would be for them when it was discovered that he was missing. He could only leave such considerations to his rescuer.

Lord Mardone left the building first and soon disappeared from his sight. As he was about to follow, it occurred to Ranauld to wonder if Mardone might play him false. He didn't hesitate for long. If he was any judge of character, such an outcome was not worth considering.

He slipped through the door and headed for the gates of the city. A few people were still abroad at that hour, but none approached him. When he arrived at the gates he found them open, even though the sky was almost completely dark. He was not challenged as he left the city.

Before he had reached the other end of the bridge, a man leading a horse approached him quietly. He handed the reins to Ranauld without a word, and the count mounted the horse and rode across the bridge into the countryside surrounding the city.

As soon as he found a road that appeared to be heading roughly in the right direction, he steered his horse onto it.

Ranauld rode steadily throughout the night. When the sun rose, it found him far from the capital.

25

Count Ranauld kept an eye on the sun as he rode, remembering to use roads that headed in a northeasterly direction. By late morning he could clearly see a range of mountains in the distance. Lord Mardone had told him to keep the mountains on his right, and he soon decided to rely on the mountain range as a guide.

Lord Mardone had promised to send men to watch out for him from a distance, but thus far Ranauld had not noticed anyone tailing him. Nor had he seen any sign of pursuit from Castelan soldiers. Apart from farm wagons, Ranauld had seen no one on the road except occasional travelers heading in the direction of the capital.

He knew he would have been missed before the morning was far advanced. Ranauld's hosts—or perhaps more accurately his jailers—had routinely brought a generous breakfast to his room not long after dawn each morning, and his absence would have been discovered then if not sooner.

The count did not doubt that he would be pursued. His captors would most likely expect him to set out for Arvenon, and that gave him hope that pursuers would head in the wrong direction. But he couldn't ignore the possibility that trackers would be sent to the coast as well.

Whether or not soldiers were coming for him, at that moment he was entirely alone, and after his confinement in the capital it felt exhilarating to be riding freely under an open sky.

Grateful as he was to Lord Mardone, he couldn't help wondering how the Castelan nobleman hoped to benefit from giving him his freedom. Even if he reached Varacellan and explained the situation to King Steffan and Queen Essanda, what could they do about it? Regaining control of Arvenon presented them with more than enough of a challenge, and until they found a way to achieve that there was little they could do to help Castel. And what could King Delmar be expected to do? Invade Castel by sea?

Nevertheless Ranauld knew that if the roles had been reversed he would have done the same as Mardone. Perhaps no further explanation was necessary.

Ranauld pressed on until he was saddle sore and weary. When he paused for a break, he discovered that generous supplies of food had been placed in the saddlebags, along with skins filled with wine and water. Lord Mardone had planned the escape carefully.

The road ran through a couple of villages and one moderately sized town, and Ranauld wasted far too much time finding a way around them. Apart from these diversions, the day passed without incident, and after pushing his horse hard throughout the daylight hours Ranauld decided to rest until dawn. Turning aside into a large forest, he picked his way through the trees until he found a suitable spot to camp well away from the road.

Nothing disturbed his rest, and he set off again in the morning after breaking his fast and refilling his water skin from a stream.

None of the roads seemed to lead directly to the coast, and he often found himself heading in the wrong direction for a time. Three days passed without any sign of pursuit, and he began to weary of the effort of working his way around every settlement that appeared in his path. After riding through a couple of villages without drawing attention to himself, he began to grow more confident.

One afternoon he turned a sharp bend in the road to abruptly find himself almost in the outskirts of a small town. The road ahead of him bustled with people, and he realized at once that it would attract undue attention if he turned and rode away. Deciding he had little choice but to risk riding through the town, he kept his head down and urged his horse forward, riding as quickly as he dared.

The road led directly through the market square, and the noise and energy of a rural market soon enveloped him. Townsfolk thronged the square, wandering happily among the stalls and sampling the wide selection of food laid out to tempt them.

A few people looked curiously at the stranger as he passed, but no one made any attempt to waylay him. Nearing the far side of the market square, his attention was captured by the smell of fresh bread. Loaves steaming from the oven had been spread out beside large rounds of cheese. Ranauld reined in his horse almost without thinking, peering down at the loaves. The woman keeping the stall was busy serving a customer and seemed not to notice him.

Among the food supplies in his saddlebags, Ranauld had discovered a small pile of Castelan coins folded into a piece of cloth. He had immediately transferred the coins to his own pouch, and they were readily to hand. He knew that a single coin would be worth more than a fresh loaf and a round of cheese.

Glancing around and seeing no obvious sign of danger, Ranauld decided to take a risk. He slipped down from the horse and approached the seller.

"One of each, please," he said quietly, holding out a coin with one hand while pointing first to the loaves and then to the cheese with the other.

The woman took the coin eagerly, although she seemed in less of a hurry to hand over the goods. "I'm sure I detect an accent, good sir," she said brightly. "We don't often see visitors in these parts. Where might you be from?"

The woman had a penetrating voice, and Ranauld felt his cheeks go warm as heads everywhere turned in their direction.

"Beyond the capital," he mumbled, waving vaguely toward the

south. He reached out his hand, impatient to take the bread and the cheese and be gone.

The woman shook her head slowly, her brows puckered. “I felt certain you must be from somewhere foreign,” she said loudly, a tinge of wariness in her voice.

After eyeing the coin suspiciously for a moment, she selected the smallest of the loaves and the least attractive of the cheeses and held them out. She didn’t offer any change.

Ranauld took the food without comment and remounted. After nodding curtly to the woman he nudged his horse forward, forcing himself to ride away slowly and steadily.

The moment he was clear of the town he urged his horse into a gallop. At the first opportunity he veered off the road onto a trail, ignoring the fact that it led west, away from the mountains. After riding for an hour he turned onto a different trail that headed north again.

He berated himself fiercely for his foolishness. He had managed to make a spectacle of himself, and he harbored little doubt that the woman, and others in the market square as well, would readily be able to describe him to any inquirers.

By the time he paused in a secluded location, he felt weary and frustrated. The bread was no longer fresh, but he tore at it hungrily anyway. The cheese was surprisingly tasty, and considering the risk he had taken to procure it, he might as well enjoy it as much as he could. When his belly was finally full, he sat back with a contented sigh, almost willing to conclude that his foolishness had been worthwhile.

Remounting, he rode hard until it was almost too dark to find a secure place to spend the night. By the time he lay down, he was tired of self-recrimination and weary from a day in the saddle. He quickly dropped into a deep sleep.

Waking with the dawn, he struggled to identify the vague sense of disquiet that washed over him as awareness returned. Memories of his visit to the market square came flooding back, and he grimaced for a moment before clambering unsteadily to his feet.

He glanced around him slowly. Something else didn't feel right. Where was his horse? He remembered slipping a halter onto the animal and securing it nearby among some grass. He could see no sign of it anywhere.

Feeling suddenly vulnerable, he concealed himself behind a tree and peered warily toward the trail he had ridden in on. No other person was anywhere in sight.

It was hard to believe that his horse could simply have wandered off. His pursuers surely hadn't caught up with him, either—he would have been recaptured immediately if they had.

After assuring himself that he was entirely alone, he headed to the place where he had left the horse. He was astonished to find a bundle wrapped tightly in cloth lying on the ground. He cautiously removed the cloth to find a generous quantity of food within it.

The situation was baffling, to say the least. After wrestling with his bemusement for some time, he finally concluded that Lord Mardone's men had taken his horse and left the food.

If Mardone's people were involved, two questions remained. If they saw a need to remove his horse, why hadn't they spoken to him directly about it? And if they didn't want to speak with him, why hadn't they left a note?

It occurred to him that the second question was probably easiest to answer—either they saw it as too risky to leave a written message, or they were unable to read and write. As to why they hadn't spoken to him, they'd probably been instructed not to.

He tried to remember exactly what Lord Mardone had told him. The nobleman had said he would send men to tail Ranauld, and that they would try to direct trouble away. He hadn't offered a reason why the men would be tailing him rather than traveling with him.

It probably wasn't difficult to understand, though. Someone would be sure to see them if they traveled together, and sooner or later Lord Mardone would be implicated in the escape. The Castelan no doubt had excellent reasons for wanting his men to remain at arm's length at all times.

Ranauld was left with a decision. Should he stay where he was and wait, or should he set out for the coast on foot? In the end he decided to stay and wait, at least until the following morning.

Remaining in one place for a whole day quickly became wearisome, especially after an extended period in the saddle. Once the sun had set he lay down as usual, but he struggled to get to sleep, spending the first few hours tossing and turning uncomfortably on the hard ground.

Eventually he must have drifted off though, because he woke to discover that his horse had been returned. The animal was grazing peacefully where he had originally left it.

A quick investigation showed that the food in his saddlebags had been replenished too, so he broke his fast before riding out.

He could only wonder if Lord Mardone's men had seen signs of danger and decided it would have been hazardous for him to travel on the previous day.

Perhaps his pursuers had been drawing close. If so, where were they now? Were they far enough ahead that it didn't matter, or had they headed in a different direction? The thought that they were ahead of him was especially alarming. If they had guessed his destination, they'd be waiting for him.

He set off immediately, intent on staying especially alert. The day passed without incident, and he began to notice signs that he was at last approaching the sea. Unfamiliar birds flew high above him, and he watched them curiously, confident that they were seabirds.

As dusk approached he spotted a lone farmer working in a field. Seeing him approach, the man stood and waited for him.

Ranauld halted his horse a few paces away. "Pescadere?" he asked simply.

After peering curiously at him for a moment, the man pointed off to the northeast.

Ranauld nodded his thanks and rode away immediately without looking back.

With night almost upon him and Pescadere apparently still some distance away, Ranauld decided he had little choice but to find a place to spend the night. Eager to put distance between him and the farmer, he rode until the light had almost faded from the sky.

Since leaving the capital he had mostly ridden beside forests and cultivated land. He now found himself among low hills covered with bushes and scrawny trees. Finding a suitable place to camp in such terrain was considerably more difficult. Coming upon a ramshackle abandoned cottage, barely visible in the deepening dark, he decided to spend the night there.

Ranauld slept restlessly and rose before dawn. The farmer had indicated that Pescadere lay to the northeast, and the inland road continued in that direction. As soon as it was light enough to travel he decided on a more indirect approach to the town. He would ride due north instead, heading for the coast. When he reached the sea he would turn right and make his way into Pescadere from its western end.

He didn't even consider circling around to the east. That would have required a longer journey, and any approach from that side was uncertain given that a mountain range lay to the east.

After traveling for a couple of hours he reached the sea. A steep cliff towered above the water, and he dismounted before approaching the edge. Waves crashed onto the rocks below, and seabirds wheeled above him, their harsh cries carried away by the stiff breeze. He caught a distant glimpse of a single boat sailing east. Expecting to find Pescadere in that direction, he remounted and headed away from the cliffs before turning east and riding parallel with the coastline. Within a couple of hours the cliffs had given way to extensive sand dunes. The sea now broke across a rocky shoreline, with the rocks punctuated by occasional stretches of sand.

A small boat, most likely a fishing vessel, stood out to sea just off one of the sandy beaches, and Ranauld paused to peer curiously at it. As he watched, the boat approached the shore, continuing until it was beached on the sand. A man climbed out of the boat and began waving furiously at him.

After a moment's hesitation, Ranauld rode down onto the beach.

"Are you Ranauld?" called the sailor.

"Who wants to know?" he called back suspiciously, bringing his mount to a halt several horse lengths from the man.

"I am a fisherman, and my name is Carpis," the man replied. "I am here to take you to Varacellan."

26

Dismounting from his horse, Ranauld approached the boat. "How did you know to find me here?" he asked.

"I didn't exactly," Carpis replied with a crooked smile. "Put it mostly down to luck."

When the fisherman smiled, Ranauld noticed that a number of teeth were missing from one side of his mouth. He had apparently lived a rough life.

"You are fortunate you stayed away from Pescadere," Carpis told him. "Yesterday especially. The place was swarming with soldiers." He raised an eyebrow, poking a finger in Ranauld's direction. "All of them looking for you."

The missing horse now began to make sense. Lord Mardone's men must have been aware that pursuers were close behind him. Perhaps realizing that he would not reach Pescadere soon enough to avoid being caught, they had decided to delay him. In the process they had made him more alert than ever. Even without making direct contact they had managed to steer him away from trouble.

"Why did you come here?" Ranauld asked the fisherman.

Carpis shrugged. "If you were stupid, you would have blundered into Pescadere and been taken. If you were smarter than that, you would have decided to approach along the coast. The coast on the eastern side of the town is rocky and inaccessible. That left the western approach. So here I am."

Ranauld nodded. "What about the horse?"

"Mardone's people won't be far away. They'll take care of it."

Ranauld peered around him. No one was visible. He could see at a glance, though, that the sand dunes and low hills in the area offered many possible points of concealment. People could be observing him from almost anywhere.

Removing the bridle from the horse, Ranauld replaced it with a halter which he tied to one of the more sturdy bushes. Then he clambered into the boat beside Carpis.

The fisherman tossed him a large coat that felt oily to the touch. "Put this on," Carpis commanded. "It will keep you dry."

As Ranauld obeyed, the fisherman began pushing them back into the swell. The count clung to the side of the boat, eyeing its frail timbers uncertainly. Pitting such a tiny vessel against the remorseless ferocity of the ocean seemed like madness, and an unreasoning dread flooded over him, coupled with a reckless desire to leap from the boat and dash for his horse.

He shook his head fiercely, determined not to give way to such craven impulses. Carpis knew what he was doing. Fishermen took to the sea every day—their livelihoods depended on it.

And what choice did he have? He knew of no other way to escape from Castel.

Carpis dipped a pair of oars rhythmically into the sea until the boat had cleared the shore, then he raised the sail and took his seat at the tiller. Spray splashed repeatedly over Ranauld as the boat plowed through the waves, and he shrank back, trembling involuntarily.

As the boat sailed further away from the land the breakers gave way to a rolling swell and the spray diminished. The waterproof coat had kept his body dry, but Ranauld's head and face were now wet enough that he began to shiver in the steady breeze. Carpis tossed him a dry piece of cloth he retrieved from somewhere, and Ranauld caught it gratefully, using it to dry his face and hair as best he could.

Carpis now headed his boat east, and the bare shoreline was soon interrupted by a town that swung slowly into view. A few boats, appearing tiny at this distance, were anchored near the shore. Other vessels had put to sea, and one or two appeared to be heading in their direction.

"Get down! Quickly!" ordered Carpis sharply, waving his hand urgently toward the middle of the boat.

Ranauld obeyed at once, lowering himself until the whole of his body was positioned below the side of the boat.

The fisherman pointed to a large piece of sail lying across the bottom of the boat. "Get under that sheet, and stay there until I tell you otherwise!"

After a few moments Ranauld heard a loud splash. He guessed that Carpis was throwing a net overboard.

"A boat is heading in our direction with a couple of soldiers in it," Carpis said, speaking quietly. "Be ready to slip over the side if I tell you to."

"But I can't swim!" hissed Ranauld.

There was a brief pause while Carpis mumbled fiercely to himself. Ranauld couldn't hear what he was saying, but the general sense of it wasn't hard to guess.

Everything went quiet for some time. Eventually a voice called roughly, "What are you doing?"

"What do you think I'm doing?" barked Carpis. "I'm a fisherman. Can't you see I have my net out?"

More anxious moments passed.

"What's under that sail in the bottom of your boat?" the voice demanded.

Sweat began to trickle down Ranauld's face. He didn't dare wipe it away.

"Too much water, and not a single fish," growled the fisherman. "Or were you hoping for a glimpse of the naked wenches I'm hiding in the bilges?" he asked, guffawing loudly.

Ranauld heard no immediate response. He scarcely dared to breathe. Would the soldiers board the boat? Would they demand Carpis throw back the sail? If they did, all would be lost.

The voice started up again. "We're looking for a man. A foreigner. Have you seen anyone?"

"No foreigners have been fishing around here," snarled Carpis, "and they'd better not try it! Anyone who elbows in on our fishing grounds will have my gaff hook in their guts!"

Everything went quiet. Ranauld breathed shallowly, too frightened to move a muscle. Before long he started to seriously wonder if he would go mad.

When he almost thought he couldn't bear it any longer, Carpis's voice called to him. "You can come out now. But stay down out of sight!"

Relief flooded over Ranauld as he slithered out. It was difficult to resist the temptation to stand up, but he did whatever he could to stretch his aching limbs. He peered over the side. No boats could be seen anywhere nearby.

Carpis was hauling in the net. A few fish flapped helplessly in it, but the fisherman ignored them, hastily setting the sail instead. Before long they were gliding across the water once more, heading east.

They sailed on through the day, and Carpis eventually indicated to Ranauld that he no longer needed to hide. They often caught sight of other fishing vessels and occasionally ships with two masts.

The sun was drawing near to the horizon when Carpis finally steered the boat into a broad channel. Other boats were heading in the same direction, most of them undoubtedly sailing home, and peering ahead Ranauld caught sight of an expansive harbor. Tall ships lay at anchor, and many fishing boats headed for their own moorings.

Carpis sailed the boat to a largely empty pier and secured two lines at each end of his boat to metal cleats on the pier. As Carpis was climbing out of the boat a harbor official approached. The two men had a brief conversation, and Carpis handed over a couple of coins.

The official left them after waving toward the dock area. It appeared to Ranauld that they now had the freedom of the port.

"Come with me," said Carpis. "Don't say a word to anyone. If anyone approaches us, I'll do the talking."

He steered them toward the most heavily trafficked areas of the docks, although he carefully avoided the taverns that dotted the area. They began to climb, heading toward the main part of the city.

Before they had cleared the docks a couple of rough looking men approached them. One of them had a hook nose. "Not thirsty today, friends?" he asked, jerking his head toward the nearest tavern.

Carpis looked the man up and down without offering comment. Ranauld kept his mouth shut as instructed.

"Well?" the man leered at Carpis, leaning in threateningly. He was clearly daring the fisherman to challenge him.

"Any prow is improved by a painted lady," Carpis finally responded.

The hook nosed man narrowed his eyes. "You smell of fish," he sneered. "Who do you think you are to be mouthing the code? I say you overheard it."

Faster than Ranauld's eye could blink, Carpis drew his knife and had it at the man's throat. He sneered back at Hook Nose.

"And who do you think you are?" Carpis asked. "I wonder what the Peerless Mariner might have to say about your attitude. Do you think you're better than him?"

Hook Nose glared back at him, not daring to move with the knife at his throat.

Other men had begun to gather. Ranauld noticed them stealing glances at one of their number, looking for direction. Seeing who Carpis was, the leader waved his fingers. The other men dispersed immediately, leaving the leader with Hook Nose and his original companion.

"Is there some kind of problem?" the leader asked Carpis evenly. "I know who you are, but I don't take it kindly when someone holds a knife to the throat of one of my men."

Carpis nodded respectfully to him before lowering his knife and stepping back. "Ask your man here. I gave him the code, but he only seemed interested in trouble."

The newcomer directed a sharp glance at Hook Nose, who began to squirm uncomfortably. The leader then directed his attention to the other man, apparently seeking confirmation of Carpis's story.

When Hook Nose's companion inclined his head slightly, the leader's face hardened. "The Peerless Mariner would wish to extend his apologies," he told Carpis. He glared at Hook Nose. "The issue will be dealt with," he added.

Hook Nose scowled at Carpis, but Ranauld saw fear in his eyes as he followed his companions away.

No one remained to block their path, and Carpis immediately resumed their journey.

They soon cleared the docks, and Ranauld found himself walking between rows of dilapidated cottages. "What just happened there?" he asked Carpis.

Carpis looked at him for a moment as if weighing him. "The docks are controlled by a person known as the Peerless Mariner. He's someone who doesn't answer even to the king. No one can go to the docks or move through them without permission from the Peerless Mariner. I've got a passcode—a very special one—that lets me go anywhere in the docks. That's for your ears only," he added with a frown.

"How did you get the passcode?"

"Let's just say I did something for the Peerless Mariner that mattered to him."

Ranauld nodded, more grateful than ever to have Carpis as his guide. He would never have made it through the dockside without him.

After several more minutes of walking briskly they entered a broad avenue lined with stalls selling food of various kinds. Bustling crowds thronged the stalls, people spilling out onto the avenue as soon as they had made their purchases. Everywhere he looked, Ranauld saw men and women laughing and chattering happily as they strolled together.

In his brief exposure to Varacellan, the city had presented Ranauld with a curious mix of carefree exuberance and veiled menace. He knew that similar contrasts could be found in any city. One significant difference between Varacellan and Arnost stood out —not being a port, Arnost had no dockside district.

Above the avenue towered the castle, and Carpis led Ranauld to its gates. After arriving there, the fisherman named one of the king's aides, and asked the guards to send him a message.

The aide arrived surprisingly quickly, reinforcing the influence enjoyed by Carpis. After thanking the fisherman sincerely for his help, Ranauld followed the aide into the castle.

He was taken immediately to King Steffan and Queen Essanda.

They were overjoyed to see him. Having just sat down for their evening meal, the monarchs insisted that he join them. After learning that he had not eaten a solid meal for many days, the king commanded him to take his fill before attempting to pass on news of any kind.

Ranauld yielded without hesitation. Sitting down at once, he ate ravenously, paying no heed to the entertainment he was providing others at the table.

STEFFAN CALLED TOGETHER the entire contingent from Arvenon to hear Ranauld's report. He also invited King Delmar.

Will and Rufe's actions in regaining control of the army outside Steffan's Citadel had seemed almost effortless. That experience had raised Steffan's expectations of Ranauld achieving something similar with the larger army camped outside Castel. He was therefore frustrated at Ranauld's complete lack of progress in winning back control of those men. He needed that army. He also needed to clip Pisander's wings in every way he could.

Steffan didn't openly express his disappointment—it was obvious to him that Ranauld was embarrassed enough already. He was soon grateful for his own restraint. His chagrin was overshadowed by his growing astonishment as Ranauld laid out his visit to Castel Citadel, his insights into the growing influence of Eisgold, his meeting with King Rupert, and his subsequent escape with the active help of a dissident faction within the local nobility.

Eisgold's return to Castel came as no surprise to Steffan—the reports of King Delmar's agents were now fully confirmed. Nevertheless he was shocked to discover the extent of Eisgold's sway. And he was almost as alarmed and distressed as the queen to hear of the vulnerability of the young King Rupert.

Both Arvenon and Castel were now subject to the malign influence of men with no regard for the best interests of those kingdoms. The only possible winner would be Agon of Rogand, and time was growing short to prevent Agon from taking full advantage of the situation.

Only Varas remained truly free. Steffan knew as well as King Delmar that without decisive changes in Arvenon and Castel, Varas was unlikely to stay that way for long.

27

In the days that followed Agon's visit to Chalno, the king considered many times ordering his men to return to the mystic's dwelling to relieve the fool of his head. He restrained himself admirably.

Even the faintest possibility of achieving unending life made it worth putting up with a lot. That didn't mean Agon would ever forgive the peremptory way in which Chalno had dismissed him, instructing him to return in four weeks. No one ever treated Agon that way and got away with it. As soon as he had everything he wanted from the mystic, Agon intended to settle the score once and for all.

The four weeks had almost elapsed when Lady Ona returned to Rog and gave Agon a full report on the situation in Arnost.

"Pisander is barely holding things together," she concluded grimly. "The incompetents who surround him only make his task more difficult."

As she was speaking Agon had been slowly turning white with fury. He finally erupted. "I give the idiot every advantage! Every resource he could possibly require! And this is how he squanders my wealth?"

He stormed about the room, shouting at the top of his voice and smashing every breakable object within reach.

Lady Ona could not help but be shaken by his reaction. Her rosy cheeks were considerably more pale than usual. The king noted it with satisfaction. Nevertheless he was also impressed to see that she was largely managing to keep her poise. Lady Ona was herself an unusually valuable resource, and Agon promised himself he would not lose sight of that fact.

Having exhausted his rage at least for the moment, he resumed his seat. "I will be departing for Arnost within the week," he announced calmly.

If Lady Ona was at all taken aback by the sudden transformation, she showed no sign of it. Agon couldn't fail to be impressed by her unusual ability to tolerate his forthright expression of his passions.

"You will accompany me," he said. "I will have need of your particular talents."

She bowed her pretty head respectfully, and he dismissed her.

Lady Ona's report had demonstrated to Agon yet again that if he wanted something done properly, he needed to do it himself.

He called for one of his aides.

"I will be leaving for Arnost in seven days' time. Make sure that everything is ready for my departure by then, or suffer the consequences. And get Lord Krasmir in here. I want to speak with him."

Krasmir was not long in arriving. An aide ushered him into Agon's private apartments.

"I am calling the Great Council together," Agon told the nobleman. "We will meet in six days. I will be informing them of my departure for Arnost, and announcing your regency in my absence. I expect you to remember all of my instructions," he added in a growl.

The nobleman nodded dutifully, his face impassive. He left the moment he was dismissed.

Agon gazed scornfully at his departing back before turning to Ennawi with a frown.

"Krasmir isn't even suitable for the regency, much less ready for it," he told the slave, shaking his head. "I have no one else, though.

Lady Ona might have made for an amusing alternative, but I need her in Arnost."

He scowled. "Of all of my nobles, the only one who would ever have made a capable regent was Drettroth. I could never have trusted him of course, so it could never have happened.

"As it is, I'm only able to trust Krasmir thanks to the Stone of Authority. I can't help wondering what might have happened if I'd become aware of the stone earlier. I could have used it on Drettroth. A lot of things would have turned out very differently." He shook his head at the thought of what might have been.

The king left his apartments, aware that more pressing matters demanded his attention. He had no more time to waste on fanciful daydreams.

As he left he called back over his shoulder, "You'll be coming to Arnost with me, Ennawi." His lips twisted in the semblance of a smile. "I'm sure a change of scenery will be exactly what you've been hoping for."

Once the king had gone, Nistinaa appeared. She came to Ennawi and fed him in the usual way.

"It seems as if we'll all be going on a journey," she told him. "If the king's taking you then I need to come, as well."

She peered into his unresponsive eyes. "Not that he bothered to let me know, of course—he probably doesn't know I exist, and I can't say I'm sorry about that. One of the servants overheard him talking and passed it on to me."

She finished her work and stood back for a moment. "What will become of us, Ennawi?" she asked.

No answer was forthcoming, and she expected none.

Raising her hands in a helpless appeal to the heavens, she turned away and left the king's apartments.

Exactly four weeks had elapsed when Agon arrived at Chalno's dwelling once more. He was in a foul mood.

Early that morning a dispatch had arrived from Arnost. Pisander was asking him to come as soon as possible and to bring an army. He already knew from Lady Ona's report that there were problems thanks to Pisander's mismanagement, but clearly there had been a further deterioration. Why hadn't the imbecile stated the issues directly?

Soon he would find out for himself. In the meantime, he needed to focus his attention on Chalno.

What am I? Madman? Or genius? the mystic had asked, referring to himself. The king had been wrestling with the question ever since. At that moment he was no closer to an answer, but he would not be returning to Rog without one.

The question Chalno had directed to the king had been easier to answer. *What are you? Wolf? Or prey?* Agon was the wolf, as Chalno would soon discover if he failed to deliver on the king's expectations.

The mystic appeared at the door of his rude hut moments after his royal visitor arrived. Once again the guards checked him for weapons, then discreetly moved away to allow the two men to converse undisturbed.

"Well?" Agon demanded.

Chalno bowed. "Great King, may you live forever," he said, an ironic smile curling his lips. "Perhaps we will now be able to attach an extra layer of meaning to these words," he added.

Agon frowned. Was the mystic suggesting he had made progress?

"Come with me, Your Majesty," invited the mystic, pointing into the forest behind his dwelling.

The king followed without hesitation. His guards scrambled along behind them, frantically trying to strike the right balance between protecting their monarch and respecting his demand that they maintain a discreet distance.

Chalno led the king to a small clearing in the forest. A rough pile of stones stood in the middle of the clearing, capped by a large flat rock with a smooth surface. A dark residue covered the rock and had run down its sides. A sickly sweet smell filled the air.

Agon realized that he was looking at an altar, and that the dark residue was dried blood. It reminded him of the temple in Rog, and he screwed up his nose in distaste.

"There is life in the blood," intoned Chalno.

A shiver traveled up Agon's spine at the sound of the words. "The blood. Which creature is it from?" he asked.

"A fox, a hare, and a stoat. And my blood with it of course," the mystic replied, nodding wisely.

The thought of blood spilled for sacrifice caused the king to shudder. From his earliest days he had felt uncomfortable with such rituals. He said nothing, waiting for Chalno to speak.

"The scroll you brought to me offered hints," the mystic began. "Hints that would make sense only to a priest, and even then only to a priest willing to think beyond the narrow confines of our religion's teachings. There were still pieces missing though. I spent two weeks striving to understand them."

"And did you?"

Chalno looked at him blankly.

"Did you understand them?" Agon repeated.

The mystic's eyes glazed over. "Who can plumb the unfathomable? How can the incomprehensible be understood?" he droned.

The king's eyes narrowed in anger. As always, the fool refused to be pinned down. He gritted his teeth, once more leaving it to Chalno to break the silence.

Eventually his patience was rewarded. "I found myself faced with certain...metaphysical leaps," the mystic said, speaking as much to the air as to his visitor. "I leaped across a chasm to be faced with an abyss. Spanning the abyss I was confronted with a rift. Crossing these divides brought me to where I am today."

"And where is that?" demanded the king.

"I find myself standing on the threshold of eternity," whispered the mystic, awe in his voice.

"And how do you cross that threshold?"

"It is not necessary to cross it. It is enough simply to have reached it."

A part of Agon wanted to simply dismiss the mystic as a madman. Another part of him couldn't help but be impressed.

"So you have achieved unending life?"

"I believe I have," the mystic answered simply.

"Unending life on earth?"

"For as long as earth endures."

"You believe. But are you certain?"

The mystic shrugged. "The passage of time will reveal it soon enough, Your Majesty. I am an old man. I will not need to ask you to wait long."

"You expect me to wait until you grow old?" asked the king, scowling in disbelief. "I am not young myself. Nor am I a patient man."

The mystic had unbelievable gall to claim success without offering some means of verifying his claims. Chalno might be content to bide his time, but Agon refused to wait years to see if old age made a fool of them both.

It had already occurred to the king that he might need a way to assess the effectiveness of Chalno's supposed agreement with the dark gods.

"I could kill you right now," Agon suggested with a cruel smile. "What better way to test your achievement?"

Chalno looked horrified. "Any covenant with the dark gods has its limits, Your Majesty. Do you imagine they would care about preserving my life once my head had been removed from my shoulders?" The mystic shook his head anxiously. "This ritual does not offer a way to shield a person from the consequences of violent death, whether it be by execution, misadventure, or other means. Physical protection is still a necessity, and it must be achieved by more traditional methods."

The mystic's words made sense, and they had saved his life, at least for the moment.

"I can offer one small piece of evidence, Your Majesty," the mystic asserted.

"Well?" demanded the king.

Chalno pointed to his leg. "I have long been troubled by a weeping ulcer on my leg. Since the ritual, the ulcer has healed."

Agon remembered the ulcer—it had been disgusting. There was no further sign of it. He was impressed, although he would never admit it openly.

"What is required to achieve this covenant?" he asked.

"I will explain the requirements in detail," Chalno replied. "But blood sacrifice is needed. And in your case the price will be very high indeed. Thousands of souls will be required merely to open your account."

Agon glowered at him. "You used a couple of rabbits. Why should it be so different for me?" he demanded.

The mystic shrugged. "The price is determined by the value of the service rendered, Great King. Since your life is infinitely more valuable than mine, it will cost more to preserve it."

The king understood that well enough. Nevertheless his brows drew together in a scowl. The idea of paying his fair share had never appealed to him in the slightest.

Chalno apparently saw that he wasn't satisfied. "Think of a leaf on the river, Your Majesty. It floats without assistance. Your sword, being much heavier, could never float without support. The sword is more weighty than the leaf in other ways, too, given its greater potential to impact the lives of others." Seeing that the king understood, he continued. "The life of the king of Rogand is weightier in so many ways than the life of a poor and unheralded hermit."

Agon's life was clearly valuable beyond measure, while Chalno's life counted for nothing. The mystic's words were incontestable.

Agon pondered the possibilities. Was it truly possible that with the mystic's help he would finally be able to prolong his own life indefinitely? If so, sacrificing lives would be the least of the challenges.

"I can think of a quick way to build some credit, without even leaving my own borders. And it will prove rewarding in more ways than one." Agon rubbed his hands together in anticipation. "What else will I need to do?"

Chalno lowered his voice and leaned closer, his foul breath filling the king's nostrils. The man's ulcer might be healed, but his teeth were still just as rotten as they had been on the king's previous visit. "I will explain what is needed, Your Majesty," he said.

Agon had to force himself not to draw away in disgust. He gritted his own teeth while the mystic explained in simple terms everything that would be required.

The king knew he would find the rituals harrowing, but it would be worth it. "I will be leaving Rog for a time," he told the mystic. Then his voice became a growl. "When I return I will be expecting something much more convincing than an ulcer to verify your claims. If you fail to satisfy me I will devise a test of my own."

The look on Chalno's face made it clear that he understood the king's meaning perfectly.

The king strode back to the mystic's hovel and mounted his horse, his guards trailing dutifully behind him.

Agon felt unexpectedly buoyant as he rode away. Having waited for weeks, he at last had something to show for his patience. Any possibility of a bargain with the dark gods was worth any kind of delay. Of course everything hinged on whether the mystic was offering something more than just an illusion.

Either way, it was the work of a moment to decide on his first victims. There were more than enough of them to satisfy the dark gods, and they were long overdue for eradication. The very thought of it brightened him enormously.

The day had started badly with the arrival of the missive from Pisander. Now the mystic was pointing him to a way of extending his life indefinitely. His day was definitely improving.

As THE KING rode away Chalno finally yielded to the trembling that had threatened to take control of his entire body. Agon terrified him. Whenever Chalno found himself in the presence of the king, he could barely manage to keep the shaking at bay.

For a long time he had told himself that he held life loosely. He discovered the truth only when he was confronted with death. King Agon was not a man to toy with, yet Chalno had dared to do just that. He had taunted the king with word games, pretending he was far-sighted and wise beyond other mortals. Having almost paid with his life, Chalno had discovered he was not yet ready to die.

He had convinced himself that mortality held no terrors for him. It was hardly surprising. Raised in a poverty-stricken home environment, life had been a misery from his earliest years. Ejected from the priesthood because he didn't fit in, or more accurately because he didn't measure up, his situation had not improved when he returned to the secular world. Normal people soon made it clear they didn't want him around. So he had become a mystic—cut off from the world, and desperately trying to convince himself he was above the rabble.

Then, after years of barely subsisting in the forest, he had been sought out by none other than Agon, High King of Rogand. Finding himself taken seriously by the king, discovering that the king actually needed him—it had been a heady experience. So he had played along, like the fool he was.

It had been nothing short of madness to string along someone as dangerous as Agon. Miraculously, he had survived, so far at least.

He didn't honestly know what to make of Drettroth's scroll. He had not been lying when he said that only a priest would be able to make sense of its contents, or that it was missing crucial information. He had also spoken the truth when he suggested that the scroll required a mindset that would be unacceptable to any true priest.

So, as best he could, he had enacted the rituals hinted at by the scroll. Having done so, perhaps he really was now standing on the threshold of immortality.

Had the dark gods healed his ulcer? The ulcer had persisted so long that he had given up hope of ever being free of it, but he couldn't entirely rule out the possibility that it had healed of its own accord. If it had been the dark gods who healed his ulcer, did that mean they had agreed to prolong his life?

He couldn't be certain.

Could a mortal negotiate with Malzakh the Destroyer and Nehrvina the Awful? Or were they toying with him as he had toyed with the king?

Chalno had no doubt that the dark gods would be more than willing to receive any blood sacrifice that he or Agon offered. That didn't mean they would keep their end of the bargain.

Time alone would tell, much as Agon didn't want to hear that.

He needed to decide what to do in the meantime. His home wasn't much, but he would be sorry to give it up. Nevertheless, fleeing his home was the price he must pay if he couldn't come up with better proof for Agon than a healed ulcer.

He faced a bigger question. Did he have more to fear from Agon, or from the dark gods themselves?

He sat down with a weary sigh. Any attempt at answers could wait until the following day.

28

Agon had little opportunity to dwell further on his interaction with Chalno. Pandemonium filled the palace as he prepared to set out for Arvenon with his retinue. Given the number of people and the resources involved in the journey, a logistical nightmare was guaranteed.

The king had decided that a large detachment of mounted soldiers would set out first, followed by foot soldiers. He would come next, riding his horse or sitting in a comfortable carriage, depending on his mood. Carriages would be provided for Lady Ona and any other travelers of note. They would follow the royal carriage. Ennawi would also have a carriage of his own, since a man without hands could hardly be expected to ride a horse. Agon was proud of himself for considering such an insignificant detail.

A small army of servants would follow, with wagons laden with food and other supplies. More soldiers, both on foot and on horseback, would bring up the rear.

Whenever the column stopped for an overnight stay, servants would set up a veritable tent city, prepare food, and serve it to the other travelers. In the morning, food would again be prepared and served, the tents packed up, and the column would set out again. A lengthy break would be taken around noon to allow food to be served in portable pavilions.

The entire journey was expected to take weeks.

Agon was unwilling to ever rely upon foreign soldiers for his protection, so the large contingent of Rogandan soldiers traveling in his column would remain with him when he finally reached Arnost.

The multitude of servants accompanying the king presented an entirely different problem. A plentiful supply of servants would undoubtedly be available in Arnost when he arrived, and that left Agon with a dilemma.

The first option he considered was to send his servants home from Arnost and rely on local replacements. The difficulty was that the unwanted servants would need to be fed and guarded on the return journey. They would consume a mountain of supplies, and a contingent of his soldiers would be needed to ensure they completed the journey and returned to their duties in Rog.

The second alternative was to retain the servants once he arrived in Arnost. Housing them within the city would present a new set of logistical challenges, and locals would undoubtedly need to be turned out of their homes as a result. Pisander would need to deal with the complexities.

Agon had settled on the second alternative, not least because he expected his daily routines would proceed more smoothly with servants who understood his mother tongue and were familiar with his way of operating.

A less benevolent ruler might have simply disposed of the unwanted servants when he arrived in Arnost. Agon congratulated himself that he was too enlightened to seriously consider such an option.

None of that would matter until they reached Arnost, and the chaos surrounding the preparations was rapidly raising questions about whether they would get there at all. Finding an effective administrator to leave behind as regent had been enough of a struggle. Agon now found himself desperately in need of another one.

In the end Lady Ona's frustration with the lack of progress

bubbled over. Stepping into the heart of the confusion, she took charge herself. Agon looked on with amazement as order miraculously began to emerge from the chaos.

For reasons he couldn't articulate, her success made him extremely uncomfortable. Fortunately, he found much to criticize.

As the day progressed, he took her aside. "Lady Ona, I can't help noticing a number of glaring shortcomings in your coordination efforts," he told her loftily. "Fortunately I am able to provide guidance. Follow my instructions closely, and everything will begin to run smoothly."

He then proceeded to give her the benefit of his superior wisdom.

Lady Ona waited restlessly for his monologue to conclude, then she bowed stiffly. "Please pardon my presumption in becoming involved at all, Great King. I am more than willing to defer to your more expert judgment." With that she departed, without waiting to be dismissed.

Intensely annoying as Lady Ona's lack of cooperation might be, Agon reminded himself that he needed her in Arnost. Shrugging dismissively, he put her out of his mind. He had come up with satisfying solutions for each of the problems he had observed. It was time to step into the breach himself to implement them.

Less than an hour had passed before Agon remembered why he hated administration. Superior as his skills and insights undoubtedly were, the process of chasing down the details bored and irritated him. It suited him much better to oversee the efforts of others. He always had flawless instructions to offer. Sadly, he had never yet found an administrator capable of effectively understanding and implementing his instructions.

In the end he sent for Lady Ona, determined to ignore her provocations. She duly arrived and bowed low.

"Organization bores me," he told her. "I have decided to allow you to do it."

She offered no response, simply staring pointedly at him.

He rolled his eyes. "Do it your way," he said irritably. "I have decided to ignore your shortcomings."

She bowed again. "As you wish, Your Majesty."

He dismissed her with a lazy flick of his fingers.

Lesser mortals were such fragile creatures. Would he ever find someone truly satisfying to work with? The idea of unending life seemed almost abhorrent at times like this.

In the end two more days went by before Agon's procession was finally ready to leave for Arnost. Under Lady Ona's direction, the number of travelers and the wagonloads of supplies had diminished considerably, but Agon didn't argue. He held to his promise and remained aloof from the details.

Late one afternoon the king was informed that Lady Ona had appeared with a request for an audience. He made his way into the small audience chamber adjoining his private apartments.

"Show her in," he ordered.

Lady Ona came in and bowed low.

He stared at her through narrowed eyes. Her garments were surprisingly modest. She would never be able to hide her beauty entirely, even if she tried, but on this occasion her customary flirtatious and provocative demeanor was nowhere to be seen.

"Great King, may you live forever," she offered humbly, before bowing low again. "Your servants are ready to depart," she told him. "We await only Your Majesty's command."

So she had done it. And without his guidance. He stared at her without speaking, observing casually the telltale signs that she was beginning to squirm. It was a familiar ritual, one he had performed many times over the years with an endless stream of servants and hopeful petitioners.

When he finally decided she had sweated enough, he addressed her curtly. "We depart at dawn tomorrow. You are dismissed."

She bowed deeply and turned to leave. She glided away with stately and measured steps, but Agon was not deceived. She desperately wanted to run, and she was not successful in hiding it.

He glowered after her shapely figure as it slowly disappeared from view. It was time he lay down for a while—his head was beginning to pound.

29

King Steffan stood with Queen Essanda in a pleasant meeting room in Delmar's castle, gazing out beyond the city of Varacellan to the tall ships anchored in the bay. The sun was shining, and a gentle breeze caressed the king's face. The scene before him betrayed no hint whatsoever of the troubles that beset him on every side.

King Delmar joined them, and Steffan nodded a welcome, somehow conjuring up a half-hearted smile to go with it.

The Varasan monarch gazed at him steadily for a moment before clapping him on the back. "There's sure to be a way through it all, Steffan. We'll find it together."

"Thank you, Delmar. I can't imagine where we would be without your support."

Ranauld entered, with Will, Rufe, and Jonas close behind him. Steffan waved the men to a conference table in the middle of the room, and the monarchs joined them there.

Essanda looked distracted. Elena had offered to take care of Prince Aiden whenever needed, and Thomas and Brother Ander had also promised to help Elena out. On this occasion the queen had taken her up on the offer. Essanda was confident that their son was in good hands, but Steffan knew that she never found it easy to detach herself from Aiden.

Refreshments were brought in by two servants who bowed and closed the door as they left.

"I have called this conference to consider our next steps," Steffan began.

He couldn't keep a frown from his face. "Arnost and much of Arvenon is controlled by Pisander and his henchmen. Castel has declared war on Arvenon, and has increasingly come under the influence of one of the plotters behind the assassination. Thanks to Count Ranauld we now know that King Rupert believes that King Delmar and Will are responsible for the attack that led to King Istel's death.

"We have an army stationed outside Castel. Count Ranauld was prevented from making contact with the men in that northern army, so its status is unknown. But we have to assume it is still under the command of men loyal to Pisander.

"On the positive side, we have regained control of the army originally stationed outside Erestor. That western army is now led by Lord Burtelen with the help of Rellan, and we expect it to have been bolstered significantly by the addition of soldiers from Erestor. We have instructed them to close the border with Rogand."

He nodded to Delmar. "The support we have received from King Delmar is the only other thing worth celebrating in the midst of this madness."

"After the help you extended me during the Rogandan invasion, it is my pleasure to return the favor," Delmar replied. "And there is further news. I have just learned from my agents that Agon is preparing to set out for Arnost. He is apparently traveling with enough people to populate a modestly sized town, so it seems unlikely that he will be traveling quickly."

"That is significant news, Your Majesties," said Will. "In light of it I have a suggestion to offer."

The king raised an eyebrow. "Why do I always feel anxious about your well-being whenever I hear those words from your lips, Will?" he asked. "The truth is, though, we need ideas, and yours are always worth considering." He extended his palm, indicating that Will had the floor.

"We cannot allow King Agon to establish himself in Arnost," began Will. "It will be extremely difficult to remove him if that should ever happen."

Steffan nodded grimly. "I agree. But we have sent an army to prevent him crossing the border."

"That is true," Will agreed. "But what if Pisander decides to redeploy the army currently on the borders of Castel? He might send it to the Rogandan border in support of Agon. The outcome is not easy to predict if Lord Burtelen and Rellan should find themselves surrounded, with Agon's Rogandans before them and Pisander's army behind them."

"Are you suggesting that the men in Pisander's army would be willing to fight their own countrymen?" asked Steffan.

"It is difficult to predict," Will replied. "They have been fed so many lies. If they believe you and the queen are dead, it's hard to know how they might respond."

Steffan frowned. "But what can we do? If we leave the border unguarded, Agon will walk in unopposed."

"I agree, Your Majesty," said Will. "I am not proposing to withdraw our army. We just need to prevent Pisander from sending his army against them."

"What are you proposing?" Steffan asked bluntly.

"Two suggestions," said Will. He turned to King Delmar. "The first will depend on your assistance, Your Majesty."

"I'm listening, Will," Delmar told him.

"I understand that Pisander has no significant force stationed at the border with Varas," said Will.

"That is correct," confirmed Delmar. "He has scouts, but little more."

"My proposal is that you invade Arvenon, Your Majesty," Will told King Delmar. He hurried on before anyone could object. "Your men would be accompanied by King Steffan and Count Ranauld. The goal would be to force Pisander to send an army to counter the invasion.

His only available force is the northern army currently stationed outside Castel."

Steffan could scarcely believe his ears. "Pisander's army mainly consists of men loyal to me. Are you proposing we ask the Varasans to fight my own soldiers in my name?"

"Certainly not, Your Majesty," Will replied. "As soon as Pisander's army arrives, the Varasan army would withdraw to the border. Pisander is neither strong enough nor foolish enough to invade Varas. I would expect a stalemate, with both sides observing each other from a position on their own side of the border. Meanwhile the men would have come within easier reach. Count Ranauld and Rufe are well known to the men, as are you, Your Majesty. Between you all, another opportunity might present itself to turn them against Pisander."

Steffan was still frowning. "I notice that Ranauld and Rufe feature in this proposal, but not you. What is your other suggestion?" he asked.

"I propose to go to Rogand."

"For what purpose?" asked Steffan, his frown deepening.

"With the goal of distracting Agon, possibly even intercepting him."

"How do you propose to do that?" Steffan growled. He shook his head. "I've learned to take you very seriously, Will, but your boldness does border on the reckless at times. I'm sure you're honest enough to admit that."

Will offered no immediate response.

"You seem to have been drawing from a boundless well of luck," Steffan continued. "But sooner or later that well is going to run dry. Don't expect me to agree to anything that will hasten that day—you're far too valuable to me."

Will had been listening patiently, but Steffan's little speech had clearly failed to make an impression on him. Steffan had been frustrated before by the unshakable confidence his commander showed in his latest plan. Apparently this occasion would be no exception.

"I appreciate your concern for me, and I freely acknowledge that risk will be involved," Will finally conceded. "But all of us are aware of how much is at stake. Our options are likely to dwindle over time, and dwindle rapidly. We need to take our chances, however fragile those chances might appear to be. If we don't, Varas will become our final refuge. And how long can Varas stand once Arvenon and Castel are in the hands of Agon?"

Steffan passed a hand wearily across his face. Will was right of course. As always.

That didn't mean he needed to agree to Will's proposal. The king knew he should be grateful for his commander's astuteness when it came to strategy, but he could sense where this was heading. It wasn't the first time that Will had been drawn to a high risk scheme, one that dangled an impossibly big payback. Steffan was determined to avoid being maneuvered into agreeing to any such scheme. Not when he had so much to lose.

"So what is your plan?" he asked. He was aware that his voice carried an edge, but he didn't care.

Will didn't hesitate. "I have been speaking to some of King Delmar's agents. They have learned that many of Agon's noblemen are deeply unhappy about his new foray into Arvenon. All of them were required to contribute significant manpower to Drettroth's invasion force, and all of them have suffered heavily as a result of Drettroth's losses. With fewer peasants to work the land, crops have diminished greatly. Agon has already demanded a new round of soldiers, and the nobles are expected to train and equip them before releasing them. Another bad year is looming due to these distractions.

"The nobles have no desire to continue on this path, especially when they see little purpose in it beyond bolstering Agon's ego. We believe that Agon has been made aware of this unrest, although there is no sign that he is taking it seriously.

"I believe we can provide him with a nudge. Agon's likely path to the border will take him past an area I visited more than once with my uncle during my youth. Over the centuries the kings of Rogand have given the people of that region abundant reason to hate them."

"I know a little of the Aen-ur," Steffan told him. The blank faces around him confirmed Steffan's suspicion that few in Arvenon had even heard of the Aen-ur.

Clearly Will knew of them. Steffan knew he shouldn't be surprised. It was never wise to assume anything about Will, and the king had seen more evidence than most of the folly of underestimating him.

Will continued. "I plan to go to the lands of the Aen-ur and use the area as a base. Now that I know many of Agon's nobles are unhappy, I will take any available opportunity to fan the flames. If there is any way to disrupt or delay Agon's progress to the border, I will do so. That should give Rellan and Lord Burtelen as much time as they need to get their army in place to prevent Agon from crossing the border.

"If possible, I will try to create confusion behind him. Either way, I hope to give him good reason to reconsider his plan to set himself up in Arnost. It will be worth it even if it buys us a temporary reprieve."

Steffan shook his head. "The risks far outweigh any likely benefit. You would be almost unprotected—you know how few soldiers we have with us."

"I wouldn't take soldiers. I would not be going there to fight. A smaller party is much better suited to the purpose—the last thing I want is to attract attention. Haldek's mother country is Rogand, and I will take him if he is willing to go. And I will ask Thomas to accompany us. He is reasonably proficient in Rogandan now—Haldek has been teaching him."

"You can't ask Thomas to leave Elena and Tamara, Will," the queen protested. "He isn't a fighting man. It wouldn't be fair."

Steffan's brows furrowed. "Why would you want him with you anyway?" he asked. Will seemed to place a surprising reliance on Thomas, and the king had never understood the reason.

"We will avoid fighting entirely, Your Majesty," Will told the queen. Then he addressed himself to the king once more. "I value

Thomas because he is not a soldier. He often notices things—important things—that I have missed."

"I can confirm that, Your Majesty," said Rufe gravely.

The king shook his head. Even Rufe seemed willing to take Will's plan seriously. Steffan was far from convinced, but there were far more important issues to consider, and he wasn't going to allow himself to be distracted by such details.

"I can see merit in your first proposal, Will," said the king, "and I will discuss it further with King Delmar. I can't help wondering, though, if any of my predecessors ever proposed that a foreign power invade Arvenon," he added wryly.

"As for your second proposal, I see so many problems with it I'm not ready to even consider it at this point."

King Steffan thanked everyone for their participation, then he closed the conference.

He left in a grim mood. Will's proposals might be hard to stomach, but Steffan knew that his commander was only trying to make the most of the limited options available to him. The options had narrowed so severely because Steffan had become little more than a refugee, dependent on the beneficence of a foreign ruler.

As Will was leaving the conference, Jonas swung in beside him.

"I won't hesitate to join you on your mission to Rogand if you want me to come," said Jonas. "I hope you know that."

"Thank you, Jonas," Will replied. "That's no surprise to me. And I don't want you to think I'd leave you behind because of any lack of confidence in you. As the king immediately recognized, the mission is a fool's errand. I wouldn't be doing you any favors by asking you along. But the bigger reason is that I need you to stay with the king. He will need competent commanders by his side, and I'm trusting you and Rufe to fulfill that role in my absence."

"We will do our best," Jonas told him.

Will stopped and faced Jonas. "There's something I've been wanting to ask you, Jonas. You grew up on a farm, didn't you?"

"Yes," Jonas replied.

"When all of this is over—assuming we survive—I've been wondering if you would be willing to consider the role of steward on my holdings in Erestor. I know it would be asking a lot. It would be a very different role from being a leader in the army, but you've seen for yourself that I'm not the most popular noble in Erestor. The role calls for an organizer who understands farming, but it may well involve fighting sooner or later."

Jonas's eyes had gone wide. "I accept!" he said, without hesitation. "I can't imagine anything that would suit me better!"

Will beamed at him. "Good! That's settled, then!" he said, clapping Jonas on the back.

A meal awaited them, and they headed off together to enjoy once more the bounty of King Delmar's provision.

LATER THAT DAY Will received a summons to attend King Steffan. He arrived to find the king in a pensive mood. He bowed respectfully. "Your Majesty?"

"I have something I've decided to entrust to you, Will." The king removed something from the pouch at his belt and held it out. "Take it."

Will reached out and received from the king a small shiny object. He turned it over in his hand. It appeared to be a small glazed tile with a brightly painted surface. He guessed it had once been part of a mosaic, but he couldn't imagine what the mosaic might have depicted. Several lines of writing in a language unknown to him had been scratched on the reverse side of the tile. The lettering was so tiny it was barely distinguishable.

A story clearly lay behind the object. "What is it?" asked Will, intrigued by its mystery and curious to understand its hidden meaning.

"It was a gift from a long-dead king of the Aen-ur to one of my ancestors," the king replied. "It was given to me by my father, just as it was handed down to him by his father. My father convinced me of its value. Perhaps that's why I still carry it with me. That and its small size." He shrugged. "I've been forced to leave so much else behind."

"It's fascinating," said Will.

The king nodded. "Sadly, the details of the story have been lost over the years, but it seems that my ancestor rendered a significant service to the Aen-ur king. In return he was given this token. It might still mean something to the Aen-ur, but I can't say that with any certainty."

Will looked at the king questioningly.

The king frowned back at him. "You'll undoubtedly conclude that I'm sanctioning your visit to Rogand," the king said irritably. "I'm not happy about it, Will! Not happy at all!"

"I understand, Your Majesty," Will replied quietly. He held up the stone. "Thank you for entrusting this to me. I hope one day I will learn the story behind it."

King Steffan dismissed him abruptly. The king might have handed over the tile, but he was clearly far from persuaded about Will's proposal.

Will hurried away to begin serious preparations for the journey to Rogand.

"Will! We haven't seen you for a while. Come and join us." Thomas grinned a welcome.

"Thanks, Thomas," he replied. "Elena," he added, nodding in her direction. He smiled at Tammi, but the smile seemed forced. Thomas couldn't remember seeing Will so distracted before.

"You look as if you have something on your mind, Will," he offered tentatively.

Will nodded. "I need to ask you something," he said.

Glancing at Elena, Thomas saw that she had tensed. It was

unlikely that Will would have noticed any difference in her demeanor, but the change was obvious to Thomas.

Both of them waited for Will to continue.

"I am planning to go to Rogand," he told them.

Thomas frowned. "That sounds dangerous."

Will nodded. "It is. But I have little choice. Time is not on our side."

He sighed. "I'm sure I don't need to explain the realities to you both. Agon intends to annex Arvenon and Castel, and he will almost certainly succeed—unless we can find a way to stop him. Soon only Varas will remain free. King Delmar won't be able to hold out for long. The consequences for everyone in the three kingdoms are too awful to think about."

Thomas nodded mutely, stealing another glance at Elena. She caught his eye, and he noticed that her face had gone pale. Neither of them had forgotten Will's comment after their visit to the former Lord Tarestel in the dungeon. Will had said at the time that they needed to get close to Agon, because the Stone of Knowing would be able to answer all their questions about his intentions.

Both of them could undoubtedly guess what was coming next.

"I'm not sure how much I can achieve by moving against Agon," Will admitted, "although I have a few ideas. But it would help enormously if you were with me, Thomas."

Now that Will's request was out in the open, Thomas experienced a strange sense of release. The uncertainty was finally over. His momentary flicker of relief was short-lived, though. A heavy feeling of dread slowly settled over his spirit.

"I won't let Thomas go to Rogand without me," Elena said firmly.

Will lowered his eyes. He didn't speak, although Thomas could guess what he was thinking.

Thomas turned to Elena with a sigh. "I wouldn't want to go to Rogand without you either," he said. "But taking Tammi would be impossible. And I can't imagine us both going and leaving her behind."

An uncomfortable silence followed.

Will was the first to speak. "I'll leave you to discuss it," he said. "I'm sorry to have raised it at all. I wouldn't consider going myself if the need wasn't so great."

It occurred to Thomas to ask an obvious question. "Has the king agreed to this?"

"Not precisely," Will admitted. "He needs some time to think about it. I expect he'll come around before long."

So the king was no more excited about this plan than Thomas.

Will didn't linger. He said his farewells and was quickly gone.

The moment he was out of sight Elena rounded on her husband. "You can't do it, Thomas!"

"How can I say no to Will?" he asked her miserably. "He hasn't ever held himself back. He's always given everything he has."

"But he doesn't have a wife and a daughter!"

Thomas found no answer to that.

Elena's voice became steady. "We could lend him the stone."

Thomas looked at her in stunned amazement. "We can't do that!"

"We can't?" she asked, a resolute look on her face. "Or we won't?"

He could only stare wide-eyed at her.

Abruptly she softened. "I'm sorry, Thomas. It isn't fair for me to pressure you about the stone. You've shared it with me willingly, but the responsibility for it has always rested on your shoulders. That's been true since long before I met you."

Thomas shook his head firmly. "You're right to ask me to question my motives." He sighed. "We can't lend Will the stone though. Have you forgotten my conversation with him at Newhaven? I told you about it at the time. He let me know why he's so willingly left the stone with me all these years."

"I haven't forgotten," she told him. "Will has his reasons for never asking for it himself or expecting you to give it to the king. He thinks the stone is safer with you."

Thomas nodded. "Will never does anything without a reason."

"And you're right of course," she said despondently. "Even if you offered it to him he wouldn't take it."

Tears came into her eyes. “I know you’ll need to go with Will. But I’m frightened, Thomas! I’m not sure if I could bear to lose you.”

He reached out and drew her close. He didn’t say it aloud, but he felt just as miserable and frightened as she did.

It had felt like such a relief when Will made it clear he was content to leave the stone with Thomas. But it also meant there was to be no release from the burden.

He felt trapped. The stone seemed like a monster of the deep that had wrapped its tentacles tightly around him. It was suffocating him.

How could he ever break free of it?

30

A gentle swell pushed the flat bottomed boat onto the sand. Sailors jumped out and led three restive horses onto the beach. Thomas followed, with Will and Haldek close behind, and each of them took a halter from the sailors.

The sailors had no desire to delay their departure for a moment longer than they needed to, and they wasted no time returning to their ship. They were keenly aware that it would be some considerable time before they cleared Rogandan waters on their journey back to Varacellan.

Thomas watched them go with mixed feelings. Delighted as he was that his world was no longer bucking and swaying unpredictably, he was sorry to leave the relative safety of the Varasan vessel. The prospect of riding into Rogand filled him with unease.

Not long after Thomas and his companions waved the sailors off, they moved inland. The beach might have been deserted, but Will apparently wanted somewhere less exposed to spend their first night on Rogandan soil. The sea had long since disappeared behind them by the time the sun sank below the hills to the west.

After leaving Varacellan, the Varasan ship had headed out to sea, staying well clear of land as it sailed past Rog, not making landfall until they reached a small bay far to the southeast of the Rogandan capital. They were now planning to ride southwest across mostly barren country until they intersected the main road south from Rog. The trading route had been established along the western edge of Rogand, in the shadows of the Blue Mountains that ran from Varas in the north down into Arvenon further south. The road traced almost the entire length of the mountain range before cutting west through a pass into Arvenon.

Their destination was a region beyond the main road that reached up into the lower slopes of the mountains. Will had said they would need to ride hard for several days before they reached it.

The horses had quickly become unsettled when they were led into the hold of the ship. Thomas had remained with them throughout the voyage, and for the most part he had done a successful job in keeping them calm. No one could be sure how rough the seas would be or how the horses would cope with it, so Thomas had selected six animals to accompany them. In the end all six of the animals had arrived in good condition, and Thomas chose three of them at random. It hadn't been easy for him to leave the other horses on the ship knowing they would be forced to endure the return journey.

Back on solid ground once more, the three horses were already looking more settled. Come the morning they would be running beneath an open sky.

After a brief discussion with Haldek, Will decided to light a fire. Thomas was grateful. Warmth and hot food were more than welcome after their time at sea.

Thoughts of Elena and Tammi filled Thomas's mind as he lay down to sleep. Elena had put on a brave face when he left, but she hadn't been able to hide the fear in her eyes. He had stroked her hair as she embraced him, whispering a promise that he would try to be careful.

Then he had lifted Tammi, holding her tightly until the moment he needed to board. She had clung to him despairingly when he tried to hand her to Rubin, and the sound of her tears had chased him up the gangplank.

Determined to get some sleep, he rolled over and tried to shut it all out. He guessed he would have plenty else to worry about on this trip.

The following morning Will called a brief conference before they set off.

"Now that we're in Rogand, we need to avoid any situation that requires you to speak, Thomas," he said. "Your accent will give you away, not to mention your grammar."

"Along with the so, so many words he still must learn," said Haldek. He chuckled and gave Thomas a wink.

Haldek was right of course. The two of them had continued to work on Thomas's Rogandan, but there was still a great deal for him to master. And he didn't have Elena's ready facility with foreign languages.

"If anyone asks why you're not speaking, we'll say that you're mute," said Will. "Don't forget. It will be a problem if you suddenly start speaking."

Thomas nodded.

"How much Rogandan do you understand?" Will asked him.

"Some," Thomas replied. "I have been working on it with Haldek. I understand a lot more if people speak slowly."

"Don't expect them to speak slowly, because they won't," said Will. "But you'll get plenty of opportunity to practice. After this conversation none of us will be speaking anything except Rogandan. We'll try to remember to talk a lot, to help you get used to it."

They rode steadily across rolling hills on the first day. Vegetation was sparse, and the entire region seemed vast and barren. They found no sign of paths and no hint of habitation. Thomas saw no sign of wild animals either. If any creatures larger than rodents inhabited this area, they were keeping out of sight.

Will once again built a fire that night. "The fire is as much for protection as for warmth," he said. "You may not think so, but dangerous creatures are prowling all around us."

That seemed to be pretty much what Will had said, anyway. As promised, he was speaking only in Rogandan now. He had tried to speak slowly for the sake of Thomas, but unfamiliar words were still unfamiliar, however carefully articulated.

When they woke in the morning Will handed Thomas a small leather pouch. In it was a thick paste, oily to the touch. "Smear this on the exposed areas of your skin, Thomas," he said. "It will make you look darker, and you won't stand out as much."

Will had a pouch of his own, and he applied the paste liberally to his own skin.

When they had both finished, Haldek eyed them critically. He shook his head in disgust. "Neither of you look like Rogandans!" he exclaimed. "And as for your hair..." He pointed disdainfully at Will's red locks.

Thomas winced when he examined their leader more closely. The color of Will's hair looked strange and unnatural against his newly darkened skin.

Will pulled two larger pouches from his saddlebag and tossed one of them to Thomas. "This is for your hair," he said. "I'm afraid it isn't going to smell pleasant." By way of translation, he touched his nose before screwing it up uncomfortably.

Thomas couldn't help grinning. Opening the pouch soon wiped the grin from his face though. The smell was indeed putrid.

"We'll only need to apply it every few days," Will promised him. "As long as we don't wash."

Thomas apparently didn't look mollified, because Will added, "The smell does fade quickly."

Thankfully Will was right about the smell. And Thomas soon had plenty else to distract him anyway.

They'd been riding steadily all morning without seeing another human. Occasionally they came upon sheep that scattered in fright as the horses approached. Eventually they crested a ridge to find themselves among a group of shepherds. The men were sitting around a large fire pit, and they sprang to their feet when Will's party appeared.

Will pulled his horse to a stop, calling out a greeting. The men stared at them suspiciously at first, but to Thomas's eye their gaze soon became calculating. One of the shepherds at once invited them to dismount and join them in a meal. He spoke in a jovial tone, but he made it clear he wouldn't take no for an answer.

Haldek had said very little, but Thomas could see he was itching to be gone. Will was polite but firm. He explained that their friend—and with this he pointed to Thomas—had become very sick, to the point where he was no longer able to speak.

Claiming to be a healer, another of the shepherds loudly insisted on examining the sick man. The shepherds began to spread out around the horses, smiling and nodding eagerly. Their cheerfulness seemed forced to Thomas. He sensed a confrontation looming.

Will called a sharp command, and all three of them urged their horses forward, riding down anyone who tried to block their path.

Apparently deciding that Thomas was the easiest target, a couple of them attempted to pull him from his horse as it sprang away. They partially succeeded in dragging him from the saddle, but his horsemanship far exceeded their expectations. Breaking free, he swung effortlessly back into the saddle and quickly rode out of reach.

"Follow me!" Will called urgently, leading them over the crest of a small hill and racing across the low-lying ground beyond it.

Only when the shepherds were far behind them did Will rein in his horse. He patted its steaming neck as it snorted.

"Shepherds have a bad reputation in Rogand," he told Thomas, lapsing into Arvenian. "And they're armed with slingshots. They use them against predators of all kinds, and they're deadly with them. We were fortunate. Things might have ended very differently if we'd still been in their line of sight when they retrieved them."

After that they became much more alert. They caught glimpses of other people in the distance a couple of times but managed to avoid further contact.

After the sun set they found a sheltered place to spend the night and shared a simple meal together. As Thomas sat absently chewing his food his thoughts wandered to Elena and Tammi far away. What had they been doing that day? Were they thinking of him right now as he was thinking of them?

By the time he lay down to sleep Thomas felt exhausted, although his weariness wasn't primarily physical. His experiences were taking him back to his wandering days during the Rogandan invasion. He had witnessed his share of fighting, and it had been terrifying. That hadn't been the only thing that sapped his energy though. He had been worn down by the constant uncertainty—the feeling of never knowing what might be lurking over the crest of the next hill.

His experience of Rogand was beginning to feel uncomfortably like that.

He thought back to a simpler time when life had offered nothing more complicated than the daily chores of a stable hand. Could such a life ever satisfy him now? Challenging as his path had been at times, it had led him to Elena and to Tammi, and he could never wish them away. He knew he had a great deal to be grateful for.

At the same time he faced an uncertain future, wandering through a foreign land surrounded by enemies. Restless and on edge, he tossed and turned for several hours before finally managing to get to sleep.

LONG AFTER THE three men had ridden away from the beach, a fishing boat pulled in to the same bay. Carnwill swam ashore, annoyed at having fallen so far behind the men he was pursuing.

The stay in Varacellan had become increasingly frustrating for Carnwill. With Thomas accommodated in the royal castle, the tracker had been unable to keep him in sight at all. Then he had almost failed to notice when his target set sail at dawn on a Varasan ship with Will Prentis and a Rogandan companion.

Thomas had left Varacellan too soon for Agon's agents to abduct him. Who could say where he was headed now?

Against the odds, Carnwill managed to quickly find and hire a sleek fishing boat. It was reputed to be the fastest in Varacellan, but by the time they put to sea the Varasan ship had long since left the port.

Carnwill didn't know for certain which direction the ship had taken once it left the harbor. Following his instincts, he had instructed the fisherman to head northeast. Many hours had passed before his guess was confirmed. When the fisherman eventually caught sight of the Varasan ship far ahead of them, Carnwill could barely contain his relief.

Both vessels were far from land when they sailed past the harbor at Rog, the fishing boat staying far enough behind to avoid alerting the sailors on the Varasan ship. Eventually they approached the shore once more, the fisherman anchoring his boat behind an island while the ship unloaded its cargo.

Once ashore, Carnwill saw at once that the men had ridden away, heading inland. Where they were heading and why, he couldn't say. Without a horse of his own, all he could do was set off after them on foot, tracking the horses.

Several days passed before he finally accepted that he had lost the trail, and with it any chance of finding Thomas.

Carnwill could think of no good reason for Will Prentis and his companions to travel to Rogand and put ashore so far from human habitation. His instinct told him that Prentis planned to intercept Agon, perhaps in the hope of assassinating the king.

He had little choice but to find a horse and seek out the king himself. Changing direction, he began walking northwest, heading for Rog.

THE COUNTRYSIDE gradually changed beneath the hooves of their horses as Thomas and his friends made their way through the heart of Rogand. Increasingly they found themselves riding through farmland, with roads, villages, and even towns beginning to appear. Not surprisingly, human contact also became markedly more frequent.

Will skillfully managed any interactions that proved impossible to avoid, and they weren't threatened again.

"The farmhouses look different," Thomas said during one of their breaks from riding.

"Farmhouses in this region are mostly made of straw," Haldek told him. When Thomas looked surprised, he added, "Straw is readily available and inexpensive. The builders start with a wooden frame, then pack in straw bales. Straw thatching is used on the roofs. The straw keeps the cold out in the winter."

"Straw houses catch fire easily too," Will added dryly.

Haldek shrugged. "Accidents happen. People learn to be careful."

"Buildings in the towns don't seem to be made of straw," said Thomas.

Haldek shook his head. "They are mostly made of cob, which is a mixture of wet clay, sand, and straw. The walls are thick, so they sit on stone foundations. The buildings stay warm in winter and cool in summer."

Rogand had always seemed so alien, so menacing to Thomas. He was caught off guard by the natural beauty of the countryside around him and surprised by how familiar the crops and the farming appeared to be. The farmhouses certainly looked different, and the towns even more so. But for the most part he could easily have imagined himself to be in a remote corner of Arvenon.

He began to see that his attitude to Rogand had been skewed. It wasn't surprising, given the atrocities carried out by Rogandan soldiers during the invasion. Yet Haldek had once been a Rogandan soldier, and Thomas knew him to be a thoroughly decent person who had come to care deeply about Thomas and his family.

Now that he found himself traveling through the heart of Rogand, Thomas realized he needed the reminder that not all Rogandans were like King Agon and Lord Drettroth.

Even so, he was masquerading as a Rogandan, having come to Rogand to subvert its king. He knew he could reasonably expect no mercy if he was caught.

. . .

THE DAYS ROLLED STEADILY by as Will and his companions rode inland. Eventually they caught sight of a distant mountain range that Will named the Blue Mountains. The border hugged the mountain range with the mountains themselves being located in Arvenon.

After they crossed a large river Will seemed to get a more accurate reading on their location. "I've led us further south than I intended," he said. "We will head north for a while as soon as we reach the main road."

By the afternoon they were heading north in the direction of Rog.

"King Agon is heading south on this road, isn't he?" Thomas asked. "What if we meet him?"

Will didn't seem at all concerned. "He'll be traveling with a very large party," he replied. "We'll see the dust from their column long before we see any of his people."

Thomas tried not to think about it, but from that point his sense of imminent danger began to increase.

When night came Will kept them moving forward for several hours. The moon was almost full, and the road was plainly visible. The conditions made it easy to continue to ride as long as the horses could reasonably carry them. They eventually stopped for the night only after Will had found a suitable sheltered location well away from the road.

They rose before first light and continued their journey north. Will was plainly eager to reach their destination well before Agon arrived there if at all possible. After almost another day's travel they paused briefly to rest the horses.

"I am beginning to recognize a few landmarks," Will told them. "We will continue to ride until dark, then we will find a place to camp. The place I am seeking cannot be far off. I expect we will reach it not long after we set off in the morning."

"Where are you taking us, Will?" asked Haldek.

"We're heading for Aen-irac," Will replied.

Haldek looked horrified. "That is a name of ill omen," he said, his voice tight.

"Its reputation is what makes it useful to us," Will said calmly.

"Are you certain you know what we will find there?" Haldek asked him.

"If you are referring to reports of phantoms and monsters, I give little credence to such things," Will replied with a shrug.

Thomas had been working hard to suppress a growing sense of alarm. "Will we be safe there?" he finally asked.

"Nowhere in Rogand is safe for us," Will told him.

No one spoke until Haldek eventually broke the silence.

"It is time for me to remind you of a conversation we had in Varacellan, Will. I spent years at Agon's castle in Rog. King Agon is an evil man, and he is bad for Rogand. For that reason I will support your efforts to bring him down. But it stops there. I will not fight my countrymen."

Will nodded. "I have not forgotten, Haldek. I would never ask you to fight your countrymen. I am just as eager as you to avoid fighting. I suspect there are a few too many of them even for me," he added with a lopsided smile.

Will became serious again. "King Steffan only agreed to let us come to Rogand on the understanding that we would take no part in any conflict," he said.

Nothing further was said. When they resumed their journey, Will once more kept them riding until it was almost dark. Then they rode their horses into the forest, picking their way among the trees until the road lay well behind them.

Haldek appeared uneasy, casting glances about him nervously. Until that moment, Thomas had been curious about the stories the others had referred to. Now he was grateful he hadn't asked.

They ate silently. When they had finished Will quietly arranged for them to take turns watching through the night. He could scarcely have found a more effective way of saying that danger now surrounded them on every side.

Thomas took the first watch. The time passed uneventfully. Nevertheless, a sense of foreboding had settled over him, and his stomach had twisted itself into knots. When he handed over the watch to Will in the small hours of the morning, he did so with considerable relief.

Late as the hour was, sleep eluded Thomas when at last he lay down. When he eventually surrendered to it, he dreamed.

Thomas found himself standing on the porch of a large cabin in a secluded section of a vast forest. A lake stood before the house, and trees stretched out behind it far into the distance. Elena stood beside him, and Tammi played nearby. There was no sign of either Rubin or Haldek.

A strange creature with an unnaturally large fish-like head emerged from the water and stood dripping for a moment on the shore of the lake. The creature transformed into a woman. To all appearances she was perfectly normal. She seemed to be about the same age as his mother. Leaving the lake, she came and stood before him. Elena seemed untroubled by her. Tammi ignored her entirely.

She captured his gaze, and as Thomas stared into her eyes he felt himself sinking rapidly into their depths. A dizzying array of scenes raced toward him, flooding his senses. He was reminded of the sensation created by the stone when it bared a person's memories before him. The only difference was that the lives of many people swirled around him now. Some scenes emanated joy, but pain and loss issued from others.

In spite of the intensity of the experience he was not frightened. Immersed as he was, he experienced it dispassionately.

The woman somehow gathered him up, blanketing him with a warm sense of compassion, and he felt himself buoyed up as he was gently ejected back to his position beside the lake.

When the woman held out a hand to him, he somehow knew what was expected of him. Without hesitation he withdrew from around his neck the chain that held the Stone of Knowing and placed it into her outstretched hand.

Nodding a simple acknowledgment, she turned and retraced her steps to the lake. As the woman waded into its depths, she transformed once more before his eyes into the creature that first emerged from the lake. He stood watching as the woman-creature slowly sank beneath its surface. He remained unmoving until the final ripples had died away.

Thomas woke from the dream with a start. Everything around him was still and quiet, and stars peeked down through the trees overhead. He lay in silence, lost in his thoughts, until the sky slowly lightened.

Haldek had taken the final watch, and a sharp cry from the Rogandan roused Thomas to sudden alertness.

Leaping to his feet, Thomas glanced around him wildly. A ring of spears surrounded the three men, and a circle of grim faces confronted them.

No way of escape remained. They had been taken.

31

Even before his hand reached for his sword, Will saw the futility of any such response. Twenty men had encircled them with a ring of steel, and only he and Haldek could claim to be fighters. He forced himself to relax.

Something struck him as unusual about the men surrounding them. Peering forward with a puzzled frown, he saw in the dim light of the pre-dawn that it had not been Agon's soldiers who took them by surprise.

A young woman stepped into the circle to his right. He could not make out her face in the semi-darkness, but he sensed the confidence that radiated from her. She called out a few words in a fluid language that he did not understand. He nevertheless recognized that the words had been spoken in the tongue of the Aen-ur.

He turned to face the speaker. Everything was slowly becoming more distinct in the growing light, and he saw a slim figure clad in dark earthy colors. A wicked looking knife lay strapped against her side, but she was otherwise unarmed.

"Aen-usul aen-uwe!" he called back.

Her eyes seemed to go wide for a moment, and she trained her gaze upon him. He felt unaccountably exposed as she coolly looked him up and down.

A new set of sounds escaped her lips, and he could only shrug in response. He had quickly exhausted his paltry knowledge of the language of the exiles.

She stared at him for a moment longer before redirecting her scrutiny to Haldek. Switching effortlessly to the language of Rogand, she demanded, "Why does a Rogandan trespass in the forests of Aen-irac?" Her voice betrayed no sign of an accent.

Haldek made no reply, nervously turning his gaze to Will instead.

The woman once more fixed her attention on Will, her eyes narrowing. She jerked her head in the direction of Thomas to include him. "Neither of you are Rogandan," she said, "in spite of the dye in your hair and the oil on your faces."

She was now speaking in Arvenian, and Will stared at her in surprise. Her mastery of languages was impressive. It was also obvious that very little escaped her notice.

He inclined his head to acknowledge the accuracy of her assertion, but otherwise held his peace. It seemed wisest to avoid speaking until he needed to.

One of the spearmen spoke to her in his own language, and she replied in the same tongue, bowing briefly in respect. It appeared that the spearman was leading the soldiers, and that her role was that of spokesperson and interpreter. Whatever her actual role, she was clearly possessed of unusual confidence.

The spearman jerked the head of his spear toward the forest, and his companions reformed into a loose column with the three intruders positioned in the middle. The horses were led along behind them.

As they headed deeper into the forest, Will reflected on their situation. He had set out for Aen-irac with the intention of making contact with the exiles, and they had succeeded in doing just that. It hadn't been at all clear to him how such a connection might take place, or how their arrival would be received. The likelihood of enlisting the aid of the Aen-ur against Agon was even less certain.

Many questions remained to be answered. There was always going to be risk involved in this initiative, though, and he felt no reason to be dissatisfied with the outcome thus far.

He couldn't help being curious about the young woman, and he took the opportunity to steal glances in her direction when he was confident she was looking elsewhere. Who was she? Her facility with languages made it difficult to identify her race. She didn't look like one of the Aen-ur, and her hair wasn't dark enough for her to be Rogandan.

He was no closer to an answer several hours later when the party crossed a plank bridge suspended by ropes over a swift flowing river. A small settlement lay on the far side of the bridge, nestled among the foothills that led into the mountains. Trees had been cleared to construct a small cluster of sturdy wooden buildings.

Will and his companions were led to one of the buildings and ushered inside. Food and water were brought to them, but it was very obvious to them that they were regarded as captives. Will saw no reason to be unduly alarmed, and he sat down on what appeared to be a low bed and proceeded to enjoy his food.

Thomas did not appear especially concerned. He would undoubtedly have learned a great deal about the intentions of their captors from the stone, and Will was looking forward to an opportunity for a quiet word with his friend.

Haldek looked considerably more anxious.

"I don't think you have any reason to be alarmed, Haldek," Will began. "I don't think these people intend us any harm. Not yet, anyway."

He looked at Thomas with raised eyebrows, hoping for some kind of confirmation.

Thomas nodded. "I don't think they've decided on any course of action—they mostly seem curious about us. I imagine they'll wait until they've heard what you have to say, Will."

A question about the young woman hovered on the tip of Will's tongue, but he pushed it aside, acknowledging to himself it was little more than idle curiosity.

Darkness had fallen when the door opened. The young woman was standing outside, flanked by several armed guards.

"Come with me," she commanded them sternly, speaking in Rogandan. "You must answer for your actions in trespassing on these lands."

Thomas glanced at Will nervously. Haldek was tense, but his face was calm.

Will was not unduly concerned, and he followed her without hesitation. Thomas seemed willing enough to follow his lead.

Haldek was giving nothing away. Given Rogandan attitudes to the Aen-ur, though, Will could readily guess what he might be thinking.

The woman led them to a depression in the ground that formed a natural amphitheater. Roughly fifty men and women sat around the rim of the depression, and Will and his companions found themselves positioned at the center of the gathering. Although it was dark, many torches burned brightly among the gathered throng, illuminating their faces with flickers of light.

"Do you all speak Arvenian?" the woman asked the three of them, speaking in that language.

When they nodded, she said, "That is good. I strongly advise you to avoid the Rogandan language. The people here understand it, but they use it only at great need and even then reluctantly. Out of respect for them I will translate between their language and Arvenian."

She bowed to a man in the circle who wore a simple circlet of wood on his brow. He spoke a few words, and she bowed again.

She turned back to Will and his companions. If she sensed that Will was their leader, she gave no sign of it. Turning first to Haldek, she asked him, "Who are you, and why are you here?"

"My name is Haldek. I came here at the request of my friend," he replied, nodding toward Will.

She glared at Will as she spoke in the Aen-ur tongue. Then she turned to Thomas, a frown on her face. "And who are you?"

"My name is Thomas Stablehand. I am here for the same reason."

Once more as she translated she fixed a glare upon Will. "It seems you are responsible for this intrusion," she said, finally addressing him. "What reason can you offer?"

"Where I come from it is customary for strangers to exchange names and greetings when they first meet," he told her.

She flushed slightly, but he paid no attention to it, bowing respectfully first to her, then to the gathered people around them.

"My name is Will Prentis, and I bring you the greetings and best wishes of King Steffan and Queen Essanda of Arvenon."

"And who are you, Will Prentis, to speak on behalf of kings?" she asked.

A strange sensation prickled Will's spine hearing his name on her lips. He ignored it.

"I am also known as Lord Torbury," he said with another bow. "I command the armies of King Steffan of Arvenon."

She looked around dismissively. "And where are these armies?" she asked mockingly. "Have you come to shield us behind a wall of steel?" Her eyes narrowed. "Or have you come here to beg for help?"

Will, painfully aware of how near to the truth she had come with her shrewd guess, offered no response.

Her translation had not kept pace with their interactions, and without waiting for an answer she turned away from him and spoke rapidly to the silent watchers.

Then she turned to Thomas. "My name is Amyra," she said with a graceful bow. Next she faced Haldek and bowed once more. Finally she turned to Will. After gazing expressionlessly at him for a long moment, she bowed stiffly before turning her back on him.

Facing the man with the circlet, she spoke a few words. The man was clearly a leader among these people. He spoke again, for longer this time, then went silent. She bowed respectfully, then focused her attention on Will.

"What has brought the commander of the Arvenian armies so far from his homeland?" she asked bluntly.

Taking a deep breath, Will allowed his body to relax. "I am here because King Agon is once again on the move," he began. "It is only a few years since Arvenon, with the help of its allies from Castel and

Varas, broke the power of the invading Rogandan armies. Sadly, the peace has proven to be short-lived. Agon sent assassins into Arvenon with the goal of weakening the kingdoms that had resisted him so successfully. The assassins struck when the kings of Arvenon, Castel, and Varas were meeting together to confer. The king of Castel was killed, and King Steffan of Arvenon was severely wounded. Agon is eager to take advantage of the weakness of his enemies. He is once again heading west with an army."

While Amyra was translating, he slowly pivoted until he was directly facing the leader wearing the circlet.

The moment her voice trailed off, Will began speaking again. This time he spoke in Rogandan, ignoring the angry glare immediately directed at him by Amyra.

"You may be asking yourselves why the Aen-ur should care about such matters," he said forthrightly. "You may think that the world no longer has any awareness of your existence, nor any interest in it. And perhaps you are right, at least in part. The history of your people is not a secret to everyone though. It is no mystery to me. I know that all of the land that is now Rogand belonged to you at the time when the first of Agon's people pushed north two hundred years ago. The people of Lestanor resisted their passage ferociously, and they hurried on until they found themselves in the broad and fertile land of your predecessors. The Aen-ur received them peaceably and helped them find places to settle.

"But more and more of them came, and when they grew strong enough they turned on those who had welcomed them. They burned your fields and laid siege to your fortresses. Bitter years followed, and the songs of joy gave way to dirges lamenting the long, slow defeat of the Aen-ur.

"The remnant of your ancestors retreated at last to Ishitar Ataye, the mightiest and most magnificent of their strongholds. Their resolve was strong as the final siege began, but hope slowly faded as supplies dwindled and the attackers relentlessly wore down their defenses. Two terrible years had passed when Agon's forefathers at last breached the walls and tore down the fortress, slaughtering all who sheltered there. The once mighty and prosperous Aen-ur became fugitives, hiding away in the forests, hoping they would not be noticed."

Some of the men and women before him had gone pale. Others had begun to mutter in anger.

"How dare you speak to them in this way!" hissed Amyra in fury.

Will ignored her, raising his voice until his words echoed back from the surrounding trees. "I make no apology for confronting you with the painful history of your ancestors," he called. "You might believe that these events belong to the distant past, but you know from your own recent history that unfinished business from the past has a way of coming back to haunt you."

He stood tall, summoning every ounce of his authority as he continued. "Nor do I apologize for speaking to you in Rogandan. I know you understand the language well enough, and soon enough it will echo once more throughout your forest refuges—if you choose to turn your faces away from the unpleasant realities of the world around you. All of you here know what to expect, because you are old enough to have witnessed the carnage firsthand."

He paused, fixing his gaze intently on them. "I am aware of Agon's personal history with your people. While he was still a young man he singled out the Aen-ur as the first targets of his cruelty. He hunted your people through the forests of Aen-irac and massacred every man, woman, and child unlucky enough to fall within his reach. Perhaps you think he has forgotten about you. If so, you are wrong. Dangerously wrong."

He pointed at Haldek. "My companion here is Rogandan by birth, although he now lives in Arvenon, and he bears you no ill will. He will readily confirm that Rogandan children are raised on nursery tales of Aen-ur monsters that prey on the unwary at night—demons that will come for them in their beds if they misbehave. No Rogandan will ever sleep entirely comfortably while the imagined threat of the Aen-ur hangs over them. Not while the remnant of your people still linger in the land to lend it credibility."

He glanced at Haldek, who met his eyes briefly before nodding once. Haldek then lowered his gaze, clearly unwilling to meet the eyes of the people around them.

Will turned back to the leader. “Agon was nurtured on the same prejudices. Right now he is heading to Arnost, intent on subjugating the three kingdoms that lie to the west. If he is allowed to crush all foreign opposition, he will remember the Aen-ur. He will come here again, and next time he will finish the job.”

Will paused. The people before him had gone silent. He waited, allowing his words to sink in.

He had one final thing to say, and he switched once more to Arvenian to say it.

“I know that, hidden from the world, you have quietly gathered your strength since the dark days when Ishitar Ataye fell. When last Agon came after you, you were able to conceal your true numbers from him. Agon would move against you at once should he ever discover the truth. What has not been hidden from inquirers like me will become plain to him as well, sooner or later.

“Agon will soon pass close to the forests of Aen-irac. Nevertheless, I have not come here to ask you to oppose him directly. I fully understand the wrath you would bring down on your heads.”

Amyra translated once more, although he saw that her brows were furrowed in anger as she glanced at him. He saw in her eyes that she considered his bluntness an insult to the Aen-ur. He knew that he had also shown her disrespect in her role as translator.

He had no desire to arouse her displeasure, but what choice did he have?

He fell silent while Amyra translated his words. Then he stood quietly, waiting for a response.

When he finally allowed himself to relax, his shoulders slumped. He discovered that his heart had been racing, and he had been breathing hard.

Finally the leader stood to his feet. “My name is Faluye-Atae,” he said, speaking fluently in the language of Arvenon. “You may call me Atae.” He offered a stiff bow, and Will acknowledged it with a bow of his own.

"You claim to know a great deal about us, Will Prentis of Arvenon," said Atae. "Why should we pay attention to you and your words? You say you will not call on us to oppose Agon directly. Why then are you here?"

"These are matters I would gladly discuss with you, Atae, although I believe they would be better suited to a conference. First, though, I have promised to convey an offer on behalf of King Steffan of Arvenon. His offer is addressed to you all, and it is not dependent on anything you might do to aid me. This seems an appropriate forum in which to present it."

After a moment's hesitation Atae nodded, caution evident on his face.

Will glanced at Amyra to catch her attention. Then he continued in Arvenian. "You may be aware that the border between Rogand and Arvenon runs along the eastern fringes of the Blue Mountains. It may not seem obvious, but the legal reality is that all of us are currently in Arvenon, not Rogand. I understand your strong historical connection to Rogand, but Rogand has also been the source of your troubles and your persecution. King Steffan extends to you an invitation to relocate to the other side of the Blue Mountains. The land there is almost completely unsettled, and you would be welcome to make it your home. You would be well within the borders of Arvenon, and shielded by a significant natural barrier from any in Rogand who might wish you harm."

As Amyra translated, the listeners began to stir, and a buzz of animated conversation arose.

"Any such relocation would represent a significant upheaval for our people," Atae replied, still speaking in Arvenian. "And it would be of no value to us if Agon succeeds in his attempt to annex Arvenon."

Will waited for Amyra to translate before responding. "That is undeniably true," he acknowledged. "But he hasn't succeeded yet."

Atae considered Will for a few moments. Then he said quietly, "You will have your conference in the morning."

He spoke more loudly in his own language, and people rose from their seats, all of them speaking at once to each other in animated tones. Will could not readily tell from their demeanor how they had reacted to his words.

Amyra turned to him, her eyes still smoldering. He saw plainly that she had no intention of overlooking his offenses, either against her or against the Aen-ur.

"Atae has invited you all to join us for our evening meal," she said coolly.

Then she turned to the armed men who had escorted them to the amphitheater and spoke rapidly to them in their own language.

She turned back to the three men. "You may prepare for the meal in your own way. These men will escort you."

Then she bowed stiffly and turned away.

32

Torchlight flickered around Thomas as he sat with Will and Haldek enjoying the meal prepared by the Aen-ur.

After Amyra had left them, they had been led once more to their assigned dwelling. Fresh water stood beside the dwelling in a large barrel, and after washing themselves they had changed into the cleanest clothing available in their saddlebags. They were now sitting in the hall of a large building, the space illuminated by many torches and warmed by huge fires crackling at both ends of the room.

The meal could almost have been called a feast, except that the mood of the people around him was noticeably subdued.

As they were leaving the amphitheater earlier he had turned the clasp on the chain around his neck to prevent the stone from coming into contact with his skin. It had been an easy decision to leave it that way when they arrived in the banqueting hall. He had no wish to intrude on the thoughts of his two friends, and quite apart from that, the flood of sensations coming to him from the stone would have been overwhelming in a crowd this size. He didn't need magical help to sense the underlying tension in the atmosphere around him though. It had been obvious to him as Will was speaking that his words had touched on a raw nerve. The unease had not diminished; if anything it had grown.

Amyra had joined Thomas and his companions, intending to act as translator whenever that was needed. She made it clear to them that Will's stubborn insistence on speaking in Rogandan earlier in the day—against her explicit advice—had been highly inappropriate. Any repetition would be a serious affront to the Aen-ur.

Thomas sensed that her concerns were well founded. Nevertheless he had the impression that Amyra had been considerably more irritated by Will's action than Atae.

Will had shown surprising insight into the Aen-ur and their history, and Thomas wondered how he had come to know so much. He intended to ask him about it as soon as an opportunity presented itself.

"So you have a wife," Amyra was saying. "You must be missing her."

"Very much so. And my young daughter as well," Thomas replied wholeheartedly. "Are you married, Amyra?"

Her face became suddenly unyielding. "I have not been so fortunate."

He raised a questioning eyebrow.

"Opportunities have arisen," she acknowledged with a shrug. "I have been told more than once that I am difficult to please."

He gazed at her thoughtfully. Amyra seemed very different from his own wife. She did not exude the gentle graciousness of Elena—he had yet to meet another woman who even came close to his wife in that respect—but she was both intelligent and accomplished, and by no means unattractive.

"I'm sure it is obvious to you that I am not of the Aen-ur," she said frankly, "even though they choose to embrace me as one of their own. I suppose the truth is that I'm not entirely sure where I do belong."

He nodded. Most of the Aen-ur seemed sallow of complexion, differing from both Arvenians and Rogandans. Their hair color, though, matched the black tone of the Rogandans. So far he had not seen individuals with hair that was distinctively different.

With her hazelnut brown hair, and skin that was darker than an Arvenian's and lighter than the native inhabitants of Rogand, Amyra presented a marked contrast to everyone around her. Her appearance didn't clearly mark her as a member of any of those races. Her heritage was almost certainly mixed.

Thomas couldn't help being curious about her background. He had caught significant glimpses earlier thanks to the stone, but other people had been in sight at the time and he hadn't felt any need to focus particular attention on her. His main interest had been to discover if she represented any kind of threat to them. He'd seen no obvious sign to suggest it.

"How did you come to be among the Aen-ur?" he asked.

She smiled. "They welcomed us when we came here many years ago and encouraged us to make a home among them. I was a small child, but I know from my mother that we were vulnerable and friendless at the time. Their warm acceptance changed our lives. My mother soon found a role as a healer—she is much respected."

"You seem to have a position of authority here yourself," he noted.

She shook her head firmly. "I have no actual authority here, except perhaps as a senior translator. Most of the Aen-ur learn no languages beyond their own. Rogandan is an exception, although they do not speak it unless absolutely necessary." She aimed a dark look in Will's direction. "They deal routinely with traders of every nationality, including many from Arvenon, Castel, Varas, and Lestanor. Some among the Aen-ur speak the languages of these kingdoms, but few have achieved mastery in them. I am fortunate to have inherited from my mother a facility with languages."

She smiled grimly. "Foreign traders tend to be shrewd in their dealings. A few are unscrupulous—more than willing to exploit anyone they perceive as weak. The Aen-ur have come to appreciate my involvement because I stand up to them."

Her account did not surprise Thomas in the least. She had spirit, and it was already obvious that she was very protective of the Aen-ur. He could easily imagine her negotiating and advocating vigorously on their behalf. Thanks to Will, they had already seen her in action. He threw a quick glance in his friend's direction.

He was confident she meant them no harm, in spite of her prickliness toward Will in particular. And he'd spent enough time with Amyra for her to become a person rather than just another nameless individual. He'd reached a point where he was not willing to use the stone to pry into her mind and memories, at least not without a compelling reason.

Amyra had been conversing at some length with Thomas. She had spoken to him exclusively in Arvenian, and he was grateful for her consideration. His companions had restricted themselves to Rogandan since the ship deposited them on the beach, and he was enjoying a break from the constant effort of translating every thought before he could speak.

When they first arrived for the meal Amyra had initiated a polite conversation with Haldek. Engaging with a Rogandan clearly cost some effort on her part, but she seemed intent on seeing beyond his origins. Nevertheless, it hadn't been long before she turned her attention to Thomas, and she had seemed content to remain locked in conversation with him ever since. Perhaps, having soon discovered that he was already spoken for, she decided she could afford to relax and enjoy his company. Perhaps she simply saw nothing offensive about him.

Will was a different matter entirely. After aiming a frosty nod in his direction when they entered the building, she had completely ignored him. Will had noticed her aloofness, and Thomas caught him shooting occasional glances in her direction throughout the meal.

Will had clearly managed to upset her, and Thomas wondered what exactly had elicited such a strong reaction from her.

Almost at that moment she jerked her head in Will's direction. "It seems your friend—His Lordship, Commander of the armies of the world, or whatever he is—imagines himself as someone very special."

Thomas's brows drew together in surprise. "Will?" He shook his head emphatically. "He's less concerned about his own importance than almost anyone I've ever known!"

"That certainly wasn't how he came across to me," she said disdainfully. "Trumpeting his titles, lecturing the Aen-ur about their own history." Her hazel eyes flashed angrily. "Insisting on speaking to them in Rogandan—after I'd explained they would find it offensive!"

So that was it. Seeing the fire in her eyes, Thomas felt thankful that he hadn't been the one to provoke her.

He gazed at her in fascination. Her face seemed to acquire an elfin quality when she was agitated. She was an intriguing person.

He shot a glance at Will, wondering if he was aware of her displeasure. He caught his friend studying Amyra curiously, although he looked away nonchalantly as soon as he noticed Thomas glancing in his direction.

Amyra shook her head dismissively, sending her chestnut brown hair dancing. "Why should I care?" she asked with a shrug. "He seems to think he can bend the Aen-ur to his will. Let him try."

Thomas decided to change the subject to a less personal topic. "Do the Aen-ur have much contact with the outside world?" he asked.

"As little as possible," she said, "although they are well aware of what goes on around them. All of them learn Rogandan from a young age—they regard it as a necessary concession to the harsh realities of their situation. You have also seen that Atae speaks Arvenian, although he is unusual in that regard."

"Do they trade with the rest of Rogand?"

She nodded. "Indirectly. They trade with visiting Arvenian or Lestanorian merchants, who then sell their products throughout Rogand and beyond."

Thomas knew that Will had grown up with his Arvenian uncle who was a merchant. Perhaps he had traded with these people. That might at least partly account for Will's knowledge of the Aen-ur and their history.

"What do they sell to the merchants?" Thomas asked curiously.

"There are mines in the mountains," Amyra told him, waving a hand vaguely toward the peaks. She seemed unwilling to be more specific.

Shortly after that Amyra excused herself and left the banquet hall, leaving Thomas wondering if he had asked one question too many.

They found their hut strongly guarded when they were escorted there after the meal. Will didn't seem concerned at the implied lack of trust.

"You've upset Amyra," Thomas told him.

"I'm not here to impress her," Will replied with a shrug.

Thomas raised an eyebrow. He had a feeling that Will might care about her opinion more than he was letting on. Whether that was true or not, Thomas was very certain about one thing—Will would never allow such considerations to distract him from his purpose.

"What are you planning?" Thomas asked him.

"I expect we will be invited to a conference tomorrow, with a smaller group of people," Will replied. "I am hoping the Aen-ur will agree to do something to at least slow Agon down for a while. I'd like to get you an opportunity to take a closer look at Agon," he added, giving Thomas a significant look. "Of course that isn't the reason I'll give them for asking them to do it."

Thomas's heart beat a little faster. Getting close enough to see the Rogandan king was certain to be dangerous. But it was the reason he had come here.

"I'm also wondering if there might be an opportunity to examine their oldest records," Will added, "assuming any have survived. They might have an intact copy of your scroll."

Such a prospect captured Thomas immediately. The copy of the scroll that had been read to him and Brother Vangellis at the monastery had been torn and incomplete and offered no detail about either the Stone of Authority or the Stone of Vitality. Knowing more about the Stone of Authority might prove crucial to thwarting Agon's plans. The writer had also promised a more complete explanation of the behavior of the stones later in the scroll, and Thomas had often wondered what he might have written.

THE FOLLOWING morning Will received the invitation he had been waiting for. Atae had promised him an opportunity to explain why they had trespassed on the lands of the Aen-ur. Will was hoping to convince their captors to become their allies, although he was aware that other less encouraging outcomes were also possible. While it was too early to say whether they had found their way to help or to trouble, all uncertainty was likely to be resolved before long.

Amyra came to meet them, greeting Haldek formally and offering Thomas a muted smile. She eyed Will dispassionately, looking him up and down briefly. She was not rude, provided that complete indifference didn't count as rudeness.

Following her to a smaller building, they found Atae and four other men of the Aen-ur waiting for them. A silver-haired woman also stood beside Atae, and Will immediately guessed that he was looking at an older version of Amyra. The woman directed a searching glance at each of them, but reserved her most careful scrutiny for Will.

Atae greeted them noncommittally. "You asked for a conference," he told Will, speaking in Arvenian, "and we are here, although I promise you nothing. We have treated you with courtesy, perhaps more than your bluntness has earned. Whether we come to regret our forbearance will be largely up to you."

He indicated the woman. "I have invited our friend Dahra to join us since we value her wisdom."

Dahra bowed briefly to each of them. "Unfortunately I was not able to join you yesterday," she said, speaking fluently in Arvenian. "I am a healer for this community, and I was called to assist a young woman in her first childbirth. We found ourselves confronted with a number of complications, but I am glad to say that both mother and baby are well."

Will bowed respectfully to her, observing her curiously. As they were seating themselves, his attention was distracted by a sharp intake of breath at his side. He glanced around in time to see Thomas fiddling with the chain around his neck, a thunderstruck expression on his face. His young friend quickly lowered his head to hide his discomposure, but Will saw that Dahra had also noticed his reaction, and she was studying Thomas with considerable curiosity.

The stone had clearly revealed something that startled Thomas. Interested as he was to know more, Will knew he could not afford to allow his focus to be diverted.

"We are listening," Atae said. His demeanor suggested that his patience might have limits.

Will had no desire to waste his time. "I will be frank with you," he said. "At the time we left King Steffan and Queen Essanda, the Arvenian capital Arnost was occupied by mercenaries controlled by an Arvenian traitor, a man who has been financed by Agon and owes allegiance to him. This man took control when King Steffan was severely wounded, and at the same time he also took command of the two Arvenian armies on active duty. We have already regained control of one of those armies, and the king was working to do the same with the other. Meanwhile, although Castel is ruled by the young son of the murdered King Istel, his most powerful advisor is a Castelan traitor who is also working on behalf of Agon.

"King Steffan and Queen Essanda are currently in Varacellan, working closely with their ally King Delmar of Varas. Their immediate goals are to prevent Agon from crossing the border into Arvenon, and to regain control of all Arvenian army forces. Regaining control of Arnost will come later.

"I am telling you this because I do not wish to overstate the strength of the forces arrayed against Agon."

Atae's expression left no doubt about his conclusions from Will's summary. "Given the strength of Agon's support within Arvenon and Castel, it sounds as if he has every chance of succeeding," he said grimly. "He isn't a man to forgive and forget. When he completes his conquests, he will not hesitate to turn the full force of his wrath on anyone who dares to move against him now."

Will was not deterred. "Agon may appear to have everything going his way. He is relaxed and confident, but his opponents are far from defeated. He knows that his assassins struck down King Steffan of Arvenon, and he may well still believe him to be dead. Whether or not Agon is already aware of it, the king has recovered from his wounds, and King Delmar of Varas is gathering forces to resist Agon. King Delmar will stand with King Steffan, and together they will oppose Agon with all their might.

"Meanwhile, Agon's nobles are not pleased at all about Agon's new invasion. They bore the brunt of the losses from the last invasion. Most of their peasants were called away from the fields to bolster Agon's army, and the greater proportion of them did not return. Agon emptied his treasury to fund the invasion, and he has since multiplied the troubles of his nobles by taxing them harshly in an attempt to replenish his coffers. None of the nobles have been bold enough to openly oppose Agon. Not yet. But they are restless."

Will could see that Atae was far from convinced. "And what kind of contribution do you imagine the Aen-ur making toward your cause?" Atae asked. "Before you answer the question, you should know that we see no reason why we should take you seriously, Will Prentis," Atae told him bluntly. "Or why we should believe anything you say."

In response, Will reached into the pouch at his belt and retrieved the tile entrusted to him by King Steffan. He had no idea whether it would have any meaning to Atae, but this was clearly the time to find out. He glanced at it briefly, once more entranced by its beauty and mystery. Then he handed it to Atae.

The leader's eyes narrowed as he took it in. Flipping it over, he squinted as he scanned the tiny writing on the other side. His eyes were wide as he handed it to his countrymen. Each of them examined it before passing it to Dahra. She in turn showed it to Amyra. The young woman examined it almost defiantly before returning it to Atae.

"Do you know what this is?" the leader asked Will sharply.

Will shook his head.

"It is a princely gift," Atae told him. "How does it come to be in your possession?"

"King Steffan entrusted it to me," Will told him. "It was given to one of his forebears by a king of the Aen-ur in return for a service he rendered to that king. I know little more than that. I was given to understand that the details have been lost in the intervening years."

"The ancient gifts of the Aen-ur always had great potential for abuse if they fell into the wrong hands," Atae told him. "For that reason such gifts were always issued with a key. Do you have the key?"

Will looked at him blankly. "I know of no key," he said. He paused for a moment. "King Steffan did tell me, though, that his father pressed him to memorize a phrase when he passed it down to him. King Steffan entrusted the phrase to me when he was bidding us farewell, and I committed it to memory." He closed his eyes and took a deep breath. "Sinowe isakhi wazihe alwa ishae-nixi," he intoned. Opening his eyes, he looked at Atae. "Does that mean anything to you?"

The expression on the faces of the Aen-ur astonished him. All of them appeared stunned. Not one of them said a word.

Atae finally spoke. "You have just provided the key," he replied. Seeing the confusion on Will's face, he added, "The key is not an object, it is a spoken phrase. It is independent of the writing on the stone, and it must be memorized. The writing on the stone is incomplete without the key."

Will was still confused. Perhaps aware of it, Atae added, "You would need to understand our language to fully comprehend the wordplay involved in such messages. But a simple example in your own language might give you the sense of it. Suppose I were to say, 'The food served at last night's banquet was sumptuous.' That might convey the impression of lavish feasting. If I were to add, 'The hungry went to bed hungry,' we might begin to understand that food was not served equally to everyone. The second statement has become a key to understanding the first."

Will nodded slowly.

Atae continued. "Suppose the original statement included both sentences. 'The food served at last night's banquet was sumptuous, but the hungry went to bed hungry.' We might understand a deeper meaning if the key were, 'Those who refused the invitation to the banquet feasted only on their folly.'"

Atae hadn't finished. "We might form a very different conclusion if the key were instead, 'Each person attending the banquet was served exactly what they deserved.'"

Will thought he was beginning to understand, at least in part.

"The tile your king received was originally part of an elaborate mosaic in the floor of the throne room at Ishitar Ataye. The mosaic suffered a similar fate to the fortress. Very few pieces survived, and every one that is still preserved is precious to us. I will not attempt to explain the meaning of the message of the writing as clarified by the key. Suffice it to say that a great debt is owed to your king by my people. As his representative, the debt is owed to you."

Atae handed the tile back to Will. "Keep this, and return it to your king. The debt will not be erased by anything we can do to help you at this time."

Will's mind was spinning as he returned the tile to his pouch. Dahra was watching him with an inscrutable smile playing on her lips. Amyra appeared thoroughly disconcerted.

"Our resources might be limited," Atae told him. "But we will do whatever is within our power to help you."

33

Will stared at the Aen-ur. His prospects had changed in a moment, thanks to a small glazed tile. It was hard to comprehend, but now was not a time for guessing.

"I have two requests," he told Atae. "Are you aware of Agon's column?"

"We are closely monitoring his progress," Atae confirmed, "especially as he draws nearer to our lands."

"Am I right in thinking that he is still some days away?" Will ventured.

Atae had a rapid interaction with one of his countrymen. He nodded agreement. "They are traveling slowly. They are setting up what amounts to a small town every time they camp for the night. The head of the column is not likely to reach this area for another five or six days at the earliest."

Will nodded in satisfaction. "Arvenian forces are moving into position to prevent Agon from crossing the border. Any time we can buy them could prove significant. Suppose a natural disaster were to bring his progress to a temporary halt? A forest fire at a point where the trees fringe the road, for example, or a flash flood caused by the temporary redirection of a river. It could take place well away from your lands to ensure that the Aen-ur come under no suspicion."

Once more the Aen-ur ignored their visitors to converse in their own language. It had more the appearance of a debate this time, and from time to time the participants became very animated. Will glanced at Amyra. She had not joined the conversation, but she was following it closely, a frown slowly deepening on her face. She seemed uneasy with the direction the interaction was heading, and for some reason Will found that encouraging.

Glancing at Dahra, he discovered the older woman studying him intently. He stared calmly back at her, untroubled by her scrutiny. Everything about her radiated gentleness, although he sensed a sturdiness beneath it all.

Something about her made Will think of Brother Vangellis as he had come to know him in the latter days of his life. The monk had been battered by pain and grief, and for a time crippled by his own shame. In Will's experience people were often hardened by such experiences, but the buffeting seemed to have softened the monk. Brother Vangellis had by no means been weak though; a surprisingly tough resilience had underpinned his gentle compassion.

Dahra reminded him of the monk. Will liked the little he had seen of her, and he found himself hoping he would have the opportunity to get to know her better.

He turned his attention back to Atae. The conversation was still in progress, but much of the heat had gone out of it, and heads appeared to be nodding.

After a couple more minutes Atae turned to him. "Any action will involve risk. But there is a place to the north of here where it might be possible to do something along the lines of what you have requested. The location is in the direction of Rog, which means Agon's column will reach the site sooner. Many of my people live in close proximity to it—we can ill afford to act unless our intervention can be made to appear entirely natural."

Will nodded his understanding. "It has never been my desire to expose your people, Atae, and I thank you for even considering my request. I know my king and queen will greatly appreciate whatever help you can give."

"You said you had a second request," said Atae.

"Yes. The Aen-ur have been in the land since ancient times. I have been wondering if any of your older records have survived."

"What is the reason for your interest?" Atae asked.

"There is some suggestion that King Agon is making use of an ancient artifact to enhance his power. I wish to examine your records in case they might mention such an object."

Atae showed no sign of taking seriously any talk of ancient artifacts, but Dahra immediately directed a sharp glance at Will.

Atae once more conveyed the request to the others. After a brief conversation, he turned to Dahra. She glanced at Will before turning back to Atae with a definite nod. He addressed the others, and all of them either nodded as well or simply shrugged. He asked a question of Amyra, and she replied briefly. Will studied her face, but she was giving nothing away.

"Some of our records survived the fall of Ishitar Ataye," Atae told Will. "You may visit with your companions provided you are willing to accept the supervision of one of our number."

Will nodded immediately. "Of course," he replied.

Atae pointed to one of his countrymen, who nodded a greeting. "This is Kaemin. He speaks no Arvenian, but Amyra has agreed to accompany you as translator." He glanced at Dahra. "Dahra would also accompany you gladly if other commitments did not prevent her from doing so."

To Will's eye, Dahra looked very disappointed, but he heard a sigh from Thomas at his side. It sounded a great deal like relief. Will was surprised—he could not imagine that Dahra presented any kind of threat. He promised himself he would pursue it with Thomas once an opportunity arose.

"Our records are located within the ruins of Ishitar Ataye," Atae told them. "It should be possible for you to visit the library briefly and still reach the place where we plan a distraction to delay Agon. But you will need to set out immediately."

Atae was as good as his word. Horses were brought, and Will and his party were mounted within the hour. Accompanied by Kaemin, Amyra, and four armed soldiers, they headed north, led by one of the four men who had joined their party.

Will felt certain that the Aen-ur must have a way of traveling quickly through the forest. He never imagined for a minute that they would be willing to use the main road to Rog. His guess was confirmed after only a few minutes.

Picking their way through the trees they emerged onto what appeared to be an ancient road. Stray leaves blew across it, and the forest had encroached on it in places, but it had survived the rigors of time largely intact. Broad enough for two carriages to travel side by side, it ran as straight and true as the flight of an arrow on a still day. No end to the road was visible to Will. It disappeared into the far distance beyond his sight, rising and falling with the contours of the ground.

As soon as they were on the road they made excellent time. They passed other Aen-ur travelers heading in the opposite direction; during the time they were riding, they passed ten such groups before Will stopped counting. Most of the groups were quite large in number and invariably traveling with heavily laden wagons.

The surface of the road was still firm, and it allowed them to continue riding safely until well after night had fallen. After they had been riding under the stars for about an hour, their guide led them off the road a short distance until a large and sturdy cabin came into view in the moonlight. One of the soldiers disappeared inside and soon reappeared with a burning torch.

A large stack of firewood lay nearby, and the soldiers set to work building a fire in the cabin's fireplace and preparing a simple meal. They shared the food as soon as it was ready to eat.

While they were eating, Will directed a question at Amyra. "Are there other cabins like this?" he asked.

She looked down her nose at him for a few moments before deigning to answer. "Yes," she finally confirmed. "They were built at regular intervals along both sides of the road. People are assigned by the Aen-ur to maintain them for the use of travelers."

"Are the Rogandans aware of all this?" he asked, indicating the cabin and the road.

"They do not come here," she said simply. "They are fearful of venturing beyond the borders of Aen-irac, and we are far from the borders here. Even traders are granted access only to the outer fringes of Aen-ur territory."

Will absorbed this information with considerable interest. Her reply matched his own experience—his uncle had traded with the Aen-ur a number of times in his presence, but their business had never taken them far into Aen-irac.

The traffic on this road had exceeded his expectations. The Aen-ur were clearly numerous and organized. He was beginning to suspect that the full extent of their trade might far exceed the expectations of anyone who didn't know them intimately.

The cabin was large enough to easily accommodate their company, and people began spreading out bed rolls after finishing the simple meal. It was apparent that the soldiers had no plan to post sentries. This remote corner of Aen-irac was apparently regarded as safe by the Aen-ur.

Desiring a few moments alone with his thoughts, Will headed outside. The Aen-ur ignored him. Apparently they had decided he was no threat.

The cabin stood on the edge of a small clearing, and Will moved to the center of it, gazing up at the night sky. He thought of his previous visits to Aen-irac. His uncle's business as a trader had required him to travel widely, and Will had visited many stranger places as a result. His late uncle had certainly hoped Will would follow him in his vocation, and Will wondered briefly if he would have been disappointed with his adopted son's eventual choices. He shrugged off such thoughts. He had learned many useful skills from his uncle, but the prospect of a life as a trader never held appeal for him.

Absorbed in his thoughts, he barely registered that someone had joined him until the lithe figure of Amyra appeared beside him. She followed his gaze into the heavens, and the two of them stood side by side without speaking for a time.

"Your presence in Aen-irac disturbs me greatly, Will Prentis," she finally said. Her tone was pitched somewhere between a purr and a growl, and it made him think of a tigress, poised to pounce.

She stood close enough that they were almost touching. Her presence discomposed him for reasons he didn't understand. He shook his head involuntarily, irritated at his own reaction.

With no response forthcoming, she spoke again. "These people are vulnerable enough already without you putting them at risk. It is clear that their safety and security mean nothing to you. But it matters to me."

He shrugged. "I spoke truthfully to Atae. I have no desire to see the Aen-ur exposed to Agon's attention."

"Then why don't you just leave? It would be the best thing for their sake—for the sake of everyone."

A hint of pleading had appeared briefly through her fierceness. Was it possible that she was finding him a little unsettling?

A sudden desire came over him to say something witty. His life had exposed him to an unusual variety of experiences, and he had never lacked boldness when facing the unknown. Nevertheless, engaging in light-hearted banter with a woman was unfamiliar territory.

He accepted the challenge, his mouth twisting into an ironic grin. "I seem to have occupied more than my fair share of your attention, Amyra. I'd never thought of myself as attractive."

She glared at him scathingly. "Perhaps you've managed to convince yourself that a scarred face and a limp are attractive to a woman, but don't expect me to pander to your delusions."

He winced, surprised by how much her words stung. He'd been a fool—he should have kept his mouth shut.

After an uncomfortable silence, Amyra sighed. "I have no desire to fight with you," she told him. "I just wish you would take your ambitions somewhere else." The cutting edge had vanished from her tone, but she left her earlier remarks hanging.

Standing beside an attractive young woman who apparently regarded him with complete disdain, Will felt uncharacteristically awkward. He'd never possessed the ability to charm women, and for the first time it brought him a twinge of regret. The spitfire standing at his side was equal parts mysterious and exasperating, and he knew himself to be poorly equipped for the challenge of trying to make sense of her. And what would be the point anyway, when she so obviously despised him?

He reminded himself why he had come here. With his mission yet to be accomplished, he had more than enough to occupy his attention. He could not afford distractions.

"I did not come here to further my ambitions, whatever you might think," he said coolly. "If Agon is allowed to succeed, the way of life you seem to find so agreeable won't long survive. The Aen-ur will be swept away, along with everything they value."

He fixed her with a steely gaze. "I am at least trying to prevent that. What are you doing, apart from working against me?"

Without waiting for an answer, he turned and made his way back to the cabin. He made no attempt to disguise his limp.

34

A fork in the road took them deeper into the mountains. They had been riding for almost an hour when the trees parted. All of them simultaneously drew their horses to a halt.

Ahead of them lay a deep gorge. The noisy roar of a rushing river carried clearly on the morning air. On the far side of the gorge lay the shattered remnants of a once mighty fortress. Most of its walls had been torn down, and only the broken fragments of towers still climbed skyward to hint at its former glory.

There was something eerie about its whispered grandeur, but even in its ruin Ishitar Ataye was still magnificent.

A broad bridge had once spanned the gorge, but surviving pieces of its crumbling stonework were now visible only on the far side. Glancing downriver Will noticed a flimsy rope bridge suspended across the gulf.

Amyra's voice sounded over the tumult of the water. "We must leave our horses on this side," she called.

She had been avoiding him, and Will was thankful. He had felt more awkward than ever in her presence after their exchange outside the cabin.

Two of the soldiers remained with the horses. Haldek accompanied them to the bridge, but it was obvious he had no interest in joining them. Will knew he had no fear of heights after his years patrolling the battlements of Agon's castle. It seemed more likely that he was reluctant to view more closely the ancient destruction wrought by his countrymen. Either way, Will was content to leave his friend in peace. Haldek would no doubt rejoin the two soldiers if he found himself alone for any length of time.

Flimsy as the bridge appeared to be, Amyra climbed onto it without hesitation and began crossing, placing her feet carefully while holding on firmly with her hands. One of the soldiers was not far behind her, and Will quickly followed their example. When he was halfway across he looked back. Thomas and Kaemin were already on the bridge and the other soldier was poised to take his turn.

With multiple people crossing at one time, the bridge began to sway alarmingly, and Will was forced to focus all of his attention on finding the next place to plant his foot. When he finally reached the end he looked up to find that Amyra had been staring at him. She glanced away before he could meet her eye.

As each person reached the end of the bridge she leaned forward, holding out a hand to steady them as they stepped once more onto solid ground. She hadn't offered him the same courtesy, although he decided not to dwell on it.

Kaemin now took the lead. The older man wended his way through the ruins until he reached a small section of ground that had been cleared of the rubble strewn everywhere. Following him behind a fallen column, Will came upon the cleverly concealed entrance to a low building. Anyone not already aware of the entrance would have been fortunate to find it.

As he entered, Kaemin called out a greeting. An answer sounded from somewhere inside the building, soon followed by a face fringed with gray hair. The man emerged and greeted Kaemin warmly.

After a brief conversation, all of them were invited into the building, and they followed him down a flight of steps into an underground room of vast size covered with shelves. Scrolls and parchments could be seen everywhere.

Their guide turned to them with a friendly smile. "I am Inyaet," he told them, speaking in Arvenian, "and I am the chief librarian here. I normally have two other helpers, but they are currently away visiting family."

Will introduced himself and Thomas.

"I understand you are looking for old scrolls that speak of ancient artifacts," Inyaet continued. He led them to one end of the room and pointed to a single shelf covered with old scrolls. "I have spent many years sorting through our older documents and records," he said. "This shelf contains everything we have that could be categorized as myths, legends, and fantastical stories. Personally, I find such tales fascinating and often informative as well. From the limited range of documents, though, you might reasonably guess that content of that kind was not granted a high priority by past librarians."

"May I?" asked Will, pointing to the shelf.

"Perhaps I can hand you documents for your perusal," Inyaet replied. "Some of the older scrolls are extremely delicate and require special care."

"I will treat them with the greatest respect," Will assured him.

"Shall I begin with documents written in Rogandan or Arvenian?" asked Inyaet.

Will shrugged. "I'm not sure."

"Perhaps we will start with our Arvenian collection, since there are fewer of them."

The librarian carefully selected a dozen scrolls, glancing at each of them in turn before handing them gingerly to Will, one at a time.

Will opened the first. "Reliable lore concerning draggonnes and other winged serpenttes of fearsome mien," he read aloud. He glanced at Thomas, who rolled his eyes heavenward.

Most of the other documents contained similar nonsense. Inyaet had almost reached the end of the Arvenian documents when Will unrolled the latest scroll and read out, "*Three talismans of great potency are abroad in the world, uncelebrated, unrecognized, and hidden from any certain knowledge.*" Even before he glanced up to see the troubled look in Thomas's eyes, Will knew they had found what they were seeking.

He turned to Inyaet. "We would like to examine this scroll more closely if you are willing."

The librarian came to Will's side and bent over the document, scanning it briefly. "Ah, yes. I remember it. The writer seems to imagine a circumstance where tiny objects—objects with magical properties, of course—can be used to influence the destiny of kingdoms. An intriguing fantasy. You are most welcome to examine it, for whatever it's worth."

He straightened again, smiling at Will. "I don't imagine that my services will be needed—you seem to be an unusually capable reader."

Hearing the admiration in the librarian's voice, Will couldn't resist a glance in Amyra's direction. Her face was unexpressive.

Inyaet pointed to a table surrounded by three stools, and Will carried the scroll carefully to it. Thomas and Amyra joined him there.

Will slowly unrolled the scroll until all the writing was visible.

"Is it all there?" Thomas asked breathlessly.

Will ran his eyes to the end of the scroll and nodded. "I think so. It ends like this: '*My account ends here. May the scholar who stumbles upon it derive greater benefit from this lore than I have myself. Randolf of Clerbon.*'"

Glancing at Thomas, Will saw that his face had gone pale.

The librarian apparently felt no need to sit with them as they read the scroll together. Instead he turned his attention to Kaemin, who spoke no Arvenian and was probably much less interested than the librarian in myths, legends, and fantastical stories. The two men were soon engaged in an energetic conversation in their own language.

Will turned his full attention to the scroll. Taking a deep breath, he began to read aloud.

. . .

'Three talismans of great potency are abroad in the world, uncelebrated, unrecognized, and hidden from any certain knowledge. Perhaps I alone know their true history, long forgotten with the passing of many scores of years. I once learned of an ancient parchment, lost and mayhap forgotten by all save only an aged hermit. The old man had glimpsed it in his youth, and he described it to me as well as his failing memory served him.

Long did I search for it, and bitter and fruitless my labor seemed. Dark and tiresome would be the full tale thereof. At last, hope having deserted me, I stumbled upon it, the greatest treasure in my possession. Even now I have it before me, a faded manuscript, crumbling with age and arcane in script. Many candles burned to naught ere I found a way to decipher it.

Hear, then, the testimony of a scribe whose witness has been silent for many an age:

Long years have passed away since Goodman Tomas walked upon the earth. A poor farmer and simple he was, yet greatly beloved by all who knew him. He lived in a rude hut in but a small village.

One day his fortunes turned. Though his back had been bowed down with much labor, yet was he seen to stand again straight and tall. Tales grew up around his wisdom, and people journeyed from afar to seek his counsel. His insights failed him not, and his sayings gave birth to a bountiful supply of proverbs.

It came to pass that his village became a town, and the town a city, and he the mayor. His family prospered likewise.

Late in life offered he a gift unto the king of his country. Rude in appearance was the gift but great in effect, and the king, who was a good ruler, handled it wisely. His fortunes likewise changed, and he became powerful even as his kingdom prospered.

The story sprang up and spread abroad that Tomas had received a star from heaven that fell from the sky and landed in the form of a rock beside his hut. Great and manifold were the gifts bestowed by this rock upon its owner—gifts of insight, good health and influence among men. And behold, having received it freely from Tomas, the king rejoiced also in the selfsame gifts. Nor were the benefits denied to Tomas when he yielded up the rock. He continued as before until he had attained a great age.

So Tomas died, full of years, and in time the king also slept with his fathers. The son of the king prospered, too, and increased yet more in power. A subtle, but alas, not a wise king was he, and many enemies gathered themselves against him. The neighboring kingdoms rose up, bound together in hatred for the king and desire for the rock. Nevertheless, try as they might, they could not overcome him, such was his might in arms and his shrewdness in council. Finally, by treachery alone was he brought low, slain by the hand of one he trusted.

Thus lost the son of the wise king his kingdom and his life, all through foolishness and pride. The ruler who wrested control of his kingdom laid hands upon the rock, lusting to command every virtue of which he had heard so much. It benefited him nothing. Years of bitter fortune and failing prosperity passed, until in anger he caused the rock to be smashed into a thousand fragments and cast outside his palace.

And lo, it came to pass that certain peasants, chancing upon the pieces, found them pleasing to the eye. Taking them up, they bore them unto their dwellings. Anon it was seen that some of the virtue of the rock had passed into three of the pieces. One brought health and vitality, a second, great authority, and a third, insight into the hearts and minds of men.

Long and illuminating would be the history that chronicled the fortunes attending those who found the stones. Time revealed that the stones, as likewise the rock vouchsafed to Tomas, lost their virtue entirely when taken by force, at times remaining dormant for a generation. Only when a stone was gifted freely, or found by chance, was the virtue bestowed. The stones together were like the original rock in every respect but one—once a gift had been made of a stone, its virtue was thereafter withheld from the giver.

Some stones passed as heirlooms from father to son or mother to daughter. In time the gift was always squandered through pride or folly, or lost through violence or misadventure.

None can say where the stones are today. Long years have passed since last I heard aught of them. Many say they are lost forever, and some rejoice in their vanishment. Some say they are a gift from God to the wise. Others say they are a tool of the Devil to curse and ensnare all who receive them.

There was a time when one of the stones lay in my hand for a moment. Young and foolish I was, and greatly desirous of possessing it, though every opportunity was denied me. Now I am old, and wiser, and content with my lot in life. Who could envy those who bear the burden of such a gift?

THE WITNESS ENDED THUS. My account concerning the ancient manuscript is accurate in every particular and my translation faithful and true. I, Randolf of Clerbon, swear it on my life.'

'In the unrelenting passage of years since the scribe lived and breathed, many things have changed, and some remain the same. The role of the rock in shaping kingdoms, revealed in the manuscript, has never ceased. The true history of Arvenon and the surrounding kingdoms is incomplete without reference to the stones of power.

Such fateful talismans—how they haunt my dreams! Ever have I sought them, but alas, thus far to no avail. Much lore have I gathered concerning the three—the Stone of Vitality, that grants well-being and life beyond the span of other men, the Stone of Authority, that bestows power and influence for good or for ill, and the Stone of Knowing, that lays bare the hearts and motivations of others. I record here but a small part of this lore, in order that my labor shall not prove entirely vain, that my research shall not crumble to dust with my mortal body.

What, then, can be said of these stones? They respect neither rank nor status. They surrender their power impartially to saint and sinner alike. Certain boundaries do, however, encompass those who bear them. The potency of a stone is diminished by afflictions of the body or the spirit, especially when a stone is new to the bearer. Familiarity increases their virtue, though bearers assume fearful risks with overuse.

Such is the witness of those who lay greatest claim to discernment about the stones.

Nevertheless, overuse has never been chief among the perils confronting those who bear a stone. The principal danger has ever been the lust of others who desired the stones for themselves.

A stone fails of its purpose if a bearer has been killed to acquire it, no matter who carried out the murder. The same failure ensues if a stone is taken without consent.

Such limitations have never deterred the unscrupulous, though. The most cunning among them have ever recognized the futility of force, and sought instead to obtain the stones using fear and intimidation. That history must needs be told.

First, though, it is necessary to faithfully chronicle the properties of the stones. I will describe each in turn, for though their lineage is common, their likeness and behavior vary considerably.

The Stone of Knowing is said to be little bigger than a man's fingernail, smooth to the touch, and colored brightly with azure and magenta tones. The stone grants admittance—full and unfettered—to thought, intent, and motivation of every person upon whom the eye of the bearer falls. Certain parchment fragments, perplexing in nature, hint that even animals and birds lie within its reach, at least in small measure.

No memory from the past is safe—every secret buried deep must be surrendered to its power. The stone may offer glimpses of what is to come, but with no certain assuredness, since many a fork in the road awaits the traveler who journeys to the future.

An extraordinary weight bears down upon the hand that cradles this stone. It is said that, of the three, the Stone of Knowing holds the greatest potentiality for good or evil, depending only on the character of the one who bears it.'

WILL PAUSED, shooting a glance at Thomas.

"The other scroll ended there," Thomas told him, his voice taut with emotion. "It had been torn."

Will didn't respond. Bending down to the scroll once more, he continued to read aloud.

. . .

'The Stone of Authority, likewise tiny in size, is reported to be colored gray with flecks of red, and in shape round like the sun and flat like a thick strip of leather. The stone bends all created things to the will of the bearer. Of things living, humans are most to be feared, and they have ever been the chief targets of its power.

The human will can gradually be bent by the stone, shaped to the will of the bearer. All are susceptible, though none can be compelled to act against their deepest beliefs or their own character.

No fool is made wiser, nor do the wise become fools. Leaders lead, workers toil, and soldiers fight as ever before. The will alone is affected. The will is neither expunged nor obliterated, rather it is tutored to new purposes. A crowd is impervious to influence; wills must be tutored one at a time. Most claim that two weeks is sufficient.

The Stone of Authority is a perilous stone to possess. The tight link between the bearer and the person influenced by the stone is broken if the bearer dies or loses the stone. Where this is understood, the bearer of the stone quickly amasses enemies among those determined to release the ensnared.

The Stone of Vitality is unremarkable in appearance, dark gray in color and resembling a crescent moon in form. Unlike the other stones it has no direct or indirect impact on anyone but the bearer. It conveys long life, good health, and extraordinary vigor, although it cannot offer protection from death or disfigurement by violence. Such strange tales surround this stone. Rumors of improbable healings and even resuscitations abound, to the point where it is impossible to separate fact from hearsay.

Having described the stones, a final task remains. I undertook to record a history of the dangers faced by those who possess a stone, and I do so now.

At first, those who possessed the stones made no attempt to keep them secret. They perceived no cause for nervousness, since reports had spread abroad that to take a stone by force was wasted effort. A stone becomes available to another only when received as a gift from the bearer, or when found after the bearer has lost it or died. As already noted, the bearer's death must not have resulted from an attempt to acquire the stone.

Thanks to these protections, anyone fortunate enough to possess a stone openly enjoyed its benefits without consideration of consequences, just as the wealthy have always flaunted their riches in full sight of the poor. This state of affairs could not long persist. The stones awaken a hunger that is fiercer and far more dangerous than any lust for riches.

Taking a stone by force was impracticable, but incidents arose to test the boundaries of the forbidding. I learned of a father who gifted a stone to his son. After witnessing the use to which the gift was put, he repented of his decision and wrested the stone away, wholly against the will of his son. As expected, the stone thereafter failed to work reliably on his behalf. Nevertheless, at occasional moments of particular need it did indeed function as before, even if in lesser measure. Outcomes were alike for other individuals in similar circumstances. Such reports encouraged the unscrupulous to probe every limit with ruthless fervor.

Men and women without conscience, perceiving they had nought to lose, multiplied threats and intimidation in their lust to gain possession of a stone. In time it was seen that almost any abasement could be visited upon stone bearers to induce them to yield up their prize, without compromising the power of the stones. The solitary constraint was one of volition—the bearer must be allowed to retain the stone until they wearied of duress and handed it over willingly. If the bearer was stripped either of the stone or of their life at any moment before agreeing to relinquish it, then the transfer proved of no more value than an extraction by force.

Not surprisingly, any bearer possessing the tiniest ounce of wisdom soon went to considerable lengths to conceal their possession of a stone. The effect of the stones, though, is surpassingly difficult to disguise. How can such power be reliably hidden? None with insight could mistake the obvious signs, provided only that they were acquainted with the history of the stones and their behavior.

In time it became impossible, even for those with wealth and power, to long possess a stone with any expectation of security. Such conditions must persist until the stones are altogether lost to memory, forgotten by the world.

Surely that situation has arisen even now. Where are the stones today, and who among the living remembers them still? Though I yet seek them with unwavering fervor, hope has long abandoned me.

My account ends here. May the scholar who stumbles upon it derive greater benefit from this lore than I have myself.

Randolf of Clerbon.'

WHEN HE HAD FINISHED, Will put down the scroll and took a deep breath. It was obvious to him that he had barely begun to understand the complexities resulting from possession of the stones.

Thomas sat silent, lost in his thoughts.

Will's musing was interrupted by Amyra. "Such nonsense!" she scoffed. "I hope we came here for a better reason than this." When neither of her companions responded, she stared at them strangely. "Surely you don't take this seriously!"

Will and Thomas exchanged glances. The expression on Thomas's face seemed unusually guarded, and Will guessed that he was anxious to avoid his secret being exposed.

A frown slowly appeared on Amyra's face. "Even my mother wanted to hear anything we discovered about small stones," she said, apparently speaking to herself. "She can't have meant fables—she would never be taken in by such idiocy!"

Thomas directed a sharp look at her, but she didn't notice. Pushing herself purposefully to her feet, she shook her head in disgust. She marched out of the building, her chestnut brown locks dancing furiously about her face.

Carefully rolling up the scroll, Will returned it to the librarian, thanking him politely for his help.

Realizing that his guest was preparing to leave, the librarian ceased his conversation with Kaemin abruptly. "Surely you cannot have finished!" he exclaimed to Will in dismay. "We have so much of interest here to a scholar like yourself. Some of our historical records date back hundreds of years! They are more valuable by far than the fables you have been studying."

"I'm afraid I am not the scholar you imagine," Will assured the librarian with a smile. "Arvenon does have true scholars and librarians, and I don't doubt they would gladly explore your treasures for as long you would allow them to. I'm sure they would be pleased to return the favor, too, if you were willing to travel to Arvenon."

After waving Thomas out of the building, Will quickly followed him. The librarian was still pressing them to stay as they emerged into the sunlight.

It was painfully obvious that Inyaet was starved of human companionship. Will wasn't surprised. He would have gone mad this far from human habitation, perched on the edge of a ravine, and spending every day among the rubble of a ruined citadel.

Inyaet looked on glumly as they climbed once more onto the rickety bridge. They inched their way out across the void, trying not to look down at the raging torrent below.

As soon as he reached the other side Will looked back for a final glimpse of Inyaet. The librarian seemed small and pitiful standing alone at the base of the derelict fortress, surrounded by the debris of a forgotten age.

Raising his arm, he sent a farewell wave. When Inyaet's arm rose in response, Will turned away.

Haldek appeared before they reached the horses. "I'm sorry for not joining you, Will."

Will didn't mind at all. The fewer people who knew about the scroll the better. "Don't concern yourself, Haldek," he said, smiling and slapping his friend lightly on the back. "The bridge was already rickety enough without you on it as well."

Will's thoughts were racing as he swung into the saddle. The scroll had given him plenty to think about.

He pulled his horse alongside Thomas. "Based on what you and Elena learned from Tarestel before King Delmar executed him, it seems likely that Agon has the Stone of Authority," he said.

"I agree," Thomas replied. "I've always believed that Drettroth saw a copy of the scroll. If Agon has seen it too, he will have been using the information to full effect."

Will nodded. "It did offer one potential encouragement. If Agon loses the stone, whatever he's done to Pisander and Eisgold will immediately be undone."

35

The soldiers led Will and the others back to the main road. When they reached the junction, Kaemin bade them farewell. After they had thanked him he rode away with one of the soldiers, returning to the place where they had met.

The remaining three soldiers then led them in the opposite direction.

Amyra preempted Will's question by announcing, "We are heading to the location where a diversion is being prepared."

Her tone made it clear that she wasn't at all pleased about the Aen-ur placing themselves at risk in response to his request.

Will held his peace. It was hard to suppress a wave of irritation at her attitude though. None of this was intended to benefit him personally. Why did she continually feel the need to resist him?

They rode until daylight faded slowly around them and the trees were reduced to dark masses. Then the soldiers spotted a marker that pointed to another of the wayfarers' cabins, and they turned aside from the road to find it.

Thomas had been noticeably restless since they left Ishitar Ataye. After the soldiers had shared around some food, Will invited Thomas to join him outside.

"Did the missing section of the scroll answer any questions for you?" Will asked him.

"It completely explained what I experienced after taking the stone from Simon," Thomas replied.

Will decided to be direct. "Something's bothering you, Thomas."

Thomas stared into the dark. "Hearing the scroll in full wasn't easy. It's clear that things didn't end well for anyone who had one of the stones. There was nothing vaguely hopeful about it."

It wasn't hard for Will to guess what his friend might be feeling. Thomas had a family now. He wasn't responsible only to himself.

"And the stone has brought you to Rogand. You're in danger again because of it," said Will.

Thomas said nothing.

"I'm the one who's responsible for putting you at risk," Will acknowledged.

"No," said Thomas, shaking his head, "I'm responsible. I'm the one who's always insisted on keeping it." Thomas met his eyes. "You're not asking me to do anything you're not doing yourself. You've faced danger more than anyone."

It was Will's turn to shrug. "There have always been compelling reasons."

Both of them fell silent.

Will wanted to promise that he'd never call on Thomas again. Just as soon as this crisis was over. But he couldn't do it. He knew better than anyone that another crisis would always be lurking around the corner.

"Let's get some sleep," he said. "We'll be glad of it in the morning."

Thomas nodded, and they headed back into the cabin.

NO ROAD HAD EVER BEEN BUILT to connect the ancient road of the Aenur with the current main road from Rog. Accordingly the pace of Will's party slowed painfully once they left the ancient road and headed into the forest. From time to time they came upon animal trails heading in the right direction, but for the most part they were forced to pick their way through the trees. Many dreary hours lay behind them before they eventually broke free of the forest.

After a brief consultation with the soldiers, Amyra came to them. "The main road is not far to the east. We will head north for a while until we reach the bridge."

It was the first time Will had heard any mention of a bridge, and he wondered if the Aen-ur were planning to use it as their way of slowing Agon's progress. With no further information forthcoming, Will decided to hold his questions until they arrived.

The riders traveled along the tree line, staying out of sight of the main road. The day was almost spent by the time they finally came to a halt. One of their number rode forward until he disappeared from sight. He eventually returned with another man.

Amyra translated as the new arrival introduced himself to Will. "I am Rhillyon. I have been tasked with slowing Agon for you."

Will dipped his head. "I am Will Prentis. How far away is Agon's column?"

"They are not likely to arrive tomorrow. It will be the following day."

Rhillyon indicated that they should follow him, and the whole group set off behind him, heading north.

The riders didn't stop until they came in sight of a large stone bridge spanning a river.

The source of the river lay in the mountains away to the south. After flowing east through the forest, it bent north, skirting the foothills of the mountains. Agon was traveling in the opposite direction—south from Rog along the main road, heading toward the place where the river bent toward its origin.

For many leagues the road and the river ran side by side—the mountains on one side, the river on the other, and the road in between. As the road continued south, the ground between the mountains and the river became rocky and impassable. At that point the road followed the bridge across the river.

South of the bridge, the road continued beside the river, although the river now lay between the mountains and the road. The road and the river eventually diverged, with the road continuing south beyond the source of the river.

Rhillyon led them to a ridge among a stand of trees where they could clearly see below them the road and the bridge. The position allowed them to observe traffic on the bridge without being visible to prying eyes.

"Where is Agon positioned within the column?" asked Will.

"A large group of soldiers is leading the column," Rhillyon replied through Amyra. "Agon follows close behind. We are planning to collapse the bridge before any of them arrive. Agon will be trapped on this side of the river, so we will need to be careful."

"Who is traveling behind Agon?" Will asked.

"Mostly servants. Another large group of soldiers is bringing up the rear."

Will thought for a moment. "Could we disable the bridge after the first group of soldiers has already passed? It would make our task easier if Agon could be temporarily separated from a large proportion of his guards."

Amyra didn't immediately translate the message. She glared at Will. "You are asking these people to put themselves at great risk!"

Will gazed back into her flashing eyes, trying not to notice how attractive she was when animated. He recaptured his focus with difficulty. "I'm not expecting them to take all the risks. I'll do whatever I can myself."

Both Thomas and Haldek looked alarmed at his statement, but Will was not moved by their concern. He had never been inclined to ask others to face danger on his behalf.

Amyra's eyes narrowed, but she translated his original message. She spoke for long enough that Will was left in no doubt that she was adding plenty of her own thoughts as well.

"It might be possible," Rhillyon replied. He seemed more fascinated by the suggestion than alarmed, apparently seeing it as a challenging problem to be solved.

Will liked Rhillyon already.

The bridge was built with stone and featured a single arch. "It looks very old," Will said after studying it closely.

"It is," Rhillyon replied. "Almost three hundred years old. My people designed it."

Will pursed his lips and gave out a low whistle. "It looks different from bridges I'm accustomed to," he said.

Rhillyon nodded. "It uses a segmental arch design. The arch is curved, but it doesn't form a complete semicircle."

Will nodded. "It stands much higher above the river than bridges in Arvenon."

"The design allows the span to remain clear of the water even when the river is heavily in flood," Rhillyon told him.

Will nodded in appreciation. "How badly will it damage the interests of the Aen-ur if the bridge becomes unusable?" he asked.

"It will have no real effect on us," Rhillyon replied. "We stay within our own territory. It isn't safe for us to travel in the open, so we avoid the road. That also means we don't use the bridge."

Will raised his eyebrows. "So your people built it, but the Rogandans get the benefit."

Rhillyon acknowledged his remark with a shrug of resignation.

"How can you collapse it?" asked Will. The bridge looked very solid—it must be since it was still in good condition after three hundred years. He wondered how anyone could possibly manage to collapse it.

"We will need to remove a few of the key wedge-shaped stones that support the arch," Rhillyon replied.

Will was impressed. "You seem to know a lot about bridges."

"Our skills have not been entirely lost."

"Is the bridge going to collapse immediately once you remove the stones?" Will asked.

"Not if we are careful. We will attach metal hooks to the bottom of some of the stones. Then we will loosen the stones and tie ropes to the hooks. We will need to do it at night when there is no traffic on the bridge, so no one observes us."

Will nodded.

"Pulling on the ropes will remove the stones. They will fall into the river and sink to the bottom with the ropes. The bridge should quickly begin to collapse. The challenge will be to conceal both the ropes and the people pulling on them. If we can do that, it might appear that the stones fell out as a result of age and wear, and that the bridge collapsed naturally."

He peered down at the river. It was broad, and it was surging rapidly under the bridge. It would be dangerous to slip into the water after the bridge collapsed, but he could see no obvious place to hide nearby.

"It's going to be risky," Will acknowledged. "I will help with the ropes."

Clearly it would be much safer to remove the stones before Agon's column arrived. But the confusion would be greatest if the bridge came down just before the king crossed it. Agon would then be separated from the leading group of his soldiers by a swiftly flowing river. Thomas would probably never find a better opportunity to take a close look at Agon with less risk.

Figuring out a way to avoid detection was a challenge, but they still had time to do it.

The sun set not long after they arrived, and a cold wind sprang up. Clouds covered the moon entirely. It was not a night to be abroad, and traffic on the road gradually ceased as travelers found somewhere to camp for the night.

After posting men to keep watch for unexpected arrivals, Rhillyon directed his engineers to start work on the bridge. Ropes were secured to the sides of the bridge, and men were suspended on them. Soon the sound of hammers and chisels rang in the night.

On two occasions a sentry hurried in to warn them that someone was approaching, and all went quiet for a time. Work quickly resumed the moment the travelers had gone.

Will perched himself on the bridge to allow him to observe the work closely as it progressed. It wasn't easy to see what was happening in the dark, but he saw enough of the energy and effectiveness of Rhillyon and his men to be enormously impressed.

As dawn approached they moved off the bridge and hid themselves among the nearby trees.

"The work is almost completed," Rhillyon told Will. "We'll rest during the day and finish it after the sun sets again." He glanced back at the bridge. "We've completely removed some of the wedge stones already. Not enough to make the bridge unstable, but it will make our task easier next time."

"I'll join you under the bridge tonight," Will told him. "I want to be clear about what I need to do to remove the wedges."

Rhillyon nodded as Amyra finished her translation. Then he yawned widely.

Will gave him a friendly slap on the back, and both of them moved away to rest. Almost the moment Will lay down he fell asleep.

It was late afternoon when he woke once more. Rhillyon and his team were stirring too, and all of them gathered to look down at the bridge. No sign could be seen of their work the previous night, and people were crossing the bridge as usual in both directions.

"Are you sure the bridge will be weak enough to collapse?" Will asked Rhillyon.

The man grinned back at him once the question was translated, contenting himself with a single emphatic nod.

Will moved away and found himself some food and water. Then he sat down to enjoy it. Looking up after a few minutes, he found Amyra standing nearby staring at him. She didn't look happy.

"What have I done now?" he asked.

His question seemed to discomfort her momentarily, but she quickly recovered. "Are you determined to go through with this?" she demanded.

"I've explained why it's necessary," he said reasonably.

She didn't respond.

"You seem to have convinced yourself I'm doing this for my own sake. That isn't what's happening here."

She still offered no response.

He sighed. "Do you think I enjoy putting people in danger? Do you think I enjoy putting myself in danger?"

"You seem to live for it," she told him decidedly.

He stared at her for a moment, then he burst out laughing.

She frowned back at him, her face flushed. "Why is that so funny?"

"I'm just struck by the absurdity of our situation. Here I am, in the heart of Rogand, about to attempt something that might cost me my life. These might be my last few hours. I'm spending them with you, and neither of us can think of anything better to do than argue."

She didn't seem at all amused. She took a breath and opened her mouth, no doubt intending to tell him what she really thought. Then she seemed to think better of it. Turning on her heel, she swept away from him.

He watched her go with undisguised admiration, unable to deny any longer that he found her both extremely attractive and utterly fascinating.

He shook his head. There was no point in entertaining daydreams that involved Amyra. Even if he survived this latest venture, he would be wasting his time directing attention to her. She had made it perfectly clear what she thought of him.

It took an effort, but he dragged his mind back to the problem at hand.

AMYRA STOOD AMONG THE TREES, peering down at the bridge. She could make out very little in the dark.

Will Prentis and Rhillyon stood somewhere beneath it, no doubt fingering the ropes that lay in their hands. More wedges had been removed throughout the night. Rhillyon's engineers were satisfied that the span, while still safe to cross, was almost at the point of collapse. The removal of a few more wedges should destabilize it completely.

Rhillyon had decided that two men should be able to complete the task at the right moment. He insisted on being one of them, and

Will Prentis had insisted on being the other. They would need to remain in place until the king had almost reached the bridge.

She knew that the road was visible from their position below the bridge. They had been told that the king was traveling either in a carriage or beside it. As soon as any of the royal carriages came into sight, the two men would tug on the ropes and remove the loosened blocks.

As soon as the bridge had collapsed, they were planning to slip into the river and swim away in the confusion. Some of Rhillyon's people would be waiting to retrieve them downstream.

Amyra had protested that any number of things could go wrong with this scheme, but she had no better plan to offer. Will had told her that if something unexpected happened, they would respond to the situation as it developed.

He was clearly accustomed to being in command, and it didn't seem to greatly trouble him that his actions put others in peril. That irked her.

The Aen-ur had been dragged into an extremely risky plan that had enormous potential to rebound on them. All because Will had called in an old debt. He believed the price was worth paying, and she could only hope it was truly as necessary as he claimed.

She had to at least admit that he didn't shy away from danger himself.

Of late she had taken to resisting him at every turn. She invariably reacted to him with annoyance and often sarcasm. He would never have guessed it, but she was expressing irritation with herself as much as with him.

Her own reactions baffled her. She had never met someone like Will Prentis. He was annoyingly sure of himself—far more so than could possibly be reasonable under the circumstances. He'd been like that from the moment she first clapped eyes on him. She'd always thought of self-assurance as a good thing, but in his case she found it irritating. And yet as much as she wanted to simply dismiss him as over-confident, she had a nagging feeling that he might still prove to be right.

His restless energy astonished her. He was so driven—he seemed unable to rest. He always seemed to be pursuing something pressing, and she felt constantly off balance as a result.

His drivenness wasn't the only reason she found it unsettling to be around him though. It was obvious that he admired her, and she was aware that he'd noticed and appreciated her abilities and self-confidence. There was nothing new about that—plenty of other men had admired her in the past. But there'd always been a catch. Sooner or later every one of them had begun to feel threatened by her. It wasn't her they wanted—it was a dumbed-down version of her.

Not Will Prentis. He didn't seem at all intimidated by her. He didn't seem the kind of man who needed to reduce her so he could feel good about himself.

She had no idea how it had happened, but somehow he'd managed to get under her skin. He was constantly on her mind, and of late she'd frequently caught herself staring at him. Alarmed at her growing obsession, she'd decided to stop thinking about him entirely. That hadn't been working at all. The previous night she had even dreamed about him. And such dreams—her cheeks warmed at the memory.

There was nothing especially attractive about him. Well, not his face, anyway. Even with a limp, his physique was not lost on her. He seemed oblivious to the rippling muscles beneath his tunic. But she had noticed.

She had even been reduced to quizzing Thomas and Haldek about him. It shocked her that she could stoop so low.

After they left Ishitar Ataye she had cornered Thomas. "So is it true that Will Prentis commands an army?" she asked skeptically.

Thomas had looked affronted. "He doesn't just command *an* army," he corrected her. "He commands the entire Arvenian army. And he commanded the combined armies of Arvenon and Castel during the Rogandan invasion. Everyone who knows anything about military strategy gives him most of the credit for defeating the Rogandans. Their army was much larger than ours!"

Once she'd got him started, Thomas warmed to his subject. "You should see the way his men respond to him!" He shook his head in wonder. "Just a few weeks ago I was with him after a battle. His men almost worship him. I've never seen another leader vaguely like him."

She turned up her nose. "No wonder he's so full of himself. They undoubtedly think he's so wonderful because everything has always gone well for him. And he's a noble, too—noblemen grow up expecting to be in charge."

Thomas had frowned at her. "No! You're completely wrong about him, Amyra! He's forever facing situations that everyone else sees as hopeless. His luck is certainly legendary, but he's never relied on luck. His decision making is uncanny. He seems to find a way of turning situations around, no matter how bad they are. And he might be a noble now, but he was born a commoner. King Steffan only made him a nobleman out of gratitude after he defeated the Rogandans."

Amyra was more than a little taken aback by this account of Will Prentis.

Thomas was a countryman of Will Prentis though. A Rogandan might be expected to form a more realistic assessment. Choosing a moment when Haldek was riding apart from the others, she positioned her horse alongside him.

"How did you come to know this Will Prentis?" she asked him, speaking quietly in Rogandan so as not to offend any of the Aen-ur.

Haldek gazed at her narrowed eyes, and for an uncomfortable moment she wondered if he guessed more about her motives for asking than she wanted to admit.

"He rescued me," he replied. "I was with a group of Rogandan soldiers fleeing Arvenon after we lost the battle at Torbury Scarp. Will and his men came upon us. He let the others go, but he kept me with him. Somehow he saw that I had nothing to go back to, and he asked Thomas and his wife, Elena, to take me in. The years of living with them and Elena's father have been the best years of my life."

Haldek had glanced ahead at Will, riding near the front of the group. "He is undoubtedly the greatest general of our times. But he is also one of the most compassionate people I have ever known."

Amyra frowned. “If he’s so compassionate, why has he led you here?”

Haldek had shrugged. “He has never put his own interests before his responsibilities. Perhaps that’s one reason why others are so willing to follow him into danger. His men will do anything for him. He’s unlike anyone I have ever met.”

Shaken by these assessments, she could think of nothing to say in response. Nodding to him, she had moved her horse away.

If these men were to be believed, almost every one of her initial impressions of Will Prentis had been entirely mistaken. He constantly managed to surprise her.

She gritted her teeth. She had no desire to become infatuated with him, yet thinking about him had almost become a compulsion. It was maddening.

After her conversations with Thomas and Haldek she reminded herself that she had decided not to think about him anymore. This time she was determined to follow through with it.

Now, a couple of days later, she found herself standing above the bridge waiting for the dawn and thinking about him again. She frowned in frustration at her own weakness.

A voice spoke softly beside her, speaking in the tongue of the Aen-ur. “The dawn—it comes.”

She raised her eyes to the heavens. The speaker was right. The sky was indeed beginning to lighten slowly.

As she watched, the light grew stronger. The bridge was now clearly visible. She could see no sign of the two men beneath it.

King Agon’s tent city had not been visible from their current position, but the previous evening scouts had informed them that it had been pitched not far away. It must have taken a couple of hours for the tents to be taken down and stored, because the morning was well advanced before Agon’s horsemen appeared on the road to the bridge.

Amyra held her breath as they rode closer. Soldiers on foot followed them, hundreds strong, and she watched anxiously as the seemingly endless stream poured across the bridge. Their tramping feet did not appear to affect the span in any way, and for the first time she wondered if Rhillyon and his men had done enough to destabilize it. What if Agon's whole column simply crossed the river and disappeared up the road? She noticed that she had begun to sweat.

The irony of her own reaction was not lost on her. She had been so adamantly opposed to Will Prentis's plan. Now she was worried that it wouldn't succeed. She shook her head, unable to comprehend herself.

The seemingly endless stream of soldiers finally came to an end, and several carriages at last appeared behind them. Agon himself was approaching. Her heart began to race.

As the carriages drew closer she tried to picture Will and Rhillyon pulling at the ropes. She strained her ears for the sound of wedge blocks falling into the river, but she was too far away to hear, and the marching of the soldiers would have blotted out the sound anyway.

Finally she noticed what appeared to be a puff of dust near the top of the bridge. The soldiers marched on, oblivious to it. More dust appeared. A low rumbling sound reached her ears. The top of the bridge appeared to tremble. Then the entire span collapsed, disappearing into the river with a mighty splash. Cries carried to her as soldiers were plunged into the raging river. She saw heads bobbing as men were swept away by the current.

She tried to peer down through the confusion. Were Rhillyon and Will Prentis swimming to safety as they had planned? Frustration rose within her at the impossibility of finding out anything that was happening.

A part of her was tempted to get up and run down there—to help them, or even just to observe the situation for herself. Recognizing her impulse for the folly it was, she restrained herself.

Not all of the soldiers had crossed the bridge before it fell, and men were now lining both banks of the river. A small number of soldiers had been pulled to safety from the water, but most had probably either been swept downriver or drowned.

She could see no sign of either Rhillyon or Will Prentis. She could only hope they had managed to swim away in the confusion as planned. They would surely be discovered if they lingered under the remains of the bridge—there was nowhere there to hide.

The thought of Rhillyon falling into the hands of the Rogandans filled her with alarm. It would be a disaster if Agon's people suspected the Aen-ur of an attempt on the life of the king. He had to find a way to escape.

As for Will Prentis, she felt certain he would be captured, and the very idea of it chilled her to the bone. The force of his personality might have provoked and aggravated her, but, perverse as she might be, she had come to eagerly anticipate the latest clash of their wills.

The world she had known before he appeared had always seemed rich and full to her. Now it felt strangely routine and colorless; his arrival had added unexpected spice to her life. She had come to count on him being around, and the likely future that stretched out before her now seemed unaccountably bleak.

Her mind became numb as she fully acknowledged the truth for the first time—she could not face the thought of losing him.

36

Catching his first glimpse of a carriage on the road, Will touched Rhillyon's arm and pointed. Both men had positioned themselves on the near side of the bridge to simplify their escape. Rhillyon nodded, and both of them shifted focus to the ropes beside them.

Will picked up a rope and began to tug with all his might. After almost a minute, the first wedge began to slide. As he continued to strain, he had the satisfaction of seeing the wedge pull loose and plummet down into the river.

The sound of the splash made him wince, but there was no indication that it had been heard by anyone on the bridge.

Another splash immediately followed, and Will saw Rhillyon toss the rope into the river and grasp another. Soon both of them were pulling and discarding, pulling and discarding, as fast as they were able.

Another wedge-shaped block pulled free, and Will saw the first sign that the span above was beginning to give way. A spray of dirt came down as an adjoining block fell into the water of its own accord. Looking up, he saw other blocks poised, ready to fall.

Then abruptly the span collapsed. Stones and men came crashing down together to disappear into the boiling water. Heads began bobbing in and out of the water downstream as soldiers were carried along by the current.

Men were already gathering along the banks of the river, and it was immediately obvious to Will that their position was now exposed.

Rhillyon must have seen it, too, because Will saw him hastily throw the last of his ropes into the water. He did the same, aware of the importance of discarding all evidence of their interference.

A splash sounded as Rhillyon dived into the water. When his head bobbed to the surface again, he was already far downstream. He was now far enough away that Will was hopeful that he would escape capture entirely. For Rhillyon's own sake, and for the sake of the Aen-ur, such an outcome was crucial.

Will quickly followed him into the water, allowing the current to take him.

He had barely begun to swim when loud cries alerted him to a woman who had just pulled herself from the river downstream. She was searching the torrent, calling out frantically for her daughter. Almost immediately he spotted the child nearby, struggling helplessly in the water.

He groaned. He hadn't noticed a family approaching the bridge, but they must have been crossing at the moment it collapsed. Striking out vigorously, he headed for the girl. He barely reached her in time. She coughed and spluttered feebly as he held her head clear of the water.

Will swam her to the bank, and hands reached out to pull them both in. The mother appeared and clutched the girl to herself, tears of joy streaming down her face.

Rogandan soldiers had hurried to the riverside to help, and several of them now clustered around Will. "Who are you?" one demanded roughly.

"He's no Rogandan," another growled accusingly. "Look at his hair!"

Will had carefully renewed the black dye in his hair and recolored his skin before joining Rhillyon under the bridge. Now he noticed black dye dripping from his head, staining his garments. The water must have rinsed away the dye and exposed his red hair.

"He's a filthy Arvenian," a soldier spat. "I skewered enough of them during the war."

Men quickly crowded in and began striking him. He was hard pressed to keep his feet, and he knew if he went down he would be kicked and trampled to death.

A voice suddenly rang out with authority. "Move away from him immediately! We need him alive. Lady Ona will want to question him."

The pummeling came to a reluctant end. Hands grabbed him roughly, and he was dragged away and thrown down beside a tree. Several men with drawn weapons gathered around him.

Will's body felt like one massive bruise. As far as he could tell, none of his bones had been broken. That was something to be grateful for.

People were milling aimlessly around the road now that their progress had been blocked. He imagined that Agon's men would be trying to decide how best to get across the river. No suitable fords were located anywhere nearby, and the terrain was difficult to navigate on this side of the river. They would need to somehow find a way to repair the bridge. That wasn't going to be completed anytime soon, and the knowledge gave him considerable satisfaction. How Thomas might contrive to get a glimpse of the king he didn't know. But the king would certainly be here for some time.

Several hours passed before he saw any sign of order emerging. Tents were starting to appear beside the road, stretching back along the way the column had come. Agon's tent city was appearing before his eyes. It would undoubtedly be situated here for however long it might take to repair the bridge.

Before nightfall his guard was changed, and he was led to a different location. He now found himself well within the camp, almost certainly inaccessible to anyone who might want to rescue him. Two iron stakes were driven into the ground, and the guards chained him between them. After tossing him a water skin and a small lump of bread, they ignored him completely. It was becoming clear that he was being left to spend a cold night in the open.

When the dawn came, Will greeted it without enthusiasm. Throughout the night the cold had gnawed away at him, and his bruises left his entire body in a state of constant pain.

He wondered if Thomas would find a way of getting close to the king. It wasn't easy to see how it might happen, but the disruption might offer at least some kind of opportunity.

Amyra was not far from his thoughts either. She had warned that their escape plan could easily go wrong, and she would no doubt feel completely vindicated by what had just happened. He could well imagine her disdain when he failed to appear and it became obvious that he had been captured.

Dubious as his own prospects might be, it would be a disaster for the Aen-ur if Rhillyon had been captured. That outcome seemed improbable to Will. Rhillyon's chances would undoubtedly have been good as long as he survived the river. His own people should have been on the lookout for him, and after the drama of the bridge collapse, Agon's men had been completely disorganized and distracted. It seemed unlikely that the Rogandans would have reached him first.

The morning was not long advanced when a group of guards came and unchained him from the stakes. After tying his hands roughly, they led him to one of the larger and more elaborate of the tents. Four guards stood on duty outside the tent, and their leader instructed his escorts to wait with the prisoner until he was summoned.

A succession of people came and went from the tent, and Will could occasionally hear snatches of conversation from inside the tent, especially when the voices were raised. The most easily distinguished voice was that of a woman. Sometimes she purred, and sometimes she growled, but from the demeanor of people leaving the tent, he was left in no doubt that she was a force to be reckoned with.

Eventually his turn came, and he was unceremoniously dragged into the tent. Before him stood an unusually attractive woman.

She might be attractive, but he couldn't help noticing that she didn't have flashing hazel eyes and restless brown locks dancing carelessly about her face.

"Bow before Lady Ona, you dog!" exclaimed the guard, and rough hands forced Will to his knees. He was left wincing at the pressure on his bruises.

Lady Ona's beauty was real enough, but Will saw at a glance that she was also exceedingly dangerous. She had the look of a person not accustomed to having her will thwarted.

"And who might you be?" she demanded.

"Just a humble merchant, My Lady," he replied respectfully.

"You were near the bridge when it collapsed. What were you doing there?"

He bowed his head humbly. "My business partner and I had just begun crossing the bridge when it collapsed, and we fell into the water. My donkeys and my business partner were swept away in the river. I had just reached the bank when I was apprehended by your guards—I have no idea why they seized me. I have been left with nothing, and I am worried about the fate of my friend."

Will had adopted a worried tone, and he was not entirely faking. He allowed his concern about the fate of Rhillyon to flood his thoughts as he was speaking, and he felt sure that he sounded convincing.

Lady Ona, though, was studying him closely, a shrewd look on her face. "What is your name?" she asked in a silky tone.

"I am called Ronald, My Lady," he replied.

"Well, Ronald, I want you to come for a little walk with me," she said.

Her delicate hand swept out, indicating the entrance to the tent.

He headed outside with Lady Ona following close behind. Several guards swung in beside him, maintaining a respectful distance from their mistress. They apparently had few concerns about her safety, and Will was left in no doubt about her ability to handle herself.

She pointed toward the remains of the bridge, and he headed obediently in that direction.

They had gone no more than a few paces before she appeared to change her mind. "That's far enough!" she called, pointing back toward the tent.

Will shrugged, and retraced his steps.

When they were inside the tent once more, Lady Ona turned to the guards. "Untie his hands," she ordered, "and then leave us." Seeing their uncertainty, she added, "You need not concern yourselves. I'm well able to handle him."

Bowing, they cut Will's bonds and left as she commanded.

"Take off your tunic and your top," she ordered Will.

A frown of determination came at once to his face. Seeing it, she waved a hand dismissively. "Don't be ridiculous. It's obvious that you're covered in bruises. They need to be treated."

After a moment's consideration, he shrugged and complied with her request. She pointed him to a stool, and he positioned himself on it while she opened a trunk and rooted through it. Eventually retrieving an expensive looking white container, she removed the lid to expose a fragrant smelling paste. Scooping large dollops of it onto her fingers she gently smoothed it over his skin.

The soothing effect was immediate.

"Thank you," he said noncommittally when she had finished.

"It's my pleasure," she purred, a coquettish smile on her lips. "You're so strong." She ran a finger across his shoulders, setting his skin tingling and his face glowing.

"It's a strange thing," she told him, shaking her pretty head. "Sometimes we see only what we expect to see. We can completely miss the unexpected, however obvious it might be."

She smiled daintily. "Take yourself, for example. For many months I've been longing to meet the famous Will Prentis in the flesh. But he was the last person I expected to be brought to me in my very own tent this morning!" She gave out a laugh of pure elation, a sound overflowing with triumph and with relish.

Will looked at her with narrowed eyes.

"I can imagine you must be surprised. It was the scars on your face that first alerted me, along with your distinctive red hair under the dye. I simply had to take you for a little walk, just to confirm that you had the characteristic limp I'd heard about."

She smiled. "It's so good to meet you, Will. Or should I call you Lord Torbury?" She paused for a moment, musing. "No, I think it has to be Will," she finally concluded. "The title is much too formal, too stuffy. Not at all appropriate between friends. And we *are* going to be friends, Will—very special friends."

She looked at him in a way that sent heat flooding into his cheeks and up into his forehead. His reaction to her brazen provocativeness seemed to please her enormously.

Coming up behind him, she ran her fingers through his hair. "It's obvious that you have yet to be tamed by a woman," she breathed. "That is so much the better—for me as well as for you. You will not be disappointed, I promise."

Leaning over him, she ran a finger along the scar on his right cheek. Her perfume flooded his senses, and he felt his face glow hot once more.

"I know exactly what's going through your mind," she said softly. "You can relax. Your bruises are looking very angry right now. Your education can afford to wait a while."

She smiled sweetly. "Cases like yours can be surprisingly delicate, and I've never been one to ruin the moment with over-eagerness. I want to make sure you're fully able to appreciate the adventure," she crooned.

He swallowed. He had no intention of being seduced by Lady Ona, but he was painfully aware that he had very little experience dealing with women, and none at all dealing with a woman like her.

Amyra had presented him with more than enough of a challenge. He might have responded clumsily to her, but he sensed that he was stumbling toward the opening movement of a timeless dance. He would have been willing enough to be drawn in if she had ever allowed it, for all that it felt awkward and unfamiliar.

Lady Ona was another matter entirely. She was dancing to a very different rhythm. He couldn't pretend he didn't feel its allure, and he could see from the look in her eye that she was more than confident she had his measure. He was determined never to yield to her, but he didn't doubt for a moment that she intended to make it very difficult for him to resist.

She tossed her head, allowing her lustrous hair to fall forward across her shoulder. Every movement was enticing. She seemed well aware that men found her irresistible.

He tore his gaze away. Seeing it, her full lips formed a smile. It was a predatory smile, and she flaunted it.

Then she sighed, and the spell was broken. "I do have one small obstacle before me. One way or another, the king will soon learn of your existence, and he will be furious if he believes I have tried to withhold you. The problem is that once he finds out who you are, he will undoubtedly want to kill you. He will see your arrival as an ideal opportunity for a spectacle. If I can forestall that, he may over time be persuaded to change his mind. The king is very unpredictable though."

A look of determination came to her lovely face. "Never fear, Will Prentis. I will do whatever it takes to save you." She slowly eyed him up and down, a smile of eager anticipation playing across her face. "I have the feeling that you will be well worth the effort."

Will felt unaccountably exposed and vulnerable.

"Dress yourself," she commanded.

Calling for the guards, she jerked her head toward her prisoner. "Bring him. We are going to the king."

She set off toward the largest of the tents, with the guards pulling Will along behind.

The sound of angry yelling reached Will's ears even before they reached the tent. He saw Lady Ona wince slightly, then she made her way to the guards outside the royal tent. Singling one of them out, she spoke quietly into his ear.

He nodded, before directing a hard glance at Will. Then he seemed to steel himself before stepping inside the tent. He soon emerged, a new round of shouting chasing him outside.

Taking a deep breath, he nodded to Lady Ona.

She came to Will and took his arm. "Leave the talking to me," she said firmly, guiding him into the tent.

King Agon was sitting on a small throne within the tent, and he glared balefully at Lady Ona as she approached. She bowed low before him. He then switched his gaze to Will. Will contented himself with a nod of the head. He saw alarm flash across Lady Ona's face, and perversely it gave him at least a small measure of satisfaction.

Curiously, the king did not react. "Who is this bold fool you have brought before me?" he demanded.

"Great King, may you live forever," she replied. "This man was found near the bridge when it collapsed. The soldiers suspected him of involvement and brought him to me."

The king's eyes narrowed. "His head will not be long on his shoulders if that is true," he said. "Perhaps even if it is not true," he added with a nasty smile. "Who is he?"

"His name is Will Prentis, although he is also known as Lord Torbury. He is Arvenian."

The king's eyes went wide with surprise. "*The* Will Prentis?" he demanded. "The man who presided over the destruction of Dret-troth's army?" A gloating look came into his eye. "And here he is, completely in my power."

"I am willing to interrogate him, Your Majesty," said Lady Ona. "I have ways of uncovering the truth. If you will give him to me for two or three days, I am confident I can expose his true intentions."

The king turned his gaze on her. Then he threw back his head and laughed. "My Lady Ona, you are so boringly predictable! All this talk of uncovering and exposing—you think of nothing but your unbridled lust." His face turned suddenly cold. "Your appetites mean nothing to me," he spat. "I will do as I please with this prize."

He returned his gaze to Will. "Will Prentis! What an unexpected opportunity you present me with. What a messy spectacle I could arrange, with you as the centerpiece. Sweet revenge! It has been far too long coming, and I would be able to savor it to the full."

He paused, and went silent for a full minute. "Delicious as it might be, I have a far better idea. A man like you offers unusual potential. You and I are going to become very well acquainted. You have served your king loyally, I'm sure." His lips peeled back in a vague semblance of a smile. "Who knows, though? Perhaps even the most loyal of subjects can undergo a change of perspective. I dare to imagine that you might gradually find yourself coming around to my point of view."

Agon gazed at his captive, a smirk of satisfaction on his lips.

Will kept his face impassive.

Agon laughed. "I see you are skeptical, but you may yet surprise yourself."

"Guards!" he called. Several men clustered around his throne snapped to attention. "Tie this man's hands behind his back. Tie them securely but loosely, and don't harm him. I merely want to ensure that he can't interfere with me in any way."

He turned to Lady Ona. "You are dismissed," he said coldly, flicking his fingers toward the entrance of the tent.

Lady Ona looked as if she was sorely tempted to speak, but she held her peace and withdrew.

It was perfectly obvious to Will what Agon had in mind. As he looked at the king he noticed his hand straying to a hidden fold in his clothing. No doubt the Stone of Authority lay secreted there.

He had escaped the web of Lady Ona, only to fall into the hands of a ruthless tyrant with the power to magically bend the wills of other people to his own.

What could he do to resist? The scroll had offered no insights whatever, but there had to be a way.

He wasn't going to stand by and allow himself to be transformed into the compliant puppet of a monster. He would rather die.

37

After four harrowing days in close proximity to the Rogandan king, Will had long since learned to stay well clear whenever Agon worked himself into one of his rages. It happened all too frequently. Ennawi usually bore the brunt of it.

Agon's eyes bulged, and the veins in his neck stood out as he harangued his mute slave. "I should have reached Arnost long ago. Why am I thwarted at every turn?"

In spite of his fury, he kept his voice low, apparently well aware that he could expect no privacy in his royal tent, surrounded as it was by dense clusters of the tents of his servants.

As usual, Ennawi showed no reaction to the tirade. Will had long since ceased to be amazed at the slave's ability to remain unresponsive.

Will had observed that Agon spoke to Ennawi as if they were holding a conversation, and that the king seemed to say whatever was on his mind. Sometimes when Will was standing nearby, Agon whispered conspiratorially in the slave's ear. Ennawi apparently suited the king perfectly—he was the ideal listener, and he was the soul of discretion. The king's secrets were safe with a man who could neither speak nor write.

Will had met Ennawi on the first day of his imprisonment with Agon. It was far from obvious how a slave without hands managed to feed himself, and Will was not surprised when he caught his first glimpse of the slave's carer. The king had disappeared off on some errand, and Nistinaa soon arrived to feed and tend to Ennawi as usual. Seeing Will in the room, she had observed him doubtfully for a while before apparently deciding she had little choice but to take the opportunity presented by the king's absence.

Since then he had contrived to speak to her several times, and she had gradually relaxed in his presence. Ennawi's situation appalled him, and he told her so directly. It left him speechless when she told him the slave had been enduring such abuse from Agon for years.

The king spoke, attracting Will's attention once more.

Agon had finally mastered himself. "For all the frustrations, a new source of delight will soon present itself," he told Ennawi. "As I have already told you, I have at last found a use for the Aen-ur. I won't need to wait much longer now." A gloating smile played across his lips.

Will had heard no previous mention by the king of the secretive people who had offered their help, and Agon's words made him uneasy.

Some part of him recognized that even a couple of days ago this information would have chilled him to the bone. Others before him had come under the influence of the Stone of Authority, and he wondered how many of them had understood exactly what was happening to them. Perhaps his situation was unique. But it made no difference. He had been resisting the power of the Stone of Authority with all his might, but nevertheless he knew he was slowly succumbing to it. The process was already well advanced. Agon's agenda, not to mention his moods and attitude, still seemed sour and distasteful to Will, but he felt vaguely aware that everything about the king should be inspiring a much stronger negative reaction from him.

Through the fog that seemed to be clouding his volition, Will sensed that Agon's reference to the Aen-ur was significant, and that something needed to be done, and done quickly, to protect them.

If Thomas could get a glimpse of Agon, all would be revealed. It suddenly occurred to him, though, that there might be another way.

It hadn't taken long for Will to decide he could trust Nistinaa, and they often conversed quietly whenever they found an opportunity. Eventually he gathered his courage.

"Is there any way you could get a message to my friends?" he whispered.

Immediately she became guarded. "I will do nothing to put Ennawi at risk," she told him firmly.

He made no attempt to press her. He would need to choose the right moment.

There was little he could do other than to bide his time.

HALDEK HAD POSITIONED himself as near to the royal tent as he dared, contriving to look busy while surreptitiously observing the people who came and went from Agon's presence. To a casual observer he was just another Rogandan soldier. Thanks to Rhillyon's men he had been clad and equipped appropriately—everything he was wearing had been pilfered from unwary guards.

He had taken fearful risks to get near to Will. After watching the area for some time he had boldly claimed the guard duty for a supply tent located quite close to Agon's own. His years of sentry duty allowed him to put in a very creditable performance. So far he had not been exposed.

He soon came to recognize Nistinaa as a frequent visitor to the royal tent. He often caught glimpses of her through the entrance to the royal tent, and more than once he saw her whispering with Will. Their body language suggested they were comfortable in each other's presence.

Mustering his courage, he decided to speak to her next time a suitable opportunity arose. In the end he didn't need to wait long.

She had been hurrying past when he called softly to her. “Excuse me! Can I speak with you?”

Startled, she paused long enough to peer in his direction. When it became obvious that she wasn’t planning to stop, he decided to fall in beside her.

“Could you give a message to the man you were talking to in the tent? His name is Will Prentis.”

She looked at him mistrustfully.

“I’m a friend of his.” Conscious of the risk he was taking, he nevertheless decided he had little choice but to trust her. “All I want you to do is to let him know that I’m nearby. Could you do that please?”

The suspicious look on her face gave him little hope that she would follow through.

“Just tell him that Haldek spoke to you,” he said.

Then she was gone.

Haldek returned to his guard duty. Knowing that the woman could turn him in whenever she chose, he found it almost impossible to relax. It was therefore an enormous relief when she quietly approached him the next evening, jerking her head toward a quiet corner behind a nearby tent.

“I told him,” she said. “He wants to know what you’re planning.”

Haldek exhaled in relief. “We want to get him away from here as soon as possible. Come to me again tomorrow—I’ll let you know the details then.”

She left after giving him a brief nod.

That night and the following day were extraordinarily tense for Haldek.

The king’s camp was surrounded by sentries, but with no one expecting trouble the guards were unusually lax. Before Haldek first entered the camp, he’d carefully monitored the approaches from the forest, finally selecting a location where the guards appeared to be especially inattentive. Since that time he had been safely using the same entry point to come and go from the forest.

In preparation for getting Will, Haldek first returned to the forest and arranged for a party to be on hand to spirit them away. He then returned to the camp and found his way to a cluster of supply tents.

The supply tents were more heavily guarded than the camp itself. Knowing the reputation of Rogandan soldiers, Haldek didn't find it particularly surprising.

To extract Will he needed to get one of the sentries drunk, and to achieve that he needed a wineskin. Wineskins were the most desirable of prizes for thieves, so the penalties for anyone caught stealing them had always been severe. Nevertheless, he decided to steal more than one to allow for contingencies.

Two hours stretched to three as he stood near the supply tents watching for an opportunity. By the time the afternoon had almost worn away, he was reaching a point of desperation.

He began to wonder if he should have instead asked the Aen-ur to supply him with wineskins. There wasn't time to go back now though, and their wineskins might be very different from the ones supplied to the Rogandan army. He couldn't afford to rouse suspicions.

He was almost ready to abandon hope when a large group of men came to collect supplies for the evening meal of the king, Lady Ona, and other senior leaders. They rummaged through the tents noisily, eventually leaving with a large quantity of food and alcohol.

Once they had gone, Haldek decided to risk everything on a gamble. Waiting until they were well out of sight, he hurried toward the supply tents, approaching from the direction in which they had gone.

"They didn't get enough of the good wineskins!" he told the guard. "The king will have our hides if we don't get it right!"

After looking doubtfully at him for a moment, the guard shrugged and waved Haldek to one of the tents. Wasting no time, Haldek dashed into the tent and carefully selected the three most expensive looking wineskins he could find. Then he hurried away, waving his thanks to the guard as he headed back the way he had come.

The moment he was out of sight he came to a halt. His heart was pounding, and he was panting from nervous energy.

It was too soon to relax though. His next task was to steal a couple of dark cloaks with hoods. Fortunately that proved much more straightforward. After hiding the cloaks near the king's tent, he returned to his guard duty and waited for darkness.

Not long after sunset, the woman appeared again, just as he had requested. Having instructed her to send Will to the same current location in four hours, he slipped away.

His final task was to deliver the wineskin to the guard at the perimeter of the camp. He knew from experience which guard should be on sentry duty that night. Haldek had previously spun him a yarn about hunting in the forest, even returning with a small boar on one occasion to support the deception. After a few days Haldek had come and gone often enough that the sentry simply ignored him.

On this occasion Haldek wanted to make sure the man was thoroughly inebriated when the time came to slip out of the camp with Will. One wineskin should be more than enough to do the job.

When he approached the sentry post, Haldek was shocked to find no sign of the regular guard. Another soldier was there in his place. Dismayed at the setback, he backed away to consider his options. Time was not on his side.

A bold approach had secured him the wineskins, and he decided to risk a final gamble.

Staggering up to the sentry with the three wineskins clutched to his chest, he peered at the sentry through blinking eyes. "Wheresh the king's tent?" he slurred.

The sentry snorted. "That way," he pointed. "From the state you're in, you'd better stay well clear of it."

"Thank you, sho much," he replied.

Spinning unsteadily in the direction indicated, he lurched forward, apparently failing to notice that one of the wineskins had slipped from his grasp and fallen to the ground.

Haldek stumbled on until he was out of sight, then he crept back to observe the sentry. To his relief the man had already started on the wineskin. It was now simply a matter of time.

Hope began to stir for Will when Nistinaa told him about meeting Haldek. He assured her that Haldek could be trusted, and after some initial hesitation, she agreed to meet with him again.

Time seemed to crawl while Will waited for the next contact to take place. He sensed that his independent will was slowly ebbing away, and the urgency of escaping from Agon had become pressing. It needed to happen soon if he expected to leave with any of his volition still intact.

At the same time, he found himself increasingly struggling with any idea that required him to go behind Agon's back. A part of his being had slowly retreated to a hidden inner sanctuary, and that hidden core affirmed the importance of removing himself from the presence of the stone. But another part of him was bent toward Agon and his priorities, and that part had been growing ever stronger.

The war within him continued to rage unchecked, but his independent core somehow managed to rise up to assert itself. It allowed him to reach an agonizing decision.

The next time Agon left the tent, Nistinaa appeared again. "I met with Haldek again!" she whispered excitedly. "They're going to try to get you away from here—tonight. They told me the details. You need to..."

"No!" he replied, cutting her off. "Don't tell me any details. It's important that I don't know them."

As she stared at him in bewilderment, he dug deep, drawing upon every reserve he could summon, willing himself to respond only out of the inner core of his being, weakened though it was.

"I'm going to explain to you what needs to happen," he told her. "You and Ennawi will be the ones going with them, not me. Follow their instructions. As soon as you are safe, find Thomas Stablehand

and let him spend time with you, and especially with Ennawi. Thomas Stablehand—don't forget! Nothing else matters."

She looked back at him wide-eyed.

"Do you understand?" he insisted.

She nodded.

"We must not speak of this again."

She opened her mouth to protest, and he shook his head emphatically. "It's already too late for me," he told her with a frown, turning away.

The hidden core of his will had chosen to abandon his own interests, favoring instead a path that might save the Aen-ur. And the remnant of his independent self was not idle even now. Working tirelessly, it positioned the interaction with Nistinaa as a matter of no relevance to Will's conscious awareness. *I am not responsible for these two people—they don't answer to me. Whatever they might be doing is none of my business. I must be careful to ignore them. Any involvement from me would be an intrusion.*

Nistinaa slipped away, and Will felt a sudden need for fresh air. Following her to the entrance of the king's tent, he paused, peering out with uncharacteristic timidity.

Lady Ona stood nearby, watching the tent. Her eyes narrowed at once when she saw Will.

He groaned. The king had banned Lady Ona from both his tent and his presence as soon as he had Will in his power. Agon had no intention of sharing his prize with anyone.

She had obeyed, but more than once he had seen her prowling nearby like a lioness, ready to pounce the moment her prey came within reach.

In his reduced state he simply couldn't face her—he could no longer summon the resources.

His head began to pound, and reaching up unsteady hands, he ran them through his hair. Then turning away from the relative freedom of the open air, he stumbled back to the suffocating confinement of his prison.

38

"Where's Will?" hissed Amyra. She had barely been able to restrain her eagerness as the moment of his escape approached. Now there was no sign of him. Her brows were furrowed in vexation.

The nearest sentry was drunk and snoring loudly. Haldek had slipped past him without difficulty, and not one but two people had followed him—a woman and a younger man. There was no sign at all of Will.

The woman stared back at Amyra anxiously. "He wouldn't come. He insisted on sending us instead. I am Nistinaa, and this is Ennawi." The man she pointed to was completely unresponsive.

Amyra glared at her suspiciously. "Did you pass on Haldek's message?"

Nistinaa nodded, but Amyra wasn't at all convinced.

"She's telling the truth," Thomas whispered insistently. "I know why Will sent them."

Rhillyon drew closer. "We can't stay here," he told them. "We'll need to find a way to rescue Will later."

He led the little party swiftly away, toward the safety of the forest.

They didn't pause until they were far from Agon's camp. Ennawi had to be helped every step of the way. In the end a soldier stood on each side of him and took an arm, guiding him forward and even carrying him at times.

When they finally stopped, Nistinaa faced them, tears glistening in her eyes. "Thank you," she said. "I never dared allow myself to believe this day would ever come."

A look of determination came over her face. "I made a promise to Will. He wanted us to meet with Thomas Stablehand. He said that nothing else mattered."

Amyra glared at the woman. How could meeting with Thomas possibly be more important than freeing Will?

Thomas did not seem at all surprised. He approached Nistinaa. "I am Thomas Stablehand," he said gently.

He studied her for a few moments, then his face grew grave. He turned to Ennawi next, and his eyes quickly grew wide with alarm.

"Thank you," he said to Nistinaa. "I will meet with you again soon."

He turned to Amyra. "I must speak with you. It is extremely urgent."

She frowned at him, still struggling to overcome her frustration at the outcome of their attempted rescue.

Seeing her hesitation, he reached out a tentative hand.

She pulled away instantly. "Don't touch me," she snapped, more irritated than ever. She glared at him, refusing to budge.

Thomas sighed. "I wanted him back as much as you did," he said quietly. "I'm truly sorry about what happened."

She felt a flush rising to her cheeks at the implication of his words. If he thought this approach would win her over, he was badly mistaken.

His face hardened. "There was a reason why Will sent them instead of coming himself. He decided that the reason was more important than his own safety. Do you want to hear what it was, or not?"

She glared at him for a long minute. "Very well," she said sullenly. He'd have been wasting his time if he appealed to anything except her curiosity. Perhaps he was smarter than she'd thought.

Thomas turned and headed away from everyone else. She followed him, although she didn't do it with any grace.

He didn't stop until the others were well out of hearing range. Then he turned to face her. He stared awkwardly at her for long enough that she began to feel uncomfortable, then he shook his head and slowly released a long breath.

She frowned at him in bewilderment.

"I have something to tell you," he said. "You won't want to hear it, and you definitely won't like it. But I'm doing it for Will—he would want you to know. If you care about him at all, you'll hear me out."

She glared back at him defiantly for a moment. But she nodded. She was skeptical about what he was going to say, and she made no attempt to hide it. But he had succeeded in getting her attention.

"I need you to promise you won't tell anyone what I'm about to reveal to you."

"If you insist," she said.

"I do."

She shrugged. "Get on with it, then."

"I'm sure you must have wondered why the three of us came here," he began.

"I've never made any secret of that," she snorted.

"And you must have wondered why Will brought me in particular."

She didn't bother to deny it.

"You were there when Will read the scroll aloud," he said.

She frowned. "Are you talking about that old scroll at Ishitar Ataye?"

He nodded.

"That was utter nonsense," she scoffed.

He sighed. "You agreed to hear me out," he reminded her.

She scowled at him, but she subsided.

"The scroll talked about three stones of power. One of them was the Stone of Knowing. Will knows where that stone is, Amyra. He knows that I have it. He sent Nistinaa and Ennawi to us for one reason—so that I could use the stone to discover everything they know about Agon and his plans. Ennawi can't speak, and he can't write, so the king has known he's safe. He's been confiding in him for years. Will knew that I could use the Stone of Knowing to find out everything that's passed between them."

She rolled her eyes and shook her head. "Surely you don't expect me to believe any of this."

He ignored her reaction. "I don't use the stone to pry on people I know, and that means I've avoided using the stone to discover your thoughts. But I can use the stone anytime I choose. If you want proof, I can offer it right now."

Amyra's eyes narrowed as she considered this. She didn't believe him of course. But even the idea of having her thoughts exposed gave her pause. "Are you claiming you can find out something I'm thinking?"

His eyes bored into her. "Not just *something* you're thinking, Amyra. Everything. Past and present. Your hopes and dreams, your memories, your secret desires. All of it."

She blushed scarlet, unable to prevent herself.

"Choose any topic you like," he said boldly. "I'll pick you clean. You can try to hide your thoughts if you want. It won't make any difference."

She stared back at him, and he didn't blink. She faltered, suddenly unsure what to think. She reached a decision very quickly though. It wasn't a risk she was willing to take. Not under any circumstances.

"Go on," she said warily. "I'm listening."

"I've done what Will wanted me to do. I examined their thoughts, and now I know what Agon is up to."

Her eyebrows drew together. "Come on, Thomas! You can't have looked at either one of them for much more than a minute!"

"I didn't need longer than that," he told her. He took a deep breath. "Look, I can well imagine that you don't want me poking around in your mind. But if it's the only way you'll believe me, I don't see that we have much choice."

"Go on with whatever you were going to say next," she said stiffly. "Like you would if I believed you."

He looked at her hesitantly for a moment, then he shook his head. "It won't be useful to continue if you don't believe me." He took a deep breath. "I told you that I've avoided using the stone on you, and that's the truth. But I did use it when we first encountered you."

Her shock turned to anger before she could blink.

"Why should that be a problem?" he asked pointedly. "You don't believe any of this is true." His tone was mild, but she saw the intensity in his eyes.

"What did you see?" she asked breathlessly.

"That you were no real threat to us," he replied. "That was my main purpose in checking."

"And what else?" she insisted.

He gazed at her hesitantly for a moment. "Your father," he finally offered.

Her eyes narrowed. "What about my father?"

"You feel abandoned by him."

She didn't respond.

"He loved you, Amyra. He died to protect you and your mother."

Tears came unbidden to her eyes. "How dare you?" she asked furiously. "How could you possibly know anything about my father?"

"You don't remember him—you were too young. But the memories are there, locked away in your mind. I saw him when he left you for the last time. You were wailing, and he kissed you on the forehead. He had tears running down his cheeks."

She was sobbing now. "It can't be true. I wasn't thinking about him when I first saw you."

"You didn't need to be thinking about him. It stood out, because it's such an important issue in your mind."

He was trying to be gentle, and she could see he was feeling wretched himself. It didn't help. She shook her head in angry denial.

"Let me try again," he said with a sigh. "When we first met the thing uppermost in your mind was the man who had been trying to woo you. He'd been pestering you for weeks, and you find him intensely annoying. He tried to give you a valuable gift—a horse—and you refused it. He thinks you need to become submissive."

Her tears ended abruptly. She stared wide-eyed at him. "What was his name?"

"I don't remember. But there was something about a pig."

A snort escaped her lips. She wasn't sure if it was laughter or astonishment. "That is his name. It sounds a little like the Aen-ur word for boar." She screwed up her face. "Far too close for comfort in his particular case."

She ran a trembling hand over her eyes, and her breath hitched as she mastered herself. Then she faced him. "I believe you, Thomas."

He looked shamefaced. "I'm sorry I did that to you, Amyra. I'm truly sorry. I know it's a violation, which is why I avoid using the stone around people I know." He glanced up at her face apologetically. "My wife is much better at this kind of thing. I mainly rely on the stone to find out people's motives and intentions. She's able to use it to help people. She's a lot like your mother..."

"What about my mother?" she asked sharply.

"Never mind," he said, his expression suddenly guarded.

He seemed to recover himself. "That isn't all. There's more you need to know."

"I'm not sure how much more I can take," she said unsteadily.

He shook his head. "I don't mean like that. The scroll talked about another stone—the Stone of Authority."

She'd been so ready to scoff at the scroll before, but her ridicule had dissolved like the morning mist. "It supposedly lets you control other living things, especially people."

He nodded. "Agon has it."

She looked at him in alarm, hoping he could somehow be mistaken. "How do you know?" she asked.

No hint of sarcasm remained in her tone. Impossible though all of it was, she no longer doubted him.

"From Ennawi's thoughts and memories."

She frowned, more from surprise than skepticism. "It's hard to imagine anything meaningful going on in the mind of that one."

Thomas shook his head firmly. "Don't let appearances deceive you. He's both intelligent and aware. He's only like he is because Nistinaa drugs him."

Her eyes narrowed in disapproval.

"There are reasons why she does it. None of that matters though," Thomas insisted. "The scroll suggested that it takes two weeks to completely bend someone's will. Will has been with Agon for almost a week now, and the stone has begun to have an impact on him." He eyed her uncertainly for a moment, then he seemed to reach a decision. "You might as well know the truth. I was able to witness his interactions with Nistinaa in her memory. He's already been badly affected."

Her eyes grew wide again, this time with horror as the implications began to sink in. And she wasn't alone in her concern about Will—Thomas looked pale enough to be ill.

"What's worse is that Will knows what's happening to him," Thomas continued. "That's why he sent them instead. Even if we could get him away from Agon right now, he wouldn't be himself. He'll never be himself again—not until Agon loses the stone or dies."

Her heart had begun to pound. She stared at him, speechless.

"It doesn't end there either," he told her miserably. "Agon is planning to attack the Aen-ur. And he'll soon be in position. Once he crosses the river he'll be very close to Aen-irac."

"But why attack them? Because of the bridge?"

"No! He has no idea who's responsible for collapsing it. He hates the Aen-ur for reasons that aren't important right now. His motive is that he believes he's found a way to live forever. He intends to do a deal with the dark gods. His end of the bargain is to provide rivers of human blood, and he's planning to start with the Aen-ur. He'll have them rounded up and slaughtered. That will only be the beginning—the people of Arvenon will be next."

It was all so much to take in.

Thomas continued with barely a pause. "Will went to great efforts to make sure we would find out. The Aen-ur need to be warned!"

A look of determination came to his face. "Somehow we need to stop Agon and find a way to free Will."

39

The column stretched far ahead of Will and even further behind as he rode beside the king. The enforced delays lay behind them at last.

A makeshift bridge had been erected over the river, allowing horses and their riders to continue the journey. The wagons filled with provisions were another matter. The column had been obliged to wait while an endless line of new wagons, all of them fully laden, were assembled on the other side of the river. It had been enough of a challenge to replace the food and drink and other supplies left behind. Replacing the tents was going to take much longer. The king, Lady Ona, and a small number of others would sleep under cover that night. Everyone else would be camping in the open.

As was frequently the case, Agon was restive and disgruntled. Both the delays and the disappearance of Ennawi had contributed strongly to his irritation.

Ennawi's disappearance was especially baffling. An exhaustive search had failed to find any trace of the slave. He posed no threat, but he was Agon's property. Whether he had wandered away or fallen in the river and drowned, he had no business doing it without the king's permission.

None of this troubled Will. Although the circumstances of Ennawi's departure were known to him, he was firmly convinced that it was not his business to intrude in the matter. As for the king's moodiness, that wasn't his concern either. His purpose was only to further the king's interests.

His current state of compliance had not been reached overnight, and he knew that even now a part of him still fiercely resisted any notion of bowing to the will of the king. It wasn't as if his objections had gone from his mind—it was rather that his former reasoning no longer seemed compelling.

The king guided his horse alongside Will's. "It is a glorious day, is it not?" asked the king, a savage smile creasing his lips. "Very soon I will carry out final judgment upon the Aen-ur devils," he said. "My soldiers will burst upon them unawares. They will be herded together, and I will watch with delight as they are slaughtered."

"How will such bloodletting further your cause?" asked Will bluntly.

The look on Agon's face turned rapidly from astonishment to anger. The anger soon faded, though, to be replaced by a smug smile. "You cannot imagine how satisfying you are, Will Prentis," he said. "At last I have someone capable whose only goal is to further my cause." Then his face grew harder. "I will be lenient this time, but never question my plans again. It is enough for you to know what I wish to do."

Will nodded. It was true that he didn't need reasons. As long as he understood the king's will, nothing further should be necessary.

At the same time, the king's plan raised uncomfortable questions for him, questions that would persist even when the resistant part of his will had finally been suppressed. He had never countenanced the indiscriminate killing of non-combatants, and he could not stand by while women and children were slaughtered. Yet if he had understood Agon's words correctly, the king was planning exactly that.

Will shook his head in confusion. Not having ever been confronted with a conflict between his duty to his sovereign and his convictions before, he had yet to decide how he should handle it.

. . .

A BRUTISH SOLDIER was ushered into the king's tent, and Agon bared his teeth in a semblance of a smile.

He turned to Will. "Will Prentis, I want you to meet the commander of my soldiers," he said. "This is Wannyk."

Wannyk bowed stiffly. Will greeted him with a non-committal nod. He had already encountered enough Rogandan army commanders to last a lifetime.

The king addressed Will. "My commander has been considering how to respond should my enemies attack us on our journey. He would like your thoughts and opinions."

Will stared back at the king cautiously.

"Do you hesitate to take any necessary measures to protect your sovereign?" snapped Agon irritably.

After a moment's hesitation, Will shrugged, nodding his acceptance. What harm could there be simply in protecting the king?

Wannyk pulled out a parchment, and Will saw that it was a crudely drawn map. No writing appeared on it anywhere, so it was impossible to tell which region it depicted.

"Suppose our forces were deployed here, and the enemy here," began Wannyk. "What would you do?" He eyed Will skeptically.

Will glanced at the map for a moment. He pointed at a particular location. "They would expect you to deploy your main defenses here." He pointed again. "And they would attack here."

Wannyk was unimpressed. "That is obvious," he grunted.

Situations like this were child's play for Will, and he found himself rising to the challenge. "You would instead carry out a preemptive attack here," he said, stabbing a finger at a different location. "They would be forced to move soldiers to that location to counter the attack. It would only be a feint. Your main attack would be carried out here." He pointed once more.

Wannyk's eyes went wide.

"Well?" demanded Agon. "Get onto it immediately!"

Wannyk scurried from the tent.

Will frowned. “What just happened, Your Majesty?”

“Don’t trouble yourself, Will,” said the king loftily. “It was nothing more than a training exercise.” Agon’s smile seemed even more false than usual.

Had Will just given Agon’s commander a strategy for attacking the Aen-ur?

He gritted his teeth in annoyance. Acting against his convictions had never been an option for Will. But he wasn’t used to working with a sovereign who deviously manipulated his subjects, and he couldn’t escape the feeling that he had just been played.

He would need to be doubly on his guard, because it surely wouldn’t be long before he faced a similar situation again. And he had no doubt that the stakes would be higher next time.

THE ROAD along which the column was traveling still ran parallel to the foothills of the Blue Mountains. Outliers of the forest that covered the slopes stood to the right of the road. No trace of the river remained; it had long since bent sharply away from the road, stretching up into the mountains where it had its source.

To the left of the road lay a series of rolling hills leading to vast expanses of grazing land.

A distant rumble caused Will to glance upward. No storm clouds had gathered in the sky, and he drew his horse to a halt in bemusement as the rumble continued to grow in volume. The column moved on, but others had also noticed the sound, and many of them were beginning to peer around nervously.

The noise grew abruptly to a deafening roar as the hills to Will’s left burst suddenly into life. A vast mass of stampeding cattle thundered across the nearest ridge, charging straight toward the column. Long horns flashed ominously, picked out by rays of the late afternoon sunlight.

Panicked screams filled the air as men and horses fled for their lives. Any semblance of order vanished in an instant as the column descended into a chaos of fleeing forms and flashing hooves.

In the confusion a cart was overturned just behind Will. Fighting for control of his horse, Will somehow managed to steer the terrified animal behind the cart. The cattle flowed around them, trampling everything in their path.

Peering around in the dust and the turmoil, Will spotted the king and half a dozen of his guards sheltering behind the royal carriage. As he watched, the carriage began to wobble under the strain of pressing cattle. Abruptly the carriage came crashing down onto its side, the king and his men barely scuttling back to safety in time. The fugitives quickly hurried forward again to shelter behind the overturned carriage.

The flow of cattle slowly began to diminish, but before it ceased entirely a lean figure dressed in black rode up. Leaping from his horse, he landed on the overturned royal carriage, a sword flashing in his hand.

By the time the startled guards had drawn their own swords, two of them lay dead. The remaining guards outnumbered their attacker four to one, but they were soon fighting for their lives.

The king watched the battle with wide eyes, bellowing for more guards. He had picked up a fallen sword and was preparing to defend himself, but the ashen appearance of his face suggested he wasn't optimistic.

By the time Will finally managed to reach them only one of the guards was still fighting. Will's weapons had been taken away when he was made a prisoner, so he reached down for a discarded sword.

A quick glance at the king suggested that Agon was not entirely sure what his captive would do now he was armed. Will ignored the king, facing the intruder instead. He wasn't a moment too soon. The last guard finally went down.

The attacker engaged him without hesitation, and Will marveled at the stamina of the man. The black clad fighter had been battling without pause for several minutes, but he moved as if he had just begun.

A couple of minutes were all it took for Will to wonder if he had finally met his match. The man was simply too skilled, too fast, and too determined.

More of Agon's guards arrived before the attacker could finish Will off. A lucky jab by one of the guards took the intruder in the leg, distracting him enough that Will was finally able to penetrate his defense with a thrust to his torso.

Reaching for his belt, the attacker withdrew a knife and threw it at Agon. Out of the corner of his eye Will saw the king twisting to one side away from its path.

Throwing the knife was the final act of the dark clad intruder. Thrust through by several swords, he fell to the ground and lay unmoving.

Will saw at a glance that the king had survived the attack. Apart from nicking Agon's arm and drawing blood, the knife had missed him entirely.

A piece of cloth lay nearby on the ground. It appeared to be relatively clean. Will tore off a couple of strips and moved to bandage the arm of the king. Agon glared at him while he worked, but made no comment.

If Will had been expecting gratitude from Agon, he would have been disappointed. Certainly King Steffan would have responded differently. Having never been motivated by the need for praise, Will ignored Agon's stony silence.

"Call for the royal physician," Will told a guard calmly. The man hurried away to do his bidding, apparently choosing to ignore Will's status as a prisoner.

Agon appeared to be slowly emerging from shock. "Who was he?" he demanded, pointing at the body of the attacker. The king moved closer, poking at him with his foot. As he did so, Will noticed what appeared to be a parchment tucked within the man's clothing.

Bending down, Will pulled the parchment free.

"Give me that!" demanded Agon furiously. Stepping forward he snatched it from Will's hand. A frown came to his face as he scanned its contents. "Impossible!" he finally snorted, before thrusting it back into Will's hand.

Will read the parchment. His brows furrowed together. He turned to the king, lowering his voice. "So this man was an assassin? And Drettroth hired him to attack you?" He shook his head, glancing at the chaos around them. "I imagine we have the assassin to thank for the cattle."

Agon glared back at him. "Drettroth always hated me. I should have killed him myself instead of leaving you Arvenians to do it for me!" He scowled. "Drettroth was a failure when he was alive." Then he gave out a mad laugh. "Now he's failed again!"

Before the king could say any more, a guard arrived, accompanied by the royal physician.

Seeing the flustered look on the physician's face, Agon snapped at him. "Well, don't just stand there! Get on with it!"

The physician bowed briefly before unwrapping Will's strips of cloth and examining the wound. His brows knit together in a frown. "This wound..." he began tentatively.

"Stop fussing!" Agon snapped.

"But Your Majesty," sputtered the physician.

"Bandage it!" roared the king.

Fumbling awkwardly, the physician rewrapped the wound with fresh bandages, his fingers trembling. Then he hurried away.

The king watched the retreating back of the physician for a moment, then he took a breath and cast his eyes around. What he saw caused him to shake his head in anger.

Will followed his gaze. Most of the cattle had vanished in the direction of the forest, although a few still wandered nearby, lowing mournfully. The devastation left behind them was staggering.

The column would be delayed once more, and this time the king had the long dead Drettroth to thank for it.

Agon would not be happy. Having seen more than enough of what that looked like in practice, Will turned aside, allowing his feet to drift. He saw no reason to be around to witness the storm.

Wandering back down the column he noticed the first signs that order was beginning to emerge from the chaos. Men were scurrying about, righting upended wagons and rounding up horses. Supplies were being retrieved from the mess and placed in orderly piles. Curious, he stepped behind a wagon to observe.

It quickly became clear that the driving force behind the efforts was Lady Ona. Will had never seen the king lift as much as a finger to organize anything, yet somehow the practical needs of the column were met each day. Tents were set up, food was prepared, horses were provided for, supplies were replenished, and everything ran remarkably smoothly. It seemed likely that the king largely had Lady Ona to thank for it.

Being himself an organizer by nature, Will watched with considerable curiosity as she went about the task. There was much to admire about her approach. She was clearly an effective communicator as well as a skilled manager, and she didn't entirely neglect little compliments and words of encouragement.

As he watched, a young servant approached her carrying two heavy bags. He appeared extremely tentative as he put them down in front of her.

"Where have you been?" she demanded, her eyes flashing dangerously. "You're late—as usual! I expected you long before this."

The servant bowed his head, but didn't dare to reply.

Pulling open the neck of one of the bags she peered into it. "This isn't what I told you to bring!" she shouted.

She stood with her hands on her hips, glaring at him for a moment. "Take off your tunic and your shirt," she commanded, her voice now controlled and even.

He obeyed, trembling violently.

She approached him, casually running a finger across his bare back. "It upsets me when my people disappoint me," she said smoothly. Then she turned to one of the soldiers. "Flog him. Twenty strokes."

Soldiers took each of his arms and dragged him away.

"Don't dare to disappoint me again," she yelled after him.

Will looked on, appalled by her behavior. Perhaps her servant had failed to bring what she wanted in a timely fashion, but she made no attempt to explore the reasons. She had simply erupted.

Perhaps this was how she relieved her own tension. Perhaps she used such opportunities to keep her subordinates alert and responsive. Either way, after the demonstration he had witnessed, her underlings would undoubtedly work doubly hard to satisfy her demands. Every servant in sight was certainly scurrying about frantically.

Lady Ona's cruelty left Will cold. Unwilling to watch her any longer, he slipped quietly away.

He wandered aimlessly, going wherever his feet happened to take him. How could he find his place in this new environment?

By a strange sequence of circumstances he had become attached to King Agon's column, and serving the king's interests had become his main focus. He had a new purpose, and he would find ways of fulfilling it. Being fully committed to Agon's cause, he intended to follow through with all of his energy, in whatever ways the king permitted him.

Nevertheless, other changes had crept into his life, sneaking in behind his new focus. The changes disturbed him, and he had no desire to pretend otherwise.

Satisfying reasons for his change of purpose had never presented themselves. But his new commitment was not founded on reason, so what was the point in trying to understand it?

One issue weighed heavily on him. He already knew how he would respond if asked to do something he didn't believe in. But he had an uncomfortable feeling that his principles had already been put to the test and that he had been found wanting.

Unshakable though his commitment to King Agon might be, it felt profoundly wrong. A new and unfamiliar fault line had opened inside him.

Difficulties and challenges weren't new for him—throughout his entire life he had been confronted by adversity. Yet he'd somehow discovered what he was made to do and found a satisfying way of doing it. Since reaching his adult years he had been given almost unlimited opportunity to fulfill his calling, always in support of a cause he believed in.

With that had come an underlying sense of contentment, a serenity that sustained him through the darkest times.

He was contented no longer. He wondered if he ever could be again.

40

Thomas huddled with Amyra, peering out at Agon's camp. Fires twinkled in the night between the tents that now straddled the road.

The havoc wreaked by the cattle was obvious even from a distance. The observers had no idea what to make of the stampede. Did it have a natural cause, or did others besides the Aen-ur have a motive for disrupting the king's progress?

Whatever its origin, the disruption had given the Aen-ur valuable breathing space.

They had taken seriously the warning delivered through Ennawi. The most vulnerable among them had already been removed from the area likely to be targeted by King Agon's soldiers.

Those trained to fight were another matter. Their leaders had decided that the Aen-ur would no longer allow themselves to be lightly pushed aside. They were ready to do battle for their homes as well as their lives.

Aen-ur soldiers had taken up positions facing a river, and they did not intend to make it easy for the Rogandans to cross the natural barrier. If Agon's men succeeded in spite of their best efforts, they planned to lead the attackers away from their dwellings and into an ambush.

Thomas and Haldek had been invited to offer suggestions for the defense. Haldek had excused himself from the discussion, and the Aen-ur respected his unwillingness to fight his own countrymen. Thomas had declined simply because he knew he had nothing to offer.

Amyra had told the Aen-ur she was willing to fight alongside them. She had been rebuffed. They insisted that the fighting be left to those trained for it. The defensive preparations of the Aen-ur were well advanced, and it seemed Amyra had little more to contribute toward them than Thomas.

The person the Aen-ur really needed was Will, and Thomas found himself hoping fervently that Agon wasn't planning on using Will's strategic genius for his own purposes.

Thomas returned his full attention to Agon's camp. Amyra crouched beside him, restless and agitated.

"How are we going to get him out of there?" she asked fiercely.

With little else useful to do, it was not surprising to Thomas that her attention was now fully absorbed with Will's predicament. Crucial as the information delivered via Ennawi had been, it still rankled with Amyra that their careful plan to extract Will had failed. She had been especially baffled by Nistinaa's assertion that Will himself had refused the rescue.

Thomas guessed that Will believed himself to be already ensnared by the Stone of Authority. Amyra understood the implications of that as well as Thomas did. Nevertheless, the logic of switching the rescue to Nistinaa and Ennawi failed utterly to satisfy her.

"I'm going in there," Amyra abruptly announced.

Thomas stared at her in alarm. "What do you mean? You'll end up captured yourself!"

"I don't care. I'm not going to just sit here waiting for something to happen."

She got up purposefully. "Where's Haldek?"

Thomas jumped up himself. “Wait! Let’s think this through!”

But it was too late. She had already gone, looking for Haldek.

It left Thomas with a huge dilemma. Should he go with her?

Will had brought him here so he could use the stone to discern Agon’s plans. Thanks to Ennawi, he’d already been able to do that. He could think of no further compelling reason to venture into the Rogandan camp with the intent of using the stone. And he had no skill with weapons, so he would be of little use if it came to a fight.

Taking the stone within reach of Agon would be a huge risk, and it didn’t take him long to conclude that the risks far outweighed any likely benefit he could offer Will.

His decision was made. If Amyra did go to the camp, he wouldn’t be going with her. He could only hope that his decision truly had been based on common sense and not simply on cowardice.

Before long his self doubts were interrupted by the arrival of Amyra. Haldek was following in her wake, but he didn’t look comfortable.

“Are you sure you want to do this?” Thomas asked Amyra.

“Yes,” she said impatiently. “And don’t try to talk me out of it.”

“I won’t be coming with you,” Thomas said awkwardly.

She frowned at him. “Of course not! What would be the point?”

Seeing his reaction, she softened immediately. “I didn’t mean it like that, Thomas. Both of us know there are plenty of reasons why you shouldn’t even consider a risk like that.”

He nodded his agreement, but she had already turned away.

“Haldek is going to get me past the sentries.”

“I will *try* to get you past the sentries,” Haldek corrected her. “I want to see Will rescued as much as you do, but I need to say again that I think this is a bad idea!”

“I fully understand that,” she replied, waving a hand dismissively. “But the Aen-ur can’t help—they’re distracted planning their defense—and neither of you have any better ideas. I’m going.”

“What will you do if you do find Will?” Thomas asked.

“I’m taking a couple of cloaks.” She showed them a dark bundle she was carrying. "We'll put them on and wait for an opportunity to slip past the sentries."

It sounded more like a rough idea than a plan to Thomas. "They'll be on high alert, especially after the stampede. And they're expecting to go into action soon as well," he protested.

"They won't have fully recovered from the chaos of the stampede," she countered. "There will never be a better time."

She was determined, and Thomas could see no way to persuade her otherwise. Nevertheless, he made a last ditch attempt. "What does your mother think about you doing this?"

Amyra immediately became guarded. "She isn't here to ask. But it's my decision."

Thomas could think of nothing further to say. He wondered if little Tammi might one day grow up to be a firebrand like Amyra. He had mixed feelings about such a prospect.

And then they were gone. Thomas stared at their departing backs with deep foreboding.

DAWN HAD BARELY BROKEN when a group of guards appeared at Lady Ona's tent calling for her attention.

"What is it?" Lady Ona asked irritably. The effort of organizing the clean up after the previous day's stampede had kept her up well into the night, and even when she did go to her bed she had slept badly.

Two of the guards stepped into the entrance of her tent. A young woman was struggling between them, but they held her firmly in their grasp.

"We found her snooping around the camp, My Lady," one of the men reported. "She can't give any account of what she's doing. She was carrying these." He held up a couple of cloaks in his other hand.

The young woman had now transferred her baleful gaze to Lady Ona, and the noblewoman examined her thoughtfully.

"Do you understand me?" Lady Ona asked in Rogandan.

The young woman hesitated before nodding once.

"Are you prepared to be sensible if I tell these men to release you?"

Once more she paused before nodding.

"Release her," she told the men, "but remain outside the tent. If she leaves without my permission, kill her."

The young woman's eyes went wide, indicating clearly that she had understood. She stood there quietly enough when the guards released her.

"So who might you be, and what are you doing here?" Lady Ona asked her curtly.

No answer was forthcoming.

"Do you have a tongue in your head? Or are you mute like Ennawi?"

At the name of the missing slave a flicker of recognition passed across the young woman's eyes before she could prevent it. So she knew something of Ennawi. Lady Ona betrayed no indication of having detected the response, but she noted it with considerable interest.

Apparently her captive had little ability to hide her reactions. Lady Ona decided to take a gamble. "I suppose you've come to rescue Will Prentis," she said casually.

A deep blush came instantly to the face of the young woman.

Lady Ona burst into delighted laughter. "You're adorable!" she said. "You must surely be the most satisfying person I've interrogated in months. Your answers are written all over your face, even without you uttering a word."

Once again the young woman's face was flushed, this time with anger.

"Why should we be enemies?" Lady Ona asked soothingly, beaming her most charming smile. "I'll tell you my name—I'm Lady Ona. What's yours?"

Her initiative was greeted with disdain by the young woman.

"Very well, then," Lady Ona said coldly. "In that case I might as well have you executed immediately. Guards!"

"Wait!" the young woman called hastily.

The guards had appeared at the entrance to the tent once more, and Lady Ona held up a finger indicating they should wait.

"My name...is Dahra," the young woman said hesitantly.

Lady Ona dismissed the guards with a flick of her bejeweled finger.

"That's better," she purred. "There's no need for unpleasantness between us. So, Dahra, what brings you to King Agon's camp? And before you answer, I already know you've seen Ennawi, and you're here looking for Will Prentis. So don't imagine you can treat me like a fool."

"I do know Ennawi, although I can't imagine how you might know him," she replied. "We grew up together in the same village. It's true that he doesn't have much to say, although I certainly wouldn't call him mute."

Lady Ona watched her performance with real admiration. She was smooth. "And what about Will Prentis? Did you grow up with him too?" This time she spoke in Arvenian.

'Dahra'—it almost certainly wasn't her name—answered fluently in the same language. "No. I met him on the road. My family are traders. I heard he was somewhere here in the camp, so I came looking for him."

"And is he a trader too?" This time she had switched to the language of Lestanor.

The girl followed the language switch without missing a beat. "So he told me." She shrugged. "In case you were wondering about my language skills, traders need to be fluent in many languages."

She was smooth indeed.

"And who is Dahra?" asked Lady Ona. "Your best friend?" No response. "Your sister?" She paused again. "Your mother?"

Once again the girl gave herself away.

"So your mother, then. And what's your real name?"

The young woman sighed in resignation. "It's Amyra."

This time she was telling the truth. "A lovely name," affirmed

Lady Ona with a smile. The poor girl had no idea who she was dealing with.

The nature of the girl's relationship with Will Prentis was not yet clear, but there were ways to answer that question too.

"How friendly have you become with Will Prentis?" she asked innocently.

The girl did not respond, which was itself telling.

"I found him to be a good lover," Lady Ona offered breezily. "At first, anyway. I soon tired of him."

Amyra had almost gone purple. She was barely containing her rage.

This situation was becoming more interesting by the minute. Lady Ona had failed to get access to Will Prentis, and she never satisfied herself with failure. The more she pondered it, the more promising the girl's arrival appeared.

"You came to see Will Prentis," she said. "Let's go visit him."

The girl still hadn't recovered from Lady Ona's earlier announcement. The noblewoman ignored the wide-eyed look that came to her face and headed to the entrance of the tent. "Follow us," she told the guards. "Kill her if she tries to get away."

Turning back to Amyra, she beckoned with a hand. "Follow me."

Then she set off toward Will's tent. She knew exactly where to find it.

Normally his tent was pitched beside the king's, but since the cows appeared nothing could be said to be normal.

Lady Ona herself had survived the stampede as much by luck as anything. After her carriage had been overturned, a couple of hefty cows crashed into it, breaking it apart. Somehow managing to avoid their writhing bodies, she had crawled free of the carriage and cowered between its rear wheels until the danger had passed.

Amyra caught up to her as they walked. "Where did the cows come from?" she asked boldly. Lady Ona smiled to herself, guessing that the girl was attempting to recover her poise before they reached Will Prentis.

"An assassin arranged it," she said matter-of-factly. "He planned to take advantage of the distraction to kill the king. He failed."

The look on Amyra's face made it clear this was news to her. She clearly had no awareness at all of the plot.

"Will Prentis defended the king himself. In fact he was the one who eventually killed the assassin," she added.

Lady Ona couldn't resist a self-satisfied smirk when she saw Amyra's reaction. There was little doubt that any remaining poise had now deserted the girl completely.

Will Prentis had already risen when the two women arrived, but he hadn't left his tent. His eyes went wide when he caught sight of Amyra, and both of their faces turned scarlet. Will's reaction in particular was more delicious than Lady Ona had dared hope. It was plainly obvious that he would do nothing to put Amyra at risk.

She couldn't resist gloating. The situation promised to be very interesting indeed.

"I believe that you and Amyra are good friends, Will," she began.

He tore his gaze away from the girl with difficulty, his eyes narrowing when he turned his full attention to her captor.

Lady Ona's heart skipped a beat when their eyes met. Will Prentis was not her usual helpless conquest. This was the man who had overseen the destruction of the Rogandan army. She realized abruptly she'd needed a reminder of that. She would need to tread delicately.

He would become a dangerous enemy, the more so if she was ever foolish enough to let him conclude he had nothing to lose. She couldn't threaten his life either—Agon would never tolerate her having him killed.

At the same time danger was not a deterrent to Lady Ona. High risk behavior had always excited her.

"I'll have her killed in a heartbeat," she told him casually. "Whenever it suits me. You know I'm not bluffing."

She paused to let her words sink in. "I'm willing to give you an opportunity to save her though." She gave him her best coquettish smile. "Let me have you for the night, and she'll still be alive in the morning." Then she let her face go hard. "Refuse and she dies right now."

Will Prentis stepped toward Amyra, his face calm. "I'm sorry, Lady Ona," he said, "but any decision about her fate is not in your hands. The king alone will decide."

With that he took Amyra's arm and led her away, heading for the tent of the king.

Lady Ona watched them go, too stunned to respond. It had never occurred to her that Will Prentis would risk taking Amyra before the king. Apparently he intended to do just that.

AMYRA HEAVED a sigh of relief as they walked away from Lady Ona. "I was a bit worried back there, Will," she admitted with a shudder.

"You had good reason to be," he replied. "Lady Ona is a dangerous woman."

He glanced back over his shoulder in the direction of the noblewoman. "I've seen enough to know she is also a self-serving liar. Don't believe anything she told you."

She stole a glance at him, hoping it was true.

Will seemed so normal. And he had rescued her from Lady Ona. "What will we do now?" she asked.

He eyed her sternly. "That depends on why you came here."

She grinned back at him. "To help you escape of course."

"I was afraid you might say that," he replied sadly.

She stared at him, struggling to grasp the import of his words. Her eyes grew wider as she saw the look on his face and began to fully understand at last how the Stone of Authority had changed him.

"You're not committed to the interests of King Agon," said Will. "You've come here to undermine him."

Her heart began to pound in her chest. She opened her mouth to speak, but no words came out.

"I'm taking you to the king," he told her, "and he will pronounce judgment over you. I will plead on your behalf for leniency, but you will have no choice but to submit to his decision, whatever it might be."

41

Amyra followed Will with dragging steps, overcome by the horror of his transformation. She paid no attention to where they were going, and she dared not imagine what the outcome might be when she stood before the king.

Barely a few minutes had passed when an elaborate structure rose up before them. Guards stood outside at attention, and there could be no doubt that they had reached the royal tent.

The guards ignored Will, and he walked in without waiting to be announced. That simple act set the seal on Amyra's despair.

She lifted her chin defiantly, determined not to go meekly.

King Agon stood before her, but he was not what Amyra had expected. He appeared afflicted.

Seeing Will, he managed a wan smile. "Ah, Will Prentis. I have just issued the order to finally destroy the Aen-ur. You were not here to witness the moment!"

The king's words snapped Amyra completely out of her misery. Fierce anger rose up in her as she thought of the fate in store for the peaceful men, women, and children of the Aen-ur—people she had come to love and respect.

Agon's voice had slowed as he spoke. He appeared exhausted, and when he spoke again his speech had become slurred and erratic. "My men have already moved into position," he said, "and the local barons have added to their number. They have been waiting only for their commander, Wannyk, and he has now ridden away to join them. The attack will begin...a little before noon."

The king finally seemed to notice her. "You have brought someone. A woman. She must wait...I am ailing." He passed a shaky hand across his brow.

Amyra's brows drew together as she peered at the king. He had been swaying unsteadily, and he sank abruptly onto the small throne positioned behind him.

"What is happening to me, Will?" he asked. "You must help me. There are so few I can trust."

Will bellowed immediately for the guards. One of them quickly bustled into the tent. "Fetch the royal physician! Urgently!" Will commanded. "Hurry, man!"

The guard bolted.

Will approached the king. "Your arm, Your Majesty?"

Agon held out an arm that appeared swollen almost to twice its normal size. Will began unwrapping the bandage that covered the arm. Careful as Will was, the king cried out in pain more than once before the arm was released.

Amyra gasped when she caught a glimpse of what had emerged. Black and blue flesh surrounded an enormous weeping sore. The king blanched at the sight of it; only Will appeared unshaken.

A man hurried into the tent. The look of relief on Will's face suggested he was the royal physician.

The king's head had begun to loll drunkenly from side to side.

The physician went pale when he saw the arm. "It was the assassin's knife," he murmured to Will. "I fear it was tipped with some kind of slow-acting poison." He raised his arms in frustration. "I wanted to treat it at the time, but he would only let me bandage it."

Will nodded reassuringly. "What can you do for him?"

The physician checked the king's vital signs carefully. Then he stepped back and slowly shook his head. "Nothing," he whispered. "Nothing at all. It won't be long now."

Agon took a shallow breath then released a slow sigh. His head sank to his chest, and his arms slumped by his side.

Amyra looked on in stunned amazement. From her earliest memories, the very name of King Agon of Rogand had struck terror into the hearts of his enemies and his subjects alike. Absolute ruler, dreaded tyrant, persecutor of the Aen-ur—he lay dead before her. Once all-powerful, he had suffered the same fate as the most wretched of his subjects.

Everything seemed to happen at once. The physician reacted first, turning on his heel and scampering out of the tent.

Two of the guards peered curiously inside to see what was happening. Seeing Agon slumped on the throne, they ventured further into the tent. Amyra saw their eyes go wide when they saw his arm.

Leaning toward them, Amyra said in a tense voice, "The plague has taken the king. It is highly contagious! The physician has fled."

The men looked first at the body of the king, then at her. Then they dashed from the tent in terror, shrieking at the top of their voices. "The plague! It's the plague! Run for your lives!"

The growing commotion outside suggested that chaos was spreading quickly.

Oblivious to it all, Will stood unmoving, holding his head. A stricken look had appeared on his face. He looked up into her eyes. "Amyra!" he said shakily, as if he had just noticed her. "I've just woken from a terrible nightmare."

Ignoring him, she hurried to the king and began running her fingers over his clothing. She tried hard not to notice his bloated arm.

"Whatever are you doing?" he asked. He sounded as much dazed as bemused.

"I'm making sure none of this happens again," she replied tersely.

Several anxious minutes passed before she straightened again, a triumphant look on her face. "I have it!"

In her hand she held up a thin gray stone colored with flecks of red. She didn't doubt for a moment that it was the Stone of Authority.

It suddenly occurred to her that Will might put it to better use. "Would you like to have it?" she asked him.

He shuddered. He didn't need to speak to make it clear what he thought about that idea.

"We need to go!" she told him firmly. "Agon might be dead, but his soldiers are still planning to attack the Aen-ur. We have to stop them somehow."

Amyra strode purposefully from the tent with Will trailing along behind her. It was apparent that he had yet to fully emerge from his stupor.

No guards remained at their posts outside the tent, and few people were visible anywhere nearby. Then a familiar figure swung into view around the side of a nearby tent. It was Lady Ona, shadowed by four guards. Amyra's hand closed instinctively over the stone.

"What's this about the king dying of the plague?" Lady Ona demanded suspiciously.

Amyra jerked her head in the direction of the royal tent.

The noblewoman's guards looked decidedly restless. She glared at them. "Wait here. And don't let these two out of your sight!"

The guards dutifully clustered around Will and Amyra. Lady Ona disappeared into the tent.

"It's highly contagious!" whispered Amyra to the guards. "The royal physician fled in terror, and so did the royal guards." She pointed into the tent. "If she goes anywhere near him, she'll catch it, and you will too. None of you will see another dawn."

That was enough for the guards. All four of them turned and ran.

Amyra saw no reason to wait around either, and she grabbed Will's arm to urge him forward. Before they had gone more than a couple of steps, Lady Ona reappeared. Amyra turned to face her.

She regarded them coolly. "It was the assassin, wasn't it? I have some experience of poisons myself."

Amyra stared back at her impassively.

"So where did this story of a plague come from?" the noblewoman asked, her eyes narrowed.

Amyra didn't bother to answer.

Lady Ona's gaze flicked over Will, still trying to master himself after his sudden reawakening, and settled on her. "I see," she said.

A knife appeared in Lady Ona's hand. Amyra flushed with anger when she saw that it was her own weapon, taken from her when she had been captured. She glared at the noblewoman.

"This situation is by no means a disaster. It raises such interesting possibilities," said Lady Ona, advancing toward her. "The king has no offspring of course. Someone entirely different will need to ascend the throne. Someone energetic and capable. Someone like me."

Amyra peered frantically around for a weapon to defend herself. A discarded shield caught her eye, and she grabbed it, slipping her arm hastily through the straps. She barely managed to raise it before Lady Ona reached her.

The noblewoman clearly had extensive training with a knife, and Amyra saw that even if she'd been armed herself, she wouldn't have survived for long. The shield was all that saved her in the first frantic moments of the struggle.

The shield was almost certainly a ceremonial item—each of the guards had been carrying one when Amyra arrived at the royal tent—and it was lighter and smaller than the shields carried by regular soldiers. Nevertheless, it had been fashioned from metal and was solidly constructed. With it she was able to keep Lady Ona at bay, and even to push her back. But she could think of no way to disable her opponent or finish the fight.

The noblewoman abruptly turned aggressive, thrusting forward in a series of lunges that forced Amyra back. Unable to risk looking anywhere except at her attacker, Amyra tripped on something behind her and fell heavily to the ground.

Before she could move a muscle, Lady Ona was standing over her, one foot firmly planted on the shield to prevent her from raising it.

A cruel look covered the noblewoman's face. "You were pathetically easy to manipulate," she gloated. "Your interference was beginning to annoy me, but it ends here."

She raised Amyra's knife for a killing stroke.

Waiting helplessly for the end, Amyra heard a dull thud. Lady Ona slumped senseless to the ground.

Will appeared in her place, his eyes clear at last. Reaching down a hand, he helped her to her feet.

Amyra stared down at her enemy. "Is it safe to simply leave her?" she asked, making no attempt to soften the hostility in her tone.

Will shook his head. "No, it isn't. She's a dangerous woman, and she could do a great deal of harm if she did manage to ascend the throne."

"Is that likely?"

He shrugged. "She's immensely capable, and I've met few people so devious." He stared down at her prone form. "But even so, I couldn't bring myself to knife her in the back when I could easily disable her. And I won't kill her now when she's defenseless."

Unable to think of a suitable response, Amyra reached down for her knife and wrenched it from the noblewoman's hand. She felt anything but satisfied, but she was no more willing than Will to kill a person while they were unconscious.

She shot an awkward glance at Will as she turned away. "You didn't, did you?" she asked.

"Do what?" asked Will, a puzzled frown on his face.

"Bed her. She told me you did."

"Never!" he replied vehemently.

The revulsion on his face answered her question as plainly as his words. Embarrassed at having asked, she felt her face coloring deeply.

Will didn't notice. "We need to find horses," he said, his eyes roving among the tents.

In their haste to escape the plague someone must have released the horses, because a few of the animals could be seen nearby. Approaching one of them, Amyra found it already saddled. Having secured the reins, she reached forward to shorten the stirrups.

"Amyra!"

The warning shout caused her to spin around. She found herself confronted by the vengeful face of Lady Ona, her hair matted with blood and a crazed look in her eye. Once more she held a knife, raised high and ready to strike.

The killing blow never came. Her eyes went wide with surprise as the knife dropped from her fingers. Blood seeped slowly through the clothing below her ribs.

Amyra stepped nimbly aside as Lady Ona pitched forward. She lay still with a knife protruding from her back. The horse threw back its head and stamped its feet in alarm.

Will sprinted up. "I would never let her kill you," he said breathlessly. He stared down at Lady Ona for a moment, then knelt to examine her. "She's dead," he reported.

Amyra gazed at him unsteadily. One of her hands still enclosed the Stone of Authority, and the other tightly gripped the reins of the horse. She was leaning heavily on the horse for support.

She wanted to throw herself into his arms, but an uncharacteristic timidity paralyzed her, and she couldn't move.

His brows drew together tightly as he stared at her. "Did she harm you?" he asked fiercely.

She shook her head.

He gazed into her eyes. What was he thinking and feeling?

Her heart knew what she wanted, but her limbs had let her down. She stared helplessly at him, desperately hoping he would take the step for her.

He was the one who looked away first. "I'll find a horse," he said at last. "We don't have much time."

42

Amyra and Will rode as fast as they dared, skirting the fringes of Agon's army as they headed for the river where the Aen-ur intended to make their stand.

Amyra's thoughts were a confused jumble. Everything had started going wrong almost from the moment she blundered into the Rogandan camp. And yet—impossibly—she had achieved her goal. Will Prentis was free, and riding beside her. More than that, King Agon, the scourge of the Aen-ur, was dead, along with the manipulative schemer Lady Ona.

The Stone of Authority disturbed her the most. She had glimpsed its terrible power—she remembered vividly the despair she had felt the moment Will decided to turn her over to Agon. The look in his eyes still haunted her.

Now he was free of it.

She had every reason to feel exhilarated. Instead she felt strangely deflated.

The stone now rested in a tiny leather pouch she had discovered at Agon's camp. She had tucked the pouch into her bodice. Apparently she was the stone's new guardian. What did that mean? She tried hard to remember anything at all from the scroll read to them by Will, but details eluded her. She hadn't taken the scroll seriously enough to commit any of it to memory.

Thomas had believed every word, and so had Will. How must it have felt for Will to know he was coming under the power of the Stone of Authority, knowing he was slowly being bent to the will of a man like Agon?

Stray thoughts came unbidden to her mind. Could the bearer of the stone use it to compel someone to love them? She blushed at the thought, immediately rejecting it as the dangerous fancy she knew it to be. Whatever she might do with the stone, she knew she could never use it on another person. Not for any reason. She had seen the effects all too clearly.

The sound of water could be heard ahead, and Amyra's thoughts were drawn back to their immediate circumstances. She was leading them to a location upriver from the place where the two armies would confront each other. It wouldn't be possible to cross the river at her destination of choice, but the elevation would afford an excellent outlook of the entire area.

Only a few minutes passed before they emerged at the top of a series of rapids. Below them they could clearly see Aen-ur soldiers spread out on the opposite side of the river.

They had apparently arrived barely in time, because horns sounded, and the first of the Rogandans came into view across the river from them. It took no more than a glance to see that the Rogandans far outnumbered the Aen-ur.

"I recognize this place," Will said grimly. "Agon tricked me into giving his commander a battle plan."

"What can we do?" she asked miserably.

He studied her quietly for a moment. "You have the stone," he suggested.

"How will that help?" she asked.

"You won't be able to influence any of the people," he replied, "it takes too long. But the scroll did say that the stone bends all created things to the will of the bearer."

"What does that mean?"

He shrugged helplessly. “I don’t know.”

“Does *created things* only mean things that are *living*?”

He raised his eyebrows. “You’ll have to find that out for yourself.”

Retrieving the stone, she held it in her hand, trying to imagine how it might be possible to use it.

As she glanced down at the rival armies, it struck her that something wasn’t right. Amyra knew that cheers and battle cries could usually be heard as men prepared for battle. Both armies were completely silent. She knew this fight was deadly serious for the Aen-ur. That might account for their silence. But the Rogandans?

She looked at Will quizzically. “Why are they so quiet?”

“The Rogandans haven’t come for a battle,” he replied grimly. “They’re here to carry out a massacre.”

As he spoke, the Rogandan lines began to move forward, quickly reaching the river. The first of the soldiers were already wading in.

Something rose up inside her. The Aen-ur did not deserve this. They were a people of peace. She and her mother had come to them vulnerable, and the Aen-ur gave them a home and a future, pointing them to hope.

This must not be allowed to happen. She shook her head in denial.

The water below her lurched and swayed in response to her agitation, and she stared at it in amazement. She raised a hand, and water sprayed into the air.

Clearing her mind, she moved her hands about randomly. Nothing happened. As soon as she focused her will on the water once more, it responded to her intent.

She was painfully unpracticed, and there was no time to experiment. Gulping in great breaths of air, she tried to steady herself. Then she thrust out both hands as if holding back the river. The flow slowed at once to a trickle, water welling up as if a dam had suddenly appeared in the river. Water was soon spilling out over the riverbank, splashing around their legs.

Downriver the Rogandan soldiers paused, peering upward to find out where the water had gone.

Amyra abruptly dropped her arms, and water thundered down over the rapids in a flash flood that swept down the river.

The Aen-ur fighters were far enough back from the river to be largely unaffected. The Rogandan soldiers were forced to scramble to safety. She could only imagine what they must be thinking. Swooping her hands toward them, she sent a howling wind that pushed them further from the river. The Rogandans must have withdrawn immediately, because none of them at all were now visible along the river. Stilling the wind abruptly, she began to wave her hands back and forth, focusing on the trees.

She had no way to see what was happening, but if she was achieving her purpose, the trees were waving their branches violently, slapping at any soldiers who wandered within reach. Creepers would be winding across every path, tripping the soldiers as they fled. Even the wild creatures of the forest would be haranguing the soldiers as they passed, snarling or howling as if demented.

After half an hour of this she collapsed in total exhaustion.

Returning her attention to her surroundings with an effort, she noticed that water was flowing normally across the rapids as if nothing had happened. Her wet feet, though, still provided a tangible reminder of the climactic events that had taken place.

Glancing at Will, she saw open awe on his face. "What have you been doing since the water and the wind?" he asked.

She closed her eyes and took a few unsteady breaths before responding. "I've been using the trees, the bushes, the creepers, and the animals," she said wearily. "To eject the Rogandans from the forest. If I did it right, all of them will have survived. But they'll be convinced the forest is haunted. I'd be amazed if they're ever willing to go anywhere near the Aen-ur again."

Admiration shone in his eyes. "You're remarkable, Amyra!"

She returned a weak smile, too spent to respond.

He shook his head in wonder. "You routed an army with nothing more than the Stone of Authority."

She was no less bemused. How was it even possible?

"We need to find Thomas and Haldek," he said. "And Rhillyon.

They'll be worried about us. As soon as you think you're capable of riding, I'll help you onto your horse."

"CAN I SPEAK WITH YOU, DAHRA?" Thomas had been dreading this moment, but he knew he could put it off no longer.

The older woman looked at him curiously before nodding and leading him to a quiet place among the trees. She sat down on a fallen log and gazed up at him.

The laughter of children and the sounds of normal life penetrated faintly to their location, but Dahra had chosen a setting that seemed to radiate tranquility.

With Agon dead and the Rogandans repelled, the Aen-ur had celebrated wildly for a couple of days. Since then everything had quickly returned to normal.

For some, nothing would ever be the same.

"You've been working with Ennawi," he ventured.

She nodded. "He's a sad case. His spirit was broken a very long time ago. Nistinaa has been trying to help, but there is only so much I can do for him."

"You were able to help people in the past," he said. "Much more than you can now."

She gazed at him in her quiet way, but she didn't speak.

"I think you've guessed, haven't you?" he said. When she still didn't reply, he added, "Would it help if I call you Sheylha, the Seer?"

Her face went pale.

"I have the Stone of Knowing now—the stone you once called your own."

He took a deep breath. "I didn't know you existed before we came here. I was touching the stone when I first saw you, because I wanted to understand people's intentions. I saw that you'd held the stone for many years. Until you got rid of it."

She didn't seem able to speak.

"I tried to tell Amyra, you know," he said awkwardly. "Ahnya as she was. I tried to tell her that her father didn't abandon her. I'm not sure that it helped."

The anguished look in her eyes made him wince.

"I'm not very good at this kind of thing," he said remorsefully. "My wife Elena is much better at it. It's remarkable how much she's achieved, even with so little practice." He shook his head. "But she isn't here."

He took another deep breath to steady himself. "You, though—you are here, and you're a master. You worked with the stone over many years, and it's astonishing how much you were able to do for people."

All trace of expression had vanished from her face, and her eyes were guarded.

He sighed. "I'm not using it right now," he assured her. "When I first found it I abused it badly. Eventually I decided not to use it on people I know. Everything I discovered about you was from our first meeting—I haven't used it on you since."

He passed a hand over his eyes. "What I saw shook me to the core though," he admitted. "I haven't been able to get it out of my mind."

Her face had grown calm again, but still she found nothing to say.

He knew what he needed to do. For so long he felt trapped by the stone, bemoaning his inability to break free of it. Now an opportunity had come. Why did he feel like he was about to lose a vital organ?

He shook his head and set his jaw. This wasn't about him. He had seen into Ennawi's mind, witnessed the full extent of the abuse the slave had endured over the years. No one apart from Dahra had even a chance of helping him. Thomas could never live with himself if he refused her the opportunity.

The choice was clear—he could play his part in repairing a lifetime's worth of abuse, or he could selfishly hoard the stone, to use or not use as he saw fit.

He sighed deeply. Reaching for the chain, he withdrew it from beneath his clothing and pulled it over his head. As his hand closed over the stone he was careful to look away.

Heart pounding, he opened his hand and held it out.

Out of the corner of his eye he could see that she hadn't moved.

"Take it!" he insisted.

After an agonizing delay she slowly stretched out her hand.

He took one more deep breath in a futile attempt to calm himself. "It's yours," he said firmly. "I want you to have it."

As she took the stone from his hand, his eyes found their way to her again. He felt suddenly naked, and heat rose up to cover his face.

Her eyes had closed briefly when she took the stone. Opening them again, she stared directly at him. He steadied himself under her gaze, finally managing to bring his racing heart under control.

After a long moment she abruptly dropped the stone into her lap. A flush came to her face.

"You can have it back now," she said, although she made no move to return it.

He shook his head. "You know why I've given it to you. You need to help Ennawi."

Slowly her face grew calm again, and she nodded her head.

He opened his mouth to explain how she could rotate the clasp to control the contact of the stone with her skin. Then he remembered that she didn't need to be told.

"I didn't entirely believe you, Thomas," she admitted. "About not using the stone once you got to know someone." Her face briefly reddened once more, and she wouldn't meet his eyes. "You've been much more respectful of others than I ever was. But then you already know that."

He shook his head. "You only ever used it to help people. You never abused it the way I did."

Her face was noncommittal. "Perhaps not. But I intruded constantly on people's thoughts without their knowledge. I didn't even spare my own husband. Almost until the end he had no idea what I was doing."

She shook her head. "It was still a form of abuse, for all that I tried to use it for good. I've had many years to reach that conclusion for myself, but until you came along I couldn't see it. Perhaps I wasn't willing to."

Her face set in determination. "I will try to help Ennawi. But starting from now, I won't knowingly intrude on people again."

HAVING RECEIVED a request from Dahra to join her at her hut, Will made his way there with considerable curiosity. She met him at the door and ushered him inside.

He studied her furtively as he followed her in. Her daughter's resemblance to her was striking, although he decided that Amyra had fire and she had grace. If Dahra had ever been as fiery as her daughter, she had long since mellowed.

"Please!" said the older woman, waving him to a seat.

He obediently sat where she directed him.

"Tell me about your limp, Will," she said.

He shrugged. "It's an old battle wound. The lower half of my body was crushed under a horse."

"Does your back cause you pain?"

He nodded.

"Constantly?"

He shrugged again.

She rolled her eyes. "Men! Some of you seem to think a battered body is a virtue. The more damaged, the better."

He didn't respond.

"Can I examine you?"

He gazed at her uncertainly for a moment, then nodded.

"Take off your top, and lie face down on that table," she told him, pointing to a flat surface covered by a blanket. It stood just below waist height.

He hesitated for a moment before doing as she requested. The situation brought back uncomfortable memories of his introduction to Lady Ona, and he felt unusually vulnerable.

A large pot of steaming water stood by the fireplace, and she gingerly drew a blanket from it. After folding the blanket many times, she placed it into an empty tub between two thick pieces of wood and squeezed out the hot water.

After a couple more minutes she brought the still steaming blanket over to him. After touching it to her face to test the temperature, she placed it carefully across his back. After the initial shock, the warmth felt very soothing.

She lifted the blanket to expose the lower part of his back. “This is going to hurt,” she warned. “Probably quite a lot. Rest assured that I won’t be doing you any damage.”

She was soon prodding and pressing around his lower spine. Her warning was not overstated—some of the probing left him clenching his teeth to manage the pain.

Eventually she slapped him lightly on the back. “You’re a tough one,” she told him jovially. “You can dress again. I want to see you again in three days.”

She briefly described a few exercises. “Do each of them once a day. And don’t come back with excuses about why you didn’t find the time!” She gazed at him with an eyebrow raised threateningly.

“Thanks,” he said. “I think.” He nodded to her, then turned to go.

“Will!” she called softly.

He looked back over his shoulder.

“Follow your heart,” she told him, an unreadable look on her face.

He faced her again, frowning. “What does that mean?”

A wry smile came to her lips. “You do know what your heart is, don’t you?” she teased.

When he didn’t respond, she sighed. “You lead men, Will Prentis, and you devise strategy. You’re very good at it. But a different kind of skill is needed for matters of the heart.”

He felt himself blushing like an awkward youth. Was it possible she’d somehow guessed his feelings for her daughter?

She looked at him seriously. “You’re actually much more capable than many men. You know how to build effective partnerships with difficult people, people who have very different backgrounds and purposes from your own.” She grinned knowingly at him. “That particular skill happens to have very broad application.”

He didn't know what to say.

"There's just one other thing you need to master," she told him, serious once more.

She had his full attention, and he tried hard not to look too eager.

"You need to learn to say what you're feeling. Women like that."

He stared at her wide-eyed.

"It isn't exactly *what* you say that matters," she assured him. "The fact that you're making the effort will count for a lot."

He stood unmoving, his thoughts whirling chaotically.

"Off you go!" she ordered firmly, waving her hands to shoo him out.

Jolted unceremoniously back to reality, he spun around and hurried out of her hut.

BACK PAIN HAD BEEN part of Will's daily experience for years. Like his limp, he had come to accept it as normal. Although Dahra's efforts had left him wincing, he didn't actually feel worse when he left her. And after a day or two he began to feel noticeably better.

After his second visit he began to catch glimpses of a quality of life he had long forgotten, one he had believed gone forever. And her efforts had already begun to improve his limp.

She was changing his life.

"Dahra, I don't know how to repay you," he told her seriously.

"Nonsense," she replied. "No repayment is necessary." She paused. "There might be something you can do for me though."

He gazed expectantly at her.

"I'll let you know when the time comes," she told him vaguely.

He left her with a shrug.

Spending time with Dahra inevitably set him thinking about her daughter.

He had completed everything he came to Rogand to do. Far more, thanks to the contributions of Rhillyon and others. Amyra, too, had played a key role at the end.

No Rogandan army would be attempting to force the border with

Arvenon now. No further reason remained to delay his return to King Steffan.

No reason except Amyra. He would not leave Rogand without making an attempt to win her. He couldn't pretend he felt confident, but he had never been one to shy away from difficulties. And he wasn't entirely without hope. She had pursued him into Agon's camp, almost with disastrous consequences for herself. Did that mean anything?

He knew one of the biggest challenges of his life lay before him. Dahra could say all she wanted about following his heart, but he had more basic problems to overcome first. From his first meeting with Amyra he had succeeded in alienating her, ignoring her advice and bypassing her as translator. Opportunities for irritation had only multiplied from there. And while he found her hopelessly appealing, she had made a point of telling him to his face that she found him unattractive.

A much bigger problem had been weighing heavily on him though. Almost immediately after taking the Stone of Authority, she had discovered how to bend it to her purpose. She made it appear effortless—the memory of her mastery still filled him with awe. With the stone she had rallied nature to end a battle before it began.

The invaders had been routed without loss of life on either side, and her achievement confronted him with a difficult truth. If he had been the one to awaken nature, he would not have hesitated to turn it against the Rogandans.

He was a man of blood. Multitudes had died as a result of his mastery at war. Not just his enemies—his own men had drunk deeply from the same chalice.

It wasn't that he thought he should have acted differently in the past—he could see no other options. But Amyra, faced with the destruction of the people she loved, had conceived of a different way and imagined it into being.

How could a man like him ever hope to win such a woman?

43

For better or for worse, the time had come for Will to find out if he had any hope of a future with Amyra. He knew she liked to spend time alone in the forest when she could, and having once glimpsed her horse in the distance tied to a tree, he thought he had a rough idea where he might find her. Mounting his own horse, he gathered his courage and headed for the location.

Her horse was exactly where he expected it to be. After securing his mount beside it, he picked his way through the trees in search of her.

Not far in he came upon a small clearing. The sight he saw there took his breath away.

Amyra stood on the far side of the glade. One of her arms was raised high, and a host of brilliantly colored butterflies filled the air around her.

He watched wide-eyed as she slowly weaved her arm back and forth through the air. Glimmers of blue, red, purple, and every color of the rainbow danced before his eyes as the fluttering insects swirled about her in a delicate cloud, imitating her every movement. She swept her arm majestically in a circular motion, down and up again, and the butterflies dipped and soared smoothly in response. He stood entranced, oblivious to all else.

How long it went on he couldn't say, but a wave of disappointment washed over him when the spectacle finally came to an end. She dropped a small object into a leather pouch; he didn't need to be told what the object was. Then she stood quietly, watching as the colorful cloud slowly dispersed.

All this time he'd scarcely dared to breathe. As he shifted position she finally noticed him. A delicate blush tinged her cheeks when she realized he'd been watching her.

Stepping into the open, he approached her slowly. "How did you learn to do that?" he asked in wonder.

Her slender shoulders lifted in a shrug, setting her hazelnut brown tresses swaying. "It was a chance discovery. The stone seems to have a gentler side," she said with a faint smile.

In her hands, the stone was presiding over creativity rather than coercion. It came as no surprise to him.

His breath hitched as he gazed down into her face. He'd always seen the fire that flashed in her hazel eyes, but how could he have failed to be captivated by how beautiful they were?

She was no ordinary woman. Could he really do this?

He checked himself. He needed to stay focused. A challenge lay before him, but he would find a way through it. He always did.

"What brings you here, Will?" she asked quietly.

He sucked in a breath, telling himself it couldn't be that hard. "I want to speak with you," he finally managed.

She raised her eyebrows questioningly, watching him far too intently for his comfort.

In an attempt to collect himself he looked beyond her, into the trees. "I've been thinking," he began. "About a lot of things. The stone —in Agon's hands—it got me to do things. Things that made no sense."

He looked back into her face and almost lost his way again. Diverting his eyes once more, he tried again. "It got me wondering— are there other things I've been doing? Things that make no sense?"

Had he repeated himself? This wasn't working. He needed to change course before it turned into a complete disaster.

He thought he had rehearsed what he was going to say when he talked with her, but the words had become a jumbled mess in his mind. Releasing a heavy sigh, he gave up any attempt at delivering a speech.

In the heat of battle he had sometimes been forced to abandon caution entirely and follow his instinct. He decided now to do something he couldn't ever remember doing before. He would just talk—about himself.

He began at once, before he could change his mind.

"I never knew my parents," he said. "I was raised by my uncle and his Rogandan wife. I think my uncle cared about me in his own way, but from the beginning my aunt never liked me, and she took every opportunity to abuse me. I had no siblings, and they never had children of their own. I was their only child, but it never felt like we were family."

She stood completely still, her big eyes fixed on him.

Now that he was underway, the words were welling up inside him. "There was no reason for me to stay. I had no idea where I belonged, but I knew it wasn't with them. All I wanted was to make my mark in the world, and I decided the best way to do that was to become a soldier. I don't see it that way now, but it was all I knew at the time. Things just happened after that. I think I ended up in the right place at the right time."

He had no idea what she was thinking. But it was too late to stop. He'd set his course, and he would follow it to the end. "Once I started leading the army, life became overwhelming. I never found time to think about anything else. After the invasion, the king made me a nobleman and granted me holdings in Erestor—I have no idea why. But I can see now I was being given a chance at a new beginning. I didn't take it. The idea of settling down never even occurred to me.

"So here I am, years later, still wandering the world in a vain attempt to fix it." He smiled, but there was no mirth in it. "You already know how that's been working out for me. If it hadn't been for the assassin, I'd still be under Agon's power." His chin dropped to his chest. "I even turned you over to the maniac," he added miserably.

Amyra gave no response.

How could she remain silent for so long? He'd hardly known a woman to be lost for something to say.

"I never thanked you for coming to rescue me," he blurted. "It was incredibly brave!" He frowned at her. "Incredibly foolish."

Still she held her peace.

He threw up his hands in frustration. "I'm no good at this," he exclaimed, shaking his head. "There's a reason for it, too—I grew up without a woman's influence. It's left me tongue tied when it comes to feelings. I care about things, and about people. I truly do! But I don't know how to talk about it. I always thought it's the way I was made. But maybe it's just another thing I've been doing that makes no sense."

He heaved a deep sigh. For better or for worse, he'd managed to get something out.

"Thank you," she said, her voice gentle. "That can't have been easy. It means a lot that you've shared it with me."

He stole a quick glance at her. "My face will always be scarred," he said awkwardly. "But my limp is gone at least."

She stared at him blankly.

"It was your mother," he explained. "She's been working on my back."

Her eyebrows twitched together in a puzzled frown. She clearly had no idea what he was talking about.

He shrugged in resignation. "You told me that a scarred face and a limp are not at all attractive to a woman."

Merry laughter burst out of her. "And you took me seriously? Oh, Will!"

He stared back at her, completely nonplussed.

She took a step closer, and his heart began to pound.

"There's a lot more to you than your scars, Will Prentis. From the very beginning, it was obvious to me what you have up there," she told him, delicately placing a finger on his forehead. His whole face tingled at her touch. "You have a sharp mind, and you use it to great effect."

She paused for a moment. "You're self-sacrificing, too—I've seen that for myself."

A delicate flush tinged her cheeks. "You need to know that I quizzed Thomas and Haldek about you," she confessed. "You're a strong leader, but I'm well aware that you're also humble and compassionate."

She nodded solemnly. "Yes, Will, I'm afraid your secrets have been exposed." Her hazel eyes twinkled mischievously.

"But until today I hadn't glimpsed anything at all of what's going on in *here*." Amyra touched a finger to his heart, setting it pounding even harder. She lowered her voice almost to a whisper. "I must say, I like what I've been seeing."

Her beautiful eyes settled on his, and he swallowed, barely able to think straight.

She stepped closer. "Did you come here today to woo me, Will Prentis?" she asked him softly.

She was beautiful, she was beyond amazing, and she was everything his heart could possibly desire.

He could bear it no longer. Reaching out, he swept her into his arms, clasping her to himself almost with desperation.

Her face turned upward to him, and he bent down instinctively, pressing his lips onto hers. She kissed him back with a passion that sent fire racing through his veins. He cradled her head tenderly in one hand, and in response she stretched up her arms to send fingers snaking through his hair.

Time seemed to stand still as he lost himself in the miracle of her embrace.

When eventually they drew apart he stood breathing heavily, holding her at arm's length and gazing into her eyes. He couldn't speak—his heart was too full. It was more than enough just to soak her in. She gazed back at him in silence, a smile playing across her lovely face.

Dahra had been right about what he needed to say. He hadn't

planned what had come out though—he'd simply done the best he could, and somehow they'd found their way together.

"I had no idea what I was saying," he finally confessed. "I've faced major battles feeling less nervous."

"The fearless commander, quaking before a woman?" she teased.

"I've never met a woman like you," he said. "I never dared to believe I had any hope of winning you."

"You underestimate yourself, Will," she said with a shake of her pretty head. "My heart has been in your keeping almost from the day I met you, even though I stubbornly refused to admit it to myself."

He gazed at her in wonder. Then he drew her close once more, heaving a sigh of complete contentment.

When at last they walked hand in hand from the clearing, he discovered that the whole world had changed. The birds sang more brightly, the snatches of blue in the sky above were more brilliant.

Will stole glances at her as they walked, unable to keep the smile from his face. Then they mounted their horses and rode to the settlement side by side.

WILL WASTED no time seeking out Dahra, Amyra at his side. The older woman didn't need to be told what had happened between them. She took one look at their faces and burst out laughing.

"You look like you've figured out the meaning of the word 'happy,'" she told Will. "As for you," she said, turning to Amyra, "you look like you've finally discovered how to relax. Not before time!"

Will glanced self-consciously at Amyra. She treated him to a beguiling look intended for him alone.

Dahra raised an eyebrow. "I do hope you realize what you've taken on, Will," she warned. "She might be all smiles and sunshine now, but she's feisty enough for the two of you."

Then she grinned at them. "Your lives will never lack drama. But I have to say I'm confident you're going to make each other very happy."

44

The following day Will found himself heading to Dahra's hut with Amyra once more. Amyra would have nestled comfortably into his shoulder if he'd let her. He wanted it as much as she did, but Thomas had joined them, and Will was feeling extremely self-conscious.

In spite of Will's self-restraint, Thomas was clearly aware that something was up. Will turned to Dahra, eager to divert attention elsewhere. "I'm sure I'm not the only one who would like to know how Ennawi is," he said.

He chose the right topic, because Thomas immediately redirected his full attention to Dahra.

"I'm happy to tell you," said Dahra. "Before I begin, it might be helpful for you to know that Amyra has told me all about the scroll. I know how Thomas was able to discover Agon's plans through Ennawi. And he has been a great help in my attempts to better understand Ennawi."

Will nodded. He glanced at Thomas, who for some reason appeared to be carefully studying the floor at his feet. Will guessed he must have used the stone to study Ennawi, and passed on to Dahra whatever he learned.

"So how is Ennawi?" asked Will.

"I feel more hopeful than I would ever have imagined," she said. "He has a long road ahead of him, but he has taken some promising initial steps."

"What have you discovered about his background?" asked Amyra.

"It wasn't easy to get to the bottom of it," she sighed, "but between us we have been able to dig it out in the end. Nistinaa helped too, of course," she added hastily.

Her eyebrows drew together. "His situation is so complex and so incredible you could be forgiven for refusing to believe it. Lord Drettroth was the one who organized for him to be placed with King Agon, although the king had no awareness of who'd done it."

She waited for the expressions of amazement to fade away.

"It was also Drettroth who arranged an abundant supply of the potion that enabled Ennawi not to react to Agon's abuse. The supply never failed, even after his death. The potion is the only thing that kept Agon from killing him—that and Ennawi's inability to pass on anything he heard the king say. Where the potion came from I don't know, but apparently Drettroth made quite a study of poisons and their effects. This seems to have been one of his more unusual concoctions. What made it hard for Ennawi is that the drug allowed him to remain fully aware of everything that was happening, even though he never showed any sign of it. The abuse has been wearing away at him for years."

"And Ennawi had no way of striking back," said Will.

"No," agreed Dahra. "Ennawi had plenty of reason to want to harm Agon, even without the abuse. The king was the one who ordered his hands and his tongue to be cut off. I'm sure Agon wasn't aware of that when Ennawi joined him, though. Sooner or later he would have said something to Ennawi if he'd known."

Ignoring their astonishment, she pressed on.

"It happened when he was young. Word reached Agon that Ennawi's father had spoken against the king, so Agon ordered in a rage that the tongues of everyone in the family should be cut out. He demanded to be told if any further trouble surfaced in the region.

Some time later he was told that a child had repeatedly been caught stealing bread, and he apparently ordered the child's hands to be cut off.

"I imagine that Agon had no way of knowing that the same child had been affected by both actions. He probably forgot even giving the orders. But the first punishment led directly to the second. Once the family had been marked, the father couldn't work. All of them began to starve, so the young son turned to stealing.

"After the second punishment was carried out, Drettroth somehow found out about it. He took the family in and arranged for them to be cared for, perhaps wanting to make himself look good in comparison with Agon. Then he had Ennawi placed with Agon. A drugged Ennawi would have made for an ideal listener—one with no way of passing on anything he heard. Drettroth had known Agon since childhood, and he must have guessed that Agon could never resist blurting out all his secrets to such a person."

A look of horror came to Amyra's face. "So Agon was abusing Ennawi every day. And the whole time Ennawi knew that Agon had been responsible for his condition, but Agon didn't?" she asked.

Dahra nodded. "That's a good summary. You can imagine how much Ennawi has been damaged by everything that's happened."

The revelations appalled Will. His own newfound happiness seemed almost obscene when seen alongside the relentless and seemingly endless blows that Ennawi had endured.

"How did it benefit Drettroth to place him with Agon?" asked Will.

Dahra turned to Thomas.

Thomas sighed. "It's one of the first things I discovered from Ennawi," he said. "Drettroth was quite open about his reasons. One of his greatest ambitions was to acquire the Stone of Knowing. He was anticipating a day when he had taken possession of it. He would be able to read Agon's thoughts himself through direct contact, but if Agon ever refused to see Drettroth for any reason, Ennawi would provide an alternate way of discovering Agon's plans. Ennawi did eventually prove useful in exposing Agon's thoughts and plans, of course, even if not in the way Drettroth intended."

Will frowned. "And that was all there was to it?" he asked.

Thomas shook his head. "There was more. Drettroth was a subtle and devious man, and I'm not sure I fully comprehend all of his reasons. But the depth of his hatred toward Agon came through clearly in what he said to Ennawi. Agon was cruel to Drettroth from their earliest years, and it came to a head when Drettroth stumbled on the Stone of Authority while they were both still young. Neither of them realized what the stone was at the time, but Agon tricked him into handing it over, and Drettroth never forgave him. When Drettroth later learned about the true value of the stone, he hated Agon even more.

"After that incident, the young Drettroth decided to devote himself to bringing Agon down. He was canny about it. To all appearances he was Agon's strongest supporter. All the while he was making sure he strengthened himself through everything he did for the king."

"What did that have to do with Ennawi?" asked Amyra.

"Drettroth told Ennawi all this," Thomas replied. "He also told him that he was going to arrange for Agon to be killed, but he didn't provide details. If Drettroth failed and Agon got the Stone of Knowing, Agon would have discovered Drettroth's intentions from Ennawi. Agon would always be wondering what Drettroth might have planned. And Drettroth arranged that the assassin wouldn't be hired until well after his own death. By then Agon might have thought he could relax."

"It sounds bizarre," said Amyra, a baffled look on her face. "Why would he go to so much trouble for a reason like that?"

"I think I can guess at the answer, at least in part," said Will. "Drettroth captured me during the Rogandan invasion of Arvenon when I tried to infiltrate his camp posing as a priest. He had plenty else to do at the time, but he found time to taunt me. I think he derived pleasure from taunting his victims."

Thomas nodded. "I'm sure you're right."

"Ennawi might not have known what Drettroth was planning, but we do now," said Will.

"The assassin," said Amyra.

"Yes," agreed Will. "Drettroth might even have made other plans as well that we don't know about."

They all fell silent, musing.

"Drettroth must have hated Agon with a bitter passion," said Amyra finally.

"Yes, he did," Thomas agreed. "His hatred lasted a lifetime and beyond."

Dahra shook her head in disgust. "The two of them were as bad as each other," she said. "Both men were responsible for the years of abuse Ennawi suffered at the hands of Agon. They hurt him so much, and he needs to find a way to forgive them, or he'll be eaten up with bitterness for the rest of his life."

Will couldn't help but be relieved when the conversation gradually turned to less harrowing topics.

Eventually Dahra addressed herself to him directly. "When will you be leaving?" she asked.

"Soon," he replied. "King Steffan and Queen Essanda need to know what's happened here."

Dahra glanced at Amyra. "I imagine you'll be accompanying Will," she said.

Her daughter nodded. "We're planning to get married in Arnost. Once control of the city returns to King Steffan, of course. You will come for the wedding, won't you?" she asked anxiously.

Dahra grinned. "Nothing could keep me away," she assured them.

"Would you ever consider relocating to my holdings in Erestor?" asked Will hopefully.

"There's only one thing that could possibly induce me," Dahra replied.

"Grandchildren," said Amyra, rolling her eyes.

Dahra laughed, but she didn't deny it.

Thomas had been listening to the conversation with open astonishment on his face. Will leaned in close to him. "If you don't close your mouth soon, Thomas, a bird might decide to make a nest in there," he whispered. Then he clapped Thomas on the back with a wink.

As they were leaving Dahra's hut, Will turned back to her. "You said there might be something I can do for you," he reminded her.

"You've already done it," she assured him with a smile.

THE DAY of their departure had finally arrived. After so long away from his family, Thomas was impatient to be reunited with Elena and Tammi and Rubin. He was also aware that Haldek was barely less eager to see them again, even though his return to Arvenon might well mean his final farewell to the land of his birth.

As for Thomas, his own future was uncertain. He was planning to suggest to Elena that they join the community at Newhaven, along with Rubin and Haldek. They should be able to remain safely hidden there. He also thought they could invite his parents to join them.

It had briefly occurred to him that without the stone there was little reason to hide away anymore. But the people who had been searching for him wouldn't know he had given it up. Even without Agon paying them, they might decide to pursue him anyway in the hope of robbing him of whatever the king had been searching for. He concluded that Newhaven was a good choice even without the stone.

Now Will and Amyra were to be married, and Thomas imagined they might locate themselves on Will's holdings in Erestor. Newhaven wasn't impossibly far away from there; perhaps the two families could visit each other from time to time.

Will had told Thomas that Amyra now held the Stone of Authority and had described what she'd done with it. He also spoke openly of his love for the young woman. Thomas still hadn't decided which revelation astonished him the most.

Thomas had never glimpsed the vaguest hint of a romantic side to Will, and he was still coming to terms with the relationship between Will and Amyra. It seemed all the more remarkable given the way Amyra had appeared to despise Will. Appearances could certainly be deceptive.

Thomas was delighted for them both, and he had been trying to tell himself that nothing was more important than Will's news. As they prepared to leave, though, little else occupied his mind except the missing chain around his neck. He hadn't yet found a way to tell Will that he no longer had the Stone of Knowing. He had decided to wait until they left Aen-irac.

Atae, Rhillyon, and others among the Aen-ur had assembled to wish them well on their journey, and especially to bid their final farewells to Amyra. Thomas noticed more than one young man among the crowd directing dark looks at Will.

At that moment Dahra and Amyra were locked in a tearful parting embrace. Dahra had finally opened up to Amyra, revealing the details of her life before she met her husband, Kalvor, describing their years together, and recounting the events that led to his death. The two women had talked far into the night with many tears on both sides.

Dahra herself had told Thomas about it later. He wondered if he had precipitated the interaction by his comments to Amyra about her father, and he apologized to Dahra for raising the subject. She assured him that he'd done both of them a favor.

Dahra and Amyra might be parting now, but their separation was expected to be short-lived. Dahra intended to travel to Arnost as soon as it was safe to do so, and Will had promised to send an escort when that moment arrived.

None of the travelers had any idea what they might find across the border. Will expected Rellan and Lord Burtelen to be stationed there with an army. The status of the other Arvenian army was still unknown, but Arnost was almost certainly still occupied, and Castel remained to be freed from the influence of Eisgold. However, Agon's death meant that no further support would flow to either Pisander or Eisgold, and Will was confident that a way would be found to deal with them both. They would be dealt with permanently this time.

Amyra finally mounted, and all of them waved their farewells. As

Thomas was about to ride away, Dahra hurried up to him, beckoning him to bend down to her.

Dahra reached for his hand as he did so and pressed a folded piece of cloth into it. Something firm lay hidden within the folds.

"I'm giving it back," she whispered, a sober expression on her face. "It belongs to you again."

Thomas was too astonished to reply.

"I never really wanted it," she told him. "I've done what was needed with Ennawi, and I want to be rid of it. After all these years without it, the insights have felt oppressive. You and your admirable wife will be much better guardians of it. I'm very much looking forward to meeting her, Thomas!"

She stepped back into the crowd, giving him opportunity to do no more than wave an acknowledgment.

The moment Thomas found himself riding apart from the others, he opened his hand and unfolded the piece of cloth. Inside he found the chain and the clasp with the stone. Slipping it back over his head, he concealed it once more beneath his clothing.

He took a deep breath, then released a long sigh. With the stone around his neck once more, the familiar feelings of ambivalence had returned in full force.

The situation had changed, though. It somehow comforted him to know that the Stone of Knowing was no longer the only arcane influence in his world. The Stone of Authority was also heading to Arvenon, and in safe hands at last.

And he was going home. With Elena's help he had always found a way to deal with the unnerving predicaments presented by the stone. New challenges would not be long in coming, of that he was certain. When they did, he and Elena would face them together.

THOMAS WAS STARTLED out of a dream by a weight that squeezed the breath from his lungs. A rag covered his mouth, and a knee was pressed hard against his chest. Thomas struggled to open his eyes.

"Get up! Quietly!" whispered a harsh voice.

The knee was removed, and he was hauled to his feet. The fire at their campsite flickered low, and everything around him was quiet. He glimpsed the motionless forms of Will and Haldek, apparently soundly asleep. He couldn't spot Amyra, but he knew she was sleeping nearby, on the other side of the fire.

Bustling him away from the firelight, his captor pulled him to a halt among the trees.

"Agon wanted you badly, Thomas," growled the voice. "Badly enough to drag me to Rog to put some kind of spell on me. And you actually left Varas and went to him! I never reached him in time to tell him. And now he's dead."

Thomas's heart raced as a blade pressed against his throat, cold on his skin.

"I'm my own man again now," the intruder continued. "And I didn't go through all this for nothing. You've got his heirloom, or whatever it is, and I'm not leaving without it. Hand it over without a fuss, and I might even decide to kill you quickly."

"Let him go!" commanded a woman's voice. Thomas's eyes flicked up to see Amyra poised at the edge of the campsite.

"Come a step closer and he dies immediately!" warned Thomas's captor. The pressure of the knife increased at Thomas's throat. "Hand it over, Thomas," snarled the voice, "then I can go kill her too."

Thomas's mind spun, his body frozen.

Before he could respond, a screech shattered the night. Something dark glided above them, descending rapidly toward the two men.

The intruder cried out in alarm as dark wings beat about his face. "What *is* that?" He crouched low, slashing his blade wildly above his head.

Finding himself suddenly free, Thomas stumbled hastily away from his captor.

A knife flew through the air, burying itself in the body of the writhing man. He went down hard, falling directly onto the knife. He didn't get up.

Haldek appeared, rolling the intruder over to retrieve his knife. He grimaced as he examined the body. "He was going to kill you," he said to Thomas. "And her next," he added, jerking his head toward Amyra.

The young woman stood rooted to the spot, her face pale.

Will hurried to her side, not relaxing until he had assured himself she was unharmed. "You used the stone," he said softly.

She nodded unsteadily. "There was nothing nearby I could call on apart from the owl."

Thomas was struggling to master the trembling that shook his body. "You saved my life," he breathed. "Thank you."

Amyra shook her head. "It was nothing," she protested dully.

Haldek had returned to the fire and built it up again, and soon all of them had gathered around it, staring silently into the flames.

They were still huddled there when dawn broke. Working distractedly, Thomas helped Will and Haldek pile rocks over the body of his attacker. Even with the threat behind him he couldn't relax. Not with the fresh memory of the knife at his throat.

His would-be killer had been sent by Agon, and he had even known Thomas's name. The man's words echoed hauntingly in his mind.

"I imagine there's a story behind him," said Will.

"I don't want to know it," Thomas returned emphatically.

He felt nothing but relief when they mounted up once more and rode away from the campsite, continuing their journey toward Arvenon.

Thomas's mind was numb. Once again the stone had almost cost him his life.

Would it never end?

45

Lord Mardone watched covertly as Lord Eisgold stumbled along a corridor of Castel Citadel. Hidden in the shadows beside Mardone stood Count Gordan.

"Something's happened," Mardone ventured. "Eisgold is blundering about as if he's in a fog."

"The time has come," Gordan responded. "It will be too late for the king if we don't act soon."

"How many of the others are with us?" Mardone asked.

"We can count on two or three of them," Gordan told him. "The rest are still wavering. We're wasting our time pursuing them further."

They continued to observe Eisgold until he disappeared from their sight.

Mardone turned to his friend. "So we move tonight?"

Gordan nodded. "Tonight."

King Rupert lay in his bed, groaning softly. The pounding in his head and the twisting in his gut had prostrated him once more.

When would it end? He was only seventeen years old, much too young to die.

At first he failed to notice the four men who burst into his bedroom. He became aware of them when they appeared at his bedside and began lifting him bodily from his bed. When he opened his mouth to protest, they thrust a gag into it.

Every fiber of his being cried out, "Treason!", but the gag in his mouth prevented him from uttering a sound, and he was too weak to struggle. They bustled him out the door of his bedchamber—a door that should have been secured by his royal guards. No guards were anywhere to be seen.

He was hurried along an empty corridor, only to scramble down another corridor and another, until he had lost all sense of direction. All he knew was that they were traveling through rarely trafficked corners of the castle.

He had the presence of mind to recognize that they could have knifed him at any time, with no one to witness it. He could only conclude that they didn't intend to kill him. Not yet, anyway. That was some consolation.

Eventually they turned into a dark room, and the motion stopped. The youthful king was placed into a chair and his gag removed. A man he couldn't recognize in the dim light bowed low before him.

"I apologize for the abduction, Your Majesty," said a voice he knew. "We have done it only for your protection."

"What is the meaning of this treason, My Lord?" he demanded.

"Have you ever had reason to suspect me of disloyalty to the crown, Your Majesty?" Mardone asked, bowing respectfully again.

Rupert frowned. After the events of this evening, he wanted to answer in the affirmative. But he couldn't honestly do it. "Before tonight, no," he replied.

"You have no reason to doubt me now, Your Majesty! I am fiercely loyal to you, as I was to your father. Would you be willing to trust me, just for a few minutes? I want to invite you to observe something."

Annoyed as he was, Rupert was at least a little curious. Why had Mardone risked everything to bring him here?

"Very well," he grunted. "It had better be worth my while!"

"We must be very quiet, Your Majesty." The nobleman led him to a wall and uncovered a couple of peepholes. Rupert found himself staring down into a section of the royal kitchens. A maid was preparing food on a tray. He recognized the tray and some of the dishes. The food was intended for him.

Two men approached the maid. "Move aside, woman!" one of them ordered.

"Not so, sir! This is the king's meal. You cannot tamper with it!"

The second newcomer delivered a stinging blow to the maid's face, knocking her to her knees. "Don't talk back," he spat. "This is the king's medicine, prescribed by the royal physician. Don't interfere if you know what's good for you."

He pulled a vial from within his clothing, and shook a few drops into the king's wine.

The first man pulled the maid to her feet. "Now take this to the king, and don't make a fuss if you know what's good for you."

The second man shook his head as the maid hurried away. "Where's the usual girl?" he growled. "Eisgold will have our heads if word of this gets out."

The king looked on, too stunned to speak.

He continued to watch wide-eyed as royal guards appeared in the kitchens and dragged both men away.

"As Your Majesty can see, the traitors are being dealt with," said Lord Mardone with satisfaction. He covered the peepholes once more, and candles were lit in the room.

"I'm sorry you had to witness that, Your Majesty," he said. "The usual maid is in the pay of these men. We arranged for her to be replaced tonight so that you would see them in their true colors."

Rupert stared at the nobleman, aghast at what he had seen. The rumors that he was being poisoned were nothing new, but he had steadfastly refused to believe them. And yet all of them were true.

And the poisoners had named Eisgold as a conspirator.

Some of his noblemen had tried to warn him about Eisgold, and he had turned on them. A flush of shame came to his face as he recalled the rage he had directed at Count Gordan when the count dared to assert that pardoning Eisgold was dishonoring the memory of his father.

"Please read this, Your Majesty," said Lord Mardone, handing him a partially burned parchment. "One of our people rescued it from the fireplace in Lord Eisgold's apartments."

He skimmed through the scorched remnants of the parchment, barely able to believe what he was reading. The document was addressed to Lord Eisgold and signed and sealed by Agon of Rogand. It reminded Eisgold forcefully that Agon expected an early return on the generous payments he had advanced to Eisgold.

Rupert looked up into the concern on Lord Mardone's face. He knew he did not deserve the nobleman's sympathy. He could only be appalled by his own blindness and ashamed of his foolishness.

"Eisgold must be arrested at once!" he said.

Lord Mardone nodded to his men, and two of them left the room at once. "It will be done, Your Majesty. In the meantime, it is safest if you remain here with us."

Several hours passed before Rupert heard a knock at the door. The person admitted was none other than Count Gordan. The count came and knelt before him, kissing his hand.

"I owe you the most abject of apologies, Gordan!" the king told him.

"Your Majesty was deceived and imposed upon," Gordan replied.

"What of Eisgold?" Lord Mardone asked.

"He is dead," Gordan replied. "When we arrived we found that he had poisoned himself. He must have had hints of what was coming. Perhaps his end was fitting in view of his actions toward the king. He lived long enough to insist that he had been bewitched by Agon, and that he never intended harm either to Castel or to the king."

"How could he have expected such a story to be believed?" asked Rupert, shaking his head incredulously. "And what of his lackeys? My blindness seems to have been lifted at last, and it is now apparent to me that he has been spreading his parasites throughout the capital."

"The traitors will be rounded up, Your Majesty," Lord Mardone assured him. "When it becomes known that Eisgold is dead, any waverers will quickly fall into line."

"I don't know how to thank you both," the king told them. "You have saved my life and restored my kingdom to me."

"No thanks are necessary, Your Majesty," Count Gordan replied. "We are doing no more than our duty as loyal servants of the crown."

PISANDER PACED SULLENLY in the castle's main reception hall, waiting impatiently for his deputy.

When Lygell arrived, he was nervous and fidgeting. "Armies are approaching the city from two directions! The one from Varas is almost at the gates," he said, his voice quavering.

Pisander stared at him contemptuously, slowly shaking his head. "Yes," he agreed, "the king is coming to reward his loyal subjects."

Lygell just stood there, wild-eyed.

"I hear you've been arguing with your lackeys," Pisander growled.

"Some of them dared to question my authority!" Lygell replied, his face petulant. "At a time like this!"

The former earl just stared at Lygell until his deputy began to be indignant. "Why are you looking at me like that? You appointed me as your deputy—I deserve your support!"

"You deserve to be hanged!" spat Pisander. "This is a time for decisive action, not for squabbling over the scraps left on the table." He shook his head again. "What did I ever see in you?"

"Jarah!" he called. Jarah stepped forward and bowed. Pisander jerked his head toward Lygell. "Hang him in the market square. Do it now."

Jarah waved over four of the guards. They surrounded the panicked deputy and grabbed hold of him tightly.

Lygell's struggles forced them to lift him bodily as they carried him away. "No! Wait! You can't do this!" The screams grew ever fainter as they dragged him from the castle.

Pisander put it out of his mind. Everything was rapidly falling apart around him. He had seen it coming from the day his mind had suddenly cleared. He'd been acting on Agon's behalf under compulsion; he understood that clearly only when the compulsion ceased.

Pisander had never been a man who readily succumbed to pressure, so how he had been coerced was a great mystery to him. But his thoughts returned again to his abortive search for the youth who'd intruded on the council meeting so long ago. Jarah had made real progress before Pisander called a halt to his search. It was regrettable, but he had needed the hunter in Arnost.

His investigations hadn't been limited to the youth either. He had also sent an agent to Rog in the hope of gaining insight into Agon's persuasiveness. Having heard nothing further from the man, he sent another agent with no better success. After that he'd become too distracted to pursue it further.

His thoughts were interrupted by the arrival of one of his aides. "I've been asked to pass on a message, My Lord," the aide told him, bowing low.

"I am expecting no message," Pisander told him with a frown. "Who was the messenger?"

The man bowed again. "I don't know him, My Lord, and he didn't wait around."

"Well? What's the message?" Pisander asked impatiently.

"He's heard that you are looking for reliable men, and he believes he can help." The aide hesitated. "He said he would sign on with you for the right price. He claims he knows where to find plenty of others as well. A man is waiting outside the city gates to guide you to a meeting place."

Pisander frowned at the aide. A meeting location outside the city sounded very suspicious.

"The messenger said if you weren't sure whether to trust him, you should bring as many guards as you thought you needed," added the aide. He looked at Pisander uncomfortably. "Those were his exact words."

So the invitation had come from someone who was either extremely bold or had nothing to hide.

Pisander couldn't ignore the truth—he needed all the help he could get. Executing Lygell only highlighted the problem. And he had never been in the habit of turning away mercenaries willing enough to hire out their services. If Agon was no longer in the picture, the flow of resources had already ended, of course. But he had plenty in reserve.

Pisander hesitated only for a moment. He had never hesitated to take the main chance, and it had carried him further than he could ever have dreamed. Now was not a time to begin playing it safe. Nevertheless, he was no fool—twenty men rode with him when he headed for the city gates.

The man waiting outside the gates was unknown to Pisander.

"My Lord," he said with a bow that bordered on the insolent. "Could you all please follow me? We don't have far to go."

The man's brazenness didn't alarm Pisander. He would have been more suspicious if the man had feigned respect.

After only a few minutes their guide turned aside and dismounted. "Follow me," he said.

One of the men stayed with the horses. Pisander and the others followed along behind.

A second man was waiting for them, and he bowed obsequiously as Pisander approached. "My Lord," he said.

"Well?" Pisander asked. "If you want to join me, well and good. But make it quick. Two armies are about to arrive on our doorstep."

"I have a slightly different proposition," the man replied with a sneer.

Fighting immediately broke out all around him. He should never have come without Jarah at his side.

Men swarmed around Pisander's guards, so many of them—fifty at least. Whoever set up the ambush had not skimped on resources.

The struggle was over in a few minutes. Only Pisander was left standing.

"What do you want?" he asked the man facing him.

"I only ever wanted what was due to me," growled a different voice at his back. "If only one royal died in the barn, that was on your head. You wouldn't pay me what was needed to get the job done properly."

Pisander felt the knife go in as he twisted his head to confront the speaker. Even through the agony he recognized the face of his attacker.

A voice whispered in his ear. "Remember me, Count Nothing? I attacked the kings in the barn for you, but when I came to collect you cheated me. You were so very, very pleased with yourself. No one cheats Alfic and gets away with it."

The knife twisted in Pisander's back, and pain flooded over him. Everything went black.

THE MAN who remained with Pisander's horses frantically remounted and galloped back to the city the moment the fighting started. As soon as a large enough group of armed men could be assembled, he led them back with Jarah at their head.

The bodies of Pisander and his men were still lying where they had fallen. No trace of the attackers could be found.

"What now?" asked one of the men.

"Pisander and Lygell are both dead, so who's going to pay us?" asked another.

"Don't look at me," Jarah retorted, "I won't be paying anyone."

"The army from Varas is getting close!" another voice piped up. "Rumor says it will reach Arnost in a matter of hours. And there's another army almost as close, coming from the direction of the Rogandan border."

Jarah mounted his horse. "I'll be long gone when they arrive," he assured them.

He threw them a parting glance as he rode away. "Do whatever you want," he called. "You're on your own now."

46

Lord Krasmir, Acting Regent of Rogand, stood with his wife Deka staring out at the city of Rog beyond the palace grounds. Krasmir had chosen a small set of apartments within the palace for his use as regent, and he did so partly for the view. He had always found the squalor of the capital city confronting, and he didn't want to lose sight of it.

Deka studied him with a concerned eye. "How are you coping with the role of regent, my beloved?" she asked.

He smiled at her. "I've been finding it surprisingly manageable. I expected unrelenting opposition, and it's been a pleasant surprise to discover how many people are willing to be reasonable."

"It's no shock to me," she replied, one eyebrow lifted ironically. "You're standing in for a heartless monster given to violent rages."

"Be careful what you say, my dear," he chided. "I won't hear you speak badly of the king. I fully support him, which is no doubt the reason he appointed me."

Deka shook her head in bewilderment. "It's a complete mystery to me how anyone can fully support him, much less you." She threw up her hands. "It isn't as if you've ever lacked opinions about how the kingdom should be ruled."

"I have priorities of my own," he acknowledged. "I'm making it clear to anyone who asks that my focus is the stability and economic well-being of the kingdom." His brows furrowed. "I'm hoping we don't have a repetition of Drettroth's invasion."

"Especially since the king's done nothing whatever to ease the burden the invasion placed on every family in Rogand," she grumbled.

She ignored his dismay at her continued disrespect. "Do any of the barons want to keep the war going?"

He frowned at her for a moment longer before giving up with a sigh. "No," he said. "Thankfully not. None of them see any benefit in attacking our neighbors. As long as the Arvenians don't attack us, they'd prefer to let them be."

She said nothing for a while, but he could see she was eyeing him sternly. "What?" he eventually asked, throwing up his hands in exasperation.

"The fact that you're agreeing with the king now is bad enough. When are you going to abandon this ridiculous pretense about being no better than an animal?" she asked him bluntly. "You might have been able to get away with it when you were just Lord Krasmir, but you're the regent now!"

He snorted. "I've had my reasons. None of the factions among the nobility have ever bothered trying to recruit me."

"I know," she said with exaggerated patience. "It means you don't owe favors to any of them." She sighed. "You're certainly odd, but I won't deny that you're canny. These people don't know how well off they are. One day the nobles, the administrators, the priests, the common people—the whole lot of them—will wake up and discover you're the most even-handed and reasonable ruler Rogand has ever seen."

He grinned at her, blowing her a kiss.

KRASMIR STUMBLED about his apartments in a daze, groaning loudly.

"Whatever's the matter?" asked Deka in alarm. "Shall I call for the physicians?"

He ignored her question, continuing to moan.

"What is wrong with you?" Deka demanded. Her tone made it clear he needed to respond, and he needed to do it immediately.

"Something happened," he said. "It was like I woke up from a nightmare. Except it was full daylight."

He held his head in his hands. "I don't understand it!" he wailed. "How could I ever have thought that anything about Agon made sense? I must have been mad!" He paused, scowling. "Either that, or he used some kind of sorcery on me!"

She stared at him wide-eyed, probably convinced he had gone mad. He didn't care.

"A lot of things are about to change!" he said, a look of unshakable determination on his face. "If Agon was fool enough to make me regent, he'll have no one but himself to blame for the consequences. He isn't going to recognize his kingdom when he gets back."

KRASMIR FELT weary beyond words when he finally dragged himself back to his apartments. Deka was waiting for him there, concern in her eyes.

"You need to sleep!" she told him.

"How can I sleep?" he asked. "Rogand hasn't faced a crisis like this in generations! The king is dead, and there's no heir. The situation is unprecedented!"

"There's a simple solution," she said calmly. "One of the nobility needs to be anointed as king."

"Who? None of them will tolerate a king from a rival faction. We'd end up with a civil war on our hands!"

"Of course," she said reasonably. "Everyone understands that. The solution is obvious. They need to crown you as king."

Seeing the look on his face, she planted her hands on her hips impatiently. "Why must you be the last person to see what's obvious to everyone else?"

Then she relaxed, gazing at him smugly. "The wives are in complete agreement, which means there's no doubt it will happen."

JONAS SHIFTED UNCOMFORTABLY in the saddle. After another day of riding he felt hot and dusty.

From the moment Will offered him the position of steward on his holdings in Erestor, the appeal of life as a soldier had diminished greatly for Jonas. Already thinking ahead, he had approached Breysen about joining the estate as the blacksmith. When he made it clear that Breysen's family would be welcome to relocate permanently to the holdings, Breysen accepted at once.

Breysen understood that the offer was conditional both on Will returning safely from Rogand and on King Steffan and Queen Essanda being restored to undisputed control of Arvenon. No one could say with any confidence when either of those events might take place.

Considerable progress had been made toward the goal of restoring the kingdom to its rightful rulers though. The western army camped outside Steffan's Citadel on the border of Erestor had already been restored to the control of the king. That army had been placed under the leadership of Rellan and Lord Burtelen, and sent to the border of Rogand to prevent King Agon of Rogand from entering Arvenon.

The northern army, originally camped outside Deadman's Pass on the border of Castel, had been moved by Pisander and his henchmen to Varas to block a short-lived Varasan invasion of Arvenon. Once this second army came within reach, Rufe and Count Ranauld managed to induce the soldiers to turn on the leaders appointed by Pisander. The situation was resolved only after a vicious battle, but Rufe and Jonas prevailed with the help of loyalists in the army along with several units of Varasan soldiers.

With both armies now firmly under King Steffan's control, only Arnost remained in the hands of Pisander. The second army was marching south for Arnost, led by Rufe and Jonas. A strong detachment of Varasan soldiers from King Delmar's army was marching with them. Messengers had been sent to the first army under Rellan and Lord Burtelen to inform them of King Steffan's plans.

Arnost was now no more than a couple of days' march away. Scouts reported that Arnost was shut tight and still under the control of Pisander.

Jonas sat daily in conference with Rufe and King Steffan, and he knew that the idea of attacking his own capital did not appeal to the king at all. The only alternative was a siege. Starving out the defenders would spare the besiegers at the cost of everyone in the city.

Neither option was attractive. Nevertheless, the hour of decision was fast approaching.

ARMED SOLDIERS APPEARED abruptly on the road ahead, startling Amyra into sudden watchfulness. She had felt especially tense since the attack on Thomas.

"Who are you, and why are you entering Arvenon?" demanded a rough voice. It appeared that Will's party had reached the border at last.

Hearing the challenge, all of them reined in their horses.

Will stepped his horse forward. "I am Will Prentis," he called.

"Did he say Will Prentis?"

"Is it really him?"

"Will's arrived!"

Soldiers appeared from everywhere, racing forward and surrounding Will eagerly, all of them talking at once. Somehow word spread, and soon they found themselves at the center of an enthusiastic crowd of milling soldiers. One of the men began chanting, "Will! Will! Will!" The others quickly took it up until the air rang with their shouts. The noise was deafening.

Will held up a hand, and the din gradually faded away. "It's good to be with you all again," he said. "Thank you for defending the border for the king!"

"Are the Rogandans coming?" someone called. "We're ready for them!"

"No," Will replied. "I won't be needing to ask you to fight. King Agon has just died, and none of the Rogandans seem to be looking in this direction right now."

Cheering erupted, and Will had to hold up his hand again.

"Where are Rellan and Lord Burtelen?" he asked.

"I'll take you to them, Will," one of the soldiers offered.

Amyra had been looking on in awe. Now that she had witnessed for herself the adulation with which Will was greeted, she felt completely confounded. How could she ever have imagined herself worthy of him?

Then he rode close to her, and she saw the love in his eyes. "I need to go for a while," he said. "You'll be safe with these men. One of them will lead you back to their camp."

He turned to the men. "Can you please take care of my friends? This is Thomas, and Haldek," he said, pointing to them in turn.

"The horse master!" someone called as Will pointed at Thomas, and she saw Thomas color.

"And this is Amyra, my betrothed," he said with a grin. A mock frown came over his face. "Treat her well, or you'll answer to me!"

At Will's reference to his betrothed, more cheering erupted. Every eye turned in Amyra's direction, and some of the men began to whistle noisily. Will aimed a wink at her as he rode away.

"I'm one of the captains of this rabble," a cheerful voice called over the din. "Let me lead you to our camp. We'll find some warm food for you there."

AMYRA SAW VERY little of Will over the next couple of days.

He came to her one evening just after nightfall. "I'm sorry I haven't been able to spend time with you, Amyra," he said apologetically.

She smiled at him in the dark. "I completely understand—you have a job to do. There'll be plenty of time for us later."

"I'm going to be distracted for the foreseeable future," he told her. "But once we're married I will take you to my holdings in Erestor. We can build a life for ourselves there."

"It sounds very cozy," she said, leaning in to him. "Just you and me."

"And the Stone of Authority," he added wryly. "I've seen enough to know that the stones have an uncanny way of attracting trouble."

"Whatever comes, we'll meet it together," she promised with a smile.

He left her after stealing a kiss, and he went reluctantly.

The following morning the soldiers packed up the camp around them, and the army set off marching in the direction of Arnost.

Will himself stopped by in person later that day.

"We've received a message from King Steffan," he told them. "He's left Varas with Rufe and Jonas. They're leading an army to Arnost."

"Are they expecting a fight when they get there?" asked Thomas.

"No one knows exactly what to expect," Will replied. "We're planning to link up with them outside the city. We'll do whatever it takes to arrive at Arnost roughly at the same time."

WILL WAS LED to the tent of King Steffan, with Amyra, Thomas, and Haldek close behind him.

With the two armies already beginning to merge, confusion reigned supreme. Will had been overseeing the process of coordination before turning aside to seek out the king.

When they were announced, King Steffan himself appeared at the entrance to the tent. "Will! You've arrived at last! It is good to see you. Please, come and join us. Thomas and Haldek, you are very welcome too, and your lovely friend."

After sending a soldier in search of Rufe and Jonas, the king stood aside to usher the new arrivals into his tent. The tent was spacious, and it needed to be. Will knew that the king routinely used it to host conferences while on the march.

Will caught a glimpse of the queen at the far end of the tent, attended by Elena and Brother Ander.

The moment Elena spotted Thomas, she ran to him with a glad cry. After embracing him eagerly—much too briefly if the look on Thomas's face offered any indication—she turned to embrace Haldek as well. Elena called over a servant, then whispered in Haldek's ear. At her words he brightened immediately, setting off after the servant without delay. Will guessed that Elena had arranged for Haldek to be taken to Rubin and little Tamara.

Elena turned to Will, greeting him warmly.

"I'm glad you traveled with the army, Elena," he said. "Thomas was becoming very restless."

Thomas raised an eyebrow ironically. "Will has barely seen us in the last few days, so don't believe a word he says," he retorted with a smile.

Rufe and Jonas arrived in the tent just as Queen Essanda appeared at Elena's side to greet the new arrivals.

"And who is this?" asked the queen, turning to Amyra with a smile.

Will bowed. "King Steffan, Queen Essanda, Rufe, Jonas, Elena, Brother Ander, this is Amyra, my betrothed."

The occupants of the royal tent greeted his announcement with no less enthusiasm than Will's soldiers had shown and with equal astonishment.

Amyra had dipped into a curtsy when he introduced her, and Will saw that she was blushing furiously as she rose. Taking her hand, he gave it a gentle squeeze for moral support.

"Thank you for your kind welcome, Your Majesties. And Rufe, Jonas, Elena, and Brother Ander," she said. Her face might have betrayed her, but she demonstrated admirable command of her voice.

Congratulations flowed freely, and Will felt both delighted and humbled at the warmth of their response. Several of the men were unable to resist wisecracks at his expense, and several minutes passed before the laughter began to die away.

"There is a tale worth the telling here," said King Steffan with a pleased smile. "We will defer it until we can give it the attention it deserves. In the meantime, what news do you bring us from Rogand, Will?"

"King Agon is dead, Your Majesty—killed by an assassin hired by Lord Drettroth if you can believe it. We no longer have reason to expect a Rogandan army at our border. I imagine that the Rogandans will be distracted for some time by the question of the succession. What will happen when a new king emerges in Rogand remains to be seen."

Astonishment greeted his report.

"Did you have a hand in what happened, Will?" asked the king.

"Each of us played a part," he replied, "including Amyra. But none of us can rightly claim credit for the final outcome. And that is undoubtedly a good thing. I imagine the Rogandans would not take it well if their king had been assassinated by an Arvenian."

Will pulled a small object from the pouch at his belt and handed it to the king. "This tile played a key role," he said. "Keep it safe, Your Majesty. It is exceedingly valuable."

The king took the tile, shaking his head in surprise. "Once more, we must wait to hear the full details," he said regretfully. "The immediate task before us is to retake Arnost from Pisander."

"Pisander's days are numbered," Will replied. "His plan always depended on killing you both, Your Majesties. If he'd succeeded, we would have had no one to rally behind."

Rufe nodded. "We were able to retake control of the two armies because the soldiers were still loyal. They just needed to be shown the truth."

"Now that Agon is gone," added Will, "the supply of resources—to Eisgold in Castel as well as to Pisander—will come to an end."

"The reach of these traitors is greatly diminished," agreed the king. "Once Arnost has been freed, their day will be over in Arvenon. I'm confident they won't long survive in Castel either."

The king's voice took on an expectant tone. "Agon's schemes and manipulations are almost at an end, and a new day is about to dawn," he said. "All of us have endured a time of peril and grief. That time is almost behind us, and we will emerge stronger and more resilient than ever."

EPILOGUE

Undisputed master of its domain, the eagle soared high on the currents above Arnost.

Serene and majestic, it ignored the clanging of the cathedral bells and the little figures that swarmed around the city gates. The monarch of the air glided effortlessly over the city, pursued faintly by the sound of cheering as the king and queen of the surface dwellers rode in astride their mounts.

The noise and commotion fell swiftly away in the wake of the hunter's silent wings. Climbing the thermals, it wheeled westward in search of prey.

The saga continues and concludes in
The Stone of Vitality Complete Set
(The Stone Cycle Complete Sets Book 3)

NOTE FROM THE AUTHOR

Thank you for reading *The Stone of Authority Complete Set*—I hope you enjoyed it. Please consider leaving a review. Reviews make a huge difference to authors as well as benefiting other readers. I also very much appreciate feedback from my readers.

The Stone Cycle saga continues in *The Stone of Vitality (The Stone Cycle Book 5)*, described below.

When the abduction of an imperial princess sparks a tense standoff between Rogand and the distant Empire of Ahr, the dispute threatens to engulf Arvenon and its allies.

Hurrying to the Rogandan capital with an Arvenian delegation, Will joins the kings of Rogand, Castel, and Varas to plan a response. The upheavals that overtake them quickly thrust all else aside.

While the Grand Vizier of Ahr ruthlessly pursues his secretive agenda, mystery and suspicion swirl around the long-lived High Priest of the Rogandan Dark Gods.

No one is prepared for the emergence of the Stone of Vitality.

Note: The Stone of Vitality *is Book 5 of* The Stone Cycle, *a multi-part saga. The story will continue and conclude in Book 6,* The Hope of Vitality.

To be kept up to date on new releases, sign up to my mailing list at www.allanpacker.com. New subscribers will receive an exclusive bonus novelette, available in ebook, audiobook, and print format. The novelette, *The Rending: A Prequel to The Cost of Knowing*, is a complete story. It provides the background to Anneka's story without introducing spoilers for other books in *The Stone Cycle* series. The novelette is described below.

Endings may be beginnings in disguise

Anneka is comfortable and confident, a noblewoman of consequence living a life of privilege. Until the day her world is torn apart.

After losing everything she most cares about, she must abandon her home and her way of life in an attempt to secure the future of those who depend on her.

No one, least of all Anneka, could anticipate a deeper significance to her struggle. Yet her journey will one day influence the fate of kingdoms.

ACKNOWLEDGMENTS

As always, I owe a huge debt to my wife, Merilyn, who is not only my most enthusiastic supporter, but has become increasingly effective as my alpha reader. It's no exaggeration to describe her role as that of a developmental editor. Her patience is awesome, and her feedback unfailingly valuable. *The Stone of Authority* is dedicated to her.

The Struggle for Authority is dedicated to my sister, Julie, and brother-in-law, Chris. I've been blessed to share life's journey with them, and I hope I never take them for granted.

Special thanks to my beta readers, Deborah, Ray, Andrew Menzies, Jen Neal, Alison George, Cherilyn White, and Stephen. Their feedback makes a difference and encourages me to keep writing.

Mary Novak did her usual outstanding developmental edit. I continue to find her feedback invaluable. Deborah followed up with her typically thorough proofread.

Karri did another superb job on the cover. I appreciate her patient persistence.

I am indebted to Brian Plush for his wonderfully detailed map. The map beautifully illuminates the pathways throughout Arvenon and the surrounding kingdoms.

2020 was a challenging year for us all, wherever we were living in the world. At a time of great uncertainty and social upheaval, I am grateful to God, my rock and my place of safety.

ABOUT THE AUTHOR

Allan Packer writes epic fantasy, and the novels and novelettes of *The Stone Cycle* are his first published fiction.

Allan grew up surrounded by books and became an avid reader during his childhood. In his university years fantasy displaced science fiction as his favorite genre, thanks primarily to J. R. R. Tolkien. He later shared this love with his four children by reading *The Lord of the Rings* to them aloud—a three-month marathon he completed twice during their formative years.

Born in Australia, Allan has lived and worked on three continents, and spent one quarter of his working years abroad. Having worked as an IT professional throughout his career, he was first published as a technical author.

Today he lives with his wife in Adelaide, South Australia, near their children and a small but growing band of grandchildren.

Allan is currently working on his second epic fantasy series.

PART III

LIST OF CHARACTERS AND RESEARCH NOTES

THE STONE OF AUTHORITY

LIST OF CHARACTERS

- *Agon* - king of Rogand
- *Ander* - Arvenian soldier who traveled with Will and later commanded soldiers at the Battle of Torbury Scarp; decided to become a monk after the death of Brother Vangellis
- *Andri* - respected member of the Clan
- *Ava* - handmaid to Queen Essanda
- *Axel Stablehand* - master of the Arvenian royal stables at Arnost, and the father of Thomas
- *Alfic* - mercenary leader
- *Anneka* - former noblewoman who leads a community hidden away in the forest near Erestor
- *Bottren* - high-ranking Arvenian nobleman and close confidante of King Steffan; liaison to Will Prentis at the Battle of Torbury Scarp
- *Burtelen* - high-ranking Arvenian nobleman from Erestor who is a close confidante of King Steffan; played a crucial role in bringing an army from Erestor to the Battle of Torbury Scarp

- *Delmar* - king of Varas, a neighboring kingdom to Arvenon, and ally of King Steffan of Arvenon
- *Drettroth* - high-ranking Rogandan nobleman who commanded the Rogandan army during the invasion of Arvenon; known as Vilkami during his childhood
- *Duke of Erestor* - the uncle of King Steffan of Arvenon, and the regent during the king's absence during the Rogandan invasion; the senior member of the nobility in Erestor
- *Dunnridge* - nobleman who later became the Earl of Pisander (see *Pisander*)
- *Eisgold* - Castelan nobleman formerly commanding the Castelan army; exiled after the Battle of Torbury Scarp for ignoring orders at a crucial moment in the battle
- *Elena* - young woman living in hiding with her father Rubin in the forests of Arvenon
- *Elias* - abbot at the Monastery of St. Rodrig the Martyr where Brother Vangellis was hiding away
- *Ennawi* - slave of King Agon of Rogand
- *Eravitt* - Castelan nobleman
- *Essanda* - queen of Arvenon, formerly a princess of Castel
- *Gareth* - mercenary leader
- *Gerome* - monk at the monastery led by Brother Elias; close friend of Brother Ander
- *Haldek* - former Rogandan soldier who unwittingly helped Will on significant occasions; living in a tiny forest community with Elena, Rubin, and Thomas
- *Hazor* - mercenary leader
- *Hender* - young bowman living in Anneka's forest community
- *Istel* - king of Castel, a neighboring kingdom to Arvenon, and father-in-law and ally of King Steffan of Arvenon
- *Jobin* - mercenary leader
- *Jonas* - senior army leader and close confidante of Will Prentis; fought at the Battle of Torbury Scarp

- *Karevis* - Varasan nobleman and commander of the Varasan army; played a key role at the Battle of Torbury Scarp
- *Krasmir* - wealthy and powerful Rogandan baron
- *Kuper* - Arvenian soldier from Erestor who led a cavalry force to the battlefield at Torbury Scarp with his twin brother Rellan; killed at Torbury Scarp
- *Lonnigen* - Arvenian count with holdings in northern Arvenon
- *Lygell* - nobleman directing mercenaries from Arnost
- *Marya* - wife of Axel Stablehand and mother of Thomas
- *Nestor* - Arvenian soldier heading Will Prentis's spy network; traveled with Will's small band during the Rogandan invasion
- *Nilsean* - Varasan nobleman and senior army commander under Lord Karevis
- *Nistinaa* - slave who cares for Ennawi
- *Pisander* - earl and former head of King Steffan's foreign spy network who remained in Arnost during the Rogandan siege; imprisoned for treason during the siege, but bribed his way out of prison before his execution
- *Ranauld* - Arvenian count and a senior leader in the army at Torbury Scarp; a close confidante of King Steffan and a friend of Will Prentis
- *Rellan* - Arvenian soldier from Erestor who led a cavalry force to the battlefield at Torbury Scarp with his twin brother Kuper; connected with Anneka's forest community
- *Ronya* - member of the Clan
- *Rubin* - father of Elena
- *Rufe Sarjant* - respected and physically imposing Arvenian soldier; a close friend of Will Prentis and a key leader in the army
- *Scar* - respected leader in Anneka's forest community
- *Steffan the Second* - king of Arvenon

- *Tamara* - daughter of Thomas and Elena
- *Tarestel* - Varasan nobleman who became puppet ruler of Varas after the Rogandan invasion; exiled after the defeat of the Rogandan army at Torbury Scarp
- *Thomas Stablehand* - possessor of the Stone of Knowing; son of Axel and Marya
- *Torbury* - title granted to Will Prentis by King Steffan; Will Prentis was elevated to the Arvenian peerage as Lord Torbury in honor of his efforts in defeating the Rogandans
- *Vangellis* - Arvenian monk who became a key mentor to Thomas; killed at Lord Drettroth's stronghold
- *Vilkami* - noble-born Rogandan who became Lord Drettroth
- *Viggor* - leader of the Clan
- *Will Prentis* - commander of the Arvenian army, greatly respected by his soldiers as well as King Steffan due to his remarkable qualities; fluent in Rogandan and widely traveled

THE STRUGGLE FOR AUTHORITY

LIST OF CHARACTERS

- *Agon* - king of Rogand
- *Aiden* - prince of Arvenon, son of King Steffan and Queen Essanda
- *Amyra* - young woman living with the Aen-ur; daughter of Dahra
- *Ander* - Arvenian soldier who traveled with Will and later commanded soldiers at the Battle of Torbury Scarp, before becoming a monk following the death of Brother Vangellis
- *Ashar* - Rogandan fighter willing to accept dangerous assignments for the right price
- *Atae* - leader of the Aen-ur
- *Ava* - handmaid to Queen Essanda of Arvenon
- *Axel Stablehand* - master of the royal stables at Arnost and the father of Thomas
- *Alfic* - mercenary leader
- *Anneka* - former noblewoman who leads a community hidden away in the forest near Erestor
- *Belac* - mercenary under Lord Redfass
- *Bottren* - high-ranking Arvenian nobleman and close

confidante of King Steffan; liaison to Will Prentis at the battle at Torbury Scarp

- *Breysen* - member of Hazor's mercenary force
- *Burtelen* - high-ranking Arvenian nobleman from Erestor who is a close confidante of King Steffan; played a crucial role in bringing an army from Erestor to the battle at Torbury Scarp
- *Carnwill* - tracker in the pay of King Agon of Rogand
- *Carpis* - well connected Castelan fisherman
- *Chalno* - mystic and former priest of the Rogandan dark gods
- *Dahra* - healer living with the Aen-ur; mother of Amyra
- *Delmar* - king of Varas, a neighboring kingdom to Arvenon; ally of King Steffan of Arvenon
- *Drettroth* - high-ranking Rogandan nobleman who commanded the Rogandan army during the invasion of Arvenon; known as Vilkami during his childhood
- *Duke of Erestor* - King Steffan's uncle, and the regent during the king's absence during the Rogandan invasion; the senior member of the nobility in Erestor
- *Dunnridge* - nobleman who later became the Earl of Pisander (see *Pisander*)
- *Eisgold* - Castelan nobleman formerly commanding the Castelan army; exiled after the Battle of Torbury Scarp for ignoring orders at a crucial moment in the battle
- *Elena* - young woman living in hiding with her father Rubin in the forests of Arvenon
- *Elias* - abbot at the Monastery of St. Rodrig the Martyr where Brother Vangellis was hiding away
- *Ennawi* - slave of King Agon of Rogand
- *Eravitt* - Castelan nobleman who survived the assassination attempt in the barn at Paradise Valley
- *Essanda* - Queen of Arvenon, formerly a princess of Castel
- *Gareth* - mercenary leader

- *Gerome* - monk originally at the monastery led by Brother Elias, later living at the Newhaven forest community; close friend of Brother Ander
- *Gordan* - Castelan nobleman and confidante of the late King Istel
- *Haldek* - former Rogandan soldier who unwittingly helped Will on more than one significant occasion; living in a tiny forest community with Elena, Rubin, and Thomas
- *Hazor* - mercenary leader
- *Inyaet* - chief librarian of the Aen-ur
- *Istel* - king of Castel, a neighboring kingdom to Arvenon, and father-in-law and ally of King Steffan of Arvenon
- *Jace* - assassin with an unequalled reputation
- *Jarah* - mercenary and hunter in the employ of Pisander
- *Jaxin* - retainer of the Duke of Erestor familiar with the dockside district of Maranelle
- *Jonas* - senior army leader and close confidante of Will Prentis; fought at the Battle of Torbury Scarp
- *Kaebon* - nobleman commanding the Castelan army at Deadman's Pass
- *Kaemin* - elder and senior member of the Aen-ur
- *Kantor* - member of Hazor's mercenary force
- *Karevis* - Varasan nobleman and commander of the Varasan army; played a key role at the Battle of Torbury Scarp
- *Kernon* - mercenary leader
- *Krasmir* - wealthy and powerful Rogandan nobleman
- *Kuper* - Arvenian soldier from Erestor who led a cavalry force to the battlefield at Torbury Scarp with his twin brother Rellan; killed at Torbury Scarp; son of Rellan and Anneka, named for his late uncle
- *Lygell* - deputy to Pisander and most senior nobleman in Arvenon
- *Mardone* - Castelan nobleman
- *Marya* - wife of Axel Stablehand and mother of Thomas

- *Namor* - mercenary leader
- *Nistinaa* - slave who cares for Ennawi
- *Ona* - Rogandan noblewoman and trusted associate of King Agon of Rogand; proficient in multiple languages
- *Pisander* - earl and former head of King Steffan's foreign spy network who remained in Arnost during the Rogandan siege; imprisoned for treason during the siege, but bribed his way out of prison before his execution
- *Petar* - hunter and bowman living at the Newhaven forest community near Erestor
- *Ranauld* - Arvenian count and a senior leader in the army at Torbury Scarp; a close confidante of King Steffan and a friend of Will Prentis
- *Redfass* - self-styled Arvenian nobleman; mercenary leader
- *Rellan* - Arvenian soldier from Erestor who led a cavalry force to the battlefield at Torbury Scarp with his twin brother Kuper; husband of Anneka
- *Rhillyon* - leader among the Aen-ur
- *Ronya* - member of the Clan
- *Rubin* - father of Elena
- *Rufe Sarjant* - respected and physically imposing Arvenian soldier; a close friend of Will Prentis and a key leader in the army
- *Rupert* - king of Castel following the death of his father, King Istel; brother to Essanda
- *Scar* - respected leader in Anneka's forest community
- *Steffan the Second* - king of Arvenon
- *Tamara* - daughter of Thomas and Elena
- *Tarestel* - Varasan nobleman who became puppet ruler of Varas after the Rogandan invasion; exiled after the defeat of the Rogandan army at Torbury Scarp
- *Thomas Stablehand* - possessor of the Stone of Knowing
- *Torbury* - title granted to Will Prentis by King Steffan; Will Prentis was elevated to the Arvenian peerage as Lord Torbury in honor of his efforts in defeating the Rogandans

- *Vangellis* - Arvenian monk who became a key mentor to Thomas; killed at Lord Drettroth's stronghold
- *Vilkami* - noble-born Rogandan who became Lord Drettroth
- *Viggor* - leader of the Clan
- *Will Prentis* - commander of the Arvenian army, greatly respected by his soldiers as well as King Steffan due to his remarkable qualities; fluent in Rogandan and widely traveled
- *Yordin* - captain of the Nomad Lady

RESEARCH NOTES

THE STONE OF AUTHORITY

Spoiler Alert!

The reader is advised to avoid this section before finishing *The Stone of Authority*.

Head Injury

Modern medicine would likely describe the head injury suffered by Thomas as a subdural hematoma. Information about signs and symptoms can be found at:

https://en.wikipedia.org/wiki/Subdural_hematoma

Poisons

Gretchen's poison of choice was strychnine, a poison in use since ancient times. It typically takes effect ten to twenty minutes after being administered. More information can be found at:

https://en.wikipedia.org/wiki/Strychnine_poisoning

www.ingramcontent.com/pod-product-compliance
Lightning Source LLC
Chambersburg PA
CBHW021958040826
48979CB00045B/2321/J
* 9 7 8 1 9 2 3 2 1 8 1 0 9 *